Kur of Gor

Gorean Saga:

01 - TARNSMAN OF GOR
02 - OUTLAW OF GOR
03 - PRIEST-KINGS OF GOR
04 - NOMADS OF GOR
05 - ASSASSIN OF GOR
06 - RAIDERS OF GOR
07 - CAPTIVE OF GOR
08 - HUNTERS OF GOR
09 - MARAUDERS OF GOR
10 - TRIBESMEN OF GOR
11 - SLAVE GIRL OF GOR
12 - BEASTS OF GOR
13 - EXPLORERS OF GOR
14 - FIGHTING SLAVE OF GOR
15 - ROGUE OF GOR
16 - GUARDSMAN OF GOR
17 - SAVAGES OF GOR
18 - BLOOD BROTHERS OF GOR
19 - KAJIRA OF GOR
20 - PLAYERS OF GOR
21 - MERCENARIES OF GOR
22 - DANCER OF GOR
23 - RENEGADES OF GOR
24 - VAGABONDS OF GOR
25 - MAGICIANS OF GOR
26 - WITNESS OF GOR
27 - PRIZE OF GOR
28 - KUR OF GOR
29 - SWORDSMEN OF GOR
30 - MARINERS OF GOR
31 - CONSPIRATORS OF GOR
32 - SMUGGLERS OF GOR

Kur of Gor

John Norman

OPEN ROAD
INTEGRATED MEDIA
NEW YORK

978-1-4976-4488-5

This edition published in 2014 by Open Road Integrated Media, Inc.
345 Hudson Street
New York, NY 10014
www.openroadmedia.com

Kur of Gor

Prolegomena to the Tale

The thing was a monster, of course.

There could be no doubt about that.

Some of you, naturally enough, might suppose that the Kurii themselves were monsters, but that is distinctly unfair. That would be similar to regarding, say, leopards, or lions, as monsters. They are merely another life form. There is no symmetry involved here, incidentally. Kurii, for example, do not, at least on the whole, regard human beings, in their varieties and configurations, as monsters, no more than human beings would regard sheep, rabbits, squirrels, goats, and such, as monsters. The human being regards such life forms as simply inferior forms of life. And so, too, do the Kurii, on the whole, regard human beings, such small, fragile, weak, vulnerable, slow, fangless, clawless, hairless life forms, as merely an inferior form of life. And, one must admit, a case might be made along those lines, though it might pain one somewhat to recognize or acknowledge it. In some respects, attempting to assume a posture of objectivity in the matter, however briefly, this typical Kur view has much to be said for it. It is doubtless substantially justified, if not in all respects correct. The Kur does recognize, of course, that the human being has certain features worth noting, for example its two prehensile appendages, its upright stature, increasing scanning range, its binocular vision, its occasionally exercised cunning, and such, but these features are not unprecedented, and, indeed, characterize a number of rational and semirational species. The Kur itself, for example, possesses similar features, though perhaps with a keenness and ferocity which constitutes a dimension less of degree than of kind. The human being does possess languages, and cultures and traditions, the latter often alien and inimical to one another, and numerous

3

devices and tools, and even technologies, of an incipient type. These are, however, the latter in particular, inferior to those available to the Kur, when it chooses to make use of such things. The Kur, in many respects, retains, celebrates and cultivates, as a matter of tradition and choice, a number of rituals, habits, responses, and practices which one might, if one did not understand them as the Kur does, be regarded as excessively cruel and barbaric, such as the contests of the rings, and such. But the Kur, which is often eight to ten feet in height, if it should straighten its body, which it seldom does, and several hundred pounds in weight, and is clawed, and fanged, and long armed, and agile, and swift, often moving on all fours when it wishes to move most rapidly, and that is far faster than a man can run, prizes such things as its strength, and its speed, and its sensitivity, that is, in this case, its capacity to be easily aroused to rage. It does not apologize for its strength, its speed, its formidableness, such things. Nor does it attempt to conceal them. The Kurii, as humans, have produced several civilizations, some of which, as those of humans, have survived. But they have taken care to see that what we might tendentiously call their bestiality, or animality, or such, should not have been lost in these civilizations, at least in the surviving ones, to the frictions and abrasions of socialization. If there were Kur civilizations of a passive or benign nature, their historical records have not survived. Whereas the human being is commonly trained to suspect, regret, denounce, and officially repudiate his animal nature, sometimes even to the point of pretending it does not exist, and that he is a mere societal artifact, of whatever sort is currently recommended, the Kur has not cared to avail himself of such extreme and dubious stratagems. To be sure, the animal nature of the human being, driven underground, despising the facades of an acculturated hypocrisy, continues to prowl within, and, by means of a thousand twistings and subterfuges, will have its say. Surely it would be difficult to explain human history without some attention devoted to slaughter, envy, passion, greed, deceit, hypocrisy, ambition, lies, theft, corruption, assassination, murder, contempt, hatred, betrayal, and a large number of such attributes.

The Kur, in a variety of ways, you see, for better or for worse, openly acknowledges and expresses, and fulfills, his animal nature.

I report this. I neither denounce it nor commend it.

I suppose this would count as a difference between the Kur and the average human being. To be sure, if one lacks fangs and claws it is seldom to one's advantage to grapple with those who possess them. The average Kur on the other hand could best, unaided with weaponry, a typical forest sleen, and might seriously tear and bloody even a larl, though the larl would doubtless be the last to feed.

The human being is not really a tame animal, but it pretends to be. Indeed, in its effort to appear tame it may even poison and destroy itself, or, alternatively, and more usually, it may lend its animal nature to others, who will direct it in their own interests. Under the aegis and anonymity of an ideology, for example, what crimes might not be perpetrated with a conscience as clear as distilled venom?

Life exists largely, one notes, of predators and prey, though sometimes these relationships are politely, if not modestly, veiled. Perhaps you have noticed this. Certainly the Kurii are well aware of this and do not feign to ignore it. Nature poisoned, they understand, does not cease to exist, but will thenceforth exist in a deranged and malevolent manner. One of civilization's problems, you see, is to give nature its due and still survive.

The Kurii, in their ugly ways, manage this.

The Kur, in its surviving civilizations, then, gives nature its due, willingly, eagerly. That is why, perhaps, the Kur is what he is, as quick, as formidable, as dangerous as he is. Those who were not did not survive.

The Kur, then, is not a tame animal. It prides itself on its nature, its strength, its agility, its terribleness. It understands itself as a predator and would have it no other way. Daintiness of sensibility does not bring a species to the summit of a food chain.

Like many aggressive, dangerous animals, the Kur, interestingly, has its sense of propriety, and even honor. To be sure these things are normally limited to intraspecific relations. Men, for example, seldom include insects, vermin, cattle, and such, within the community of, say, honor. And the Kur seldom includes the human being within its community of honor. It would be absurd for it to do so.

For generations human beings slew their foes. Later, a great advance in civilization took place, and its name was slavery. For example, women of the enemy, particularly if young and beautiful, might now be kept about, rather as domestic animals, for the pleasure of new masters. Women, throughout human history, have counted as prizes, acquisitions, loot, spoils, and such. And one would be naive not to recognize that this pleases their vanity, even as they might writhe helplessly in their bonds. And things are not really so different now, one supposes, on some worlds, though the rituals of their pursuit and claimancy are subject to considerable variation. The Kurii, on the other hand, do not commonly practice slavery. Most often they eat their foes.

It is alleged, and we suppose with good reason, certainly we have no reason to doubt it, that the Kurii once had a world, a planet. We do not know what world that was, nor what might have been its star. But apparently that world no longer exists, at least as a viable habitat. The ambition, territoriality, aggression, and greed of Kurii groups, coupled with a remarkable technology, apparently resulted in its desolation or destruction. One can imagine the axis of such a world being explosively shifted, disastrously, perhaps even accidentally, producing lethal, global tumults of storms and climates. One might speculate on mines capable of blasting continents into orbit, and, then, consequent upon diminutions of mass, oceans being sucked away into space. Perhaps, too, the world as a whole was literally fragmented, broken into hundreds, perhaps thousands, of irregular, tumbling planetoids incapable of holding an atmosphere. Or perhaps its orbit was explosively affected, merely hurling it too close or too far from its primary, exiling it from a habitable zone. Or perhaps there was a braking of its rotation, perhaps suicidally intended, designed to produce two hemispheres, one a world of unrelieved light and heat, a scalding, furnacelike world, the other a world of perpetual darkness, a silent, polar waste. Perhaps, on the other hand, there was merely a radiological sterilization of the world, perhaps one rendering it progressively incapable of supporting life.

Whatever the particular stimulus or etiology of their migration, the Kurii long ago left their world. They may have voyaged for generations. But it is possible, too, they did not have so far to go. They currently inhabit a set of steel worlds, perhaps hundreds of them, mingled within, shielded within, what we, or you, I suppose, call the asteroid belt. The asteroid belt is perhaps the debris of what was once a planet. It is not impossible, though I do not think it likely, that it is the debris of what was once the planet of the Kurii.

Though it might once have been the world of a similar species, an animal capable of, say, destroying its habitat, of rendering itself extinct.

Such species doubtless exist. Perhaps you are aware of one.

Even the fiercest of enemies may upon occasion unite in a common project, willing to suspend their inveterate hostilities in order to achieve a common goal, say, that of discovering and acquiring a world suitable for the purposes of their life form. Should they acquire such a world they may then, as they wish, and as they probably would, return to their ancient ways, and contest it amongst themselves. It seems a plausible supposition that whatever world the Kurii might claim and conquer they will eventually allot its acres according to the measure of the sword. It would not be the first time a planet was turned into a battlefield, and its continents became fields of blood. But one must first have a world, a mat, a terrain, an arena. One needs a coliseum in which to so entertain oneself, in which to so fervently practice such enviable skills, and sports.

And so, despite their many internal divisions, their ancient prejudices and hatreds, Kurii are quite capable of uniting in a temporary, dark brotherhood, in a brotherhood with a particular object in view, that of obtaining a world.

This world should be small enough to lose hydrogen and large enough to retain oxygen; it should be neither too close to its primary nor too far; it should have a star of suitable longevity; it should rotate and have an inclined axis, these things to assure a periodicity of seasons; and it should have large amounts of water, accessible water, water in a liquid state. In short, it should be rather like Earth.

And so the Kurii, their provisional habitats nestled within, lurking within, the asteroid belt, wait.

And they are not a patient species.

Too, it offends their sense of propriety, or natural justice, that an inferior life form, such as the human, should have, much to itself, so precious a habitat. Surely they have done nothing to deserve so splendid a house within which to conduct their trivial, nasty affairs, their prosaic slaughterings unredeemed by poetry and glory. They did not earn their world. They did not build ships and beach on alien shores, and carry their flags and standards into new sunlights. They found themselves no more than born into a plenty, amongst treasures so circumambient and familiar to them they were unaware of their value. They did not realize the rarity, the excellence, of such a world. They were indigenous to the place, an accident, like bacteria and rodents, their location and their precedence no more than an undeserved fortuity. They did not measure themselves against a foe capable of resisting them. Too, it seems incomprehensible to the Kurii, as well as infuriating, that the human has seemingly so little respect for his world, which they see as so precious, that he has so little respect for that world that he could dirty it, and foul it, and place it in jeopardy.

It would be a fair question, then, though one founded upon a mistaken assumption, as we shall see, to ask why the Kurii, with their inclinations and capacities, and their sense of natural rightfulness, have not undertaken an action seemingly so obvious and one for which they are so eminently qualified.

The seizure of a world.

Surely the will is there.

Have they not come far for such a world? And perhaps, if so, is their search not now ended? Have they not now found the long-desiderated prize? Indeed, are they not now feasibly in its locality, lurking in the darkness, concealed amongst boulders, amidst drifting, floating forests of metal and stone, scrutinizing its unsuspecting lights from afar, through the porous ellipse of its borders? Are the reports of their scouts not cataloged and studied? Are they not, even now, at the gates, so to speak?

Certainly the wells and circles of space and time can be conveniently bridged.

There is no scarcity of technological expertise.

There is no shortage of power, nor of materiel, for the debris within which they conceal themselves is rich with chemicals, metals, and trapped gases. It could supply thousands of steel worlds for thousands of years, and be scarcely diminished.

Why, then, has the hand of the Kur not yet reached forth to seize so charming and vulnerable a prize, such a world, so coveted a treasure? Why have the words not yet been spoken, the orders not yet signed? Why have the ports and locks of the steel worlds not opened long ago, freeing the ships, that they might emerge like dragons, as silent as moonlight, from their caves? To what enchantment have they been subject? What incantation could hold such beasts bound? What spells might have forged their chains?

The answer to these questions is clear to the Kurii, and they have little to do with magic, except in the sense that a cigarette lighter, a hand grenade, a flashlight, would serve to an aborigine as evidence of sorcery.

The mistaken assumption of the question is that the Kurii have never undertaken such a venture. A better question would be, why do they not do so now.

Consulting the annals of the steel worlds, it seems that the paw of the Kurii, four times, did stretch forth to bury its claws in the pelt of a world, but, too, four times, it was drawn back, lacerated and bloody.

Something, you see, stands between the Kurii and their coveted world, a power, a form of life as far advanced beyond the Kur, as the Kurii are beyond those of Earth, as far as those of Earth would be beyond primitives beginning to learn pottery and weaving. The nature of this power is not clear to me, but it is seemingly quite real. It has its own world, I am told, a world not wholly unlike Earth. It is, in a sense, a sister world of Earth, though I gather it is not an offspring of the sun, as we suppose Earth to be, but rather entered its system long ago, following a search for a suitable star, much as nomads might have searched for lush grazing or fertile fields. It is spoken of in ancient records as the *Antichthon*, or Counter-Earth. Its name amongst some, amongst one or more of the rational species which inhabit it, is a strange one, one that is unclear to me—It is "Home Stone." But this mysterious word, so unintelligible and obscure, is perhaps best left undeciphered. So, we will, as occasion arises, obviate any distractive, attendant difficulties of exegesis by using, untranslated, its most common native name, which is *Gor*. The world will then be spoken of as *Gor*. The most common name for its primary, in the same most common native tongue, is *Tor-tu-Gor*, or "Light-Upon-the-Home-Stone." It would be doubtless fruitless to digress upon these semantic anomalies.

The utter masters of that world, which we will call *Gor*, are alleged to be the *Sardar*, an expression commonly translated as *Priest-Kings*, a word, we suppose, which tells us less of their nature than of the awe they inspire. Certainly it is a word suggesting power, perhaps of an unusually potent and unnatural sort, and mystery. One gathers the Priest-Kings are worshipped as gods, which flattery, if they have taken note of it, they apparently tolerate, and perhaps, for their own purposes, even indulge, and encourage. Priest-Kings, it is alleged, have mastered gravity, a force they can use for purposes as mighty as the forming, moving, and destroying of worlds, and purposes as trivial and convenient as visual and gravitational concealment, transportation, flight, work, and weaponry.

The nature of the Priest-Kings seems to be obscure. It is said by some that they are without form. This seems unlikely. Others claim they are invisible, and others, yet, that to see them is to die. Contradictions abound. It seems humans cannot get on without them. I see no reason to suppose that they are invisible. To be sure, it seems they are seldom seen, but this feature they share with many forms of life. Further, I see no reason to suppose that to see them is to die, though one might conjecture that they might be concerned to protect their privacy, with perhaps some severity. On Gor a caste exists, which we may refer to as that of the Initiates. The Initiates, in virtue of the study of mathematics, the adoption of various abstinences, such as the eschewing of beans, and a variety of spiritual exercises, and such, claim to be on intimate terms with the Priest-Kings and to be potent in their influence on them, for example interceding with them on behalf of generous clients, and such, say, calling down blessings, averting poor crops, prospering businesses, calming stormy seas, assuring success in warfare, and so on. They are also skilled in deciphering the secret messages encoded in the entrails of sacrificial beasts, prognosticating the meanings of the flights of birds, seen over one shoulder or another, interpreting the bellows and rumblings of flatulent tharlarion, and so on, all feats beyond the average layman. Their offices and efforts are invariably successful, and their predictions and prophecies are infallible, save when unforeseen factors intervene, which occurs not infrequently. My own suspicions in these matters is that the Initiates know as little of the Priest-Kings as anyone else, but they have hit upon an economic niche which may be profitably exploited. There are many ways to make a living and superstition affords a vein easily mined. It has much to commend it over honest labor. To be sure, one supposes the simpler of the Initiates take their nonsense seriously. Let us hope so. Too, doubtless they fulfill a need, if one which might seem to be something of a source of embarrassment for a putatively rational creature. Too, the average human might feel deprived, if not actually lost and lonely, if deprived of his superstitions. He is, after all, well aware of his vulnerability and the hazards of fortune. He is likely to appreciate any help he can get, or thinks he can get, or hopes he can get. And, too, who can prove that there are no secret messages lurking in the warm, bloody livers of slaughtered verr? And if the Priest-Kings choose to invest their intentions or reveal their will in the flights of birds or the emanations of discomfited tharlarion who is to gainsay them?

Human beings tend to assume that the Priest-Kings are rather like themselves, that they are human, or, at least, humanoid. Perhaps their vanity prompts such a speculation. Kurii, too, incidentally, assume that the Priest-Kings must be somehow akin to them. Surely the terror of their ships and the accuracy of their weaponry suggests that. But let us not waste fruitless speculation on this matter. Whatever may be the nature of the Priest-Kings, it is clear, as does not seem to be the case with many gods, that they exist.

The Flame Death, with which they commonly enforce their laws, if nothing else, mitigates against agnosticism in this matter.

One thing about the Priest-Kings puzzles the Kurii, and that is why this mysterious life form seldom behaves otherwise than defensively. They will react sharply if not inevitably to border crossings, but they will not pursue the rebuffed invaders; they will not seek them out, and destroy them in their lairs.

Indeed, Priest-Kings are tolerant of the presence of Kurii on Gor itself, provided they respect their technology and weapon laws.

One supposes the Priest-Kings have a different sense of civilization than, say, humans, or Kurii, who will commonly pursue and exterminate an enemy.

Perhaps the Priest-Kings recognize the Kurii as a life form, rather as the human, and, as such, as something of interest, perhaps of value, if only scientifically.

But let us proceed. Our account, after all, has little to do with Priest-Kings, whoever or whatever they might be. It has more to do with Kurii and humans.

Indeed, our story, in particular, as you may recall, has to do with the monster. It begins, in its way, on a moon of Gor, one of its three moons, and its smallest, that called the "Prison Moon."

And, interestingly, our story begins not with the monster, but with a human being.

Yes, one of those, a human being.

And a rather unusual human being, as it turned out.

Before we begin, however, as it will prove informative, we might briefly reference the common Kur attitude toward the human, other than understanding it as an inferior life form. In some steel worlds humans are kept rather as cattle, fattened, crowded, and used for feed. Kurii are fond of meat, particularly freshly killed meat. Some Kurii however keep humans as pets, and even grow fond of them. Certain other humans, selected humans, are raised to be work animals, or prey animals. The human makes an excellent prey animal, from the Kur point of view, as it can be bred for agility, elusiveness, and cunning. It can also be dangerous, and thus, consequently, is the sport of the hunt improved.

But now to the "Prison Moon," where our story has its beginning.

The Tale Begins

Chapter, the First:

The Containment Device

He thrust violently against the close, curving, transparent walls, howling with rage.

We can understand such emotions.

They are not strange to us.

In his own language his name was said to be Tarl Cabot.

Such things do not really much matter, with such creatures. Nonetheless, to themselves, and to some of their kind, they seem of much importance. I do not know, of course, whether it was important to him, or not. Perhaps some microorganisms arrange their cilia in some bizarre fashion, and then understand themselves as being somehow thereby exalted. Are names so important? Perhaps. But is that which is named not more important? One does not know with such creatures. I think they are strange.

They cannot tell themselves from their names, nor do they care to do so. They name themselves, and things, and think thereby to acquire them. They do not do so.

They have names; reality does not.

How is it, in any event, that they so invest themselves with such importance? What a piteously naive arrogance is therein displayed.

Are they truly so unaware of their small place in the yard of existence, so ignorant of the length of space and the breadth of time, of the flight of galaxies, of the journeys of streaming light, perhaps touching nothing for a hundred thousand years; are they unaware even of the patience of stone, cogitating its memories of a molten youth? It is hard to accept that they are the offspring of stars, a freshened reconfiguration of antique components long ago expelled into the darkness, but are we not all such?

They are so tiny, and so generally useless, an active rash on quietude, a small noise, perhaps brave in its way, in the night.

But are we not, in our way, as well?

When the Nameless One stirred the cauldron of stars did it intend them? Are they not a lapse of sorts? Might it have been distracted at the time? But in what workshop or cauldron was formed the Nameless One itself? From what unseen seas was it itself cast forth, beached on shores burnt by drifting, incandescent tides, and from whence came these, the tides, the continents, these, too, children of the mystery?

Before the Nameless One, you see, is the Mystery.

It is that which was, and that which is, and that which will be. And none have lifted its veil.

I suppose it is offensive to conceive that we are brothers to that woeful life form, the human, one so disgusting and treacherous in its diverse paths, one so despicable in its intolerable vanity. How absurd, how repulsive, one supposes, that we are siblings in virtue of the parentage of stars.

But then we may console ourselves that we are siblings, too, to the diatom, to the smallest living thing, to the worm in the sea, the mote in the air.

But how small, how trivial, is the human.

How easily might he be struck by some astral debris, not noticing him. Or fall prey to a prolific, invasive mite, a thousand mutations from an eye or claw, a mite not even visible to his eye.

And how despicable, how contemptible, is the human!

A spawn of greed, an embracer of comfort, a seeker of ease, a blemish on the world, a wart of vanity, a stranger to honor.

One who guards his mind, fearing it will awaken.

One who guards his mind, as one might guard a prisoner.

One who so treasures his mind that he dares not use it.

His bulwark is stupidity.

And what labor is not expended in its preservation!

How mighty is the sweet shield of ignorance!

How fearfully and carefully he burnishes it!

He is a herd animal. He is unworthy of the stars.

Yet there is in that life form a spark of awareness, for all its frivolity and frailty, for all its egregious contumely and its hideous ineptitude, a flicker of mind, however reluctant, in a largely oblivious, somnolent world. It is one of the rare places the universe has stirred, and awakened, and opened its eye, and looked upon itself, startled to learn that it exists.

Does it recoil, seeing itself in the human?

Surely it rejoices, seeing itself in us, we who are worthy of it.

It is conscious in countless minds, of course, in that of the mouse, and cat, in that of the urt and verr, in that of the barracuda, in that of the viper and leopard, in that of the hith and larl.

But we are most worthy of it.

In us is its nature most fully manifested. Are we not the outward form of its inward horror, or essence? Are we not the choice fruits of its inward terrors, the splendid robes of its dark, shrieking soul? In us, it finds its fangs, and talons, its hunger, its indifference, its terribleness, its sublimity, its rage, its glory.

And it is through our eyes that it sees the stars.

One day, perhaps, the human will disband his herds and be free. One day, perhaps even the human will lift his head, and see the stars.

They are there.

I am personally, you see, not ill disposed to the human.

If I were I should not tell this story, which deals primarily with some humans, and something not human, with the monster.

And, of course, with the Kurii.

I wonder if you know of them.

They know of you.

You could not understand our name for the human with whom we will begin. In fact, you would not even know it was uttered. One might use our name for the human, of course, but you could not pronounce it. For example, if a leopard or a lion, or a larl or a sleen, had a name for you you would doubtless not recognize it as a name, let alone as your name. We will, accordingly, refer to that individual with whom we shall begin by that name by which other humans might know him, namely, as Tarl Cabot, or, as some will have it, Bosk, of Port Kar.

He pounded again, and again, at the transparent walls, until his hands bled.

Bruised, and bewildered, he sank down then, naked, inside the bottlelike container. Such containers taper toward the bottom, that wastes may drain from them. They taper, too, toward the top.

Near the top a tube descends periodically, automatically, through which liquid, if the occupant chooses to live, may be drawn by the mouth into his body. The entire facility is automated, though one supposes some supervisory personnel may be in attendance, if only by means of olfactory devices, listening devices, cameras, or such. Certainly one seldom sees them. The tube's descent is indicated by an odor. The corridors are commonly empty and silent. One may conjecture, occasionally, from the outside, that within the containers there is sound, this being surmised from the expressions of the occupant, the motions and configurations of his mouth, the gestures of his limbs, such things. The container is rather oval, or ovoid, rounded, ascending rather vertically, but narrowing, rounded, toward the top and bottom. The diameter, in measurements likely to be familiar to the reader, would be something like four feet, whereas the container, as a whole, is something like eight feet in height, though much of this space is not conveniently utilizable, given the tapering at the top and bottom. In such a container one sleeps as one can. Indeed a soporific gas may be entered into the container remotely, which suggests there is some actual surveillance of the containers. Too, the air in the container may be drawn from the container, should one wish, say, to terminate an occupant, clear the space for a new occupant, and so on. Too, it might be noted that the corridor itself, as most of the structure, is airless. This contributes to the incarcerational efficiency of the facility.

Various life forms may be kept in such containers.

From where he was contained, the human in question, Tarl Cabot, could see several tiers of similar containers, several of them occupied. He did not realize at the time the absence of air outside the container, as the container itself contained a regulated, breathable atmosphere. And probably some of the other life forms did not understand that either. One supposes, incidentally, that there were diversities in the container atmospheres, as, upon inspection, there appeared to be substantial dissimilarities amongst their occupants.

In the human species, aside from some unusual specimens, there are two sexes. Commonly both collaborate in replication. Interestingly, the biological functions of conception, gestation, and nurturance in the human species are all centered in a single sex, that of the female. Among the Kurii, on the other hand, the procedures of replication are conveniently divided amongst three, or, if you like, four sexes. There is the dominant, the submissive, and the nurturant, who gestates and nurtures, until the child is mature enough to chew and claw its way free. At that point it is ready for meat. It is not clear if the nurturant was a naturally evolved entity or if it was the result of biological engineering long ago, in the Kurii's original world, or one of its worlds, for it may have destroyed more than one. Indeed, the technology of the nurturant might have been obtained from another species. It is not known. These thing are lost in the prehistory of a species, so to speak, or at least in the time from which no histories remain. The fourth sex, if one may so speak, is the nondominant. Under certain unusual circumstances the nondominant becomes a dominant. It is very dangerous at such times, even to dominants.

The individual, Tarl Cabot, doubtless called out a number of times, angrily, requesting an explanation or justification for the predicament in which he had so unexpectedly found himself. That would be only natural. From outside the container, of course, given the container and the near vacuum of the corridor, he could not be heard, nor, it seemed, was there anyone there to listen. He may not have recognized this, or, if he suspected it, he might have supposed that somehow sounds from within the container might be conveyed, doubtless by means of some listening device, to some point at which they might be audited, or recorded, for future audition. On the other hand, given the emptiness of the corridor, and the absence of intelligible communication from an outside source, he had no assurance that his demands, protests, or such, were anywhere registered, or even that they might be of the least interest to anyone or anything.

Needless to say this can be unsettling.

Indeed, it can derange certain sorts of minds. The instincts of many caged animals, on the other hand, are more healthy. Understanding themselves trapped, they are patient, and wait. Beyond a certain interval they do not exhaust their resources, but conserve them, almost lethargically, for a given moment, for the sudden movement, for the lunge, the movement to the throat. So, after a time, Tarl Cabot, who was not particularly disanalogous to such beasts, became quiescent, at least as far as external observation might detect. This was in conformance, incidentally, with certain recommendations of his caste codes. One can learn much, even from the codes of humans. He was, as we learned, of what on Gor amongst humans is referred to as the scarlet caste. This is a high caste, doubtless because it is armed. Individuals of this caste are of great value to their cities, their employers, their princes, so to speak. Indeed, they are indispensable in their way; have they not, however unintentionally, secured the foundation of law; have they not, however unbeknownst to themselves, raised from the mire of brutishness, insecurity, and terror the towers of civilization? Surely it is they who must man the walls and defend the bridges, who must police the streets and guard the roads, and who will in sunlight, or in darkness and storms, carry forth the standards. They are unusual men and seldom understand their own nature, nor need they. Perhaps it is better that they do not. Let them laugh and fight, and drink and quarrel, and seek their slaves in conquered cities and taverns, and chain them and put them to their feet, and not inquire into the dark and mighty processes which have bred them, which have made them so real, and necessary. And so they are encouraged to emulate the stealth and savagery of the larl, the cunning and tenacity of the sleen, the vigilance and swiftness, the alertness, of the mighty tarn. They are companions to discipline; they are hardened to short rations, long watches, and the march; they are inured to the exigencies of camp and field; and trained to fight, and kill, preferably swiftly and cleanly. They do not know how they came to be, but they would not be other than they are. They are more beast than man, and more man than beast. They are, so to speak, dangerous beasts with minds. And such have their utilities. We may laud them or despise them. They are called Warriors.

Life is very real where they live it, at the edge of a sword.

The reader may be interested in obtaining an account, however superficial, of certain events antecedent to the incarceration of the individual, Tarl Cabot.

It is rumored that within recent years certain tumults or transitions have taken place in the realm of Priest-Kings. I do not know whether that is true or not. Who is to say what thrones may have been toppled, what crowns seized? Surely such things, coups, insurrections, fatalities, suppressions, and such, are not unknown even within the benign civilizations of the habitats. And are they not useful in subverting stagnation, and improving bloodlines? And if such things occurred, it is not impossible that they may have had a role in this business. Again, one does not know. On the other hand, such things, such conjectured events, bloody or otherwise, are not strictly germane to this history.

The individual, Tarl Cabot, had, it seems, upon occasion proved to be of some value to Priest-Kings. In some eyes, though not in his, we may conjecture, he was even taken as an agent of Priest-Kings. And certainly, whether this be so or not, one may well suppose that any behavior of his which might have been deemed counter to the interests or policies of those mysterious beings would not have been likely to be generously countenanced.

We can understand these things.

In this respect I do not think we are so unlike the Priest-Kings, whoever, or whatever, they may be.

In the north of Gor, in its polar regions, inhabited sparsely by tribes of humans known as the Red Hunters, recognizable by the small blue spot at the base of their spine, it is said that he, this Tarl Cabot, once encountered a great war general of the Kurii, Zarendargar, whose name, for convenience, we have transliterated into phonemes hopefully accessible to at least some readers of this tale, certainly in this translation. Colloquially, doubtless with a certain crudity, he, Zarendargar, was spoken of as "Half-Ear." And, of course, few of the Kurii who ascend high in the rings will be without certain blemishes. A certain area of the polar region was at that time being used as staging area, under the command of the aforementioned Zarendargar, a staging area with munitions and such, for an attack on the Sardar enclave, destined to suddenly, decisively, and irremediably terminate the rule of Priest-Kings, destroying them in their own most-favored haunts or lairs. It had taken better than a century for this materiel, bit by bit, to be secretly assembled. One can well understand then its preciousness and importance to the Steel Worlds, its relevance to their projects, and such. The staging area, however, was destroyed, and somehow, in some way, Tarl Cabot seems to have been involved in its destruction. It was supposed at the time that Zarendargar was destroyed in the explosion, or conflagration, or such. But this turned out to be mistaken. When it became clear that Zarendargar had survived the destruction of the staging area, a death squad was dispatched from the Steel Worlds to hunt him down and kill him, for he had, after all, failed the people. The policies and decisions connected with the transmission of the death squad were controversial, incidentally, in the councils of the Steel Worlds, and the decree of termination, some months later, would be rescinded. This, of course, could not have been anticipated by the personnel of the Death Squad. Representatives of the Death Squad contacted Samos of Port Kar, clearly an agent of Priest-Kings, and Tarl Cabot, for assistance in hunting down and executing Zarendargar. It was assumed naturally that this assistance would be readily tendered for Zarendargar was well understood to be significant amongst the Kurii and a relentless, dedicated, and dangerous foe of Priest-Kings. The putative location of the at-that-time-fugitive Zarendargar was the vast prairies of the Gorean Barrens. Tarl Cabot, however, instead of lending his assistance to the Death Squad, himself entered the dangerous Barrens to warn Zarendargar and, if possible, protect him. This effort, of course, was not only contrary to the desires of the Death Squad, but, too, seemed clearly to be an act not in the best interests of Priest-Kings. On whose side, so to speak, was this mysterious, unpredictable, ungoverned Tarl Cabot? Was he an agent of Priest-Kings? Was he an agent of Kurii? If he was an agent, it seems he was his own agent, or an agent of honor, for, long ago, it seems, he and Zarendargar had shared paga.

In any event Tarl Cabot, having returned from the Barrens, and having learned later of his putative outlawry, resolved to leave the maritime city of Port Kar, only to return when it might be safe to do so, this intelligence to be gathered from agreed-upon secret signals to be displayed on the holding of his friend, Samos, of Port Kar.

Tarl Cabot remained at large, so to speak, for some time.

The surveillance of Priest-Kings is rather efficient, as we have reason to know, but it is also, as we have reason to know, far from perfect, particularly so in recent years. Perhaps this has to do with transitions or dislocations in the Sardar, such as have been occasionally rumored. But perhaps not. It is hard to know. Surely small ships, at least, manned by humans, have frequently enough, of late, penetrated the atmosphere of Gor. Many, apparently detected, have been ignored. Others, pursued, have eluded their pursuers. I personally suspect that this lapse of attentiveness or this seemingly tolerant permissiveness, or this seeming lack of zeal, on the part of Priest-Kings, and their ships, presumably mostly automated and remotely controlled, has less to do with technological limitations than with some reordering of priorities in the Sardar, perhaps even with an acceptance of the general harmlessness of the ships involved, and a disinterest in their common cargoes. It may be a simple matter of balancing costs. It is hard to know. Our information is clearly incomplete, and conjectural. On the whole, Priest-Kings seem tolerant of other life forms, their activities, partialities, and such. Indeed, they may even look with approbation, given the apparent current infrequency of their voyages of acquisition, or collection, on the introduction of additional human life forms to the world. To be sure, the chains of human females brought to Gor might conceivably, eventually, in some centuries, depress certain relevant markets. At that point presumably only carefully selected, high-quality merchandise would be brought to her shores. But one knows little about such things.

Eventually, however, we may conjecture that the presence of Tarl Cabot was detected. This may have been a matter of chance. On the other hand, he may have been sought for ardently, perhaps because of the heinousness of his offense, his treasonous concern for the welfare of an enemy. Perhaps he was to be used as an example. It is not known.

We now find him, at any rate, naked, in his container, in perfect custody.

He is completely helpless, and fully at the mercy of his captors, or keepers. In this respect he is not much unlike the human females whom men of his sort, on Gor, are wont to keep for their work and pleasure. They, of course, are not at the mercy of captors or keepers, but of owners, and masters. They are owned, you see. They are properties, possessions. Also, they are legally, and in the eyes of all, animals. And as such, as any other form of such an animal, an owned animal, for example pigs or verr, they are subject to barter, exchange, gifting, sale, and such. They are spoken of as slaves.

Whereas Kurii may own humans, and several do, they do not

think of them as "slaves," no more than men of Gor would think of their verr and kaiila as slaves, or those of, say, Earth, would think of their pigs and horses, or cattle, as slaves. They are simply domestic animals. The slave, then, from the Gorean view, is a domestic animal, but a particular type of domestic animal, one different, obviously, from other types, such as the verr or kaiila. Thus, not all domestic animals are slaves, but all slaves are domestic animals. Too, many Gorean men seem to be as fond, or even more fond, of their slaves than of, say, their sleen or kaiila, animals commonly much more expensive. To be sure, they master them with firmness, and do not let them forget that they are only slaves. That is seemingly the Gorean way.

Tarl Cabot was not certain how long he had been incarcerated in the heavy, narrow, glassine container. Nor are we. It was perhaps some days, or weeks. Given the absence of clocks, the unknown periodicity of feedings, if they were periodized, the nature of the soporific gas, and such, it would be hard to say.

The gravity in the venue, the Prison Moon, was currently indexed to that of its mother world, Gor, to which it was a satellite. We are not clear, given the small size of the moon, a mere several pasangs in diameter, how this was managed. It is done differently, certainly, and perhaps more primitively, in the cylinders and spheres, in the Steel Worlds. The capabilities of the Priest-Kings, whoever or whatever they may be, are not well understood. Certainly it would not do to underestimate either their power, resolve or sagacity. Four times the Kurii erred in this regard, and their mistakes were costly. That such, the Priest-Kings, have form, and can interact with matter, however, seems obvious. The Prison Moon, for example, seems to make that clear, as it is obviously an artificial moon, with its architectural steel, its absorbing cells, its focusing and power mirrors, its shielding, and such, one perhaps once used for purposes of extra atmospheric observation, perhaps low-gravity experiments, and such. It seems unlikely that it was originally designed as a facility for the retention and storage of life forms, or, if you like, as a maximum-security prison for, say, particular prisoners.

Shortly before the unexpected disruption, one which seems to have taken even Priest-Kings unawares, this seemingly adding indisputable and welcome evidence as to their limitations and vulnerability, two human females were entered into the container in question.

It is clear they were females, as the human species is characterized by an obvious and radical sexual dimorphism.

It is seldom difficult to tell a human female from a human male.

Their sexes are quite different.

Too, as is common in the human species, these two females were considerably smaller than the average male, and considerably weaker.

That tends to be a characteristic of the human female.

Size and strength are common features of the human male, and accordingly the human female, smaller and weaker, often seeks to secure and protect herself within the shelter of these features.

These two females were in some respects similar, and in other respects quite different. Both were, as we understand it, of the sort which would be attractive, even excruciatingly so, to a human male. One was darkly pelted, with brown eyes, and the other was lightly pelted, or blondishly pelted, with blue eyes. Both were young, the darkly pelted one perhaps a bit older than the other. Each was, as tests later demonstrated, healthy and fertile. Each, too, was characterized by delicate, even exquisite, features, of a sort so clearly different from the coarse type found commonly in the human male. This has perhaps to do with several millennia of sexual selection. Too, both were, as humans understand such things, deliciously figured, this, too, doubtless having to do with generations of sexual selection. Indeed, the figures of both were nearly, if not quite, at what merchants in these matters refer to as the optimum block measurements for their size and weight. Block measurements, taken presale, are commonly, and in some cities this is required by law, included in a female's sales information. They are often available, as well, before the female is put on the block, hence the name 'block measurements'. Needless to say, too, given the female's subjection to severe regimens of rest, diet, and exercise, it is almost assured, as is desired, by attention to these "block measurements," that she will come to the block in excellent condition, healthy, vital, and well-curved. That is the way she is to be sold. She is, after all, merchandise, and, hopefully, good merchandise. Too, we may suppose, being healthy, each had the needs and desires of a healthy female, and, considering their selection, may have had these drives, and such, in an acute fashion, even uncomfortably so, which would render them particularly sexually vulnerable. Gorean slavers, for example, often pay close attention to such things. After all, most men buy women for pleasure.

Both of these females were of the sort, then, which, on Gor, would be of interest to buyers. They were typical of the females found in Gorean markets, and were perhaps, we suspect, given their insertion into the container, somewhat above average. Presumably both would have gone for a good price, and certainly so if they had been brought within suitable block measurements, to which, as noted, they were already in close approximation.

At the time that these females were entered into the small compass of the container Tarl Cabot was sedated, and thus unaware of their insertion into his small world.

They, too, at the time, must have been sedated.

The corridor was doubtless pressurized prior to their insertion into the container, and then returned to its near-vacuum condition.

This was done shortly prior to the disruption, as well.

That was seen to.

I have mentioned that the females were quite different, and you must understand that these differences pertained to far more than their pelting, eye color, and such. Before I discourse, however briefly, on certain of these differences, I mention something you, or some of you, may find of interest. That is that the human female, and the male, as well, for that matter, is relatively hairless. This may be an adaptation to facilitate heat loss in long-distance pursuit and pack hunting, or, again, it may have to do merely with preferences involved in sexual selection, or both. It is hard to know about such things. A consequence of this lack of hair, or fur, is that the species, in its wanderings and migrations, certainly into colder areas, must clothe itself. This seems to have been done first by taking the skins and fur of other animals, with which the Nameless One, if it was concerned at all with such matters, had refused to provide them, and later particularly by the utilization of plant fibers, and such. Clothing also, it seems, interestingly, is often worn by the species even when it is not climatologically indicated, and, indeed, sometimes when it is even uncomfortable. It can serve, of course, as a decoration, a symbol of status, a concealment of provocative or vulnerable areas, and so on. The harnesses and accouterments of the Kurii are presumably not dissimilar, at least in some of these respects. Female slaves may or may not be clothed, of course, as the master pleases. This increases their sense of vulnerability, and dependence. The female slave is seldom unaware of her condition but, too, interestingly, seldom does she wish to be. Her bondage may be her terror, but more often it is her meaning and joy. This apparently has to do with a variety of genetic antecedents and endowments, dispositions and complementarities, selected for in the long and interesting course of human evolution. One does not note with surprise that such complementarities should occur in a species so sexually dimorphic. Indeed, one would expect them. When they are clothed, the female slaves, it is often minimally, and provocatively. This reminds them, too, of their bondage, and is sexually stimulatory not only to the masters but to the chattels, as well. The pelting of the Kur female, of course, on the other hand, is thick, abundant, rich, and glossy, and, in season, heavy. How could a human female even begin to compare with a Kur female in beauty, let alone in power or ferocity? Her fangs for example, are negligible. The human female could not, for example, in three or four Ihn, tear loose a limb from a terrified, struggling tabuk.

But now to the more important aspects which characterized the new additions to Tarl Cabot's container.

Neither, in effect, at least as yet, was Gorean.

One, the darkly pelted female, was from an area on Earth not unfamiliar to Tarl Cabot himself. It is called an England, of which there are apparently more than one. He himself, we have learned, was from a seaport in that country or world, called Bristol. He attended an institution or institutions in this England, institutions of what they think of as "higher learning." But one suspects they are, as yet, as a species, scarcely capable of what one might call "lower learning." This supposed learning, as it is spoken of, took place, it seems, in a place where cattle were once wont to ford. That seems a strange place to build. At least they have a world. The female, who is intelligent and quite articulate, at least until she was taught silence and the appropriateness of petitioning for an opportunity to speak, was also a supposed learner, or student, in that very same place, though not exactly in the same place. These things are hard to understand. Her background was rich and her family had standing in that world. She would have counted as having been of the high classes. But I do not think her family earned its class or wealth honestly or honorably, for example through the rings, but then that is not unusual amongst humans. She was a student of "anthropology." Here the translator is less than helpful. It is presumably a sort of history or literature, perhaps having to do with chants and songs. Perhaps it has to do with knowing the traditions, but the traditions are different in diverse worlds. How could one know them all? Too, they may guard their traditions. Is it appropriate to inquire into such things? If dogs or pigs had such studies, their anthropologies, or such, who could find them of interest? Perhaps a biologist? Perhaps a dog or pig? But such things are now behind the female. Her life has changed. It is interesting to note that her background is in some respects similar to that of Tarl Cabot. That may be important. She was apparently obtained by Priest-Kings for some purpose or another. I suspect the reason. We may learn later. In any event, she was not acquired by our human confederates, though it is also clear, from their assessments, that she was quite capable of satisfying their usual criteria. Indeed, I have been informed that had they been aware of her she would have been entered on their acquisition lists. In such a case she would have eventually found herself on a Gorean slave block, being auctioned to the highest bidder.

Accordingly one gathers she is a most excellent example of human female, highly intelligent, healthy, nicely curved, and quite beautiful, at least for the species, and acutely sexually needful. Too, she is tormented by the restless, uneasily sensed suspicions and yearnings, so alien to her acculturation, which afflict so many such women, longings which frighten her, and into which she fears to inquire. These longings have to do with her nature, and her identity, with what she is, most profoundly, and what she should be, absolutely. They are the longings of an acutely needful but as-yet unmastered slave.

The blondishly pelted female, certainly culturally, is quite different.

She was hitherto from one of the Steel Worlds, one of the animals kept there, she for the purpose of grooming her master. The tiny fingers and nibbling teeth of such females are well fitted for this task.

It was not perfectly clear at the time how she came into the possession of Priest-Kings. One supposed it might have been a matter of bartering at an exchange point, between our humans and those of Priest-Kings, for such interactions occasionally occur, however illegitimately; or she may have been taken to the surface by our human allies as, so to speak, negotiable currency, to be there exchanged unobtrusively for local coin. That is sometimes done. Too, there might have been a crashed or downed ship. Perhaps then she had been retrieved from her cage, perhaps drawn from fiery or smoking debris. Her master or keeper in the meantime might have made good his escape, or perhaps failed to do so, was apprehended by Priest-Kings, and routinely destroyed.

You might suppose that we could have easily solved this problem, how she came into the keeping of Priest-Kings, by simply asking her, but that would be incorrect, for she, as a typical Kur human, had never been taught to speak. Would you, for example, teach a dog, or pig, to speak?

That they can be trained for simple tasks is more than enough.

It is interesting to consider how easily the continuities of tradition or civilization may be broken.

Absent a species for a single generation from socialization and we have not even barbarians, only animals.

Clever animals, but animals.

This done, let us return our attention to the slight, but shapely, occupants of the container in question.

Both of the females, of course, were naked.

It is thus that Priest-Kings commonly keep their prisoners.

It was not originally clear for what reason the females were introduced into the container. Perhaps, one supposed, they were merely gifts for him, rather as might have been food, for another of his appetites. Certainly it seemed clear, at least at first, they were not used for purposes of torture, for then they would have been placed, presumably, in an adjacent container, where they might have been deliciously exposed, but inaccessible, rather as hot, savory food might have been placed just beyond the reach of a chained, starving man. One supposes, too, they were not placed with him in the container for purposes of breeding, for that would make little sense under the circumstances. Presumably Priest-Kings, if interested in such matters, would select appropriate seed and eggs, fertilize them, and then tend the consequent embryos, at least for a time, in a secure laboratory environment. They might then be raised for a time in containers, several months, say, or implanted in the bodies of various host mothers, of various suitable species, human or otherwise, for a natural birth later. Some Goreans breed slaves, of course. This is commonly done by agreement amongst masters. There are, too, of course, the slave farms. Some members of the caste of physicians, incidentally, concern themselves with such matters, for example, by implanting fertilized eggs in host mothers. In this way, a prize slave may be used to produce numerous offspring. The same thing is done routinely with other domestic animals. On the whole, however, this is rare with Gorean humans, who tend to be traditional in such matters and accordingly are inclined to refrain from such practices. In this respect, they are much like the Kurii, who are also reluctant to avail themselves of such devices, and who, indeed, interestingly, profess to find them unnatural and distasteful. The Kurii, for example, when they wish to breed humans, commonly chain them, left wrist to right wrist, right wrist to left wrist, left ankle to right ankle, right ankle to left ankle. After a time, this works rather well. I mention this in passing. One does not know the views of the Priest-Kings on these matters. In these respects, the Sardar is silent.

We supposed, originally, then, that they were placed in the container for his pleasure, for human males commonly derive great pleasure from the females of their species, a pleasure of which they avail themselves avidly and frequently, a pleasure not limited to certain hours or seasons, but one sought, it seems, at any hour, and in all seasons. On the other hand, as it turned out, and as we should have surmised, as the male was a prisoner, this was not the case. Rather a most insidious form of torture was intended, at least for a male of his particular type.

In order to understand the nature of this torture, one might note that the two females involved had not been selected for their role in this matter at random. They had been selected with great care. Both had, of course, been selected for their unusual desirability as human females. They were both of the sort which could drive a human male mad with desire. The girl from the Steel Worlds, of course, was no more than an animal, but she was doubtless familiar with, if contemptuous of, human males, whom she knew, of course, too, as animals, speechless animals like herself. She had been, after all, the grooming pet of a Kur master, and held herself, accordingly, superior to others of her species. Certainly she had not been bred, nor did she wish to be. She was special, in her way. She knew her name in Kur and could respond to certain commands in Kur. She could not speak it, of course, as her vocal apparatus was unsuited to the formation of its phonemes. As the pet of a Kur she had an unusual status amongst the few humans in the Steel Worlds. Doubtless she was somewhat aware of her effect on males, and was not disinclined to take pleasure in their discomfiture. She was a vain little thing, not unaware of her charms, and the pleasures of utilizing them to taunt and frustrate weak and helpless males, from whom she had nothing to fear. On the Steel Worlds she would have had the protection of her collar, which was wide and locked on her neck. It identified her master in Kur, and gave her much standing amongst those of her species. It was not a slave collar, of course, as she was not a slave, but merely an animal. It served much the same purpose as might a collar on, say, a dog on Earth. She was an animal, of course, but a very clever animal, a sly, cunning, vain, shapely, little animal. It is supposed she was included with Tarl Cabot and the other female not simply for her attractiveness, which was considerable, but for at least two other reasons. First, there was her basic raw animality, and, in its way, its associated simplicity and innocence. She would be unfamiliar with the touch of men. In this she had something of the charm of a virgin and the fascination of an unacculturated, primeval, shapely beast. Such, it is supposed, would present a normal male with an interesting, unusual, and naive object of desire, one which could be interestingly exploited, and conveniently and ruthlessly ravaged, doubtless to her bewilderment, and consternation, rather like the young female slaves who are raised in isolation from men and do not even know men exist, until, after being drugged, they are rudely awakened, to shouts and music, to find themselves in a collar, and being seized at feasts of victory, to be well ravished, afterwards to be distributed to favored officers. The second reason she was included in the container was doubtless to complicate the social interactions, so to speak, even to the point of hatred and anguish, in the small environment she shared with her fellow prisoners. This would have little to do, of course, with any initial indecision which might perplex or trouble the male, however briefly, confronted with such riches, for he might eventually, surely, enjoy either as he might please, and in any order or frequency he might find interesting or convenient.

For example, it is not unknown for a Gorean man to have more than one slave, that they may desperately compete with one another, each striving zealously to please him more than the other, that she may become his favorite. To be sure, this is a situation commonly productive of misery, jealously, and hatred amongst the slaves. Which female wishes to found inferior to another? Even a female not yet broken to her collar will strive to be found not less pleasing than another. Her own womanhood insists on this, as does her pride, her self-image, her concern for her own desirability, her sense of her own worth and value as a female. How intolerable to be found less a female than another! But then perhaps, at a moment, one even unexpected, kneeling, she looks up, into his eyes, and sees suddenly that he is her master, in a sense a thousand times more profound than the indisputable and perfected legalities in which she is irretrievably enmeshed, and wholly helpless to alter or qualify. Then perhaps the other woman is marketed, who may hope then to find a private master, as well. She who has been kept is now the single slave of a private master. She is humble and grateful. She is zealous to be such a slave to him that he will not desire another. She lives to love and serve. She fears only that he may find her in some way insufficiently pleasing. She rejoices. She has been found worthy of a man's collar. What a dignity, to wear a man's collar! What a badge of selection and excellence is that insignia, proving that she is lovely enough and desirable enough to be a slave! How free women, pretending to despise her, and her radiance, and happiness, envy her that distinction!

The anguish, the tumult, the distress, the rage, the conflict, the jealousy, in the container, as disturbing and irritating as it might be to the male, would be largely, doubtless calculatedly, consequent upon the interactions of the two females. Which female might be chosen, so to speak, or favored, and what would be the consequences of that choice with respect to the other female, and the male? Females, of course, compete for the attention of males, as would be biologically anticipated. They dress for them, they concern themselves with their appearance, their posture, their speech, and behavior. They wish to be found attractive to males.

Men, of course, compete for females, sometimes with the sword. But females, too, in their way, compete for men. Who has not seen the difference in the behavior of even veiled free women when in the presence of men, how they stand, how they hold their heads, how they speak, with such pretended, insouciant indifference? And, too, who has not seen the even more obvious competitions amongst the girls on a slave shelf when a handsome fellow is in the vicinity, their languorous poses, as though unaware of his presence, or, say, their smiles, their vivacity, or perhaps even, with the rustling of chains, the lifting of their small shackled limbs to him, begging that a bid may be made upon them?

The female from the Steel Worlds may have seldom seen another human female, unless perhaps to drive her away from the vicinity of her master, with hissing, and teeth and nails, lest she should attempt to groom him. But she would certainly in any case be acutely aware that the lovely stranger in the enclosure with her was another female, and thus an enemy, or competitor. And the English girl, aside from her confusion and consternation at finding herself as she was, unclothed, not even a thread upon her body, inexplicably confined in the small, narrow, glassine, ovoid container, within an arm's reach of a similarly confined male, would be only too aware not only of the presence of the male but of the other female, as well, who was startlingly young, beautiful, and desirable. Too, there was something about the other female that seemed somehow incomprehensibly different from the women with which she was familiar. There was something somehow animallike about her. She seemed untutoredly, rawly, primitively, radically female. Never had she encountered such a female. How could she, as a civilized creature, even stripped, compare with such a sensuous little beast? In her presence, she was acutely sensitive of her own deficiencies, her deficiencies as a female animal, one reduced to its biological essentials. A hundred transparent, inhibitory wrappings swathed her about, constricting her; a culture's tendrils and trammels had been tightened about her; she had been shaped by frowns, images, propounded exemplars, small remarks, sneers, customs, and scoldings for years, subtly taught, by a multitude of cultural stratagems of which she was scarcely aware, to belittle and discount, if not despise, the very substance of herself, the very core of her being. She had been taught that her femaleness was a matter of historical idiosyncrasy, a societal convention, a social construction, and one perhaps somewhat regrettable. It was to be understood as a fabrication peculiar to a locality, a particular place and period, something of no more than transitory significance. At best it was an unimportant contingency, irrelevant to important matters such as advancements, politics, and promotions, a contingency to be ignored, if not deplored, as much as possible, saving perhaps as it might be politically utilized to obtain unearned advantages.

And now she was naked in a container.

What a simple refutation of absurdity is nudity.

The girl from the Steel Worlds, and the girl from England, as indicated, had not been selected at random.

In particular, however, we should note that the English girl had been selected by her captors, the Priest-Kings, with particularly great care, and with all the expertise and wisdom of their advanced science, to be a match with the male in question. Each would be intensely, irresistibly attractive and desirable to the other. She would be exactly the sort of woman he would relentlessly bid upon to bring into his collar, and he would be exactly the sort of man into whose collar she would long to be locked. This matching, of course, was scarcely accidental, or gratuitous. It had its role to play in what would prove to be an interesting and remarkable, if duplicitous and guileful, gambit of Priest-Kings. Each would seem to be a gift to the other, in the most profound modalities of male/female relations, but a gift, as it turned out, which had its ulterior purposes, one intended to further the designs of Priest-Kings.

The blondishly pelted female from the Steel Worlds was the first to recover consciousness. It seems probable that she was the most lightly sedated of the three, doubtless that this might occur.

She awakened something like an Ahn before the disruption.

As she was essentially an animal she, as most animals, accepted her surroundings rather as a given, as no more or less explicable than a great number of other possible givens. A dog, on Earth, for example, accepts electric lighting without amazement, or inquiry into its nature. It is just the way his world is, in that time and place. He will, of course, as would a sleen, take cognizance of his surroundings, familiarize himself with this new territory, and such. He does not, however, wax hysterical, doubt his sanity, or such.

The first thing the little beast did was flare her nostrils, perhaps trying to catch the scent of her master. Then, gingerly, slipping, putting her hands out, she examined the peculiar barrier through which she could see, but could not pass. She examined, and took the scent of, the male confined with her. He was much larger, and somehow much different, it seemed, from the few males of her species with which she was familiar. He was quite different, of course, from her master. In her blood there were stirrings with which she was unfamiliar. Her lip wrinkled, and a canine was visible, as she inspected the other female in the container. A slight, tiny hiss of displeasure escaped from betwixt her well-formed lips. There was no pan of food or water in the container, she noted, nor could there have easily been, given its curvature. These things did not please her. There was a hoselike tube near the top of the container, but it would be difficult for her to reach it. Too, she did not understand its purpose. She put her hands to her throat, feeling for her collar, but it was not there. This puzzled her, for her master had always kept it on her. It had had a ring on it, to which he sometimes attached a leash, when he walked her. She was very proud to be walked by her master, and she did not wish to be confused with others of her species, inferior sorts, whom she despised, strays, scavengers, and such. In particular she would not wish to be confused with the cattle, crowded and fattened in their pens, for she knew they were eaten. It made her uneasy to be without the collar. Indeed, she was afraid. Sometimes catchers, small Kurii, badly pelted, only four or five hundred pounds in weight, prowled the habitat, searching for loose humans, escaped or strayed, usually to be hamstrung and put back in the barred pens, then unable to walk, unable then to do much more than feed at the troughs, fatten, and wait, usually ignorantly, for the butchers. But she was not ignorant. She was apprised of the usual fate of such. It would not do, at all, to be mistaken for one of them. It would be one thing to lead them to the knife, they following unsuspectingly, docilely, and quite another to be confused with one of them. That would not do at all. Where was her master? She wanted her collar. She felt understandably uneasy without it. Her master had had only one pet, her. Hopefully she still belonged to him. Certainly, too, she would not wish to share her importance and status with another pet. She looked angrily at the other female. She, too, of course, must be a pet. What else, as she was, could she be? She did know there were other pets. That must be one of them. She resented the other female, and feared her, and what she might mean. She snarled, softly. Her fingers crooked. Her master had had her nails clipped and filed, but even so, even had they not been, they were poor weapons, certainly compared to the claws and fangs of the masters. There could be no doubt as to the relationships involved, nor as to the rankings of species, nor as to her own nature, and the appropriateness of it, that of a harmless, caressable pet. But surely not harmless to such as herself. She could scratch and bite, and hiss, and she had, more than once, to the amusement of her master, driven other females, bloodied and shrieking, from his vicinity.

But the master was not here?

Where was he?

She did sense the maleness of the larger human in the container, and this maleness intrigued her, and fascinated her. She also had strange feelings in his presence, feelings which she had not experienced in the vicinity of the few males she had encountered in the habitat. It never occurred to her that he might have speech, for only the masters, the Kurii, had language. Animals, such as she, and others, were incapable of such things, just as they were incapable of building pens, making rooms light and dark, burning objects at a distance, and such.

They could not even make the chains and shackles in which they were sometimes so helplessly placed.

She, at least, had not yet been chained to a man.

But clearly the male in the container was the nearest thing to her master, and thus she, as any smaller animal would, had a lively sense as to where lay the power in this small world, and, accordingly, in which direction lay her best interests. It would be with the larger animal. She was unfamiliar with larger animals who had been turned against themselves, who were hampered, crippled, neutralized and vitiated by the knives of social engineering. She would not have understood them. She was certain then she must ingratiate herself with him, and appease him, and certainly so with the other female in the container. She could not drive her off, of course, given the peculiar enclosure in which she found herself, but she could certainly warn her off, and, hopefully, so terrify or intimidate her that she would not dare to offer the least challenge to her priority. The male was to be hers; the other must not be permitted to intrude; accordingly, she must, in one way or another, be eliminated, physically or psychologically, or both, as a possible competitor or rival. The female from the Steel Worlds regarded the other female. She did not think it would be hard to teach her terror, and her place. If the male were a Kur, she would groom him, smoothing and licking his fur, and searching for insects. Sometimes her master permitted her to wipe and dry his teeth with her hair, in which activity she could scavenge for meat particles. Too, not unoften he permitted her to clean his nails and claws with her tongue. These were largely hygienic pursuits. Little of a symbolic nature was involved here. She was simply a docile pet serving her master. It was quite unlike the practices of the Red Savages of the Gorean Barrens who not unoften put their white female slaves naked on their bellies before their lofty, silken mounts, the kaiila, in helpless, servile prostration to the mere beasts of their masters, whose paws and nails they must then clean with their lips and tongue. This is because of what, in their traditions, is called the Memory. Few white men are allowed in the Barrens. Commonly they are ridden down and killed. Lovely white women, on the other hand, are accepted as slaves, and are sometimes, at trading points, bartered for, usually with the skins of the Pte, or Kailiauk. Occasionally, too, they are raided for, and then carried deep within the Barrens. Sometimes they are kept in herds, guarded by boys, but normally, in their colorful, beaded leather collars, they serve in the lodges. The native women, unless prevented, treat them with great cruelty. The slaves perform much work in the Barrens and give their masters much pleasure in the lodges. Some white women flee to the Barrens, that they may become the slaves of such men.

The girl from the Steel Worlds studied the sleeping male, puzzling over her sensations.

She had never yet been chained to a man.

She wondered what it would be like, to be chained to a man.

She had seen the relevant devices, of course, on posts and

hanging in sheds, dark, stern, heavy, close-fitting shackles, breeding shackles.

She wondered what it would be like to be put in them, to be locked in them, to feel them on her body, their weight, and that of their short chains, and to be aware of their close, unslippable clasp on her small wrists and ankles, then so helplessly confined in their designed encirclements, and then to be led before a male and fastened by their means to him, himself their prisoner, as well.

She would be helpless, of course, so near to him, so close as to feel his breath, the heat of his body.

The methods of the Kurii are traditional, and perhaps primitive, but, too, they are clever and efficient.

She looked again at the male.

She did not think she would mind being chained to him.

Suddenly the girl from the Steel Worlds made a tiny, angry sound, for the other female had whimpered, and stirred, and put out her hands, as though feeling for some familiar surroundings, the edge of a bed, a pillow, a layer of covers. The other female's hand slipped on the descendent, glassine surface of the container. Her shapely legs moved, sought purchase. She squirmed. A foot moved, slipping, toward the bottom of the container. Suddenly her eyes opened, wildly, and she tried to stand, abruptly, and slipped down, toward the bottom of the container. Her belly was to the outside of the container, and, struggling to stand, but slipping, she, confused, astonished, disoriented, bewildered, shocked, pressed her hands against its thick, enclosing, transparent surface. Then suddenly, half kneeling in the container, unable to stand, she uttered a wild, incoherent scream, a cry of utter incomprehension and dismay, and shook her head, as though to awaken herself. She even struck herself on the cheek, sharply, and tore at her forearm with her nails, even to bring blood. This sudden hysterical activity and outcry on the part of her lovely container mate startled the girl from the Steel Worlds, who drew quickly back, alarmed, then perplexed, then resentful. She could not understand the distress, the consternation, the bewilderment, of the other girl. She was not behaving as would one of her species, as the Steel Worlds' girl understood such things. This was not the way a pet would be expected to behave. Presumably a master would not care to have a pet behave in such a fashion, and would punish it. She was perhaps a poor pet. Surely she was an unusual pet. She did not even snarl at the Steel Worlds' girl or attempt to challenge her. She seemed unaware of her surroundings save in so far as her occupancy in the container was concerned. She struck against the sides of the container, and pounded on them, sobbing, with her small fists, and cried out, as though in protest, or disbelief, or to attract someone's attention. But the corridor, of course, was empty, and silent.

Whereas the surprise of the Steel Worlds' girl at this seemingly unmotivated and unaccountable behavior on the part of the other female is understandable, given her background and experiences, I think that it will be in general comprehensible for most of us, and presumably for the majority of our readers, particularly those in the habitats. It was not unusual, at any rate, for a civilized female, to the extent that such are civilized, suddenly confronted with a seemingly inexplicable transformation in her circumstances and condition, to behave in a manner which suggests bewilderment and alarm. Although we are not certain just how the Priest-Kings manage these things, we may presume they are not altogether unlike the practices of our human confederates. Whereas they enjoy utilizing a number of securing devices, ropings, thongings, traps, and such, and a variety of interesting psychological techniques, in acquiring and orienting their wares, some of which are extremely enjoyable and sophisticated, their most common procedure is a simple one, merely to sedate the unsuspecting female while sleeping, and then to strip and bind her, and then transport her to the collection point, for shipment in her waiting capsule. She is not revived, commonly, unless they wish to enjoy her on the voyage, until she is on Gor, commonly in the house of a slaver. In short, she retires, unsuspecting, in the midst of her familiar surroundings, and awakens in a quite unfamiliar reality, both ambient and personal. This pertains not only to the women of Earth, of course, but may pertain as well to the women of Gor.

There is much to be said, I am told, for both varieties. Gorean men enjoy both. Originally, Earth females on Gor tended to have about them something of an aspect of luscious exotica. Barbarians, the stupid sluts could not even speak Gorean, the language. To many Gorean males this seemed almost incomprehensible, but, we note, many languages are spoken on Gor, though obviously, because of the standardizations agreed upon by the caste of Scribes, meeting at the great fairs, Gorean is the most common. Also, it is thought that the Priest-Kings wish to have a single language at their disposal by means of which they can address themselves to almost any human likely to be encountered on their world. Now, however, with the relative commonness of Earth females in the Gorean markets, they have lost much of their erstwhile exotic flavor. Often they are now regarded, and particularly by slaves of native Gorean origin, as merely an inferior sort of slave. But men like them. That is doubtless the reason they are not as rare on Gor as formerly. They sell well. Too, it seems they make superb slaves, grateful, devoted, sexually helpless, passionate chattels. On Earth it seems their sexual needs were suppressed in favor of various neuterisms and political expediencies, and sacrificed to a variety of peculiar societal imperatives. They were, in short, for whatever reasons, taught to suspect and deny their sexuality, and see it, if at all, in terms of guilt and fear. They were taught, too, to see men as weaklings and inept adversaries, not surprising given the crippling social engineering to which most Earth males were subjected almost from the cradle, and not as their natural masters. They sensed, of course, the meaninglessness and emptiness of their existence, the tragic, profound lacunae in their lives, that a female can obtain the wholeness of her nature and being only in relation to a dominant male, and that she can find her ultimate sexual fulfillment only in the earthquakes and blasts of a helpless, surrendered slave, one writhing in the arms of her master. On Earth women were starved; on Gor they are fed, be it only on scraps of food thrown to a slave. It is the paradox of the collar; in it, a helpless slave, she is most free. To be sure, the lot of an Earth slave on Gor, as that of any slave, is not an easy one. Too, it might be noted that some Gorean men, apprised of what is termed the "Second Knowledge," have some understanding of what is done to men on Earth and how they are commonly treated. Accordingly, their treatment of Earth females is likely to be excessively severe, requiring of them, however irrationally, an atonement for the faults and crimes of their sex on their former, sorry world. Such girls are swiftly apprised of the nature of their collars. They soon learn they are no longer on Earth, dealing with the men of Earth, but are on Gor, at the mercy of Gorean men. They are now no longer a woman of Earth but merely a female on Gor and a man's helpless, perfect, and complete slave.

Different techniques are used to introduce women to their new life, and these often depend on the house. Sometimes they are revived in slave wagons en route to one destination or another, that they may have time to adjust; or the tiered cages might be used; or a simple chaining, with others, in a keeping room. Some are awakened to the lash. Others are given time to adjust, even days, in a darkened cell, chained by the neck, with water and gruel. It should be remarked that few women are promptly sold. Most are given some training first. That helps them to survive. Many Earth women, for example, do not even know how to lace a man's sandals or bathe him. It would seem absurd to lash them for such ignorances as their culture has not prepared them to perform such tasks. To be sure, such deficiencies must be quickly rectified, and the whip will be utilized to encourage diligence.

Sometimes, however, our human confederates, for their amusement, alert the quarry, sometimes months in advance, and perhaps hint by hint, of her ineluctable fate. Most commonly this is done with a quarry which is unpleasant, smug, nasty, insolent and vain, and who has, too, say, an overweening sense of her own qualities, importance, and superiority. To be sure, she must be intelligent, beautiful, healthy, and so on, or she will be ignored. Too, as would be expected, she must also be the sort who can be easily made the writhing, helpless victim of her profound, if initially suppressed, sexual needs. Such a quarry, at first, usually, misinterprets the clues she is given, however obvious they may be, with respect to the network of plans within which she is already enmeshed. Perhaps a set of measurements, her own, is slipped beneath her door, interestingly pertaining in particular to her wrists, ankles, and throat, or perhaps, even more obviously, she is sent a tunic in the mail, a slave tunic. To be sure, at that time she understands it only as a brief, revealing garment. Perhaps she dares to don it secretly, and then, startled at how she appears in it, and flushing with embarrassing, unaccustomed heat, she hides it away. To be sure, it may later be thrown against her body. In time, however, as the net tightens, things will become ever more obvious. She will receive messages, and calls, which are quite clear, but will be interpreted, naturally enough, as impostures, jests, and hoaxes, or even insults. Examples would be such things as "Simple custodial hardware consists of ankle and wrist rings, and, of course, a collar. We have your measurements for such," "The tunic you received in the mail was a slave tunic. You may find yourself in one, if your master permits it," or even things as obvious as, "You may begin, even now, to think of yourself as a Gorean slave," or "Be careful in your diet and see that you exercise well, that you may be more likely to obtain an affluent master when you are sold, from a slave block on the planet Gor." To be sure, she believes that there is no such place as Gor. It is embarrassing to bring these things to the attention of the police, but she eventually does. But they are more bemused than helpful. She does, of course, inquire into the nature of Gor, and begins to have a sense of the nature of the fate which might await her there, a young, beautiful female of Earth. Her beauty she had always until now bartered to her own advantage, utilizing it, with its smiles, and gestures, and turnings, to obtain the perquisites of Earth. Now she begins to suspect that its value might substantially accrue to the benefit of others, that others, and not she, might have their profit upon it. It would seem to have little value to herself now, save as it might procure her a better master or a lighter bondage. But she has learned in her reading, to her consternation, that Gorean men are not lenient with such as she would be, an embonded Earth female. Might her charms then, and her tricks and wheedling, so irresistible on Earth, be unavailing on Gor? Might they even bring her an impatient stroke of the switch or lash? Finally, one morning, she awakens, discreetly attired in her lovely night gown, just as when she retired, though it is now thrust up to her thighs, to discover that her ankles have been tied widely apart, with leather thongs, to the bottom bedposts. She frees herself, though with tears of frustration and difficulty, and rises, and rushes about, frantically, but she finds that she is alone in the apartment, and the doors and windows are locked. There is a note on the dresser. With a trembling hand she opens and reads it. It is written in a powerful, cursive masculine script, suggesting severity and the nonexistence of compromise:

Female:
Rejoice. In spite of your many deficiencies and your

unworthiness, it has been decided that you will be taken to Gor, there to be sold as a slave.

We trust that you enjoyed having your legs tied apart. You will grow used to such things on Gor.

You belong in a collar. Therefore, you will be put in one.

Flee, if you wish.

You cannot escape.

In the field, in the early morning, you will remove your clothing and kneel, and lift your wrists to us, to be braceleted.

Hasdron, of Gor.

In such a case the female often does, as was so in this case, flee. Then began a nightmare of fear and pursuit, when time and time again she thought herself secure, and having escaped, only to be confronted with a new evidence of the proximity, seemingly ever more closely, of those who followed her. At last, early one morning, in an open field, trembling, shaking, chilled, exhausted, unable to run further, she sees them about her, discernible in the half light and fog of the early morning. Defeated, she numbly removes her clothing and kneels in the cold grass, frightened, lifting her wrists to them. It is the first time she has worn slave bracelets. A collar and leash is then put on her and she is drawn to her feet and led to a waiting van. In this vehicle her leash is attached to a sturdy wall ring, only a few inches from the floor, and she is put to her side, to be given the injection which will render her unconscious, an unconsciousness which will be ended only with her awakening on Gor.

But let us return now to the container of Tarl Cabot.

The English girl continued, for a time, to pound on the obdurate side of the container. Too, she tried to call out, for a time, but, being highly intelligent, soon realized that her cries might not be heard outside the thick glassine barrier within which she found herself enclosed.

Shortly thereafter, she seemed to understand, perhaps in part from her distraught reflection in the barrier, with a sudden, poignant and alarmed fullness of realization, her complete lack of covering, and she became, too, then, perhaps for the first time, more acutely aware that she was not alone in the container. She turned about and looked wildly at the unconscious male, who had just begun to stir, perhaps aroused by her actions and cries, which might have seemed far off to him, and at the blonde female. She tried to put her legs together and cover herself with her hands, frenziedly, an activity which puzzled the blonde. Perhaps she was trying to protect herself from blows, not yet delivered? The blonde could understand that. She began to speak to the blonde but the blonde, of course, had no language, and her noises would have been unintelligible to her. Doubtless, trying to cover herself, she must have been demanding at the same time some sort of explanation from the blonde, an account of their common predicament. The blonde however, to the brunette's dismay, and trepidation, wrinkled her lip and snarled at her, much as might have an animal, a displeased, threatening animal. She shrank back, and this pleased the blonde, who raised her hand, menacingly, clawlike. The brunette shrank back then even further, frightened, until her back was against the glassine wall. Clearly the blonde was in some way less than human, or mad. The blonde made a rumbling noise in her throat, reminiscent of a Kur's warning growl, and the brunette, alarmed, pressed back even more tightly against the wall. There was something inhuman about the blonde, something feral, and dangerous. She tried to smile at her, but this brought forth only a more intense warning noise. She began then to speak soothingly to the blonde, as one might attempt to pacify a beast, perhaps an ocelot or small leopard, but this merely elicited an angry hiss. The brunette then remained very still, watching the blonde, fearfully. The blonde, for her part, was pleased that the other creature was intimidated. Indeed, she had expected a counterdisplay of hostility, and an exchange of hissings, and spittings, as with others, until they were beaten and torn, and fled away, bitten and bleeding. The other pet then, from the point of view of the blonde, was an unbelievably poor thing, spiritless, and without fight. Was she not confined in the container the blonde would have fully expected, with another snarl, that she would have fainted, or backed away, and then suddenly turned about, and fled. That pet, she was sure, would not be worth a collar. Better to put her in with the cattle, in the pens. She could imagine her, looking out through the bars. To be sure, she might count as a tender morsel for her master.

The blonde had not even understood that the brunette had tried to communicate with her in a language. Only the Kurii, as far as she knew, had a language. The other pet just made strange noises. Did she not even know how to whimper, for food, or a caress, or for mercy?

The blonde thought she would show her mercy, if she would stay out of her way, and have nothing to do with the male.

Otherwise she might lose her eyes.

The blonde was not the sort of pet who would happily share a food pan, or a master.

The brunette was confused, disoriented, frightened, and sick with misery.

Also, she was terrified of the blonde, who did not seem human, but something different, something wild and feral in a human form.

Too, she had never encountered anything so innocently, and rawly, so naively, and so primitively female before. The creature exuded a sexuality which she could scarcely comprehend. The brunette was, of course, too, a female, but, aside from her dreams, in which she was often well and callously handled, and as a female, and in some of which she even wore a slave collar, she chose, on the whole, save for certain gratifying, manipulative ambivalences, some of which may be noted later, to see herself, and to behave as, and strive to be, a witty, clever, urbane, discriminating, tasteful, lofty, superior, refined, educated, largely, it must be admitted, sexless entity, a person to whom sex then was meaningless, or, at least, irrelevant and unimportant. She was an individual, then, of staid culture, tedious civility, tiresome refinement, and an insufferable, snobbish gentility. She refused the attentions of men, or boys, when they were offered, unless they were of an acceptable, suitable background and class. One must be careful about such things. On her rare dates she would remain aloof and remind her companions, when necessary, in quite clear terms, to their chagrin, of her dignities and their correspondent duties. Sometimes, however, she wondered what it would be to be in their arms. But such thoughts were soon thrust away, indignantly, or almost indignantly. She was quite pleased with her social station and irritatingly vain concerning what she took to be, mistakenly, as it turned out, the excellence of her breeding. To be sure, in some respects, her breeding was indeed excellent, for it had been selected out by the Priest-Kings, for, in particular, certain of its dispositions and helplessnesses. For their purposes, then, at least, it was an excellent breeding. Too, of course, it was an excellent breeding for general human purposes, as well, as suggested, for she was highly intelligent, beautiful, and such. Too, she would prove to have sexual latencies of a sort which, once ignited, once commanded forth, would put her helplessly, beggingly, needfully, ungovernably, uncontrollably, at the sexual mercy of men. She would need their touch and attentions. But that is not uncommon with a certain sort of woman. Goreans are familiar with them. They are called slaves. I think I mentioned that had our human confederates known of her she would have been selected for their purposes, and would eventually have found herself suitably auctioned, as would be appropriate for her. Her diction was precise, but distant and aloof. One had the sense that they were being talked down to. She would later learn to speak softly, modestly, and humbly, when she was given permission to speak. She commonly dressed with a seemingly understated but yet all too obvious elegance. She was cool, prim, priggish, and formal. Yet, beneath her clothing, if one looked closely, it could be discerned that she might be attractive. And when she was stripped, this became clear.

The brunette, shuddering, put her face in her hands, tears streaming through her fingers, and wondered if she had gone insane.

At this point, only several minutes before the disruption, the male in the container, the prisoner, Tarl Cabot, opened his eyes.

We do not know how long he had been awake, but presumably it had not been long. Yet we are sure he was awake somewhat before he permitted this to be understood.

He was, after all, of the Warriors.

He had an active mind, and was, of course, by now quite familiar with the nature of his confinement. Therefore he would not have been startled or dismayed at finding himself as he was, in the container, but would have doubtless been more surprised had he not found himself so. His concerns, therefore, had more to do with trying to fathom the designs of his captors. For what reason was he now not alone in the container, and why with these two particular creatures?

He had not been informed, of course, by Priest-Kings of his

inadvertence, error or crime. This is not unusual. Would you inform, say, an insect, or small animal, found annoying, of the reasons for your displeasure? You would, presumably, simply deal with it, and as you pleased. Surely the Flame Death does not explain itself, but simply strikes. But in certain cases, with rational creatures, this lack of communication is deliberate, and calculated to unravel, so to speak, its victim, who, perplexed and frightened, is denied an accounting of his alleged faults or charges. He is plunged then into confusion, dismay, and, not unoften, is overcome by a sense of unlocalized, nebulous guilt. Such techniques, incidentally, are not unknown on Earth, or in some of the Steel Worlds. But Tarl Cabot had, it seemed, surmised, and correctly, that his predicament was occasioned by his intervention in the strife between the Steel Worlds and the world of the Priest-Kings, Gor, an intervention in which he had sought to warn and succor a Kur, Zarendargar, or "Half-Ear." Too, largely on account of this intervention, it was supposed, and certainly with some plausibility, that he was an agent of Kurii. And such things are not condoned by Priest-Kings, nor, indeed, would their like be condoned by Kurii, who have a variety of interesting techniques for dealing with supposed traitors, techniques which we shall omit to delineate, on the grounds that they might be found disturbing by readers with whom they might be unfamiliar. Doubtless the Priest-Kings have their techniques, as well. And we suspect they could hardly be inferior in effectiveness to those of the Kurii. To be sure, given his codes, Tarl Cabot would be less encouraged to indulge in fruitless speculation and laborious self-searching than biding his time, attempting to obtain a weapon, plotting an escape, and such. The codes encourage attention to the future and action, rather than to the past and speculation. The exceptions commonly have to do with matters of honor and vengeance.

Largely, certainly after the few first days, or was it hours, in the container, Tarl Cabot had been curious as to why he was being kept alive. He had not yet been slain. Why? Indeed, had they wished to slay him, they might have done so long ago, doubtless within moments of his discovery. Certainly he was totally at the mercy of his captors. He might have been denied the liquid food dispensed now and then through the tube, a poisonous gas might have been introduced into the container, rather than the sedating gas, the air might have been simply drawn from the container, and so on. Indeed, a number of things might have been done to him. Who knows, say, what might have been introduced into the container while he slept, which might have satisfied the sense of vengeance of outraged Priest-Kings, perhaps a coil of squirming osts, a live sleen, successions of urts each time he slept, which he might try to kill, and on which might feed, until eventually, from pain and loss of blood, days later, unable to resist, he became the feed. Perhaps, even, the container might have been slowly filled with mud or sand, or with fast-growing poisonous molds, or with dark water, in which swam the tiny, razor-teethed eels kept in large pools at the palatial villas of some Gorean oligarchs, both as a delicacy, and as a standing admonition to slaves, to which swift, snakelike, voracious creatures they may be thrown. He was being kept alive for some reason, but for what reason?

The Priest-Kings, it seemed, were not yet done with him.

Perhaps he was being saved for some holiday, some celebration, in which he might be used as a spectacle.

Certainly they had not forgotten about him, as is sometimes the case with prisoners in Gorean dungeons.

They were Priest-Kings.

Too, he was now not alone in the container.

Clearly he was recollected.

For what purposes were the females introduced into his tiny world, and why these particular females?

The blonde whimpered, and licked at his shoulder.

The brunette, trying desperately to keep herself covered, as she could, gasped. She had witnessed this simple act in utter disbelief. Her inadvertent exhalation had been one of astonishment and shock, of indignation and disapproval, one of protest, even outrage. And yet the act frightened her, because she felt its reality, and physicality. It seemed one of the most real things she had ever witnessed in her life. It spoke not of ideas and theories, or verbalisms, or of the fencings and cant in which she had sought to perfect herself, of the skills which brought status in her world, but of a different world, one of which she knew but little, one in which she had little part, one in which she did not belong, one in which she would be neglected and ignored, a world of rain and wind, and grass, and beasts, and sunlight, one of life, not of its contrived substitutes.

Whereas she was doubtless shocked at what she had seen she was also, in a sense, moved. Perhaps she thought of herself, as in one of her dreams, so licking a male's shoulder, perhaps commanded to do so, in precisely that subservient manner. Several times she had awakened in her bed, from such dreams, twisted in the covers, heated and thrashing, tormented by sensations that seemed to enliven and enfire every cubic inch of her, and turn her skin into a mottled sheet of living flame. At such times the smallest touch of a male, or even a smile, would have brought her begging to his feet. Sometimes she had fearfully, so awakening, felt her wrists and ankles, and her throat, making certain that her small, fair limbs were not thonged, and her lovely neck not encircled by a man's claiming collar.

The slut clearly had promise.

The Priest-Kings had done their job well.

The male seemed not to notice her, not truly then, but turned to the blonde, and apparently spoke to her. Doubtless he did so in Gorean. She seemed startled that such seemingly articulate sounds should emanate from a human. She tried to imitate them, but managed, one supposes, to do little more than replicate a handful of disjointed phonemes. He seemed puzzled at her response. He did not understand, of course, at that time, that she, whatever might be her native intelligence, which was surely considerable, lacked speech, and for a very obvious reason. It had never been taught to her. Presumably he first thought her simply differently spoken, and that they had no language in common. But he soon discounted this speculation as she did not seem to speak to him in a different language, hers, but seemed rather to be trying to make his own sort of sounds. He did not think she was retarded because she had a lively, seemingly perceptive sense about her, and she repeated a number of his sounds with an alacrity and accuracy that suggested, rather, an agile, quick mind. Too, she could not be deaf, or a mute. Clearly she was not mute for she could utter sound, and she could not have been deaf, for she produced many of his sounds, though not all, with surprising fidelity. He then supposed, as we later learned, that she must be a Gorean exotic, in this case a slave who has been raised without a language. It did not occur to him at the time that she was from the Steel Worlds.

He then turned his attention to the brunette who, frightened, not meeting his eyes, flushing scarlet, every inch of her, turned frantically away from him, her side to the glassine barrier, covering as she could the sweetness of her bosom with her small hands.

She was well-curved.

He assumed she must be a slave, as she was enclosed with him. Certainly her curves were worthy of an auction block, at least in a minor city. He did not understand why she strove so mightily, essentially so futilely, to conceal herself from him. That was not like a slave. No slave, aware of the lash, would dare such a thing. Yet here, surely, the pretty thing, the nicely curved little slut, must be a slave.

He had looked, of course, upon many slaves. But this one seemed unusual, in many respects. Her demeanor was odd. She was trying to shield herself, however ineffectively, from his scrutiny. She could be punished for that. And she had not performed an obeisance, nor had she addressed him in Gorean. As she was in the container, it had not occurred to him that she might be a free woman. It had not even occurred to him to see her as a free woman, robed in dignities, a citizeness, entitled to respect and deference. He saw her instantly, doubtless as the Priest-Kings had intended, in terms of the brand and collar, in terms of shackles and the whip, in terms of the auction block and cage. She was the sort of woman a man would put joyously, triumphantly, to his feet. She was far too beautiful and desirable to be free. Freedom was not for such as she. She was the sort of woman a man would not accept, except upon the terms of absolute and complete ownership.

You could look upon her, and see she was a natural slave.

The man who does not see natural slaves as slaves is a fool. They are slaves, and are whole only at a man's feet.

She decided she would turn her head to him, pleadingly. Surely he must understand her distress, her fear, her confusion, her consternation, her predicament!

The blond uttered a menacing, soft growl.

The brunette shuddered, frightened of the other female.

But, too, suddenly, instinctively, she understood where might lie her one hope, her single protection, from the hostility of the other girl.

It would lie with this taciturn, supple, naked, powerful man.

Never before had she depended on a male for anything.

She was acutely conscious of her nudity.

Perhaps she could smile at him.

She was in no way unaware of her effect on males, and had often, shamelessly, pleasurably, made use of her sex to tease, torment, and exploit them, even while pretending to a sexless neutrality, putting forth then a charade of impartial personhood which was only too obviously, to an astute observer, belied by the subliminal signals she was at pains to project, and the tumults and furies they inevitably kindled, to which she would then, were they manifested, react with surprise and indignation.

We earlier alluded, as I recall, to such aspects of her persona.

The males with which she was familiar were easily manipulated. A clever woman, particularly if lovely, could do with them rather as she pleased.

They were, of course, not Goreans.

Suddenly their eyes met.

Directly.

Fully.

She did not smile, as she had intended. She could not. Her lower lip trembled. She was profoundly startled.

She had not expected this.

What manner of eyes were these?

She trembled, and if she had tried to speak, she would have stammered, helplessly.

But she could not speak.

And she felt that if he had spoken to her in some settings, the rug in a Tuareg tent, the tiles of a Roman villa, she would have instantly knelt before him, and pressed her lips fervently, placatingly, to his feet.

She found herself looking into the eyes of a dominant male, for the first time in her life, into the eyes of a man who was by nature the master of such as she, a woman.

This could not be, she thought, a man of Earth.

These surely did not seem the eyes of a man of Earth. In them reposed resolution, and power.

Before them she felt small, helpless, vulnerable, female, and weak.

Never before had she felt like this before a man, so graspable, so weak, so female.

She felt him a thousand times her superior.

And what only could such as she be to such as he?

She suspected she knew.

Where had she seen such eyes before?

Could it have been in her dreams?

Then she sensed herself surveyed.

She shuddered.

But certainly more was involved here than merely the eyes of a dominant male, regarding a female.

To be sure, that in itself might have been shocking to her, to find herself looked upon as one might look upon a property, something desirable that one might own, and would be appropriately owned, but a great deal more was involved. We recall that she had been selected as a match for the particular male in question, and that, thus, they would find themselves irresistibly and excruciatingly attractive to one another. She was, in effect, a slut he might pursue in dreams, and he was to her, too, in her dreams, one to whose feet such as she would hasten, to kneel, and press her warm, moist lips upon them, hoping to be found pleasing. She seemed to him one for whose throat was made his collar, and he to her as one for whose collar her throat was made.

She found these moments, these sudden sensations and feelings, unprecedented and inexplicable, suffusive, shocking, overwhelming.

She had the sudden sense she belonged in a collar, a slave collar, and that such as she was the rightful property of such as he.

And he, too, though this was much concealed, looked upon this frightened, shapely, stripped beast with remarkable intentness.

There was little doubt as to her suitability.

Such women are made for the slave block.

It is wholly right for them.

They belong upon it, to be taken from it by masters.

What would it be to have her at his feet?

How startling, he thought, that so extraordinarily attractive and luscious a slut should be before him.

And how unique and special she somehow seemed!

He was pleased with the look of her.

She had promise.

The limbs of such women call for chains, their throats for collars. They are whole only at the feet of a man.

And here, as she was, she must be a slave!

He must have her, he thought.

On the outside he would doubtless have brought her quickly to his chains.

But then, suddenly, he grew suspicious.

How unlikely that this female should be in the container! Many were beautiful slaves, and it would not be hard to find them on Gor. He had been a man of wealth and power, even a captain, with many ships, in Port Kar, and had lusted for and possessed many branded beauties, acquiring them and discarding them in the markets as he pleased. But this female was surely amongst the small number of those he had found most tormentingly desirable. She was one of the most exciting sluts he had ever seen. Everything about her seemed to beg to be possessed, to be mastered. The Priest-Kings could have placed any of thousands of collar sluts in the container. But this one seemed special to him, as though tailored from his dreams. Perhaps, he thought, she had been! Might not the Priest-Kings, with their wizardry, have inquired into such things, and perhaps, in the female's case, too, might they not have accessed her own needs, fantasies, and dreams?

This match, he suddenly suspected, is too close, too well done.

In this, he speculated angrily, is seen the hand of Priest-Kings.

I must be on my guard!

The girl, meanwhile, was struggling to regain her former sense of self, somehow lost before this man. But it seemed dashed, and irrecoverable.

She thought of herself in his arms and had the sudden sense she would oil and leap within his arms as no more than a helpless, manipulated toy, as not other than a meaningless slave.

Then she strove to discard such radical and disturbing thoughts.

All the shallow, torrential, withering blasts of her former life rose up before her, outraged and denunciatory.

She had always had power as a female. She would now exert it. Men were weaklings.

She smiled at the brute in the container.

Clearly he might protect her from the other female, whom she feared.

He did not smile back.

This disconcerted her.

Her smiles had always proved a successful coin on her old world, easily purchasing accommodations and favors.

But he seemed to see through its falseness.

He spoke to her, it seemed not pleasantly, and doubtless in Gorean, for she shook her head, negatively, indicating her lack of comprehension. Then she spoke to him, hoping doubtless that she might somehow be understood. She doubtless spoke to him in an English, that of one of the Englands aforementioned. For the first time she detected a distinct reaction in her reticent, supple interlocutor. He had clearly not expected her to be conversant in that language, which is seldom heard on Gor. It was in his own native language, as it turned out, much to his astonishment, that he was addressed. This instantly exacerbated his suspicions. Tarl Cabot is not, we note, natively Gorean. I am told he speaks Gorean with an accent, but such subtleties seem to me neither here nor there. There are many accents, I am told, too, even amongst native Goreans. In any event, the fact that the female spoke his native tongue, as well as the hitherto noted excellencies of her face and figure, which seemed customized, so to speak, to his own tastes, informed him, as he had suspected, that her presence, and doubtless, too, that of the blonde, in the container, was not a matter of mere happenstance, but had some role to play in the designs of Priest-Kings. Certainly he did not think, as we had originally supposed, that they were some sort of gift to him, or even a mere concession to one of his appetites.

The woman meanwhile, finding herself understood, shook with emotion, and, sobbing with unspeakable relief, eagerly, gratefully, neglecting to request permission, began to speak, enunciating what must have been a torrent of solicitations, questions, inquiries, demands, protests, and such, which was surely understandable. She was doubtless trying to explain, too, that some terrible mistake had been made, that there must be someone to whom to appeal, and so on. The fact that she had not requested permission to speak, at least at such length, doubtless seemed anomalous to Tarl

Cabot. It was almost as though she might be a free woman, and not a slave. But he was tolerant, at least for a time, of her effusive excesses, doubtless taking into consideration her confusion and dismay, given her presumably recent entrapment and her present circumstances. There is a time, of course, to show a woman kindliness, compassion, and understanding, and then a time to put her to her knees and remind her that she is only a slave. Tarl Cabot, as he could, tried to answer the woman's questions, and apprise her to the best of his ability of the nature of her location, the identity of her captors, and such. There was much, to be sure, that was unknown to him, as well. At one point, she shook her head wildly, and then, a few moments later, apprising herself of the gravity, and more clearly of the nature of her surroundings, she threw back her head and apparently screamed in misery and terror, though one could not hear her outside the container. It had been made clear to her, it seems, that she was no longer on Earth, but was a captive of beings alien to her, in an artificial satellite of a planet she had not even known existed, the Prison Moon. She then began to sob hysterically, trying to keep herself covered, as before. Tarl Cabot could not only see her, but, now and then, given the lighting, could see her reflection, as well, in the barrier behind her. Gradually, despite the improbability of the matter, he began to suspect that she might not be a slave. To her horror he pulled her hands apart and placed them, fingers locked, behind the back of her head. She immediately removed them from this location but when he lifted his hand, irritably, and was obviously prepared to cuff her, sharply, as though she might be naught but a recalcitrant little brute, she quickly replaced them, putting them into the position he had prescribed. Her eyes were wide. It was doubtless the first time she had ever been subjected to discipline. She had strange feelings, being under a man's will.

She was then handled, and turned about, for he was looking for slave brands. The most common site for such, recommended in Merchant Law, is high on the left thigh, under the hip. But there are other sites, as well. As the polities of Gor are largely scattered and independent there is, as would be expected, some variation in brands. The most common types are the staff and fronds, and the Dina, resembling a small and common flower of that world. Various cities, too, have their brands, such as Treve, and Ar, and some populations, as well, such as those of the nomadic Wagon Peoples. The white female slaves of the Red Savages of the Barrens are not branded. Being white in that area, it is understood they are slaves. Their colorful, beaded collars, however, identify their masters.

The brunette was not accustomed to being handled so, as might be a slave. But she did not object, perhaps for fear of being struck, or perhaps for another reason, having to do with surprising and unexpected sensations. He did not test her slave reflexes, though, had he done so, he might have found them such as would considerably raise her price in a market. To her misery and chagrin she found herself waiting and hoping that he, this unusual man, would touch her intimately, but he did not do so. Had he done so, she feared she might have cried out, softly, gratefully, and squirmed with pleasure, and was this so different from a slave?

The blonde, while all this was proceeding, had been profoundly puzzled. It seemed that these two humans, members of her own species, actually communicated with one another, rather as did the Kurii. That such creatures should be able to do this, that they should have a language, had been hitherto beyond her ken. Now, enflamed with curiosity, and sensing amazing and unforeseen horizons, she longed to speak, as well. When Tarl Cabot had positioned the brunette the blonde, instantly, to please him, had straightened her body and placed her own hands, fingers interlocked, behind the back of her head. Too, when he turned toward her, she did her best, of her own accord, to turn about for him, that he examine her as he had the other.

Tarl Cabot indicated that the blonde might lower her hands, and she did so. She tried to press herself against him, but he gently pushed her back. She uttered a small protestive whimper, but drew back.

The brunette, too, lowered her hands, but, at the male's frown, returned them to the position behind her head.

He was not too pleased with her.

It annoyed him that she would attempt to cover herself. It was too much like a free woman.

The brunette blushed, wholly, but kept her hands, fingers interlocked, behind the back of her head.

It is a common examination position. It lifts the bosom nicely, and keeps the hands from interfering with the examination, in both its visual and tactile dimensions. If she had been standing on an examination platform it would be usual for her legs to be placed widely apart.

He regarded her, and she looked away.

She tried to look away, as though indifferently, but we fear she failed to do so. She recalled his hands on her body, handling her as though she might have been an animal. Never had she had an experience of that sort. And she had dared not protest. She had the sense that he would do with her as he wanted. He had handled her as though she might be the least, the most worthless, the most unimportant, the most contemptible, the most meaningless, and the most desirable, of human females, the female slave. Too, she was well aware of how she might appear to him, in her present position. The thought crossed her mind that the men she had known on earth, and had so despised, would have been delighted to see her so. She thought of herself placed so before them, helpless, completely subject to a masculine will. Would they have rushed to afford her succor? No. How amused rather, and pleased, they would have been! What a pleasant vengeance on her they would have found in this! And she was aware, displayed, too, that she was now suffused with unfamiliar feelings and sensations. She found them disturbing and, in their way, frightening. She feared to speculate on their nature.

Tarl Cabot crouched in the container, and reflected. It had seemed clear to him that the two females, given their attractiveness and their placement in the container, must be slaves.

Yet, clearly, they were not collared, nor, as far as he could discern, were they branded.

Commonly a slave is both branded and collared. The brand identifies its wearer as a slave; the collar also identifies its wearer as a slave but it, too, commonly, bears a legend, or identifies the master, or such. A typical legend might be something like "I am Margaret, the slave of Rutilius, of Venna."

Not all slaves, of course, are branded and collared.

Tarl Cabot supposed that the blonde might be an exotic, in this case a slave raised without a language.

He was more puzzled, and a great deal more uneasy, in the case of the brunette.

Surely she must be a slave!

But there were so many anomalies in her behavior, her attempts to cover herself, the absence of lovely symbolisms of servitude, such as obeisances, her failure to request permission to speak, her general lack of deference, and so on.

Slaves may lie, of course, but it is extremely dangerous for them to do so. It is expected that they will speak the truth. They do not have the liberty of the free woman to deceive and dissimulate, to conceal the truth, or twist it and deny it, as they please.

It then occurred to him, in fury, what must be the plan of Priest-Kings.

Neither woman, he then suspected, was a slave!

He had been placed in the container with two beautiful free females, and his codes, his honor.

It seemed likely to him, you see, at that point, that the blonde, too, must be free, perhaps a freed slave.

The Priest-Kings doubtless counted on this natural surmise.

He was to be torn then between his nature and his codes, between his passion and his honor.

Sooner or later, rather as a starving man put in with food, he would feed, and would then in this way betray his codes.

Then, humiliated, lost to honor, broken as a warrior and man, shamed and degraded, mocked, they might do with him as they pleased, perhaps doing away with him in some grisly, amusing fashion on some holiday, or even turning him loose, if they wished, naked in some wilderness, to live as he could with himself and his dishonor, a dishonor doubtless to be broadcast, from city to city, amongst those of the warrior caste.

He then, in anger, addressed his question to the brunette, who, for a time, scarcely understood its import. The question seemed to her incomprehensible. Her world had not prepared her to even understand such a question. On her world, as far as she knew, slavery did not even exist, or certainly not, at least, in areas with which she was familiar, and certainly not with such as she. Had she not made clear to him her wealth, her standing, her position, her class, her breeding? Too, could he not see that she was fair? She was not such as would be enslaved! She was not such as could be enslaved! Her, in a collar, never! She was not a brown or dusky lass!

He then let her lower her arms, and she covered her lovely breasts, and turned away from him. She was furious and shamed, but, too, she then thought of herself as a slave, and what it might be to be a slave. Had she not, in her dreams, in thongs and chains, often enough, lifted her body fearfully, beseechingly, to strong, silent men bearing whips?

So, she was not, and presumably neither was the other, the blonde, a slave.

The brunette's denials of her collaring, and her insistence on her status as a free woman, once she even understood what he was asking, had been violent and intense, even hysterical. The very thought that she might be a slave, such an abjectly debased and degraded thing, had seemingly been found insulting, demeaning, and outrageously offensive.

Tarl Cabot leaned back in the container.

He had not expected the intensity of her response to his question. It had been surprisingly emotional, the tearful hysteria of her denials of bondage, the agitation and near frenzy with which she enunciated her claims to be a free woman.

He found such things of interest.

He smiled.

Clearly a nerve had been touched. Some sensitivity, seemingly, had here been somehow engaged.

But he thought no more of it at the time. It was the sort of thing which might well be left to an inward dialogue, say, that between a girl and her pillow, or her secret self.

It was not that he accepted uncritically the brunette's denials of bondage, of course, so much as that the supposition of her freedom seemed to best explain, and best cohere with, a hundred small details of her temperament and behavior. And even more to the point, if she, and the other, were free, this suddenly illuminated why they should have been inserted into his small, glassine world. They were neither gifts nor commonplace sexual provender, but torture devices, wherewith to despoil him of his honor, and perhaps his sanity.

Slave girls may be used as men please. It is what they are for. But these were free women.

There were the codes.

Female slavery is quite common on Gor, for men enjoy owning

women, as they might other domestic animals, but not every woman at every time stands for every man within the rights of the capture loop.

A female, for example, who is within the rights of the capture loop for one man may well not be within such rights for another.

For example, whereas I am not clear on the nature of "Home Stones," or their meaning, if any, it would be unusual, as I understand it, for a woman to be enslaved by a man with whom she shares a Home Stone. She might, of course, be enslaved for vagrancy, misdemeanors, or crimes. Too, it is generally accepted that a man may enslave a woman who has insulted him or in some way treated him badly, but this option is seldom acted upon, it seems, if a Home Stone is shared. Interestingly, Gorean free women are commonly proud, haughty, insolent, arrogant and outspoken. They often treat males with contempt and ridicule. One supposes then that they are relying on the assumed protection of a common Home Stone. Or perhaps it is their way of, as it is said, "courting the collar." In any event there are considerable differences between the Gorean free woman and the Gorean slave girl, for example, in attitude, speech, garmenture, and behavior. For example, Gorean slave girls must be pleasing to their masters. If they are not, they will be punished.

Warfare among polities, not always declared, is common on Gor, and the women of one polity in such a case are regarded by those of the other as objects eminently suitable for apprehension, as prizes, as loot, they, as well as rugs, jewels, coin, art works, fine cloths, draperies, saddles, harnesses, kaiila, and such. When a city falls her women, stripped and chained, are herded to the conquering city, to be sold, or, if kept, to serve and please the victors. Such depredations pertain, of course, to the seas, and to the roads, as well. Sometimes wars are fought to obtain slaves, for men desire them. It is supposedly delicious to capture a woman of the enemy, and enslave her, and publicly display and humiliate her, leashing her and marching her about, and such, this making clear that even the high-caste women of the enemy are worthy of no more than being abject slaves to the victor.

Gorean women are always at risk of the collar. It is strange that more Gorean free women do not seem to understand this.

Doubtless it becomes clearer to them when they are stripped and chained.

They are relatively safe, usually, only within the walls of their city, and amongst those with whom they share a Home Stone, but not always, as suggested, even then.

To make this matter more clear, and to be fairer to the customs of Gor, it should be noted that any woman, any woman whatsoever with whom one does not share a Home Stone, is understood to be fair game for the capture loop. This does not entail, of course, that one is under any obligation to bring them within one's chain, but only that one is entitled to do so. The cities need not be at war. They need only be different. To be sure, some deference is usually accorded to allied cities, which, however, are few, as Gorean polities tend to be mutually suspicious of, and often hostile to, one another. Accordingly, slave raids are a common pastime amongst young men, raids in which not only slaves, but free women, as well, may be taken as booty.

A common Gorean saying has it that all women are slaves. It is only that some are in collars and others are not.

Free women hear such sayings with trepidation.

And there are, of course, slavers, who specialize in these matters, and brigands, and bands of brigands, who frequently engage in these activities.

Travel between cities is usually accomplished in caravans, which affords some protection, both to goods, and females.

Goreans, as Kurii, have their senses of propriety, and what is to be permitted and what is not to be permitted. For example, it is understood that free women are not permitted in paga taverns. Some, however, curious, or bold, or such, disguise themselves as boys, or even as slaves, and dare to enter such forbidden precincts. If they are discovered, they are not unoften enslaved. If they would be in such a tavern, let them be so appropriately, bringing paga to the tables and serving in the alcoves, in their own collars, locked on their necks, slaves. Similarly, should a free woman impersonate a slave, which is frowned upon, it is thought suitable that she be made a slave. If she would appear a slave, let her be a slave. It is, in most cities, incidentally, a capital offense for a slave to impersonate a free woman. It is understood that there is a vast and unbridgeable chasm between the priceless free woman and the worthless slave. To be sure, some slaves are quite expensive, and some free women, displayed, would not be likely to receive a bid.

As a last remark, it might be noted that it is generally understood that any woman who becomes a slave should be kept a slave.

As an extreme example, let us suppose that the daughter of a household is captured, carried away, and enslaved. Then, let us suppose that she, say, through exchanges, buyings and sellings, and such, is recovered by her family. They will not free her, but, disowning her, will keep her as a slave, as any other slave in the house. She will serve as any other slave, and, as any other slave, if her work is not satisfactory, will be lashed. Eventually, once she has fully understood how she has shamed and humiliated her family, she will sold out of the house, as might be any other slave. Cast her into the markets. She is now only goods. It is the Gorean way. Similarly, let us suppose a woman of a given city falls slave and eventually finds herself once more in her native city. There she will remain a slave, and may well be kept in a slavery more grievous than what was hers outside the city. Her bondage, that she has served others, rendered obeisance to them, cried out and leapt, collared, in their arms, and such, has shamed her city. Too, for such despicable activities, she is an insult to free women. To them she is an abomination. She has been a slave. Thus, she will remain a slave. Sometimes a fellow, who was once a spurned suitor, discovers a woman whom he had earlier courted in vain is now a slave, and buys her. He will see to it that she serves him splendidly.

Let us consider again, briefly, the "daughter of the household." As we recall, as we left her, she had been cast into the markets, and was only goods. To be sure, interestingly, the girl, herself, is not displeased. Perhaps it would not do to tell her family, but she loves her collar. She is, of course, acutely aware of how she had shamed and humiliated her family, and perhaps, to some extent, regrets this, but, too, she felt a certain rightness in kneeling before her brothers and sisters, in her rag and collar, and serving them, and such. Similarly she dares not meet the eyes of her offended, scornful parents. How could she, once their daughter, now a slave, do so? In the kitchen and halls, where she scrubs and cleans, she accepts as her due, as any other slave, her reprimands and switchings. Sometimes, at night, after humbly, head down, assisting in serving dinner, she is sent upstairs, and is chained to the slave ring at the foot of a visitor's couch, as might be any other slave, for his pleasure. This is fitting. She is now no different from any of the other house girls. But usually at night she clutches her threadbare blanket about her, and lies curled in her kennel, awaiting dawn, when she will be summoned forth to new labors. But she is pleased, surely, when, her lessons learned, her family's reproach suffered and accepted, its displeasure ventilated upon her, with abuse and switch, to its satisfaction, she is hooded, and taken to a slaver's house, where she is sold for a pittance, that her worthlessness may be made clear to her. There, in the slaver's house, in the pens, she will await her vending. If convenient, it will doubtless take place on the next sale day. Interestingly, she is not disconsolate, but happy. She knows she is excellent female meat. She has been found worthy of a collar. How beautiful and exciting then she must be! She looks forward to her sale. She hopes some of her scornful brothers and vengeful sisters might come to see her sold. She will then have her vengeance on them! She will pose, writhe, and dance as the slave she is, and knows herself now to be. Let them flee from the auction house, in rage and shame, as she is taken from the block with a fine bid. It is her hope, now, to find a kind, strong master, who will be strict with her, and well command her, and well fulfill her womanhood, one whom she may then, in gratitude, selflessly love and serve.

One thing that is apparently difficult for free Goreans to understand, and perhaps for others who are free, or enjoy the semblance of freedom, is the reveling of the slave in what they conceive of as her degradation. Does she not know she is a debased, worthless creature, unworthy to lace a man's sandals? Does she not know she is a rightless, domestic animal, subject to buying and selling, her thigh branded, her throat encircled with its locked, debasing insignia of bondage? How is it that she can sing at her work, or step so lightly, toss her head as she does, and smile, and kneel and belly as the subservient creature she is, so contentedly, so happily? Does she not know she may not even place a thread of cloth upon her body without the permission of her master, and that she is subject to the very whip she licks and kisses so gratefully? How is it that she can lovingly kiss the chain that fastens her to her master's couch?

Civilization has its imperatives and priorities and surely high amongst these are the pretensions and indoctrinations which prescribe and evaluate the perceptions of its occupants. These pretensions and indoctrinations often have in mind, so to speak, primarily the persistence of the civilization, and not the happiness of its occupants, or inmates. The inmates are taught to commend some things, and emulate certain exemplars, and so on. There is not always an easy congruence between what a civilization insists on as true, and what is, in fact, true. Consider, as an example, the view that a woman is essentially similar to a man, and thus what is appropriate for a man is appropriate for a woman. It is not obvious that this is true. It may be taught, and insisted upon, and such, perhaps even hysterically, but that, I think you will see, does not make it true. Consider, for example, matters pervasive within higher, or more complex, species, such as the ratios of dominance and submission, and then consider, too, in particular, the human species, which is clearly and radically sexually dimorphic, and in a thousand ways. Would it really seem so surprising if amongst sexes so different there might not be diverse rightnesses? What if, say, in a given species, for example, the human, nature had chosen to breed not neuters, but, say, dominants and submissives, or, to speak more clearly, masters and slaves. What a falsification of nature it would be then to teach natural masters and natural slaves that they were, or, at least, must pretend to be, neuters, or identicals, or such. They are not. The human male is best fulfilled in the mastery. And the human female does not come home to herself until she is on her chain. She relishes being conquered and subdued, being given no choice but to obey. In the ancient genes of her she lives for, hopes for, and craves male dominance. In her heart she has been bred for the pleasure and service of the male. She wants to be herself; she wants to be mastered. At the feet of a male who will have from her what he wishes, she understanding this and knowing herself choiceless in the matter, as she wishes to be, she finds her fulfillment. In the collar, she is, then, most free. The female who knows herself as a natural slave, and longs to be a slave, will not be fully happy until she has found her master, or he her. She belongs on her knees before a man. She kisses his feet.

Civilizations differ. The Gorean civilization is a complex, high civilization, comparable to various others, and its height is not a little associated with the fact that it is on the whole compatible with nature, rather than incompatible with her; it constitutes less of a contradiction to her, than an acceptance, and, indeed, in its way, an enhancement, of her.

Once collared, you see, a woman is never the same. How radiant are the slaves, and how fulfilled, and how envied they are by the bitter free women!

But now let us return to Tarl Cabot.

Presumably to many men the alleged dilemma in which he found himself would have been nonexistent, or, at least, ignored.

Why should one not feed when hungry? Why should one not drink when thirsty?

Many men, doubtless, and not the worst, might simply have rejoiced in their good fortune and, so to speak, enjoyed the repast with which they had been unexpectedly provided. Indeed, many Warriors might have done so. And one does not doubt but what a member of that other, though rarer, Gorean martial caste, though not held a high caste, the Assassins, might have done so. If one, anyone, were squeamish concerning the legalities, or etiquette, of the situation, he might have simply enslaved the women, and then put them to his pleasure.

Too, one supposes many men might, if only as an assertive effrontery to Priest-Kings, a way of mocking their subtleties, of refusing to suffer, might have made prompt use of the goods placed at their disposal.

Cabot, of course, unwisely or not, was not such a man.

The codes do, you see, recommend respect for the status of the free female, if not for the female herself. To be sure, the codes make it abundantly clear that this pertains only to females with whom one shares a Home Stone. Cabot, however, as some Warriors, tended to generalize this recommendation to free women more generally, saving, of course, those who might be insolent or abusive, or of an enemy city. Whereas there are clear cases in which the codes apply or do not apply, they, as most recommendations, rules, principles, and such, perhaps unavoidably, were occasionally afflicted with a regrettable penumbra of obscurity. More acutely, a personal sense of honor, one which seems to me misplaced and overly sensitive, seems to have been involved, one clearly exceeding the parameters of the codes. One suspects this might have been the consequence of a personal idiosyncrasy, or even a residue lingering from an unnatural and ridiculous acculturation, one to which he had been subjected in the innocence of his childhood or adolescence.

In any event both females were helpless and at his mercy.

And yet he refrained, perhaps unconscionably, at least for the time, of making use of one, or both.

If the Priest-Kings thought that his fellows in the caste of Warriors would scorn him for dealing with the goods in the container as one might expect, it seems to me they were incorrect. Too, if Cabot was of this opinion, he, too, in my view, was mistaken. On the other hand, if they did not know humans that well it seems they did know this particular human, Tarl Cabot.

Whereas it is true that Warriors might scorn a fellow of their caste who had lost his honor, it is not at all clear that they would have regarded the usage of two females, neither of whom had a Home Stone, as it turned out, as in any way involving a loss of honor. Indeed, not making use of them would doubtless have been viewed as an inexplicable peculiarity, calling for some justification or, at least, an explanation.

Tarl Cabot was surely not eager to be shamed in the eyes of other men. On the other hand, he was most concerned not to be shamed in his own eyes.

There are such men.

As there are such Kurii.

In any event, the Priest-Kings surely knew how to torture this particular individual, Tarl Cabot.

He was confined with two lovely specimens of the human female animal, one of which was acquiescent, sinuous, eager, and rawly sexual, and the other, educated, articulate, and urbane, stripped, was one of the most excruciatingly desirable women he had ever seen, one who seemed made for his collar, one matched to him as slave to master.

And, as we have noted, this was no coincidence, no accident.

It had been seen to by Priest-Kings.

Yes, they clearly knew how to torture this particular individual, our friend, Tarl Cabot.

The English girl, despite the strange, unfamiliar feelings in his presence, feelings which frightened, warmed and delighted her, did not understand, of course, that she had been selected out for him, that she had been chosen for him with great care, that she had been matched to him most exquisitely, as slave to master.

And, indeed, so naive was she that she was not even fully aware that she was such as, in general, aside from the specifics of a given situation, are rightfully put to the feet of men, as properties.

To the practiced, discriminating eye of the professional slaver, who is skilled in reading women, their beauty and their needs, it was clear she belonged in a slave collar.

There are many such.

Despise them if you wish.

But they belong on their knees before men, and their necks belong in collars.

The English girl was one such.

Indeed, had our human confederates known of her, as earlier indicated, she would have been long ago acquired and disposed of, suitably, in the Gorean markets.

The English girl, shrinking back against the confining, glassine barrier, and continuing to cover herself, as she could, regarded Tarl Cabot reproachfully.

She would expect, and would demand, that he behave toward her as what, in her world, and his former world, was known as a "perfect gentleman." Surely the other men she had known had done so. She had seen to it that they had not dared not do so.

Cabot was well aware of her expectations in these matters and he, a male, found them irritating. Was she unaware that she was beautiful and naked? Was she unaware she was a woman and he was a man? Did she not know he was of the Warriors, and that she, with all her loftiness and pretensions, luscious and unclothed, easily within his grasp, did not even possess a Home Stone?

But he growled, and did not touch her.

The sinuous little blonde beast looked up at him, and licked at his thigh, but he pressed her gently, firmly, back.

She whimpered, reproachfully.

For the first time in her life she was afflicted with imperative, unaccountable sensations.

She was in heat.

He did not touch her. She looked balefully at the brunette, who, still covering herself as she could, looked away, frightened.

Tarl Cabot rested back, against the wall of the container, and looked out, into the empty hallway.

The container was transparent, and had there been wardens or guards, visitors or bystanders, the container's occupants would have been in public view.

Tarl Cabot had no doubt that the Priest-Kings, or others, properly situated, could see and hear all that might occur within the container. That would be important for them. The hallway might be empty, and silent, but there were doubtless, somewhere, surveillance devices, cameras, microphones, or such, to them undetectable, perhaps no more than a few microns in width.

Tarl Cabot lifted his head, for he had detected the feeding signal, the odor connected with the liquid food dispensed through the tube at the height of the cylinder.

Given its consistency and its tension within the tube, it must be drawn into the mouth, as one wishes, until one is satisfied, or until the quantity allotted is consumed. Any residue not imbibed is retracted.

Cabot was hungry.

Were the two females encased with him slaves, he would of course feed first. Even in a normal household the master takes the first bite from the bowl proffered to him by the slave. She must clearly understand, as his property, that she is dependent upon him for food, as for other things. Often then they eat together. Sometimes he feeds her by hand. Sometimes, he takes what he wishes, and then, later, puts the bowl on the floor for her and she then feeds, head down, on all fours. She may or may not be clothed for meals, just as, within the household, she may or may not be clothed. She is commonly clothed outside the household, usually in a brief tunic.

In no way is she to be confused with her glorious superior, the free woman. She is merely a degraded, worthless beast, a domestic animal, a property. Still, it must be admitted, she is attractive, chained to a slave ring.

He wondered if the interval between feedings had been longer than usual.

His hunger suggested that it had been.

Surely his warders, or guards, knew of the additional occupants in the container. Would there then be additional food? He supposed so. Neither female could get her mouth to the tube. It had apparently been adjusted to his height, if he stretched somewhat.

He wondered if they were hungry.

He supposed so.

As they were free women, he should feed them first.

He wished they were slave girls. Slave girls may be forced to beg, and perform, and well, for their food. Slave girls may be used as men please. It is what they are for.

But these were not slave girls.

He did not think so. He was sure they were not.

And they were not.

The blonde was looking about, alert, quizzical. She, an exquisite little animal, was very sensitive to a variety of odors, a variety of sounds, and such. She was unfamiliar with this odor, but it suggested food. She looked about, and whimpered. She is hungry, thought Cabot.

He lifted himself to the tube and drew some feed into his mouth. He did not swallow it, but took the blonde by the hair and gently pulled her toward him. He then, holding her head back, placed his mouth over hers. She sensed the food almost immediately, squirmed a little, and, excitedly, took it from him. He repeated this action twice, and then he thought that she had had enough. Too, he was not sure how much feed would be available. While he was engaged in feeding the blonde the brunette had watched, at first in horror, and then almost pathetically. She is hungry, thought Cabot, very hungry.

He took more of the liquid food into his mouth and looked at her, but she shook her head, wildly, negatively. But there were tears in her eyes. She is very hungry, thought Cabot. Had she been a slave he would have left her hungry. Had he been rather as many other men, he might have seized her, lifted her, and held her to him, helplessly, her head held back by the hair, and then, placing his mouth over hers, permitted her to feed. In such a case, the girl would have been left in no doubt that she was a female.

The thought crossed Cabot's mind that she would much profit from a taste of the lash.

The lash is efficient in humanizing a female.

But he expelled the gelatinous provender into his cupped hands, and held them to the brunette.

Gratefully, she put down her head and, still covering herself, as she could, fed. Something within her realized that her head was bowed before him. Too, as she moved her hands, she must have been aware, given his stance and her posture, he so close, that he was nicely positioned to assess the sweetness of her figure. Surely, despite her efforts, the softness and fullness of her bosom could be but ill concealed. But surely he was a gentleman, and would not do so. He must avert his eyes. But she looked up, and saw his eyes full upon her, and she put down her head again, quickly feeling a flush of heat.

Never before, she was sure, had she been so looked upon.

What sort of man could look so upon a woman?

And what sort of woman might be so looked upon by a man?

She shuddered.

She was not a slave! She was not a slave!

But was it not as a slave might be looked upon?

Again then she shuddered, but this time with a strange pleasure.

She was sure he was pleased with what he saw.

This both disturbed her, and pleased her.

And so might a slave have been pleased, understanding that her beauty was such that it might meet with a man's favor.

Too, she thought then to herself, perhaps I can make use of this. I am a female, and he is only a man.

Then she continued to feed.

He liked the way her hair now fell to the sides of her neck. He could see the base of her bowed neck, with the short, fine hairs there. He considered what it would look like in a slave collar. It is there, at the back of the neck, incidentally, that the collar commonly closes and locks. If the collar is to be changed, the male does so from behind the girl. This helps her to keep in mind that she is a slave. If a new collar is to be placed on the girl this is commonly done before the old one is removed. If a girl is between collars, or is being fitted, or such, she is commonly bound hand and foot. Her limbs may be freed, of course, once she is again in a collar. Aesthetic and psychological features are commonly involved, as well, in these matters. With the lock in the back, as the girl, and others, might be most commonly expected to see the collar, the enclosing, encircling aspect of the band is most prominent, this suggesting an uncompromising security and irremovability. The common Gorean slave band, incidentally, even in its simplicity, flat, narrow, and close-fitting, is quite beautiful on a woman. In certain cultures one supposes women might pay a great deal of money to obtain such a device, though perhaps one more akin to those one might expect to find on high slaves, say, colored, enameled, ringed, bejeweled, of precious metals, and such. On Gor, of course, these collars, at least the simple ones, sell for a pittance, and even common slaves are routinely fastened in them. Indeed, this is required by Merchant Law. Clearly, all in all, the collar is an attractive device which much enhances the beauty of a woman. But doubtless its most significant aspect is its meaning, that its occupant is a property, that she is owned.

He again gave her food.

Her hair was not short, but it was not of a common slave length either. But, he thought, it will grow out.

Then, he fed her again. Then he desisted, despite her plea for more. In his view she had fed sufficiently. The diet of slave girls is closely supervised, as that of any other animal one wishes to keep in prime condition. She was not a slave girl, of course, but it pleased him to decide when she had had enough. Also the blonde had had only three helpings, too, so to speak. Indeed when the blonde had understood that the brunette was asking for a fourth helping she became quite agitated, bared her small canines, and hissed menacingly. Tarl Cabot growled softly at the blonde, who then subsided. She understood the purport of such noises. The brunette, pleased at this, requested more food, again, but was denied her wish. Seldom one supposes had she failed before to obtain her way. But this was not her familiar world. Things here were quite different. She did, however, rejoice that the male, at least as of now, stood between her and the frightening little thing with which they were sharing the container.

She watched the male then, as he fed.

It did not seem there was much left. He wiped his mouth with his right forearm. She wondered if, the next time, were there a next time, the food might be rationed differently.

How lean and strong seemed the male to her.

She would have muchly preferred that the blonde had not been there, of course, for she feared her, but there may have been another reason, as well, one that she might have been more reluctant to acknowledge.

Too, she would not have cared to have discovered herself alone in the container. Bewildered, confused, she might have literally lost her mind. In her present situation there was in her proximity at least another human, for the male clearly was human, who was similarly incarcerated, and, moreover, one who could speak her language, who would try to comfort her, assuage her fears, and such.

Too, in his presence she felt strange sensations.

He seemed to her stronger, and more powerful, than any male she had hitherto met.

He is crude, and rugged, but not unattractive, she mused.

Indeed, in some moments, she felt herself absolutely weak before him, and had sensed that she would be helpless in his arms.

Indeed, had she not had dreams in which she was helpless, eager, and begging in the arms of men less than he, strange dreams in which she had found that the throat of her heated, mottled, thrashing body had been confined, however inexplicably, within a close-fitting, irremovable metal circlet?

She regarded the blonde.

She would certainly fear to be alone with the feral little savage, but, happily, she was not alone with her. Had she been alone with her, and unable to flee, she would have made herself small, groveled, whimpered, and begged for mercy. She would have done her best to assure her, cringing, terrified and pleading, not only that she constituted no threat to her but that she would try to avoid her to the best of her ability and, in any disputed matters, would instantly retire and yield her first place. Such behaviors, though the brunette might not have cared to recall the point, given her class, her social background, the excellence of her education, the quality of her diction, and such, were common in the animal kingdom. But she had little fear of the blonde now, for the male, she was sure, would protect her. She needed only to ingratiate herself with him, and that should not be difficult. She had always had her way with men, and, too, had she not sensed, though to her indignation, how he had viewed her while feeding her? She knew she was a female of high intelligence, and she was quite well aware that she was also one of unusual attractiveness. Yes, he would protect her. Any male, she was sure, with a bit of attention on her part, and perhaps a little thought, and a smile, or two, could be entangled helplessly within the net of her wiles. She had always had whatever she wanted of men, and he was a man. He would be no different.

Perhaps she might even permit him to kiss her.

She might find that interesting.

She wondered what it might be to be kissed by him.

She had been kissed before, of course, once or twice, by men of Earth, as much as an experiment as anything else. In both cases she had pretended shock and indignation.

That had disconcerted them, and taken them off guard. Both had stammered, and apologized.

Secretly she had been much amused.

What inane twits they were!

She could have had both well in hand after that, but neither had any longer been of interest to her.

Their subsequent invitations were declined.

She had found the men of Earth weak and boring.

She was certain that he with whom she was incarcerated was not physically weak, but then, too, some men of Earth were physically strong, irritatingly so. But even the strongest men of Earth, she had discovered, were psychologically weak, presumably as a consequence of their conditioning programs, designed to thwart and tame them, or, with some effort, she was sure, could be made so, even pathetically so. She wondered if her fellow prisoner was psychologically weak. If not, she was sure she could soon make him so, by turning his own strength against him, by dividing him emotionally, and by arranging self-conflicts which would bring him, his own confused enemy, to an uncertain and anxious balance, where she might, by as little as a breath, so to speak, move him to her will.

Were men not made to be wrapped about the smallest finger of a beautiful woman?

And was she not beautiful?

At that time she was not familiar with how common beauty is on Gor, and how it may be easily purchased in the markets.

She smiled to herself. She had always had whatever she wanted of men, even as a pretty little girl, even before her face and body, advancing through its teens, had become, as now, disturbingly, tormentingly, desirable, suitable for fastening in a slave coffle.

Always she had been able to manipulate and control men, by a word, a tone of voice, a smile, a frown, a tear.

It would be no different with this male, he with whom she shared this inexplicable, eccentric, bizarre confinement.

Her sex, and her beauty, had always proved reliable instruments, and weapons.

They would so now.

The male in the container was a man, and he would be no different from the others.

She did not understand, of course, that he, despite his familiarity, as she had discovered, with her language, was unlike the men with whom she had hitherto been acquainted.

He was of the Warriors; he knew battle; he knew the sea; he knew the great bow, and the blade.

Too, she was quite unfamiliar with Gorean males, and how they viewed women, in particular those with whom they do not share Home Stones.

Their acculturation had not been that of Earth, but one quite different, one far more consistent and healthy, one far more natural.

Nothing had prepared her, you see, for the men of Gor.

And this large, strong man was no longer of Earth. He was now of Gor.

How could it even occur to her that Gorean men would look upon such as she and see her not in terms of her breeding, education, position, and background but in terms of the slave tunic and chain, in terms of the whip and collar?

Did she not know that such as she were put barefoot and naked on the sawdust of the slave block and routinely auctioned to the highest bidder?

Comfortable with her assumed power, and confident that she would be protected by the male in the container, she cast a glance of lofty disdain at the blonde. Did the blonde not even know enough to cover herself, as did the brunette, at least to the extent possible?

Many facial expressions and bodily words, so to speak, in the human species are presumably genetically coded, at least with respect to their templates, as they are amongst other Earth primates, for they seem, for the most part, to be easily interpreted amongst diverse linguistic and cultural groups, for example, expressions of contentment, of jealousy, of pride, of pleasure, of satisfaction, of suspicion, of anger, and so on. In any event, whether in virtue of these species characteristics, or in virtue of her experiences in her Steel World, the blonde took instant umbrage at the brunette's expression, and bared her canines and hissed viciously at the brunette, who drew back, frightened.

The male put out his hand and pressed the blonde back who, hands raised, and fingers crooked, was clearly on the verge of attacking the brunette.

The male apparently made soothing sounds to the blonde, as she had no language, who then crouched down beside him, docilely, looking up at him.

He shook her head, good-naturedly, and she put her head gently against him. She had done this often with her master.

Then, looking at him, timidly, she licked his knee.

The brunette looked upon this display of tenderness with severe disapproval, but the male did not deter or punish the little animal.

Rather he smiled at the brunette, who gasped in indignation. Apparently the brute had no intention of prohibiting the blonde from engaging in such disgusting exhibitions of ingratiation.

What sort of man could he be?

Was he even a man, as she had known men?

Perhaps he was something far more masculine, more virile and dangerous, more dominant?

What then might be the relation of such a man to a woman?

Perhaps he was the sort of man who would simply master a woman?

She thought of herself as mastered, and shuddered, with pleasure.

Then she cast such thoughts from herself, indignantly.

Surely she was not such that she could be mastered! She was educated, and civilized, and such!

But what if it was done to her?

Her dreams had left her in no doubt that it could be done to her, and with perfection.

Surely she would fear the whip.

She would be choiceless.

Never before had she encountered such a man.

Could she be longing for a master?

Was that what it was to be a woman, to be a slave?

Then she, a civilized beauty of station, position, and class, the young, spoiled, pampered, proud, self-righteous scion of a pathological acculturation, put aside such thoughts as offensive and absurd, and considered her present predicament and vulnerability.

She was imprisoned, helplessly, perfectly, why or how she had no idea. She had no evidence, even, of the number or nature of her captors, or owners.

She looked at the heavy, glassine walls, closely curving about her, within whose compass she and the others were confined.

She was a member of a miniscule social group, in a tiny, inescapable environment, subject to a technological ecology she was incapable of altering. What might be the social relations in such a world, in such a small, stout, encircling, transparent world?

And what might be the consequences to herself of these social relations?

She became extremely frightened. What if she were marginalized, or neglected? What if the little animal should become, so to speak, his favorite? How would this affect her plans, her role, in this tiny space? There was a single male, and two females.

Must she not somehow compete for his favor?

At this point, she seemed to speak to him, but in response she received only his smile, which disconcerted her.

She then drew back, miserably, against the wall of the thick, glassine barrier, and, for some time, watched the little blonde, with her soft, pink tongue, licking at the male's knee.

She became more and more agitated.

She seems then to have said something to Tarl Cabot, which displeased him, for he seems to have spoken back to her, sharply.

She then, upset, drew back, again.

Perhaps no man had spoken to her in that fashion before.

She began to cry.

He paid her no attention.

Later, she seems to have said something to him again, but he only shrugged, noncommittally.

She tried to plead with him, it seemed, but he looked away.

Tears stained her cheeks.

Had she been found displeasing?

Never had that happened before.

Clearly then she understood, perhaps as never before, save in her dreams, her femaleness in relation to a male's maleness, that she was a female, and that she, if she would please, or even survive, had best relate to the male as a female.

She was startled.

He was dominant.

Never before had she sensed a male dominant over her, but she sensed it now.

He controlled the container, or could, if he wished.

It must have been clear to her then that she might be isolated, excluded, that her standing in this tiny world might be in jeopardy.

What if she were not fed?

Then, after a time, the brunette, covering her breasts, as she could, with one arm, put out her hand and took one of the hands of Tarl Cabot.

Looking at him, she drew it timidly to her mouth, and, putting her head down, began to lick at its palm, perhaps to obtain any residue of the gelatinous provender which it had hitherto held.

Then she looked up at him, frightened, and then, again, submissively, put her head down and licked his palm.

Could she at one time have even conceived of herself doing this?

Could it be she, behaving so?

Oddly, she felt sexually enflamed.

She was trying to please a male.

How would the males she had hitherto known react to this, those she had treated with such coolness, with such contempt and condescension, whom she had routinely disdained, belittled, and spurned, whom she had treated as so much beneath her, to whom she had postured herself as their lofty, haughty superior, seeing her naked, fearful, degraded, attempting to please a male? Would they not have cried out with pleasure, and perhaps removed their belts, that they might have served as whips?

Tarl Cabot did not withdraw his hand, but he looked at her, closely. Slaves sometimes try to call themselves so to the attention of their master. It was a slave's gesture, a slave's act. Cabot wondered if she knew what she was doing. It is erotic, of course, to feel that soft tongue in the palm of one's hand. It, too, this gesture or act, is often used not simply as a device of placation, but as a way of petitioning to be caressed.

The blonde, half asleep, contented, did not even object to the brunette's solicitation, her apology, and begging for forgiveness.

The brunette was then, in her view, no more than another pet. And she was not concerned at the moment, in her own contentment, with driving her away.

The male put his left hand on the brunette's forehead and, holding it in place, gently drew his right hand away.

The brunette looked up, timidly.

He smiled at her, and she put her head down, quickly, beside his leg. He then gently drew her hands apart that she, kneeling now beside him, need no longer prolong her pretense of modesty, so out of place in their tiny world, that she need no longer struggle so absurdly to hide her beauty from him.

She did not then grasp herself as before, in that preposterous fashion, trying to conceal herself from him, for he had seemed to discountenance it, but she did press herself against his leg, putting her head down, so that he could not see the full slave of her.

This amused him.

Did she not know that he could seize her, and hold her, and turn her, and examine her, minutely, and then, his assessment done, discard her, casting her to the side of the container as one might a slave?

But he recalled she was a free woman.

She looked up at him, timidly, tears in her eyes. And then put her head down and softly licked the side of his leg. She then put up her head again, timidly, to see his reaction.

It was the sort of thing a slave might do.

Would her solicitation be accepted, or might he be annoyed, and cuff her from his leg?

He put his hand gently on her hair, and then she felt, in a moment, his hand close within her hair, holding it, tightly.

She was helpless.

She winced.

He seemed to struggle with himself. He wants me, she thought, trying to hold her head very still, quite aware that if she made any sudden movement or made the least attempt to escape, it would hurt even more, and that he, if he wished, with a mere tightening or twist, could subject her to the torment of hundreds of tiny scalding knives of pain, to avoid which she would do anything. Then he released her hair. She was, after all, a free woman.

She crouched as she could in the container, against his leg.

She was startled, confused.

He could have done with her what he wanted, but he had not.

She put down her head.

She kissed his leg, again.

She had strange, unaccountable sensations.

This is what it is, she thought, to be a female.

Then she thought, I want him to claim me. I want to wear his collar. Lash me, she thought, prove to me you own me.

But he did not touch her.

She was free.

She grappled with her feelings. Had women felt this way, in a thousand years, she wondered, or two thousand, perhaps in Baghdad, Damascus or Byzantium, in Athens or Rome, in Thebes or Corinth, in Gaul or Britain, or in the German forests, or in Persia or Egypt, or in Nineveh or Babylon, or in the great muddy river valleys, or in horse-haunted grasslands, the dominion of bowmen, or in clustered huts where metal was new or in fire-illuminated caves where flint was patiently shaped?

What would it be, she wondered, to struggle in the thongs of a prehistoric lover.

Where have the gods gone, she asked herself.

We no longer hear them call to one another.

What has become of us? What have we done to the world?

She felt herself touched then, you see, however softly, by the fingers of a world alien to her, a natural world of meadows and moisture, of damp rocks and blades of moist grass, a world rather like her own might once have been, unspoiled, a world quite different from the world she had known, an artificial world, a sly world, one of lies and pretense, of hypocrisy, and artifices, of convention and deception.

Am I a slave, she asked herself. Is this my master?

She looked up at him, and he smiled.

He is reading my body, my expressions, she thought. He knows, he must know, what I am thinking!

So he reads women, does he? Well, he is mistaken in the case of such as I! Perhaps there are low women who would grovel and place a man's foot upon their head, but I am not one such! My knees do not seek the tiles! My tongue is not for the feet of masters! My limbs are not for the chains of owners, my throat is not for their collars!

I am not such, she thought. I am not such.

I am not a slave, she thought. No, no, I am not a slave, not a slave!

Then suddenly, angrily, she thrust away from him, and thrust herself back against the obdurate transparent barrier which so closely confined them.

He smiled at her, and she lunged forth to strike him but he grasped her wrists and he held her helplessly before him, her struggles as futile as might have been those of a child, until tears of frustration streamed down her cheeks.

He then released her.

She regarded him angrily.

I hate you, she thought. I hate you! Then she subsided, frightened, for he had frowned.

I have displeased him, she thought.

Why does he not discipline me? Because I am a free woman, of course. She shuddered, as he looked away. If I were a slave, she thought, he would punish me. Why does he not make me his slave?

But I fear that I am not worthy to be his slave!

But clearly he desires me!

I think he would not mind having me at his feet!

Then why might he not make me his slave?

Where is Earth? Where is my old world! Where is the world where I understand myself? What is this place, or world, where I cannot understand myself, but where I am other than I was, and am hopelessly, needfully so?

I must never understand myself as I truly am, she thought, for that is forbidden!

But why, she asked herself, is it forbidden?

Teach me who I am, she thought, teach me myself! Release me! Free me, to be myself, and yours—*Master*!

She then cried out at him, angrily.

It was at that point that the disruption occurred.

Chapter, the Second:

The Disruption, and
What Occurred Shortly Thereafter

For whatever reason, she had cried out angrily at him.

Then, suddenly, each of the tiered containers in the long hallway shook, and several broke from their stems, and tumbled, rolling from the tiers which, themselves, were twisting from the walls. Had there been air in the hallway there might have been much screeching of metal, and the ringing of ovoid containments striking the floor, rolling, crashing into one another.

The container with which we have been concerned tilted eccentrically, as had several others, this container toward the center of the hallway. Doubtless there was much consternation within its confines. Air began to hiss from it, and Tarl Cabot thrust his hand against the aperture through which this complex gas was escaping, rushing outside. Within the container its occupants began to suffer, almost immediately, from the diminution of its atmosphere. The human life form, as many others, requires oxygen, in one form or another to survive. Commonly, this is imbibed from an atmosphere, in an exchange of gases. One life form, for example, will exude a waste product, its poison, into the atmosphere which is, interestingly, necessary for the life of a different life form, and that life form, in turn, expels into the atmosphere another waste product, poisonous to itself, yet benign, even necessary, to, say, the first life form. It is thus by means of an exchange of poisons that the gift of life flowers. The wheels turn. The ways of the Nameless One are obscure. Kurii, incidentally, require oxygen for life, as well, as does the cobra and ost, the leopard and larl. This may, too, be the case with Priest-Kings, but one knows little about them.

The blonde, gasping, scratched at the inside of the container, wildly, as though she would scratch through it and obtain air outside, but there was, at that time, no air outside. The brunette had her hands pressed against the inside of the container. Her face, viewed from the outside, was distraught. So might be that of a small animal contained in a jar from which the air was being removed. Tarl Cabot removed his hand from the aperture through which the atmosphere was escaping, and lunged against the transparent barrier, three times, but his efforts, as he should have realized, would be ineffectual. Within the container they could probably hear the air hissing out. Outside a ripple might have been noted, but little else. He again tried to block the aperture, but with indifferent success. Too, as they breathed, the atmosphere within the container, now tenuous, became ever more toxic.

The cause of this disruption was, of course, at the time unknown to them, nor, at the time, would it have been of great interest to them. Their concern was with its effects.

The brunette was the first to lose consciousness, and, a bit later, sinking toward the tilted bottom of the container, the blonde was the second. Both were in their way small animals, small, lovely animals.

Tarl Cabot shook his head, and tried to keep his hand against the aperture, but, in a bit, his hand fell to the side. There was no longer the hiss of escaping gas, for, if any remained in the container, it was not enough to call attention to its exit. His knees buckled, and he tried to brace himself against the slanting wall of the damaged vessel. It seems likely he would have shortly lost consciousness when he became aware, dimly, that one of the loose containers was suddenly moving about, and it seemed a wind of tiny particles, like a dry blizzard of dust and scraps, invaded the corridor. He thrust his face to the small rupture in the container which he had tried to seal with his hand. There was surely there, at that small, opened gate, a welcome entrant, a whisper of air, an indisputable, salubrious freshening, within the tiny world. He saw the particles outside subsiding. He heard the sound of one of the cylinders shifting its position. Outside there was air.

At the same time he saw at the end of the corridor a red line, like a knife, slowly describing a large circle, bubbling and hissing, as it moved, in the steel. Then, as the circle was nearly completed, there was a sound as of a single blow, abrupt and impatient, on the other side, perhaps a small explosion, and the steel protruded into the hallway, as though it had been struck by a fist, and then there was another such blow, or explosion, and there was a screeching of metal, and then a large clanging sound, as the large circle of steel, with its diameter of ten feet or more, collapsed, rocking and shimmering with sound, into the hallway.

In this opening there suddenly appeared, harnessed and alert, enweaponed, ears erected, eyes blazing, head turning from side to side, a gigantic form.

Behind it, visible in the opening, some half crouched, were similarly accoutered forms.

Air was moving into the capsule rapidly; in moments the atmosphere in the capsule was in equilibrium with the circumambient atmosphere.

The blonde stirred and lifted her head, and then, pressing her hands against the glassine barrier, began to squirm and utter excited sounds.

Into the hallway now emerged ten or more of these large forms, in the hands of some were rifles, in the hands of others heat knives and double-bladed power axes. They were large-eyed, these creatures, now with verticalized pupils, in the light, pupils which could, as those of the sleen and larl, swiftly adapt themselves to anything short of total darkness. Their ears, large, pointed ears, several inches in width at the base, were erected, ears which could rotate nearly 180 degrees without the head moving, ears so keen that they could detect the movement of an urt in the grass at a hundred and fifty feet. Their nostrils in the large, flattish faces were wide and flared. In some of the faces, as the beasts, some of them hesitating briefly, entered the hallway, the nostrils contracted and distended, scanning for scents, rather as one might look, or one might listen. Their sense of scent was well developed, and useful in the hunt, and war. Their jaws were large and powerful. Those of a male could wrench the head from a tabuk in a single motion. Had they stood fully erect those of this group, carefully selected, would have averaged some ten to eleven feet in height. They were large specimens, even for their breed, having a width of three to four feet, and a weight, I conjecture, of some sixteen hundred pounds. The fur of two were erected, increasing an aspect of size and fearsomeness. And four had earned their way to the second ring.

The brunette had awakened, and, lifting her head, groggily, looked outside the container, and then, suddenly, she flung her hand before her face, and, eyes wide with horror, uttered a long, shrill scream, and fainted.

Tarl Cabot, angrily, with his foot, thrust her out of his way, to the bottom of the container.

She was useless, and a woman.

And no better, he thought, though free, than a slave, but, assuredly, one nicely curved, who should bring a good price. She would look well curled at a slave ring, he thought, where she belonged.

Let them hide behind men, he thought, whose they are, and to whom they owe their lives.

Do they not understand that, really?

They are slaves, he thought. Let them learn that, and strive to be pleasing. Free, they are without identity; free, they are meaningless and worthless; free, they are egotistical bothers, haughty nuisances, arrogant annoyances, self-alienated creatures removed from both biology and themselves, unhappy, pathetic, miserable, casting-about, frustrated creatures who do not even understand the meaning of their own malaise. But collared, marketed, and such, they are quite nice. Subject to buying and selling, and the lash, they are pleasant to have about the house. They work well, and from their thrashing, squirming bodies one may derive inordinate pleasures, pleasures not even within the ken of free women.

And is it not pleasant to have them coming to one's feet, helplessly, needfully, piteously, their slave fires ignited, to beg yet another caress?

We must not think too harshly of the brunette. We must remember that she was from Earth, and the environment in which she found herself was now quite different from that to which her upbringing, her education, and such, had accustomed her. Too, we must understand that she was weak, and a female. Too, she had never before seen Kurii.

The blonde, agitated, excited, was pounding on the glassine wall.

Had I only a weapon, thought Tarl Cabot. But, too, he was astonished at the appearance here, in the Prison Moon, of Kurii.

Why were they here?

What did they want?

Would the glassine walls not dispermit their access to the container, as effectively as it imprisoned its occupants?

Surely the Kurii had no keys, or signals, to open these sturdy cells.

But they had weaponry, surely, and if it could burn through walls, and blast steel apart, make doors where there were no doors, why should it not, cared they to do so, melt or cleave away the glassine walls which confined them?

But were they of interest?

And might they not perish in the destruction of the cell, blasted into ashes or deliquesced into boiling fluid?

One of the gigantic, shaggy creatures came to the edge of the container and peered within.

The blonde pounded on the wall, uttering eager sounds.

The jaws of the beast opened, revealing fangs.

He means to kill and eat, thought Cabot. To its sort we are food.

The blonde continued to utter eager sounds.

To Cabot, at that time, the expression of the beast seemed naught but a hideous grimace, but it was not. He would later learn that that movement of the mouth, the exposure of the fangs in that fashion, without the laying back of the ears, without the warning rumbling, was not a sign of hostility, at all. It was rather, in its way, an expression of recognition, of pleasure. I suppose one might speak of it, if it is not too absurd to do so, as a smile. And is the human smile not, in its way, similar? Is it not a baring of the teeth, a way of saying, I could bite you, and tear you, but I will not, because I like you? Is it not in its way a threat behavior revoked, withdrawn, as a sign of good will, perhaps even affection?

The long, dark tongue of the beast moved about its left fang, and then slid back into the cavernous jaw.

He will eat her, thought Cabot.

Did the blonde not understand the danger in which she stood?

The beast examined the container.

Cabot moved back within it, trying to shield the women.

The beast then slung its rifle behind its left shoulder, to a harness hook, and seized the container with its long arms, but could not fully encircle it. Its grip slipped. It then went behind the container and, bracing its back against the wall, pressed its feet against the container. Cabot heard its claws scratch on the container, outside. Then it had a better leverage. Then it exerted itself against the container, and, after a moment, broke it fully from its stem, and tubing, and wiring. Cabot and the others were thrown to the side of the container as it struck the floor, and rolled momentarily. Then it was still, on the floor.

This movement and shock awakened the brunette, who now lay immobile, terrorized, on what had been the vertical side of the container, but was now its flooring, lying as it did on the floor of the corridor.

Again she lost consciousness.

The beast then, others gathered about, unhooked his rifle, a stubby, cylindrical fire tube, and directed it toward what had been the top of the container. Cabot pushed further back, to what had been the bottom of the container, forcing the blonde behind him, she squirming and protesting, back to where the unconscious brunette lay.

A blast of force rocked the container.

Cabot, shaken, could feel the residue of the heat. There were numerous glassine droplets scattered about.

The container was open.

The blonde tried to squirm past him, but Cabot held her back.

The brunette, probably from the concussion of the blast, the movement of the container, had again recovered consciousness.

She was now on her knees, wide-eyed, trembling, behind the blonde, whose advance Cabot had arrested.

The Kur who had opened the container, as though his work was now done, returned his weapon to its hook, behind the left shoulder, and turned aside, to one of his fellows.

It was as though he need do no more.

Things, it seemed, might now take their course.

Another Kur motioned that the occupants of the container, who were back within the container, should come forth.

"Stay back!" said Cabot to the women, though only one could understand his import.

The blonde struggled.

"What are they?" begged the brunette.

"Kurii," said Cabot. "They feed on humans."

The brunette moaned.

"I am afraid," she said.

"Be afraid," he said, angrily.

"Do not be angry with me," she begged.

"You do not deserve patience," he said. The thought crossed his mind that she should be lashed. No, he thought, she is free.

"Where are the men?" she asked.

"What men?"

"Their masters!"

"These are a rational life form," he said.

"They have no masters?"

"If so, only of their own species," he said.

"There are no men?"

"No," he said, angrily. "If there were men, you would be in little danger."

The blonde continued to squirm.

"I do not understand," said the brunette.

"If there were men," he said, "you would be collared and sold."

"Collared?" she gasped. "Sold?"

"Certainly," he said. "It is all you are good for, if that."

The blonde suddenly squirmed loose and darted from the container. "Come back!" cried Cabot.

He scrambled from the container, to recover her, but he was seized by a Kur, and held up short.

He struggled, futilely. The strength of a human is small, compared to that of a superior species, such as that of the Kur.

The Kur who had opened the container, once the container was open, had turned aside to a fellow, and then, after a moment, as though he had finished whatever work was to have been done, had moved down the hall, toward the still-warm wound, that improvised, burnt gate, at the end of the hallway, through which the Kurii had effected their ingress.

There, before that opening, he stopped.

His back was to the length of the hallway.

The blonde, once she was free of the container, stopped, and stood in the center of the hallway. The Kurii stood about her, but did not attempt either to deter her, or apprehend her.

They did not seize her and begin to feed.

This surprised Cabot, for the species enjoys living meat.

It is not unusual for Kurii, incidentally, to quarrel over prey, fighting for it, tearing it apart, each withdrawing then with its secured portion, to crouch down and feed, alert, watching the others.

But, to Cabot's astonishment, she stood unharmed amongst them.

The large Kur who had opened the container then turned about.

He uttered a Kur sound, and the blonde stood absolutely still, as if frozen in place. She whimpered, and tears ran down her cheeks. But she did not move.

She understands him, thought Cabot. She is under discipline!

The Kur then uttered another sound, and she fled to him, and, to Cabot's amazement, leaped into his arms. She then crawled happily to his shoulder and began to nibble and bite at his fur. He stroked her with a paw, gently.

That is why she cannot speak, thought Cabot. She is not an exotic, denied speech. She has never learned to speak. She is not of Gor. She is of the Steel Worlds! She belongs to the beast! She is his pet! Had he come to the Prison Moon, with all the attendant risk, merely to recover a pet? Cabot found this hard to believe. She may believe it, thought Cabot, but I do not.

He regarded her, she contented, elated, on the shoulder of the beast, her master. She, with all her beauty, he thought, is a Kur pet! She would sell well on Gor, he thought. But here she is only the curvaceous, sleek little pet of a Kur! And then he realized even more the insidious cleverness of the Priest-Kings. Of course, he would assume she was a freed exotic. It would never have occurred to him that she might be a Kur pet! He had not even known that such as she existed. He regarded her, on the shoulder of her master. What a loss, he thought, to the sales platform.

Cabot awaited the tearing of his body.

There are a variety of ways in which this might be done, and much depends on the individual beast. Sometimes the head is bitten free and the spurting neck is covered with the predator's mouth, which is then drenched with the imbibed, flighted blood; another way is shared by certain other forms of predator, such as the larl or forest panther, in which the prey is seized, say, at the shoulder, and then, as in a frenzy, disemboweled with the hind legs; sometimes the victim is merely held and, after a few moments, as it struggles, the throat is torn open; a clean fashion is simply to bite through the base of the neck; perhaps the least attractive Kur feeding is to torment the quarry, biting and licking here and there, perhaps a finger, a hand, a foot, and so on. The victim's pain is supposed to improve the taste of the meat. When the victim is dead, some of its choice parts, the organ meat, usually, is eaten first by some of the Kurii, particularly if others are about, but others of the Kurii, usually when alone, will save it for the last, finishing their meal with the most savory morsels. Lest we be led to think the less of the Kurii in these matters, it is only fair to point out that most of the meat eaten in the Steel Worlds is not human. It takes a long time to raise a human for meat, even a child. Even to produce a human, we note, takes most of a year. Accordingly, most of the meat raised in the Steel Worlds is verr, tarsk, vulos, and such. It might also be mentioned that many Kurii do not even enjoy human meat. It is, it seems, a matter of taste. Too, it should be noted that much of the meat available in the Steel Worlds is not obtained in the hunt or live kill, but is processed from slaughtered animals, the meat of which is then dried, salted, or frozen, for future consumption. Too, although the Kurii are well thought of, in your presumed vocabulary, as carnivores, there are a number of processed food stuffs which have been engineered to be compatible with their digestion and fit for their nourishment. This will not be surprising to anyone familiar with the same sort of thing elsewhere, say, on Earth, where, for example, natural predators, and carnivores, such as the dog and the cat are often supplied with such alternative forms of nourishment.

What are the Kurii doing here, Cabot wondered.

One of the Kurii looked into the container, to its back, to where the brunette, kneeling, bent over, trying to make herself small, as though this would somehow make her presence in the container less conspicuous, was trembling, uncontrollably. He said something, in his tongue, peering within.

Cabot had heard that noise, or one much like it, but a moment ago, a noise which had been uttered by the large Kur who had opened the container, that noise to which the blonde had responded by rushing to him.

He is calling her, thought Cabot. She was a female, naked in the container, like the blonde. He is supposing she is a Kur pet, he thought. Such females, being highly intelligent, he supposed, doubtless make excellent Kur pets. Highly intelligent, they would doubtless train quickly.

The Kur seemed puzzled that she did not emerge from the container, and repeated the noise.

He was then spoken to by one of his fellows.

He then motioned that the brunette, kneeling in the back of the container, should emerge. There was no mistaking the sweep of that mighty paw. Not surprisingly, however, this invitation was declined by the brunette, who shook her head negatively, wildly, a gesture which may have been surprising to the Kur but was clearly not an act of compliance.

The beast uttered a displeased growl.

It went to the floor, and reached its long arm within the container, but it could not reach the brunette, who whimpered and drew back even further.

The opening in the container was wide enough for the beast to enter it, but Kurii are cautious beasts and it did not understand the container, or the wiring and tubing about. Many animals are reluctant to enter small confines with which they are unfamiliar, confines which do not have a clear second exit, confines in which unseen dangers might lurk, confines in which they might be trapped. The container was transparent, and a human would have thought little of entering it, but the beast was not human; and perhaps, more importantly, it was acutely aware, as a normal human might not be, of the subtlety and power of Priest-Kings. In any event it was reluctant to crawl into it. What if there should be some sort of field which might be activated by anything of its size, or genetic constituency?

It backed away from the container, and stood up, again, as such beasts commonly stand.

Two or three of the beasts looked about, uneasily.

They cannot stay here long, thought Cabot. This breach of the Prison World must be detectable in the Sardar. They must, after sealing themselves to it, or by means of protective gear of some sort, doubtless to be reassumed later, have burned through a lock, or even the shielding of the satellite. In any event Cabot had little doubt but what Priest-Kings would even now be apprised of the presence of unauthorized Kurii in the Prison Moon.

Perhaps even now investigatory ships were rising swiftly, silently, from the Sardar.

The Kur who had reached into the container now spoke to two of his fellows, who went to the container and began to lift it, between them, tilting it toward the floor.

The brunette shrieked piteously, and tried to brace herself within the container, to keep from slipping forward, and downward.

They know she is not a pet, thought Cabot. Pets obey instantly. If they do not, they are doubtless punished, or done away with.

She will be eaten, thought Cabot.

The container was tilted further, and shaken, and the brunette, screaming piteously, was tumbled out onto the metal flooring of the hallway.

She rolled to her back and lay there, looking up at the beasts gathered about her. "Please, please," she screamed, "do not hurt me! Do not hurt me! Please, Sirs, do not hurt me!"

How she addressed the Kurii as "Sirs"!

She had perhaps never even used that expression of the males of her world, but now it came from her in her terror, addressed not to men but to these fanged, clustered beasts looking down upon her.

Did she think they would understand what she said?

Doubtless not, but surely her terror, her plaintive mien might be intelligible, perhaps even to a lion or larl! But did she think her pleas might move such beasts, prepared to feed?

Cabot struggled, but could not free himself.

He thought she looked well on her back, in what is referred to as the "capture position." In this position, the captive locked in the arms of the captor, the captor can assess and enjoy the least nuance of expression in the captive's countenance. This position, too, is enjoyed by many masters with their slaves. The gasping, begging, countenance of a slave, wholly surrendered, helpless, sobbing herself his, is often not displeasing to a master. Too, as a male, he could not help but suppose she would also look well on her belly, either looking up to him for mercy, or facing away, that she may the more clearly understand that she is his domestic animal.

Should he have noticed these things?

Certainly, for he was a male.

It is natural and healthy to do so.

And he was now Gorean, and Goreans see the females of their species as, literally, the females of their species.

Too, we recall that she had been selected by Priest-Kings to be excruciatingly desirable to him.

In conversations within the container, not reported in this narrative, she had learned that his name was Tarl Cabot, which name, of course, meant nothing to her, nor was she even aware that Tarl, a name which seemed strange to her, was a not uncommon name on Gor, and one, we may suppose, originally, of Torvaldslandian origin.

Her name, for at that time she had a name, was Virginia Cecily Jean Pym. She was, I think we mentioned, English, sophisticated, educated, and such. Due to family position and wealth, we would have had to account her of the English upper classes, though her origins, in actuality, as nearly as we can determine, were not to be traced through traditional aristocratic lines, at least as far as legitimacy is concerned. A female ancestor, it seems, had caught the eye of a duke of York, though well before certain wars associated with that house and another. In Tarl Cabot's view, whose origins, being mercantile, were perhaps less imposing, she was an insufferably spoiled, snobbish brat. To be fair to Cabot, however, rumors had it, at least, that he might have had some connection with that Venetian John Cabot, or Giovanni Caboto, a Fifteenth-Century (Earth Chronology) mercenary sea captain who sailed for England, in the time of Henry VII, and was the first European after several Viking explorers, mariners, pirates, or such, to make landfall on the coast of North America, which is a portion of Earth's northern hemisphere. But this connection appears dubious, for a number of reasons, primarily having to do with the lack of evidence. There were, however, Cabots in Bristol at the time of Caboto's sailing on May 2, 1497 (Earth Chronology) and that doubtless, human vanity being what it is, sufficed to embellish family lore.

It will help to make certain subsequent developments in our narrative more clear if we add in a further remark, or two, pertaining to the brunette, at that time Miss Virginia Cecily Jean Pym. She had, largely through her upbringing, primarily by servants, occasionally abetted by a distant father and a supercilious, frigid, unhappy mother, and a desire to be faultlessly *au courant*, quite ambivalent attitudes toward the male sex of her species. They did trouble her, for she was raised to suspect and detest them, but, too, to her unease, she found them troubling. She found them both attractive and repellant, such large, crude creatures. Fortunately, they were weak, easily led about, instrumentalized, and so on. In her dreams she wondered if there were other sorts of males, and, at least in her dreams, somewhat to the embarrassment of her waking hours, she discovered them. It is important to understand that her natural needs, drives, and desires were extremely strong, unusually strong, even, dare we suggest it, slave strong. Had she been a scion of a simpler time, with a more natural upbringing and environment, we hazard a conjecture she might well, herself, have captured the eye of a nobleman, as allegedly did an ancestress, a nobleman who, in those days, in one way or another, might pretty much have whatever women, or wenches, he wished. She would surely have run happily to his stirrup. The blood of a needful, yielding female ran deeply in her veins. Genetics had formed her thigh for the kiss of the iron, her throat for the encircling clasp of the collar. Lastly, recall that the Priest-Kings had selected her out, perhaps from thousands, for their purposes, and that our own esteemed confederates, who are specialists in such matters, would have, had they discovered her, unhesitantly entered her on their acquisition lists. She was the sort of woman who belonged in a cage on Gor, from which she might be extracted, to be sold. She was then, in short, a natural slave, who had not yet encountered masters. And recall, as well, that not only had she been selected out to be excruciatingly desirable to Cabot, as a slave, but that he would be to her, in virtue of the same matchings, excruciatingly desirable to her, as a master. He would see her in terms of blood-stirring, virile claimancies, and she would find herself weak and helpless before him, as no more than a begging, pathetic slave.

Would he see fit to satisfy her?

Lastly we might note that Miss Pym, despite ambivalences with respect to the male sex, enjoyed being attractive to them, as she knew she was. She was quite different from those beautiful women who, for some incomprehensible reason, do not think that they are beautiful, perhaps through a failure to fulfill some transitory stereotype of female beauty, one idiosyncratic to a particular time and place. Some of them, nicely curved and naturally bodied, do not understand that they are beautiful until they find themselves in Gorean slave chains. But Miss Pym, whether from vanity or not, was under no delusion with respect to her attractiveness. She might have been a bit shorter or more slender than some slaves but Cabot effected nothing critical on that score, nor, I think, would have many men. To be sure, in a pleasure garden, in virtue of this lack of height and weight, as trifling as it might have been, she would have been subject to several of the other, larger girls, who might have beaten her when they wished, subject, of course, to the intervention of the attendants. Such women long desperately for a private master, but this is not unusual, for any slave. A well-stocked pleasure garden is doubtless pleasant for the master but it is likely to be less pleasant for its inmates, given the boredom, the intrigues, the competitions, the tense, shifting alliances, and such. Too, such gardens are often little more than a vanity amongst rich Goreans, as might be, say, the well-kept gardens surrounding a villa or estate. Wealthy Goreans not unoften strive to rival one another in such matters, as they might in dwellings, stables, walks, parks, and colonnades, in hunting sleen, racing tharlarion, aviaries, art collections, pools, and such. Fashions, too, can change, for example, in the color of grasses favored in pleasure gardens, the hair and eye color of its slaves, and so on. In any event, Miss Pym was under no delusion as to her own attractiveness. Indeed, she probably overestimated it, somewhat, as she had never had any experience of the relevant markets, nor any understanding of how her beauty might rank with that of others, many of them doubtless her superiors. The markets, of course, sort out the beauty of women, on a monetary scale, according to what men are willing to pay for it. But, as of now, perhaps in her vanity, and surely quite complacently, Miss Pym regarded herself not only as an extraordinarily beautiful woman, but, indeed, quite possibly, as the most beautiful woman she had ever seen. And we must admit, certainly given the women she had seen, who were numerous, of course, there was some justification for this view. Certainly she had found it confirmed in her mirror. In any event, she was pleased with her attractiveness, which was of considerable quality, and enjoyed noting its effect on men. It pleased her to trouble and torment them. That is, we suppose, a pleasure natural to beautiful women, to which it would be boorish to object. It is, of course, a pleasure more safely indulged in by free women than slaves, for, in the case of slaves, men, rather than spending their time being troubled and tormented, may simply buy the slave and bring her home, collared and braceleted.

The brunette squirmed on the metal flooring. "Please do not hurt me, please, Sirs!" she cried.

She put her small hands before her face, wildly. Cabot thought they would look nicely in slave cuffs. Were not such small, lovely wrists made for a master's steel?

"Please, Sirs!" she cried. "Do not hurt me! Do not hurt me!"

What are they waiting for, Cabot wondered. Will they not feed now, perhaps even fighting for scraps?

Where are the Priest-Kings, Cabot wondered, wildly.

They must know the security of the Prison Moon has been breached. How long does it take to bring ships to this orbit, with their technology, the closest of the three moons?

"Do not hurt me, Sirs!" she wept.

Did she think the shambling brutes could understand her, other than her fear, her distress? Perhaps they could sense she was begging for mercy. That should be clear enough.

Cabot saw no translators. He knew such devices existed. Indeed, he had had the experience of one in the northern polar regions of Gor, when he had been entertained by Zarendargar, war general of the Kurii. Too, Kurii, most at any rate, would need such devices, surely so, for communicating with their human confederates. Too, there might be different languages spoken in the Steel Worlds. Some humans, incidentally, can make out carefully spoken Kur, but they are unable to reproduce the sounds. Some Kurii, on the other hand, can not only follow carefully spoken Gorean, but are able, in a rough, guttural, rather frightening fashion, to produce a facsimile of, or a form of, Gorean. To be sure it is seldom easy to make this out. With respect to translators more generally, one supposes that the Priest-Kings themselves, whoever or whatever they are, must have such devices in order to communicate with humans, and perhaps, too, with Kurii. But of such things I have no personal experience. Mysterious, one supposes, are the ways of Priest-Kings.

"Please do not hurt me, Sirs!" cried the brunette.

One of the Kurii lowered his head to her body.

It begins, thought Cabot, first the girl, who is small, soft, and tender, and then me, tougher, more sinewy.

"Don't eat me!" she wept. "I will be good. Keep me! I will be very good! I will be obedient! I will serve you! I will do whatever you want!"

You are less prissy and proud now, aren't you, Cabot thought. Would that the males whom you belittled and abused on your world, whom you treated with such disdain and insolence, whom you teased and tormented, could see you now, naked, groveling and begging, before beasts!

Why have the Kurii come to the Prison Moon, Cabot asked himself.

Surely not to rescue a pet.

Why then? For what? To probe the defenses of Priest-Kings, to test equipment, to train and season pilots and task squads, to enact a trial of courage, to fling before Priest-Kings some sort of an act of defiance, what?

Where are the Priest-Kings, Cabot asked himself.

"Masters!" cried the brunette, suddenly, squirming in terror, on the metal floor, and drawing up her legs, the breath of the beast hot on her body, "Masters!"

Cabot was startled.

Had he heard what was said?

Had she said that—what he had thought he had heard?

"Please, Masters!" she screamed, "do not eat me! I will be your slave! Keep me as a slave! Make me your slave! I will be a slave! No, no, I am a slave! I am a slave! Keep me for yourselves, or sell me to men! Do not eat me! Keep me, or sell me! I beg to be your slave, to be kept or sold, as it might please you!"

These words came from her as though from her dreams, wild, tearful, and unutterably heartfelt, but they were cried out in full consciousness, in full waking reality, as she writhed, terrified, on the metal flooring of the hallway, at the clawed feet of fanged Kurii.

She is a slave, thought Cabot. The beautiful, curved, petty, snobbish thing is a slave! Excellent! Does she not know those words cannot be unspoken? She has bespoken herself slave. In all legality the little slut is now a slave. Does she understand that? The words have done it. She is now subject to claimancy. She is now no more than an unclaimed slave!

The closest beast to her, who had put down his head, probably merely to smell her sweat and terror, and the lingering, offensive odors of the container, for most Kurii are less fastidious in such matters than many humans, extended his long, dark tongue and ran it over the side of her body on the left, and she shrieked in terror.

He put his large paw over her face, to silence her, and one could see her eyes, wild, over that hairy appendage which covered most of her face.

She seemed paralyzed with fear.

It then removed its paw from the mouth of the former Miss Virginia Cecily Jean Pym, now, unbeknownst to herself, no longer a free woman, but now only a nameless slave, subject to claimancy.

It stood up.

It wanted salt, thought Cabot.

The Kurii looked about, uneasily.

One of them said something to his fellows, and several of them turned toward the burned, torn metal at the end of the hallway.

They are leaving, thought Cabot.

He remained motionless in the clutch of the Kur who held him, not struggling, passive, seemingly docile, seemingly resigned to his fate, whatever it might be.

One of the Kurii reached down and seized the brunette by the right ankle, lifted it, and, by its means, turned her to her belly. Her eyes were frantic, her ankle lifted and held behind her, and she stretched out her hands to Tarl Cabot, piteously.

He remained inert.

"Mr. Cabot!" she cried. "Mr. Cabot!"

How dared she, a slave, so speak a man's name?

She was half lifted from the floor, facing him.

He did not move, nor gave he any indication he was concerned with her plight.

"Mr. Cabot!" she wept. "Mr. Cabot!"

Again she had dared to use his name!

A girl once collared would fear to do so. A slave addresses free men as Master, free women as Mistress. She would use their name, normally, only when kneeling, and in response to interrogation.

"Slave."

"Yes, Master?"

"What is your name?"

"Margaret, Master."

"Who is your master?"

"Rutilius, Rutilius of Venna, Master."

The Kur who held her ankle turned about and, the ankle retained in his grasp, began to follow those who had already departed the hallway.

"Help me!" screamed the brunette, being dragged away, backwards, on her belly, by the grasped ankle, over the metal flooring, down the hallway, toward the opening. "Help me!" she cried. "What are they going to do with me? What are they going to do with me?"

"They must leave," said Cabot. That seemed obvious to him, given their unease, their behavior.

"What are they going to do with me?" she shrieked.

"You are being saved for later," he said.

"What are they going to do with me!" she cried.

"Presumably you will be eaten," he said.

She shrieked, wildly.

At this point Cabot, who had hitherto for some time remained inert, seemingly crushed and defeated, reconciled to whatever might lie in store for him, in the grasp of his captor, suddenly lashed back with his elbow, striking sharply, heavily, as an ax, into the ribs of the Kur who held him, who, startled, grunting in pain, released him.

A common principle of warfare is surprise, others being such things as concealment, deception, and so on.

In a moment Cabot, perhaps foolishly, had raced after the Kur who was drawing the sobbing, hapless brunette toward the opening at the end of the corridor. It turned suddenly, aware of the sound on the flooring, and threw up its arm before Cabot's thumbs could gouge through its eyes. Such slaves as the brunette belong more properly, after all, to human males, not to Kurii.

Cabot was smote back, and sank groggily to the flooring.

He was aware of the beast reaching for a heat knife, and saw it glow white, almost instantaneously. At the same time he heard the rapid scrape of claws on the flooring behind him, and an enraged bellowing, as of fury and pain, as the Kur he had eluded rushed forward.

Too, he became aware of a large shape, like a boulder of fur, in the doorway, behind the Kur he had attacked.

The brunette screamed in misery, crawling to the side.

He could feel the blistering heat of the knife, and his vision was blinded with its light, which was wildly reflected about, leaping on the walls of the corridor.

One is not to look at the blade of a heat knife, for that is one of its features, and advantages, that it may temporarily blind its target.

Cabot tried to leap up, blindly, but, at that moment, before he could regain his feet, the Kur behind him seized him, lifting him, and holding his arms helplessly to his sides.

Scarcely could Cabot see through the whirlpool and chaos of light which seemed to blaze before him.

He did see the arm with the knife approach.

It will be the heart, he thought, sought within the cavern of exploded ribs, severed from its vessels, and extracted with a paw, to be crammed into a fanged mouth.

But a large paw rested gently on the arm that held the knife, and the knife suddenly turned red, and then gray.

Cabot struggled, weakly, unable to escape the grip of his captor.

He shook his head, trying to restore his vision, trying to resist the saberlike afterimages which seemed to slide and glow, and emerge again and again, on the walls and surfaces of the world before him.

He became aware that a Kur had taken the brunette by the hair and pulled her to her feet, and that she then, bent over, her hair grasped tightly, cruelly, in a paw, was being conducted rapidly, she running beside him, sobbing, from the hallway.

It is a common slave leading position, thought Cabot. A slave's hair is not only beautiful, and may be used for a number of erotic purposes, and, if long enough, for custodial purposes, as well, but it also makes it easy to control her, punish her, and such. When a girl is put into such a leading position, in which she is humiliated, mortified, and helpless, and knows her least recalcitrance may bring her excruciating pain, she is well reminded that she is not a free woman, but a slave.

It was doubtless the first time that the brunette had been put in slave leading position.

It would not be the last.

Cabot struggled to free himself, to pursue the beast in whose keeping was the former Miss Pym.

One really wonders about the rationality of the human species. What could he, alone, weaponless, have done in her behalf, or in his own?

Perhaps there are genetic predispositions to madness in the human species. To be sure, Kurii, too, can be guilty of such indiscretions. Are we not dark brothers?

Cabot shook his head, to clear his vision.

From somewhere he heard a sirenlike whine. It was a signal, doubtless, perhaps of warning, of alarm, perhaps a sign of urgency, perhaps a signal for recall, for regrouping or retreat.

Cabot became aware of a large, shaggy head peering at him, but inches from his face.

The massive, fanged jaws before him seemed twisted into some contorted configuration. Was it meaningless, or did it betoken menace, or was it a smile?

"Half-Ear!" exclaimed Cabot.

He was then cuffed into unconsciousness.

Chapter, the Third:

The Stall

"Why am I on a chain?" she asked.

Cabot shook his head, and tried to bundle his thoughts together, trying to piece a number of diverse shreds and particles into a coherent picture of reality.

He sat up in the straw.

The gravity, he sensed, was much like that of Gor, and much the same as on the Prison Moon. But he did not think he was on Gor, or on the Prison Moon.

He found himself in an open, but low, some four feet in height were the walls, three-sided, boxlike enclosure. It had a wooden floor, which was covered with a heavy layer of straw. It was an enclosure such as might have been used for the bedding of animals, and perhaps, in its way, it was. Following one of the selections of our translator, we shall refer to it as a stall.

A dim light was provided by lamps. They are akin to the energy lamps of Gor, he thought.

Cabot looked across the stall at the brunette, who was kneeling, her knees and thighs obscured by the straw, to his right.

On her neck, closed, was a sturdy metal collar. On this collar there was a heavy collar ring, and to this collar ring there was attached a heavy, black chain, which presumably was fastened to a ring or mount under the straw.

She held the chain near the collar ring and jerked it twice, angrily, against the collar ring. "Explain this!" she demanded. "What is the meaning of this?"

"It is a collar, and chain," said Cabot.

"I am well aware of that," she said. "What is its purpose?"

"To keep you where you are," said Cabot.

She pulled at the chain, angrily. "I am well aware of that!" she snapped.

"Why then did you ask?" said Cabot.

She made an angry noise.

"Perhaps to keep you safe," he suggested.

"From what?"

"I do not know," he said.

"You attempted to rescue me," she said.

"But failed to do so," said Cabot.

"Obviously," she said.

"At least you have not been eaten, at least as yet," said Cabot.

She turned white.

"Do you think—?" she asked.

"Possibly," he said.

"But not yet?"

"No," he said. "I think they have other purposes in mind for us, at least as of now.

"What purposes?"

"I do not know."

"Why are you clothed?" she asked.

"I do not know," he said. He wore a brief, gray tunic, a Gorean man's tunic. He had no weapons.

He regarded her.

Women look well on a chain.

She reddened. She covered her breasts. "Do not look at me!" she said.

"I will do as I please," he said.

"You are not a gentleman!" she said.

He looked away.

"Thank you," she said, coldly.

He looked back at her. It was pleasant to look upon her, particularly as she was on a chain.

"Please!" she protested.

Cabot shrugged. He supposed he might not be a gentleman. It was not of great concern to him. Too, what had gentlemanliness to do with this? She was a slave. She was a domestic animal; she might be chained in a public market, for the inspection of all and sundry.

She had bespoke herself slave.

She was slave.

"What do you suppose your beauty is for?" he asked.

Angrily, she tightened her arms and hands against her body. She does not know she is a slave, he thought. That is all right. She can always learn later. A slave may not conceal her body from a master, of course, without his permission. Her beauty is not hers; it is owned by the master.

Cabot went to the foot of the chain, as she drew back, and ascertained that it was fastened to a heavy ring bolt, anchored in the floor.

"Yes," she said, irritably, "it is fastened quite securely."

Did she not know she could be lashed for speaking in that tone of voice to a free man? Did she think she was a free woman. Yes, thought Cabot, of course, she thinks she is a free woman.

"I am not clothed, and you are," she said.

"Yes?" he said.

Did she not know that she was beautiful, and he was not? And she was, of course, a slave, a chained slave.

"I will see," he said, "if I can arrange some clothing for you."

"Thank you," she said, acidly. "I would be extremely grateful."

He smiled. Did she not know the clothing he would arrange? He thought she would look quite well in a brief slave tunic. Certainly the fellows she had known on Earth would think so.

A slave tunic can be quite fetching on a woman. To be sure, they are designed for that purpose. They display the legs, usually generously, and often the thighs, and do little to conceal the bosom, and her soft, fair shoulders. They leave little to the imagination, and what little they leave calls attention to what is concealed in so delightful and provocative a fashion that the tunic is almost an invitation to its own removal. Some feel that a slave tunic can make a woman look even more naked and vulnerable than when she is stripped. Such tunics, too, despite their brevity, lack a nether closure. In this way, the slave is reminded in yet another little way that she is to be always at the convenience of the master.

"You are not chained," she said.

"No," he said.

"Why?"

"I do not know."

"Please stop looking at me!" she said.

"Why?"

"'Why'!" she exclaimed.

"Yes."

"Beast!"

"Yes," he said.

She gasped, and drew back, clenching her arms yet more tightly about her. After a time, she said, petulantly, sullenly, "You are no gentleman."

"No," he said.

"What are you?" she asked, angrily.

"Gorean," he said.

"What is that?"

"If you live long enough," he said, "you will be taught."

She looked at him, for a moment, quizzically, but did not pursue her question. She knelt back, on her heels.

Excellent, thought Cabot, excellent.

She did not remove her arms and hands from her body, but she straightened her body, and lifted her head, and shook her head a little, to throw her hair behind her.

Good, thought Cabot, good.

She smiled a little smile, at him. He supposed it was to be taken as a shy, rueful, resigned smile. Surely it was artful.

He found her tormentingly attractive to him, but had she not been selected to be so?

She is playing her little game, he thought. She is sensing her power. Doubtless such things in her past well served her purposes. They are less likely to be effective now.

He considered how she would look in a collar, and was pleased. In it her beauty would be much improved. But does not the collar enhance the beauty of any woman, the contrast with her softness, its irremovability, and its meaning?

It is little wonder, he thought, that Merchant Law prescribes that the fair throats of female slaves will know the collar, that their fair throats be clasped within such lovely, indicatory, uncompromising, irremovable, possessive encirclements.

"I suppose," she said, lightly, "you are looking at me because I am beautiful."

"You will do," he said.

"'Do'!" she cried.

"Yes," he said.

"Am I not the most beautiful woman you have ever seen?" she demanded.

"No," he said.

"I have been told by many men," she said, angrily, "that I was the most beautiful woman they had ever seen!"

"They had not seen the women of Gor," he said. To be sure, beauty is more than a mere combination of external relationships, the eyes to the hair, the thigh to the forearm, and such. Beyond such things, of course, it is difficult to define but then, so, too, is almost anything of importance. It is perhaps more analogous to an illumination, or a whisper, or a kiss, than a measurement. Slavery, incidentally, often brings a woman to beauty, for a variety of reasons. Most trivially, within it she is seldom permitted the straining, disfiguring uglinesses common to the free woman, nastiness, arrogance, brassiness, and so on. Such unpleasantries can be lashed out of her, for they are not pleasing to the master. More importantly, more profoundly, in slavery she finds herself in her place in nature, at her master's feet; in slavery she finds herself returned to her womanhood, to her mastered femininity. Perhaps such things explain the common contentment of the slave, so incomprehensible to many free women, her devotion to the master, her instant obedience, her zealous service, her happiness, her love, and so on, and, doubtless, too, her helpless, spasmodic yieldings to his peremptory possession of his property. The slave, perhaps even roped or chained down, may be used in many ways, as the master might please, perhaps tantalized for writhing hours, until she begs for release, or perhaps, if he wishes, merely put to his purposes briefly, perhaps, her tunic torn away, simply flung to the floor, there to be subordinated as the property she is to his authority. Free women sense, perhaps to their rage, but cannot fully comprehend, the pervasive and profound sexuality of the slave, which irradiates and suffuses her entire existence, even in such small things as the touching of a collar, the feel of a tunic, the touch of tiles on her knees or belly, the leathery taste on her tongue as she slowly, humbly, softly, gratefully licks the whip, the sense of fulfillment in kneeling, and bowing her head before her master. It is beyond their ken, unless they should one day find themselves in the collar.

"Gor?" she asked.

"Yes," he said, "a world, one quite different from that with which you have hitherto been familiar."

"This is not Earth," she said.

"No," said Cabot.

"Is this—Gor?" she asked.

"I do not know," he said.

"I demand to be returned to Earth!" she said.

"If they wanted you on Earth," he said, "they would have left you there."

"Perhaps I am being held for ransom?" she said.

"They could have kept you on Earth for that, were it their purpose," he said.

"I want to go back to Earth," she said.

"Earth is behind you," he said.

"Behind me?"

"Yes."

"—Forever?"

"Yes."

"Then I am now—of Gor?" she said.

"Yes," he said, and then added, thoughtfully, "or elsewhere."

"But what is to become of me—on Gor?" she asked. "What could I do on Gor? What could I be on Gor?"

Cabot smiled.

"I do not care for that smile," she said.

How easy it would be, thought Cabot, to simply cuff her, and position her, and begin her training!

He thought it might be pleasant to train her, the haughty little bitch, the supercilious, smug slut.

"Do they speak English on Gor?" she asked.

"No," he said.

"But you speak English."

"I am from England," he said, "Bristol."

"I am from Mayfair," she said.

"Do you wish to live?" he asked.

"Certainly," she said, uneasily.

"Gorean," he said, "from the name of the world, is the most commonly spoken language on Gor. At least that is so in those areas with which I am most familiar, and certainly it is so in the high cities."

"High cities?"

"Ar," said he, "Turia, Ko-ro-ba, Thentis, Treve, Venna, and such."

"Those are cities?"

"Yes," he said. "Most are tower cities, but less so Turia and Venna."

"What are tower cities?"

"The name is presumably because of the architecture of the primary defensive structures, keeps, usually reached by means of unrailed, narrow bridges."

"Why did you ask if I wished to live?" she asked,

"Because," said he, "if you do wish to live, it will be in your interest to learn to speak Gorean, as quickly and as fluently as you can."

"I see," she said.

"Even if this is not Gor," he said, "and I am not sure it is, if there are humans here, humans who have speech, it is probably the language they would speak. Too, if there are translators here, translation devices, many would presumably be devised to deal with Gorean."

"And if I do not care to learn some unusual, strange, and barbarous language?" she asked.

"Gorean," he said, "is a complex, subtle, beautiful language, with a large and sophisticated lexicon."

"Even so," she said, irritably.

"Then, I suppose," said Cabot, "you will be destroyed."

She moved, and the chain dangling from the heavy collar made a tiny sound, against the collar ring.

"You speak Gorean?"

"Yes," he said.

"Teach me," she said, "teach me Gorean."

"You must learn," he said, "five hundred words a day."

"So many?"

"I do not know how much time we have."

"Very well," she said. "Begin."

"You are prepared to say your first words in Gorean?"

"Yes."

"Very well," he said. "Say '*La kajira*.'"

"*La kajira*," she repeated.

"Excellent," he said.

"I am good at languages," she said.

"Excellent," he said.

"*La kajira*," she said. "What a lovely sound."

"Yes," he said, "the word '*kajira*' is a lovely word, with a beautiful sound."

"I like it," she said.

"You are, incidentally," he said, "*kajira*."

She laughed. "I'm happy," she said, "that such a lovely word applies to me."

"It does," he assured her. "It applies to you in fact, and with great aptness."

"Does it mean 'beautiful'?" she asked.

"Not exactly," he said, "but it often suggests female beauty."

"Good," she said.

See her straighten that beautiful body, thought Cabot. Men have bred such as she for generations, for their collars.

"It means 'a beauty' then," she smiled.

"Not exactly," he said, "but many *kajirae*, that is the plural, are beautiful."

"And I am beautiful," she said.

"You will do," he said.

"So, I am *kajira*," she said. "Lovely! What does it mean?"

"You will learn later," he said.

"I suppose," she said, "that we may have to spend some time together."

"Perhaps," he said. "I do not know."

"We have not been properly introduced," she said.

"Did we not do that in the container?" he asked.

"There was no third party," she said, "at least no appropriate third party."

"There was little help for that," he said. "There still isn't."

"No matter," she said. "We must make do, somehow. I am Miss Virginia Cecily Jean Pym, of Mayfair, London."

He smiled.

She no longer had a name. Masters had not yet given her one.

"And you are," she said, "Mr. Tarl Cabot, of Bristol."

"Once so," he said.

"Once so?"

"Yes," he said. "But, too, I have been known as Tarl of Bristol, and Bosk, captain, of Port Kar."

"Considering how we have been so inexplicably and lamentably thrown together," she said, "I think we may as well dispense with certain formalities. I shall refer to you, if I may, as Mr. Cabot."

"And how would you have me refer to you?" he asked.

"Miss Pym will do," she said.

Cabot thought she might make a better Tula, or Tuka, or Lita. Those are common slave names on Gor.

"Miss Pym," he said, "seems somewhat inappropriate, perhaps a bit prim, perhaps even pompous, does it not, for someone in your current circumstances, one who is kneeling in straw, one whose entire ensemble consists of a collar and chain?"

"Very well," she said. "I shall call you Tarl, as though we were better acquainted, and even of the same social class. I shall concede such things. And you may call me 'Virginia.'"

"I will call you 'Cecily,'" he said.

"I prefer 'Virginia,'" she said, coldly.

"I will call you 'Cecily,'" he said.

"Why?" she asked.

"Because I wish to do so," he said.

"I do not care for 'Cecily,'" she said. "I never have. In my view, it is too ordinary a name, too common a name. It is a name less fitting for me than for a shopgirl. It is insufficiently refined."

Whether a name is ordinary or not seems to depend on time and place. For example, 'Cecily' might have been an ordinary name in one of the Englands, hers, at the time, at least in her opinion, but it might have been far less common in, say, another of the Englands. Too, in her own England, at one time, it might have counted as indisputably aristocratic, enough so even for her to have found it acceptable. And once again, who knows, it may again, if it is not already there, ascend the stairs of specialness and regard. Fashion seems to exercise its whimsical rule in such matters. Too, a name which is regarded by one person as ordinary may, by another person, be regarded as quite unordinary. Consider a name such as 'Jane'. That name, as I understand it, surely a beautiful name, is commonly regarded on Earth as an ordinary name. On Gor, on the other hand, it is an unordinary name. It is not unknown, for example, for that name to be given to Gorean slave girls, and not simply because of its convenient brevity and beauty, properties suitable for a slave name, but also because, on Gor, it has an attractive exotic flavor, suggesting foreign places and goods. Earth feminine names, in general, are commonly regarded on Gor as slave names. This is not surprising as Earth females are regarded as slave stock, suitable for the collars of Gorean masters.

"I will call you 'Cecily,'" he said.

Cabot had seen more than one girl from England chained in a Gorean market whose name had been Cecily. It was a not unprecedented name for Gorean slave girls from that part of the Earth. So, too, I am told, are names such as Jane, as suggested, and others, Jean, Joan, Margaret, Helen, Elizabeth, Marjorie, Allison, Corinne, Constance, and such. Those may not have been their original names, of course. Masters name their girls as they please. To be sure, such names are also not unknown, as I am informed, in the colonies, or former colonies, of that place, too, one of the Englands. Perhaps in her present predicament, naked and chained, she reminded Cabot of one or more of the girls he had seen in the markets. Or perhaps he just thought it would be a name acceptable for her, at least temporarily.

"What if I do not choose to respond to that name," she said.

"Then I will beat you," he said.

"Beat me?"

"Yes."

"I am Virginia Cecily Jean Pym!" she said. "—Beat me?"

"Yes."

"You would not dare!"

"You are mistaken."

"You are, of course, larger and stronger than I."

"Yes."

"You would beat me?"

"Certainly."

"You may call me 'Cecily,'" she said.

"It is what I *will* call you," he said.

"Very well," she said. She drew back, abashed, uncertain of her feelings.

She put her hands on the chain, and pulled it a little against the collar ring. She was well fastened in place.

She would be addressed as men pleased. This, thought Cabot, is a good lesson for her. She is not having her own way. She is unaccustomed to being under male discipline. To be sure, she had been positioned in the container, when he had been examining her for slave marks. And later, for a time. She is trying to understand her feelings, he thought. She is sexually aroused, and she does not clearly understand how it has come about. Women respond well to male domination. They are, after all, females. She would make an excellent slave, thought Cabot. And Cabot, of course, at that time, did not well understand that the female had not only the profound sexual needs and drives of a lovely, helpless, vulnerable slave, and remarkably so, but that she had been chosen for him, and for him in particular, with exactly such things in mind.

How helplessly she would find herself his!

Are the Priest-Kings not cruel?

"May I call you 'Tarl'?" she inquired.

"For now," he said.

It would be time enough later, to let her know what she had done on the Prison Moon, that she had bespoken herself slave, and in so doing had renounced her freedom, irrecoverably, that it had been an act which it was now wholly beyond her power to revoke, amend or qualify in any way. It would be time enough later to let her know that she was now property, merely unclaimed property.

He did not think the fellows she had known on Earth would have objected to this.

Would they not have liked to have her kneeling naked at their feet, collared, fearing the lash, if she were found in the least displeasing?

Tarl Cabot rose to his feet, and looked about himself.

"What do you see?" she asked.

Curiosity, he thought, is not becoming in a *kajira*. Yet they tend to be persistently, delightfully, sometimes annoyingly, incorrigibly, curious.

"More stalls," he said. "A passageway, wooden, between them. This is, I think, a stable."

"A stable!"

"Surely, does it not seem so?"

"I, in a stable!"

"It would seem so," he said.

He then turned about.

"Where are you going!" she called. She stood up, frantically, clumsily, and found herself partly bent over, for the length of the chain did not permit her to stand erect. She must have felt she looked absurd, for she quickly knelt, again.

She clutched her arms about herself.

So might a lovely tabuk doe be tethered in the straw, thought Cabot, though for such, lacking hands, a light strand on the neck might do.

To be sure, a much lighter chain would have held her. She was a female.

How lovely they are, he thought. They are so different from us. They are made by nature to be our slaves.

To be sure, they can be nuisances, until they are collared.

"Do not leave me!" she cried.

"Are you afraid?" he asked.

"Of course not!" she said.

"Then you are stupid," he said.

"Are you afraid?" she asked.

"Yes," he said.

"I am afraid," she said.

"Good," he said.

He turned about, again.

"Do not leave me alone!" she cried.

He moved toward the opening of the stall.

"Don't go!" she cried. "If you leave me I shall scream!" she said.

He turned back, toward her.

He had at his disposal no convenient means with which to bind her, hand and foot, and gag her.

He read her body.

Binding and gagging a woman, and leaving her alone, for an Ahn or so, can be instructive to her.

He had little doubt but what the former Miss Pym would find it so. She was clearly highly intelligent.

But he had no convenient means for such at his disposal.

He regarded her, closely.

She knelt before him, looking up at him.

Again he read her body, her slave body.

She does not know it, he thought, but she is ready, nearly ready, for the mastering.

"I would not scream," he said. "You do not know who or what might hear."

"I am prepared to accept that risk," she said.

"I am not," he said.

"Do not leave me!" she said. "What are you going to do!" she cried, drawing back, alarmed, as he approached her.

He took a large handful of dry, bristling straw and placed it, crosswise, in her mouth. He then stood up, and looked down at her, she looking up at him, disbelievingly, her eyes wide, her mouth filled with the stallage. "Do not expel that," he said, "until given permission. Do you understand?"

She nodded.

He then left the stall and began to make his way down the passageway between stalls, for there were several in the structure.

After a time he returned.

He knelt beside the brunette and drew the damp, partly crushed straw from her mouth. Then she put her head to the side, and, fingering within her mouth, and spitting, she ridded herself of the residue of the straw.

Then she looked at him reproachfully. "What you did to me!" she said.

"We had little but straw to work with," he said. "I regret that."

"I am not prepared to accept your apology," she said.

"I do not apologize, nor should I," said he. "It is only that I regret that proper materials were not at hand. I think you would have looked quite nice, bound, hand and foot, and gagged, lying in the straw on your chain."

"What manner of man are you?" she asked, angrily.

"Gorean," he said. "And you are a female."

"What did you learn?" she asked.

"I looked about," he said. "There is no escape. There are bars. The stable is of wood, but it is within what seems to be a housing of iron or steel. I could see very little outside the stable."

"Are we—on Gor?" she asked.

"I do not think so," he said.

"Are we to starve here?" she asked.

"I would not think so," he said.

"What is to be done with us?"

"I do not know."

"Must you look at me so?"

"You have nice curves," he said.

She looked away, angrily.

"Do you know what such curves are called, on Gor?"

"No," she said.

"Slave curves," he said.

"How vulgar, how horrid!" she exclaimed.

"Not at all," he said. "You have a lovely body, lovely enough to be that of a slave." He continued to scrutinize her. "Yes," he said, "you have an excellent body, a slave body."

"Beast!" she exclaimed.

"You would probably bring a good price in a market."

"A market!"

"A slave market, of course."

"Never!" she cried. "Never!"

He saw that she was sexually stimulated, muchly aroused. Clearly, and not only in her dreams, she had often thought herself a slave, and had perhaps foolishly suffered and struggled against her body and its needs, her heart and its needs, against the primitive depth and helpless wholeness of her slave needs.

Doubtless often, in her dreams and otherwise, she had stood upon the slave block, in sawdust, in the light of torches and lamps, exhibited, and had been auctioned to the highest bidder. Doubtless, often, she had been led from the market, back-braceleted, and leashed, perhaps hooded, led as might be any other newly purchased animal, to her new home. Doubtless, too, she had often knelt before masters, or kissed their feet, in gratitude and love, in reverence or supplication. Perhaps she had sometimes been bound to an overhead whipping ring and had been switched, or lashed, for some miniscule fault or shortcoming. Perhaps, often, she had striven in chains, desperately, fearfully, to give her master inordinate pleasures.

"I wonder if you have had your slave wine, or some similar substance, something with the same consequences or effects," he said.

"What is slave wine?" she asked.

"Never mind," said he.

Slaves, as domestic animals, are normally bred only as the masters please.

"Are you a virgin?" he asked.

"That is my business!" she snapped.

"A determination might be made," he said.

"Yes," she said, angrily. "I am a virgin!"

Strange that she, a virgin, he thought, should be so soon on the verge of begging for sex. Already thought Cabot she feels the warmth of slave fires in her belly. He did not think it would take long before she became their piteous, begging prisoner.

Perhaps it is the chain, he thought, the chain, binding fiber, such things, which hasten such things, which bring a female so rapidly, so pathetically, so needfully, so openly and honestly, to her knees.

"What are we to do now?" she asked, uneasily.

"We shall continue with your lessons in Gorean," he said.

She put down her head, her small hands on the chain dangling from her collar. "Very well," she said.

"But," said he, "we will try to do a thousand words a day."

"I think I cannot do so much," she said.

"We will do the best we can," he said.

"Why so many?"

"I do not know how much time we have," he said.

"No," she said. "This has to do with something you saw, something you saw outside the stable."

"Perhaps," he said.

"What was it?" she asked.

"Doubtless in time you will learn," he said.

"I want to live," she said.

"We will do the best we can," he said.

"*La kajira!*" she said.

"Excellent," he said.

"You see," she said. "I remembered!"

"Excellent," he said.

"Those are my first words in Gorean!" she said.

"And appropriately so," he said.

"Why?"

"It does not matter now," he said.

"They mean I am a beautiful female!" she said.
"Something like that," he said, "or usually."
"I did not forget them," she said.
"Good," he said.

Chapter, the Fourth:

The Interlocutor

"What are you?" asked Cabot.

"The result of an experiment," he said.

I think I have made clear the difficulties of replicating in a human tongue the phonemes of Kur, as we shall refer to the language of this particular habitat, one, actually, of several in the worlds, and, correspondingly, naturally, the difficulty of reproducing in Kur the phonemes of typical human languages. These difficulties index almost entirely to anatomical dissimilarities. To be sure, it is somewhat easier for a Kur to utter noises which, allowing for considerable distortions, or, shall we say, accent, better approximate human phonemes than the reverse. It is possible, of course, for a Kur to recognize certain sounds in, say, Gorean, and for a human to recognize certain sounds in Kur. I think I mentioned, for example, that the blonde pet from the container could recognize her name in Kur, certain commands, and such. It is one thing, naturally, to recognize a sound and another to replicate it. Consequently, most communication between humans and Kurii is accomplished by means of translators. This note is largely to remind any reader unfamiliar with Kur that in the interests of intelligibility we must either devise names for individual Kurii, or have recourse to descriptions, or such. It would be difficult or impossible to replicate the actual phonemes. The reader is familiar with this already in the case of Zarendargar. Accordingly, various Kurii will be herein referred to in terms hopefully intelligible to, or at least pronounceable by, readers unfamiliar with Kur. I think we have no practical alternative to this procedure, and, accordingly, we beg the reader's indulgence with respect to this liberty, accompanied as it must be by its concomitant distortions.

"You are not Kur," said Cabot.

"I am Kur," he said.

Cabot's interlocutor surely wore Kur harness, though he was not armed, not even with the small throwing ax, or night ax, commonly used in approaching isolated sentries, and such.

"No," said Cabot.

This conversation was at the time being conducted by means of the interlocutor's translator, clipped to the harness. The device may then be carried or not, as one desires, and, when carried, does not impede movement. This particular model was disklike, and with a diameter of less than two hort. It would fit easily into the palm of even a human.

"Why do you say that?" inquired the interlocutor.

"I think," said Cabot, "you could speak Gorean."

"I am not to blame for my defects," he said.

You see the interlocutor's voice was somewhat other than that of the Kur, though surely Kurlike.

But that had been part of the experiment.

The first time the brunette had seen the interlocutor she had screamed and scrambled back, to the end of her chain, as close as she could to the rear wall of the stall.

Cabot had stood, to greet him, lifting his hand, and saying, "Tal."

The interlocutor had then, in its shambling way, put down the bowl of food and the bota of water. Later he had brought a wastes bucket. Neither time did he speak, either verbally or through the translator.

"It is hideous!" had said the brunette, when their keeper, or keeper's helper, had departed.

"It is different, surely," had said Cabot.

"It is the sort of thing that brought us here," said the brunette.

"Similar," said Cabot, "not the same, not exactly the same."

"Animals! Beasts!" said the brunette.

"They are Kurii," said Cabot. "One would be spoken of as a Kur."

"It is one of them," she said. "Can you not see that?"

"I am not sure," said Cabot.

"It is very much like one," said Cabot.

"The same!" she exclaimed.

"Much the same," agreed Cabot.

When the next day he came again with food and water, and to replace the wastes bucket with a cleaner vessel, the brunette crouched down in the straw, but did not scream.

The interlocutor had brought food, and water.

Naturally she wished to eat and drink.

Interestingly he had put the bowl of food and the bota beyond her reach.

Cabot wondered if the Kurii who had been on the Prison Moon had informed him of the brunette's words in the hallway, those words which had in no more than a moment changed her into marketable goods.

"I am hungry," said the brunette.

Cabot let her feed first.

Let her think, thought he, she is still a free woman. She can learn later she is *kajira*. Besides, we may soon be eaten. Yet, thought he, I do not think we are to be eaten, certainly not yet, for we have not yet been eaten, and, too, if we were to be eaten, would we not be fattened, or such, not given this gruel, these pellets, and water?

Cabot noticed that she had left him less than half of the food.

He said nothing about this.

It is perhaps an inadvertence, he thought.

Such things should not happen with a slave, of course. She will feed after the master or under the supervision of the master. In any event, the master would be the first to partake of the food, be it only with so little as a finger lifted to his tongue.

She took, in English, to abusing the quiet interlocutor in his attendance, treating him shortly, and with contempt.

She referred to him as "Caliban," which is apparently a reference to the literature of one of the Englands. From the reaction of Cabot one gathers the reference was not complimentary, nor was it intended to be so.

"He cannot understand me," she said.

"Much can be gathered from expressions," said Cabot, "the tone of one's voice, the attitude of one's body, such things."

"He is stupid, a beast," she said.

"He is much like a Kur," said Cabot, "and many Kurii are of high intelligence."

"He is a Kur," she said.

"Perhaps," said Cabot.

"They are stupid beasts," she said.

"I would show him more respect," said Cabot.

"Why?"

"He might take you off your chain and eat you," said Cabot, "or eat you on your chain."

"Oh," she said.

"Perhaps you should think of him less as Caliban," said Cabot, "and more as Grendel."

The translator is of little help here, but one gathers this was a reference accessible to the brunette. One takes it from the context that a Grendel might be less patient, or more menacing, or more dangerous, than a Caliban, whatever such things might be.

Also, interestingly, as clarified later, Cabot conjectured that an entity spoken of as "Grendel" had once existed on the Earth, and might have been Kur. Similarly, it was his speculation that certain other entities alleged to exist on Earth, particularly in remote mountainous or forested areas, might have been Kurii. We make no judgment on this matter, but it is true that occasionally Kurii were abandoned or marooned on Earth, usually for insubordination, or as a consequence of mutiny, or such.

"Why does he put the food by you first," she asked, "where I cannot reach it?"

"I do not know," said Cabot.

"He is a weakling," she said.

"I do not think so," said Cabot. "Let us continue with your lessons in Gorean."

"Is it male?" she asked.

"I think so," he said.

"I despise males," she said, "—present company excepted, of course."

"You need not except the present company," he said.

"Very well," she said.

Cabot thought she would look well on her belly, licking and kissing a man's feet, hoping to be found pleasing.

He supposed that she had had little experience of a certain sort of males, namely, men.

He considered the interlocutor. He was sure he was male, but was perhaps a nondominant, a male who was forbidden to express his maleness, who does not practice it, who has not fulfilled it, such things.

He wondered if many of the males of Earth were nondominants.

Little wonder then, he thought, that so many of the women of Earth languish, deprived, in sexuality's polar wastes, that so many suffer seemingly inexplicable chronic ailments, that so many are mired in boredom or depression, that so many are twisted in neurosis, that so many are frustrated, miserable, petty, irritable, and nasty, that so many are unfulfilled and tragically unhappy.

Send the better ones, he thought, to a Gorean slave block.

Consider the former Miss Pym, he thought.

She would much profit from a slave collar and a taste of the lash.

"What are you thinking about?" she asked.

"Let us continue with your lessons," he said.

"Very well," she said.

"I think," said Cabot, to the interlocutor, "you do not need the translator."

The interlocutor did not respond, but turned, and left.

"Of course it needs a translator," said the brunette.

"I am not sure of that," said Cabot.

"It is a Kur," she said.

"It is much like one," said Cabot.

"Kur," she said.

"The eyes," said Cabot, "seem different."

"I do not know that much about Kurii," she said. Certainly they do not look human."

"You are right," said Cabot.

She sniffed. "When next he comes, use the translator," she said, "and demand more and better food, richer food, and more of it, and something other than water to drink, and demand proper clothing for me."

"What would you consider proper clothing?" he asked.

"I do not understand," she said. "Why are you smiling?"

He had perhaps in mind a slave strip, or a slave rag, or perhaps a nice tunic, or part of one, and, doubtless, a close-fitting, suitable collar.

"Something appropriate," she said, "indeed, a wardrobe, casual wear, street wear, sports wear, perhaps even evening wear, such things, a wardrobe of high quality, one compatible with my social position. Why are you smiling?"

"You are learning Gorean," he said. "Why do you not insist on these demands yourself."

"My Gorean is not yet that good," she said.

"I am afraid our friend," said Cabot, "does not always turn his translator on."

"I am afraid," she said, "he has little authority."

"I think you are right," said Cabot.

"But he could surely nonetheless convey my demands, our demands, to his superiors," she said.

"Doubtless," said Cabot.

"Speak to him," she said.

"If you wish," he said.

The next day Cabot brought the wishes of his stall mate to the attention of the interlocutor, making quite certain, in a civil and polite manner, of course, but not in an obsequious manner, that he understood that these were the insistencies, or demands, of the brunette, and he was acting as a mere intermediary.

Cabot, you see, was well aware that he and his lovely stall mate were in no position to make demands.

He was grateful that to this point, at least, they had their lives.

The brunette did not follow the conversation well, given the current status of her Gorean.

At one point the interlocutor turned to the brunette and looked at her, as though for the first time, and looked at her rather intently. The brunette, disconcerted, drew back on the chain, and covered herself, as well as she could.

"She is pretty, is she not?" inquired the interlocutor.

"Yes," said Cabot.

"I know one that is much prettier," said the interlocutor.

"Oh?" said Cabot.

"They are so smooth," said the interlocutor.

"Yes," agreed Cabot. Too, that smoothness felt well within one's arms, warm, soft, alive, squirming, vulnerable.

"There are others, some others," said the interlocutor, "some with the men."

"There are men here?" asked Cabot.

"Some," said the interlocutor, "and not those in the pens, but the allies, those who have the small ships."

"Confederates of your people?" said Cabot.

"Yes," said the interlocutor, looking at him, closely, "of my people."

He looked back at the brunette, who regarded him, angrily.

"She is *kajira*, is she not?" asked the interlocutor.

"Yes," said Cabot.

The brunette, hearing this word, straightened her body a little.

How vain she is, thought Cabot.

The interlocutor then turned about, and left.

"What did he say, about our demands?" asked the brunette. "Is he going to convey them to his superiors?"

"Your demands," said Cabot. "And he did not say anything about it, one way or the other."

"What a stupid beast!" she said.

"I do not think so," said Cabot.

"Next time," she said, "you must be more firm, more insistent."

"You may speak yourself, next time, if there is a next time," he said.

"My Gorean!" she protested.

"Speak in English," he said.

"He would not understand," she said.

"No, he would not."

"Then what would be the point of it?"

"There is no point to it," he smiled.

"My demands are meaningless?"

"Yes," said Cabot. "Now kneel there on your chain and think about that."

"I did hear the word '*kajira*'," she said, pleased.

"Yes," said Cabot.

"He thinks I am beautiful," she announced.

"Pretty, at least," said Cabot.

"'Pretty'!" she said. "Beautiful!"

Cabot smiled.

"You at least," she said, "can see that I am beautiful, extraordinarily, remarkably beautiful!"

"You will do," he said.

"Beast!"

"I told you, did I not, that I thought you would bring a good price—in a market, a slave market."

"Beast! Beast!" she said.

But Cabot could see that she was pleased. What woman has not wondered what she might be worth, what men would pay for her?

If a female wishes to understand what she is, let her consult her fantasies, her dreams.

"He thought that I was pretty?" she asked.

"I think so," said Cabot.

"But what would a beast, such a beast, know about female beauty?" she asked.

Cabot shrugged.

"—You don't think?" she said. She jerked at the chain, frightened.

"I do not know," he said.

"How long have we been here?" she asked.

"I think five days," he said.

"The light here is dim, but constant," she said.

"I have frequently gone to the barred portal, through the passages, sometimes while you slept, and there have been there five lights and five darknesses."

"Day and night!" she exclaimed. "Then we are on a world!"

"We are on a world," he said. "I am sure of it."

"Then it is a natural world, a planet, for there is day and night!" she said.

"In a way, I suppose," he said.

"I do not understand," she said, "the rotation of a planet in its orbit, about its star."

"Things, I think, might be managed differently," he said.

"I do not understand," she said.

"I noted something of interest," he said, "about our friend, something I should have noticed before."

"What? The eyes, the voice?"

"The hand," said Cabot, "certainly you saw the powerful digits."

She shuddered.

"It is clearly the match for a Kur hand," he said.

"It is a Kur hand," she said irritably.

"Certainly not a typical Kur hand," he said.

"Why not?" she asked.

"The Kur hand, or paw," he said, "has six digits. The hand, or paw, of our friend has five digits."

Chapter, the Fifth:

The Steel World

"Ai!" cried Cabot, who was startled, for he was not accustomed to such things.

In the cylinder it seemed there were four long valleys, in one of which they stood; some yards outside the stable, and on the left and right, far off, on each horizon, as though in the sky, there was another valley, and another, dim, far off, lay directly overhead. Between these valleys there were mountains and forests. And Cabot, too, could see, here and there, like a silver thread, a meandering stream.

"There," said his guide, whom we shall call Arcesilaus, pointing to the left, into the distance, and sky, "is Lake Fear. There is good fishing there, as there is in the streams, and pools."

"Why is it called Lake Fear?" asked Cabot.

He was aware that Kurii were not fond of water.

"Because of the saurians there," responded Arcesilaus, "descendents of saurians from the Home World."

"And you fear them?"

"Yes."

"Where is the Home World?" asked Cabot.

"It is gone," said the second Kur, whom we shall call Pyrrhus.

"But we shall have another," said Arcesilaus.

"It is called Gor," said Pyrrhus.

"What is above us does not fall upon us," observed Cabot. It seemed strange to him to see above him, so distant, what he took to be trees, and dwellings, viewed as though from overhead, and yet he was clearly below them, or, perhaps, equivalently, above them.

"This habitat, as many, is a cylinder," said Arcesilaus, "but many, too, are spherical."

"The gravity surrogate," said Pyrrhus, "is achieved by rotation."

"It seems much like that of Gor," said Cabot.

"Intentionally," said Pyrrhus.

"One can arrange a variety of gravities," said Arcesilaus, "depending on the speed of the rotation."

"I did not understand such worlds to be so large," said Cabot.

"This is far from the largest," said Arcesilaus.

"How large is it?" asked Cabot.

"In measures with which you are familiar," said Arcesilaus, "some sixteen hundred square pasangs."

"The territory of Venna," said Cabot, "is not so great."

"I do not know," said Arcesilaus.

"It is very large," said Cabot.

"Far from the largest," said Arcesilaus.

"It is the size of a small country," said Cabot.

"I suppose so," said Arcesilaus.

"There is day and night here," said Cabot. He had ascertained this while still in the stable. The brunette had been left behind, on her chain. With the group, other than Cabot, Arcesilaus, and Pyrrhus, were the interlocutor, whom we shall call, following an earlier conversation between Cabot and the brunette, Grendel, and one or perhaps two others, depending on how one wishes to count. We must certainly count at least one, for he was a male human, a Gorean, a confederate of the Kurii, whose name was Peisistratus, who was of Cosian origin. He was not armed, for humans are not permitted arms in the habitat, save in the areas reserved for them. He did, however, carry a switch. It was some two feet in length. It was clipped on his belt. It was of slender, black, supple leather. It was felt that his presence might be useful if difficulties arose in communication with the human, Tarl Cabot. Also, as we know now he was a spy for the Eleventh Face of the Nameless One, who was Theocrat of the Steel World in question. When necessary, we shall refer to the Eleventh Face of the Nameless One, not inappropriately we trust, by the name of a powerful war leader and king, Agamemnon. The Agamemnon of whose name we have availed ourselves may, as we understand it, have been mythical. I suspect not. The Eleventh face of the Nameless One, however, is not mythical. Its presence we are told is everywhere. I do not know if that is true or not. I doubt it, however, for if it were true, why would it make use of spies? It does, however, upon occasion, assume bodies. I have seen more than one.

The other entity in our small group, which may or may not be counted, as one wishes, was the leashed pet of Arcesilaus, an unspeeched blonde human female, indeed, she whom we encountered earlier in the container. She was very pleased to have been allowed to accompany her master, even into the stable, where he, Pyrrhus, the interlocutor, and Peisistratus, the human, had come to fetch Tarl Cabot, who had, upon their arrival, risen to his feet, and saluted them, with an uplifted hand, and the word "Tal," to which greeting Peisistratus had responded, similarly. "Tal" had come, too, from the translators of Arcesilaus and Pyrrhus. The blonde had snarled at the brunette, for she remembered her with hostility from the container, and the brunette, on all fours, had drawn back, pulling to the length of her chain.

Her discomfiture amused the human, Peisistratus. "She is *kajira*?" he inquired of Cabot.

"Yes," said Cabot.

"Why is she not in position?" inquired Peisistratus.

"She does not know she is *kajira*," said Cabot.

"Position her," said Peisistratus.

"She is still learning the language," said Cabot. Among Goreans when one speaks of "the language," it is always Gorean, as though no others existed.

"She is not speechless?" asked Peisistratus.

"No," said Cabot.

"She is a barbarian," he said.

"Yes," said Cabot. Goreans often think of those who do not speak their language as barbarians. Indeed, that is the usual definition of a barbarian in Gorean, "one who does not speak the language."

"Earth?"

"Yes," said Cabot.

"I have gathered fruit on Earth," said Peisistratus.

"You are a slaver?" said Cabot.

"Yes," he said. "What is her language?"

"English," said Cabot.

Peisistratus turned to the brunette.

He spoke to her in English.

"Girl!" he said.

"I beg your pardon," she said, startled.

"Slut!" he snapped.

"Sir!" she protested.

"Are you a female?"

"I do not understand," she said.

"Are you a female?" he inquired, again, patiently.

"Obviously!" she said.

"And how should a female be before men?" he asked.

"I do not understand you," she said, frightened.

"Are you *kajira*?" he asked, harshly.

She looked wildly at Cabot, who nodded.

"Yes," she said, nodding, "I am *kajira*."

Peisistratus looked to Cabot. "I thought you said she did not know herself *kajira*."

"She does not know the meaning of the word," he said. "She thinks it means she is beautiful, or a beauty, such things."

Peisistratus then turned again to the girl.

He removed the switch from his belt.

She regarded the implement disbelievingly.

"Kneel," said Peisistratus to the girl, "now, instantly! Back on your heels. Spread your knees!"

"My knees!" she cried.

"Yes," he said, "widely. More widely! Straighten your back, place your hands, palms down, on your thighs, lift your head, look straight ahead!"

"Never!" she cried.

And then the switch fell savagely upon her, twice.

She screamed in misery.

She looked at Cabot, startled, disbelievingly, in pain. She had felt the switch. Cabot supposed it might have been the first blow she had ever received. This was true, as she had been, for most practical purposes, reared by nurses, maids, and governesses, none of whom would have dared risk their positions by more than a suggestion or a gently reproving word, easily ignored. "Help me!" she cried. There were two marks on her body. Doubtless the blows stung. He had struck her only twice. He had shown her indulgence, doubtless because he sensed her ignorance. A more aware *kajira* would have doubtless been punished seriously for her lack of instant obedience. But then a more aware *kajira* would not be likely to have been punished at all, for she would have obeyed instantly. Aware *kajirae* are seldom punished, for there is no reason to punish them. They know, of course, that they may be punished for the least failure to be fully pleasing. Indeed, they know, as well, the master needs no reason to punish them. They may be punished at any time, at his pleasure, with or without a reason. He is master.

"No," he said.

"Up, slut, position, position!" said Peisistratus.

Wildly, frantically, sobbing, tears streaming from her eyes, in pain, the brunette knelt before Peisistratus, in position, as required.

"Keep your hands on your thighs!" snapped Peisistratus, for she had dared to move to cover herself.

She complied instantly.

Cabot was pleased to note this alacrity.

Too, he was pleased to see her in position.

She looked well in position, in the position of a Gorean female slave, indeed, rather, in the position of a Gorean female slave of a particular sort, the Gorean female pleasure slave.

Indeed, Cabot thought, she might make a nice pleasure slave.

He supposed that her former male acquaintances would have enjoyed having her kneeling so, before them.

"Do you speak Gorean?" Peisistratus inquired of the girl.

"A little," she stammered. "A few words, some simple sentences!"

"What were your first words in Gorean?" he asked.

"*La kajira!*" she said.

Peisistratus then turned to Cabot, and he spoke in Gorean. "You did well," he said.

"She bespoke herself *kajira* on a satellite of Priest-Kings, the Prison Moon," said Cabot.

"I had heard this," said Peisistratus, who glanced at Arcesilaus, who nodded.

The two men then returned their attention to the girl on the chain, kneeling before them, in the straw.

Yes, Cabot thought, the former male acquaintances of the former Miss Virginia Cecily Jean Pym would have doubtless enjoyed seeing her as she was now, frightened, and obedient, in the position of a Gorean pleasure slave, subject to masculine discipline and direction.

"You are a professional slaver, are you not?" said Cabot.

"Yes," said Peisistratus.

"What do you think of her?" asked Cabot.

"Less than a half tarsk," he said.

"So little?" said Cabot.

"She is a barbarian," he said. "She knows little Gorean. She is new to her condition. She is ignorant, untutored, untrained. She does not yet know how to drive a man out of his mind with pleasure."

"But we are thinking in terms of silver, I trust."

"Yes, silver."

"Then you think she has promise?"

"They all have promise," he said. "The collar brings out their beauty. Her slave curves could be worse."

Cabot nodded. To him, of course, somehow, she was maddeningly attractive. Had not the Priest-Kings seen to that? But, too, he did not doubt that she was, objectively, an incredibly beautiful young woman, who would be of interest to almost any connoisseur of her form of merchandise. And he did not doubt that several of the men she had known on Earth might very well have considered her, as she had claimed, the most beautiful woman they had ever seen. And she, in her unweening vanity, may well have held this view herself. Her mirror, surely, had not lied. On the other hand, her mirror, too, had not been familiar with, other than its owner, women of an excellence sufficient to be brought to the marking irons and the clasping collars of Gor.

"What do you think, with training, and such," asked Cabot.

"Perhaps as much as three silver tarsks," he said, "perhaps as much as four, or five."

"Excellent," said Cabot.

In a market where beauty was commonly cheap that was an excellent price. But had he not assured her that he thought she would sell well, that she would bring a good price in market of the right sort, a slave market?

"Do you have any objection," inquired Peisistratus, "to

enlightening this stupid little vulo, this ignorant little tasta, as to what she is?"

Cabot shrugged. "No," he said, "she must learn sometime."

"I think it will be much to her advantage to come to a realization of this as soon as possible, particularly if she should be outside the stable."

Cabot regarded the former Miss Pym, who had wisely retained position.

"I think so," said Cabot.

Women well understand the switch, the whip, the rope, the chain, such things, often from the very first sight of them.

Outside the stable, a slave, not knowing herself a slave, she might inadvertently behave improperly, and find herself subjected to reprimands which might place her very life in jeopardy. Too, in many milieus it is far safer for a woman to be a slave than to be free. The free person might be simply slain; the slave, as a valued domestic animal, would be far more likely to be spared. Similarly, one would not slay valued kaiila but would add them to one's herds.

Peisistratus then spoke to the brunette in English.

"Repeat," he said, "firmly, and clearly, the first words you learned in Gorean."

"*La kajira!*" she said.

"Again!" he snapped.

"*La kajira!*"

"Keep your knees apart!"

She complied, frightened.

How soft, and inviting, were her thighs, and how sweet the secret gate to which they led.

"Again!"

"*La kajira!*" she cried.

"It is true," he said.

"Sir?"

"What do they mean?" he said.

"I do not know," she sobbed. "That I am a beauty, that I am beautiful, I do not know!"

"You are vain, are you not?"

"I do not know!" she wept.

"You are," he said.

"Yes, Sir," she sobbed.

"But that is quite all right, for one such as you," he said.

"For one such as I?"

"Yes," he said, "for one who is *kajira*."

"It does mean then that I am beautiful?"

"No," he said, "but it is seldom that one who is not beautiful is *kajira*."

She regarded him, frightened.

"You suspect, do you not?" he asked.

"No," she said. "No! No!"

"Yes," said he. "It means 'I am a slave girl.'"

"No!" she cried. "No! No! No!"

"Do not break position," warned Peisistratus.

"You bespoke yourself slave on the Prison Moon," said Cabot. "The words were spoken. The thing was done."

"I was frightened!" she said. "I didn't think! I didn't know what I was saying!"

"Slaves may not lie," said Cabot. "Do not lie. You knew well what you were saying. Do not lie. You are not a free woman. They may lie, you may not. Do not lie. You are now subject to discipline, and may be whipped."

"Whipped?"

"Yes," said Cabot. "The words were spoken. That is sufficient. It was done. Clearly, too, you meant what you said. It was obvious. But that is not important. It does not matter whether you meant what you said or not. The words were spoken. The thing was done."

"I was then a slave?"

"Yes."

"I am a slave?"

"Yes."

"You knew this all the time!" she said to Cabot.

"Yes," he said.

"But you did not tell me!"

"Of course not," said Cabot. "I was amused by your arrogance, and such, how you carried on as though you might be free."

"You were playing with me!"

"Yes," said Cabot.

"Beast!" she wept, but feared to break position.

"Yes," said Cabot.

"Free me!" she cried.

"Free yourself," he said.

"How, how?" she asked.

"There is no way," he said. "You are slave. There is no way you can free yourself."

"I despise men!" she cried.

"I do not think so," he said.

"I do, I do despise them!" she wept.

"You now belong to them," he said.

"I do not want to be a slave!" she cried.

"You will commonly kneel in the presence of free persons," said Cabot. "You will address free men as "Master," free women as "Mistress." Instant and unquestioning obedience is expected of you. Commonly, you are not to speak unless you have been given permission to do so. When you speak you will speak with softness and deference. You can own nothing. It is you who are owned. You are a property, an animal, subject to buying and selling, trading, and such. You are completely at the disposal and pleasure of your master, in all ways."

"In all ways?"

"Yes."

"—Even?"

"Yes," he said, "and particularly so."

"I do not want to be a slave!" she cried.

Peisistratus lifted his switch, but Cabot placed his hand gently on his arm, and stayed his hand.

She had not requested permission to speak.

"You do want to be a slave," Cabot informed her.

"No, no!" she said.

"But it does not matter one way or another," he said. "You are a slave."

"No," she wept. "No, no!"

Arcesilaus, who was large, even for a Kur, had witnessed the preceding exchanges with a certain degree of tolerance. Kurii, as I may have mentioned before, do not make slaves of humans, no more than, say, humans make slaves of dogs or cats. They tend to regard humans, on the whole, as food. Indeed, in Kur there is a generic word for "food," and it is understood that it covers a wide variety of edible organisms, for example, verr, tarsk, vulo, human, and so on. Similarly, in many of the Earth languages I am informed there is a similar generic word which refers to a wide variety of edibles, vegetables, fruit, nuts, meat, and so on. Kurii do, of course, recognize that humans may serve several purposes beyond those commonly associated with food, that they may, for example, have uses as workers, pets, confederates, and so on.

Arcesilaus then gave a slight shake to the blonde's leash, and she, who had been curled on the wood at his feet, quickly stood up.

"Would you like to see our world?" inquired Arcesilaus of Cabot, through the translator.

"Very much so," said Cabot.

Pyrrhus, much smaller than Arcesilaus, no more than four or five hundred pounds, who was in the ring hierarchy subordinate to Arcesilaus, was looking at the brunette, who was still in position. That movement of the features which Cabot was learning was a Kur smile, appeared about his jaws.

Peisistratus replaced his switch on his belt.

"Follow us, if you would," said Arcesilaus.

The group then prepared to leave.

Cabot turned to the brunette.

"Cecily," he said. Then he repeated the name, firmly, not unkindly. "*Cecily.*"

He wondered if she would understand what was required.

"—*Master?*" she whispered.

He saw she was highly intelligent.

"When we leave," he said, "you may break position." Then he continued to look at her, obviously awaiting a response.

"Yes, Master," she said.

He continued to regard her.

"—Thank you, Master," she whispered.

Yes, he thought, she is quite intelligent. Doubtless with some training much might be expected of her in the furs, at the foot of one's couch.

He then turned to leave, and followed the others, who had preceded him a bit down the passageway.

As he left he heard her sobbing behind him, and wildly pulling at the chain, trying to free it from its fastening.

She would not, of course, be successful in this endeavor.

* * * *

"I have noted, from the stable," said Cabot to his guides, "there seems to be an alternation of day and night."

"It agrees," said Arcesilaus, "with that of Gor, adjusted seasonally, to the middle latitudes of that world."

"Intentionally," said Cabot.

"Surely," said Arcesilaus.

"I would have thought," said Cabot, "it would have been adjusted to that of your Home World."

"Much has been lost," said Pyrrhus, "pertaining to the Home World."

"It is important to index these things to Gor," said Arcesilaus.

"Of course," said Cabot.

"It is similar in several of the other worlds," said Arcesilaus. "We wish to ease as much as possible the transition to Gor for our people."

"An invasion?" said Cabot.

"An immigration." said Pyrrhus. Cabot noted that grimacelike smile that betokened Kur pleasure, or wit.

"There are those spoken of as Priest-Kings," noted Cabot.

"Tell us about them," said Arcesilaus.

"They are powerful, and considered mysterious," said Cabot, carefully.

"They imprisoned you, for you are their enemy," said Arcesilaus.

"We are your friend," said Pyrrhus.

"They imprisoned me," said Cabot, "but I am not their enemy."

"But you are our friend," said Pyrrhus.

"Perhaps," said Cabot. "But how can a mere human, no more than a simple beast, be a friend to those as mighty and noble as Kurii?"

"Do you think you are speaking ironically?" asked Arcesilaus.

"Yes," said Cabot.

"You are not," said Pyrrhus.

"Where is Zarendargar?" asked Cabot. It was, after all, he who had doubtless planned and brought to fruition the raid on the Prison Moon.

"He is your friend?" inquired Arcesilaus.

"Yes," said Cabot.

"Interesting," said Pyrrhus.

"We shared paga," said Cabot.

"A great honor," said Arcesilaus. The translator pronounced these words precisely, clearly, unemotionally, in accents of Ar, but Cabot could tell that Arcesilaus deemed this an intelligence of some moment.

"Where is Zarendargar?" asked Cabot.

"Doubtless safe and well," said Arcesilaus. "And perhaps you will see him soon."

Cabot was not reassured by this communication, as benign as it seemed. He was sure that his rescue had been brought about through the resourcefulness and daring of Zarendargar. Why then had he not seen him?

"Tell us of Priest-Kings," said Arcesilaus.

"How do you arrange day and night here?" asked Cabot. He looked up, at the valley overhead.

"It is done," said Arcesilaus, "by an arrangement of mirrors outside the habitat and automated shutters within the habitat, utilizing the light, of course, of this system's primary."

"That light is constant," said Pyrrhus, "and it supplies us with not only light but, by means of large absorbers and transformers, enormous energy, constant energy, almost unvarying energy, which may be utilized in a variety of forms, directly and indirectly."

"The habitat," said Cabot, "would lack an atmosphere."

"An external atmosphere," said Arcesilaus. "Obviously there is no difficulty with our internal atmosphere, which, too, incidentally, is much like that of Gor."

"What could protect you from radiation," asked Cabot, "or from debris, of the sort which might be destroyed and scattered in a normal atmosphere?"

"The habitats are shielded, of course," said Arcesilaus, "with several yards of slag, steel, stone, and such."

"Objects of sufficient menace," said Pyrrhus, "such as those approximating the mass of the habitat itself, can be detected, years in advance, and no more than a small energy, at that distance, is required to move them from their course."

"Is there no danger from smaller debris?" asked Cabot.

"Very little," said Pyrrhus. "You must understand that the light and energy is introduced into the habitat indirectly, by means of mirrors and reflective devices. Occasionally a particle, weighing no more than man or tarsk, rebounding, or such, punctures the habitat, in the vicinity of the shutters. This rupture is soon detected and repaired. Even were it not, it would take several days for the atmosphere to be reduced to levels of discomfort."

"Have you factories, farms?" asked Cabot, who, from his vantage point, could see little that suggested such things.

"Certainly," said Arcesilaus, "but we would not wish to clutter the habitat with such miscellaneous utilities. Accordingly, they are isolated, usually only a few Ehn journey from the habitat. We have two agricultural satellites, or cylinders, and one devoted to industry."

"In the agricultural satellites," said Pyrrhus, "a number of crops are grown, not blood food, but crops from which, suitably processed, nourishment may be obtained. We may arrange growing seasons, temperature, soil nutriments, light and darkness, and such, as we please. Thus we may have crops all year around in any fashion desired. There are no noxious insects, or such, either, to compete for the food, as we have not allowed their entry into the areas. Only such bacteria as are beneficial are admitted."

"The farms are largely automated," said Arcesilaus, "though conditions must be monitored. Our people who work in the farm areas often wear protective clothing, for the heat, the humidity, and such, of some of the areas, particularly those of a tropical nature, would be uncomfortable."

"Out industrial cylinder," said Pyrrhus, "has several divisions in which work may be efficiently accomplished, some of it, when appropriate, under degravitized conditions."

"Where," asked Cabot, "do you get the raw materials for these things, the shielding, the chemicals, and such?"

"The habitat swims in the midst of plenty," said Pyrrhus.

"But oxygen?" said Cabot.

"Oxygen is abundant in the silicate of our neighbors," said Arcesilaus. "It is one of the commonest elements in the universe. So, too, with carbon, nitrogen, hydrogen, and such. Ferrous metals, phosphates, water, sulfur, and so on, abound. All of these materials are obtained and processed."

"You have all you need for life here," said Cabot, "food, water, raw materials, comfort, territory, abundant energy, all such things."

Arcesilaus shrugged, a movement of large muscles moving like living rope beneath the skin, moving the shimmering fur in turn like wind in the water.

"You have little to fear," said Cabot, "other than the demise of the star."

"We would then seek another," said Pyrrhus.

"You can move the habitats?"

"Of course," said Arcesilaus.

"Of course," said Cabot, "that is how you came here."

"We are not sure, now, from how far," said Arcesilaus.

"Records are lost, and some remaining are inconsistent."

"Wars," explained Arcesilaus.

"With all due respect," said Pyrrhus, glancing at the blonde, who lay at the feet of Arcesilaus, "the universe belongs by right to the Kurii. We are the highest and noblest life form in the universe, its noblest and supreme accomplishment. Has it not been designed to produce us and abet our projects? It is accordingly our duty to seed the universe with our kind and to spread the light of our civilization throughout the cosmos."

"Have you already begun to do so?" inquired Cabot.

"Yes," said Pyrrhus. "Some of the worlds are already aflight."

"You shudder?" inquired Arcesilaus.

"I felt cold," said Cabot.

"You have seen enough for one day," said Arcesilaus. "Let us return you to the stable."

"There are some other cylinders, as well," said Pyrrhus. "There is a hunting cylinder, muchly forested, where we may go for the pleasures of hunting, and we maintain, for our human confederates, a pleasure cylinder, such things."

"It seems you have everything you need here," said Cabot.

"Yes," said Arcesilaus.

"But you are not satisfied?"

"No."

"Why not?"

"This is not a natural world," said Arcesilaus.

"It is not Gor," said Pyrrhus.

"What of Priest-Kings?" asked Cabot.

"Yes," said Arcesilaus. "What of Priest-Kings?"

"Perhaps you will tell us about them some day," said Pyrrhus.

"Perhaps," said Cabot.

Arcesilaus then gave a tiny shake to the blonde's leash, and she stood, happily.

She was very pleased to be back in her collar.

You may recall her unease in the container, when she had awakened uncollared, her touching her neck, and such, her fear. You may not have understood her anxiety at the time, or fully, but would have, had you known more of the Steel Worlds. We tried to explain her concern at the time, at least to some extent. For example, apprehended by the patrollers, with their catchpoles and ropes, as a stray, she might have been remanded, perhaps hamstrung, to the cattle pens, later to be dragged to the butchering table.

In any event, it is not surprising that she was pleased to be back in her collar, with all the security it afforded her, but, more importantly, now, she was forward and even arrogant in wearing it. It indicated, after all, her particular and enviable specialness, her status, amongst humans in the habitat. She was a Kur pet.

Had she not, just now, in effect, posed before Cabot, touching the collar with both hands, pointing to it with both hands, looking up at him, indicating it, displaying it?

The collar itself was attractive on her, of course, as collars are on women. Surely she was becomingly collared, and it well set off her sleek, raw nudity, as a collar will. It was a typical pet collar, for such as she, high, to keep her head up, leather, closely fitting, locked in the back, with a ring in front, to which a leash might be attached, a chain, or such.

Cabot did not doubt but what her owner's name was on the collar. That is typical, at any rate, of Gorean slave collars. The slave's name, too, is often included, as in, say, "I am Susan. I belong to Michael of Treve," "I am Linda, the property of Emmerich of Harfax," "This slave is Phyllis. She belongs to Rufus, of Ar," and so on.

Cabot smiled at her.

She moved her face in such a way that suggested she was trying to smile. Babies smile, thought Cabot, but perhaps they learn to smile.

At this point the interlocutor, Grendel, as we have chosen to speak of him, who had silently accompanied the group until now, uttered a low, menacing growl.

Arcesilaus then said something which was not picked up by the translator, and the blonde immediately went to all fours, the leash dangling up to her master's hand, or paw. Women look well on all fours, thought Cabot. I wonder if her master knows how this sight might affect male humans, seeing lovely human females so, particularly slaves, not that the blonde was a slave. She was a pet. Cabot would have preferred that she was a slave. There is something special about slaves. He had not unoften had his own slaves approach him so, sometimes bringing him the switch, or a whip, in their teeth.

The blonde looked up at him, happily.

Again the interlocutor growled, but a word from Arcesilaus, not transmitted, rebuffed him, and he put his shaggy head down, angrily, sullenly, on his chest. But two paws remained clenched.

"Our compatriot," said Arcesilaus, indicating Grendel, "will see you to the stable."

"Why was I brought here?" asked Cabot.

"It is getting late," said Arcesilaus.

Grendel surlily indicated that Cabot should precede him to the stable, which was not far. When they arrived there, Cabot entered the stable, and Grendel closed and locked the gate behind him. Cabot turned and said "Tal." In this way he greeted Grendel. Grendel appeared surprised, but, after a moment, said, "Tal." He had not used the translator.

Cabot then returned to the stall.

The brunette was gone.

Chapter, the Sixth:

A Conversation with Grendel

"It is here," said Grendel, "in this vestibule, that you are to await the summons of the Eleventh Face of the Nameless One, Theocrat of the World."

"Of this world," said Cabot.

"Is there another?" asked Grendel.

"It is not necessary to pretend to be stupid with me," said Cabot.

"But I am stupid," said Grendel, "a mere beast."

"Switch off your translator," said Cabot. "You can speak Gorean."

Grendel shook his head, and did not move to touch the translator.

"I have a thousand questions," said Cabot, angrily. "I would know their answers."

"I shared a stall, days ago, with a dark-haired slave," he said. "She is gone. Where is she? I have been brought here, to this world. Why? Where is Zarendargar? Who is Agamemnon? What is a Nameless One? What is the Eleventh Face of a Nameless One? How are there humans here? What do you do with them? Who are your confederates? How many have you? How do they figure in your plans? There is purpose in all this, I am sure. You do little or nothing without purpose. Why am I here? What do you want of me?"

Grendel turned off his translator, and turned away.

"You know the pet of Arcesilaus!" called Cabot.

Suddenly Grendel stopped, but did not turn to face him.

Cabot had well recalled the menace in the beast's attitude, its growls, several days earlier, when he had smiled at the pet of Arcesilaus.

Cabot was not stupid. He was not certain, but there seemed something there he might be able to exploit.

"She is a pretty thing," said Cabot. "And clever. We were in the container together, on the Prison Moon. Perhaps you know of that."

Grendel turned about and crouched down. His hind legs were bent, tensed. The knuckles of his hands were on the tiles. There was moisture at his fangs.

If he charges, thought Cabot, he may slip on the tiles. They are smooth. But if he is clever he will approach more carefully, but swiftly.

He is furious.

I think he will lunge.

But he is clever.

Then Grendel retracted his claws.

He does not have permission to kill me, thought Cabot.

"She is a lovely pet, and very clever," said Cabot. "In the container she was trying to learn to speak. She could repeat sounds well. I thought I would mention this, for you might teach her to speak. That might be pleasant, and think how interesting a pet she would be, if she could speak. Would not Arcesilaus be pleased? You could use the translator."

"I am teaching her to speak," said Grendel.

Cabot was startled.

"For days, since you came to us," he said.

"Does Arcesilaus know?" asked Cabot. He was reasonably sure that Arcesilaus, despite what he had suggested, would not wish his pet to learn to speak. Presumably Kurii would not wish their humans, save, say, their confederates, to be able to speak. Surely they would prefer for their humans, their pets, their cattle, and such, to remain without speech, to remain simple speechless animals. That is the way they would want them.

"Yes," said Grendel. "And it is by his command that I am teaching her."

"I speculate that she is an apt pupil," said Cabot.

"She is apt, and zealous," said Grendel.

"Then you are much together?"

"Yes."

"You like her?"

"She is only a human," said Grendel, "an animal."

"You like her?"

"She is a lovely pet," said Grendel.

"But you like her?" said Cabot.

Grendel turned away.

"Wait," called Cabot. "Why is she being taught?"

"To be more pleasing to you," said Grendel, without turning about. "She is to be a gift for you."

"I do not want her," said Cabot.

Grendel turned slowly to face Cabot. He was like a rounded boulder of fur. He lifted his head. "You do not want her?" he said.

"No," said Cabot.

"But she is human," he said.

"So, too," said Cabot, "are you."

"No!" cried Grendel.

"Look at your hands!" cried Cabot.

Grendel, in dismay, lifted a paw before his face. Its digits were massive, but of them there were only five.

"Your voice," said Cabot, "is not full Kur, nor your eyes!"

Grendel suddenly rolled on the tiles howling in pain, and scratched at them, and then was still, crouched down, head moving from side to side, moaning.

"You told me you were the result of an experiment," said Cabot.

"It turned out badly," said Grendel.

"No," said Cabot, "it was outstandingly successful."

Grendel regarded him, puzzled.

"Who was your father, your mother?" demanded Cabot.

"My fathers were Kur," he said, "how many I do not know, perhaps a dozen, nor do I know their properties, whose hereditary coils were meshed with the matrix."

"The matrix was the egg of a human female," said Cabot.

"I was not placed in the adhering wombs," said Grendel. "Nor did I feed on the womb and tear it, and drink its blood, nor did I bite and claw my way free when it was time."

"You were carried within a human female," said Cabot, "and brought to term."

"Yes," said Grendel, "and it was her own egg with which the hereditary coils were enmeshed, the egg then replaced in her body."

"The biological mother and the birth mother were then the same," said Cabot.

"Many interventions of a subtle nature were required to bring this about," said Grendel.

Cabot then understood better the standing of Kur science.

"What was the point of the experiment?" asked Cabot. "Was it merely to advance a science, an effort to ascertain its possibilities, its limits?"

"They wished to produce something," said Grendel, "which might mediate between Kur and human, something that might speak easily with them, understand them, relate to them, be less feared by them, and by means of which they might be the better enlisted in the projects of the worlds."

"They wish humans as allies?"

"Certainly, to abet our projects, to advance against Priest-Kings, to help us, properly armed, to win Gor."

"To fight your battles?"

"Certainly," said Grendel. "Is it not better to use humans, a lesser life form, to probe for us, to do war for us, than to risk Kurii?"

"Doubtless," said Cabot.

"It is clearly so," said Grendel. "It is indisputable."

"If this project were to be successful," said Cabot, "then the territories and resources of Gor would be shared equally by humans and Kurii, as victorious allies?"

"Humans are a lesser life form," said Grendel.

"I see," said Cabot.

"They would then be no longer necessary," said Grendel.

"But they might retain uses," speculated Cabot, "as food animals, and such?"

"One supposes so," said Grendel.

"But you are here, on the Steel World, this Steel World," said Cabot.

"I have been tested with humans," said Grendel. "I am too different. They fear me. They dread me. They do not trust me. They see me as Kur, which I am. So the project was abandoned. I am thus the useless consequence of a misguided experiment. I am the only one of my kind. I am left over. I am a mistake. I am worthless."

"You are not worthless," said Cabot.

"True," said Grendel. "I am swift, I am strong, even for Kurii. And I can kill."

"You are fond of the pet of Arcesilaus," said Cabot.

"She is pretty, is she not?" he asked.

"Yes," said Cabot, "very pretty, even beautiful."

"She is to be given to you," he said.

"Why?" asked Cabot.

"Many things may be given to you," said Grendel.

"Why?"

"Perhaps you might succeed where I have failed," he said.

"How is that?"

"You are human," he said.

"I do not want her," said Cabot.

"You would be wise to accept the gifts which are offered to you," said Grendel.

"Where is your mother?" asked Cabot.

"She is dead," said Grendel.

"I am sorry," said Cabot. "How did she die?"

"She saw me," he said. "I was brought to her. She killed herself."

Chapter, the Seventh:

Cabot Learns Something of Agamemnon,
The Eleventh Face of the Nameless One

"If you would accompany me, Warrior," said Peisistratus, "I will conduct you to the audience chamber of Agamemnon, who is the Eleventh Face of the Nameless One."

"You know that I am of the Warriors," said Cabot.

"Yes," he said.

"How would you know that?"

"You carry yourself as one of the scarlet caste," he said.

Grendel had left the vestibule.

"Where is the brunette slave?" asked Cabot.

"The pathetic, ignorant slut of the stable?"

"Yes."

"I do not know."

"How is it that you, a human, are here?"

"I am well paid," he said.

"The Kurii pay well?"

"Very well," he said.

"In what tender?"

"Power," said he, "and precious metals, and jewels, and slaves. To those who serve them well the Kurii are generous."

"And to those who do not serve them well?"

"To them," said Peisistratus, "they are less generous."

"What is your role here, in this moment, now?" inquired Cabot.

"It is supposed that I may be of assistance in your meeting with the noble and exalted Agamemnon, the Eleventh Face of the Nameless One. Amongst Kurii and humans communication is often difficult, even with translators."

"Agamemnon is Kur?"

"I am not sure," said Peisistratus.

"How is that?"

"I have seen only his bodies," said Peisistratus.

"I do not understand."

"He does not care to be kept waiting," said Peisistratus.

"Let him wait," said Cabot.

"That is not wise," said Peisistratus, uneasily.

"Who is the Nameless One?" asked Cabot.

"A principle, a force, something inexplicable, something beyond human comprehension," said Peisistratus. "It is eternal, neither coming into being nor passing out of being. It scatters worlds like the petals of flowers, it shapes dimensions and brews stars."

Cabot listened, uncertain of what he heard.

"You do not understand?"

"No," said Cabot.

"Nor do I," said Peisistratus, "but the words flicker in the darkness, affording to some an illusion of understanding, a measure of comfort."

"Do they not, rather, in their futility, make the darkness yet more obscure?"

"And behind the Nameless One," smiled Peisistratus, "lies the Mystery."

"I prefer a sword," said Cabot, "and something before it, friend or foe."

"And perhaps hot paga," said Peisistratus, "and ships, and tarns, and a wallet of gold, and at your feet, in your collar, beautiful women?"

"Yes," said Cabot.

"Let us be on our way," urged Peisistratus.

"How is this Agamemnon the Eleventh Face of the Nameless One?" asked Cabot. "What does that mean?"

"The Nameless One," said Peisistratus, "is beyond human comprehension, but it speaks through many masks, conceals itself behind many veils, and manifests itself through a thousand faces. It moves in the wind, in the churning sea, in the sheetings of rain, in the cry of lightning, in the tremors of the earth; it whispers in lava scalding the affrighted air; it prowls with the panther; it soars with the tarn; it bounds with the startled tabuk."

"And Agamemnon?"

"Is one of the faces of the Nameless One," said Peisistratus.

"Surely you do not believe all this," said Cabot.

"It does not matter what I believe, or what you believe," said Peisistratus. "Many Kurii believe such things, and, I fear, so, too, does Agamemnon."

"Then he is insane," said Cabot.

"The singleness and indivisible will of the insane, coupled with great intellect and ambition," said Peisistratus, "have not unoften been the route to unusual power."

"He thinks, as I understand it," said Cabot, "he is a face of the Nameless One."

"Yes."

"Then he is insane," said Cabot.

"Unless, of course," said Peisistratus, "he is correct."

"Yes," said Cabot, "unless he is correct."

"To the audience chamber?" said Peisistratus.

"Yes," said Cabot.

Chapter, the Eighth:

An Interview with Agamemnon,
The Eleventh Face of the Nameless One

"Where is he?" asked Cabot.

The audience chamber, reached by a long passage leading from the vestibule, was quite large. It was rounded and domed, and, high in its walls were narrow windows, through which the interior was dimly lit. The floor was smooth, and red, and formed of large, fitted tiles. The encircling walls were of yellow stone. At one end of the room, opposite the portal through which Cabot and Peisistratus had entered, was a low, stone dais. On it was no chair. Behind this dais was a curtained opening.

"This might be the audience chamber of a Ubar," said Cabot.

"I think not," said Peisistratus. "Such a chamber would surely be more ornate, better lit, crowded with servitors and guards, furnished ostentatiously with precious vessels, statuary, display slaves, a sampling of nude chained beauties, preferably of high caste, ideally the daughters of Ubars, taken from conquered cities, and such."

"Still, it is similar," said Cabot.

"Doubtless it is intended to resemble a Ubar's audience chamber," said Peisistratus.

"The common housing, and domiciling, of Kurii, as I understand it," said Cabot, "is far darker, and more cavelike."

"Yes," said Peisistratus, "they have excellent dark vision, and often feel more secure, more comfortable, in such surroundings."

Cabot supposed that the Kurii might originally have been a species which sought out lairs, dark places, caves, and such.

"This is then to impress humans?"

"Perhaps," said Peisistratus, "but, too, perhaps it is intended to make them feel less closed in, more at ease."

"So where is our host?" inquired Cabot.

"It seems," said Peisistratus, "he is letting you wait."

Cabot smiled.

Shortly thereafter the curtains at the end of the room, behind the dais, were drawn open by two Kurii.

From down the hall, beyond the curtain, Cabot heard a sound as of metal, a step, and then a scraping, and another step, and a scraping. It was very slow, and very methodical, as though something were accustoming itself to an unfamiliar housing of some sort.

Peisistratus said nothing.

Cabot stepped back, for he saw in the parting of the curtain a wide face, a broad form, a long form, the end of which he did not discern.

"It is a tharlarion, a river tharlarion," said Cabot.

It was a creature of metal, but it did muchly resemble a large river tharlarion of the sort which might terrorize the Ua, and such rivers, predominantly those of tropical Gor.

It crawled slowly onto the dais, on which it crouched. Its mouth, which it opened, as though yawning, was spiked with rows of thick, nail-like metallic teeth, some inches in length. Cabot could see no face within the opening. It is a machine, thought Cabot, but where is its operator? Is it remotely controlled? The metal beast had, like the river tharlarion, a long tail, in this machine of diminishing, overlapping plates. It also had hornlike projections aligned on its metal spinal column. Cabot conjectured the jaws could shake and cut a normal river tharlarion in two, that the tail, with a swift blow, might shatter stone or fell trees.

The two Kurii who had parted the curtains for the entrance of the metal beast now crouched near it, on the dais, one on each side.

"Behold," came from a translator, presumably that of one of the beasts flanking the object on the dais, "Agamemnon, The Eleventh Face of the Nameless One, Theocrat of the World."

This was followed by a silence.

"Are we expected to prostrate ourselves?" asked Cabot. He had, incidentally, no intention of doing so.

"Certainly not," said Peisistratus. "We are not women or slaves. We are free men, of caste."

"Tal," said Cabot, to the object on the dais.

"Tal," it said, through a translator, seemingly within the metallic body. "We welcome the noble Tarl Cabot, human, and Warrior, to our world."

With an inclination of his head, Cabot acknowledged this greeting.

"We have long been eager to make your acquaintance," came from the device. "We have waited long to have you here, as an honored, and valued, guest."

"Sir," said Cabot, noncommittally.

"Doubtless you have many questions," came from the device. "Many, I trust, have already been answered by our unfortunate Grendel, whose repellant appearance we trust did not overly disgust you, and others by our dear colleague and friend, Peisistratus, of the lovely island of Cos, in Thassa. We shall shortly do our best to satisfy any residue of curiosity which might remain. First, however, allow me to thank you, on behalf of our world, for your efforts, long ago, on behalf of our beloved officer, Zarendargar, efforts which obviously brought you into disrepute with your masters, the Priest-Kings of Gor."

"They are not my masters," said Cabot.

"Surely no longer," came from the device.

"Never," said Cabot.

"Excellent," said the device. "You recognize, of course, that they are your enemies."

"It seems so," said Cabot.

"It is surely so," came from the device. "You were put on the Prison Moon, though a free man, and a Warrior, naked, in full view, in shameful, close confinement, and in circumstances clearly designed to strain your honor, after the loss of which you would presumably be disposed of, and doubtless in a lengthy, unpleasant fashion."

"How did you come to know of such things?" asked Cabot.

"We have the benefit of informants," came from the device.

"Spies," said Cabot.

"If you like," came from the device.

"Within the Sardar?"

"Unfortunately not, but Priest-Kings deal with humans and humans may deal with us."

Cabot nodded.

"Perhaps you may tell us of the interior precincts of the Sardar one day," came from the device, "of the nature of Priest-Kings, and such."

"They are the gods of Gor," said Cabot. "Who knows the nature of gods?"

"True," came from the device, after a moment.

"Two females were enclosed with me," said Cabot, "and both were free."

"Yes, free, how unfortunate," said Agamemnon, either from within the device, or somehow, in communication with it.

"One," said Cabot, "was a nasty, spoiled brat from England, though nicely faced and well-curved, who would make a nice slab of collar meat, suitably to be bid from the block, and the other was a pet, of Arcesilaus, whom I gather is an officer of yours, she, too, nicely faced and nicely curved."

"And would she not look well in a collar, as well?" inquired Agamemnon.

"Certainly," said Cabot, "and she would bring a good price on Gor."

"With training," said Peisistratus.

Blondes were rarer on Gor than brunettes, save in the northern latitudes, and tended to bring somewhat better prices, due to this rarity. Cabot himself preferred brunettes. The most desiderated hair coloring for a female slave on Gor, incidentally, is auburn.

"As we understand it," said Agamemnon, "both of those females were of a sort likely to be sexually stimulating to a human male."

"Extremely so," said Cabot.

"How cruel are the Priest-Kings," said Agamemnon.

"I used neither," said Cabot.

"Up to the point of your release," said Agamemnon.

"Yes," said Cabot.

"But let us suppose you had been held longer in captivity."

"Then, doubtless," said Cabot, "I would have put both of them to my pleasure, variously and extensively so."

"Even though they were free?"

"Yes."

"As though they were of no more moment than slaves?"

"Yes," said Cabot.

"I see," said Agamemnon.

"I am, of course, grateful for my rescue," said Tarl Cabot.

"It was our hope that you would be pleased," said Agamemnon.

"I am, indeed," said Cabot.

"I understand," said Agamemnon, "you have been inadequately housed."

Cabot shrugged.

"Better quarters will soon be arranged," said Agamemnon.

Cabot nodded. "My thanks," he said.

"And my dear Peisistratus," said Agamemnon, "you could, if need be, could you not, arrange for some feminine companionship for our friend, Tarl Cabot?"

"Certainly," said Peisistratus. "By evening, I can send him a whip and a chain of ten beauties from the pleasure cylinder." He turned to Cabot. "Do you want them stripped or clothed?"

"Clothed?" said Cabot.

"As slaves, of course," said Peisistratus.

"Good," said Cabot.

Female slaves on Gor, if garmented, are distinctively garmented, usually briefly and revealingly. That is the way men prefer it and, too, of course, they must under no circumstances be confused with free women, who are of course infinitely beyond them in dignity and worth. The slave is worth less than the dirt beneath the sandals of a free woman. Cabot supposed similar customs would obtain in the Steel Worlds. In this he was, of course, correct.

"But I am not yet ready to accept gifts," said Tarl Cabot.

"How wise you are," said Agamemnon. "Let us speak plainly."

"Please do," said Cabot.

"You are perhaps aware of the experiment, whom you refer to, and we have followed your initiative in the matter, Grendel."

"Yes," said Cabot.

"To us," said Agamemnon, "he is hideous. Consider the nature of the pelt, the shape of the eyes, the tonalities of its utterance, the monstrosity of a five-digited hand."

"I have a five-digited hand," said Cabot.

"Yes, but you are human," said Agamemnon, "and what is appropriate for you is not appropriate for a different life form."

"It seems a small thing," said Cabot.

"Not to Kurii," said Agamemnon.

"I understand," said Cabot.

"Some humans find the appearance of Kurii frightening," said Agamemnon.

"That is true," said Cabot.

"We hoped that Grendel might be acceptable to your species, being taken, in effect, as human, and might well serve us in our relationships with humans, as an intermediary."

Cabot said nothing.

"But, unfortunately," said Agamemnon, "that seems not the case."

"No," said Cabot.

"But he does seem human, does he not?"

"Not really," said Cabot. "And certainly not in size, shape, and appearance."

"Doubtless he seems far more human to us than he does to you."

"That is quite possible," said Cabot.

"In any event," said Agamemnon, "human males tend to be uneasy in his presence, and human females cry out and withdraw, often screaming and sobbing, to the length of their chains."

Cabot nodded.

"So our experiment proved unsuccessful," said Agamemnon, "and we realized we must rethink matters."

"You have human allies," said Cabot.

"Some, surely," said Agamemnon, "but not thousands, not armies."

"You wish armies?"

"Divisions, regiments," said Agamemnon.

"To destroy Priest-Kings and seize Gor?"

"To free Gor," said Agamemnon.

"I see."

"And to labor on behalf of humans, our oppressed brothers," said Agamemnon, "to liberate them from the tyranny of Priest-Kings."

"It seems a noble endeavor," said Cabot.

"Too," said Agamemnon, "our human allies would not be forgotten in the morning of our victory, but would be well repaid for their efforts, efforts which, in large part, were exerted on their own behalf."

"You would assist humans in winning Gor?"

"Arms, direction, such things."

"I see."

"Kurii can be generous," said Agamemnon.

"Riches?"

"Certainly."

"Gold, land, power, tharlarion, kaiila, women?" asked Cabot.

"Certainly," said Agamemnon.

"A world?"

"Perhaps two," said Agamemnon. "Once the Priest-Kings are destroyed, we would have two worlds at our disposal, one desirable, the other less so."

"Earth?"

"Yes."

"Gor, I take it," said Cabot, "would be shared equally, its land, its riches, and such, all, equally, between Kurii and humans."

"Certainly," said Agamemnon.

"How might I figure in these plans?" inquired Cabot.

"I see that you are interested," said Agamemnon.

"Who would not be?"

"Kurii must be involved subtly in these campaigns, at least at first," said Agamemnon. "The assistance, guidance, wisdom, direction, and counsel they provide must be veiled, at least at first. Humans must believe it is their battle, a battle waged to win their own freedom, a struggle to claim what has been denied to them, and is rightfully theirs, Gor."

"Such things have often taken place on Earth," said Cabot, "though the collusion, the veiling, and such, has not been between species."

"On the Steel Worlds, as well," said Agamemnon.

"Doubtless exploitation is common amongst rational beings," said Cabot.

"Let us speak not of exploitation but of common interests, and brotherhood."

"And what would take place on this morning of victory?"

"Gor would belong not to Priest-Kings," said Agamemnon, "but to humans."

"And Kurii?"

"We would expect some land to be set aside for us, to be reserved for our use," said Agamemnon.

"I thought Gor was to be divided equally."

"We can do with harder countries than humans," said Agamemnon, "with less arable soils, with wastelands, with mountainous areas, with desolate latitudes, arid and rocky, latitudes unfriendly to humans, with deserts, and such, areas of less interest to humans."

"The division then, even were it equal in extent, would seem much in the interests of humans," said Cabot.

"Yes," said Agamemnon.

"And what would be the relation betwixt Kurii and human on this freshly achieved world?"

"One of brotherhood, of universal peace, one of eternal harmony, of endless amity and good will."

"You need human leaders?"

"Precisely, such as yourself."

"And what, precisely, am I to gain in this?" asked Cabot.

"An excellent question," said Agamemnon, "one I can well understand and appreciate, and one which reflects well on your caution and astuteness."

"I am grateful, of course," said Cabot, "for my extrication from the power of Priest-Kings."

"We had hoped you would be."

"And what might I, personally, achieve in all this?"

"What would you say to being enthroned as the Ubar of all Gor?"

Cabot was startled.

"I see you are taken aback," said Agamemnon.

"That is largess," said Cabot, "difficult to ignore."

"We anticipated it would be so," said Agamemnon.

"You wish to return me to Gor, with arms and power, with riches, to raise a revolution against Priest-Kings."

"Yes."

"I would speak of this with my friend, Zarendargar."

The metal tharlarion was silent.

"It was he, I gather," said Cabot, "who engineered my rescue from the Prison Moon."

"Yes," said Agamemnon.

"I would like to speak with him."

"Doubtless in time," said Agamemnon. "I fear he is currently muchly occupied."

"I shared a stall, days ago, with a dark-haired slave," said Cabot. "I returned to the stall and found her gone. Where is she?"

One of the Kurii flanking the metal object on the dais spoke softly to Agamemnon, or the machine through which he spoke.

The head of the metal object, heavy and broad, with a small sound, lifted itself a little, and the apertures behind which Cabot could detect no eyes, focused on him.

"She is well," said Agamemnon.

"Has she been claimed?" asked Cabot.

"No," said Peisistratus.

"I would see her," said Cabot.

"Do you want her?" asked Peisistratus.

"I would see her."

"I can send you better women from the Pleasure Cylinder," said Peisistratus, "naked, in sirik, with switches tied about their necks."

"I would see her," said Tarl Cabot.

"By all means," said Agamemnon. "And let her be a token of the goods and pleasures which might await you."

Peisistratus nodded.

"What is your decision, Tarl Cabot?" inquired Agamemnon. "Are you with us, or not?"

"I would like some time to consider the matter," said Tarl Cabot.

"Of course," said Agamemnon. "Such a decision should not be made lightly."

At this point the ponderous machine, with the small sound of rippling, overlapping plates, and the scratch of metallic claws on the dais, turned about, and left the room. Cabot saw the metal tail twisting slowly as it disappeared into the darkness.

The two Kurii then left the dais, and redrew the curtains behind them.

"Follow me," said Peisistratus, turning about.

Chapter, the Ninth:

Cabot Renews his Acquaintance with a Blonde

"The light is dim," said Cabot.

"Your eyes will soon grow accustomed to it," said Peisistratus.

They had been winding their way through dark passageways, for several Ehn. Here and there in the passageways there were openings, commonly low, and broad, to accommodate the movements of Kurii. These led, severally, to other passageways and, in some instances, to apartments, some with several rooms. Much of the food in the various valleys was prepared centrally, so to speak, and eaten at common tables. There were, however, pantries with supplies, and cooking gear, in many of these apartments, which might be utilized when desired.

"Doubtless," said Peisistratus, "you prefer the outside."

"Yes," said Cabot. For example, the small, villa-like dwelling which had been set aside for him, of some four rooms, on the side of a hill, with a veranda, was open, light, and airy. It was, of course, the sort of place that would better suit a human than at least most Kurii, who might have felt it too open, too insecure, too exposed to attack.

"You would like the Pleasure Cylinder," said Peisistratus. "Too, there are few Kurii there."

"You find Kurii disturbing?"

"Yes," said Peisistratus. "And so, too, might a verr if it found larls in its vicinity."

"Ai!" said Cabot, shielding his eyes.

"Forgive me," said Peisistratus, his hands on a portal, half swung open, "I should have warned you, the passageways occasionally lead to open ledges, tiers of caves, and such."

Cabot and his guide emerged on a path, to their left a descent, rather steep, of some fifty feet or so, and on their right a set of caves, and above them, another set, and above that several more sets.

"We will soon be again in the passages," said Peisistratus.

"Human, human, human!" they heard, an excited feminine voice, from above.

Cabot shaded his eyes and looked upward.

"I am making noises!" called the voice. "I am speaking. If you can understand me, say, 'Yes!'"

On a small ledge, before one of the caves, looking down, on all fours, Cabot saw the blonde.

"Yes," he called to her.

Behind her, emerging from the cave, large, half-standing, he saw Grendel.

The blonde scurried down the slope and reached out, to pinch at his tunic.

"That is grooming," said Peisistratus.

"Female," said the blonde, happily, pointing to herself. "Female!"

"Yes," said Cabot, smiling, "female." He was in little doubt about that. The pet collar, high and leather, set her off nicely.

Her handling of the sounds may not have been perfect, but it was comprehensible. Even in the container Cabot recalled she had managed to repeat several phonemes flawlessly.

She looked up at him, happily. The collar was, as noted, high, and she could not well lower her head without a movement of her entire body, though she could, of course, keep her eyes cast down. Some masters do not permit their slaves to look directly into their eyes, but that is unusual. Indeed, some masters use the refusal to let the slave look into their eyes directly as a discipline or punishment. In this way the slave often becomes decidedly uneasy, for it is harder then for her to read the will and mood of the master. Many masters prefer to look directly into the slave's eyes. They well understand then who is their master. Too, it makes the girl in turn easier to read. The collar had a large ring on it, now to the front, to which a leash may be attached. For common leading the ring is in front, but if the slave is to precede the master, the collar is turned, and the ring is then at the back.

"Do not become too friendly," said Peisistratus, pointing upward.

Cabot looked up and saw Grendel peering over the ledge.

"He likes her," said Peisistratus, "and he could tear your throat out with one blow of his paw."

"I do not want her," said Cabot.

"You know, of course," said Peisistratus, "why she is being taught Gorean."

Cabot did not respond.

"That she be more pleasing to you," he said. "Agamemnon is planning on giving her to you."

"What of Arcesilaus?" asked Cabot.

"She is only a beast, and he is of the rings," said Peisistratus. "Beware of Grendel."

"I do not want her," said Cabot.

Grendel, above, uttered a vocalization, in Kur, and the blonde suddenly turned white, and, turning, scratched her way quickly up the slope, to his side.

"He called her," said Peisistratus.

"I see," said Cabot.

"Beware of Grendel," said Peisistratus. "Here," he said, then, "is a portal which will return us to the passageways."

Chapter, the Tenth:

Cabot Renews His Acquaintance
with the Former Miss Pym

"This," said Peisistratus, "is the portal to the apartment of Pyrrhus, subordinate to Arcesilaus, officer to Agamemnon."

"I know him," said Cabot.

"Enter quietly," said Peisistratus. "I wish to show you something."

Within the portal, and at the end of a short hallway, they stopped, and peered within, into a large, dim room.

It took a moment for Cabot's eyes to make out the contents of the room. It was sparsely furnished, save for some chests at the walls. There was also, to the left, a low, flat box, some four feet square. It contained some cloths, some rags, or such. Near it, too, were some pans, and a bucket. At the far end of the room, there was a large assemblage of furs, constituting a divan of sorts.

On the divan was the Kur, Pyrrhus. In his arms there was a small, white figure, which was picking and nibbling at his fur.

"She is grooming him," whispered Peisistratus. "When she encounters lice, she must eat them."

A long, light chain, some thirty to thirty five feet in length, ran from a ring on the floor, near the box, to a ring on a high leather collar, which was closed closely about the neck of the small white figure, a pet collar.

Cabot watched for a time the efforts of the small figure in the arms of the beast to whom she was attending.

"She is a Kur pet," said Cabot.

The girl must have heard the sound, for she turned about, suddenly, and cried out, "Tarl! Tarl Cabot!"

She was cast to the floor, suddenly, violently, with a clatter of the light, long chain on the tiles, and she scrambled up, to her knees, and knelt there, suddenly, clearly terrified, and regarded Pyrrhus, and then Cabot, wildly, fearfully, and pressed both her hands, frantically, tightly, over her mouth.

"She is a pet," said Peisistratus. "She is not permitted speech."

Pyrrhus said something to the brunette in Kur, a half enraged, snorting exclamation.

With a sweeping scrape of the light chain fastened to her collar, the girl fled to the low, flat box, some four feet square, that with cloths, and rags, and such, in it, terrified, and, trembling, crouched down within it.

"Pyrrhus is not pleased with her," said Peisistratus. "She has been sent to her bed. She may be killed."

"In her flight," said Cabot, "the chain overturned a pan, apparently one for water." There was certainly liquid spilled upon the tiles.

She was looking at the Kur, and at the water, and, frantic with misery, was trembling uncontrollably.

"She is clumsy," said Peisistratus. "Clumsiness is not permitted in Kur pets."

"Surely she would not be killed for crying out, for spilling water," said Cabot.

"She could be," said Peisistratus.

"Surely not," said Cabot. "Would not a mere switching, or lashing, or even a scolding word, backed by the whip, be sufficient to encourage her to be less awkward, less careless? Do not females understand such things?" The deportment of slaves is to be seemly, of course, for they are in collars. It is expected that the slave will be inconspicuous, that she will serve humbly and unobtrusively, that she will be demure, refined, reticent, attentive, deferent, and graceful. She is not a free woman. She is collared. She is slave.

"Surely so," said Peisistratus, "and many have been slain or put in the cattle pens for less."

"They would then be deprived of a pet," said Cabot.

"Not really," said Peisistratus. "One pet may easily be replaced with another, for example, with a slave from the Pleasure Cylinder."

"I see," said Cabot.

"And this knowledge," said Peisistratus, "encourages our girls in the pleasure cylinder to be muchly concerned to be found pleasing to the masters."

"I would suppose so," said Cabot.

"Certainly," said Peisistratus.

"But it would be a different pet," said Cabot.

"Of course," said Peisistratus. "But it would not matter to a Kur. To them one human female is little different from another."

"I understand," said Cabot. But he wondered if this were true.

"Many times they cannot even tell one from another."

"Interesting."

"You noted, of course," said Peisistratus, "that she cried out your name, the name of a free man."

"It was an inadvertence," said Cabot.

"Pets, and slaves, are not permitted such inadvertences," said Peisistratus.

Commonly slaves are not permitted to call free men and free women by their names. It is regarded as insolence. Some Goreans feel, too, that the name of a free person is a fine and noble thing, and thus one should not permit it to be touched by the lips and tongue of a mere slave. This prohibition, too, of course, serves to remind the slave, and keenly, that she is a mere slave.

Pyrrhus left the divan of furs, angrily, and moved toward the brunette's box, or bed.

She screamed, and put her head down in the rags and blankets.

"Do not kill her!" called Cabot to the Kur, who was poised over the pet's simple bed, in which the pet cowered, the chain running to her collar.

Pyrrhus turned, and looked at Cabot.

He was hunched down, and tense, which in the Kur is commonly a sign of hostility.

Pyrrhus looked then to Peisistratus, whom he knew.

"Our friend, Tarl Cabot," said Peisistratus, "could not help himself. He is new to our world. He knows not our ways. He fears you might in a moment of indiscretion deprive yourself of a valuable pet, an indiscretion perhaps to be later regretted."

"I know you," said Pyrrhus, to Cabot. "You are the one from the Prison Moon."

"Yes, Lord Pyrrhus," said Cabot. "You were a member of the

party of Lord Arcesilaus, when I was removed from the stable, and introduced to your beautiful world."

"It is an artificial world," said Pyrrhus.

"But one which is beautiful," said Cabot. "I returned to the stable, and found the slave gone."

"I arranged to have her brought to me," said Pyrrhus. "Do you object?"

"How could one object?" asked Cabot. "She is only a slave."

At the word *kajira*, the brunette looked up, fearfully.

Pyrrhus crouched back on his haunches. He demeanor became less threatening.

"You have seen Agamemnon?" he asked.

"Yes," said Cabot.

"You are then with us?"

"I have not yet given him my answer," said Cabot.

"Why have you come here?" asked Pyrrhus.

"He wished to see the dark-haired pet," said Peisistratus.

Pyrrhus then snarled something to the brunette and she, terrified, left the box on all fours, and, at the feet of Pyrrhus, went to her belly.

"She is training nicely," said Peisistratus. "She is quite bright."

She bellies well, thought Cabot.

Another noise emanated from Pyrrhus, and the brunette began, desperately, fearfully, piteously, to press her lips upon his clawed feet.

She is lovely, thought Cabot, and a slave. She should be so at the feet of one of her own species, at the feet of a man, her master. What a pity, he thought, to waste such loveliness, doubtless not even understood, on a Kur.

Pyrrhus then, picking up a length of the chain, indicated that his pet should go to all fours, and then he led her, on the leash, head down, before Cabot.

Another command and she knelt up, looking ahead. The collar, like that of the blonde, was high, and she could not well lower her head. She did keep her eyes lowered, frightened.

Another growling rumble in the throat of Pyrrhus, and she lowered her body until her head was nearly at the floor. In this way, one in such a collar could lower her head before a master, an owner, such things.

"Nicely done," said Peisistratus.

"Oh?" said Cabot.

"She is training nicely," said Peisistratus. "See? She is showing you deference."

Another noise from Pyrrhus, and the brunette resumed her kneeling position, back straight, looking ahead. For a moment Cabot had caught a look of fleeting terror in her countenance, of mute appeal, and then she was again in the required posture.

Cabot, a human male, could not but be struck by the loveliness of the pet of Pyrrhus. Her head was held up by the collar. The chain dangled nicely between her breasts, and then looped up, to the paw of Pyrrhus.

Yes, thought Cabot, she would doubtless bring a good price. Surely men not unoften paid well for goods such as she.

I wonder if she understands, thought Cabot, that she is now goods.

On Gor slaves come soon to understand that, that they are goods, only that.

"You wished to see her," said Pyrrhus to Cabot.

"Yes," said Cabot.

"Now you have seen her," said Pyrrhus. "Now you may go."

"Perhaps," said Cabot, "I would see her for a bit longer."

"She is clumsy," said Pyrrhus.

"She is pretty on her chain," said Peisistratus, as though by way of explaining Cabot's interest. "You may not speak to her," said Peisistratus to Cabot.

"I understand," said Cabot.

"Did Agamemnon, Eleventh Face of the Nameless One, Theocrat of the world, give him permission to come here?" came from Pyrrhus' translator.

Cabot wondered if this elaboration of Agamemnon's title was intended to be ironic. It was difficult to tell from the translator, or the movements of the body of Pyrrhus.

"I did not think you would object," said Peisistratus.

"We do not require the use of humans to forward our projects," said Pyrrhus.

"Perhaps they may occasionally be useful," said Peisistratus.

"One was produced, and was useless," said Pyrrhus.

Cabot took this to be a reference to a failed experiment, the outcome of which was Grendel.

"You are of course unquestionably loyal to the Theocrat of the world," said Peisistratus.

"Of course," came from the translator.

Pyrrhus dropped the chain of his pet, but she remained perfectly immobile.

"Nice," commented Peisistratus.

"Look at my pet," said Pyrrhus to Cabot. "You wished to see her? Now you see her."

"Yes," said Cabot.

"She is now no more than a pet, only a pet."

"Yes," said Cabot.

"My pet."

"Yes," said Cabot.

"You like her?"

"She is only a female," said Cabot.

"Is she pretty?"

"She will do," said Cabot.

Pyrrhus then, with a scraping of his claws on the tiles, went to one of the chests at the side of the room, and opened it, and withdrew a small dangling pair of objects. He returned to the girl and thrust her head down to the floor, and, as she whimpered in a tiny, futile protest, he rudely jerked her wrists behind her, and, in a moment, with two small clicks, she was braceleted.

"Gorean slave bracelets," commented Cabot.

The girl's eyes were wild, and she pulled a little, helplessly, at the bracelets.

How helpless women are in such bracelets!

"Has she been braceleted before?" asked Peisistratus.

"No," said Pyrrhus.

Cabot could see how fearfully vulnerable she felt, her small wrists pinioned behind her.

Pyrrhus then, with a movement of his clawed foot, slid a shallow pan, containing some pellets, before the girl.

"You have come to see her?" he asked Cabot.

"Yes," said Cabot.

Pyrrhus then uttered something in Kur to the girl, and she bent to the pan.

"Then see her," said Pyrrhus.

Cabot observed the former Miss Virginia Cecily Jean Pym, kneeling, bent over, her hands braceleted behind her, picking the pellets delicately, fearfully, from the pan.

"It is thus that our pets feed," said Pyrrhus. "They may not use their hands."

"I see," said Cabot.

Such feeding would commonly be done on all fours, of course.

Pyrrhus looked at him, closely.

"It is commonly done with new slaves," said Cabot, "with girls who are still learning their collars, and, occasionally, as a punishment, or as a mere reminder that they are slaves."

The girl, having retrieved the last pellet, of which number there had been few, as Kurii do not overfeed their human pets, lifted her head, frightened.

"You are not displeased," said Pyrrhus, "to see her, a female of your own species, and one seemingly so important to you that you have sought her out here, so reduced, now chained and collared, now no more than a Kur pet?"

"Not at all," said Cabot. Indeed, he was not displeased to see the former Miss Pym in this way, for he thought she might profit from such things. Indeed, had he owned her, he would doubtless have put her through similar paces, enforced upon occasion with a sharp blow of the switch.

She was, after all, not a free woman.

"Is she not important to you?" inquired Pyrrhus.

"Is that why you took her?" inquired Cabot.

"I think you like her," said Pyrrhus.

"Her curves are of some interest," said Cabot, "as those of a slave."

"You like her?"

"She has promise, however minimal," said Cabot, "as a piece of collar meat."

"I think you like her," said Pyrrhus.

"On Gor there are doubtless hundreds of thousands who are her superior."

"Why then have you come here?" asked Pyrrhus.

"I was curious to see her as a Kur pet, which seems an excellent disposition for her."

"Would you not prefer to see her as a slave?"

"Perhaps," said Cabot, "if she were more beautiful."

"Is she not beautiful?"

"She will do," said Cabot.

Pyrrhus turned to Peisistratus.

"She was clumsy, was she not?" inquired Pyrrhus.

"Indisputably," said Peisistratus.

Pyrrhus then dragged the girl by the hair to where the pan of water had been overturned, and put her kneeling, bent over, head down, before the spill.

He looked at Peisistratus.

"Tell her to right the pan," he said.

The pan was large, and shallow. It had two handles, one on each side, for ease of carrying.

"She is braceleted," said Peisistratus.

"Tell her," said Pyrrhus.

Peisistratus, in English, conveyed this message, and the girl, with a small sound of her collar chain on the tiles, bent her head to the pan. She managed to grasp one of its two handles in her teeth, and lift, with a tiny sound of the chain, and right the pan. Her knees were in water, that lost in the pan's overturning.

"Tell her," he said, "to clean the floor."

"She is braceleted," said Peisistratus.

"Tell her," said Pyrrhus.

"You have been clumsy," Peisistratus said to the girl, in English. "Clean the floor."

She turned, on her knees, bent over, to regard him.

"Now," said Peisistratus.

She then began to lap the water from the floor.

"Do you like my pet?" Pyrrhus asked Cabot.

"She will do," said Cabot.

Cabot considered her lines. They were excellent. Slaves are not unoften used in such a position.

In a few Ehn the girl timidly lifted her head from the floor.

"The floor is still damp," observed Pyrrhus.

"Girl," said Peisistratus, in English, "the floor is still damp."

She put down her head and, using her hair, dried the floor, as she could.

"Behold the human, my pet," came from Pyrrhus' translator.

"She is beheld," said Peisistratus.

Were her hair longer, slave long, thought Cabot, it would be a more effective instrument. Her dark hair was rich, glossy, and nicely shaped, but it came only to her nape. It would grow out, of course, if she survived. Long hair improves a woman's price. Much can be done with it, aesthetically. Too, she can be bound with it, and she can be taught to use it in the furs to enhance a man's pleasure.

"Are you angry?" Peisistratus asked Cabot, softly, in English.

"No," said Cabot. "Why should I be?"

"The girl," said Peisistratus.

"What of her?"

"Pyrrhus is trying to provoke you," said Peisistratus.

"With the girl?"

"Yes."

"Perhaps he does not realize she is only a slave," said Cabot.

"You are not angry?"

"No," said Cabot. "She is only a slave. Too, are not Kur pets often so treated?"

"Certainly Kur pets are often so treated," said Peisistratus, "but I am certain, in this case, that Pyrrhus hopes you will be provoked, perhaps to an uncivil word, a protest, an insult, perhaps even a blow."

"Why?" asked Cabot.

"He wishes to have a pretext to do away with you," said Peisistratus.

"Why?" asked Cabot.

"I think," said Peisistratus, "it has to do with Agamemnon."

Pyrrhus then drew the girl stumbling on her chain to the foot of the divan-like assemblage of furs, and retrieved, from its surface, a switch.

"Would you like to punish the clumsy pet?" he asked Cabot.

"No," said Cabot. "She has not offended against me."

"But, if she had, you would punish her, would you not?" asked Pyrrhus.

"If she were mine," said Cabot, "it would not be necessary for her to offend against me to be punished. She would be punished if her service was in any way, in even the least way, less than fully pleasing."

Pyrrhus lifted the switch and the girl cowered beneath it.

He struck her three times, but, as she cringed and cried out, he was observing not the girl so much but Cabot. Cabot remained expressionless.

"Well done," whispered Peisistratus to Cabot, in English.

"She is only a pet," said Cabot, noncommittally, in English.

"True," said Peisistratus, "but a nicely curved one."

"She will do," said Cabot.

"I would like to see her in a collar," said Peisistratus.

"She belongs in one," said Cabot.

"Should I not kill her?" asked Pyrrhus of Peisistratus.

"I think," said Peisistratus, "she is trying to be a good pet."

"She called out, she spilled water," said Pyrrhus.

"It is doubtless my fault," said Peisistratus, "for I introduced our friend, Tarl Cabot, into your domicile with insufficient warning. If you do not wish to keep her, give her to me, and I will take her to the Pleasure Cylinder, where she may be whip-trained and, silked, taught to serve paga properly, taught to squirm in the alcove, and such."

"You are muchly favored of Agamemnon," said Pyrrhus.

"It is my hope to serve him well," said Peisistratus.

"My hope, as well," said Pyrrhus.

"Of course," said Peisistratus.

"Perhaps I will give her another chance," came from the translator.

"If you wish, Lord Pyrrhus," said Cabot, "I will take the pathetic creature off your hands."

"I will give her another chance," came from the translator.

Pyrrhus then uttered a command in Kur and the girl hurried to the furs and leapt into his arms. Cabot, on the Prison Moon, had seen the blonde leap similarly into the arms of the Kur he had come to recognize as Arcesilaus. The blonde, however, had leapt happily into the brute's grasp, and obviously the girl before him, though she had done so with fearful alacrity, had also done so with terror. How frightening it must have been for her, thought Cabot, to put herself within the grasp of those mighty appendages, within reach of those massive jaws.

She is trying to be a good pet, thought Cabot.

"We must be on our way," said Peisistratus.

Cabot looked back at the brunette, her wrists braceleted behind her, cuddled in those massive arms, her body pressed closely, obediently, pathetically against that mighty, hirsute frame.

"Let us go," said Peisistratus.

Pyrrhus, however, gestured with his left paw, that Cabot should approach. He gestured him even closer, and then moved the fur on his right shoulder, in which movement it rippled, wavelike, and uttered a soft sound to the girl. Cabot noted within the fur tiny movements, the stirring of startled, disturbed, miniscule, crawling bodies.

The girl, in her collar and chain, weeping, pulling a little at her hands, confined behind her in the bracelets, with her small, fine, white teeth, addressed herself to her task, that of freshening and cleansing the fur of her master.

"Let us go," said Peisistratus.

About the jaws of Pyrrhus Cabot noted the grimace he had come to recognize as a Kur smile.

"Let us go," urged Peisistratus.

He and Cabot then left the apartment of Pyrrhus.

"I suppose," said Cabot, in English, "I must kill him."

"Or he, you," said Peisistratus.

They continued down the passageway.

"Why would you kill him?" asked Peisistratus.

"Because he would kill me," said Cabot.

"Not for the girl?"

"No," said Cabot, "she is only a slave."

"But an attractive one."

"She will do," said Cabot.

"I do not think you need worry about Pyrrhus," said Peisistratus.

"Oh?"

"No."

"Why not?" asked Cabot. He wished he had his weapons, the mighty Gorean spear, the great bow, even the swift short blade, like part of his own hand, which could strike like the ost.

"Because," said Peisistratus, "Pyrrhus is not in favor with Agamemnon."

Chapter, the Eleventh:

It Is Like a Tavern

"They dance well," said Cabot.

"There is not one," said Peisistratus, "who would not bring three silver tarsks, even in Turia or Ar."

"I am sure of it," said Cabot. Rarely had he seen women who presented themselves so well before masters.

"You may, of course," said Peisistratus, "have your pick."

"The musicians," said Cabot, "might grace the feast of a Ubar."

"Many have," said Peisistratus.

"What is the meat?" had asked Cabot.

"Have no fear," had said Peisistratus. "It is bosk, tarsk, and verr."

"The paga is splendid," said Cabot.

"It is the paga of Temus of Ar," said Peisistratus.

"It is my favorite," said Cabot.

"We know," said Peisistratus. "That is why it is being served."

"I am muchly pleased," said Cabot.

"Good," said Peisistratus. "Agamemnon, too, will then be pleased."

"It seems you know much about me," said Cabot.

"Inquiries were made," said Peisistratus. "It is our desire that you find your stay with us comfortable and pleasant."

Cabot looked about himself. "This might be a tavern in a high city," he said, "the counter, the vats of paga, the square of sand for the dancers, the polished wooden floors, the low ceiling, the hangings, the cozy dimness, the small lamps, the curtained alcoves, such things."

"That is our intention," said Peisistratus, "that it should seem so."

"The men about," said Cabot, looking about the tables, "seem in good spirits."

"Most are drunk," said Peisistratus. "They would rather be on Gor."

The Pleasure Cylinder, as other subsidiary cylinders to the Steel World in question, those for sport, industry, and agriculture, is reached by an automated shuttle, which departs from and docks at predesignated portals. Entrance to the shuttle and departure from it is by means of a system of locks. In this fashion the occupants, or passengers, never exposed to the rigors and perils of a near vacuum, need not concern themselves with complex suiting, reaction devices, safety lines, and such. If one could conceive of swimming without water, so to speak, that gives a sense of movement within the shuttle, while it is in flight. Handles within the shuttle, which may be held, or grasped, provide leverage for staying in position, or, if one wishes, moving about within the shuttle.

"Who are the two Kurii?" asked Cabot.

"They are strangers," said Peisistratus. "Those commonly in attendance, to monitor the cylinder, are not present."

"Strangers?"

"Officers of Agamemnon," said Peisistratus.

"Why are they here?"

"Because you are here," said Peisistratus. "Doubtless they would not wish any harm to come to you."

"They are spies."

"Yes."

"As are you?"

"Perhaps."

The two in question, large and fearsome, crouched almost at the shoulder of Cabot. He could occasionally feel the breath of one on his neck.

"Do you not recognize them?" said Peisistratus.

"No," said Cabot.

"You encountered them in the audience hall of Agamemnon," said Peisistratus.

"His attendants?"

"Yes."

As the names of these two individuals are in Kur we shall refer to them, as is our wont, by choosing, almost at random, names whose phonemic nature will be accessible to readers who may be supposed unfamiliar with Kur. We shall refer to them, in this case, by names which are not unfamiliar in Ar, indeed, names somewhat common in Ar, Lucullus and Crassus.

"Doubtless," said Peisistratus, "Kurii look much alike to you."

"I fear so, many of them," said Cabot.

"Some Kurii have difficulty distinguishing amongst humans," said Peisistratus.

"Interesting," said Cabot.

"Particularly in the case of human cattle."

"I understand," said Cabot.

"We and they, however," said Peisistratus, "with more familiarity with one another have little difficulty in distinguishing amongst individuals. Indeed, Kur young must learn to distinguish amongst different members of their own species."

"Perhaps it is so, too, with humans," said Cabot.

"Perhaps," said Peisistratus.

"Perhaps one learns to see," said Cabot.

"Possibly," said Peisistratus.

"Our friends," said Cabot, indicating with a slight gesture of his head the two crouching, hulking forms behind them, "do not seem much interested in the entertainment."

"They are Kurii," said Peisistratus. "They see us primarily as food, I fear."

"Do they hear the music as we do?" asked Cabot.

"I do not know," said Peisistratus.

"They seem uncomfortable," said Cabot.

"It is too loud for them," said Peisistratus. "Have you ever heard Kur music?"

"No," said Cabot.

"It is commonly inaudible to the human ear," said Peisistratus. "Sometimes when they seem to move strangely, or meaninglessly, they are listening to their music."

"Why then are they so close?" asked Cabot.

"They are trying to overhear our conversation," said Peisistratus, "but I fear you have frustrated them, as you persist in speaking English. Their translators then are ineffectual."

"You may of course later convey to them the gist of our converse."

"True," said Peisistratus.

With a swirl from the czehar and kalikas, and a pounding of the tabors, the dancers prostrated themselves in the sand, as slaves, and then, as Peisistratus struck his hands sharply together, they leapt up, and fled from the room, exiting through a portal, it curtained with dangling strands of blue and yellow beads, the caste colors of the slavers.

Another dancer, a single dancer, then entered the sand. Like the others, she was barefoot, and bangled.

She wore bells on her left ankle.

It is not unusual for a slave to be belled.

Bells help the female keep in mind that she is a slave.

"What will she dance?" asked Cabot.

The dancer was now kneeling in the sand, her head bowed, waiting for the first strumming of the kalika. She was nicely silked, in the diaphanous dancing silks of Gor. Her hair, long and dark, fell to the sand.

"I do not mean to be importunate," said Peisistratus, "but Agamemnon is curious to know if you have reached a decision with respect to his proposal."

"I am still considering the matter," said Cabot.

"I would not consider it too long," said Peisistratus, "as Kurii are not noted for their patience."

"He may be informed," said Cabot, "that his offer is under the most earnest scrutiny."

"Doubtless he will be relieved to hear that," said Peisistratus. "If it will speed your deliberations, you might consider that a similar offer might be made to others, whose deliberations might be less prolonged."

"To you?"

"Not to one of my caste, surely," said Peisistratus.

"I see."

A whispering sentence of notes emanated from the kalika, and the dancer rose gracefully to her feet, her knees flexed, her head still bowed, her hands at her thighs.

"If you accept the offer," said Peisistratus, "the medallion of a world's Ubar might be yours, power, hundreds of cities, rivers of wealth, innumerable pleasure gardens, exquisitely stocked with game and slaves."

"Who but a fool could refuse such an offer?" said Cabot.

"Indeed," agreed Peisistratus.

"But suppose one did refuse such an offer?"

"I would not care to be he," said Peisistratus.

"I see," said Cabot.

"Paga, Master?" inquired a soft, feminine voice.

She knelt beside the table, suitably as a pleasure slave. She was red-headed, and naked, save for the collar on her neck.

Women look well so, and slaves in particular.

"Yes," said Cabot, handing her his goblet. She then rose to her feet and backed away, and then turned, and hurried to the counter, to replenish the contents of the goblet.

"Ho, the whip dance," said Cabot, returning his attention to the dancing sand.

"You like it?"

"She is lovely," said Cabot.

"She is Corinna," said Peisistratus. "She writhes well."

"Yes."

At certain points in this dance the whip snaps and the dancer reacts as though she was struck with the whip. If she does not do well, of course, she will feel the whip.

"You are tempted, are you not?"

"Who would not be?" asked Cabot. "But I think I shall soon return to my lodgings."

"The evening is young," said Peisistratus.

The red-haired paga slave then returned with the goblet, brimming, and knelt beside the low table, at which Cabot and Peisistratus sat, cross-legged. It is common for Gorean men to sit cross-legged, and for Gorean women to kneel. Chairs on Gor are commonly reserved for individuals of rank. Gorean society is muchly based on status and hierarchy. There is little attempt on Gor to pretend that obvious differentiations in such matters do not exist. On Gor that would be regarded as dishonorable hypocrisy. The slave's eyes met Cabot's and in her glance, pathetic and pleading, he read her need. And then, looking down, she pressed the metal of the goblet to her belly, and then to her breasts, and then lifted the large cup to her lips, and, looking at Cabot over the rim, kissed the cup, lingeringly. She then lowered her head between her extended arms and proffered him the goblet, which he accepted.

"May I speak, Master?" she asked.

"Yes," said Cabot.

There were tears in her eyes. Her lip trembled. "I desire to be found pleasing," she said.

"I see," said Cabot.

"Take me to an alcove, Master," she whispered, tensely, "I beg it!"

"She is needful," explained Peisistratus.

"Take me to an alcove, Master," she said. "Chain me! Make me helpless! Whip me, if you wish! But use me! I beg to be used!"

"I gather she has been deprived," said Cabot.

"Yes," said Peisistratus.

"Why?"

"She and some others," said Peisistratus, "in order to be readied for your entertainment."

"I see," said Cabot.

Slave fires, as the expression is, are cruelly and mercilessly lit within the bellies of female slaves. It is often a part of their training. It is interesting to see a slaver take a free female, complacent in her sexual inertness, even one arrogantly proud of her frigidity, and transform her into a needful, helpless, vulnerable, begging slave, zealous to serve, that she may be rewarded with even the least touch of a male. Once the slave fires flame in the belly of a woman her freedom is behind her. She is then spoiled for freedom, is beyond it, and lives instead for the attention, love, and touch of her master. Indeed, it is not unusual that one who is familiar only with free women, with their reservations, suspicions, calculations, and inhibitions, their inertnesses and frigidities, is often astonished to encounter a female slave, one whose needs have now put her vulnerably, helplessly, at the mercy of men. Sometimes a fellow encounters in an alcove a woman earlier courted in vain, now a collared slave. It is then as though there were two women, and, in a sense, this is true, for where there was once a free woman there is now a slave. Perhaps he buys her, and takes her home. Perhaps she begs him, kissing piteously at his feet, to do so.

"Go ahead," said Peisistratus. "Take her to an alcove."

"What is your name?" asked Cabot.

"Lehna, if it pleases Master."

"Tell me of your collar," said Cabot. "What does it say?"

She touched the collar. Cabot had been curious about the collars of the slaves in the cylinder. They were of a common type, a flat, light, closely fitting band, locked at the back of the neck.

"It is a standard collar, Master," she said, "but one similar to a public collar, as that of a state slave."

"What does it say?" asked Cabot.

"It says, Master," said the girl, "that I am a slave of the Pleasure Cylinder."

"Kurii are not to eat women found in such collars," said Peisistratus.

"Would you not rather, Lehna," asked Cabot, "wear a collar on Gor, and have a private master?"

She put down her head, fearing to respond.

"You need not reply," said Cabot.

"Thank you, Master," she whispered.

"Kurii prefer that we not have private slaves here," said Peisistratus. "That gives the Kurii greater control over the slaves."

"And the men?"

"Perhaps," said Peisistratus.

"There is then less bother, too, is there not," asked Cabot, "should the Kurii desire to select some out for redistribution?"

"Yes, or food," said Peisistratus.

"Lehna," said Cabot, sharply.

"Yes, Master!" she said.

"Serve another," said Cabot.

She looked at him, wildly.

"He," said Cabot, pointing across the room, toward a fellow who had only too obviously, and perhaps disgruntledly, been inspecting the flanks of Cabot's waitress.

The girl, weeping, sprang to her feet, and hurried to the fellow indicated, who cried out with pleasure, waved good-naturedly, drunkenly, at Cabot, in appreciation doubtless for the unexpected gift, and, in a moment, the girl was being dragged, bent over, by the hair to a nearby alcove.

Cabot then returned his attention to the dancing sand.

There was a final, loud snap of the whip, and the dancer threw herself, half kneeling, half sitting, to the sand, and lifted one hand, piteously, to the fellow who had conducted his part of the whip dance.

"What do you think?" asked Peisistratus.

"Of the dance?" said Cabot.

"If you wish," said Peisistratus.

"It was nicely done," said Cabot. The whip dance is a not unfamiliar component in a tavern's entertainment, which often includes slave dance.

"You are a connoisseur of slave dance?" inquired Peisistratus.

"Not really," said Cabot. "I know little of its subtleties."

"I feel that those who judge too exactly, too critically, of such matters," said Peisistratus, "the position of the hands, the perfect framing of the head and body with the arms, the angle of the head, the lightness or moderation of a stamping foot, such things, miss much of the pleasure of the dance."

"I would suppose so," said Cabot.

"Too, it is not always the most technically flawless dancer whom men wish to conduct to an alcove," said Peisistratus.

"Perhaps a dancer who is too concerned with the assemblage of minute perfections," said Cabot, "forgets the point of the dance, which is to dance her slave before masters."

"True," said Peisistratus.

"Slave dance well displays a woman," said Cabot.

"As a slave," said Peisistratus.

"Of course," agreed Cabot.

The dancer was now kneeling, and a chain was being put on her neck, some five feet in length, rather as a leash.

"And what do you think of our Corinna?" asked Peisistratus.

"A lovely slave," said Cabot.

"I am told," said Peisistratus, "she is an excellent dancer."

"One must agree," said Cabot.

"Even technically."

"Interesting," said Cabot. "But I suspect few men would be capable of forming a judicious opinion on that matter, and that even fewer would find it of the least interest."

"True," smiled Peisistratus.

"In any event," said Cabot, "putting aside her skills as a dancer, which are doubtless considerable, she is obviously a luscious piece of collar meat."

Some Goreans claim that it is the existence of beautiful women that is the justification of the slave collar. Other Goreans claim that it is the existence of women which is the justification of the slave collar.

"Behold," said Peisistratus, "she approaches."

The dancer knelt before Cabot, and, with both hands, lifted the chain to him. "I offer you my chain, Master," she said.

Cabot took the chain and jerked it against the back of her neck, and she gasped. "I take it, if I wish," he said.

"Yes, Master," she whispered, frightened.

"You like her?"

"She is lovely."

"You may take her home with you, to the hillside villa in the Steel World," said Peisistratus, "and keep her as long as you wish."

"You are generous," said Cabot.

"The Kurii are generous," said Peisistratus.

Ah, thought Cabot, Peisistratus is interested in this slave.

"She is muchly concerned to please a man," said Peisistratus.

"Does she fear the whip?"

"Very much," said Peisistratus.

"Good," said Cabot. It is useful to the master that the slave girl is terrified of the whip. Thus it seldom needs to be used. She knows, of course, that it will be used on her if she is in the least bit displeasing. Accordingly, she does her best to be found pleasing, and fully so.

Cabot noted that the slave cast a look of misery at Peisistratus, and that the hands on her thighs lifted slightly, as though she would expose her palms to him, but then she quickly returned them to her thighs, palms down.

"She has been deprived?" inquired Cabot.

"Yes," said Peisistratus, "to prepare her for you."

"Girl," said Cabot to the dancer, "return to your cage, or kennel."

She leapt up, gratefully, cast another look at Peisistratus, and hurried from the room, departing through the beaded curtain. It shook behind her.

One of the Kurii growled menacingly. It was obviously displeased.

Cabot thought that Peisistratus leaned back, a bit.

"You did not send her to another, as with Lehna?" said Peisistratus.

"Let her rest, from the dance," said Cabot.

"I see," said Peisistratus.

One of the Kurii, Cabot noticed, was looking toward the beaded curtain.

"You did not find her attractive?" asked Peisistratus.

"She is very attractive," said Cabot.

"There are others, of course," said Peisistratus. "Would you like to inspect them?"

"No," said Cabot.

"Nature has designed them all, and well, for the collar," said Peisistratus.

"I am pleased to hear it," said Cabot.

"All would sell well."

"I am sure of it."

"And all have been readied for you."

"As the paga of Temus?"

"Yes," said Peisistratus.

"I am grateful," said Cabot.

"Perhaps you are interested in the brunette from the stall, the pet of Pyrrhus?" asked Peisistratus.

"The one whose hair is too short?"

"Yes."

"Why would one be interested in her?" asked Cabot.

"Agamemnon could easily arrange for her to be brought to you," said Peisistratus.

"She is the pet of Lord Pyrrhus," said Cabot.

"He does not want her," said Peisistratus. "He only took her to anger you. Indeed, he might kill her."

"That would be a waste of slave," said Cabot.

"There are others," said Peisistratus, "from the cylinder, even from the cattle pens. Humans are cheap."

"Where is Zarendargar?" asked Cabot.

The bluntness, the suddenness, of this question, startled Peisistratus. He looked uneasily back at the two Kurii behind them.

"I do not know," he said.

"Tell me," said Cabot.

"He is not in the Steel World," said Peisistratus. "He was removed from the domain of Agamemnon, under custody, seven days ago."

"He was merely used to bring me to the Steel World?" said Cabot.

"I fear so," said Peisistratus. "He was intent to rescue a friend, with whom it is told he had once shared paga, to save him from death or dishonor at the hands of Priest-Kings, a noble endeavor, but instead he brought him unwittingly into the grasp of Agamemnon."

"I see," said Cabot. This did not come to him as any great surprise, for he had supposed as much, having neither heard nor seen aught of Zarendargar after his extrication from the Prison Moon.

"Agamemnon will want his answer soon," said Peisistratus.

"I understand," said Cabot.

"Tomorrow," said Peisistratus, "you are to go hunting."

"Hunting?"

"On the game world," said Peisistratus, "with Lord Pyrrhus."

"Are there weapons here, in the Pleasure Cylinder?" asked Cabot.

"We are not to speak of such things."

"Are there?"

"In the ships," said Peisistratus.

"Are the ships accessible, and free?"

"They require authorization to depart, to dock, and so on," said Peisistratus. "And they are not a match for the speed or armament of Kur ships."

"They are slavers' ships?"

"Yes."

"What does one hunt on the game world?" inquired Cabot.

"Animals of various sorts," said Peisistratus.

"And humans?"

"Yes."

"This is a test of sorts, I suppose," said Cabot.

"I suppose so," said Peisistratus. "They probably wish to see if you will kill humans."

"I see."

"But, too," he said, "these are unusual humans, and our hirsute friends may be interested to see if they kill you."

"Unusual humans?"

"They have been bred to be elusive, dangerous prey animals. Some have slain Kurii."

"And if these unusual humans kill me, I would thus be proven a poor choice to abet the schemes of Kurii?"

"Yes, and then they could turn to others."

"Tomorrow then I shall go hunting."

"Cabot," said Peisistratus.

"Yes?"

"Beware of Lord Pyrrhus."

As Cabot made ready to access the shuttle and return to his hillside villa on the Steel World, he heard the blows of a lash and the screams of a whipped slave.

"It is Corinna," said Peisistratus. "She is being punished."

"Why?" asked Cabot.

"Our friends will have it so," said Peisistratus.

"But, why?" asked Cabot.

"She failed to seduce you," said Peisistratus.

Chapter, the Twelfth:

The Game World

"I think there is nothing here," said Cabot.

"No," said Pyrrhus. "You are here."

There are five subsidiary cylinders easily reachable from the Steel World by means of shuttles. The largest of these are the agricultural cylinders, of which there are two; the next largest is the forest world, or game world; the next is the industrial cylinder; and the pleasure cylinder is by far the smallest.

The forest world, or game world, is essentially a sport world for Kurii, who are fond of the hunt. The forest world associated with the Steel World under the governance of Agamemnon is something in the neighborhood of one hundred square pasangs.

Cabot could see trees, as though from above, far over his head. Similarly forested areas sloped up to the curved horizons until they reached the green sky. He could see, far above him, amidst the trees, what appeared to be a lake.

"It is lovely, is it not?" came from the translator of Pyrrhus.

"Yes," said Cabot. "Where are the others, the hunting party?"

"We have come early," said Pyrrhus.

"You carry only a net, a spear, a knife," said Cabot.

"We do not use power weapons in the hunt," said Pyrrhus.

"It would not be sporting?"

"No, and if we did so, the range would soon be overhunted."

"I would have thought your claws and teeth would be sufficient," said Cabot.

"There are beasts in the forests other than humans," said Pyrrhus.

"And they prey on humans?"

"Some," said Pyrrhus, "larls, sleen."

"It was not necessary to have shown me the cattle pens before we boarded the shuttle," said Cabot.

"They would make poor game animals," said Pyrrhus.

"Doubtless," said Cabot.

Cabot had not been pleased to see the extensive pens in which the cattle were crowded, scarcely able to move about, feeding and watering at side troughs, milling about, grunting, pressing against the bars.

"I am sorry if you were distressed," said Pyrrhus, "but you must understand that your species is a food species. I did spare you the squealing at the slaughter bench."

"They are not speeched," said Cabot.

"For the most part, not," said Pyrrhus. "Occasionally we put a speeched one amongst them, who understands what will be done, but he is unable to communicate with the others."

"I see," said Cabot.

"Do not be concerned for them," said Pyrrhus. "It is the only life they know. They fear only that their food troughs will not be filled on time, that the water troughs may be dry."

"I see," said Cabot.

"Have you ever tasted human?" asked Pyrrhus.

"No," said Cabot.

"Would you like to do so?"

"No," said Cabot.

"Yet," said Pyrrhus, "humans have often eaten human."

"I suppose that is true," said Cabot.

"But you do not care to do so?"

"No."

"I do not blame you," said Pyrrhus. "I do not care much for human myself. Do you recall my pet?"

"I think so," said Cabot.

"I do not think I would care to eat her myself," said Pyrrhus, "as I do not care that much for human, but I am thinking of selling her to another who might find her tasty."

"Doubtless you will do as you wish," said Cabot.

"I thought you might be interested."

"Why?" asked Cabot.

"I see," said Pyrrhus. "I had thought you might wish to own her."

"Her hair is short," said Cabot.

"But is she not a well-shaped female of your species, of the sort that men enjoy owning?"

"She will do," said Cabot.

"I thought so," said Pyrrhus.

"You do not approve of the plan of Agamemnon, I gather," said Cabot, "to utilize humans in the conquest of Gor."

"Why should you say that?" inquired Pyrrhus.

"Because we are here, alone, at the edge of the forest, in advance of the hunting party."

"For a human, you are clever," said Pyrrhus.

"Agamemnon, I gather," said Cabot, "does not know I am here."

"Some things, it seems," said Pyrrhus, "elude even the awareness of the Eleventh Face of the Nameless One."

"An accident of some sort will occur?"

"You were curious," said Pyrrhus. "You wandered off."

"That was unwise of me," said Cabot.

"There is little point in eying my dagger," said Pyrrhus, "for the sheath is locked, and you do not know the releasing touch."

"You would challenge the will of Agamemnon?"

"Agamemnon is astute," said Pyrrhus, "but he knows little of honor. He would expend humans, swarming them into the Sardar to exterminate Priest-Kings, thus robbing Kurii of the glory of victory."

"Surely this might save many Kurii."

"But at the cost of glory," said Pyrrhus. "One might as well utilize bacilli to achieve one's ends."

"A victory ill bought is an ill-gained victory," said Cabot.

"Precisely," said Pyrrhus.

"But it is a victory."

"One unworthy of Kurii," said Pyrrhus.

"Too," said Cabot, "after such a victory you would have to share Gor with your allies."

"Surely you do not believe that," said Pyrrhus.

"No," said Cabot, "I do not."

"That deception, too, defiles honor," said Pyrrhus.

"But it evidences the astuteness of Agamemnon."

"The pledge of a Kur is sacred," said Pyrrhus.

"Perhaps it should be," said Cabot.

"The world must not be surrendered to the Agamemnons," said Pyrrhus.

"More than one world would seem to be theirs," said Cabot.

"I must not be found here," said Pyrrhus.

"I suppose not," said Cabot.

"Remove your tunic," said Pyrrhus.

Cabot slipped from the simple garment and placed it in Pyrrhus' broad, extended paw.

"Am I to be killed now?" inquired Cabot.

"Do you think I want to return to the world with your blood on my claws and teeth?" said Pyrrhus. "Or particles of your flesh on my fingers?"

"The hunting party is due to arrive soon?"

"Yes," said Pyrrhus.

"I am to escape into the forest?" said Cabot.

"If you wish," said Pyrrhus.

"I may remain here, and address the hunters," said Cabot.

"If you wish," said Pyrrhus, "but the hunting party is in league with me."

"You have left little to chance," said Cabot.

"The hunting party will not be blamed for killing and eating you," said Pyrrhus.

"A natural mistake, as humans look much alike to Kurii?"

"Yes, and no one would expect to find you here."

"And thus the plans of Agamemnon will be frustrated?"

"For now," said Pyrrhus.

"And later?"

"Who knows what may occur later?" came from Pyrrhus' translator.

"Treachery, treason, poison, assassination?"

"I depart," said Pyrrhus.

"Perhaps I may elude the hunting party," said Cabot.

"I do not think so," said Pyrrhus, lifting the tunic which Cabot had surrendered to him, "for they will have sleen."

"Little, indeed, has been left to chance," said Cabot.

"The hunters may not be your greatest danger," said Pyrrhus.

"Larls, wild sleen?" said Cabot.

"And humans."

"Humans?"

"Certainly," said Pyrrhus. "They do not know you."

"They are dangerous?"

"Some have killed Kurii," said Pyrrhus.

"I will speak to them," said Cabot.

"They are not speeched," said Pyrrhus.

Lord Pyrrhus then returned to the shuttle lock, accessed the automated vessel, and left the sport world.

And Cabot entered the forest.

Chapter, the Thirteenth:

What Occurred in the Forest

"Tal," said Cabot, lifting his hand in greeting.

He had not proceeded far into the forest when he became aware that they were about him, amongst the trees.

He was not surprised that his presence had been soon detected, as he supposed that a watch was maintained from the forest on the shuttle lock, whence would emerge Kur hunting parties.

To be sure, there were doubtless a number of shuttle locks, giving access to the sport world at different points.

Human denizens of the forest, however, would doubtless maintain a watch on each of these.

The forest had been rather silent as he had entered it, save for certain cries, as of the calls of birds.

Cabot looked about himself.

His greeting had not been returned.

Signs, however, had been exchanged. Signs can be useful, if one is within a line of sight. Thus messages can be exchanged in silence.

Cabot was reassured that these signs had been exchanged. These denizens of the forest were far from human cattle. Indeed, they had been bred for cunning, elusiveness, and, he supposed, ruthlessness.

From the Kur point of view they were ideal game animals, highly intelligent and extremely dangerous.

They wore skins, which reassured Cabot he was not dealing with simple prey animals but animals which were, in their turn, fully capable of predation. They carried pointed sticks, some sharpened as spears, others as shorter, stabbing weapons.

"Tal," said Cabot, again.

His overture was again ignored, or misunderstood.

There seemed to be some twenty or thirty of them which were now encircling him, none closer than thirty or forty feet.

How do they think of me, wondered Cabot. They may well wonder at my presence here. Too, it is quite possible they saw me with Lord Pyrrhus, in the vicinity of the lock. Do they think I have been put here to be killed, by them or others, or do they think I am here as bait, or to betray them? Presumably, if I were killed, they would have little to fear.

Too, they may eat human, other than those of their own group. That is not so uncommon amongst humans.

One of these creatures came forward a little. Instead of skins, he wore the remains of a Kur harness. At his hip was a knife, a Kur knife. It was the only metal weapon Cabot could detect in the group.

He has killed a Kur, Cabot thought.

Behind the men, in the trees, Cabot could detect several female figures, also clad in skins. They were bare-legged, and supple.

The fellow in the remains of the Kur harness, he who had approached Cabot the most closely, made several abrupt, rapid gestures to him, which were incomprehensible to Cabot. He then turned about, and signed similarly to the others.

"Are you speeched?" inquired Cabot, in Gorean. He was sure they were capable of uttering sound. Presumably when they felt secure they would do so. They would presumably have some system of verbal signals, if not a language. Cabot did not expect them to understand Gorean, but he had hoped that they would respond with something which would indicate at least that they were speeched.

Perhaps they do not wish to utter sound too near the edge of the forest, thought Cabot.

Some of the females had now come a little closer.

Their furs did not much conceal them. Doubtless they had been attired in accordance with the will of men. None were armed. About their necks, wrapped several times, three or four times, were leather strips, about an inch wide. These were knotted in front, with a variety of ties.

These are slaves, thought Cabot. They are collared. The different knots probably identify the master. It is like Gorean slave strings, or slave laces, fastened about a girl's neck, indicating her bondage and her owner. Cabot was reminded of the leather collars, beaded, in which the Red Savages of the Barrens commonly kept their white female slaves.

They keep their women as slaves, thought Cabot. Thus there is no division within the community, which might produce confusion, hesitancy, dissension, and conflict, and jeopardize the survival of the group. Too, what true man does not desire absolute power over a woman, and what true woman does not seek a man at whose feet to kneel?

Cabot smiled, and spread his hands, making very clear, ritualistically, that he was unweaponed.

The women are coming closer, he thought. They want to watch. He is going to attack.

The fellow in the remains of the Kur harness smiled, as had Cabot.

They can smile, thought Cabot.

The fellow in the remains of the Kur harness then spread his hands, as had Cabot.

It was clearly a gesture of peace, of acceptance, of friendship.

He then attacked.

Cabot had expected the attack, but not its swiftness, its agility. He broke his assailant's hands from his neck by going between the arms and forcing them apart. He then spun his startled, squirming assailant about and brought his hands under the other's arms, locked his fingers together behind the other's neck, and began to press forward. In this way the neck may be broken. Cabot spun about, not releasing his hold, to fend other blows, the jabbing of the sharpened sticks, but none of the others approached.

Cabot exerted further pressure, but did not snap the spinal cord.

His foe uttered angry noises, but there was nothing that suggested a call for quarter, a plea of mercy, even an emanation of fear.

One of the skin-clad animals approached Cabot, unarmed, and put his hand gently on Cabot's arm.

They can kill me, thought Cabot. What does it matter? He then released his hold and his foe, dazed, shaking his head, sank to his knees amongst the leaves.

Cabot saw the women exchanging wild glances, and three or four edged yet more closely forward.

Cabot thought they would sell well.

The one who had attacked Cabot crawled away a few feet, and climbed to his feet.

He reached to the sheathed dagger he wore at his hip, and Cabot prepared to defend himself, a second time.

Why had he not drawn the dagger first, Cabot wondered.

Cabot assumed a defensive stance, knees flexed, hands ready.

But the leader, as he was that, and we shall call him Archon, to utilize a Gorean title for a variety of civic officials, removed the sheath and dagger from the remains of the Kur harness he wore and handed it to Cabot.

There were grunts of approbation from the men about, and a shaking of their simple weapons.

Cabot took the sheath and dagger from Archon and tried to draw the blade. It was frozen in the sheath. Of course, thought Cabot, it is locked in place. There is a releasing touch. The touch would have to be simple, to be quickly applied, and it would doubtless be indexed to a six-digited paw.

Cabot then gestured to Archon to approach, and he held the hilt in his right hand, placing his five fingers in five of the six depressions in the hilt, and took Archon's hand and placed one of his fingers on the sixth depression. The touch, thought Cabot, cannot be a simple grasp, but it must be nearly so, to be such as could be applied with a moment's notice. He then pressed his own fingers and the finger of Archon into the depressions swiftly, twice. The dagger sprang free from the sheath and there was a cry of wonder from Archon, and the others. Cabot then held aloft the Kur blade, nice inches in length, tapered, grooved to allow slippage and a path for blood, and wickedly sharp.

Cabot looked about himself.

The men about put their weapons to the ground, the weapons facing away from him, as though he might be ringed with points arranged to defend him, or to be directed by him.

I am first, thought Cabot.

No, he thought, I shall not be first.

To Archon's astonishment he returned the blade to him, now freed from the sheath, now no more a mere symbol of authority, a scepter of sorts, but a weapon, one capable of piercing to the heart of even a Kur.

Archon lifted the blade in wonder and jubilation.

The men ringed him, and laid their weapons about him, ringing him.

He then turned to face Cabot, the knife in his hand.

Now I die, thought Cabot.

But Archon thrust the knife through a broad leather band of the Kur harness, unwilling to trust it again to its strange, recalcitrant sheath, and approached Cabot, and, putting out his arms, embraced him.

Cabot was then surrounded by the others, who clapped him on the arms and back, and uttered soft noises, seemingly indicative of acceptance and approval.

Two females were then gestured forth. Both had long, dark hair. Archon untied the leather strips at their necks, and pointed to Cabot's feet. Instantly both knelt before him, and, putting down their heads, kissed his feet. At a gesture from Archon they both then stood before Cabot. The leather strips untied from their necks were then placed in Cabot's hands. He wrapped one about the neck of each, three or four times, and then fastened it, jerking it tight with a warrior's knot. At another gesture from Archon, they both knelt again before Cabot, and again kissed his feet.

Both looked up at him, then, and then each bowed her head before him.

The leader is generous thought Cabot. He has given me two women. They are doubtless a currency of sorts in this place.

Too, they clearly understand their relationship to men, and their place.

Slaves are, of course, in any event, a form of currency. They are exchangeable, bartarable, vendible, as any other form of goods, cloth, leather, metal, kaiila, tarsk, verr, such things.

Their furs did not muchly conceal them, and it was tantalizing to consider them washed, and brushed and combed, and in rep-cloth tunics or slave silk.

Might not both serve well in a high city?

Perhaps even as lesser slaves at the feast of a Ubar?

Yes, thought Cabot, they would sell well.

The leader is generous.

Many men would be pleased to have them chained to the slave ring at the foot of his couch.

At this point a cry, as of a bird, came through the trees.

The forest people were instantly apprehensive, and alert.

Archon gestured to Cabot, and the others, and then turned about, and disappeared amongst the trees.

The group then left the clearing, as did Cabot, as well, the two women hurrying behind him.

Chapter, the Fourteenth:

The Forest Seems Quiet

For several Ehn the forest group, one of several in the sport cylinder, though these avoided one another as roving groups are accustomed to do, moved swiftly from the clearing where they had encountered Cabot, he now with them, accompanied by the two gifts which had been given to him.

They came after a time to a hilly area, where there were rocky outcroppings, and the leader, Archon, and Cabot, and some others, climbed to a point of vantage, whence they might consider the terrain behind them.

They saw nothing.

Cabot was pleased to have survived his encounter with the group, but he placed little confidence in their sharpened sticks against the spears, the nets, and the edged weapons of Kurii. Too, he knew himself to be a marked man, who would be sleen hunted by the colleagues of Pyrrhus, and he had no wish to jeopardize his newly found fellows.

The cry, as of the call of a bird, had surely been a warning, that a hunting party had entered the cylinder.

Cabot tried to bid farewell to the group, but a fellow held his arm, and Archon moved his hand, as though wiping out marks in sand.

The signification of that Cabot surmised was negation, or denial.

Cabot then tried to suggest the sound of a growling sleen and pointed to the forested terrain below them.

Archon smiled and again performed the gesture, as though wiping out marks in sand. So, too, thought Cabot, might traces of a trail or camps be removed.

Could it be that hunting sleen were not yet come through the shuttle port?

Cabot tried to convey his apprehensions to Archon, but the leader of the group again made the gesture of denial, and led the way down from the high place.

They do not understand their danger, thought Cabot, nor the risk of being in my vicinity.

That night, near a concealed cache of food and furs, one of several Cabot supposed, the group made its camp.

He was brought furs from which he fabricated a loose tunic, and was given a sharpened stick, some seven feet in length. The strips of meat he was given were from wild tarsk, and had been dried, being hung from branches. The forest people did not cook their meat, even when freshly taken. They lacked the mastery of fire, its making and control. But even had they not, they would have been sparing in its use, for its light or smoke might have betrayed their position. His gifts, the two long-haired slaves, softened the meat by chewing it for him. One, too, dug him tubers, wild suls, and the other brought him tree fruit, kernelled pods which dangle from the Bar tree, native, as we understand it, neither to Earth or Gor. After having taken a bite of the provenders afforded him, Cabot indicated, with gestures, that the slaves might feed, as well, and they did so, gratefully. Their new master had found them pleasing, and this was evident in his permitting them to feed. When those of the group not posted to their watches began to retire, Cabot's gifts lay at his thigh, making tiny noises. Archon approached Cabot, and Cabot sat up, to welcome him. Archon pressed two roots into his hands, and Cabot held them to his face, and took their scent. They were sip root. He was familiar with sip root for it is the active ingredient in slave wine. It is taken raw in the Barrens by the white female slaves of the Red Savages, unless it is decided that they are to be bred. In its raw, unconcentrated state the effects of the root last some months, but gradually dissipate. In the high cities the Caste of Physicians has produced a slave wine whose effects are terminated only by a counter substance, called the Releaser. Sip root is bitter to the taste, and slave wine is not sweetened either. The Releaser, however, is not only palatable, but aromatic and delicious. When it is given to the girl she may, to her dismay and misery, and perhaps shrieking for mercy, expect to be soon sent to the breeding sheds, to be chained and hooded, and crossed with a male slave, who is similarly hooded. Slaves, as other domestic animals, are bred according to the will of the masters. Cabot knelt his gifts, and gave them each a root, which they then, head down, shuddering, slowly, distastefully, chewed and swallowed. In his usage of them he gave them the names Tula and Lana, both common Gorean slave names.

After the contenting of the slaves Cabot remained awake.

He was sure there must be a hunting party of Kurii in the forest, perhaps not far away.

If he had understood Archon correctly, they did not have sleen with them. It must be then, Cabot thought, another party, not the colleagues of Pyrrhus, intent upon his destruction, to be construed as an inadvertence, an unfortunate misunderstanding. Too, it seemed possible that Pyrrhus would not wish his group to enter the forest too soon after his return to the Steel World. Too, he might have hoped that after a suitable interval his colleagues' work might prove unnecessary, for Cabot might in the meantime have succumbed to other terrors of the forest, presumably wild beasts of one sort or another, perhaps even to those dangerous prey animals of his own species.

The watch was changed twice before Cabot fell asleep.

When he awakened, Tula and Lana were gone.

Chapter, the Fifteenth:

How Kaissa Came to the Forest

There is no mistaking the sound of slave bells.

But these were not the proportioned janglings of such bells, measured to the step of a slave who well knows their effect on men, and uses them to present the slave of her. Just as women of one world may use attire, perfume, cosmetics, and such, or another robes, and sandals, and veils, to call attention, while haughtily pretending not to do so, to the flesh she is offering to a man, or the slave she is dangling before him, so a slave, who is owned, may use her bells variously, perhaps their sudden flash and sparkle to announce her presence in a room, perhaps their provocative and subtle whispering to accompany her labors, see me, Master, I am yours, perhaps that insolent jangle on the street which is unmistakably a brazen and proud proclamation of her bondage, that she has been found suitable for belling, perhaps that tiny sound, and moan, at the foot of her master's couch, which calls attention to her need. She hopes she will not be cuffed.

Cabot leaped to his feet.

Into the camp area, half running, came Tula and Lana, each carrying a supple switch, formed of a narrow, green branch, dragging between them a double leashed, pathetic, gasping, stumbling figure. The figure was in a slave tunic, probably that it be made clear to Kurii that she was not to be eaten, before or after the bells were affixed. About her wrists and ankles, and neck, which wore no collar, were several strings of bells. Their sound could be easily picked up by Kurii at several hundred yards. Her small wrists had been bound tightly behind her back. There were bruises on her face where she had been struck, and one eye was half closed, and there were many stripes and welts on her

200

body where the switches of Tula and Lana had done their work, expressing their displeasure with the prisoner, and hastening her to the camp. Her calves and thighs, too, had been scratched and cut by the brush through which she had been dragged. Tula and Lana threw their prisoner to her knees before Archon, on whom, her head held back by the hair, she looked with undisguised terror.

"Ai!" thought Cabot!

It was the first time he had seen the blonde in a slave tunic.

Strange, he thought, how covering up a bit of a woman's body, particularly in a garment clearly that of a slave, can so startle and stimulate a man, can so astonishingly call attention to and enhance the attractiveness of a woman. Does it not beg to be torn away?

It is no wonder that slave raids in the high cities commonly target slaves. One can see at least what piteously thrashes within the inescapable tightness of one's capture loop. Too, of course, this mode of garmenting the slave tends to make her the likely prey of the raider, and thus diverts attention from the free woman.

They must understand, thought Cabot, that she is bait for Kurii. She is released into the forest, and her path may be followed. When humans come to investigate her, or claim her, for she is an exquisite female, the Kurii, the hunters, may close in and perhaps annihilate an entire group, or take what they wish, and perhaps ear notch the others, especially the younger ones, and leave them for a later hunt.

Archon is not a fool, surely.

Already, with swift signs, he was clearly giving orders pertaining to the breaking of the camp.

For some reason it seemed that Tula and Lana had been sent out to apprehend the girl and bring her here. Why should that be? Had men scouted the blonde and decided she would look well in the wrapping of a leather collar? If not, why would they not have killed her in the forest? Had Tula and Lana somehow discovered her, and did not know what to do with her? Did they not realize the danger of bringing her to the camp?

The answer to these questions soon became clear to Cabot, for a sharpened stick, some two feet in length, was brought forth, and a rock. The blonde's head was held back and the point of the stick was placed in her mouth. As her head was held, by the hair, she could not pull back, away from the stick. She was then thrown on her back and held down, the stick's point still in her mouth. A hand raised the rock, to use it, hammerlike, to drive the stick downward, through the back of her neck, pinning her by means of it to the ground. The blonde's eyes were wide, terrified.

It is a signal to the Kurii, thought Cabot, a clear indication, far more clear than killing her in the forest, that they understand the Kur ruse, and that they may expect such stratagems to be not only ineffective, but to result in the savage demise of a perhaps valued pet, or slave.

Cabot held the arm of the man with the rock, and made the gesture he had learned from Archon, that for negation.

Archon looked at him, puzzled. Then Archon gestured that Cabot should approach him. Archon then pointed to the blonde and pointed to the group about him with a sweeping gesture. He then drew a circle in the dirt, pointed to the blonde, and then, again, to the people about him, and then, growling, like a Kur, he pointed to the edges of the circle, moving his fingers toward the center.

Cabot nodded.

Then Cabot pointed to the blonde, and drew a circle, and made a growling noise, pointing to the interior of the circle. He then pointed to the group about them, and slashed toward the center of the circle with his finger, several times.

Archon smiled. He turned to one of his men and signed, questioningly. The man held up ten fingers.

Only ten, thought Cabot, only ten.

But even that, he supposed, would be large for a Kur hunting party.

Archon stood up, grinning. There must have been here, here in the camp, some forty males.

The Kurii will expect the humans to run, thought Cabot. They always run. But this time they are not running.

The blonde squirmed a little, in misery, with a tiny sound of the many bells. The pointed stick was still held in her mouth. It kept her in place. Cabot took it from the fellow who held it and tossed it aside. The blonde struggled to sit up, but Cabot, with his foot, pressed her back.

"Human, human!" said the blonde, on her back, looking up at him.

"Kur pet," said Cabot.

He pointed to the blonde, and tried to make it clear that he wanted some fur and leather, and Archon smiled, and guessed his intention. She would not warn Kurii.

Cabot crouched over her and wound the two leashes together, to constitute a single tether.

"Free me," she said to Cabot. "They do not understand us." She spoke in Gorean.

"You are pretty in a slave tunic," said Cabot. "It seems your Gorean is coming along nicely. Your bells are nice, too. There are a great many of them. They are slave bells. I suppose you know that."

"Free me!" she urged.

Cabot put out his hand and some fur and straps were placed in it.

"What are you going to do with me?" she said, frightened.

"We are going for a walk," said Cabot.

"You are clever!" she said. "When we are alone, free me! Return me to Arcesilaus, my master!"

"Perhaps, eventually," he said.

"What are you doing!"

Cabot fixed the wadding and straps. She looked at him, wildly.

"Is a Kur pet not supposed to be silent?" asked Cabot.

She squirmed in her bonds, and uttered frightened, muffled sounds.

Archon then lifted her to her knees and, angrily, taking her by the hair, forced her gagged mouth to Cabot's feet, where he held it for some moments, and then he, by the hair, rudely, painfully, pulled her back up, so that she knelt, as she had before.

Cabot then lifted her to her feet.

"We are going for a walk," he informed her.

Archon gestured that he would lead the way.

He knows, thought Cabot, a good place. He then followed Archon, and the blonde, unable to speak, for the straps and fur, her hands tied behind her, with a jangling of bells, followed Cabot, on her leash.

Chapter, the Sixteenth:

The Defile

Yes, Cabot thought, this is a good place.

He slipped down the side of the defile to where he had left the blonde, sitting, her ankles crossed before her, tied together with the twice-braided leash, in such a way that her head, by the leash, was drawn forward and downward, and fastened to her crossed ankles.

From the slippage on the descent, and the rattle of pebbles, she knew he, or someone, had descended to her level.

There was a small sound of the bells.

She could not well look up at him, fastened as she was.

Her wrists were still fastened behind her, as they had been since her capture by Tula and Lana.

Cabot looked to the height of the defile, to his right, and waved to Archon, who lifted his hand, and then slipped back, amongst the rocks, out of sight. The rocks rose to a height of some fifty feet or so on three sides. A shallow descent, on one side, open, led to the pitlike depression amidst the rocks.

There was another sound of the bells, angry, futile, from the prisoner.

Cabot glanced at her.

He heard tiny, angry, demanding, muffled sounds.

It seemed she had not yet learned docility and terror in the presence of a man. Such characteristics would doubtless have been elicited in the presence of a form of life with which she was more familiar. As a complacent and arrogant pet of Kurii, and priding herself as such, a species so superior on the Steel World, she was inclined on the whole to be contemptuous of her own species, which she understood, perhaps appropriately, as an inferior life form. Certainly she held the human animals of the forest, prey animals, as worthy of little respect, saving how they might constitute for her a dreadful imperilment. Surely she remembered the pointed stick, and how she might have been fixed by it to the earth of a primitive camp.

Cabot had tied her in a way acceptable for a free woman.

He had not tied her as she might have been tied, had she been a slave. In such a case she might have been knelt, and her head held down, even to the dirt, by the leash, shortened, drawn back and fastened to her crossed, bound ankles.

The thought of the former Miss Pym, now the pet of Lord Pyrrhus, crossed Cabot's mind. She was a slave. And he thought she might look well, tied as might have been a slave, bent, leash-knelt, her small hands, too, as the blonde's, fastened behind her, though, in her case, as she would have been knelt, high.

On Gor, there are many differences between the free woman and the slave, of which this difference was merely another token. When a free woman is bound as a slave, she may assume that her intended disposition is bondage. Let her then grow accustomed to what is in store for her.

It was not surprising that Cabot thought often, even irritably, of the former Miss Pym. Surely it had not been a coincidence, a simple random happening, that she had been enclosed with him in the container. Had not the selections, the machinations and subtleties, of Priest-Kings been involved in that remarkable, astonishing juxtaposition? And, too, he wondered if he might have been chosen to stand to her rather as she to him. Could there have been calculated polarities involved? Might Priest-Kings have been so cruel? Surely not.

He recalled her insistence that she despised men. Cabot doubted that this was true, but he did not doubt that she wished to convince herself of that. Perhaps she despised men as she had known them, but perhaps she did not despise men as she suspected they might be, men before whom she could be only a woman, and a slave.

There was a jangle of bells as the prisoner tried to free her hands and feet. She was not unattractive. She was clearly a sleek, sensuous, and, as of now, as she was partly speeched, a half-human creature.

Cabot thought of Grendel.

He was as strong, as swift, and possibly as ruthless, as a Kur. The heritage, and the hereditary coils, of Kurii were like cables in his blood, like steel in every corpuscle of his massive body.

And Peisistratus had made it clear that Grendel wanted the prisoner.

Cabot heard a cry, as of a bird. The hunting party must now be within the purview of those concealed amongst the rocks.

Suddenly the blonde was absolutely quiet.

She understands, thought Cabot. She now understands! Now let her be afraid. How will Kurii regard her, after this evening?

Will she be torn to pieces?

Will she be dragged to the shuttle port and eaten alive?

Will they remand her to the cattle pens, she fully aware, awaiting perhaps for weeks her turn on the slaughter bench?

Perhaps they will give her to Peisistratus, for his men in the pleasure cylinder?

To be sure, thought Cabot, this is only one party, hunting, and it is not that of Lord Pyrrhus' cohorts, for it lacks sleen. I cannot hope to elude sleen. I must distance myself from the humans. But I have tried to do something for them. If they learn to deal with Kurii, with concerted action, then perhaps isolated groups, enemies over territory, may join together, if only temporarily, for purposes of defense, or, if appropriate, aggression.

He heard again the cry, as of a bird.

It will be soon, thought Cabot.

The prisoner turned about, trying to lift her head, and regard him.

Women look well, tied, he thought, even as free women.

His thoughts strayed to the former Miss Pym.

The former Miss Pym was now a slave. It was done. The matter was concluded. It had been proclaimed openly and irreversibly. It was a consequence of her own act. It had been self-confessed, self-acknowledged, self-proclaimed. As a result of such an act a slaver might put her up, instantly, for sale. Yet he was sure that she did not understand the factual, legal actuality of her condition. Her background had not prepared her to understand, he supposed, at least fully, and consciously, the nature of her own act. He had little doubt that she was still terrified of the slave of her, the actual, natural slave of her, and would struggle to conceal her, and deny her, even frantically.

The blonde now began to make piteous noises, no longer angry, or defiant. She is trying to plead, thought Cabot, such pathetic, tiny, futile noises. See, too, how she holds her body absolutely still.

She would like to warn the Kurii, of course.

Archon would have seen to it that something of a trail, a dislodged pebble, a crushed leaf, a snapped twig, a bit of fur seemingly snagged on a branch, would draw the party in this direction. Excellent. We need now only the bells, signaling the locus of the prey, perhaps clustered about the bait. She wishes to warn the Kurii? Good. Let her do so.

Cabot bent to the tied ankles of the blonde and freed them of the leash's tether. She looked up at him, gratefully, relievedly. She awkwardly scrambled to her feet and lifted her face to him, uttering tiny, pleading sounds, that he might free her of the heavy, obdurate packing and straps which so effectively denied her speech. Cabot, instead, wound the leash several times about her throat, and tucked in one end, that it might remain in place. She turned about, lifting her tied wrists to him, but he took her by the arms, she facing away from him, and shook her, creating a jangling of bells.

She was horrified.

She tried then to stand still, absolutely still.

"You are pretty," Cabot whispered in her ear. "And you look well in a slave tunic. I wonder if you know how attractive you are in such a garment. I do not doubt but what you would sell well."

She tried to remain perfectly still.

He then gave her another vigorous shake, and there was another jangle of bells, which must have carried well into the forest.

He then hurled her from him, several feet, rolling, jangling, to the dirt, away from the opening in the defile.

She scrambled to her feet and looked wildly about.

Cabot was between her and the opening.

She turned about and tried to scramble up the steep sides of the defile, once, twice, three times, and each time, her hands tied behind her, she lost her footing, and slid, or rolled, to the pitlike depression in the bottom of the defile.

Then, on a fourth try, she managed, sliding and slipping, to attain the surface, but was there seized by one of the humans, who then thrust her back, rolling down the incline, to its bottom.

Certainly the intensity of the noise, the jangling of the bells, might suggest rapidity, and urgency, perhaps associated with fleeing prey animals.

The purpose of the bait is to cluster the prey, and keep it together, but the frenzy of the jangling must surely now suggest the need for speed in the pursuit, the noise perhaps signaling the escape and scattering of startled prey.

Cabot gestured that the blonde should approach him, and she did, in misery, terrified. He then unwound the twice-braided leash from her throat, took it in hand, and knelt her beside him, a bit behind him, on the left, where slaves commonly kneel when accompanying a master.

She uttered piteous noises.

Cabot hoped that Kurii would infer that she was guiltless in this trap, and was no more than a hapless, blameless tool in an unexpected stratagem. This, of course, too, was true. But Cabot did not suppose that her masters would necessarily see things in precisely this light.

At that point, roaring, and running, half bent over, several Kurii rushed into the defile.

Chapter, the Seventeenth:

How the Hunt Turned Out

There were ten of them, as expected.

One, he was sure, was Arcesilaus, the blonde's owner.

Seeing only Cabot and the blonde before them, the Kurii, startled, stopped. They looked about for humans. Surely they had expected to find humans, doubtless fleeing, to be rapidly pursued. They had not understood that the defile was closed beyond the opening, that there was no exit opposite the opening. Had there been humans they would have been trapped in the defile. This doubtless puzzled the Kurii, for it was uncharacteristic of cunning prey animals to allow themselves to be trapped in such a manner. It did not even occur to them that it might be they who stood in some jeopardy.

Cabot lifted his hand to them in Gorean greeting. "Tal," he said.

At that point the first large stone, hurled from above, struck one of the Kurii on the shoulder, and he spun about, howling, holding his arm, which now seemed to dangle uselessly from his shoulder. Kurii looked up, wildly, astonished, and met a rain of stones, large and small. Two were struck about the head, and one fell to the ground. They tried to fend away the stones and more than one limb was shattered. Then several boulders, rolled to the edge of the height by more than one man, were tumbled down the steep sides of the defile, and bounded into the defile. Two Kurii were struck by these objects, one squarely in the chest, and he staggered back and lost his footing, and fell against the wall, and then, scratching at the wall, and turning, he regained his feet, and, in fury, raised his arms and sought to roar, but the sound was odd, half choked, air and blood rushing from the fanged jaws. Then he seemed dazed, and disoriented, and staggered again, and then fell, and then spat blood into the dirt. And about the top of the defile were now better than two dozen humans again hurling stones downward, stones easily the size of a man's head. The Kurii were disconcerted, and surely taken unawares. Then, in the confusion, several humans, screaming, and carrying their pointed sticks, slid into the defile, and others rushed forward, through the opening. The Kurii had not encountered humans in this manner before, for humans had always fled from them. But the humans were not now fleeing, but attacking, and relentlessly, and viciously, and, moreover, the Kurii were considerably outnumbered. When one tried to defend itself from a sharpened stick three or four other humans, like sleen hanging on the flanks of a larl, drove their points deep into hairy bodies. In moments, four Kurii were dead, and there was not one other that was not bloodied, and the six remaining Kurii, snarling, and tearing and biting, and sweeping about them with their spears, broke through the opening, and the massed humans, to the forest beyond. Cabot signaled that the humans should follow them and continue to attack them. They must not be allowed an opportunity to regroup, or even, clearly, to grasp what had occurred.

It is not unusual that the hunted may become the hunter. The larl, for example, will commonly circle, or double back, and stalk its hunters.

But this was the first time that this had occurred with humans.

That night humans fed on Kur. Cabot did not join them, for he was reluctant to feed on rational animals.

He did return two slaves, Tula and Lana, to Archon, and take his leave of the humans.

He took with him the blonde, leashed and bound, and gagged, but now relieved of her bells.

Chapter, the Eighteenth:

The Ledge

One supposes that it was foolish of Cabot to return the blonde to the vicinity of the shuttle port, that she not be left to the beasts and humans of the forest, but such activities are not unprecedented amongst humans. Presumably, too, it ill behooves a member of one species to comment on peculiarities in the behavior of another. She was, of course, in Cabot's view, a free woman. Perhaps that made a difference. On the other hand it seems likely that he would have behaved similarly had she been no more than a slave. Humans are strange. They like to own, and master, their women, and fully, and even to the whip, but, too, they will commonly go to great lengths to care for them, to nurture them, and defend them. Many are willing to die for them. What men want of women is a slave; what women want of men is a master.

At the shuttle port the blonde had put down her head and rubbed it against the chest of Cabot, half in fear, half in gratitude. It was a gesture not unlike one which a Kur pet might accord her master.

Cabot then put her from him, and turned to enter the forest, but turned suddenly, angrily, back, half snarling in frustration, went to her, and, in a stride or two, seized her by the arms, and lifted her before him. He held her so for some moments, regarding her closely. She was, as I understand it, a comely female of his species. Certainly the Priest-Kings must have selected her with care, having placed her for their purposes in his container on the Prison Moon. And one suspects that there was little that Cabot could not discern of her attractions, as she was in a slave tunic. There was doubtless a call of blood to blood. Had she been a slave, or, perhaps, even fully human, Cabot might have taken her in hand,

211

and provided himself with the joy of her. She was, of course, a free woman. Perhaps that made a difference. He did not, in short, in the end, put her to his pleasure, either abruptly or violently, or with patience and leisure, as is sometimes done with a slave, as she writhes and gasps, and begs piteously in her ropes or chains that he not desist in his attentions. To be sure, she would be at his mercy, and he would do as he pleases, for she is only a slave. But he did draw her to him, as he was human, and, holding her head so she could not move or escape, he placed his lips upon hers. And then more forcibly. He drew back a little, and she looked up at him, with something like wonder. This act, which seems to be a cultural act, was not fully understood by her.

It is an act not uncommon amongst humans, or, indeed, certain other species, but it is not universal even amongst humans. Universal, of course, are sexual advances, provocations, and such, of one sort or another, uncustomary nearnesses, touchings, caressings, rubbings, postures, dances, and so on. Amongst Kurii nibblings and bitings are common, not to injure, but rather to signal that harm, which might be done, is not done. The male, for example, may close his teeth on the female, possessively, but not tear her, and the female, in response, if acquiescent, may similarly bite at the male, as though defensively, but not to the point of blood. If she is not acquiescent she can inflict serious injury. Kur courtship, so to speak, is analogous to circling, and leaping, and feigned biting, which sometimes becomes dangerous. Indeed, observers unaware of these things sometimes think two Kurii are fighting, and not courting. The Kur male, like the human male, tends to be larger and stronger than the female of the species, which may well account for the survival of the species, as the female must be impregnated with or without her consent if the species is to survive. The Kur female is large and dangerous, but the Kur male is even larger and more dangerous, and, in the final accounting, he may hold her in place, and do with her as he wishes. To be sure, much depends on the nature of the species.

The general pervasiveness of the conjunction of the lips amongst humans suggests that something more than simple cultural idiosyncrasy may be involved, presumably on a level not immediately accessible to consciousness, a level in which the act is understood as symbolic, and analogous to, and suggestive of, and preliminary to, more intimate conjunctions. This is perhaps why certain human cultures object to the meeting of the lips in the fashion in question. For example, Gorean free women are commonly veiled in public, at least in part, presumably, that their provocative lips not be publicly exposed. Indeed, one of the things most dreaded by a Gorean free woman, particularly of high caste, is that they will be face-stripped and their lips exposed to public view, as though they might be those of a slave. That slaves are not permitted veiling, and that their lips must be exposed to all, even in public, is regarded as one of the shames imposed on a slave.

One of the reasons many Goreans consider women of the world Earth as fit for slaves is because many bare their lips publicly. This initial lack of concern with facial nudity commonly arouses contempt in not only Gorean free women for Earth-origin female slaves, but the contempt of Gorean female slaves, as well. Indeed, often the Earth-origin female slave, as she grows more familiar with Gor, becomes acutely conscious of the baring of her face, that she is denied veiling, that males may look upon her as they wish, and so on. It is the same, is it not, with kaiila, pet sleen, and such? Animals are not veiled. Later, however, as she learns her collar, and realizes its proclamation of her desirability, attractiveness, and beauty, and learns the joy of bondage, and her role in, and importance in, Gorean society, she is likely to walk proudly, head high, shoulders back, and brazenly display her master's property. No longer does it concern her that free women will hate her and that other Gorean female slaves will now regard her as a serious rival. She has now learned that such as she is likely to sell as well from the auction block as they. To be sure, she will be wise to humble herself before free women, and kneel, and cringe and grovel, as any other Gorean female slave. It is not pleasant to be switched.

But to return to the meeting of lips, or the pressing or touching of lips, by one or both parties, and such, which the translator, upon inquiry, suggests may be spoken of as a kiss, we note that the slave may be kissed and must kiss whenever the master pleases, and however he pleases, for she is owned. Similarly, the master commands not only the lips of the slave, but her tongue, teeth, hair, hands, and body. All of her, you see, belongs to him. She exists for his service and pleasure. She usually cooks, cleans and launders for him, and, in general, cares for his clothing, his belongings, including herself, and his quarters. She welcomes him to his domicile, kneeling. She is no stranger to petitionings, placations, prostrations, and obeisances. She is familiar with helplessness and subordination, for she is a slave. She is not unfamiliar with chains and ropes, or hoods, blindfolds and gags. Such things liberate her sexually and remind her, and clearly, that she is not a free woman. She is likely to be trained in duties both domestic and erotic. Once the slave fires have been lit in her belly, her freedom is behind her. Henceforth, she belongs to men. Thus one should not be surprised to find her on her knees before a man, her head down, kissing his feet, in piteous supplication for his touch.

She is slave.

And so Cabot had pressed his lips, and forcibly, upon those of the grasped, startled pet of Arcesilaus.

Doubtless she found the experience to which she had been subjected puzzling, but, too, it seems, not distasteful.

Doubtless, too, it produced an unfamiliar unease within her lovely body, presumably associated with suddenly effectuated receptivities. The act may have spoken to her below the daylight of consciousness, like a whispering in the secret night of her belly, but, too, perhaps there was involved no more than a calling of blood to blood, so to speak.

It may help to understand this if we make it clear that Arcesilaus, despite several invitations, some coined, had never put her out to use, even after the reddening of her soft thighs. She had never been locked in the breeding shackles. She had, of course, given her age and health, been often stirred and troubled by scarcely understood sexual curiosities and promptings. But she could make little of these disturbing hormonal afflictions. Many she had not even understood as sexual in nature. Her master had not had her spayed. She did find herself upon occasion uneasy in the presence of human males, but there were few it seemed in the Steel World, other than in the cattle pens, who were bred largely amongst themselves, for meat and stupidity, and of those elsewhere encountered, many were pets, and of little interest, being indolent, and passive, and neutered.

Cabot angrily thrust the blonde from him, and turned to face the forest.

She whimpered.

He could hear, more clearly now, the sounds of sleen. He had been aware for Ahn of their entrance, two beasts, with a hunting party of eight, as he counted, through the shuttle port. But he had set a trail which was lengthy and circuitous to gain time, and permit him to return, after circling about, to bring the blonde to the entrance of the shuttle port. Before engaging in this endeavor he had, within the forest, placed his prisoner, still leashed and gagged, on her belly in the leaves before a lofty Tur tree, and knelt across her body. He had then freed her hands and turned her about, and retied them before her body. He had then, turning her again to her belly, with one strand of the double-braided leash, fastened her hands, already bound, closely against her belly, and knotted the holding strap behind the small of her back. With the second strand of the leash he improvised a sling and, with one loop under her arms and the other behind the back of her knees, and she behind him, he began to climb the tree. On a high branch, some seventy or eighty feet above the ground, he sat her back against the trunk of the tree, and, with the second strand of the leash, fastened her in place, by the feet, belly, and neck. The height, he hoped, and her silence, would protect her from predators, of various sorts. The branches would be likely to break beneath a larl and the sleen, a ground animal, is reluctant to climb. She might hope that hunting humans might not look upward. She regarded Cabot piteously, and squirmed a little, helplessly. She could not free herself, as she had been tied by a Gorean warrior. Such are taught the binding of prisoners. Indeed, even Gorean boys are taught the binding of women, given slaves on which to practice, of course. She whimpered, a tiny sound, muffled within the fur and straps of her gag. She looked at Cabot. In his eyes there was no mercy. She would remain as she was. She whimpered and squirmed, futilely. She looked well, bound. The brief tunic, too, left few of her charms to conjecture. Had she realized her status as a free woman, and the nature of men, she might have striven to hold her body exquisitely still. Slaves on the other hand are often inventive, and even cunning, in the use of movement and bonds, and will often strive by such means to incite the master. What slave does not know that even the slightest sound of her chain, seemingly inadvert, may stir a master to distraction.

How innocent they are! And sometimes it is a narrow margin which separates them from a ravishing and a lashing, from an affectionate, indulgent caress and the impatient, punitive sting of a switch. Cabot then descended the tree and set about creating a trail that would take even sleen some Ahn to negotiate. He would return later for the Kur pet. In the meantime she would wait for the business of men and Kurii to be worked out, appropriately helpless to interfere with or affect the outcome. This treatment of the female, incidentally, even should she be free, is not unusual for Goreans. She will await the issue of events, wait to discover whether she will be freed, to be returned in honor to, say, her city, or learn to whom she will now belong. The female from the Gorean point of view is often viewed as goods, and a prize, to be allotted, or disposed of, as men please.

Cabot left the blond at the shuttle port, to which he had returned her, listened for a bit, and then sped into the forest.

He remembered the taste of her lips.

It seemed a shame to waste her as a Kur pet. Might she not be better in a cage, preferably a tiny one, instructive for her, awaiting her sale?

He had no hope of eluding sleen indefinitely, and he did not wish to bring humans of the forest into additional jeopardy.

He had as weapon only the long, sharpened stick, some seven feet in length, a common length for a Gorean spear, which had been given to him by Archon, and retrieved at the edge of the forest, near the shuttle port.

Sleen, when wild, or released, commonly trail silently. When leashed, however, and used as controlled hunting animals, they often drag against their leashes, and harnesses, attempt to hurry the hunters, growl in frustration, and sometimes utter an angry squealing sound, as though protesting the supposed dalliance of the leash masters, the seemingly unnecessary length of the hunt, which they, released, might have terminated long ago, and perhaps even the possible further flight and possible unexpected elusiveness of a prey whose trail they have already located and are readily pursuing.

Cabot understood that he would be unable to distance either sleen or Kurii, for the sleen is a swift, tireless tracker and the Kur, particularly when descending to all fours, its accouterments fastened to its body, can easily outrun a man, either in a short race, for speed, or in one ranging over pasangs, for both speed and endurance. One notes in this, in passing, the superiority of the sleen and Kur life forms to the human. But then these superiorities are obvious to all neutral observers. And one need not, one supposes, remark further on the greater strength of the Kur, nor the massiveness of its jaws, the penetrability of its fangs, the capacity of its claws, particularly on the hind feet, to disembowel prey, and so on.

Accordingly, Cabot was not disposed to flee until, desperate and exhausted, perhaps after some Ahn, his muscles aching, his body shuddering, his lungs gasping for air, he would lie vulnerable and helpless in the path of his pursuers.

He would prefer to deal with them, or be dealt with by them, while he was in a state of strength and acuity.

Had his pursuers been unwary and unsuspecting men, or such beasts of another sort, he might have circled about and attempted, undetected, from the rear, to eliminate them one by one, certainly were they in single file and suitably separated. This is a common strategy with an unwary and unsuspecting line, but it is unlikely of success with, say, Warriors, or Assassins, as they are alert to, and familiar with, such procedures, often resorting to them themselves. And Cabot supposed, correctly or not, that the colleagues of Lord Pyrrhus would be well aware that their quarry was of the Warriors, and, accordingly, would not, thus, even though it was human, underestimate it. Too, Cabot supposed, correctly I believe, that the sense of both hearing and smell on the part of Kurii would militate against his making more than a first kill. Too, he had no metal blade with which to cut a throat, nor an ax, with which to sever a spinal cord, nor a true spear whose blade might cleave easily, even through inches of hide, hair, and flesh to a heart. In short, he supposed he might, at best, rid himself of one enemy before seven others, and excited sleen, turned about and raced toward him. He elected, thus, to climb a small escarpment, some thirty feet from the ground, which would slow sleen in their ascent, and, with good fortune, allow him to defend himself for a time with the sharpened stick or pole, were the sleen loosed. He was supposing it would be immaterial to the hunters whether he was brought down by sleen, which might have been wild sleen of the forest, one might speculate, or slain, supposedly by accident, with a cast of the mighty Kur spear.

He waited on a ledge, between rocks, on the small escarpment, and considered it was an odd place to die, but an interesting one. He could see forest over his head in the cylinder, as well as about him. Sunlight, gathered and focused, was brought into the cylinder, as into at least the main habitat, by mirrors, from Tor-tu-Gor, or Sol, as these are the same star. He was interested, too, to note, as he waited, that a film of water, a dense humidity, emerged from various concealed conduits, about him, and doubtless above him, as well, high overhead in the ceiling forest. These emanations of moisture were doubtless controlled by automatic devices, and the moisture, in turn, would evaporate to be recycled, indefinitely, rather as in a natural planetary environment. He watched with some fascination as beads of water formed on the leaves of rock-climbing Turpah, a parasitic but edible growth commonly adhering to the bark of the Tur tree. His skins, from the humans of Archon, dampened, and clung to him. The bath of moisture much accentuated the freshness and fragrance of the forest. Then, after some ten Ehn, the discharge of moisture ceased, as suddenly as it had begun. In the greenery below, as the heat became more sensible, the softened, refreshed air began to tremble and steam.

It was a quarter of an Ahn afterward when Cabot again heard sleen.

He could tell they were excited, their eagerness and agitation much increased, with the freshness of the trail.

In a moment, breaking through the greenery, he saw the lead sleen, its viperlike head to the ground.

Cabot stood up, and struck the butt of the stick on the rocks at his feet. "Up here!" he called. "Here, up here, gray friend!"

The sleen lifted its head.

Behind it was a Kur, holding its leash, who pointed eagerly toward Cabot and alerted his fellows with a bellowing roar, as of jubilation, as of triumph.

The sleen threw itself against the harness and the Kur struggled to hold it in place. In a moment the second sleen appeared. Both were more intent on the trail and its freshness than the fact that the prey was actually in view. The trail, like a trickle of scent, still obsessed them. Cabot then saw the other Kurii emerge from the trees. Two Kurii had been rather in front of the group, each with a sleen. The other six had traveled in pairs, each pair in tandem fashion behind the preceding pair. Thus Cabot realized he would indeed have been able to make only one kill, if that, as the other member of the pair would have been instantly alerted as to the attack on its fellow. Yes, thought Cabot, they were trailing a warrior. He was gratified that they had chosen in this way to show respect for his caste.

The eight Kurii were now emerged from the forest and were rather at the bottom of the small escarpment.

Six were quite large, the other two were considerably smaller, surely no more than three to five hundred pounds.

Translators were flicked on.

"Greetings," came from a translator.

"Greetings," responded Cabot.

"We thought to follow you further," said one of the Kurii.

"I trust you are not disappointed," said Cabot.

"You understand why we have come?" asked one of the Kurii.

"I think so," said Cabot.

"You led us a strange trail," said another.

"You could not escape through the shuttle port," said another. "There are codes."

"So I understand," said Cabot.

"On our return to the shuttle port, following your eccentric trail, we discovered a bait beast," said one of the Kurii.

"A female bait beast," said another.

"Interesting," said Cabot.

Where men are concerned, females make the best bait beasts. The application of the "lure girl" is familiar in many locales. One of the few times a female slave is permitted to don the garments of a free woman without being slain is when she is used in such a role. Sometimes they are put on the bridges late at night, in the light of the moons, and when a marauding tarnsman makes his strike, the city's tarnsmen may take flight and close in upon him. A common stratagem is for a group of seeming maidens to be noted sporting outside a city's walls, perhaps tossing a ball about, or such, and laughing, and chatting, with one another. When foreign tarnsmen, intent on plying chain luck, descend to acquire this seemingly vulnerable trove of loveliness, they are surprised, for numerous guardsmen emerge suddenly from concealed pits and encircle them. Free women, incidentally, are almost never used in such a role. If one were she might be likely to be soon stripped and found in her own collar, that is, in her master's collar.

"We did not eat her," said another, "as she was garmented."

"Not yet," said another.

"How do you know she was a bait beast?" asked Cabot.

"What else could she be, here?" asked another.

"True," said Cabot.

"But where is her hunting party?" asked one.

"Why did you not ask her?" said Cabot.

"You know little of us, human," said one. "Such creatures are pets, at best. They are not speeched."

"I see," said Cabot. How quick, thought Cabot, was the mind of the blonde. She would have understood Cabot was hunted. Had she not, as well as he, heard sleen? Taken as an unspeeched pet, at best, she could not be intelligibly interrogated as to his whereabouts. Too, as unspeeched, they would not fear she might inform upon them. As little might be feared on the world, Earth, from a stray dog.

The greatest danger to her, thought Cabot, would presumably be from the surviving members of the decimated hunting party, or from others who knew of it, for she, the bait girl, had not been used by Kurii to entrap humans, but by humans to entrap Kurii. Cabot had done his best, having her bound and helpless beside him in the pitlike depression, to make it clear she had not willingly betrayed her masters. To be sure, she had been used against them, willingly or not, and Kurii do not tend to be a benevolently disposed, understanding or forgiving species. If she had been used in such a fashion once, might she not be used in such a fashion again? Too, perhaps she had collaborated with humans, with intent. As she was speeched, or partly speeched, this might seem all the more possible. And certainly Arcesilaus knew she was at least to some extent speeched, as he had arranged for this, her tutoring being supplied largely by Grendel.

"We are thinking of removing her garment and eating her on the way back," said one of the Kurii.

This remark startled Cabot, for he was unused to thinking as Kurii, to whom humans are little different from verr or tabuk.

"Perhaps she has escaped," said Cabot.

"No," said another. "We braceleted her hands behind her back, about a tree, and hung the key about her neck."

"In that way the meat will stay fresh," said another.

"She is perhaps a pet," said Cabot, "and her master would not wish her eaten."

"He would not know."

"Her master," said Cabot, "is Lord Arcesilaus."

The Kurii looked about, one to the other.

"How would you know that?" asked one.

"She was not in his collar," said another.

"She was not even in a collar," said another.

"She may be a stray, who was used as a bait beast," said another.

"She may have stolen a tunic, in order to avoid being eaten," said another.

"Sometimes they will kill one another for a tunic," said another.

"I have seen her on his leash," said Cabot.

"We will be hungry, after the hunt," said another Kur.

"I am here," said Cabot. "What difference does it make, which human you feed upon?"

"The sleen will have you," said another.

"They have come this far," said another. "They have been successful in their hunt. They will want food."

The sleen, indeed, were now scratching at the earth, and had their heads raised, regarding him.

A sleen is a dangerous animal, and a hungry sleen is additionally dangerous, and one who expects to be rewarded for a successful hunt, and is not so rewarded, is extremely dangerous. Such a beast may turn upon its leash-holder. When sleen are used in hunting slaves, if the slave is to be recaptured, and not slain, the hunters usually carry meat with them, to reward the beast once the prey is in custody.

"Lord Arcesilaus will not be pleased if you eat the girl," said

Cabot. To be sure, Cabot was not certain of this, and Arcesilaus might have been, for all Cabot knew, contemplating the same act.

"He will never know," said one of the Kurii.

"Shall we release the sleen now?" inquired one of the Kurii, of Cabot, one somewhat in advance of the others, one Cabot took to be the leader of the group.

"That decision," said Cabot, "would seem to be yours, rather than mine."

"We expected you to run, until you could run no further," said one of the Kurii.

"Humans do not always run," said Cabot.

"It seems you are too stupid to do so," said one of the Kurii.

"Would you run?" asked Cabot.

"No," said the Kur, "but I am Kur."

"Perhaps he is Kur," said another of the group of hunters. Being Kur, you see, is not always a simple, descriptive term denoting a particular species. The question, "Are you Kur?" can be asked even of a Kur. There is a meaning here which transcends biological classification.

"No," said Cabot. "I am human."

One of the Kurii below him snarled viciously. The translator, however, provided the translation without passion. "You are meat," it said.

"Do you think the pointed stick in your grasp is a weapon?" inquired one of the Kurii.

"Lend me your spear, if you wish me better armed," said Cabot.

"You could not cast it," said a Kur.

"Then I must make do with my pointed stick," said Cabot.

"He is brave," came from one of the translators.

"You must understand," said one of the Kurii, he who seemed most prominent amongst them, "this does not have to do with you."

"In this there is nothing personal," said another.

"I understand," said Cabot. "You hunt on behalf of Lord Pyrrhus, who is foe to Agamemnon."

"Release the sleen," said he who seemed to be their leader.

The sleen doubtless recognized this command in Kur, and not in Gorean, for which the translators were set. In any event, they reacted instantly, even before Cabot heard the translator. They began to tremble and scratch at the ground, and they then lurched forward, and were held back, and then, again, they strained forward, eagerly, against the harness, which made it more difficult to release the catches. They both looked upward at Cabot, their eyes alight with anticipation. The two catches, and then the safety catches, were freed, with four snaps, and the two sleen sprang forward and began to scratch their way frenziedly up the short, steep slope.

One sleen fell backwards, twisted wildly in midair, snarling, and fell to the ground at the foot of the small escarpment, and turned to climb again. The other sleen was at Cabot's feet, snapping, when Cabot thrust the homely spear through its spread jaws, the point tearing through the left cheek of the beast. It slipped back, but seemed impervious to pain. The first beast leaped upward, gained a purchase on the slope, and joined Cabot on his narrow ledge, until it was thrust back, over the edge, bloodied, with the stick, to slide to the foot of the slope again. The second sleen was thrust back again, its chest blooded. When the first sleen again attacked, Cabot struck it back with the butt of the primitive weapon. Both sleen were then at the foot of the small escarpment, turning about, tails lashing, each again then looking upward.

The ledge is defensible, thought Cabot, wildly.

There was suddenly a flash of darkness to Cabot's left, and a sharp, sliding, grating sound, as one of the great spears struck against a projecting outcropping, and was then arrested, snapped in two, by the wall behind him. Cabot lunged to the side, to his right, as another spear struck into the stone behind him, marking it as though struck with a hammer. One of the Kurii was now ascending the slope. Cabot thrust at him with the pointed stick but the Kur grasped it and drew on it, and Cabot released it, lest he be dragged from the ledge. At the same time he was conscious of something like an enveloping cloud of rope which descended about him, and he tried to throw it off, to fight it, but it was cunningly whipped about him, with no more than three or four motions, and he was thrown from his feet, enmeshed in its toils. Cabot tried to roll free but one hairy foot held the net closed, and Cabot, his fingers in the strands, each better than an inch thick, was helpless. Cabot realized the net had been well cast and well handled. Begrudgingly he admired the skill with which it had been employed. This hunter, he supposed, had netted humans before. Surely it had been done skillfully and Cabot knew himself helpless. Cabot himself was not unskilled with nets, and certain arena fighters, called fishermen, used net and trident on the sand. Cabot himself had used nets upon occasion to capture slaves, and women to be made slaves. When a city falls, it is common for the slaves of the city to submit themselves to the conquerors, kneeling, head down, arms extended, wrists crossed, for binding. Some, of course, and sometimes free women who have disguised themselves as slaves, that they not be peremptorily slain, flee. Sometimes, too, house slaves, tower slaves, palace slaves, and such, unaccustomed to more demanding slaveries, will flee, hoping to avoid sharing the chains of more common slaves. In any event, Cabot was not a stranger to the netting of women. Some he would keep, who pleased him. Others he would distribute as he pleased, amongst his men, and of others he would profit from their sales.

And now Cabot himself was netted, though not in the light toils of a weighted slave net, which he might have torn open and shredded, a net unsuitable for a man but inescapable for a female, but in a mighty net, stoutly woven, thickly stranded, cast by a Kur, a net that might have held a larl.

Another Kur ascended to the ledge on which Cabot lay, enmeshed, trapped, in the toils of the net.

This second Kur carried a spear, which he handed to the net holder, who then, grasping it some four feet behind the blade, lifted it, his hands high over his head, and pointed it downward, toward the heart of Cabot, who lay in the toils of the net, on his back, looking upward.

Chapter, the Nineteenth:

The Intervention of the Steel Larl

There was suddenly above Cabot a rushing sound and a torrent of fire and Cabot turned his head away, half blinded, and was barely aware of the gigantic, headless trunk above him, the parts of arms, striking about him, and the charred particles of parts of a blackened spear, the metal head of which, half melted, struck softly onto the ledge. The trunk did not bleed as the flame had seared shut the avenues of blood within that large body, and the head, or the parts of it which remained, slid slowly downward, descending from the rock wall behind him.

At the same time he heard the hiss of power weapons below the escarpment. But such weapons were not permitted in the sport world!

There were howls of surprise and fury, some abrogated instantly, as if a machine might have been switched off. He heard Kur sounds, most discordant, some articulate, others half uttered, or blurred. The translators, several of which must have been still on, transmitted sounds in Gorean but the emanations were so disordered as to be largely unintelligible.

Cabot, struggling in the net, rolled to his side, about the large, headless trunk encumbering the ledge, to peer through the strands, down into the clearing at the foot of the small escarpment.

There was another blast of fire below him, which was reflected upward, as though a small sun had exploded, casting an ignited chemical shower against the escarpment, and he saw the residue of one of the sleen smoking below him. In the clearing below there were, too, five steaming bodies, the flesh burned away to darkened bones, and three of the hunters had flung down their weapons, in token of surrender. They were then cut down with streams of fire

225

where they stood. The eight who had hunted Cabot had all been destroyed. About the clearing, armed with weapons outlawed within the sport world, were at least fifty Kurii. Two Kurii, other than the hunters, had been penetrated by spears, with which the hunters had been armed. A heat knife lay on the ground, still blistering and flaming, which one of the Kurii snapped off. The other sleen had its back to the escarpment, snarling, and then it sprang at one of the Kurii, clinging with its jaws to its arm. The arm was torn off, and the sleen shook it angrily. Power weapons were aimed at the beast.

A Kur roar, abrupt, definitive, emanated from the forest, and the power weapons were lowered. On several of the translators of the hunters, almost simultaneously, Cabot heard, "No!"

Through the trees into the clearing emerged a machine, slowly, menacingly, in the form of a gigantic larl.

The larl is known on Gor. It is not known if it was native to Gor or, as many other forms of life, including humans, it was brought to that world by the mysterious Priest-Kings, whoever or whatever they might be. The ecological niche on the planet Earth, which is usually filled with large predators of a feline nature, such as the lion, the tiger, and such, is filled, or mostly, on Gor by the larl, and a diversity of smaller predators, primarily pantherine in form. The adult Gorean larl is usually in the range of seven feet at the shoulder and over a thousand pounds in weight. It is lithe, sinuous, agile, aggressive, ferocious, carnivorous, and, unlike the sleen, quadrupedalian. It has a broad skull, rather triangular in shape, and is fanged, and clawed. But the machine which now emerged, stalking, from the forest, must have been ten to twelve feet at the shoulder. Its weight would be difficult to ascertain without a better sense of its construction, but it was doubtless considerably heavier than a natural larl.

The living Kurii in the clearing, their weapons lowered, stepped aside, to allow the advance of the device.

The sleen, the Kur arm dangling from its jaws, lifted its head and regarded the strange new arrival.

It did not regard it as a living thing, of course, for the signals of sound, and odor, were incorrect. But it did regard it as a foreign object, inexplicable perhaps, but surely not welcome.

The machine, almost catlike, picked its way delicately amongst the bodies of Kurii, both of the hunters and the others.

The sleen crouched down, and began to gnaw at the arm, this appendage held in place by its forefeet.

The Kur who had been attacked by the sleen lay to one side, bleeding. Kurii seldom tender aid to one another in such a situation. This is a cultural matter. The common thought is that if he is Kur he will need no assistance. Rendering assistance is sometimes, as well, thought demeaning to the injured or wounded. It is, so to speak, calling attention to his need, or weakness, which can be regarded as shaming or insulting him. Pity is regarded as belittling both he who is pitied and he who pities. It is not strength. Too, there is commonly another to take the place of such a one.

"Larl," Cabot heard. He thought this sound came from the interior of the machine.

Immediately the living Kurii raised their power weapons, looking about, alertly.

"No," Cabot heard, again.

Yes, the sound emanated from within the machine.

Cabot knew that larls could be found in the sport world, as well as sleen. These beasts were hunted by Kurii with primitive weapons, as well as men. Indeed, he had reason to believe that humans not only defended themselves from such beasts, as they could, but occasionally hunted them, as well. Too, occasionally they must have slain a Kur. Archon had worn remnants of a Kur harness.

A larl, thought Cabot, might have been brought to the clearing by the smell of blood.

He then saw it, as must have the Kurii, as well, tawny and sinuous, amongst the trees, half crouching.

It was waiting, thought Cabot. Why is it waiting?

"Sleen," Cabot heard.

At first he understood this to be a reference to the beast feeding below, but this conjecture was instantly belied by the feeding beast, for it raised its head suddenly and snarled, menacingly, possessively.

On its six legs, belly to the ground, tail lashing, a wild sleen approached the hunting sleen.

It is not only the larl which can smell blood, thought Cabot.

The hunting sleen was a much larger animal, and had been bred through generations not only for its hunting skills, but for size, ferocity, and aggressiveness. Such animals are sometimes used in sleen fights, on which bets are made. There is amongst some species, including Kurii, a common belief that the wild animal is somehow superior to the domestic animal, but this is usually false. The domestic animal has been bred from the wild animal to be its superior. Wild animals are on the whole smaller, lack stamina, are malnourished, infested with parasites, and short-lived. The domestic animal is usually larger, better fed, longer-lived, healthier, and trainable, with respect to virtues ranging from stamina to patience, to restraint, to techniques of stalking, attacking, and killing. For example, the wolf hound of Earth was originally bred to kill wolves.

The hunting sleen growled at the wild sleen.

This growl was returned by the wild sleen, whose ribs could be seen within its snarled, matted fur.

It is starving, thought Cabot.

It will not be warned away.

The hunting sleen then rushed upon its wild fellow, and, in moments, after a brief, squealing, exploding, rolling, tangled bunching of fur, the wild sleen lay, eyes glazed, limp in the dirt, its throat still throbbing, discharging blood into the dirt.

It was at this point that the larl advanced.

It was waiting, I see it now, thought Cabot, for there to be but a single foe, and one perhaps exhausted, or weakened, from an earlier contest.

The meat will now be all his.

The larl did not understand of course the menace of the power weapons, and their scope, so unlike single arrows, weapons which might have transformed him in a moment into a little more than a mound of burned meat, like a small mountain, smoking and bubbling, beneath a descending, gentle scattering of drifting, burning hair.

But the machine stood between the winnings of the sleen and he who would lay claim upon them.

The sleen was now burrowing his muzzle into the body of the wild sleen, chewing out the organ meat, delicacies most prized amongst carnivores.

The larl, no more than the sleen, reacted to the machine as a living thing, no more than it might have to a rock or tree.

But the mouth of the machine, and its fangs, raked the flank of the larl as it tried to brush past.

The larl snarled with rage, and turned, and licked at its bloodied flank, and then tried to pass, again.

Again, it was torn.

The larl tried to strike the object from its path with its paw, and there was a raking, scraping sound, but it might as well have struck against a wall of iron, and there was, as a consequence of the blow, which might have struck a man yards from its path, almost no movement in the machine.

The larl, irritated, puzzled, put its muzzle closer to the machine, trying to fathom its nature, and the mouth of the machine, very gently, opened, and took the throat of the larl in its metal jaws. The larl did not understand this, for it sensed nothing alive, but then its eyes widened, and it tried to pull its neck free, but the jaws very gently, continued to close, as might have an electronic vice. Then the larl pulled and snarled, and then blood spurted from its nostrils, and then, as it twisted, ever more weakly, its head was bitten away.

Cabot noted that the Kur who had been attacked by the sleen now lay quietly to the side. The body would be left for the beasts of the forest. This, in such situations, is regarded as cultural. In this way, in Kur belief, one is reconciled with, and returned to, that nature which has spawned one. The gift of life is a loan, as the Kur commonly sees it, a loan for which one is grateful, a loan which, when due, is to be willingly repaid with the coin of death.

The machine seemed to lift its head, and turn it in one direction, and then its head, on the mechanical neck, rotated to another direction, opposite.

"There were only eight, and two sleen," said one of the Kurii.

"One sleen remains," said another.

Then the machine lifted its head, further, and Cabot knew himself discerned.

"You know me?" inquired the machine.

"I think so," said Cabot.

"Are you well?" inquired the machine.

"Yes," said Cabot.

Something was said to one of the Kurii, and it clambered upward, reached Cabot, and then lifted the net, with its prisoner, Cabot, and carried it down the slope to the level. It placed the net and Cabot at the paws of the machine, which towered above him.

"Close your eyes," said the machine, and Cabot obeyed. Even through his closed lids Cabot could sense the blast of light and heat, moving about him. Then it was shut off and Cabot opened his eyes, and stood up, unsteadily, free, the severed, burned shreds of the net about his feet.

Cabot looked up. The head of the machine, as it sat, like a larl, was several feet above his head.

"It was doubtless with this that the sleen were set upon him," said a Kur, lifting Cabot's tunic, taken from a pouch attached to the harness of one of the fallen hunters.

"Let us see," said the machine.

The Kur who held the wadded tunic threw it before the feeding sleen, who looked upon it, and then crawled toward it, and then, suddenly, as though recovering from some distraction, perhaps its experiences at the ledge, its attack on the Kur, its fight with its wild fellow, the satisfying of its hunger, looked at Cabot, and snarled. Cabot crouched down. He did not have even his pointed stick with which to defend himself. The tail of the sleen began to lash. It gathered its four hind feet beneath it. It growled.

"It is going to attack," came from one of the translators.

"I will attack," came dispassionately from the machine.

There was a flash of metal plating and joints as the device leapt past Cabot, pouncing on the startled, suddenly rearing sleen, its weight striking against it, then half crushing it, and then the machine, rising up slowly, pinned the sleen in place with its left forefoot and the right forefoot of the device began to descend, slowly, a timing reminiscent of the closure of its jaws on the throat of the larl, the sleen squirming beneath it, and Cabot heard a shriek of the animal, the splintering crack of its backbone, like the snapping of a stick, and then the rupture of ribs, one after the other, and then witnessed the flattening of the body, organs and lungs half protruded, as though disgorged, through the jaws.

The machine then, as Cabot backed away, went to the bodies of each of the hunters, and, taking the head of each in the massive metal jaws, bit it away. It went lastly to the largest of the hunters, he who had commanded the others, and he who had assured Cabot as to the lack of animosity resident in his dark mission, and bit off his head, as well.

The machine then, standing over the headless body of the large Kur, regarded Cabot.

"This," it said, stirring the body with its broad, metal-clawed foot, "was Kalonicus, cousin to Pyrrhus."

Cabot nodded.

"Pyrrhus, enemy of the world," said the machine.

"I would know little of that," said Cabot.

The machine then took up the huge body of the Kur in its jaws, held it dangling for a moment, while looking about itself, and then it shook it as though it might have been no more than a handful of rags, shook it viciously, and then flung it away, until it struck against trees, and fell to their feet, better than a hundred paces far.

The machine then turned to the Kurii about, and sat back on its metal haunches, catlike, blood on the steel of its jaws, its head up.

"Hail Agamemnon, Eleventh Face of the Nameless One, Theocrat of the World," came from a translator, and the Kurii knelt, each on a single knee.

Cabot did not kneel.

One of the Kurii noticed this and growled.

Cabot did not kneel.

The Kur raised his power weapon.

"How is Tarl Cabot, my friend?" came from the machine.

The Kur lowered his power weapon. He then, and the others, at a nod from the great machine, rose to their hind feet.

"I am well, Lord Agamemnon," said Cabot.

"How is it," inquired the machine, "that you came to the sport world?"

"May I ask," said Cabot, "how is it that you came hence?"

The machine was silent.

One of the Kurii growled, softly.

"It is to your timely intervention that I doubtless owe my life," said Cabot. "I am grateful. It seems I was mistook as a prey human by noble hunters."

"That would have been tragic," said the machine.

"A lamentable misunderstanding," said Cabot.

"We came to the forest," said the machine, "upon being apprised of your possible danger by Peisistratus, human."

"Then I must be grateful to him, as well."

"Lord Pyrrhus, it seems," said the machine, "erred in taking a human into his confidence."

"I fear I fail to understand," said Cabot.

"Do you think it is wise to trust a human?" asked the machine.

"It is hard to tell," said Cabot. "Much might depend upon the human."

"He was betrayed by Peisistratus," said the machine. "He thought Peisistratus was his human."

"I see," said Cabot.

"But he is my human."

"I see," said Cabot.

"So how came you here, my friend?" asked the machine.

"I was curious," said Cabot. "I wandered off. It was unwise of me."

"I see," said the machine.

"How is Lord Pyrrhus?" asked Cabot.

"He has been deprived of his rank, his goods, and chattels," said the machine. "He is in chains. You need no longer fear him."

"I know little of these matters," said Cabot.

"We will expect you to be present, and testify, at his trial, his trail for high treason."

"He will receive a trial?" said Cabot.

"Certainly," said the machine. "Do you think we are barbarians?"

Cabot looked about, at the sleen, the larl, the blood-soaked ground, the headless bodies. "Certainly not," he said.

"Lord Pyrrhus is not above the law," said the machine.

"No one is above the law," speculated Cabot.

"No," said the machine. "One is above the law."

"And who might that one be?" asked Cabot.

"I am he," said the machine.

"I understand," said Cabot.

Chapter, the Twentieth:

The Trial

Cabot was well bedecked, in purple robes, sashed with gold. About this neck were strings of rubies.

He refused a diadem of gold, as he felt himself no ruler, no king, no baron, no Ubar, no Administrator, or such.

Peisistratus, too in splendid robes, stood near him, on a step below the surface of the platform of the witness. This platform was twelve feet high, and railed, and stout enough to support more than one Kur. The jury was a thousand Kurii, ranged on tiers. Lord Pyrrhus, chained by limbs and neck, and fastened in a cement pit, had spoken in his own defense, but his defense, articulate and bellicose, did little more than confirm his guilt. He did protest his innocence of treason, and his insistence that he had never acted otherwise than in the best interests of the species and the world.

The testimony of Peisistratus, taken through translators, had made it clear that Lord Pyrrhus had intended to take the human, Tarl Cabot, hunting in the sport cylinder, which seemed upon the surface, if tasteless considering some of the game available, at least sufficiently innocent. Other testimony had made it clear that Lord Pyrrhus had returned from the sport cylinder without Tarl Cabot, and that, later, a hunting party of eight Kurii, three of whom were womb brothers, and two of whom were egg brothers, to Lord Pyrrhus had entered the sport world with sleen, and had been arrested in the midst of an attempt upon the life of Tarl Cabot, esteemed ally of Agamemnon.

"You are the human, Tarl Cabot?" inquired the translator of the chief prosecutor.

"I am," said Cabot.

"One supposes it is possible," said the prosecutor, "that a terrible mistake is involved in all this, for the defendant is Kur."

"Certainly," said Cabot.

"Yet it seems clear, and overwhelmingly so, that Lord Pyrrhus had designs upon your life."

"What reason could he possibly have for such designs?" asked Cabot.

"That question is to be ignored," said the judge, who was not visible, but whose presence was made known by a sound system, and whose words were picked up by the platform translator, set in the railing before Cabot. The body of Agamemnon, in this instance, Cabot supposed, was in effect the courtroom itself. He had little doubt that Agamemnon, wherever he might be ensconced, could see as well as hear the proceedings.

"We need not inquire into such matters," said the chief prosecutor, "as facts are at issue, and not motivations."

"Very well," said Cabot.

"One fact is clear, at least," said the prosecutor, "that a tunic, bestowed upon you in accordance with the largesse of Lord Agamemnon, Eleventh Face of the Nameless One, Theocrat of the World, was in the possession of the hunting party by which you were endangered, a tunic used to set sleen upon you."

"Certainly to find me," said Cabot.

"I do not understand," said the prosecutor.

"Perhaps the party was sent by Lord Pyrrhus, or someone, to locate me in the sport world, and thereby effect my rescue."

"We have ample testimony," said the prosecutor, whose movements suggested anger, though the translator spoke without passion, "that in the time of your location your life was in great jeopardy."

"That is true," said Cabot. "I fear the hunters mistook me for a game human."

"How could that be?" inquired the prosecutor.

"I fear I was clad in skins, suggesting a human game animal," said Cabot.

Several of the encircling jurors exchanged glances.

"Lord Pyrrhus took you to the sport cylinder and abandoned you there, to be hunted down and killed by his cohorts," said the prosecutor.

"Is that not speculation?" asked Cabot.

"It is fact," said the prosecutor.

"One supposes the jury must decide on that," said Cabot.

"Are you intent on trying to protect one who would have had you slain?"

"Is that not for the jury to ponder?" inquired Cabot.

"You could not have reached the sport cylinder alone," said the prosecutor. "You could not know the shuttle codes."

"I was to go hunting with Lord Pyrrhus," said Cabot. "I had codes from him, though I do not now recall them. I was to wait for him, but I went ahead. Perhaps he came later to the shuttle port, and deemed that I had declined the hunt, and thus returned to his quarters."

"What are you telling us?" asked the prosecutor.

"I was curious," said Cabot. "I wandered off. It was unwise of me."

"You would hold Lord Pyrrhus innocent in all this?" said the prosecutor.

"Certainly," said Cabot.

Pyrrhus, clothed in chains, in the pit, regarded Cabot, puzzled.

"What are you doing?" whispered Peisistratus to Cabot.

"Kaissa," said Cabot.

Peisistratus seemed content with this answer.

The prosecutor turned about, and, high in the tiers, above the jurors, a small light glowed briefly, twice. It would be noted, presumably, only by those facing it, and perhaps looking for it. Cabot, given his vantage on the platform, did see it.

"The witness may step down," said the prosecutor.

Cabot descended from the platform, and Peisistratus, who had been near to him, waiting on a step, accompanied him.

"The jury will note," sounded the voice of the judge, which seemed to come from everywhere in the room, the platform translator producing this in Gorean almost immediately, "that the guilt of Lord Pyrrhus is overwhelmingly clear, albeit largely circumstantial. The aberration of a witness, or the obscurity of its testimony, must not be permitted to distract your attention from either the charges or the indisputable and incontrovertible evidence on which they are based. The jury may now deliberate."

"Do they not withdraw?" asked Cabot.

"Certainly not," said Peisistratus. "The judge would then not know how each voted."

"The verdict need not be unanimous?" asked Cabot.

"Certainly not," said Peisistratus. "If that were the case a single madman or fool, a simpleton, a partisan or malcontent, might nullify or vitiate an entire trial."

"Is a simple majority required?" asked Cabot.

"No," said Peisistratus, "innocence or guilt must be clear, so a clear, significant majority is required, and in a trial such as this, involving charges of high treason, guilt must be exceedingly clear, this requiring that nine out of every ten jurors draw the knife."

"If more than one out of ten do not unsheathe their blades?"

"Then the defendant is acquitted," said Peisistratus.

Already in the tiers many six-digited paws were clasped about the handles of their knives, but, Cabot noted, many jurors were crouched down, knuckles on the tiers, their knives untouched.

"Hold!" called the voice of the unseen judge.

The jurors looked about themselves, but the location of the judge, as the voice emanated from a diversity of locations, was not clear.

"Pyrrhus," called the voice.

"Lord Pyrrhus," bellowed a voice from the pit, with a fierce shaking of chains.

"Did you or did you not seek the death of the human, Tarl Cabot?"

"I did," said Pyrrhus.

"So his honor destroys him," said Cabot to Peisistratus, at the foot of the witness platform.

"Perhaps not," said Peisistratus.

"You have spoken in all honesty, as Kur," said the judge.

"Certainly," said Pyrrhus.

"Let it be so recorded," said the judge.

"And let this, too, be so recorded, and I speak as Kur," called Pyrrhus, his voice rising from the cement pit, in which, to rings, he was chained, "I am guilty of no treason against the species or the world!"

This caused a considerable stir on the tiers, for it was clear Lord Pyrrhus had spoken as Kur.

"If I am guilty of treason," he continued, "it is not treason against the species and the world, but against one who would betray the honor of the species and the world, a dissembler and deceiver, an opportunist and thief, a liar and seeker of power, a true traitor to worth, nobility, and valor."

"So name such a foe," said the judge.

"He cannot," said Peisistratus to Cabot, "for it is forbidden, sacrilegious, blasphemous, to speak ill of the Nameless One, or of any mask through which he speaks."

"Let the jury draw their daggers or not," challenged Pyrrhus.

"Agamemnon may not have his majority," said Peisistratus, looking about the tiers.

"He confessed to seeking my death," Cabot reminded Peisistratus.

"You are an animal," said Peisistratus. "We can be killed here with more impunity than might a wild sleen in a Gorean forest. We are not even pets. We are not even owned. No restitution, even, would be expected for slaying us."

"Then it matters little?"

"It matters nothing, save for your interest to Agamemnon," said Peisistratus. "Your testimony clouded matters for Agamemnon. He expected to convict on its basis. You betrayed him. The jury was confused."

"That was my intention," said Cabot.

"You are interested in abetting revolution, in spreading division in the Steel World?"

"I suppose my life now," said Cabot, "will be worth little, if Lord Pyrrhus goes free."

"He will not go free," said Peisistratus. "But his party will doubtless remember your testimony."

"Is Pyrrhus not to be now acquitted?" asked Cabot.

"Acquitted, perhaps, but not spared," said Peisistratus.

"See the knives," said Cabot.

Many were unsheathed, and by far the most, and each of those daggers pointed downward, threateningly, toward the pit in which Lord Pyrrhus awaited the verdict.

"I do not think," said Peisistratus, scanning the tiers, "that Lord Agamemnon will have his needful numbers."

"Hold!" came the booming voice of the judge.

"No," whispered Peisistratus, "he would not have his needful numbers."

"Desist!" came from the speakers about the courtroom. "This matter will be decided otherwise."

"It will be the arena," whispered Peisistratus.

Daggers were sheathed, and the Kurii stirred restlessly, eagerly, on the tiers.

"Kur to Kur!" cried Lord Pyrrhus, shackled, but mighty, looking upward, fangs bared.

"Yes," said the judge, the voice seeming to ring about the gigantic chamber. "Kur to Kur!"

The Kurii on the tiers leaped up and down, howling with pleasure. Muchly were they satisfied with this outcome.

The passion for truth, and the seeking of justice, in the Kur heart, is linked more closely with victory than deliberation, with triumph than balloting, with blood than mind. The hereditary coils have cast their countless lots, and nature has made her innumerable decisions amongst them, according to her mysterious wills and ways, denominating her fortunes of extinction and prosperity, of defeat and victory, of death and life. To the Kur it is the highest court, and her judgments are nonrepudiable.

Guards even now were loosening the holding chains of Pyrrhus and preparing to lead him from the cement pit in which he had been held below the jurors, below the witnesses, below the judge.

"Will he be fed?" asked Cabot.

"Probably not," said Peisistratus.

The jurors were filing from the great chamber.

The chief prosecutor looked up toward the ceiling, but the light there did not glow. He then left the chamber.

In a few moments Cabot and Peisistratus were alone.

"It is done, is it not?" asked Cabot.

"Part of it," said Peisistratus.

"Are we to see the denouement of this matter in the arena?" asked Cabot.

"It will be required of us," said Peisistratus.

"What is the fate," asked Cabot of Peisistratus, "of the pet of Arcesilaus?"

"Are you not more interested in the fate of another?" asked Peisistratus.

"The blonde human," said Cabot, "the pet of Arcesilaus. From hunters who pursued me I learned they were contemplating feasting on her, and had left her secured, that her meat be fresh, fastened to a tree near the shuttle port, her arms braceleted behind her, the key to the bracelets on a string about her neck."

"You know Grendel?"

"Of course."

"He sought her in the forest world, and soon found her, near the port, and freed her."

"Freed her?"

"To return her to Arcesilaus, of course."

"He may have risked much," said Cabot, "for those who pursued me had secured her, as meat, I fear, to be feasted upon following the completion of their task."

Amongst Kurii meat, as amongst sleen and larls, may be fiercely contested. One does not lightly take another's food.

"True," said Peisistratus, "he did risk much, and cannot have known that the hunters might not have soon returned, or, even if later returned, would have demanded their meal."

"Interesting that he would so jeopardize himself for a mere human, put his life at risk against Kur custom," said Cabot, "and for one not even an ally, but for one the mere pet of another."

"Doubtless," smiled Peisistratus.

"One can but speculate on the motivation," said Cabot.

"But the pet is well-curved, is she not?" asked Peisistratus.

"Surely," said Cabot. "But he is Kur."

"Part Kur," said Peisistratus.

"I see," said Cabot.

"Once freed, she tried to flee from him, even into the forest, but he easily overtook her."

"Nature has seen to it that such cannot outrun either men or Kurii."

"He was forced to bracelet her in the very bonds from which he had freed her, her wrists now before her, clasp her in his arms, and carry her, by force, to the Steel World."

"Surely she understood she was to be returned to Arcesilaus."

"But not, she would wish, by he," said Peisistratus. "By anyone but he."

"Why not?" asked Cabot.

"She abhors him," said Peisistratus.

"He may have risked his life for her."

"She abhors him," said Peisistratus.

"Would she not be in danger from Arcesilaus," asked Cabot, "for she was used to bait a trap, one in which Kurii were slain?"

"Arcesilaus does not bear her ill will," said Peisistratus, "but, too, it is not now practical for him to keep her. She was used against Kurii. That is not to be forgotten. Might it not happen again? She is human. Where do her true loyalties lie? Too, she is now partly speeched, and that weighs muchly against her. Indeed, perhaps she connived against Kurii. In any event, if not he, his fellows, and others, call for her blood."

"I gather she was an excellent pet."

"Yes," said Peisistratus. "And Arcesilaus was doubtless fond of her."

"That was my understanding."

"He can obtain another," said Peisistratus.

"So she is to be slain, or sent to the cattle pens?"

"When she was brought before Arcesilaus, she flung herself on her belly before him, and, her small wrists braceleted before her, she clasped his foot, and kissed and licked, weeping, piteously, at his claws, but he remained adamant."

"And so she is to be slain, or sent to the cattle pens?"

"Arcesilaus, I think, remains fond of her, and was pleased to learn she still lived, and that she had been brought safe to the Steel World."

"By Grendel."

"Surely."

"But Arcesilaus will not keep her."

"Certainly not."

"What, then, is to be done with her?" asked Cabot.

"Grendel himself provided the solution," said Peisistratus.

"And what was the nature of this solution?" inquired Cabot.

"He purchased her, for a pittance," said Peisistratus. "She is now on his leash."

"And what was her view of this?" asked Cabot.

"She was beside herself with disbelief, with horror, and humiliation, and fury, and misery," said Peisistratus.

"But she is still on his leash."

"Of course."

"Excellent," said Cabot.

"He is not wholly Kur," said Peisistratus. "She has always hated him, loathed him, as do most of the Kurii, as a misbred monster and freak, and now she belongs to him, and the collar on her neck is his."

"He risked his life for her."

"She despises him," said Peisistratus.

"Doubtless he will keep her under an excellent discipline," said Cabot.

"No," said Peisistratus. "She puts on airs and has no fear of him."

"Though she is a mere pet?"

"Yes."

"I see," said Cabot.

"She wishes to demean and rule him," said Peisistratus. "She is haughty and petty. She treats him in ways that no Kur would tolerate. Even in public she insults him, and shows him disrespect. She does not serve him, she does not groom him."

"Perhaps she should be disciplined," said Cabot. "Women understand such things."

"He will not lay a hand on her," said Peisistratus.

"She will then grow ever more insolent, more tiresome, and troublesome," said Cabot. "She will understand his gentleness, his kindness, his forbearance, or whatever it may be, as weakness."

"Doubtless," said Peisistratus, "but, in any event, she is still on his leash."

"I see," said Cabot.

"And what of her Gorean?" asked Cabot.

"She demands that her lessons continue," said Peisistratus.

"I suppose that is to the good," said Cabot.

"She is small, petty, and thankless," said Peisistratus.

"I am sorry to hear that," said Cabot.

"But she is still on his leash," said Peisistratus.

"I wonder if she understands what that means," said Cabot.

"Probably not," said Peisistratus. "Do you want her?"

"No," said Cabot.

"You need only say the word and Agamemnon would give her to you, or any other who might please you."

"Lord Agamemnon is generous," said Cabot.

"Have you pondered the offer of Agamemnon, proposed to you in the palace?" inquired Peisistratus. "He grows impatient."

"I expect to give him my answer soon," said Cabot.

"I trust it will be the right answer," said Peisistratus.

"It will be," said Cabot.

"Good," said Peisistratus.

Cabot smiled.

"I would not dally overlong," said Peisistratus.

"No," said Cabot.

"I shall accompany you to your lodgings," said Peisistratus.

"That is perhaps wise, considering my testimony," said Cabot.

They then left the courtroom.

"It is interesting to me," said Peisistratus, "that you have expressed no interest in the fate of another."

"What other?" asked Cabot.

"The brunette, she with whom you shared a stall," said Peisistratus.

"I remember her," said Cabot. "She was the pet of Lord Pyrrhus, as I recall. But, as I understand it, he was deprived of his rank, his goods, his chattels, and such, even before the trial."

"The outcome of the trial was not in doubt," said Peisistratus, "until the unexpected vacillations and vagaries of a particular witness."

"But the trial was inconclusive?"

"The trial, perhaps, but not justice," said Peisistratus. "Justice will have its way, by one road or another."

"I see," said Cabot.

"Kur justice," said Peisistratus, "is nothing if not efficient and expeditious."

"So what happened to the goods of Lord Pyrrhus?" asked Cabot.

"I see you are interested."

"Surely," said Cabot.

"Goods and chattels were confiscated, thus becoming the properties of the state."

"Of Lord Agamemnon?"

"Yes. But one chattel was given away before the fall of Lord Pyrrhus."

"Given away?"

"Yes."

"Oh?"

"The brunette," said Peisistratus. "When Pyrrhus expected you to die or be slain in the sport cylinder, he was no longer interested in a simple slut, a mere human, one whom he had acquired primarily to provoke you."

"To whom was she given?" asked Cabot.

"To me," said Peisistratus.

"And you accepted her?"

"Certainly," said Peisistratus. "It would have been churlish to refuse, do you not think so, and, besides, what fellow would not be pleased to accept the gift of so lovely a pet?"

"She was given to you as a pet, and not as a slave?"

"Yes," said Peisistratus.

"But she is a slave."

"Every inch of her, every hair on her head, every cell in her body, every bit of her," said Peisistratus.

"Then she has not yet been claimed as a slave?" said Cabot.

"No," said Peisistratus.

"Interesting," said Cabot.

"I thought you would be interested," said Peisistratus.

"What has been done with her?"

"She has been taken to the Pleasure Cylinder," said Peisistratus.

"Then she will be safe from Kurii."

"Unless from those who monitor the cylinder," said Peisistratus.

"I trust she is worked well," said Cabot.

"She is worked excellently," said Peisistratus, "and she is becoming well apprised she is a slave."

Cabot was pleased with this intelligence pertaining to the former Miss Pym. The sooner she understood she was a slave, and no more than a slave, the better. He supposed several of the young men who had known her on Earth would not be displeased to own her.

"Few in the cylinder speak English," said Cabot.

"She is being taught Gorean, by the girls," said Peisistratus. "And she is learning quickly."

"Good," said Cabot.

It is important for a girl to learn quickly the language of her masters.

"She is highly intelligent," said Peisistratus.

"Good," said Cabot.

Goreans do not wish for the lips of a stupid woman to be pressed to their feet.

"Too, of course," said Peisistratus, "as she is a female slave, she is being taught the pleasing of men, by a switch."

"Of course," said Cabot.

To be sure, the switch is largely an encouragement to diligence and a corrective for mistakes, or clumsiness. Its applicability may also be noted where errors in Gorean grammar, phrasing, or such, might take place.

"I am surprised," said Cabot, "that she has not been claimed."

"None will claim her," said Peisistratus.

"But she is surely comely, would look well in ropes, would be nicely curved at one's feet, would bring a good price off the block, and such."

"Nonetheless," said Peisistratus, "none claim her."

"Surely the cylinder could do so, publicly," said Cabot.

"It has not done so," said Peisistratus.

"On Gor there are many slaves owned by the state, by institutions, businesses, and such."

"This is not Gor," said Peisistratus.

"There are difficulties?"

"Several," said Peisistratus. "Food, oxygen, space, the quotas, the allotments, the requirements of Kurii, and such."

"Interesting," said Cabot.

"She should be soon claimed, or destroyed," said Peisistratus.

"Why is that?" inquired Cabot.

"There is no place here for unclaimed slaves," said Peisistratus.

"I know a world," said Cabot, "where there are untold thousands of unclaimed slaves."

"I know that world, as well," said Peisistratus, "but I would say untold hundreds of thousands, perhaps millions, of unclaimed slaves."

Cabot was silent.

"But when we bring them to Gor," said Peisistratus, "they find themselves claimed, and owned, and clearly the properties of masters."

"True," said Cabot.

It is a joy for the slave to find at last her master, and for the master to have at his feet at last his slave.

"It seems she should be claimed," said Cabot.

"When sleeping in her chains, uneasy, sobbing, twisting and rolling about, she calls your name," said Peisistratus.

"Interesting," said Cabot.

"Was she not placed in the container on the Prison World with you, by Priest-Kings?" asked Peisistratus.

"Yes," said Cabot.

"Doubtless to be exquisitely attractive to you, to be even irresistibly attractive to you, one to be a perfect slave for you, one who would be a veritable slave of your dreams, one perhaps designed for your collar, one perhaps even bred for your collar?"

"Perhaps," said Cabot.

"It seems then that the Priest-Kings have miscalculated," said Peisistratus.

"It would seem so," said Cabot.

Certainly he could see little point in her being placed in the container other than to torment him, tearing him apart, betwixt his honor and his desire. But then he asked himself, how could one desire such a female, one so haughty and contemptuous, one so obsessed with her own contrived, eccentric self-image, one so naively and pretentiously, so uncritically, imbued with her vanity, and the encumbrances of an unnatural, pretentious, forlorn civilization? But certainly she had been well turned on nature's lathe, to taunt and torment men, at least until she had become their vulnerable, helpless possession.

"But she is clearly a slave," said Peisistratus.

"Of that there is no doubt," said Cabot.

"Do you think she knows she is a slave?"

"In one sense," said Cabot. "The chain on her leaves her in no doubt of it."

"But do you think she knows the chain is rightfully and appropriately on her, that it belongs on her?"

"Probably not," said Cabot.

"Do you think she will fight the understanding of herself as rightfully a slave?" asked Peisistratus.

"Probably," said Cabot.

"You are not interested in claiming her?"

"No," said Cabot.

"Here is your lodging," said Peisistratus, pausing on a step, leading up to the small villa set aside for Cabot's use, nestled in the side of a hill.

"Yes," said Cabot.

"Agamemnon awaits your answer," said Peisistratus, looking upward, after Cabot.

"He will have it soon," said Cabot, ascending the stairs.

"Cabot!" called Peisistratus.

Cabot turned, and looked down. "Yes?"

"I shall call for you at the fifth Ahn," said Peisistratus.

"The arena?" asked Cabot.

"Our presence is required," said Peisistratus.

"I understand," said Cabot.

"It will not be pretty," said Peisistratus.

"I understand," said Cabot.

Chapter, the Twenty-First:

What Occurred in the Arena

Cabot and Peisistratus were ushered into a cage, mounted on a middle tier of the encircling seats.

"We can see well from here," said Peisistratus.

The cage door was locked behind them.

Cabot was in a simple tunic and sandals. He had left the robes, the strings of rubies, behind, in the villa assigned to him.

"Why are we caged?" inquired Cabot.

"Perhaps because we are animals," said Peisistratus, "and our hosts feel it is fitting. Perhaps to prevent you, should you be so inclined, from interfering in the festivities. Perhaps to protect you, lest some here be displeased with your testimony at the trial."

"But you, too, are caged," said Cabot.

"I, too, am an animal," said Peisistratus, "from the Kur view. And would it not be demeaning to you, beloved of Agamemnon, to be caged alone, and I left free?"

"I learned from Agamemnon, in the forest, he the metal larl, or within it, somehow, or controlling it, somehow, that you are his human."

"Shall we speak in English?" inquired Peisistratus.

"Certainly," said Cabot, in English.

"I am my own human," said Peisistratus.

"Does Agamemnon know that?"

"No," said Peisistratus. Then he pointed to an entryway, high in the tiers, across the arena, with its sand. "That is Lord Arcesilaus," he said.

There were flags and banners about, and the tiers were muchly filled.

"There are venders about," said Cabot, "seemingly selling treats."

"Do not ask their nature," advised Peisistratus.

"Very well," said Cabot.

"Can you hear the music?" asked Peisistratus.

Several of the Kurii in the tiers were moving oddly, some swaying.

"I think so," said Cabot, straining. "But it sounds not like music, but rather like throbbings, like the wind in the forest, like rushing streams, subtle, distant, sometimes cries, as of seized, frightened animals, such things."

"And much is indecipherable, resembling nothing comprehensible to you?"

"Yes," said Cabot.

"The throbbings, the beatings," said Peisistratus, "suggest the beating of the Kur heart, and then the movements of wind and water suggest the suddenness of vision, and the circulation of hastened blood, and the squeals, the lamentations, the shrieks, the moans, may recall war, and the hunt. But much of it, I fear, is simply unintelligible to a human, and much literally offensive to our hearing. The rhythms are only partially shared with us. Perhaps it is configured to a nervous system, or diverse hereditary coils. How much is cultural, and how much is indexed to a different physiology, to a different hearing, a different speech, even a different sense of touch, is difficult to tell."

"It has stopped, hasn't it?" asked Cabot.

Peisistratus lifted his head. "Yes," he said. "They are ready to begin."

There was suddenly a pounding of drums, mighty drums.

"Ai!" cried Cabot, startled.

"That is not difficult to hear, is it?" smiled Peisistratus.

There were twelve such drums, each with two drummers, in the first tier of the arena.

"No," said Cabot.

"There are twelve drums," said Peisistratus. "And there are twelve digits on the two forepaws of the Kur."

"Each has two drummers," said Cabot.

"The Kur has two eyes," said Peisistratus. "Hands and eyes."

"I thought Kur music was silent, or almost so."

"Certainly not silent to the hearing of the Kur," said Peisistratus. "But the drums may not even be understood as music. Those are arena drums, but there are also drums of war, of signaling, of formation, and so on."

Cabot's blood began to race.

Peisistratus, too, was effected by the beating.

"It seems humans and Kurii share drums," said Cabot.

"Drums," said Peisistratus, "speak to the blood, to the heart. They speak of the beat and insistence of life."

"They are used on Gor to marshal and control tarn cavalries, and set the cadence of the wing beat, of the flight," said Cabot.

"Certainly," said Peisistratus.

"Is the sound not too loud for Kurii?" asked Cabot.

"Apparently not," said Peisistratus. "Nor is the crash of thunder, the rolling of waves, the breaking of ice in a frozen river, the tumbling of the avalanche, the eruption of the volcano."

"One gathers its loudness is stimulating."

"Yes, and the rhythms," said Peisistratus.

"They speak of blood, and life, and excitement," said Cabot.

"They have their drums," said Peisistratus, "and we have ours, as well."

"Yes," said Cabot, "of war, and the march, sometimes to measure the stroke of oars, occasionally to signal the opening and closing of markets, of gates, and such."

"There are subtle drums, too, demanding, insistent, maddening, exciting, sensuous drums, of course," said Peisistratus.

"True," said Cabot.

This was presumably an allusion to the use of drums, together with other instruments, we may suppose, in slave dance, a form of dance in which a type of human female, the female slave, helpless and vulnerable, as all female slaves, ornamented, and beautifully if scarcely clothed, dances her beauty, hoping to be found pleasing by masters. If she is not, she knows she may be whipped, perhaps slain.

The drums were suddenly silent.

One could now hear Kurii, moving in the tiers, eager, expectant.

"It begins?" asked Cabot.

"Yes," said Peisistratus.

"It is here that Lord Pyrrhus will attest his innocence against Agamemnon, Kur to Kur."

"Yes."

"Lord Pyrrhus is large and powerful," said Cabot. "Agamemnon must be courageous indeed to face such a foe."

"Doubtless," said Peisistratus. "Would you like me to purchase you a treat?"

"No," said Cabot.

"Look," said Peisistratus, pointing to the sand, several feet below.

There a Kur was bent under a large piece of meat, which he deposited in the center of the arena. He then exited, and the meat lay there, a mound, in the sun.

Cabot grasped the bars, angrily.

"It is tarsk," said Peisistratus.

Cabot released the bars.

At that moment, on opposite sides of the arena, from gates at the level of the sand, there emerged two large sleen.

"They are starving," said Peisistratus.

Both animals seemed to rush toward the meat. One reached it first, and thrust his muzzle into it, tearing it, ripping out gluts of meat, and gorging them, but then the other sleen was upon it, and the two animals rolled in the sand, in a frenzy of snapping, and clawing, and in moments the jaws of each were bloody, and gouts of fur had been torn from the pelt of each, and then, suddenly, one had the throat of the other, and tore it open, and then, as the torn animal crouched down bleeding, and subsided, and rolled to its side, the victor busied himself with the meat.

Cabot saw necklaces of strung coins being exchanged in the tiers.

"Ramar has taken the meat six times," said Peisistratus. "He permits the other sleen to reach the meat first, and find distraction in it, and then he attacks."

"I see," said Cabot.

A Kur, with a long pole, with a hook on its end, sunk it into the meat, and drew the meat, the sleen, Ramar, feeding and following, through one of the gates at the level of the sand.

A large Kur then entered the arena, carrying a length of rope, and crouched down, waiting.

Shortly thereafter two other Kurii, from opposite sides of the arena, entered upon the sand, and approached the large Kur, and stood some ten feet before him, and apart from one another, by some ten feet, as well.

"They are not armed," said Cabot.

"They do not need to be," said Peisistratus. "Note the larger beast. See the rings on the left wrist."

"Yes."

"He stands high in the rings," said Peisistratus. "His seed is avidly sought."

"I do not understand," said Cabot.

"Surely you see the two before him are female," said Peisistratus.

"No," said Cabot. "It is hard to tell."

"They are smaller, the pelting is smoother, glossier, less shaggy."

"I see they are differently harnessed," said Cabot.

"That, too," said Peisistratus, amused.

One might note that in the human species the sexes are radically dimorphic, anatomically, emotionally, psychologically, and so on. They are very different, and are interestingly complementary. Even a Kur can instantly see the difference between a human male and a human female. It is sometimes annoying to a Kur that some humans cannot immediately, similarly, distinguish between a Kur male and a Kur female. It is less annoying that they sometimes fail to distinguish between a typical Kur male and a Kur nondominant. To be sure, the differences there are mostly behavioral. Most humans, incidentally, have never seen a Kur womb, either of the shelf or wall type, as they tend to be hidden, and guarded. The female's egg, once fertilized, is deposited in the womb, and develops within it, the infant later to chew and claw its way free, that in something between a half year and a year. Some wombs perish after one child; some hardy wombs have produced as many as forty or fifty infants. The womb itself makes no contribution to the genetic endowments of the offspring. The womb, in historical times, at least, replicates itself, parthenogenetically, by budding, so to speak. As indicated earlier in the text, certain obscurities obtain with respect to the origin of the earlier wombs.

With a sudden screech of rage the two females flung themselves upon one another.

Kurii in the stands leaped about and called out encouragement to their favorite in what seemed doubtless to Cabot a surprising and unusual contest. The crouching male, with the length of rope grasped in one paw, scarcely moved.

The two females tore at one another, until at last one lay in the sand, bloodied, trembling, and lifted one paw, pathetically, for mercy.

"The male Kur does not beg for mercy," commented Peisistratus. "That is another difference."

"Surely that is cultural," said Cabot.

"Doubtless," said Peisistratus.

"She is going to kill her!" said Cabot.

The victor had crouched down and savagely pulled back the head of the vanquished, and set her fangs at the throat of the vanquished.

A roar of approbation coursed through the crowd. Perhaps the vanquished had not fought well enough.

Again a paw was lifted pathetically, begging for mercy.

The victor, encouraged, licensed, so to speak, widened her jaws, and thrust forward.

But a roar of prohibition emanated from the throat of the male, and the victor stopped, and then thrust the vanquished from her, contemptuously, and leaped in the sand, shrieking in triumph.

The vanquished Kur female crawled some feet away, bloodying the sand.

The victor then approached the male.

He cuffed her, half spinning her about. She was already bloodied from the fray from which she had emerged victorious.

"It seems," said Cabot, "he is not pleased with the outcome of the battle."

"No," said Peisistratus. "It would be the same with either. He is merely asserting his dominance."

"She has accepted his blow," said Cabot.

"Of course," said Peisistratus. "Were he not dominant she would despise him. She wishes his dominance. She would be insulted to submit to any other sort of male. What Kur female would? What do you think this is all about?"

"What if she had not accepted his blow?"

"I do not understand."

"What if she had retaliated, attacked him? She is surely a fearsome creature, as we have seen."

"Then he would beaten her, if not maimed or killed her," said Peisistratus. "Did you not see the rings on his wrist. He has killed male Kurii to obtain those rings."

"Look," said Peisistratus.

"I see," said Cabot.

The female now stood before the male, her head down, and her arms at her sides. The male then encircled her body several times with the length of rope he carried, fastening her arms to her sides, and then, with the length of rope left, he fashioned a leash for her, and led her toward an exit gate. She half danced in his wake, and howled to the stands.

"It is a noise of pleasure, of triumph," said Peisistratus. "She has conquered her rival, and she has been acquired, at least for some days, by the male of her desires."

"I think I prefer our human ways," said Cabot.

"Perhaps they are not so different," said Peisistratus.

"Look!" said Cabot, pointing to the sand.

The vanquished Kur female had struggled to her feet, and begun to hobble from the sand. Several Kurii would have assisted her, but she bared her fangs, and warned them away, viciously.

They regarded one another, frightened, and then looked piteously upon the torn, bleeding female.

Again they tried to approach, solicitously, but, again, with a baring of fangs and a snarl, she warned them back.

They fled back, and then, as she regarded them, one after another, they moved back further, and bent down, to make themselves smaller in her presence.

"They are cringing," said Cabot. "Are they her hand maidens?"

"They are males," said Peisistratus. "They are her attendants, assigned to serve her."

The female then hobbled toward an exit gate, before the others, alone, blood in her footprints.

The others then followed her.

"They are males?" asked Cabot.

"In a sense," said Peisistratus. "They are nondominants."

"I see," said Cabot.

The drums then beat again.

"What is that?" asked Cabot, in disgust. "What are those things?"

From several of the lower gates a number of unusual creatures, crowded together, clumsy, heavy, confused, bleating and whining, were driven by cries and whips into the arena.

"Surely you know," said Peisistratus.

"They are large, sluggish, surely well-fed," said Cabot, peering downward.

"They have been fattened," said Peisistratus.

"What are they?"

"Cattle humans," said Peisistratus.

"They cannot be human," said Cabot.

"Perhaps not," said Peisistratus. "But it is a matter of breeding. Great changes may be so wrought. Consider Earth. How many of your dogs recall in appearance and demeanor their remote, swift, hungry, far-ranging ancestor, the gray wolf?"

"We would not breed even dogs so," said Cabot, in fury.

"Because you do not raise them for meat," said Peisistratus.

"Those are small Kurii!" said Cabot, observing the entry unto the sand of a swarm of eager, shaggy forms.

"Actually Kur children," said Peisistratus. "Many have not lost their womb teeth."

The cattle creatures were whipped to the center of the arena, where they stood crowded together, bleating.

"They are frightened, and disoriented," said Peisistratus. "This is very different from the security of the pens."

The small shaggy forms, many no more than five feet in height, and perhaps no more than a hundred to a hundred and fifty pounds in weight, encircled the huddled, confused cattle creatures.

"This is how Kurii want their young to view humans, to understand humans, to think of humans," said Peisistratus.

"They would think otherwise of humans did they meet them in the field of battle," said Cabot.

"Doubtless," said Peisistratus.

"What are they going to do?" asked Cabot.

"It is a form of play," said Peisistratus. "Children are fond of games. They are pleased to frolic."

"What are they going to do?" asked Cabot.

"See the ribbons?" asked Peisistratus.

"Yes," said Cabot. "But what are they going to do?"

"Kill," said Peisistratus. "The ribbons will mark their kills. He with the most ribboned meat wins a little crown and a haunch of roast tarsk."

"No!" cried Cabot, foolishly.

Suddenly the children raced upon the huddled cattle, seizing them, lacerating them, tearing them. The cattle did not defend themselves, though several now fled wildly, clumsily, terrified, about the arena, pursued swiftly by the youthful predators with their colorful ribbons.

Occasionally an adult Kur, with a stroke of his whip, turned one of the confused cattle back toward the center of the arena.

"Do not feel sorry for them," said Peisistratus. "They are not truly human. They do not even understand what is going on. They only want to be returned to their pens, and the feeding trough."

There was a squeal from one of the cattle below, as three of the youngsters clung to it, gripping it with their yet-immature fangs.

"This accustoms them, of course," said Peisistratus, "to killing, and the taste of blood, in a convenient, economical fashion."

Cabot shook the bars of the cage.

"Caution," warned Peisistratus. "Kurii are watching."

Cabot shook again the bars of the cage, futilely.

"There is nothing you can do," said Peisistratus. "Do not concern yourself. It is only a game."

"Why do they not fight back?" cried Cabot. "They are larger than their foes."

"They are cattle," said Peisistratus.

There were howls of pleasure, of amusement, from the stands, as one or more of the cattle, inept even in flight, startled, bleating, was brought down.

"Do not concern yourself," said Peisistratus, to Cabot. "This is what they are for."

"Look!" cried Cabot. "One has turned on its attacker!"

"That is not to take place!" said Peisistratus. "That is not permitted!"

"Apparently the creature does not understand that," said Cabot.

Below, one of the cattle, half blinded with its own blood, had closed its fat fingers about a small shaggy throat.

"Is the child not to be rescued?" asked Cabot. "It will kill the child."

"Do not concern yourself," said Peisistratus. "The others do not."

The whitish, obese creature let the limp body of the youngster fall to the sand. Its throat was then, as it stupidly looked about, comprehending nothing, casually cut open by one of the adult Kurii.

"That one," said Peisistratus, "cannot be ribboned. He does not count."

"What of the child?" asked Cabot.

"He allowed himself to be caught. He failed. He will be forgotten."

"Is it not a tragedy?" asked Cabot.

"Not if it does not spoil the game," said Peisistratus.

Only one or two of the cattle were still alive.

"It is over," said Peisistratus, presently. "See, that one child is victor. The large one. He has ribboned five beasts. That is quite good, but some have ribboned more."

Cabot observed a small, golden crown, apparently of a paperlike material, being placed on the victor's head. There was applause in the stands, the rhythmic pounding of hands on thighs. Later, he would receive, Cabot surmised, a haunch of roasted tarsk, a meat generally much preferred by Kurii to human.

"When," asked Cabot, "will Lord Pyrrhus and Lord Agamemnon meet, Kur to Kur?"

"Presently," said Peisistratus. "But first there are some beast fights. May I purchase you a treat?"

"No," said Cabot.

The beast fights were largely amongst fighting humans, variously armed. Some of these were game humans who had been netted in the sport cylinder, but most were killer humans, bred for savagery, raised for the arena.

"Are they speeched?" inquired Cabot.

"Most," said Peisistratus.

"And in what speech?" asked Cabot.

"In the language to which most translators are set," said Peisistratus. "Speeching is helpful in monitoring and managing their training. Some, of course, are not speeched. Sometimes the speeched and the nonspeeched are set against one another. If the battle is team war the speeched side has an advantage."

"Undoubtedly," said Cabot. "And to what speech are most translators set?"

"Gorean," said Peisistratus.

"Good," said Cabot.

It was late in the afternoon, as the mirrors arranged the day, when, to Cabot's amazement, two figures with which he was familiar entered onto the sand. The first, broad and powerful, half bent over, alert, looking from side to side, was Grendel. The second figure, stripped and high-collared, as befits a Kur pet, and on a chain leash, was the blonde. She was led to a point near the center of the arena. Many sounds of disapproval from the tiers, encompassing hissings and snarls, had greeted this pair upon their appearance. At the center of the arena a circular cement platform, some five feet in diameter, emerged from the sand. In the center of this platform, fastened to a plate anchored in the cement, there was a heavy iron ring. The blonde's chain was fastened to this ring.

At a gesture from Grendel, the blonde went to all fours, the chain then looped on the cement, save where it looped up to her collar.

"Why is she on all fours?" asked Cabot.

"Is it not appropriate for an animal, a pet?" asked Peisistratus.

"Yes," said Cabot.

"Or a slave?" inquired Peisistratus.

"Certainly," said Cabot.

Slaves are occasionally kept on all fours, forbidden to rise, feed from pans on the floor, are led about, leashed, on all fours, and so on. This regimen or strictness is imposed upon them sometimes as a punishment or discipline, sometimes as a part of their training, or, sometimes, simply to remind them that they are a slave, their master's domestic animal. Sometimes the girl must bring the master's whip to him on all fours, the implement held between her teeth. She will later learn if she is to be caressed or struck.

"What is this about?" asked Cabot.

"Many Kurii," said Peisistratus, "want her blood. She is held accountable for the debacle in the forest, that of the hunting party of Lord Arcesilaus. In it, you may recall, Kurii were slain."

"I recall," said Cabot.

"Grendel has refused to sell her to those who wish her harm," said Peisistratus.

"Harm?" said Cabot.

"—to those who would kill her with needles, a corpuscle at a time, who would inject her with slow, agonizing poisons, who would feed her to urts or sleen, who would cast her to leech plants, who would roast her alive and eat her, and so on."

"I see," said Cabot.

"He has been offered more strings of coins than you and I would part with for a good slave."

"And she only a pet."

"Precisely."

"It seems he is fond of his pet," said Cabot.

"He is a fool," said Peisistratus. "He will now die."

"I gather he must now, if he wishes to keep her, or save her, defend her?"

"Assuredly," said Peisistratus. "And the crowd is against him."

"How is this to be done?" asked Cabot.

"He is to face seven challengers," said Peisistratus, "any one of whom might easily slay him, for they are Kur."

"Is he not Kur?"

"Part Kur."

"Perhaps," said Cabot, "he is more than Kur."

"When the combat is done," said Peisistratus, "the girl will be taken by the challengers, to be done with as they intend."

"If they win," said Cabot.

"Can there be doubt?" asked Peisistratus.

"The fortunes of war, like the rains in Anango, are difficult to forecast," said Cabot.

"I will wager a string of coins," said Peisistratus, "on the challengers."

"Against what?" inquired Cabot. "My life?"

"Certainly not," said Peisistratus. "Besides, your life, at this point, is still of interest to Agamemnon."

"A slender security," remarked Cabot.

"You would know more of that than I," said Peisistratus.

"So what should I put up, against your coins?"

"One of your strings of rubies," suggested Peisistratus.

"A string of coins against a string of rubies seems a strange wager," smiled Cabot.

"True," said Peisistratus. "I shall make it a dozen strings of coins, and throw in a pet."

"A pet?"

"The brunette."

"Keep her," said Cabot.

"Is it a wager?" asked Peisistratus.

"I think you are more aware of the value of rubies," said Cabot, "than I am of the value of your coins."

"Perhaps," smiled Peisistratus. "But is it a wager?"

"Very well," said Cabot. "It is a wager."

"It is a pity to take your rubies so easily," said Peisistratus.

"The challengers!" said Cabot, pointing downward.

From a gate at the level of the sand below and to their right, seven large Kurii, harnessed for war, entered the arena. Each carried a long, thick, metal bar, some ten feet in length, some three inches in diameter. Such an implement would have been difficult for many humans to lift, let alone wield. Kurii, however, might play with such a device as with a wand, or as a brawny peasant might with his stout, well-grasped defensive staff, a punishing implement which, well used, might overcome a blade.

The crowd stamped, roared, leaped about in place, and smote its thighs, expressing its pleasure with the number and harnessing of the challengers. Indeed, some of the challengers were well known to the crowd, from ascendancies in the rings, and more than one was accounted a champion.

The challengers turned about in the sand and lifted their simple weapons in salute to the crowd, which incited still more approbation in the tiers.

"Is Grendel to be unarmed?" asked Cabot.

"You now fear for your rubies?" asked Peisistratus.

"Is he to be unarmed?"

"No," said Peisistratus, "that would not be Kur, that would not be honorable."

"Look!" said Cabot.

An additional bar was handed to one of the challengers, by an arena praetor, or officer. That challenger then thrust his own bar down, into the sand, some four feet, with a mighty motion, and then, contemptuously, hurled the bar he had been given by the officer toward Grendel. It descended like a lance, and was arrested, tilted, in the sand, before Grendel. The cast had been more than a hundred and fifty feet.

Grendel bent to retrieve the weapon.

Amusement coursed through the crowd.

"See," said Peisistratus. "He is only part Kur. It is too heavy for him. He can barely lift it. Fear for your rubies, friend Cabot."

Cabot smiled.

One of the Kur challengers roared and raced across the sand toward Grendel, his weapon held with two hands over his head.

Many humans find it remarkable that so large a creature can move with such rapidity.

Cabot was familiar with such characteristics, of course, and so, too, one might note, was Grendel.

The blonde screamed.

The noise of the crowd was suddenly silenced.

For the challenger, its chest bloodied, staggered back, and then sat, dazed, stupidly, in the sand.

One end of Grendel's bar was soaked with blood, for better than eighteen inches from its thrusting end.

"The swiftness of the thrust, the suddenness, the ease of it!" exclaimed Peisistratus, wonderingly.

"He is as strong as a Kur," said Cabot, "perhaps stronger."

"It was a trick," said Peisistratus, reproachfully.

"Surely deception," said Cabot, "is an element not unknown in war."

"The others will now be more wary," said Peisistratus.

"Yes," said Cabot.

"And the rubies," said Peisistratus, "will soon be mine."

"It is hard to predict the rains in Anango," said Cabot.

"That it will rain in the summer is not hard to predict, in one week or another," said Peisistratus.

"In seven weeks?"

"Yes," said Peisistratus.

"May not the challengers attack *en masse*?" inquired Cabot.

"That would not be Kur," said Peisistratus. "That would not be honorable."

"Good," said Cabot.

The next Kur approached cautiously, his weapon at the ready. Grendel came forward, to place himself between the pet and his antagonist.

The crowd now leaned forward, intent upon the sand.

The matches were now of greater interest than had been anticipated.

The second challenger struck downward with his weapon, and Grendel fended the blow but in such a way as not to take the brunt of its weight, but rather to slide it aside. There was, however, nonetheless, a shower of sparks. The blonde cried out, and pulled back on her chain, it hooked to her collar.

"The beating on the bar," said Cabot, "would in time weaken the arms of he who blocks the blows, surely by the third or fourth attacker."

There were several more exchanges, each with its shower of sparks. The challenger then stepped back in the sand.

Grendel did not pursue him.

He wished, doubtless, to remain in the vicinity of the pet, lest the attacker might the more easily slip past him. The goal of the attackers was primarily the blood of the pet, to revenge themselves upon her, however irrationally, to which object the destruction of her despised defender was largely incidental.

Grendel and the second attacker then, some yards apart, crouched down, watching one another.

Cabot could see the movements of the lungs of the two beasts.

The attacker then began to groom itself, not taking his eyes off Grendel.

They remained so, almost motionless, for several minutes.

The crowd was silent, and patient. Kurii, when hunting, are very patient.

The attacker then roared and rushed forward, and, as it advanced, but feet from Grendel, Grendel setting himself to accept the charge, the attacker suddenly twisted to the side and, with one clawed foot, swept a great storm of sand toward Grendel, a blasting flight of particles that might have stunned and blinded a tharlarion. But Grendel who had anticipated this device hurled himself to the sand below this flighted granular torrent, and swept his bar across the sand, striking the now-again-turned attacker frontally across the legs, some inches above the ankles, and the attacker, with a bellow of agony, fell forward into the sand, its legs shattered, as the sand fell about Grendel and his pet, descending even onto the cement platform, and striking about the pet's back and shoulders, and coating her hair and eyelashes. Grendel then rose to his feet, slowly, deliberately, and, as the crippled attacker watched, and lifted his arms to defend himself, Grendel struck down with his bar, shattering through the fending arms, and breaking the head open as one might have beaten a hammer into a crusted larma. He then went, deliberately, to the first attacker, who sat helplessly in the sand, and punched through his skull with the bar.

"He is Kur," breathed Peisistratus.

"Or human," said Cabot.

Grendel then turned to regard the five remaining challengers.

There was a roar of anger from the stands.

"The crowd is displeased," said Cabot.

"Not with Grendel!" cried Peisistratus. "Observe!"

Four of the five remaining challengers were advancing together.

"It is, I gather, not Kur," said Cabot.

"No," said Peisistratus. "It is not Kur."

The crowd was howling with rage, but the four continued to advance, and began to spread themselves about, to encircle Grendel, and he could not, of course, defend the pet on more than one side.

She was screaming, and, with her small hands, jerking wildly at the chain. This was futile, of course, as it had been decided that she would remain in place. In Gorean arenas, beautiful female slaves are commonly awarded as prizes to the victors. They are usually chained in place, to await their disposition, pending the outcome of the contest. In the current instance, of course, it was the very blood of the female that was sought.

"The rubies are now mine," said Peisistratus, angrily.

"Consider the rains in Anango," said Cabot.

"Do not be foolish," chided Peisistratus.

Grendel suddenly left the vicinity of the pet on its chain moving with great speed toward the nearest of the attackers, it unwisely now, too eager, some yards in advance of the others. There were movements of the weapons but they did not make contact. The foremost attacker's bar struck down into the sand, and Grendel was then behind it and he thrust his weapon into the abdomen of his foe, and literally lifted the Kur from the sand, impaled, and flung his body from the weapon.

"He is strong even for a Kur!" cried Peisistratus.

"He is more than Kur!" cried Cabot.

At the same moment another of the Kurii rushed toward the pet, who screamed, his bar lifted, to strike down, but Grendel spun about and flung his weapon almost as might a lesser creature have hurled a javelin, and it struck he who threatened the blonde in the back, emerging through his chest, and his bar fell ringing on the cement to the left of the terrified pet. At the same time, a side stroke from a bar struck Grendel on the left arm, and the arm jerked, useless, for the moment paralyzed. Grendel scrambled toward the cement platform, to retrieve a weapon, his or the fallen bar of he who would have smote the pet. But there lunged between him and his goal another of the attackers, his weapon raised.

Grendel crouched on the sand.

The blonde pulled back to the length of her chain.

"He does not see the attacker behind him!" said Peisistratus.

"He sees the shadow," said Cabot. "He knows! He sees the shadow!"

"Why does he not move?" demanded Peisistratus.

"It is not yet time," said Cabot.

"The shadow is gone!" said Peisistratus.

"The mirrors have been changed," said Cabot. "Not every foe, it seems, is on the sand."

"Grendel dares not turn his back," said Peisistratus.

Had he done so the foe between him and the pet might have struck.

"He need not do so," said Cabot. "Again they underestimate him."

"How so?" said Peisistratus, grasping the bars, looking down to the sand.

"His hearing," said Cabot. "It is that of the Kur."

Whatever the clue might have been, a pressing of a paw into the sand to gain leverage for a blow, an intake of breath prior to striking, a tiny sound of harness, perhaps even the slick, shifting of a grip, to take advantage of a less-moist, drier surface, Grendel threw himself to the side and the mighty bar plunged a foot into the sand beside him. He then leapt up, turned, and seized the startled Kur who had struck at him and swung him about before him, to interpose him between himself and the attacker in the vicinity of the platform, who had quickly sped forward, but now stopped, angrily, the bar lifted.

"Why does he not strike?" asked Peisistratus.

"He needs a clean blow," said Cabot. "If the weapon is stopped, by sand, by the body of the other, it might be seized by Grendel."

"He could decapitate both with one blow," said Peisistratus.

"Grendel might," said Cabot. "But I do not think it could be done by a common Kur."

Grendel's left arm, slowly, surely, doubtless with considerable pain to himself, encircled the throat of the Kur he held, and he drew back a mighty fist, and this fist, with a blow that might have felled a tharlarion, he drove into the back of the Kur's neck, better than two inches, breaking the skull away from the vertebrae. He then cast aside the limp body of his former antagonist and turned to face the sixth challenger, the last of the four who had advanced together.

The seventh challenger had not interfered, but had remained crouched, with his weapon, near the far wall, near the gate through which he and the others had originally entered.

The sixth challenger now moved about Grendel, circling, who, weaponless, unwilling to reach for a weapon, and thus expose himself for a blow, turned, crouching, to keep his foe before him.

The challenger was then again between Grendel and the pet.

It was clearly unwilling to turn and attack the pet, for that would expose it to Grendel's attack.

They then crouched in the sand and faced one another, some four or five yards apart.

After a few moments the challenger began again, warily, to move, again circling, his clawed feet scarcely disturbing the sand, perhaps not wanting the cement shelf behind him, against which he might stumble, perhaps wanting to have both the pet and Grendel in view.

"I fear he has a clean blow," said Peisistratus. "It is only a question of the moment in which he will strike."

"It seems," said Cabot, "the rubies are yours."

"I do not think I want them," said Peisistratus.

It is, of course, next to impossible, without an object to interpose, to escape the vicious, lateral sweep of such a weapon.

"Look," said Peisistratus. "Grendel has backed near the platform. He chooses to die in the vicinity of the ungrateful, worthless thing for which he has fought, and for which he will now die."

The stands were now quiet.

And so Grendel stood, not moving, before the platform.

"He accepts his fate, and awaits it uncomplainingly," said Peisistratus.

"I fear so," said Cabot.

"He is Kur," said Peisistratus.

"And human," said Cabot.

The sixth challenger, with a grimace of pleasure, lifted his weapon and saluted Grendel.

There were in the stands noises of approval, and the smiting of thighs.

"He accepts him as a worthy foe," said Peisistratus.

"Grendel, it seems," said Cabot, "is at last redeemed."

The sixth challenger drew back his great bar and then suddenly it hurtled about in a smooth, sweeping arc within the compass of which stood Grendel.

"Ai!" cried Cabot.

The blow might have shattered walls, felled small trees.

The two beasts struggled for control of the weapon.

Grendel had grasped it in its flight. His two massive forepaws were clasped about the bar, as were those of its startled wielder.

A cry of astonishment roared through the stands.

Then Grendel drew the weapon closer and closer to himself, inch by inch.

"The Kur should loose his grip!" said Cabot. "He is being drawn too close to Grendel!"

But the Kur was unwise, and was reluctant to surrender the weapon. Did it truly think the struggle was for the weapon? Did it not understand that the struggle was for who should live and who should die?

Suddenly Grendel released the weapon and thrust out his massive clawed paw and the fingers of his right paw thrust through the left eye of the Kur and the rest of the grip, the thumb, was on its jaws, back, behind the fangs, and then Grendel turned his paw, thus lifting and exposing the Kur's throat, and then brought it forward, to his own jaws, and tore it away, and then stood crouched over the shuddering, dying body, blood smeared on his chest and about his jaws.

The blonde screamed in horror.

Grendel turned to regard her, his long dark tongue moving about, licking the blood about his fangs.

She lay down on the cement platform, covering her head with her hands, trembling.

Grendel then went to one of the fallen weapons, picked it up, returned to his kill, and there lifted the weapon, saluting his foe.

"He has accepted him as a worthy enemy," said Peisistratus.

There was much silence in the stands, and then several of the Kurii smote their thighs, acknowledging this gesture of respect to one of their species, albeit from one hitherto deemed not Kur, but no more than a malformed thing, a misbred brute, an abomination, a monster.

There was then a roll of drums, and all eyes turned to the seventh challenger, who now rose from his crouching position, to a height of some ten feet.

"He is massive," said Cabot.

"He is the champion, Magnus, Rufus Magnus," said Peisistratus.

"He is concerned with the blood of the pet?" inquired Cabot.

"No," said Peisistratus. "He has been hired."

"He has no personal interest in the matter?"

"None," said Peisistratus, "unlike the other challengers. His only interest here is to kill Grendel and collect his fee, after which the pet may be dealt with as others please."

"He is a champion?"

"A high champion," said Peisistratus. "See the two rings on his left wrist?"

"Yes."

"They are of gold," said Peisistratus.

"Look," said Cabot. "He puts aside the great bar."

"Yes," said Peisistratus.

"He will face Grendel unarmed?"

"No," said Peisistratus.

A praetor now approached the seventh challenger, and placed in his huge paws a gigantic ax, some ten feet in length, and double-bladed at each end, an ax which, in the grip of one such as he, one of such strength, might have decapitated a larl, and perhaps even, with three or four blows, Gor's mightiest constrictor, the giant hith.

"Is this honorable?" asked Cabot.

"Some higher authority has ruled on this, apparently," said Peisistratus, grimly.

"Agamemnon?"

"Doubtless," said Peisistratus.

The champion, Rufus Magnus, shifted the great ax about, easily, from paw to paw, testing its balance, and then, satisfied, he looked across the sand, to where Grendel stood, waiting.

The blonde now lay collapsed upon the platform, a tiny, pathetic, trembling figure, white against the gray of the cement. Cabot was not sure she could move, even had she wished to do so. He grasped the bars.

"You can do nothing," said Peisistratus.

"It is getting dark," said Cabot, suddenly.

"The mirrors!" said Peisistratus. "They are turning!"

The light which before had streamed into the arena was now lessening, as though night were falling, gradually, but at an unnatural pace.

"He must attack, he must run, there is little time!" exclaimed Peisistratus.

"I think there is no time," said Cabot.

"The shutters are closing!" said Peisistratus.

"I cannot see!" said Cabot.

"Nor I!" said Peisistratus.

"The shutters have closed?" asked Cabot.

"I do not know," said Peisistratus.

"If there is light I cannot detect it," said Cabot.

"Nor I," said Peisistratus.

There were anticipatory noises from the crowd.

"They can see!" cried Cabot.

"The champion is advancing upon him!" said Peisistratus. "I am sure of it!"

"Dishonor!" cried Cabot.

"True," said Peisistratus, angrily. "There is no honor in this."

There was a roaring, as though of a frightened animal below in the arena.

"Turn up your translator!" cried Cabot.

Peisistratus fumbled in the darkness.

"More! Higher!" said Cabot. "Direct it toward the sand!"

"Light! Light!" came from the translator. "I cannot see! Light! I cannot see!"

"It is Grendel," said Peisistratus. "He is terrified! He is lost! He cannot see!"

"Excellent!" cried Cabot.

"What?" cried Peisistratus.

"We see him as Kur," cried Cabot, "but they see him as human, as human!"

"They think he is blinded, helpless, forlorn in darkness?"

"Precisely," said Cabot, speaking in what for him was utter darkness.

"But he cries out in terror!" said Peisistratus.

"Does he?" said Cabot.

"Ah!" breathed Peisistratus, softly.

"And, too, it seemed," said Cabot, "he was slowed, muchly injured."

"Ai!" cried Peisistratus.

"Our large, fierce friends, I fear, have miscalculated," said Cabot.

Shutters must then have been reopened, and mirrors turned again, to gradually illuminate the sand.

"I owe you a dozen strings of coins," said Peisistratus.

Below, howling, his left arm lifted, two golden rings now on his left wrist, stood Grendel.

One of his clawed feet was on the chest of his antagonist, and the great, blunt bar he had had as weapon was thrust some four feet into the sand, first having pierced the massive neck of the antagonist, then pinning him to the sand by the ruptured throat, the body of the antagonist jerking, splashing sand about, hands and feet, and then scratching futilely at the thick metal bar.

"He could see!" said Peisistratus.

"Yes," said Cabot.

Grendel put back his head and howled in victory, a Kur's cry of triumph.

In the stands, after a silence, first one, and then another, and then thousands, smote their thighs in approbation.

"He has taken the two golden rings from the wrist of Rufus Magnus," said Peisistratus.

"They are his now," said Cabot.

"In the falling of darkness I see the hand of Agamemnon," said Peisistratus.

"The authority would have been his, indeed," said Cabot. "Surely it could not have taken place without his permission, or command, but what could be his interest in the matter, the pet, vengeance for a hunt gone wrong?"

"It is my speculation," said Peisistratus, "it has more to do with Grendel."

"How could that be?" inquired Cabot.

"The experiment, the outcome of which was Grendel," said Peisistratus, "turned out badly, Grendel failing to be such as to be accepted by humans as a leader. Such failures do not reflect well on the astuteness or stratagems of a Face of the Nameless One, and their lingering, failed residues are best discarded."

"I see," said Cabot.

"And there is unrest within the world," said Peisistratus.

"I have gathered that," said Cabot.

"In the cylinders treason lurks," said Peisistratus. "In the palace, accordingly, dark imperatives obtain."

"The winds of power sometimes blow waywardly," said Cabot.

"One who has grasped power is not easily persuaded to relinquish it," said Peisistratus.

"It is so, too, with humans," said Cabot.

"And there is another experiment, the outcome of which is not yet determined," said Peisistratus.

"What is that?" asked Cabot.

"That of enlisting a human leader, one men will trust, a warrior, a seeming champion, a seeming hero, one whom men, properly motivated, will unquestioningly, eagerly follow, one who will lead armies against the Sardar."

"I see," said Cabot.

"Agamemnon grows impatient for your answer," said Peisistratus.

"He will have it soon," said Cabot.

Grendel had now removed the great bar from the sand, and from his antagonist, and cast it aside, into the sand.

He then turned about and went to the cement platform, and freed the chain of the blonde pet from its ring. He then led her slowly from the platform, to the sand, and then across the sand, and then through one of the far gates, she on all fours.

Two attendants, with poles with hooks, came and removed the now inert body of the champion, dragging it through the sand, furrowing it, to another gate.

"The blonde pet is now safe," said Cabot.

"Here, no human is safe," said Peisistratus.

There was then a sudden roll of drums.

"What is it?" asked Cabot.

"The climax of the festivities," said Peisistratus.

From a far gate, a Kur, laden with chains, goaded by hot irons, was herded, stumbling, toward the center of the sand.

"It is Lord Pyrrhus," said Peisistratus.

"He is ill," speculated Cabot.

"More likely, faint from hunger," said Peisistratus.

The Kur's chains were removed, and it stood alone, in the center of the arena. Despite its size it seemed small there.

"Or, too," said Peisistratus, "it may be weakened from loss of blood."

"I do not understand," said Cabot.

"Drawn from his veins," said Peisistratus. "Thus there is no visible wound."

"Still," said Cabot, "he is a formidable foe. Agamemnon is not without courage to face such an enemy, Kur to Kur."

"Perhaps," said Peisistratus.

"What will be the weapons?"

"None," said Peisistratus.

"None?"

"Hand to hand, tooth to tooth," said Peisistratus.

"He is courageous, indeed," said Cabot.

"Perhaps," said Peisistratus.

"Surely it were better to send a champion against Lord Pyrrhus," said Cabot, "rather than risk himself, a Face of the Nameless One, in the arena."

"Agamemnon himself will do battle, Kur to Kur," said Peisistratus.

"A worthy World Lord," said Cabot. "I salute him."

There was then another thunder of drums, and the tiers turned to face a great part of the wall. It was below and well to the left of where Cabot and Peisistratus were held in their cage.

Two mighty doors there swung open.

The portal might have admitted tharlarion.

For some moments nothing emerged from the gate.

"Ai!" said Cabot, dismayed.

In the portal, now, some eight to ten feet in breadth, some twenty feet in height, there appeared what seemed to be a gigantic, metallic Kur, the limbs, the body, the head, all in proportion, and cunningly devised. The light flashed on the plating and fangs of the immense artificial beast. Suddenly, perhaps on released springs, sharp claws, like curved knives, a foot in length, sprang into view.

"It is a body of Agamemnon," said Peisistratus, dryly.

The huge metallic head, with eyes like fire, turned from side to side, and then halted, and inclined a foot forward and downward, peering at the figure on the sand, Lord Pyrrhus.

It then, slowly, foot by foot, heavy in the sand, approached Lord Pyrrhus, who made no move to flee, or to defend himself.

One of the metallic paws swept out, and the chest and the side of the face of Lord Pyrrhus, symmetrically lacerated, streamed with lines of blood.

Twice more was Lord Pyrrhus struck, and he struggled to retain his feet.

"He is trying to goad him to fight," said Peisistratus.

"Lord Arcesilaus, across the way," said Peisistratus, "is leaving the tiers."

Others, too, were filing out.

Again and again the metallic beast struck Lord Pyrrhus, as though growing more and more frustrated, sometimes flinging him yards, rolling, fur bloody, across the sand. Still Lord Pyrrhus, again and again, staggered to his feet, and made no effort to either flee or defend himself.

"Why does he not fight?" asked Cabot.

"He is fighting," said Peisistratus.

"He is not," said Cabot.

"There is much here you do not understand," said Peisistratus.

"To be sure," said Cabot, angrily, "what could he do?"

"Agamemnon wants him to struggle, to strike even against the metal, to howl, to scratch at the plates, however futilely."

"It is unlike a Kur not to fight," said Cabot, "whatever the odds, however improbable the outcome."

"He is fighting," said Peisistratus.

"Surely not," said Cabot.

"Surely, so," said Peisistratus. "He is defeating Agamemnon by finding such a combat beneath his dignity, by demonstrating his mockery of such an absurd contest, by making it clear to the world that Agamemnon, in assuming this body and arrogating to himself its advantages, has abandoned all pretence to, or claim to, honor."

"I see," said Cabot.

"Lord Pyrrhus strikes a great blow thusly for his cause."

"Many have left the tiers," observed Cabot.

"In disgust," said Peisistratus.

"They were to meet, Kur to Kur," said Cabot.

"But they have not done so," said Peisistratus.

"No," said Cabot.

At this point it seemed that Lord Pyrrhus was minded to attack the gigantic, armored machine which so tormented him. He raised himself from the sand and howled in rage, but then, as though recalling himself to himself, he lowered his arms and retracted his claws.

He stood there in the sand, not moving, his head lifted.

"He is showing his contempt for Agamemnon," said Peisistratus.

The gigantic machine then, as though in fury, closed its jaws about the waist of Lord Pyrrhus and lifted him from the sand and shook him, violently. Even in the tiers one could hear the bones breaking, the muscles and flesh ripping and tearing. Blood streamed from the eyes and mouth. Fur and blood spattered even to the walls of the tiers. And then Agamemnon cast the body from him, and turned about, and left the arena.

Peisistratus and Cabot regarded the remains of Lord Pyrrhus.

"He was Kur," said Cabot.

"And he won," said Peisistratus.

"The tiers are muchly emptied," said Cabot.

"The festivities have ended," said Peisistratus.

"Yes," said Cabot.

"Agamemnon will be dissatisfied with this," said Peisistratus. "He will now be trebly dangerous."

"Why is he not deposed?" asked Cabot.

"He is the Eleventh Face of the Nameless One, Theocrat of the World," said Peisistratus.

"I see," said Cabot.

"Do you salute him now?" inquired Peisistratus.

"No," said Cabot.

Peisistratus pounded on the bars of the cage. "Release us!" he demanded.

A Kur then came, and unlocked the cage, and Cabot and Peisistratus left the tiers.

Chapter, the Twenty-Second:

Paga

"Paga, Master?" asked the slave.

Cabot looked up, blearily.

"Do you not recognize her?" asked Peisistratus.

Cabot rubbed his eyes, and tried to focus.

"No," said Cabot.

"We are keeping her a virgin for you," said Peisistratus.

"A virgin slave?" smiled Cabot.

"White silk," Peisistratus assured him. "Any time you wish her, you may drag her to an alcove, fling her down amidst the chains, fasten her in place, and teach her to writhe."

The slave shuddered.

"Did I not have her before?" asked Cabot.

"No," said Peisistratus.

"I thought I did," said Cabot.

The slave regarded him, angrily. Was she no more than one slave amongst others?

But, yes, that was all she now was.

"No," said Peisistratus, "others, others."

"I do not remember," said Cabot.

"You were drunk," said Peisistratus.

"I had her?" asked Cabot.

"No," said Peisistratus.

"How long have I been here?" asked Cabot.

"You have been with us for three days now, mostly drinking, and sleeping."

"I remember the arena," said Cabot, slowly. "I was not pleased."

"Few were pleased," said Peisistratus. "You drank to forget, too much, too long, but one does not forget."

"No," said Cabot, slowly. "One does not forget."

"Perhaps," said Peisistratus, "it is time to remember."

"No," said Cabot, sullenly.

"Are you not of the Warriors?" asked Peisistratus.

"Once," muttered Cabot.

"Always," said Peisistratus.

Cabot tried to see the slave. "She is not collared, is she?" he asked, puzzled.

"Those are coins," said Peisistratus.

"For each use of her, after the red-silking of her," asked Cabot, "the coins then to her master?"

"She is not a coin girl," said Peisistratus. "If she were, the coin box would be chained about her neck and locked. She would have no access to the coins."

"Why are there strings of coins about her neck?" asked Cabot.

"They are useful, to remind her that she is a slave, that she has economic value, that she can be bought and sold, and such. Let her think of herself as, in effect, similar to the coins, an object, a property."

"I see," said Cabot.

"There are twelve strings of coins, your winnings," said Peisistratus. "From the arena."

"I do not want them," said Cabot.

"Nonetheless, they are yours."

"Why are they about her neck?"

"I told you," said Peisistratus. "I would throw her in with the coins."

"It is she?"

"Yes."

"The brunette?"

"Yes."

The slave straightened her body, and lifted her head, and looked away. She assumed an aspect of irritation, of resignation, of disinterest, of frigidity, of disdain, even of boredom.

She was determined to give masters no pleasure.

How naive she was!

Did she not understand how she could not help but give them pleasure, how even her ruthless, helpless subordination to their will would give them pleasure, and how, if they chose, in their patience, she could be inevitably transformed into a squirming, begging instrument of delight, thereafter to be vulnerably, hopelessly dependent on a man's touch?

"Beware, slave," said Peisistratus.

"Yes, Master," she said, frightened.

"I do not want her," said Cabot.

The slave gasped, and drew back.

She regarded him, startled, disbelievingly.

Could a man not want her?

She drew back, further. Her assumed mien of boredom, of disinterest, and such, was now well vanished. She now seemed confused, frightened, disbelieving. How could this be? Had she heard aright? She was kneeling, she, who, quite possibly, had regarded herself as the most beautiful woman she had ever seen, she who had known herself excruciatingly desired, who had taken great pleasure in leading males on, and tormenting them, and then rejecting them, was now kneeling before a male, utterly vulnerable, she now a slave, at the mercy of masters, strings of coins about her throat, and he had not cried out with pleasure at the prospect of her use, had not seized her by the hair and drawn her rudely, instantly, to the privacy of one of the small, enclosed, lamp-lit alcoves.

Was she lacking, was she not attractive?

Was she not such that she could make men her toys?

Or was it now that she was the toy, with whom men might choose to play, or not to play?

She seemed uncomprehending. Momentarily she was angry. Then she was afraid, terribly afraid.

She was now a slave, and helpless. What if she was not wanted? What would be done with her? Too, she now knew that her beauty, in this place, was not that unusual. Here, she was but one slave amongst others.

Slaves are chosen for their beauty, you see. The collars on their necks are not easily purchased.

Too, she was here before a man, and men, such as she had while on Earth met only in her dreams, men of will, and force, men before whom such as she, she realized, could be but a slave.

But he had not wanted her?

She wanted to be wanted.

She must be wanted!

She needed to be wanted!

She knew that she, if necessary, would beg to be wanted!

Despite her pretences from Earth, you see, clung to hitherto so futilely, she was now muchly different from what she had been.

Even in her virginal state, her belly was muchly stirred. Effusions of desire, of readiness, of desires to please, in this so unnatural, and yet so natural, a place, had begun to afflict her with intimations of submission and ecstasy.

Here, in this place, her feigning, her pretenses of bravado, her postures of indifference, and such, suddenly seemed pointless and absurd, even to her.

And what if masters chose not to accept them?

Here she was not as she had been on Earth.

These men would not be likely to be patient with her.

Here she found herself a woman, and a slave, amongst true men.

And she knew such men would expect much of a slave.

And she must strive desperately to please them!

How paradoxical it all seemed to her. Here, where her body was subject to shackles, she found her needs, long denied and desperately, even fearfully, suppressed, unshackled. Here they were allowed to emerge, and run free, into the daylight of nature. Here she could be a joyful, shameless animal, which, as a slave she was.

Indeed, those needs must emerge.

They could be commanded forth.

Men would have it so.

They would have her the helpless victim of her needs, so much then at their imperious mercy.

And what of these new desires, such remarkable consequences of the liberation of her deepest self?

Such desires!

Keen, insistent, irresistible, overwhelming desires!

How like torture, and ecstasy, they were!

Already she sensed she could become their prisoner, as much as though weighty chains had been locked upon her small, fair limbs.

Well would she be enshackled in them! How much they would place her at the mercy of masters!

For the first time in her life, other than in the joy of her dreams, she understood how a woman could kneel before a man, and place her lips tenderly, humbly, gratefully, submissively, to his feet, thanking him for his collar and the fulfillment he granted to her.

Too, she suspected how she, bound, might understand, and gratefully welcome, even the stroke of the whip, unfit for free women, but confirming for her as it would her status as object and property, as something subject to the whip, as something owned by her master.

Already, you see, she had begun to suspect, and well, what it might be, to be a woman, and a slave.

And, as the Priest-Kings, in their cruel wisdom, had chosen her for her desirability, and particularly to a man such as Cabot, indeed, had chosen her to be irresistible to him, so, too, in her way, she had been matched to Cabot, as slave to master, that he would be irresistible to her.

And now, as she knelt helpless before him, the choice wholly his, he had not accepted her. He had denied her acquisition.

She, however incomprehensibly, had been rejected! Tears of shock, of amazement, of confusion, of fear, of misery, of helplessness, sprang to her eyes, stung them, filled them, and ran down her cheeks.

"I fear you have distressed her," said Peisistratus.

Cabot shrugged. What, after all, are the feelings of a slave?

"Stop crying," said Peisistratus to the slave.

"Yes, Master," sobbed the slave.

"Would you rather I had strung the coins on a post?" asked Peisistratus.

"Do whatever you want with them," said Cabot, slowly.

"You could kill yourself, drinking like this," said Peisistratus. "Men have."

"What would it matter?" said Cabot.

"It might matter much," said Peisistratus.

"Is it truly her?" asked Cabot, trying to focus on the slave.

"We have had a collar prepared for her," said Peisistratus. "The legend says 'I am the property of Tarl Cabot'."

"I do not want her," muttered Cabot.

The girl stifled a sob.

"If unclaimed," said Peisistratus, "she must be disposed of, and soon."

It seemed the girl would cry out, or speak, but she remained silent. Several times she had been switched for speaking without permission.

It is one of the first things a slave learns, that it is not always permitted to her to speak, when and as she wishes.

She is slave.

"Let another claim her," said Cabot, sullenly.

"None will have her," said Peisistratus.

"Is she such a tharlarion?" asked Cabot.

"Her hair is too short," said Peisistratus.

"It is short," said Cabot, leaning forward.

"Set the goblet aside," said Peisistratus to the kneeling slave. "Split your knees, more widely! Straighten your back!"

"Yes, Master!" she said.

"Quickly, slut!" he snapped. "More quickly!"

"Yes, Master!" she wept.

"Move the coins to the side, with both hands," said Peisistratus, "so that we may examine your breasts."

"Yes, Master!" she sobbed.

"She is not bad," said Peisistratus.

"Perhaps not," granted Cabot.

"I think," said Peisistratus, "that few would confuse her with a tharlarion."

"I want the paga," said Cabot. "Paga!"

"Do you wish to be whipped?" Peisistratus asked the distressed, trembling slave.

"No, no!" she cried. It seemed clear she had felt the whip.

"Stand, pose!" he snapped.

Instantly the slave complied. It seemed that she had learned something of what it was to be a slave.

Such as she, slaves, obey instantly, unquestioningly. They are slave.

She had obviously been taught something of what it was to be a female slave.

Certainly she posed well.

Perhaps she had so posed in her dreams.

"Enough," said Peisistratus.

"Yes, Master," she said, and then stood before masters, waiting to be returned to position.

"She seems to understand something of her body," said Cabot.

"Use her," said Peisistratus.

"No," said Cabot, shaking his head, slowly.

"Men would pay good money for her," said Peisistratus. "Perhaps as much as two silver tarsks."

"Keep her," said Cabot.

"She is a well-curved slut," said Peisistratus.

"So, too, are thousands of others," said Cabot.

"I thought she might be special to you," said Peisistratus.

"No," said Cabot.

"As I understand it," said Peisistratus, "from Arcesilaus, and others, she was enclosed with you on the Prison Moon."

"That is true," said Cabot.

"Surely that was no mere happenstance. She would have been selected for you, selected for you by Priest-Kings, and doubtless with great care, with all their shrewdness, and science, selected to be irresistible to you, a slut of your dreams, that you might be tempted from your honor."

"Perhaps," said Cabot, angrily.

"The Priest-Kings are cruel," said Peisistratus.

"True," said Cabot.

"She is English, is she not?"

"Yes."

"Intelligent, highly educated, and such?"

"Yes."

"Nicely curved?"

"Doubtless."

"And extremely beautiful?"

"Perhaps."

"She is, too, as I understand it, a self-confessed slave."

"Yes," said Cabot, "the words were spoken on the Prison Moon itself."

"Here," said Peisistratus, "you may have her for nothing. She is goods, and honor, I assure you, is no longer in the least involved."

"True," said Cabot.

"So take her," said Peisistratus.

"No," said Cabot.

"Surely you want her in your arms," said Peisistratus.

Cabot shook his head.

"Surely you want her at your feet, on her belly, licking and kissing, whimpering, begging," said Peisistratus.

"She is a vain, cold, haughty bitch," said Cabot.

"No, Master!" wept the slave, inadvertently.

Gone surely then was her facade of disdain, of boredom, and such.

She was then much alive, and vulnerable.

She then, quickly, fearfully, put her head down, doubtless fearing to be beaten.

"Look up, slut," said Peisistratus.

The slave lifted her head.

"See that throat, and those features," said Peisistratus. "Perhaps two and a half silver tarsks?"

It is difficult to speculate on these matters, but it seems clear she was a beauty, given the limitations of her species. To be sure, she was fresh to her bondage, had received little training, and knew little, at that time, of a slave's major concern, that of serving and pleasing, selflessly, intimately and inordinately, the males of her species.

"Keep her," said Cabot.

"To be sure," mused Peisistratus. "Doubtless the slave fires have not yet been kindled in that lovely little belly."

"May I speak, Master?" begged the slave.

Peisistratus nodded.

"I fear, Master," she said, "I already feel such fires."

"And when did this first come about?" inquired Peisistratus.

"On the Prison Moon," she said, softly, "when first I acknowledged myself—explicitly, publicly—slave."

"You do not yet know what it is to feel slave fire," said Peisistratus.

"Yes, Master," she whispered.

"Have the other girls taught you nothing of interesting men?" asked Peisistratus.

"A little, Master," she said, shyly, not meeting his eyes.

"You posed well," he said.

"Thank you, Master," she whispered.

"Now," he said, "we shall see if you can dance."

"Please, no, Master!" she wept, suddenly, frightened.

Peisistratus gestured to the musicians, who reached for their instruments.

"No, Master, please!" she cried. "I do not know how to dance!"

"All women know how to dance," said Peisistratus. "Make certain the coins jangle well."

"Please, no, Master!" she wept.

"She is a pretty slut," said Peisistratus.

"I want paga," said Cabot, angrily.

Peisistratus gestured to the musicians, and they touched memories of Gor, of her rivers and lakes, her trails, her valleys and mountains.

"Dance!" commanded Peisistratus.

And the slave danced, as she could, danced for fear of the whip, for fear of her life, danced for the pleasure of men, hoping to please them, hoping that they might see how beautiful and desirable she was, and would be kind to her, and then for the sudden desperation of her awakened needs, and danced as what she was, a slave.

"Enough," said Peisistratus.

The musicians put aside their instruments, and the slave had collapsed, sobbing, to the floor.

"You are right," said Peisistratus. "She is not much good."

The slave, prostrate, wept. Her small body had tried to please. Surely they knew she was not a dancer, not a trained dancer, one whose smallest, subtlest motions might drive a man mad with desire. The coins, dangling from her throat, made a tiny sound, on the flooring.

"Paga," said Cabot.

"You have had too much," said Peisistratus.

"Paga," said Cabot.

"Paga," repeated Peisistratus, summoning the slave with a gesture.

Quickly, summoned, she hurried to the small table, knelt, and retrieved the goblet.

"You cannot even see her clearly, can you?" asked Peisistratus.

Doubtless the form of the slave, bedecked with coins, her only garment, swam before his eyes.

"It is truly she?" said Cabot, uncertainly.

"Yes," said Peisistratus.

"Why have none claimed her?"

"I have forbidden it," said Peisistratus. "I have given the orders."

"Rescind them," said Cabot.

"No," said Peisistratus.

"Why not?"

"There are the quotas," he said. "She is unclaimed."

"Surely you understand my position here," said Cabot. "I can accept no slave."

"Your position, as I understand it," said Peisistratus, in English, "is that you could become master of human Gor, that you could have armies, palaces, riches, hundreds of slaves."

"And she is part of the temptation, is she not?" asked Cabot.

"Perhaps," said Peisistratus.

"I want paga," said Cabot.

"It is a matter of honor, is it not?" inquired Peisistratus.

"There is nothing to be done," said Cabot. "There is the cage. It is like the arena."

"I am to inform Agamemnon that you decline his offer?"

"You may do whatever you wish," said Cabot.

"Drink no more, not now," said Peisistratus.

"Paga!" demanded Cabot.

"Remember the arena," said Peisistratus.

"Paga!" thundered Cabot, in fury.

Swiftly the slave pressed the goblet about her body, as she had been taught, associating the metallic, rigid cruelty of the goblet and the fire of the drink with the softness, the readiness, the warmth, and the desirability of her body, in this way making it clear that both goods were proffered, both placed at the disposal of the master, both the drink and the female. And the girl inadvertently gasped, startled, as the metal rim pressed into her belly, bespeaking the dominion to which she was subject, and she looked down into the swirling liquid in the cup, and Peisistratus smiled, for did not the fire in the goblet in its way stand token for another fire, and might she not suspect this, that which might burn in the grasping, liquid softness of a slave's belly?

The girl then lifted the goblet to her lips and kissed it slowly, humbly, regarding Cabot over its rim, and then she put down her head between her extended arms, and offered him the goblet.

"No," begged Peisistratus.

Cabot reached out, and clutched at the goblet, and some paga spilled, to the right thigh of the slave.

"How do you choose to die?" asked Peisistratus. "One who herds tarsk would not choose to die so."

"It does not matter," said Cabot. "There is nothing to be done."

"You are of the Warriors," said Peisistratus.

"Once," said Cabot.

"Still," said Peisistratus.

"There is nothing to be done."

"Look into the paga," said Peisistratus. "Do you like what you see there?"

"No," said Cabot.

"Is that you?"

"Yes."

"No," said Peisistratus. "The paga lies."

"How can it lie?" asked Cabot.

"It deceives you, it betrays you."

"Paga can betray no one," said Cabot, patiently, forming the words very slowly.

"No," said Peisistratus, "but it can show you one who betrays himself."

"I am he," said Cabot, slowly.

"You are he," said Peisistratus. "Now swirl the paga, and look again into it."

Cabot moved the fluid in the goblet, and peered into it. One supposes, in that troubled, swirling fluid, there was nothing to be seen, other perhaps than reflections, rivulets, small currents.

"What now do you see?" inquired Peisistratus.

"The arena," said Cabot, slowly.

"Then you have not forgotten it?"

"No," said Cabot. "I have not forgotten it."

He then slowly, carefully, poured the paga unto the table, and it ran from the table to the floor.

"Slut," said Peisistratus.

"Yes, Master?"

"Get out!"

"Yes, Master," cried the slave, and rose up, and, with a jangle of coins, fled from the table.

Cabot then cast the goblet from him, and it clattered on the flooring, several feet away, and rolled to the side.

He then slumped down, to the side of the table.

"Let him sleep," said Peisistratus to one of his men.

Chapter, the Twenty-Third:

What Occurred in a Glade

The grass was long and soft in the area, abundant, and green and flowing, in the soft wind.

Cabot stirred.

He was no longer in the Pleasure Cylinder.

He did not open his eyes. He felt the weight of the iron on his limbs, on his wrists and ankles.

He heard a sound of chain. Something was bending over him. He felt soft lips press against his lips. She remembered that, he thought—from near the shuttle lock.

He opened his eyes, and looked into blue eyes. She drew back a little, some inches from him.

She had been brushed and combed, washed and perfumed. She was worthy of a Ubar's pleasure garden, but he was not a Ubar.

He thrust her to the side, as he could, and she whimpered, puzzled, irritably.

He then sat up, and regarded her, his fellow prisoner, his right wrist shackled to her left, his left to her right, and so, too, with their ankles.

He shook the chains, angrily, and she cried out, in pain, for this had hurt her.

Breeding shackles, he thought. Breeding shackles!

She tried to approach him, again, and he thrust her back.

"You are a slave," he said.

"Certainly not!" she exclaimed.

"Then you are a pet, that of Grendel."

"No," she said, "I have been taken from him."

"Whose pet, then, are you?" he asked.

"I am not a pet," she said.

"Where is your collar?" he asked.

"I have no collar," she said, angrily. "I am not a pet."

"What then are you?" he asked.

"I am a free woman," she said.

"A free woman, shackled," he said.

"Yes!" she said.

"Have you been named?" he asked.

"I have chosen my name," she said. "I call myself 'Ubara'."

"That is not a name," he said. "It is a title."

"Does it not mean Great Woman, Magnificent Woman, Most Important of Women, such things?"

"Your Gorean is still lacking," he said.

"It suggests such things, does it not?" she inquired.

"Perhaps," he said.

"Then I am 'Ubara,'" she said.

"Many a Ubara," said he, "conquered, stripped, learns to belly, and lick and kiss, as the most abject of slaves."

"Then what should my name be?" she asked.

"You wish a noble, refined, dignified, exalted, priceless name, do you not?"

"Surely," she said.

"Then," said he, "what of 'Bina'?"

"Good," she said. "I am Bina!"

He thought that would be a good name for taking her off an auction block. 'Bina', in Gorean, is a common word for slave beads, usually of colored wood, with which a low slave might be permitted to bedeck herself. It is also a not uncommon name for a low slave.

She smiled, satisfied, arrogantly.

He, too, smiled, though, one supposes, at her arrogance.

"We have been chained together," he observed, "in this soft, pleasant place. And to the side I see some wine, it seems, some larmas, some grapes, some wedges of soft bread."

"We are to breed," she said.

"Why?" he asked.

"It is the will of our superiors," she said.

"They are not my superiors," he said.

"You need not fear for your honor," she said, "for I am acquiescent, and will authorize your touch."

"You are generous," he said. "But why would you do this?"

"It is the will of the superiors," she said.

"I see," he said.

"I know little of these things," she said, "of breeding, and such, but even were I not acquiescent, I gather, you might, eventually, do your will upon me, in some fashion or another."

"Quite possibly," he said. "Eventually. I am only human."

"I see," she said.

"Come to my arms," he said.

She approached him, and he enfolded her in his arms. He held her so, for a few moments. Then suddenly, surprised, she said, "Oh," and trembled.

"Is anything wrong?" he inquired.

"No," she said. "It is pleasant," she said.

Then she rubbed against him.

He touched her.

"Oh!" she said, startled.

"You are a hot little animal," he said, pleased.

"I do not understand these feelings," she said.

He then pressed her back.

She tried to approach him, again, but, again, he pressed her back.

"I do not understand," she said.

"Grendel," he said, "loves you, but you probably do not even understand that. He risked his life in the arena, for you, against great odds."

"It was his will to do so," she said. "He is a monster. Hold me, again!"

But he thrust her back, angrily.

"Often you have made him suffer," said Cabot.

"Certainly!"

"I gather you never were acquiescent with him, so to speak, nor did you, so to speak, authorize his touch."

How tragically are men at the mercy of free women, he thought, at the mercy of their vanity, their whims, their petty tempers, their cruelty, and petulance. How understandable that they make them slaves, and then do with them as they please. And how interesting that the women, brought then to their place in nature, at the feet of men, fulfilled and happy, thrive in their collars. Unlike most free women they are, in their way, muchly honored, for they have been found worthy of mastering, worthy of being owned. And they will strive to be good slaves, and, indeed, what choice have they, and this, too, pleases them, to have no choice.

"Certainly not," she said. "He is not Kur, he is not human. He is a malformed beast."

"And did he not, with the whip, see to it that you groomed him, carefully and assiduously?"

"Certainly not," she said.

"He never touched you, never disciplined you?"

"Certainly not," she said.

"But in the arena, the leash, your posture."

"Show," she said, "for the crowds, otherwise they might have swarmed onto the sand and torn us both to pieces."

"He loves you," said Cabot.

"That is his foolishness," she said.

"Yes," said Cabot, "that is his foolishness."

"I despise him," she said. "I defied his will. I belittled him, in public. I made him suffer, each day and night."

"And yet," said Cabot, "he loves you."

"He is a fool," she said.

"I think so," said Cabot, "a champion in the arena, mighty and dangerous, but a fool elsewhere, in the small, soft hands of a woman."

"I made him suffer," she said.

"Why?" asked Cabot.

"It pleased me," she said. "He is a beast. Now touch me, again, as you did!"

"You demand it?" he asked.

"Yes!" she said.

"No," said Cabot.

She tried, again, to approach, to thrust her body against him, but he, again, thrust her back, to the ends of the chains.

He must resist the beauty of her, the softness of her, the perfume of her, so heady, so like strong drink, the warmth of her eager, excited body.

"You must complete your touching of me," she said. "You have begun strange things in me. I do not understand them. Continue! Continue!"

"You are a hot little beast," he said.

It occurred to him that it was doubtless not an accident that she had been enclosed in the container with him, as well as the brunette.

Doubtless the Priest-Kings had addressed themselves to these matters with almost mathematical precision.

"Continue!" she demanded.

"Perhaps, now, you may suffer, a little."

"We must breed!" she cried.

"Why?" he asked.

"It is the will of our superiors!"

"They are not my superiors," he said.

"We must breed!" she cried. "If we do not breed," she said, "they will send me to the cattle pens!"

"At least you will go as a free woman," he said.

"Fool!" she cried.

"Why do they wish us to breed?" inquired Cabot.

"They want a killer human for the arena," she said, "another killer human."

"I see," said Cabot

"Have me!" she cried.

"I breed as I wish," said Cabot, "not as others wish."

"You have displeased Agamemnon," she cried. "You will be done with in horror, put to death in unspeakable ways."

"Not permitted to die in the arena?"

"Certainly not, not with honor, but in some lengthy, degraded fashion, one fit to satisfy the affronted pride of Agamemnon."

"I could not in honor do his will," said Cabot.

"Fool, fool, fool!" she wept.

"Yes," said Cabot, "but a fool for honor is a fool with honor, and better such a fool than Agamemnon in all his shrewdness and cunning, in all his wisdom and astuteness."

"I do not understand you!" she screamed. "You are mad!" she wept. "Mad! Mad! Were I a collared slave, beaten and cast to your feet, you would use me!"

"Doubtless," said Cabot, "if she had imbibed her slave wine. It is what they are for."

"I do not want to go to the cattle pens!" she cried.

"I do not think that would happen," said Cabot. "They would

be fools to send you to the pens. Rather they would chain you in the barracks, where you might be paired, under Kur supervision, with a succession of killer humans. They do not need me."

"You have done something to me," she wept. "You have begun something in me! I do not understand it! I have never had feelings like this! I am in misery!"

"You are aroused," said Cabot. "You do not know what is going on in your body, but there is a simple explanation. You are in heat, and apparently considerably so. It is all very natural. And it is a tribute to your health, to your vitality."

"I cannot stand it!" she said.

"Such heat, and even greater heat, is quite common amongst slaves," he said.

"I am not a slave!" she said.

"But then, of course, slave fires have been set in their bellies."

"I am not a slave!"

"Certainly not," he said.

"I cannot stand it!" she said.

"Doubtless it is unpleasant," said Cabot. "Sometimes slaves whine, and shriek, and scream in need, in their cages, before their sales."

It is common to deprive red-silk slaves of the touch of men before their sales, sometimes for days. How eager are they then to ascend the block in their chains. How they extend their small, chained wrists piteously to the crowd, begging to be purchased, to be granted a male caress. In this way, their frustrated appetition exhibited as clearly and obviously as their bared beauty, for who would buy a woman clothed, is their price often improved.

"I am not a slave!" she cried.

"Of course not," he said. "Men, too, of course, untamed men, virile men, can know such deprivation and need, as well. To be sure, they have a considerable advantage, as they may simply make use of slaves, in the taverns, and such."

"I am not a slave!"

"Of course not," said Cabot.

"I am chained to you, closely, inseparably, helplessly, in breeding shackles, in breeding shackles!" she wept. "Take me! Use me!"

Cabot regarded her.

"Take me!" she screamed. "Use me!"

"Do not," said a voice.

Cabot turned, and found himself facing Grendel.

"Why have you come?" asked Cabot.

"To kill you," said Grendel.

Chapter, the Twenty-Fourth:

What Occurred Later in the Glade

"Then do so," said Cabot, angrily.

"Have you touched her?" asked Grendel.

"Certainly," said Cabot, "and well."

Grendel's large body trembled with rage.

"Here is my throat," said Cabot, bearing his throat. "Be quick!"

"You are chained," said Grendel.

"Thus you have less to fear," said Cabot.

"I will not kill a man in chains," said Grendel. "A human could do that."

"You are human!" said Cabot.

"No," he said, "I am Kur."

"You are not!" screamed the blonde. "You are human, only human!"

"Did he hurt you?" asked Grendel, his voice gentle, anomalous in such a form.

"Yes, yes!" screamed the blonde. "He hurt me, cruelly, viciously, terribly!"

"Examine her body," said Cabot, "that you may see the bruises, the discolorings, the lacerations."

"Do not look at me!" screamed the blonde.

"I see no such marks," said Grendel, puzzled.

"It is easy to lie, once one is speeched," said Cabot.

"Kill him!" screamed the blonde, shaking her chains, pointing at Cabot. "Kill him!"

"Obey your pet," said Cabot.

"You do not love him?" asked Grendel.

"Kill him!" she screamed.

"Obey your pet," said Cabot.

"She is not my pet," said Grendel. "She was taken from me, by the command of the Eleventh face of the Nameless One, Agamemnon, Theocrat of the World."

"Then she is his pet," said Cabot.

"No!" cried the blonde. "I am a free woman! It was so said, and said by him, he himself, the Eleventh Face of the Nameless One, Agamemnon, Theocrat of the World!"

"Then how are you here?" asked Cabot.

"By his will!" she screamed. "We are all owned, even the free!"

"I am not owned," said Grendel.

"Nor I," said Cabot.

"Kill him!" she cried, pointing at Cabot.

"Do you not love her?" asked Grendel.

"No," said Cabot.

"Kill him!" pleaded the blonde.

Grendel drew forth a key from his harness. "I killed for this," he said. "I am now outlaw in the world."

He thrust the key into the shackles of the blonde and Cabot, freeing her first, then Cabot.

"I am not your enemy," said Cabot.

"The common enemy," said Grendel, "is Agamemnon. Several of us know this."

The blonde had retreated several feet, standing back in the grass. "Bring me clothing!" she demanded, "robes, regalia!"

Grendel regarded her.

"I am a free woman!" she screamed.

But she was, of course, as naked as a pet, or slave.

Grendel returned his attention to Cabot.

Cabot rubbed his wrists, and looked up at Grendel, like a boulder before him. "Now, I am free of chains," he said, "and you may kill me."

"Yes, kill him!" called the blonde.

"It would be better if I did so," said Grendel to Cabot, "for Agamemnon has conceived a thousand variations of a thousand deaths for you."

"Do then as you wish," said Cabot, angrily.

"We are all doomed," said Grendel.

"Not I, not I!" screamed the blonde.

"Perhaps not you," said Grendel. "There may be a way to save you."

"You should not have interfered!" cried the blonde.

"I thought he would take you from me, that you were lovers," said Grendel.

"No," said Cabot.

"—I love her," said Grendel.

"That is known to me," said Cabot.

"Kill him," called the blonde. "Prove you love me! If you love me, kill him! Kill him, for me!"

"Because he does not love you?" said Grendel.

She was silent, furious.

"Thousands do not love you," said Grendel. "Shall I kill them all?"

"I hate you!" she screamed.

"I would that I could hate you," said Grendel, "but I cannot. It would be easy to tear your nasty, hateful, lying head from your shoulders, but I cannot, nor do I wish to do so."

"You are bringing us all to death!" she said.

"I could not let him have you," he said.

"You will never have me!" she screamed.

"If you could stop me from loving you," said Grendel, "you would have succeeded, long ago."

"Do not love her," said Cabot.

"I do," said Grendel. "I must."

"She is not worth your love," said Cabot.

"Not worth the love of a beast!" she scoffed.

"No," said Cabot. "Not worth the love even of a beast."

"That is what I am," said Grendel

"You are less a beast than she," said Cabot.

"I am beautiful!" she cried. "I am beautiful!"

"Yes," said Cabot, "you are beautiful."

"I am Bina," she cried, proudly. "I am Bina!"

Grendel lifted his head, and regarded her, puzzled.

"Bina!" she insisted.

"As you will," said Grendel.

"And Grendel," she cried, "is the name of a monster!"

"So I am given to understand," said he.

"It was a joke," said Cabot. "Choose another name."

"I am Grendel," he said.

"As you will," said Cabot.

"You came to kill him," said the blonde. "Do it!"

"She speaks boldly for a pet, does she not?" said Cabot.

"She is not a pet," said Grendel.

"I am a free woman!" said the blonde.

"She is a hot little slut," said Cabot. "Why do you not collar her, put her to your feet, lash her, and keep her as a slave?"

Grendel regarded him, aghast.

"She might then be good for something," said Cabot. "As a free woman she is a bother. As a slave she might be pleasant in her chains. I am confident she would squirm well."

"Beast! Beast!" she cried.

"Unthinkable," said Grendel.

"Not really," said Cabot. He looked about. "Look," he said, "there is food here, and some wine. I am hungry. Let us share this small repast."

"I killed for the key," said Grendel. "Guards will discover the body. Shortly thereafter they will come to this place."

"The bread is good," said Cabot, and he seized up a handful of grapes, as well, from the dish on the grass.

"Strange things are going on in the world," said Grendel.

"The wine, too," said Cabot, wiping his mouth. "What strange things?"

"The fleet has departed," said Grendel.

"The invasion of Gor?" said Cabot, suddenly.

"No," said Grendel. "It is other than that."

"War?"

"I fear so," said Grendel.

"Amongst the worlds?"

"Between two, I think," said Grendel.

"This, and some other?"

"This world would take Gor for itself," said Grendel. "Another would oppose this unilateral seizure of a prize to be reserved for all. Agamemnon, I suspect, will strike first, to rid himself of possible rivals."

"War of Kur upon Kur?"

"There is a history of such things, a long and bloody history," said Grendel.

"Strange," said Cabot.

"And do not humans war upon humans?"

"Yes," said Cabot.

"Is it then so strange?"

"No," said Cabot, thoughtfully. "It is not so strange."

"Serve me," said the blonde to Grendel, and he bent to fetch some wine, some grapes, some bread for her.

He waited upon her, humbly.

She sat on the grass, and fed. "You need not kill him," she informed Grendel. "You are a champion. He is not worth your stroke."

"She demeans me," smiled Cabot.

"And me," said Grendel. "She demeans all whom she does not fear."

"Look upon her," said Cabot, "and think collar."

"Is that how you look upon women?" inquired Grendel.

"Often, if I find them of interest," said Cabot. The thought crossed his mind of the brunette, whom he clearly found of interest.

"She is a free woman," said Grendel.

"So, too, once," said Cabot, "were most slaves."

"Bring me wine," said the blonde, to Grendel, and he purveyed to her again the flask.

"I thought pets were not permitted wine," said Cabot.

"I am not a pet," she snapped.

Slaves are sometimes permitted wine, if they beg prettily enough for it. The slave is dependent on the master for all things, including her food. The master takes the first bite of shared food; if he should be seated, say, on a bench or chair, the slave commonly eats at his feet, kneeling beside him; sometimes she is fed by hand, particularly the first bites of food; sometimes she must eat from dishes on the floor, her head down, on all fours.

"Bread," said the blonde, and it was fetched for her, again, by the shambling hulk of Grendel.

"How came you here?" asked Grendel.

"I was drunk, in the Pleasure Cylinder," said Cabot, bitterly. "Peisistratus betrayed me. I awakened in the breeding shackles."

"You would decline the offer of Agamemnon, to arm and lead the humans of Earth against the Sardar," said Grendel.

"Certainly," said Cabot.

"Honor?"

"Certainly," said Cabot.

"How then," asked Grendel, "were you betrayed by Peisistratus?"

"I was given no opportunity to flee, to fight," said Cabot.

"Fruitless opportunities," said Grendel. "Would you wish Peisistratus to risk his own life, and that of his men, to abet a brief, fruitless escape, a gesture of meaningless defiance, on your part?"

"He is my enemy," said Cabot.

"No," said Grendel.

"He is the human of Agamemnon," said Cabot.

"He is his own human," said Grendel, "and one of us."

Cabot looked at him, puzzled.

"Those who would overthrow Agamemnon," said Grendel. "As was Lord Pyrrhus, and as is Lord Arcesilaus."

The blonde looked at him, suddenly.

"You spoke unwisely, friend Grendel," said Cabot. "She has heard, and to save her own skin, she will betray you, and Peisistratus, and Arcesilaus."

"No," said the blonde. "No, no!"

"She is speeched," said Cabot, "and speech enables betrayal."

Grendel turned slowly to regard the blonde.

"No!" she said. "I will not speak. And I heard nothing, nothing!"

"Secrets," said Cabot, "are lightly revealed by free women."

"Do not fear," said Grendel to the blonde. "I will not harm you. Though you betray me to sleen or tharlarion, to a hundred deaths, I will not harm you."

"I wish to go to Gor," she said. "I will be safe there. I will be rich there! I will win my way with beauty, for I am beautiful and men will do as I bid them. On Gor I will be Ubara!"

"On Gor," said Cabot, "beauty is found more often on the chain of taverners than on the thrones of states."

"I am not so stupid as to be a slave," she said.

"Slaves," said Cabot, "are commonly chosen not only for their beauty but for their intelligence. High intelligence much improves a woman's price on the slave block."

This is, of course, not surprising, for the higher a woman's intelligence, provided it be conjoined with profound feminine needs, the better the slave.

"I will not tell," she said.

"It would be well to take precautions," said Cabot.

"They will not be necessary," she said.

"Perhaps we could arrange ticket for you," said Cabot, "on the next transport to Gor."

"Do so!" she said.

"That is a joke," said Cabot.

At that point, in the distance, a bar began to ring, and its ringing was taken up by other bars, and the cylinder itself seemed to ring.

"They have found the body," said Grendel, "that of he from whom I obtained the key to your chains, he who managed the sheds in which the breeding shackles are stored."

"I shall wish you well then," said Cabot, "for we must go our diverse ways."

"You have plans?"

"Of course."

"I think, too," said Grendel, "that that is best, for if you are not with us, as though we were conspirators, or in league, I may purchase her life."

"How so?" asked Cabot.

"They will kill me," said Grendel, "or capture and destroy me, but if she appears innocent in all this she may be spared."

"And how shall she appear innocent?" asked Cabot.

"I have brought rope for the purpose," said Grendel.

"Excellent," said Cabot. "She will then appear your innocent, hapless prisoner."

"That is what I would be!" she cried.

"Yes," said Grendel.

"Rope me!" she cried.

Grendel turned about, and went some feet away, in the grass.

"You have never felt ropes, have you?" asked Cabot.

"No!" she snapped.

"You will find the experience interesting," he said, "the constricting, enwrapped coils tightened on your body, the specialness of the consequent sensations, they enveloping you, the feeling of being utterly helpless, the knowledge that you are then totally at another's mercy, and such."

"He will do my bidding!" she said.

"But he need not," said Cabot.

She turned white, and trembled.

In a moment Grendel had returned, with several light coils of rope. Of these supple circlets he freed some loops.

"Do not rope me!" she said, suddenly.

"It will be better," said Grendel.

"Then let him rope me!" she cried, pointing at Cabot.

She is a clever little she-sleen, thought Cabot. She has a sense of what may be done. She is still aroused. In my ropes, she senses she may be irresistible to me. And perhaps she might be! All men desire absolute power over a woman, and all women desire to be in the absolute power of a given man, one to whom they long to yield, one who will see her as a helpless, possessed female, and one in whose ropes she well realizes herself such, no more than that, a helpless, possessed female, to be done with uncompromisingly as he pleases, and one who will see to it that she yields well. The female longs to submit, and the male to master.

"Have him rope me!" she said to Grendel.

How delicious and perfect to the male is the female whom he finds in his bonds!

How beautiful she is!

And the bonds need not be of cord, nor of metal or leather, of such things. Ideally they are the bonds of slavery itself.

That is how the female is in his power, truly and perfectly, and she knows herself such, in every fiber of her well-curved, embonded being.

"Now!" she cried.

She is so clever, thought Cabot. So very clever!

Grendel looked at Cabot, loops of rope dangling from one paw.

"No," said Cabot. "Rope her."

"No!" she cried, but already the loops were being put about her, and drawn tight, pinning her small, lovely arms to her sides.

"Forgive me," Grendel begged her.

"Make them tighter," said Cabot.

"Oh!" she cried, squirming, regarding Cabot with fury.

"Now," said Cabot, "look upon her. She is yours."

"Yes," said Grendel.

"Beast!" she screamed at Cabot.

She was now well swathed with rope.

"Now make her a leash, and draw her away, behind you," said Cabot.

"Beast, beast!" she screamed at Cabot.

A length of rope was knotted about her throat.

"In the arena," said Cabot, "two Kur females fought, competing for the seed of a champion, and the bloodied winner was roped and led away, as might have been nothing, a mere female slave, and was joyful, that the seeding would be hers."

"So it is often done," said Grendel.

"Do not seed me!" cried the blonde.

"The bars have rung," said Cabot.

"Yes," said Grendel, looking about, his ears lifted.

"Lead her away," said Cabot. "Lead your pet away."

"I am not a pet!" she said. "I am a free woman!"

"A free woman, on a rope," said Cabot.

"What will be done with me?" she begged.

"If you are fortunate," said Cabot, "you will be sent to the Pleasure Cylinder, to be branded and collared, and learn to please men."

"Never!" she cried.

"Or perhaps you will be sent, chained, on a slave ship, to be sold in the markets of Gor."

"No!" she cried.

"Be of good cheer," said Cabot. "You might bring a good price, and obtain a well-to-do master."

"I, a slave? Never a slave! Not I!"

"A collar is too good for you," said Cabot.

"Beast!" she hissed.

"Do not fret, small, soft one," said Grendel. "And let us hope these coarse encirclements, doubtless so embarrassing you, and so discomforting you, will dissociate you from my crime. When you are found as you are, bound and helpless, it is possible your life may be spared."

Cabot was not sure of this, as the Kur concept of justice is latitudinal, and often deep, and guilt is seldom conceived of as an individual thing, but rather as a generic plague which must be ruthlessly extirpated. Should friends not have dissuaded the evildoer from his actions? Should they not have anticipated it, and intervened? Should they not have suspected it, and reported its likelihood to authorities? Is there not a festering hotbed of criminal potentiality somewhere to be rooted out, from which soil another such deed might spring? And should not one who carelessly provided the provocation for a deed, say, a temptress, not suffer for her role in the matter, as well? And should one risk a repetition of the crime, or a similar crime? Group guilt, of course, is a concept not unknown, as I understand it, in many Earth societies, as well, families and descendents being punished even for deeds done long ago, perhaps centuries ago. Are not even peoples accountable, down to dozens of generations?

The blonde looked wildly at Cabot.

She knew, as well as he, that her innocence, such as it was, might well be insufficient to purchase her life.

Then her expression changed, to a sudden, wild thought, one of relief, even of elation, and possibility.

Yes, thought Cabot, she has a better way to purchase her life! And she is aware of it!

"I wish you well," said Grendel, a common Gorean farewell.

"I wish you well," responded Cabot.

And the two then parted, Grendel drawing after him a small, well-formed human female, blonde.

She looked back, once, at Cabot, and then was jerked forward on her rope, by hastening Grendel.

Chapter, the Twenty-Fifth:

The Stray

"Hold!" commanded Cabot, and the two smaller Kurii, lesser Kurii, scavenger Kurii, not even worthy of the ships, stopped.

These were such as roamed about, patrolling areas for strayed, or flighted, animals, tarsks, humans, and such.

Cabot had returned to the villa which had been earlier assigned to him, from which he had fetched a tunic, some supplies, and a pouch, into which he had thrust the strings of rubies given to him earlier, before the trial of Lord Pyrrhus, in which his testimony had been so ineffective.

If these two Kurii had been apprised of his escape, they did not register that the human before them was he of whose escape they had heard. He did not seem a fugitive, and he was not collared, and so not a pet, and he was clothed, thus, presumably, a human ally, perhaps one of the men of Peisistratus, of whom they had heard. Too, humans look much alike to most Kurii. Too, he spoke to them with abruptness, and authority, seemingly unquestioned, and this startled them, for his authority might have been genuine. Certainly, if they had been informed of the escape of some human from, say, the breeding shackles, it did not seem likely this could be he, for would such a human not conceal himself from them? Would such a human not avoid them at all costs? Would such a human not have been in hiding, naked, and terrified?

But it is probable these Kurii, of the sort assigned minor duties of sanitation, the collection of stray animals, and such, did not even know of the escape of a human from the breeding shackles, two days ago.

Too, many of the guards of the cylinder, and most of its military

303

personnel, had departed with the fleet, on whatever dark mission it had embarked.

Had this not been the case Cabot might well have remained at large less than an Ahn or so.

The two Kurii had in their custody a human female.

No longer were there strings of coins about her neck.

As she was uncollared and naked it was only to be expected that she, upon being detected, would be promptly taken in charge.

Kurii are tidy in their closed, orbiting environments, as they must be, and are not patient with stray animals.

"Release her," ordered Cabot, and the two small Kurii, each of which had held an arm of their prisoner, loosened their grasp.

She looked at Cabot, wildly, half dazed. She was unsteady. Her knees nearly buckled beneath her.

"On your belly, slut!" Cabot snapped.

Swiftly the girl, terrified, went to her belly.

Did she not know she was in the presence of a free man?

"Excellent work!" Cabot commended the two Kurii, and they glanced at one another, seemingly pleased.

"We have been looking for this bitch," said Cabot. "She is to be returned to the Pleasure Cylinder immediately. You may go your way. I will take her in charge."

The larger of the two Kurii growled.

"I will commend you, of course, to Peisistratus, high human of the world, favored of the Eleventh Face of the Nameless One, Theocrat of the World," said Cabot. "What are your names?"

"Your translator will not carry our designations," said the larger of the two Kurii. "We are the Second Patrol."

"Patrol Two," said Cabot. "Well done!"

The two Kurii looked at one another, shrugged, and turned about, and left. There seemed to them little point in contesting the custody of a stray, particularly if there might be some risk in doing so.

Cabot looked down at the girl, and she inched forward, and put her lips down, humbly, on his left foot.

Her lips were soft.

It is apparently pleasant to feel the soft lips of a slave on one's feet.

It is, too, of course, a common act of deference on the part of a female slave, to kiss the feet of a master, or, indeed, of a free person. Too, we may suppose the slave was timid, frightened, and grateful.

Doubtless, too, she was concerned to acknowledge her bondage, and please the male.

In such ways, and many others, a woman's submission may be betokened.

"On your knees," he said.

She rose to her knees.

"You may speak," he said.

"You called me 'slut' and 'bitch'," she protested, tears in her eyes.

"You are less," said Cabot. "You are a slave."

He looked fixedly, critically, at her knees, and she widened them.

"Better," he said. "What are you doing here?"

"I was turned out," she said. "They would not keep me."

"They have their quotas," said Cabot. "How have you lived?"

"I hid by day," she said. "I stole food, from garbage, at night. But I was seen. Swiftly they took me. What would they do with me?"

"You are a stray," said Cabot. "Presumably they would remand you to the cattle pens, in order that some good might be gotten out of you, as food."

She shuddered.

"You rescued me," she said.

"I fear it may do you little good, in the long run," said Cabot.

"What are you going to do?" she asked.

"We are going back to the Pleasure Cylinder," said Cabot. "I have some business with Peisistratus."

"I cannot go back!" she said.

"Stand," he said. "Face away from me. Put your head down. Cross your wrists behind your back."

"You cannot bind me," she protested. "You are from Earth!"

"Do you dally in obedience?" he inquired.

Swiftly she rose, turned about, lowered her head, and put her hands behind her, wrists crossed.

"You are going to bind me?"

"Yes."

"But I am from Earth!"

"No longer," he said.

She must stand so, for a time, waiting, for he removed the strings of rubies from his pouch, and freed the rubies from their cords, and deposited them in his pouch, and then, with one of the cords, not returned to the pouch, he fastened her wrists behind her.

"Where are the coins won from Peisistratus?" he asked.

"He took them," she said.

"Turn about," he said, "and precede me."

He then gave her a thrust, to hurry her before him. She stumbled, and then caught her balance. "Har-ta!" he said. "Har-ta!"

She hurried forward.

He gave her another thrust.

"This is for show, is it not?" she asked.

"No," he said.

"You think I am a slave?"

"I know you are a slave," he said.

She gasped.

He then took her by the hair, and turned her about, to face him. He looked into her eyes, fiercely.

She was clearly frightened.

"You are hurting me," she said. "Oh!"

"Shall I call you Miss Pym?" he asked.

"You may call me whatever you wish," she said, frightened.

"Why?" he demanded.

"Because I am a slave," she whispered.

"Do not forget it."

"No," she said, frightened.

He wished that the boys and young men she had known on Earth could see her now. They would derive much pleasure at seeing her as she was now, and should be, as a slave.

"You have," said he, "as of now, a general permission to speak, rescindable at my pleasure, but I suggest you use that permission with discretion."

She was silent.

"Do you understand?" he asked.

His grip tightened.

"Yes!" she said. "Yes!"

"Is that how you address a free man?" he inquired.

"No!" she said. "No—*Master! Master!*"

She shuddered, and then he released her hair, and turned her about, again. Unbidden, she put her head down.

"What?" he asked.

"Nothing," she said. "Nothing!" She seemed piteous, shaken, open, emotionally revealed.

Cabot steeled himself against pity.

Cabot recognized the moment as important to her, a door opened, a barrier crossed, a secret confessed.

"You said something," he said. "What was it?"

"It is not important," she said. "It was nothing, nothing!"

"Perhaps it was an utterance of defiance, of rebellion, or protest?"

"No, Master!" she said.

"Or perhaps the merest breath of a possible reluctance, the smallest suggestion of a mere hesitation in your desperate concern to be prompt and pleasing in all ways?"

"No, no," she said. "No, Master!"

"Speak!" he snapped.

"Please, no!" she begged.

"Speak!"

"No, please no! Have mercy!"

"Do you wish to be lashed?"

"No, no!" she said.

"Speak," he said.

"I said," she whispered, softly, frightened, "I—I love calling men 'Master'."

"That is because you are a slave," said Cabot.

"Yes, Master," she said.

"Too, it is fitting," said Cabot, "that you call them Master, for they are your masters."

"Yes, Master," she said.

He saw that she inadvertently trembled with emotion, with pleasure.

Interesting, he thought, how women can find themselves only in bondage.

"Say now," said Cabot, "'I am a slave.'"

He was merciless, you see. But then such are masters.

"I am a slave," she said.

"Louder," he said, "more clearly."

"I am a slave!" she cried.

Again he noted her reaction, one which shook her body, suffusing it with significance and heat, with sudden emotion and pleasure.

"Say now," he said, "'I am a natural slave, and should be a slave, and am a slave.'"

"*I am a natural slave,*" she said, "*and should be a slave, and am a slave.*"

"It is true," he said.

"Yes, Master," she said.

"Again," he snapped—"'I am a slave.'"

"*I am a slave,*" she said.

"It is true."

"Yes, Master."

"You are charged and pleased, and suffused with desire," said Cabot.

"Yes, Master!" she breathed, pulling a little at her bound wrists.

"In such simple ways," said Cabot, "is your womanhood spoken."

"Yes, Master," she whispered.

"Forward!" he said, pushing her ahead of him.

"Yes, Master!" she cried.

"Hurry!" said Cabot. "To the shuttle lock, that appertaining to the Pleasure Cylinder.

"We do not know the codes!"

"Some will know them," said Cabot. "There must be frequent comings and goings."

"I dare not go there, Master!" she wept. "I was cast out. They may kill me!"

Cabot thrust her rudely forward, again, roughly, without consideration. She was a slave. One may handle a slave so. They expect it. And it is appropriate for them. They are not free women.

"Hurry!" he said, angrily.

"Yes, Master!" she wept.

"Har-ta!" said he. "Har-ta!"

"Yes, Master," she wept. "Yes, Master!"

Chapter, the Twenty-Sixth:

A Slave Will Be Put in a Collar, as Is Appropriate

"Why have you brought this slut back?" asked Peisistratus.

"Kneel, slave," said Cabot to the girl. "Head down, to the floor."

"You have coins of mine," said Cabot.

"Fetch the coins," said Peisistratus to a burly lieutenant.

"You betrayed me," said Cabot.

"They came for you," said Peisistratus. "One of the translators of a monitor was set for English. Such translators are rare. I did not realize one was in the cylinder. It was clear in our conversation, to me, and to the monitors, that you would frustrate the will of Agamemnon, a will unwise to frustrate. If we betrayed you, it was simply in not contesting your removal from the cylinder, at the risk of our own destruction."

"I have considered my hands on your throat," said Cabot.

"You could kill me, swiftly, I have no doubt," said Peisistratus. "Those of your caste, as those of the Assassins, are skilled in such things. But would you do it here, now, and die under the blows of my men, a moment later? I see no considerable advance in either of our fortunes from such a precipitance."

"It has occurred to me that you may be of use to me," said Cabot.

"You are aware that you are hunted in the world?"

"I conjectured as much."

"I am of use primarily to myself," said Peisistratus.

"Hitherto, perhaps," said Cabot.

"I do not understand."

"You know of the departure of the fleet," said Cabot.

"Certainly," said Peisistratus.

"Fewer Kurii are now in the world," said Cabot.

"Yes."

"I was freed from breeding shackles by Grendel, whom you know," said Cabot. "With me, freed as well, was she who was once the blonde pet of Arcesilaus, later the pet of Grendel."

"I know her," said Peisistratus. "Perhaps three tarsks."

"She is with Grendel, who is being sought, for the murder of a guard, and perhaps for freeing prisoners from breeding shackles."

"He is dangerous," said Peisistratus, "particularly where that little blonde animal is concerned."

"True," said Cabot. "We saw him in the arena."

"You shared the shackles with the blonde?"

"Briefly."

"And Grendel did not rip out your throat?"

"I fear the thought had crossed his mind," said Cabot, "but of greater interest to you, and one of the reasons I have sought you out, other than perhaps to kill you, is to inform you that the little blonde animal, as you think of her, and appropriately in my view, overheard him utter seditious remarks, involving a conspiracy of rebellion, implicating himself, Lord Arcesilaus, and you."

Peisistratus turned white. "She must be killed then," said Peisistratus. "Her tongue could be torn out. She does not know writing, does she?"

"When Grendel is taken," said Cabot, "as I think must soon occur, if it has not already come about, she will attempt to purchase her life by betraying his remarks."

"We must get to her first, and kill her," said Peisistratus. "If she can write her hands might be removed."

"There are other ways," said Cabot, "stumps drawing pictures in sand, even physical responses to cleverly dichotomized questions."

"Then kill her, certainly," said Peisistratus.

"Grendel will not permit her to be harmed," said Cabot. "He would have to be killed first."

"Acceptable," said Peisistratus, grimly.

"And who would do this?"

"You."

"No," said Cabot.

"We are finished then," said Peisistratus.

"No," said Cabot. "We must strike first."

"The world?"

"Certainly."

"You are joking?"

"No."

"Nothing is prepared," said Peisistratus.

"You have access to the codes to the sport cylinder, and can access the barracks of the killer humans, and the cattle pens."

"The cattle will be useless," said Peisistratus. "They will not stir from the vicinity of their feeding troughs. And the killer humans, speeched and unspeeched, are wild, uncontrollable, dangerous, vicious, undisciplined. They would kill us as easily as Kurii. The game humans will be unwilling to leave the shelter of their forests."

"Do you have power weapons?"

"Some, on the ships, not many," said Peisistratus. "But then power weapons are not generally available in the world, either, being kept in arsenals."

"You know their locations?"

"Surely," said Peisistratus.

"I assume Kurii are reluctant to discharge such weapons in the world," said Cabot.

"Certainly," said Peisistratus. "It could be extremely dangerous."

"Good," said Cabot.

"But they will seek them and utilize them to protect the world," said Peisistratus.

"Perhaps," said Cabot.

"Indisputably," said Peisistratus.

"If we were between the Kurii and their arsenals," said Cabot, "it would be difficult for the Kurii to reach those weapons."

"Not as difficult as you surmise," said Peisistratus, bitterly.

"How is that?" asked Cabot.

"The arsenals," said Peisistratus, "are not easily accessed, for they are stored at the flat termini of the cylinders, where Kurii may fly."

"Fly?" said Cabot.

"There is little or no gravity there, but an atmosphere, of course, as elsewhere in the cylinder, and thus wing harnesses, of canvas and leather, reinforced by stays, may be used to negotiate those spaces. It is not too unlike the shuttles when beyond their ports."

"I see," said Cabot, angrily.

"There would be no way for us to keep the Kurii from the arsenals."

"The great bow?"

"Certainly not," said Peisistratus. "We are not peasants."

"It is one of the most fearsome weapons on Gor," said Cabot. "How else do you suppose ten thousand small villages from Torvaldsland to Turia, from Thentis to Schendi, have retained the liberty of their Home Stones for centuries?"

"We are not peasants," said Peisistratus.

"Would that you had less prejudice against the bows of peasants," said Cabot, "for they can follow and pierce a jard in flight."

"There would be power weapons in the palace, of course," said Peisistratus. "Those alone might destroy your putative cohorts."

"Have you common weapons, on the ships?" inquired Cabot.

"For use on Gor, of course," said Peisistratus, "to be used there, that we not attract the attention of Priest-Kings nor seem to violate their laws, crossbows, blades, javelins, spears, and such."

"I see," said Cabot.

"Thus armed," said Peisistratus, "we seem to be of little interest to Priest-Kings."

"Interesting," said Cabot.

"Perhaps they take us for common merchants," said Peisistratus. "One does not know, and even if they do not do so, and understand our origins and business, they seem content to ignore us then, once we are on Gor and clearly in conformance with their laws."

"Interesting," said Cabot.

"And, of course," said Peisistratus, "we make certain that our slave coffles of stripped, neck-chained beauties from Earth, being marched to various markets, are indistinguishable from common Gorean coffles."

"Understood," said Cabot.

"Too," said Peisistratus, "there is little difference between a Gorean woman and an Earth woman once they are both on a chain."

"Certainly," said Cabot.

"I think it is important in these matters, too," said Peisistratus, "not to treat our selections from Earth otherwise than as common slaves, which they are of course, lest too much curiosity be aroused, and so, thus, we have recourse to the coffle, the wheeled cages, the chaining of their ankles about a central bar in a closed slave wagon, the lash, and such."

"I understand," said Cabot.

"Many Goreans," said Peisistratus, "think that Earth is on Gor, in a remote region, inhabited by barbarians."

"I have understood that," said Cabot.

"There are risks involved, of course," said Peisistratus, "once we have landed the cargo, our selections, the slaves, and have forgone the use of superior weapons."

"Of course," said Cabot.

"Sometimes we lose them to raiders, or bandits."

"It would make little difference to the slaves," said Cabot, "no more than to purloined kaiila, as they would then merely be sold for different prices, or in different markets."

"Yes," said Peisistratus. "Interestingly some of the girls rejoice, thinking they are being rescued."

"Until they find themselves being lashed even more cruelly in a different direction?"

"Yes," said Peisistratus.

The girl kneeling beside them, her head to the floor, her wrists bound behind her, trembled, understanding then that she was not unique, and that there was a familiar and established role for such as she on the Gorean world.

"The killer humans are trained with weapons," said Cabot.

"A limited number, used and reused," said Peisistratus, "tridents, nets, blades, small bucklers, such things."

"It seems then," said Cabot, "that there is little hope."

"The power weapons in the palace alone," said Peisistratus, "might eradicate a small army. The fire in a single holster might incinerate a hundred men, without damage to the cylinder."

"It is hopeless then," said Cabot.

"Yes," said Peisistratus.

"I wonder," said Cabot, regarding Peisistratus narrowly, "if you are one of Agamemnon's humans."

"Perhaps," said Peisistratus. "You have no way of knowing, do you?"

"I think I will kill you," said Cabot.

"And my men then you," said Peisistratus.

Cabot's hands opened and clenched. They were large hands, for a human.

"Beware that you do not deprive yourself of an ally," said Peisistratus.

"Are you an ally, or an enemy?" asked Cabot.

"An ally," said Peisistratus, "but I have no intention of dying on a flame rack to convince you of my position in these matters."

"The blonde, when acquired, will implicate you," said Cabot.

"What if I am a spy," said Peisistratus, "who has infiltrated the higher echelons of the rebellion, that I may betray you all?"

"You did not seem such, moments ago," mused Cabot.

"Perhaps I was acting," said Peisistratus.

"I will trust you," said Cabot.

"I am a skilled liar," said Peisistratus.

"I will trust you," said Cabot.

"And thus are men easily betrayed," said Peisistratus.

"Or ennobled," said Cabot.

"I think you are a fool," said Peisistratus.

"The matter is hopeless?" asked Cabot.

"Certainly," said Peisistratus.

"Leonidas, at Thermopylae," said Cabot.

"I do not understand," said Peisistratus.

"Hesius at the Pass of Boduin," said Cabot.

"Ah," said Peisistratus. "I see!"

These allusions may be unintelligible to the reader. They are not found in the lexicon.

"You can take your ships and escape," said Cabot.

"No," said Peisistratus. "When the fleet departed the locks were sealed."

"Will you join me then at Thermopylae?" asked Cabot.

"At Boduin," smiled Peisistratus.

"What of your men?" inquired Cabot.

"We are with you, Captain!" cried a man.

"And I, and I!" cried a hundred others, clustered about.

"You are all fools!" called Peisistratus.

"Dispatch them, on a hundred errands!" said Cabot.

"It will be done," said Peisistratus. "Decius! Torquatus! Henrius! Eteocles! Septimus! Tytaios! Elrik! Sarpedon!"

Men crowded forward.

"And what of you?" said Peisistratus.

"I must seek out Grendel, for he may need me," said Cabot. "And I must warn Lord Arcesilaus, if there is still time!"

"Lord Arcesilaus will be warned by another," said Peisistratus, "for you might be easily recognized."

"As you will," said Cabot.

"Grendel may have been taken by now," said Peisistratus.

"Possibly," said Cabot.

"Perhaps he had the presence of mind to strangle the little blonde beast before she could speak," said Peisistratus.

"He would not touch her," said Cabot. "He would die for her."

"Better to die for a urt," said Peisistratus.

"She is beautiful," said Cabot.

"Let her be dipped in acid," said Peisistratus. "She will be less beautiful then."

"I think he is still at large," said Cabot.

"After two days?"

"If he were not, would not guards have come to the cylinder by now?"

"Probably," said Peisistratus.

"I think so," said Cabot. "Certainly his small, well-formed companion, the small, sleek beast of which he is so unconscionably fond, has the coin of advantage and survival well in hand, information of importance to Agamemnon, and would spend it instantly to procure not only her life but his favor."

"By now," said Peisistratus, "she may be heaped with jewels and be his advisor."

"Yes," said Cabot, "with her leash attached to the arm of the throne."

"But the guards have not yet come."

"No."

"Where will you seek Grendel?" asked Peisistratus.

"Where I think he, as human, will go," said Cabot, "a place unfamiliar to Kurii, and one dreaded by them."

"In their own world?"

"Yes," said Cabot. "There is such a place."

"We know little now," said Peisistratus. "It may even be dangerous to leave the cylinder." He then turned to a subordinate. "Reconnoiter, with care," he said. "If all seems clear, go to the world, inquire, learn of matters, return, report."

"Yes, Captain," said the man and left for the shuttle lock.

"Agamemnon may be biding his time," said Peisistratus to Cabot. "It may amuse him to wait, even for a holiday or festival, to collect and display the conspirators."

"Yes," said Cabot.

"Do not go yet!" said Peisistratus.

"I must," said Cabot.

"It is unwise," said Peisistratus. "Wait, for intelligence."

"There may be no time," said Cabot.

"Torus," said Peisistratus.

This was the lieutenant of Peisistratus, a burly fellow. It was he who had been dispatched earlier, shortly after Cabot's arrival in the cylinder, for the strings of coins, Cabot's winnings from the arena, which had once been strung loosely about the throat of an unclaimed cylinder slave, who, however unworthy, had been permitted to pose and dance for Cabot, and even to kneel humbly before him and offer him paga, in a manner appropriate to her bondage. This fellow, Torus, had been standing nearby for some time. He had the strings of coins looped over his left forearm.

Peisistratus took the coins and handed them, on their strings, to Cabot.

"Of what good are these?" asked Cabot.

"I did not steal them," said Peisistratus. "I kept them for you. They are yours."

"Better one sword," said Cabot.

"We will provide one if you wish," said Peisistratus. "But I think it will be safer for you to be unarmed."

"How so?"

"An unidentified armed human might be slain on sight."

"I wonder," said Cabot, "if you are the human of Agamemnon."

"You do not know," said Peisistratus.

"Very well," said Cabot. "I will carry no blade."

"It was your mistake, friend Cabot," said Peisistratus, "to have concerned yourself with the affairs of Kurii."

"It seems," said Cabot, "they first concerned themselves with mine."

"Take the coins," said Peisistratus. "They are yours, and the silver is rare here and valued by Kurii, for ornaments, and such."

"They may be of use?"

"More so than a sword, I suspect," said Peisistratus.

"Perhaps," said Cabot, thrusting the coins and strings into his pouch.

"The gates of many cities have been unlocked with a key of silver," smiled Peisistratus.

This is, one gathers, a saying. Its origin is obscure. It may be from the "Field Diaries," an anonymous Gorean publication, often attributed to Carl Commenius, he of Argentum. It has also been attributed to Dietrich of Tarnburg, Lurius of Jad, and even, interestingly, to Marlenus of Ar. One suspects that its actual origin is lost. It, or its variations, might emerge, naturally enough, one supposes, from reflection upon a variety of historical instances.

"I wish you well," said Cabot.

"You extend your hand?"

"But you do not take it," observed Cabot.

The simultaneous grasping of hands, right to right, is a feature of certain Earth cultures, as it is of some Kur cultures. As most humans, and Kurii, favor the right hand, this grasping of hands is a token of respect or friendship, each surrendering, so to speak, the weapon hand to the other.

"Stay with us, until we have word of the outside," advised Peisistratus.

"No," said Cabot.

"Then," said Peisistratus, "I extend my hand, and wish you well."

Each then took the hand of the other, firmly.

Cabot turned to go.

"Wait," said Peisistratus.

Cabot hesitated.

"What of the slave?" asked Peisistratus.

The slave at their feet, her head to the floor, her wrists bound together, behind her back, began to tremble, and sob, but dared not change position.

"She?" said Cabot.

"Surely," said Peisistratus. With his bootlike sandal he thrust her from her knees to her side on the flooring.

"I leave her," said Cabot.

"Please, no, Master!" she cried.

"She spoke," observed Peisistratus.

"I have given her permission to speak," said Cabot, "but a permission rescindable by my will, and one not to be abused."

"You are permissive with a mere slave," said Peisistratus.

"Perhaps," said Cabot.

"I throw her in, with the coins," said Peisistratus.

"I do not want her," said Cabot.

"Please want me, Master!" she wept.

"We have kept her a virgin for you," said Peisistratus, "and have even had a collar prepared."

"Her hair is too short," said Cabot.

"Want me, Master!" she wept. "I beg to be wanted!"

"We have an eel pool in a nearby garden," said Peisistratus. "By now the eels are doubtless hungry."

The slave went to her belly and, terrified, hands tied behind her, squirmed to Cabot's feet. "I do not want to die, Master!" she wept. "Am I not attractive? Am not of interest, some interest? Want me, please! I beg to be wanted!" She pressed her lips to his feet, piteously, and covered them with kisses, and tears.

"Do you think you could be a good slave?" asked Peisistratus.

"Yes, Master! Yes, Master!" she wept. "I will love and serve, wholly, unstintingly, selflessly!"

"In all ways?" asked Peisistratus.

"Yes," she wept, "yes, Master!"

"You understand what it means," he asked, "'in all ways'?"

"Yes, Master!" she cried. "I do, I do, and I want to so serve. I will beg piteously to so serve!"

"Prepare," said Peisistratus, to his men, "to take her to the eel pool."

Before two fellows could seize her up, she scrambled wildly to her knees before Cabot, and, agonized, tears streaming down her cheeks, lifted her eyes to him, piteously, her lips trembling.

"Claim me, Master!" she wept. "I am an unclaimed slave! Claim me, I beg it!"

Cabot looked down upon her.

"Want me!" she begged. "I beg to be wanted!"

"You beg to be wanted?" asked Cabot.

"Yes, Master," she said, "I beg to be wanted!"

"It was not so on Earth, I gather," said Cabot.

"No, Master," she said. "But now I beg! Please want me, Master! Want me! I beg to be wanted!"

Cabot smiled. "Your hair is too short," he said.

"It will grow, Master," she said, smiling. "It will grow."

"Pronounce yourself slave, and unclaimed," said Cabot.

"I am a slave," she cried, "and I am an unclaimed slave!"

"You belong then," said Cabot, "to whoever claims you."

"Yes, Master!" she cried.

"You look well on your knees," he observed.

"Thank you, Master," she wept.

"I claim you," he said.

She began to tremble, uncontrollably, shedding tears of irrepressible emotion, wild tears of relief, of gratitude, of wanton, unrestrained elation, of instantaneous, irresistible joy, and it seemed, so sobbing, that she would fall. And a fellow behind her, taking her by the hair, steadied her, and forced her head up, to regard Cabot.

"You are a slave, are you not?" asked Cabot.

"Yes, Master!"

"Whose are you?"

"Yours, Master!"

"Speak it, then," said he.

"I am your slave, Master!" she said.

The men about cried out with pleasure, and smote their left shoulders in approval.

"Bring the collar," said Peisistratus.

"She has fainted," said a man.

"There is a haunch of tarsk in the kitchen," said Peisistratus. "Let the eels be fed."

"Yes, Captain," said a fellow.

Chapter, the Twenty-Seventh:

Cabot Has Delayed His Departure,
Upon the Advice of Peisistratus

"I am chained!" she said. "Chained!"

"It is common with slaves," said Cabot.

She lay back in the furs. "I am utterly helpless," she said.

"That, too, is common with slaves," he said.

It is true that she was well spread.

It was not unfitting for her, as she was a slave.

The alcove was illuminated by a single, tiny lamp, in a niche in the wall, to the left, as one would face the back of the alcove. The alcove itself, as many, was small, low-ceilinged, with curved, sloping walls, floored with heavy furs. The light of the small lamp cast its warm, soft, flickering glow about the walls. In the alcove, as is often the case, were various devices, gags, blindfolds, shackles, coarse rope, silken cords, adjustable chains, a switch, a whip, such things, convenient to masters, not unfamiliar to slaves.

The space was closed with a heavy leather curtain. This was buckled shut, on the inside.

"And I am collared!" she said.

"Yes," he said.

"You put me on all fours, my head down," she said, "and then collared me, as though I might have been a dog."

"You are less than a dog," he said. "You are a slave."

"Yes, Master."

"You trembled, as it was closed."

"The sound, Master!" she breathed. "It is a sound which surely no woman ever forgets! Is it not the most meaningful of sounds, that snap, that click, as the collar is closed on one, and one realizes that it is now on one, and that one is collared?"

"There are many meaningful sounds," said Cabot, "the snarl of the sleen, the roar of the mountain larl, the scream of the tarn, the drums of war, the clash of steel on steel, the crash of waves, the creak of a vessel's timbers, the sound of bright canvas awakening to a sudden wind after calm, the whisper of silk on a slave's body."

"I do not understand much of what you have said," she said.

"It does not matter," he said.

The collar was a common Gorean collar, of the sort favored in particular in her northern hemisphere, flat, light, sturdy, about a half to three-quarters of an inch in height, close-fitting, locked, the lock at the back of the neck.

"The legend on the collar was shown to me," she said. "But I could not read it."

"It was read to you," he said.

"Yes," she said. "'*I am the property of Tarl Cabot.*'"

"It is true," he said.

"Yes, Master," she said. "Master."

"Yes?"

"I have always wanted to be owned," she said.

"Have no fear," he said. "You are owned."

"I could not even read my collar," she said.

"It matters not," he said. "You are illiterate in the language."

"Will you teach me to read Gorean?"

"No," he said.

"I am to be kept illiterate?"

"Yes," he said, "many Earth-girl slaves on Gor are kept illiterate. They need not be literate for what the master wants them for."

"I see," she smiled.

"Free women prefer it that way, too," he said, "that the distinction between themselves and the meaningless slave be the more clearly drawn."

"I see," she said.

"Too," said he, "curiosity is not becoming in a slave girl."

"I have been told that," she laughed. "But, too, I suspect we are muchly subject to curiosity."

"Yes," said he, "sometimes to the correction of the whip."

"It is a strange feeling," she said, "being a slave, and being in a slave collar."

"The collar marks you as slave," he said, "and identifies the master."

"And," she said, "if I am not mistaken, it is extremely attractive."

"Yes," he said, "both for its aesthetics, and its meaning."

"I understand, Master," she said. "And I am sure, too, a man enjoys seeing a slave collar on a woman."

"Of course," said Cabot.

"There is something else, too," she said.

"What is that?" he asked.

"How it affects the woman," she said, "how it stimulates her, arouses her, informs her, and frees her."

"Frees her?"

"Yes," she said. "It is hard to explain, but I never felt so free, as a woman, until I was in this collar."

"Interesting," he said.

"What you did to me!" she smiled.

"It was nothing," he said.

"Nothing!" she said. "You so aroused me that I begged piteously for my own deflowering!"

"Do not use so absurd an expression," he said. "One can no more deflower a slave than a she-tarsk."

"I see," she said.

"But it is true you are now no more a virgin slave."

"I am now 'red silk,'" she said.

"As is common with slaves," he said.

"But I do not have a thread of red silk on my body," she chided.

"A red-silk slave," he said, "is red silk even if naked."

"Yes, Master," she said.

"I have arranged with Peisistratus for a tunic for you," he said.

"Oh, Master!" she breathed, delighted.

"It is a cast-off tunic," he said, "sleeveless, gray, and rather short, doubtless you will find it so, but I think you will be fetching in it."

"I will hope to please my master," she said.

"One detail must be attended to," he said, "before you receive the tunic."

"What is that, Master?"

"You must be branded."

"Branded!"

"Certainly," he said. "We would not want you to be confused with a free woman."

"I must be branded?"

"Certainly," he said. "You are a slave."

"I am afraid."

"It will not take long, only a moment or two. It is a small, tasteful mark. I will have it placed high on the left thigh, under the hip."

"Will it not disfigure me?"

"No, it will enhance your beauty."

"It is a small mark?"

"Yes," he said, "small, but clear, and, I assure you, unmistakable. It will mark you perfectly, as slave."

"We are leaving in the morning?" she said.

"Yes," he said, "Peisistratus thought it best."

"You were thinking of leaving earlier," she said.

"I considered it," he said.

"And the opportunity of bringing me to the alcove did not influence your judgment?"

"I deferred to the judgment of Peisistratus," he said.

"I see," she said.

"To be sure," he said, "the sight of you in a collar did not dissuade me."

"Seeing us in collars arouses men, does it not?" she asked.

"Of course," he said, "in a thousand ways."

"It is as though we were animals," she said, reproachfully.

"The slave girl is an animal," he said.

"Yes," she said. "And I am excited to be such."

"I learned from Peisistratus," he said, "that shortly after coming to the cylinder you were given slave wine and the inoculations pertinent to the stabilization serums."

"Slave wine, that bitter drought," she said, "that I might not be bred except as masters might please."

"Yes," he said.

"But I may be bred, as masters might please."

"Of course," he said.

"For I am a slave."

"Yes."

"An animal."

"Yes."

"What was the purport of the inoculations?"

"You do not know?"

"No," she said.

"You are familiar with the utility of inoculations in the prevention of certain diseases, surely," he said.

"Certainly," she said.

"Goreans, of the caste of physicians," he said, "long regarded ageing not as a fatality to which they must be naively resigned, but merely as another malady to which their craft might be addressed, one to be remedied."

"I have heard of such research on Earth," she whispered.

"It has come to a successful conclusion on Gor," he said.

"Forgive me, Master," she said. "I cannot believe that."

"It does not matter whether you believe it or not," he said.

"Oh!" she said.

"Your body is very sensitive," he said, "as is fitting for a female slave."

"You are going to make me cry out, and beg again?"

"If it pleases me," he said.

"I am immortal?" she said.

"Not at all," he said. "You are human, very human. You are extremely mortal. It is only that you are now, assuming the serums hold, immune to the ravages of age."

"'If'?" she said.

"They do not always hold," he said, "but, commonly, they do."

"I can understand," she said, "why free persons might avail themselves of such achievements, but why would they be bestowed on slaves?"

"Clearly," he said, "to keep up their value, in the case of a male slave, his strength, in the case of a female slave, her beauty."

She gasped.

"Your touch!" she said.

"Do you like that?" he asked.

"Yes," she said. "Yes!"

"You are an extremely beautiful young woman," he said. "And in bondage you will inevitably increase in beauty, and, as you increase in beauty, your desirability to men will increase as well, and you will become more and more valuable on the auction block."

"I do not want to be sold," she said.

"It will be done with you as masters please," he said.

"Yes, Master," she said.

"Surely you can understand," he said, "how men would not want your beauty to fade, for in such a way they would lose on their investment. Your value must be kept up, if only for the auction block."

"I am frightened," she said.

"And so your youth and beauty will be retained," he said.

"To be kept in a collar," she said.

"Of course," he said.

"I love my collar," she whispered.

Then she suddenly looked wildly at Cabot, and pulled at her chains, but she could move only inches in them.

"Touch me again so, Master!" she begged. "Touch a meaningless slave so, again! She begs it!"

"Yes!" she cried. "Yes! Again, again!"

But Cabot lay back, regarding the low ceiling of the alcove.

She reared in the chains. "Please, Master!" she begged.

"A man of Peisistratus will attempt to contact Lord Arcesilaus in the morning, in the cylinder day, openly, a fellow not to be suspected by Kur guards, as I might be."

The slave whimpered.

"Much depends on whether Grendel has been taken or not," said Cabot. "If he remains at large, the conspiracy is safe, if only for the moment."

"Please, Master," she whispered.

"I think Peisistratus is right," said Cabot, "that we wait until morning."

"Master," she whimpered.

"Very well," said Cabot.

"Master!" she cried.

"Your body," said Cabot, "is now the body of a slave."

"I am now any man's slave," she wept.

Under the hand of any man, you see, the slave is helpless.

"I am worthless," she said, miserably.

"No," said Cabot. "That is merely the absurdity of your former culture speaking. It is only now that you have any true value."

"Perhaps as much as two silver tarsks," she said.

"In your former culture," said Cabot, "only males were thought to have value, really, and thus the female was supposed to become a pretend male, with male properties and virtues, a counterfeit male, a facsimile male, and so arose all the nonsense of identity, a farce transparent even to children, but one of value in promoting an agenda based on envy and greed, an agenda of distortions, of unrelenting propaganda, of lies and law, to bring to ruination societies, societies to be so transformed then as to foster the ends of the unnatural, the disturbed, the psychologically malformed, the haters and misfits."

"This is the first happiness I have ever known," she said, "to lie as a slave at the mercy of my master."

"Rest," said Cabot.

"You are unchaining me?"

He freed the lovely slave then of her impediments.

"Do you not fear I will run away?" she asked.

"The collar on your neck would bring you back to me, quickly enough," said Cabot.

She touched the collar. "Yes," she said, softly, thoughtfully, "it would." She then understood something of the helplessness of a female slave. She then snuggled down beside Cabot, her lips at his waist. "But I do not want to run away," she said.

"Good," he said.

"And I want to be branded," she whispered.

"You will be," he said.

"I am worthless," she smiled.

"No," said Cabot, softly.

"I may be worthless," she said, "but I am fulfilled."

"No woman who is fulfilled," said Cabot, "is worthless."

"No," she smiled. "I am not worthless. I may be worth as much as a silver tarsk."

"Perhaps two," said Cabot.

"Thank you, Master," she said.

Cabot kissed her, and her lips were soft, and yielding.

"Is it permissible," she asked, "for one who is a slave, to be a slave?"

"Certainly," said Cabot.

"And then for one who is a master, to be a master?"

"Yes," said Cabot.

"What right have any to deny such truths?" she asked.

"None," said Cabot.

"Please, caress me, Master," she whispered.

"Do you beg it?"

"Yes, Master."

"As an abject, rightless slave?"

"Yes, Master."

"Very well," he said.

She leaped in her chains, crying out in gratitude.

Chapter, the Twenty-Eighth:

The Seeking of Grendel

"She is pretty," said Peisistratus.

"Yes," said Cabot.

"The tunic well sets her off," said Peisistratus. "I see there is a smear of blood on her thigh."

"She can be washed, later," said Cabot.

"You had her taste her virgin blood?"

"Of course," said Cabot. "Stand straight," he said to the slave. "You are under the gaze of a free man."

"The tunic is quite short," said Peisistratus.

"She has excellent legs," said Cabot.

"Well then to display them," said Peisistratus. "She seems prettier now than yesterday, in the cylinder."

"She has learned something of the meaning of chains," said Cabot.

"Left thigh," said Peisistratus. "Lift up your skirt."

The slave complied.

"Excellent," said Peisistratus. "She is well marked."

It was tiny and lovely. It was the common *kajira* mark.

"You may lower your skirt, and kneel," Cabot informed the slave.

She lowered her skirt, and smoothed it, delicately, carefully, and then knelt beside her burden, supplies from the cylinder, which she would bear, as her master's lovely beast.

How vain they are, and how beautiful, thought Cabot.

"Kneel more straightly," Cabot admonished the slave. "Good," he said. The slave had much to learn, but she was highly intelligent, and would doubtless learn quickly. One of the most difficult things for a female slave, incidentally, is to be under her master's discipline while in the presence of a free woman. She knows the free woman despises her for being a slave, but, also, envies her, to the point of hatred, for her bondage, and the superb, uncompromising domination to which she is subject.

"Her hair, of course, is too short," said Peisistratus.

"It will grow," said Cabot.

"Corinna is better," said Peisistratus.

Corinna, as one might recall, was a cylinder slave, one perhaps favored by Peisistratus. She was a skilled dancer. I believe we may have noted this, earlier.

"Perhaps," said Cabot.

The slave stiffened, angrily.

How vain they are, thought Cabot. And how delicious. It was no wonder that men made them slaves, and had them serve them with perfection.

One of the nicest of gifts, incidentally, is a lovely female slave. Too, they are cheaper than a kaiila, or trained sleen, and far less expensive than a tarn, one of Gor's mighty saddle birds.

A chain of twenty or more beauties might be exchanged for a single tarn.

And how, Cabot thought, they learn to compete with one another, each to be more pleasing to the masters, each to bring a higher price on the sales block. They will fight over a brush or comb, an eye shadow or lipstick, or earrings, or a ribbon. They will tear hair for a bangle.

Yes, he thought, how delicious are slaves. Who would wish to live without them?

And the love of a slave for her master!

Who can understand that love, who has not had a slave at his feet?

Peisistratus looked about.

"I think," said Peisistratus, "I should accompany you no further."

"It seems quiet," said Cabot.

"Unnaturally so," said Peisistratus.

Cabot looked up at the forests overhead. "Your men are about their errands?" he asked.

"Yes, since last night," said Peisistratus.

"You are attempting to contact Lord Arcesilaus?"

"A man is on his way to his lodgings now," said Peisistratus.

"It is strange," said Cabot, "but while it is so quiet here, elsewhere, amongst the darknesses separating the worlds, fleets may be locked in dire, fearsome war, a thousand vessels exploding and burning, casting about debris and crews, fleets maneuvering, calculating, firing, escaping, dying, withdrawing, advancing, doing what men and Kurii do, conducting their affairs as usual, affairs so momentous to transitory civilizations, the universe indifferent, not noticing, or caring, blooming and dying, again and again, never noticing or caring, according to its own long laws."

"But we have been here," said Peisistratus. "Nothing can change that."

"Yes," said Cabot. "Nothing can change that."

"I think that is important," said Peisistratus.

"I think so, too," said Cabot. "We are part of it, and we know something of it, while it knows nothing of us."

"In us," said Peisistratus, "as we are of it, it knows something of itself, and, in its way, of us."

"Perhaps," said Cabot.

"We are the torch by means of which it explores its own caverns," said Peisistratus.

"Perhaps," said Cabot.

"I wonder if Grendel has been taken," said Peisistratus.

"I do not know," said Cabot.

"If he has been taken," said Peisistratus, "his little blonde she-urt will have lost no time in uttering all she knows, to save her worthless hide."

"Doubtless," said Cabot.

"It could be," said Peisistratus, "that Agamemnon is unsure of the extent of the conspiracy, and will thus wait for the return of the fleet."

"That is quite possible," said Cabot.

"You are determined to seek Grendel?" said Peisistratus.

"Yes," said Cabot.

"Where will you seek him?"

"Where I think he will go," said Cabot, "a place where Kurii will be reluctant to follow."

"Where?" said Peisistratus.

"There," said Cabot, pointing upward, toward a shimmering

patch of silver, seemingly small at the distance, amongst the forests above."

"Lake Fear," said Peisistratus.

"Yes," said Cabot.

Chapter, the Twenty-Ninth:

A Saurian Is Encountered

It was some days later, perhaps five, for the records are unclear on the point, that Cabot and his pretty beast reached the sloping shores, and the graveled beach, against whose stones lapped the waters of Lake Fear.

Cabot sorted through the residue of the supplies brought from the Pleasure Cylinder.

There was little of an edible nature left.

"Master, may I speak?" she asked.

"Yes," said Cabot.

How nicely she is learning her bondage, thought Cabot. Although she has a general permission to speak, albeit a permission subject to instantaneous revocation, and one not to be abused, still, she had requested permission. That was judicious of her, was it not? Perhaps her master was busy, and did not care to be annoyed? Perhaps she did not wish to risk having her permission to speak taken from her.

Too, requesting permission to speak is a way of showing deference to the master, and it helps the slave to keep her bondage well in mind, and that her permission to speak is, when all is said and done, contingent on the will of the master.

"It is beautiful here," she said. "What is fearful about this place?"

"See these lines in the beach," said Cabot. "They are the traces of the movements of large bodies. I am told there are saurians here, and they will come upon occasion to the beach."

"There are none here now."

"Examine this mark," said Cabot. "See the edges, almost sharp. It may have been made last night."

"I do not see why Kurii should fear such things, on the land."

"If power weapons were permitted in the cylinder, they would have nothing to fear," said Cabot, "but they are not, and these things, I understand, are far more terrible than Kurii, though on land they do not move quickly."

"But in the water?"

"There they are formidable," said Cabot. "Many are designed for aquatic predation."

"They are reptiles, air-breathing things," she said.

"Tharlarion of a sort, as I understand it," said Cabot.

"We have seen no sign of Lord Grendel," she said, "nor of Lady Bina."

"You speak of her as 'Lady'?"

"Yes, Master, for she is free."

"We are much in the open," said Cabot, "and with purpose. I want him to see us."

"Then it is we who will be found?"

"And in our being found, he himself is found," said Cabot.

"If it be he who finds us," she said.

"Yes," said Cabot, "if it be he who finds us."

"Kurii may come here," she said.

"Probably, at times," said Cabot.

"Lady Bina has a name," she said.

"She is free, as you correctly recognized. She named herself."

"I may not name myself, may I?" she asked.

"Certainly not," he said. "You are a slave."

"'Bina' is a beautiful name," she said.

"I think it is nice," said Cabot.

"It seems short for the name of a free woman," she said.

"Perhaps," said Cabot.

"On Earth," she said, "female slaves were sometimes given meaningful names, things like Plum or Cherry."

"How would you know that?" he asked.

"I looked into such things, on Earth," she said.

"You were interested in learning of the nature and lives of female slaves?" he asked.

"Yes," she said.

"But you did not expect to become one?"

"No, Master," she said. "What free woman expects to be

collared?" She looked about. "Does 'Bina' have a meaning?" she asked.

"Do not concern yourself with the matter," he said.

"Forgive me, Master," she said.

"'Bina' is a beautiful name for a beautiful woman," she said.

"It is a beautiful name, in its way, and one appropriate one for her," said Cabot, "and she is indeed a beautiful woman."

"Is she more beautiful than I?" inquired the slave.

"Of course," said Cabot, "is not any free woman a thousand times more beautiful than the most beautiful of slaves?"

"Master?"

"That is a joke," he said. "It is, of course, the most beautiful of women who are sought for slaves, and in bondage, however reluctantly, they become even more beautiful."

"But she is beautiful," said the slave.

"Yes," said Cabot, "and she belongs in a collar."

"I do not like her," said the slave.

"She would scorn you, as the dirt beneath her feet," said Cabot.

"As I am a slave?"

"Certainly."

"And appropriately?"

"Certainly."

"I was not always a slave," she said.

"You were always a slave, at least since puberty," said Cabot.

"But not as I am now, branded and collared, a slave in the fullness of all legality."

"No," conceded Cabot.

"We were rivals, in the container," whispered the slave.

"Oh?" said Cabot.

"Each of us wished to be the most pleasing to you."

"But you were free," said Cabot.

"In your presence I was no more than a naked slave," she said.

"One would have scarcely guessed that, from your demeanor," he said.

"In the container," she said, "I first glimpsed myself as what I truly am, a woman, and a slave."

"Interesting," said Cabot.

"She, at least," said the slave, "is clothed in the beauty of a name!"

"It is a beautiful name, in its way," said Cabot.

"I have no name," she said. "I am a nameless slave."

"As of now," said Cabot.

"I may not name myself?"

"No."

"Are you going to name me, Master?"

"I may," said Cabot.

"I must hope that the name my master gives me, if he chooses to name me, will be pleasing to him."

"Perhaps," said he, "I will name you 'Miss Virginia Cecily Jean Pym'."

"That is not the name of a slave," she said.

"It was," he said.

"Yes, Master," she said.

"That seemed to me a very pretentious name," he said. "Probably it was contrived in such an extensive and absurd way to compensate for the brevity and plainness of the surname."

"'Pym'," she said, "is among the most respected, honored, and aristocratic of surnames!"

"It is pleasant to take aristocratic women and make them slaves," said Cabot, "to reduce them to begging, groveling sluts."

"And am I not an aristocrat so reduced?" she asked.

"No," he said. "Not really."

"No?"

"You were clearly not an aristocrat," he said.

"Master?"

"You may have thought yourself one, but rather, I think, despite your pretensions, you were, so to speak, a throwback."

"I do not understand," she said.

"Though you regarded yourself as, in effect, an aristocrat, you were even then, though this was unknown to you at the time, a mere slave."

"I do not understand," she said. "But it is true that I am a slave, and need to be a slave."

"It is not merely that you were not titled, for few are," he said, "but rather that you carry slave-girl genes in every cell of your body."

"How is that?" she asked, puzzled.

"I shall conjecture," he said.

"Please do so, Master," she whispered.

"Many of the female ancestors in aristocratic lines," he said, "were, in effect, slave girls, taken into households for their needs and beauty. Few would have been accounted slaves, perhaps, but that was, in effect, what they were, the lovely daughter of a peasant, sold for sheep, the orphaned beauty put to work in the stables, the pretty domestic servant summonable to the manor's lord's bed, and such, and, earlier, thousands of beauties sold in the markets of Roman Britain, and such. Women have always, in effect, been goods, of one sort or another, and men have always appropriated beauty. Do not doubt that many women in aristocratic lines once thrashed in the straw of stables, moaned in closets, obeyed in kitchens, and such. Many a woman, in effect, was dragged upward, from the collar to the coronet, and in the master's bed were never permitted to forget the collar."

"All were such women?" she asked.

"Certainly not all," he said. "And many of these women, perhaps the less beautiful, were not taken into families, but merely thrown a coin, or cast aside."

"And you think I may derive from such?" she whispered.

"I find it not hard to believe that some ancestress of yours might have been sold naked from a slave block in Roman Britain," he said.

"I only know that I am a slave, and need to be a slave, and desire to be a slave."

"Actually," he said, "the fundamental explanation here doubtless long precedes historical variations of the sort I have suggested."

"It has to do with the nature of women, and of men?"

"Yes," he said. "It would have to do with the natures favored by natural selection, in our species, interestingly, a radical sexual dimorphism, not only anatomically but psychologically, and the desire on the part of the smaller animal to submit and serve, to be owned and mastered, and that of the larger animal to own and master, such things."

"Nature would select for masters and slaves?"

"Yes," he said. I suspect this all goes back at least to the caves, and to thongs and capture, or bartering or exchanging women, buying and selling them, and such."

"We would have all been slaves," she said.

"Even a princess," he said, "has often been exchanged for land and power."

"Yes, Master."

"Kneel more straightly," he said.

"Forgive me, Master," she said.

"Slavery, in a legal sense," he said, "is a much later development. It is a sophisticated, complex social institution, one which has characterized most of the world's great civilizations. Its pervasiveness and success is doubtless to be accounted for by the fact that it has a profound natural basis. A civilization need not be antithetical to nature, a contradiction to nature, an affront to nature. It may, rather, recognize her and accept her, and, in its way, in its own complex context, celebrate her and enhance her."

"Yes, Master," she whispered.

"Of the helpless, loving slave, needing and wanting men, desiring to please and serve them, moaning and ecstatic in their arms, and the independent free woman, with her frigidity and pride, who is most likely to replicate her genes?"

"The master," she said, "would chain the slave to his bed."

"Of course."

Many Gorean couches, incidentally, have a slave ring at their base, to which a woman may be chained.

"Are all women slaves?"

"The Goreans have a saying," he said, "that all women are indeed slaves, only that some are in collars and some are not."

"I think it is true," she said.

"Certainly it is true that many are," he said, "indeed, untold numbers, restless, unfulfilled, longing for their masters."

"Yes, Master."

"The phenomenon is so widely spread, if not absolutely universal, that there must be genetic predispositions involved."

"Yes, Master," she said.

"Were you satisfied with the men of Earth?" he asked.

"No," she said. "I despised them. I would not let them near me!"

"And here?" he asked.

"Here," she said, "I have met men before whom I can be only a slave."

"They know well how to handle women like you," he said.

"Certainly," she said. "They collar and master us."

"Yes," said Cabot.

"And they move me, and thrill me," she said.

"You look well in your tunic," he said.

"A slave tunic."

"Certainly."

"Does master wish me to remove it?"

"Not now."

"It may be easily torn from me," she said.

"Perhaps, later," he said.

Cabot returned to inspecting what meager supplies remained in the pouch and bundle.

"Is there a whip amongst your things?" she asked.

"Certainly," said Cabot, "it was supplied by Peisistratus."

"Will you whip me?"

"If you are not pleasing," he said.

"Truly?"

"Certainly."

"I will strive to be pleasing."

"Excellent."

"But perhaps sometime you may whip me," she said.

"Why?" he asked.

"—That I may better know myself a slave," she whispered.

"We shall see," he said.

"Lady Bina has a name," she said.

"Yes," said Cabot.

"At least she is clothed in the beauty of a name," she said.

"Yes," said Cabot, absently.

"Will you not name me sometime?" she asked.

"Probably," said Cabot.

"I would like a name," she said.

"What you would like, or would not like, is of no interest," said Cabot. "Too, you must understand that any name put on you is like the brand or collar. It is a slave name, only that."

"Of course," she said, "for I am a slave. But, Master, would it not be better if I were named? Would it not be easier then to refer to me, to order me about, to summon me to your side, and such?"

"This matters to you, does it not?" he asked.

"Lady Bina has a name," she said.

"She is free," said Cabot.

The slave put down her head.

"Do not compare yourself with her," he said.

"No, Master."

"'Lita'," said he, "is a pretty name."

"Yes, Master!" she said.

"It is a common slave name," he said.

"Because it is such a lovely name for a slave!"

"Thousands of slaves are given the simple name, 'Lita'," he said, "as they are such names as 'Lana', 'Mira', 'Tuka', and such."

"Yes, Master!"

"I will call you 'Lita'," he said. "You are Lita. Who are you?"

"I am Lita!" she said, delighted. "Does it have a meaning?"

"No," said Cabot. "It is simply a lovely, meaningless sound, for a lovely, meaningless sort of animal, a female slave."

"Then it has that meaning, at least, in a way," she said.

"I suppose so," said Cabot.

"It is understood as a slave name, as only the name of a slave?"

"Yes," said Cabot. "Universally."

"Good!" she said.

"Certainly no free woman would have such a name," he said.

"So much the worse for them," she said.

"It would demean them, terribly."

"Perhaps not," she said.

Then she found herself, to her apprehension, under the gaze of her master. She straightened her body.

"Master regards me strangely," she said. "Am I not kneeling properly?"

"Lita!" he said, sharply.

"Master?" she said, startled.

"Your tunic," he said.

"Master?" she asked, uncertainly.

"Remove it," he said.

Swiftly, kneeling in the sand, she drew the tunic off, over her head, and put it beside her. Such garments have no nether closure, that the slave may well know herself slave.

"The first command I have been given as Lita," she said, "is to bare myself before Master."

"Yes," he said.

"And thus," she said, "the better I understand my name, that it is the name of a slave."

"Yes," said Cabot.

"I am bared before my Master," she said.

Cabot waited for a time, scrutinizing her lineaments. Gorean masters savor such pleasures.

"Master?" she said, at last.

"Perhaps you can anticipate the second command that will be given to Lita," said Cabot.

"I think so, Master," she whispered.

"Lita," said he.

"Yes, Master!" she said.

"Please me," he said.

"Yes, Master!" she said, and crawled to him.

Later the cylinder lights were lowered, to simulate dusk.

The slave returned to the place on the beach, with berries gathered in the woods adjacent to the slopes, those which led down to the beach.

There was no simulation of moonlight in the cylinder that night.

On Gor, given the three moons, and the differences in their phases, moonlight was frequent.

Cabot was standing on the shore, looking out over the waters of the lake. It seemed placid. He looked up, but could not see the overhead forests for the dimness of the light. Some days earlier they had been in that area, now above them, the more populated area of the cylinder, where were found many of the domiciles of Kurii, the arena, the palace, and such.

He heard the girl behind him.

He turned to see the slave.

Three times in the afternoon he had put her to slave use.

She smiled in the dusk, and lifted two handfuls of berries, her gleanings in the forest.

Cabot was pleased with the slave.

Each time her heat had increased.

But that is not unusual with slaves.

She put the berries down, on a flat rock.

Cabot looked to the side. There was a pile of dry wood there, chips, branches, and bark. This trove of combustibles had been fetched earlier by the slave, while Cabot had investigated the beach, and prowled within the forest, discovering however no sign of Lord Grendel or the Lady Bina.

Perhaps Grendel had not come to this place. Perhaps he had been already taken and was already slain, or incarcerated, heavily chained, in some foul pit or tiny cell.

While in the forest Cabot had procured a long, sharpened stick. It would serve as a weapon.

As yet, Cabot had kindled no fire, but expected to do so later, perhaps the next evening, and then withdraw from it, to the forest, to see who might come, if any, to inquire.

Cabot wondered if, overhead, the revolution had begun. Surely the men of Peisistratus had been about their errands.

Had Lord Arcesilaus been warned?

Presumably so, unless the messenger had been anticipated, or intercepted.

Eventually the stick's point might be hardened in the fire.

This place is muchly uninhabited, he thought.

He then approached Lita, who, seeing him approaching, knelt.

He opened his right hand, palm upward, and lifted it, slightly, and the slave stood.

He saw the glint of the collar on her neck.

"Lift your tunic," he said, "over your breasts, and hold it there."

"You stand well," he said.

"Master is close to his slave," she said.

Cabot was silent.

They were but inches from one another. He put down his head, and she felt his breath on her body.

"It is my hope to be pleasing," she said.

He put his hands on the sides of her waist.

"Oh, yes!" she said, softly, eagerly. "Yes, yes, Master!"

Gently he lowered her to the sand.

"You will not sell me, will you?" she begged.

"Certainly," he said, "if I tire of you."

"Do not tire of me!" she begged.

"We shall see," he said. "See, look, there are no stars here."

"Do not sell me!"

"You are goods," he said. "Who knows. I might get a good price for you."

She moaned.

"Do not fret," he said. "You are a slave. You will leap obediently in any man's hands."

"I cannot help what you have done to me," she wept.

"But you need it now," he said.

"Yes, Master," she said. "I need it now!"

"Be silent," he said. "Kneel beside me, and please me."

"Yes, Master!"

"Ah!" he said. "If only your young men of Earth could see you now!"

"Oh, Master!" she wept.

"They would doubtless relate to you differently."

"Yes, Master!" she wept.

Presumably this was an allusion to the effect the sight of a female slave may have upon a male, for such a sight can be so violent a spur to manhood as to transform a life, for who who has had a woman as a slave will be content thereafter to do with less?

"Continue," said Cabot.

"Yes, Master," she said.

"It is late," said Cabot, "and it is time to retire."

She lay beside him, her head at his waist.

"Do you know *bara*, Lita?" he asked.

"Yes, Master, from the cylinder."

"*Bara*," he said.

She went to her stomach and crossed her wrists behind her back, and crossed her ankles.

"I am to be bound, Master?" she asked.

He did not respond to her, but in a moment, with two short cords, whipped free, she was trussed, hand and foot.

"Open your mouth, widely," he said.

She then, in a moment, regarded Cabot, wide-eyed, the packing secured in her mouth, held in place with its straps.

"You obviously did not hear it," whispered Cabot to the slave. "It is approaching, slowly, coming out of the water."

Her body stiffened in terror.

"I did not want you to scream," he said. "We do not know who, or what, might be about. Do not fear. I will not let it come too close."

Cabot then lifted her in his arms, and turned toward the lake.

Her entire body began to squirm in terror. He could scarcely hold her.

In the tiny bit of light remaining she detected a large head, perhaps a yard across, wet, glistening from the water, on a long, thick neck, wet, glistening, the head some fifteen feet away, moving on the neck, weaving almost as might have the head of the giant hith, Gor's mightiest constrictor.

"Steady, Lita," soothed Cabot. "See the jaws. It is herbivorous, probably a grazer on lake plants, perhaps a threat to small fish."

The beast inched forward, on huge, paddlelike appendages. A long tail moved in the sand behind it.

"Do you know gag signals?" asked Cabot.

The beast came a bit closer.

The slave shook her head, negatively, desperately.

"One tiny sound," said Cabot, "for 'Yes', two such sounds for 'No'. Do you understand?"

She nodded affirmatively, vigorously. Her eyes were wide, stricken with terror, over the gag.

"Would you like to withdraw?" he inquired.

She uttered a tiny sound, desperately. In a moment, she uttered another, more fearfully."

"That is two sounds," said Cabot.

The slave squirmed in protest, in terror.

The head of the beast was something like a yard from them.

She uttered another sound, her body writhing in terror.

"That is one sound," said Cabot. He then put the slave over his shoulder, her head to the rear, as slaves are commonly carried, and bent down to pick up his stick. He turned, and hit the large head twice, lightly, playfully, on the side. "It is safer for you out here, at night, is it not, big fellow?" Cabot asked the saurian, and he then turned about and climbed the slope toward the forest edge. On his shoulder, the girl was unconscious.

Chapter, the Thirtieth:

A Slave Learns More of Gor

Cabot looked about.

"I am hungry for meat," he said.

A breeze was moving inward, gently, from the lake.

This was a function not of fans but of the differential heatings of cylinder surfaces.

The cylinder world, you see, is much like a natural world. It has its exchanges of gases, its alternations of day and night, its diversities of seasons, of temperatures and weathers. Most of the world's environment, too, was parklike, or soft with meadows, hills, and forests. Its agriculture, save for gardening and floriculture, and its industry, save for some traditional smithies and shops, is removed to its auxiliary cylinders, in particular those for agriculture and that for industry. Many Kurii had never been outside the cylinder.

Cabot looked down.

Lying at his feet was an object.

It squirmed in the sand, and Cabot put his foot on it, gently, to quiet it.

It was a female slave.

He removed his foot from the girl's belly.

He had not permitted her her tunic this morning.

Some sand from his bared foot adhered to her belly.

The slave at his feet was no longer gagged, but she was bound hand and foot. Slaves are often bound, or braceleted, or chained, or fastened in one way or another. There is, of course, a great variety of slave ties, and they have little in common other than the fact that in them the slave is absolutely helpless, and left in no doubt as to the fact that she is a bound slave.

The slave looked up at her master. She was frightened, certainly apprehensive. She squirmed a little, in the bonds, but could in no way lessen, reduce or mitigate their perfection.

"Have I displeased you?" she asked.

"No," he said.

"But I am bound, helplessly," she said.

"That is because you are a slave," he said.

"Yes, Master," she said.

He then lay on the beach, beside her, and she inched to him, and pressed her body against his.

She then inched downward, and kissed him on the thigh.

"May I confess something, Master?" she asked.

"If you wish," he said.

"I love being bound, helplessly," she whispered.

"That is because you are a slave," he said.

"Yes, Master," she said. "I am then so mastered. I am then so dominated, so much at your mercy, so helpless, so categorically yours, so uncompromisingly and categorically owned."

Masters, incidentally, not unoften caress their helpless slaves to ecstasy. It apparently amuses and pleases them.

"Free yourself," he said.

"Master well knows I cannot," she said.

"Try," he said.

She squirmed, and struggled, for a time, and then subsided. "I cannot free myself," she said. "I am helplessly bound."

"It is true," he said.

"Yes, Master," she said.

Among the instructions accorded to young Gorean males, incidentally, is the binding of female slaves. It is something with which every Gorean male is to be familiar.

"Slaves," he informed her, "are sometimes staked out, and used for bait."

She shuddered.

"Would you like that?"

"No, Master," she said.

"Do not fear," he said. "It is pot girls, and kettle-and-mat girls, such slaves, who would be used in such a fashion. Two-tarsk girls are not used for bait."

"I hope that I am a two-tarsk girl," she said.

"You are, clearly," he said.

"Thank you, Master," she said.

"Tomorrow," he said, "I think I will begin to leash train you."

She looked up at him.

"Beautiful slaves are often leashed," he said. "Masters in the cities, visiting markets, places of business and such, often take their girls along, on leashes."

"Like dogs?" she said.

"The same idea, of course," he said.

"I want to be leashed," she said.

"Of course," he said, "for you are a slave. Doubtless your young men of Earth would enjoy seeing you on a Gorean street, slave-clad, muchly bared, collared, leashed."

"Doubtless," she said.

"I may teach you, too, how to kneel and kiss the whip."

"I learned something of that in the cylinder," she said.

"It is a beautiful symbolic act," he said. "How did you feel about it?"

"At first I was terrified," she said, "but then, as I began to better understand its significance, and why I was on my knees, and kissing the whip, it moved me, and it stirred me, exciting my belly, profoundly."

"Excellent," said Cabot.

"Soon," she said, "I was eager to perform this act."

"Good," said Cabot.

"Too," she said, "I think I did it acceptably, with timidity, and tenderness, and deference, and hope, and awe, acknowledging my station as slave and the rightfulness of my submission to the might of men."

"And it continued to stir you, and excite you?" he asked.

"Oh, yes, Master," she said, "terribly so. Yes Master!"

"Good," he said.

"And eventually you might learn to do it," said he, "piteously, beggingly, supplicatingly, with tiny noises, in such a way as to drive a master mad with passion."

"And with my hands tied, or braceleted behind my back!" she said.

"Quite possibly," he said. "And you will improve in your skills, and learn the slow slave use of your tongue, and the slave use of your lips."

"Such things excite me," she said. "In my training, even with the hint of such thoughts, I could barely remain on my knees."

"There are many ways to lick and kiss the whip," he said, "tenderly and lovingly, humbly and gratefully, lasciviously and avidly, pleadingly, needfully, supplicatingly."

"Yes, Master," she said. "Yes!"

"There are skills involved in all slave acts," said Cabot, "even in so simple a thing as the kisses of slaves."

"Perhaps Master will teach me," she said.

"It would doubtless improve your price," he said.

"Oh, Master!" she protested.

"Incidentally," said he, "being skilled in slave acts, such as kissing the whip, has saved many a girl a beating."

"Yes, Master," she smiled. "I can understand that."

Many are the ways, incidentally, in which a girl learns to placate her masters. Most commonly it is no more than the placing of herself before him as his slave, perhaps putting herself to her knees, her head down, contritely, to his feet, perhaps ministering to them with her lips and tongue, perhaps placing his foot gently upon her head, perhaps approaching him penitently, on all fours, bringing him his whip in her teeth, such things.

"Master," she said.

"Yes," he said.

"I am restless, I am eager."

"You may speak," he said.

"Have me," she said. "Have me, please!"

"That sounds as though of Earth," he said.

"Then use me, Master," she said. "Please, use me! I beg it!"

"I gather," he said, "you are begging to be put to slave use."

"Yes, Master!"

"You beg slave rape?"

"How can one rape a slave, Master?" she asked. "The slave is a property, an animal. She belongs to the master."

"In the legal sense," said Cabot, "you are right. One cannot rape a slave, any more than one can rape a verr or tarsk."

"What if the slave were unwilling?"

"The same," said he. "No more than a verr or tarsk."

"What if she were seized by one not her master?"

"The same," said he. "No more than a verr or tarsk. But in such

348

a case the master might object, and take action, perhaps charging a coin for the girl's use, or perhaps killing the thief."

"The thief?"

"Surely, has he not availed himself of another's property without authorization, has he not stolen a use?"

"But one can rape a free woman?"

"Surely," he said, "and the penalties for that can be grievous, particularly if a Home Stone is shared."

"What is a Home Stone, Master?" she asked.

"You are a slave and may not have one," he said. "Do not concern yourself with the matter."

"Yes, Master."

"Free women may be raped, of course," he said, "by raiders, by warriors of foreign cities, by slavers, and such, for women are generally recognized on Gor as loot. But the rape of such women is usually no more than a prelude to their collaring."

"How humiliated they must be, and how shamed they must be, to be subjected to such a use when free."

"But after such a use," he said, "they are commonly desperate to be collared."

The girl said nothing.

"Perhaps," he said, "that is because afterwards they regard themselves, so reduced, and so stained, as never again being worthy of assuming the dignities and glories of the free woman."

"Oh, not at all, Master," she said.

"Oh?" he said.

"No," she said, "it is because they have been, doubtless for the first time, rather as a slave, in a man's arms."

"Interesting," said Cabot.

"And they sense not only the labors and terrors of bondage, but its meaningfulness, its stark significance, and its secret fulfillments, of which one scarcely dares speak to a man, and its joys, its indescribable joys."

"So I have gathered, here and there," he said.

"It is true, Master," she said.

"Surely their feelings toward their bondage, at least at first, must be ambivalent."

"Doubtless," she said, "but only at first, for later, as they learn what it is to be a female and a slave, they would not exchange their collars for all the dignities, glories, and freedoms of the world."

"I see," he said.

"They find their meaning, and joy, at the feet of a master."

"As a slave, as you are."

"Yes, Master," she said.

She was lovely, lying beside him, bound, hand and foot.

"With respect to the more general sense of 'slave rape,'" he said, "putting aside the legalities, and such, the expression, I think, is intended to suggest the rightlessness of the slave, and her subjectability to the least whim of the master. Too, not unoften, she is simply unilaterally ravished. The meaning of the locution then is extended, metaphorically, to reflect the powerlessness, the unprotectedness, the defenselessness, of the slave, how she is absolutely vulnerable, how she has not the least say over the uses to which she will be put."

"I see, Master," said the slave.

"But the term, too, I think," said Cabot, "clearly reflects something of the harshness, the ruthlessness, with which she may be handled."

"I gather she may not play the games of the free woman," she said.

"No," said Cabot.

"Nor demand, and control, the nature of her uses."

"No," said Cabot.

"Perhaps men sometimes grow impatient with the games, and play, of the free woman," she speculated.

"Yes," said Cabot.

"Games, and play, not available to the slave," she said.

"Definitely not," he said.

"I trust Master is not impatient with me," she said.

"No," he said. "If I were, you would be lashed."

"There is a broad sense of the term 'slave rape', of course," said Cabot, "in which all usages of a slave, all uses of her, are in a sense slave rape, as her usages are not at her will but solely at the will of the master."

"Yes, Master," said the slave, "and that is why she must frequently beg."

"Yes," said Cabot.

"How cruel are the masters," she said. "You make us need our rapings, desperately, and then we may not be granted them!"

"It is the way of masters," he said.

"And the misery of a slave!"

"Perhaps," said Cabot.

"But as the term is commonly used," said the slave, "it tends to betoken an uncompromised, categorical usage, does it not?"

"Yes," said Cabot.

"When I was free, I did not treat men well," she said.

"That is the prerogative of a free woman," he said.

"I no longer possess that prerogative," she said.

"Certainly not," he said. "You will now serve men, and strive desperately to please them, and as a slave, to the best of your ability."

"Yes, Master," she said.

"Surely I have much to be punished for," she said.

"Nonsense," he said.

"For when I was a free woman," she said.

"No," he said. "That is behind you."

"But sometimes, surely," she said, "a master will avenge himself on the slave who was once a troublesome free woman."

"Perhaps," he said.

"Perhaps she treated him badly, scorned his advances, mocked his courting, amused herself at his expense, ridiculed him, belittled him, and such."

"In such a case," he said, "he would doubtless see to it that she learned her collar to perfection."

"Good, Master," she said.

"And then he might well sell her."

"Oh, I hope not!" she said.

"He will do with her as he pleases."

"Of course, Master," she said.

"In any event," said Cabot, "as long as he keeps her, she will find herself no more than his meaningless pleasure object."

"Good!" she said, warmly.

"'Good'?" asked Cabot.

"Certainly," she said, "and would she not be occasionally subjected to—"

"Yes?" asked Cabot.

"What Master said before," she said.

"Categorical usages, slave rape, in the most common sense, and such?"

"Yes," she said.

"Certainly," said Cabot, "and perhaps frequently."

"Sometime you will treat me so, will you not, Master?" she asked.

"Perhaps," he said.

"As you spoke before," she said, "unilaterally, ruthlessly, with no thought of me whatsoever, but only of your own desire, and pleasure, using me without the least concern or mercy."

"Speak," he said.

"I want to be had," she said, "—unilaterally, ruthlessly, callously, as what I am—as a mere, helpless, meaningless instrument of your pleasure—*as a slave*."

"You request slave rape?"

"Yes, and of the most uncompromised, unilateral kind!"

"Is it important to you?"

"Yes," she said. "I want it. I want it!"

"I see," he said.

"It is fitting for me, is it not, as I am a slave?"

"Yes," said Cabot.

"Teach me I am a slave, Master," she begged.

"You understand that hereafter this may be done to you and will be done to you whenever I please?"

"Yes, Master!"

"Very well," said Cabot.

He then bent to untie her ankles.

Chapter, the Thirty-First:

Rubies

"Behold!" cried Cabot to the slave. "Come here!"

She sped to him, lightly, swiftly, in her tiny tunic.

Cabot was pleased with her.

Over the past few days she had progressed irrecoverably in her bondage. Her carriage, her kneeling, her subtlest movement, was now that of a slave.

In Cabot's hands she had been spoiled for freedom.

Cabot had no doubt that she would now go for at least two tarsks.

Freedom was now well behind her.

She had learned bondage.

Even if she were to be freed now she could never be more than an unhappy slave, a miserable slave pretending to be a free woman. She might attempt to imitate a free woman, true, but the farce would be hypocritical and hollow, for she had once worn a collar, a slave collar. The role of the free woman to her would now be shallow, empty, and meaningless.

She had learned herself slave.

If Cabot freed her, and cast her aside, she would doubtless have no hope of happiness other than to find a new master, a new man from whom to beg a collar, a new man to kneel before, and serve.

But, then, who would be so foolish as to free one such as she?

One would want her as what she was, a slave.

One would keep her as what she was, a slave.

So keep them for your pleasure.

It is what they are for.

She hurried to Cabot, and knelt at his side.

She was so soft, so radically feminine, and graceful.

Cabot noted the position of her knees.

How free she now was, how fulfilled, how unabashedly alive and sensuous!

Freedom was now behind her, forever, even if it meant the auction block.

She was muchly unaware of these changes in her mien, her attitudes, and her emotions.

She thought herself much the same as before.

But she was mistaken.

She was now slave.

She did not even realize how her body might betray her.

That is something men seldom make clear to a slave.

Sometimes a slave, in attempting to flee a bondage of great cruelty, perhaps that of the laundries or mills, might don the garments of a free woman, hoping to elude recapture, but, to the alert, practiced eye, even beneath the cumbersome Robes of Concealment, and the veils, might be detected the body of a slave. Woe to her if she were then picked up and remanded to free women, that her body might be subjected to a discreet, private inspection. Lo! The brand is detected, and perhaps even a collar! The free women are outraged, but overjoyed, for they then have at their mercy what they hate most, a female slave. And one who has dared to attempt to pass herself off as one of their own exalted sisterhood! The hapless, terrified slave is then stripped, held down, and lashed. She is then pulled by the hair to a kneeling position, and bound, mercilessly, and then, to the rejoicing, exultant shrieks of her nobler sisters, who find revels and festival in such things, she is pulled to her feet and driven, spit upon and jeered, muchly switched, to waiting guardsmen.

How gratefully she throws herself to her belly before them and licks and kisses their sandals.

Perhaps she may be spared?

They, at least, are men.

"Look, girl," said Cabot, pointing downward, at the sand.

She cried out, and put her hand before her mouth.

There was no mistaking the nature of the prints in the sand.

"Kurii!" she said. "In the night, Kurii!"

"One," said Cabot, "only one."

"We must flee, Master," she said.

"No," said Cabot. "Look here!" Again he pointed downward, and she rose to her feet, came to his side, and looked downward.

"See," said Cabot. "Small prints, barefoot, the prints of a woman!"

"It is Lord Grendel then," she said, "and Lady Bina?"

"Yes," said Cabot. "I am sure of it!"

"It could be a trick, to trap Master," she said. "A Kur, and a slave, or pet."

"I do not think so," said Cabot. "The prints do not come down to the beach. They come from the lake."

"How could that be?" she asked.

"A boat, a raft," said Cabot.

"It is death to be on the lake," she whispered.

"It may be death to be on the beach," said Cabot, "if discovered."

Cabot looked out, over the lake. It looked quiet. It was hard to believe that beneath that placid surface menaces might stir.

"We set the fire, as a signal, three nights ago," said Cabot. "This might be the signal that it was seen."

"The prints?"

"Surely."

"Lord Grendel would not know it was your signal," she said.

"He has come to investigate," said Cabot. "He has found the ashes of the fire, and that is not all he found."

"What else?"

"What I left."

"I do not understand," she said.

"On this stone," said Cabot, "I left rubies."

"You left rubies about!" she said, shocked.

"Do not concern yourself," he said. "You may own nothing."

"But my master!" she said.

"They are all here," he said.

"How could he find them, in the dark?" she asked.

"He has the vision of a Kur," said Cabot.

"How do you know he found them?"

"They have been rearranged," said Cabot.

"How would he link them with Master?" she asked.

"He was present at the trial of Lord Pyrrhus," said Cabot, "and might well have seen the strings of rubies given to me by Agamemnon, which I wore over my robes."

"He knows then that it is you who left them?"

"He would at least surmise such," said Cabot.

"How do you know it was he who rearranged the rubies?" she asked.

"I do not know," he said, "but I believe it was he."

"Why, Master?"

"The rubies are arranged in the shape of a letter," he said, "the fifth letter in the Gorean alphabet, Gref."

"Master?"

"The first letter," he said, "in the name 'Grendel'."

"Might not anyone have so arranged the rubies?" she asked.

"Yes," said Cabot, "but look here, to the side, in the sand. Here, the print of a hand, pressed down, firmly, deeply, into the sand."

"So?" she said.

"Look," he said.

"Five fingers!" she said.

"Not six," said Cabot.

"Grendel, Lord Grendel," she said.

"I think so," said Cabot.

"What will we do?" she asked.

"We will set a fire again, tonight," he said. "And wait."

"Yes, Master," she said.

"Gather wood," he said.

"Yes, Master," she said.

"And before it grows dark," he said, "you will please me."

"Yes, Master," she said.

Chapter, the Thirty-Second:

Cabot Receives Guests

"Ho!" called Cabot, softly. He lifted a branch, from the flames, moving it back and forth, and then replaced it in the fire.

"Tarl Cabot!" said a voice, like that of a Kur, but not perfectly so. It was a voice which could articulate, after a fashion, Gorean phonemes.

"Lord Grendel," said Cabot, relieved.

"Grendel," said the owner of the voice. "Why are you here?"

"To ascertain your whereabouts," said Cabot, "and that of a free woman whom I fear is not to be trusted."

"You came to bring me news, or succor?" said Grendel.

"News," said Cabot, "is that the revolution is imminent, and may have begun. You might therein be of valuable service. Succor, if I could be of service, and found you needful."

"I need no help," said Grendel. "And are you armed?"

"With a sharpened stick, to serve as spear," said Cabot.

In the darkness there was a snort of derision.

"Come ashore," said Cabot.

A raft, heavy, with doubled timbers, grated on the beach. Its size and weight were doubtless intended to provide stability on the lake, and provide some impediment to the efforts of large saurians who might emerge beneath it, hungrily, to tip or overturn it.

"I trust you are better armed," said Cabot.

"I have a long ax," said Grendel. "With it I have slain four tharlarion."

"Then you have meat," said Cabot.

"I know why you are here," said Grendel.

"Why?" said Cabot.

"You have it in mind to slay the Lady Bina," he said.

"I will do my best to see that she does not betray Lord Arcesilaus and Peisistratus to the palace," said Cabot.

"No harm must come to her," said Grendel, menacingly.

"Do you then come ashore to kill me?" asked Cabot. "I have no serious weapon, and I cannot outrun you."

"You are of the Warriors," said Grendel. "In your hands a tiny branch, sharpened, a length of vine, is dangerous."

"I am concerned that the Lady Bina does not reach Kurii," said Cabot. "But I have no interest in causing her harm."

"She is safer with me, on the lake," said Grendel.

"Scarcely," said Cabot.

"I will not speak!" came a voice from the darkness, that of the Lady Bina, doubtless still on the raft.

"You would speak instantly, and at the first opportunity," said Cabot.

"No," she said. "And save me from this monster!"

"If you are going to kill me," said Cabot to Grendel, "might we not eat first? Perhaps you have some meat, from tharlarion."

"Do you have others with you?" asked Grendel.

"No," said Cabot.

"'No'?" said Grendel.

"None," said Cabot, "that is, none save for a meaningless thong bitch, whom I have named Lita. Lita, come forward."

The slave came and knelt beside Cabot. She could be seen in the light from the small fire.

"I have seen her before," said Grendel. "But she is now different."

"Yes," said Cabot. "She is now different."

"There is a collar on her neck," said Grendel.

"She is nicely marked, as well," said Cabot.

"It is not just such things," said Grendel.

"No, I suppose not," said Cabot.

It was true. Many were the subtle and lovely changes which had recently been wrought in the slave.

"Disgusting!" said a feminine voice in the darkness.

The slave stiffened, and shrank back, recoiled, in fear. It seemed she would leap up and flee, but she remained on her knees. She had not been given permission to rise. She had heard the censorious, imperious voice of a free woman. There was no mistaking the enmity in such a voice, to such as she. And she well understood how much she would be at the mercy of so powerful, glorious, and exalted a creature.

Then, stepping carefully, daintily, departing from the forward portion of the raft, slid onto the sand, that her feet not be dampened, a woman had descended to the beach.

Cabot bowed, respectfully, for he was in the presence of a free woman, and such are to be treated with the courtliness due to their status.

"Tal, Lady Bina," said he.

"Tal, fellow," said she.

"Do not approach him too closely," said Grendel.

"I fear the oaf not," said she.

Lady Bina, to the extent practical, was robed. She was not sandaled, but she was robed. Cloths had been found, or stolen, with which she was now attired. She was unfamiliar with the cumbersome intricacies of the usual Robes of Concealment, their arranged foldings, the abundant drapings, and such, which vary from city to city, but she had simulated something akin to them, doubtless with the aid of Grendel, who would have been familiar with such things from his abortive venture to Gor, that in which he had failed Agamemnon, as he had not been accepted there as human. A hood was about her head, loosely, but she was not veiled, though something like veiling was about her neck, and might presumably have been emplaced as veiling.

"Do not approach him too closely," warned Grendel.

But Lady Bina came to stand before Cabot, and looked up at him.

"You are robed," said Cabot.

"Certainly," said she, "as I am free."

"I recall you," said Cabot, "as the naked, collared pet of Lord Arcesilaus, and as once clothed only in chains, in breeding shackles, as I recall."

Grendel growled, and was close at hand, a little behind the free woman.

Lady Bina regarded Cabot, fiercely, and then, with all her might, slapped him across the left cheek.

"You do not have gloves," said Cabot. "Commonly free women, or certainly those of high caste, wear gloves with the Robes of

Concealment. I might have caught a glimpse of your wrist, and noted that it might look well enclosed within a slave bracelet."

It seemed she would strike him again, but then did not do so. Rather she laughed, lightly, dismissively.

"You are not veiled," said Cabot. "Are you not afraid that your lips might be discerned, and their nature mistaken for that appropriate for a slave?"

Grendel half roared in protest.

"Forgive me, Lord Grendel," said Cabot.

In the full Gorean Robes of Concealment little of the free woman can be seen saving her eyes, over the veiling, and beneath the hood. In the Tahari region the veiling is often so complete that even the eyes cannot be seen, but must be surmised, as peering outward though a dark gauze. Certainly the body is to be muchly concealed. And the robes, with their length, and the nature of the sleeves, and the gloving, are designed to conceal as well as possible the speculative treasures which might be hidden within them.

To the Gorean the sight of a free woman's wrist, or ankle, can be powerfully stimulatory.

That the wrists and ankles, and the throat, and the lips, and face, of a woman of Earth can be commonly seen is taken by most Goreans as evidence that they are worthy, at best, if anything, of being the slaves of Gorean free persons. And certainly these barings much ease the work of the Gorean slaver plying his trade on Earth. Such acquisitions are fully bared, of course, when sold. Only a fool, it is said, would buy a woman clothed.

"No," she said. "If I were veiled my beauty would be concealed, and it is the means by which I will bend men to my will."

"We each have our weapons," said Cabot.

She laughed, merrily, and then, as though first noticing the slave, she said, "What have we here?"

"Head down," said Cabot to the slave, and she lowered her head.

"How scrawny she is," said Lady Bina.

"Scarcely," said Cabot.

"I wonder what men see in such things," said the Lady Bina.

"They have their purposes," said Cabot.

"What a skimpy garment," said the Lady Bina. "How bared she is! She might as well be naked!"

"It is a slave tunic," said Cabot.

"And there is something on her neck, is there not?" said the Lady Bina. Then she said to the slave, "Lift your head, girl!"

The slave lifted her head, quickly, frightened, looking straight ahead.

"Why it is a metal collar," exclaimed the Lady Bina, as though astonished. "And how closely it encircles her neck!" she said. She then walked about the slave, and parted the hair at the back of the slave's neck, for one may handle slaves so, and the slave, frightened, remained unmoving, absolutely so. "And there is a lock here!" she said. She then put her hands on the collar, and tried to open it. "Why it is locked on the poor thing!" she said, as though amazed. She then came about the slave, before her, and stood next to Cabot. The slave did not dare to meet her eyes. "Surely she can take it off," said the Lady Bina, as though concerned.

"No," said Cabot.

"How is that?" she asked, as though puzzled.

"It is a slave collar," said Cabot.

"Then she is a slave?"

"Yes," said Cabot.

"But would she not then be marked?" asked the Lady Bina.

"Brand!" snapped Cabot, and the slave, as she had been trained, shifted her weight, kneeling, to her right knee, extended her left leg, and drew the hem of the tunic to her hip.

"What a lovely mark!" said the Lady Bina.

A tear ran down the cheek of the slave.

"You may return to position," said Cabot, and the slave, again, knelt, and gratefully, her head down.

"Perhaps you would like one like it yourself?" asked Cabot.

Grendel growled.

The Lady Bina, it seems, did not hear his remark.

"There is a legend on the collar," she said.

"It says," said Cabot, "'I am the property of Tarl Cabot'."

"Yes," said the Lady Bina, "it was hard to read, in the light."

"What did she cost you?" asked the Lady Bina.

"In a way," said Cabot, "I owe her to your cohort and champion, Lord Grendel, for I won her, in effect, on a bet, wagering that he would be successful in the arena. I won coins in this matter from Lord Peisistratus, and he generously threw her in, with the coins."

"Then she cost you nothing?"

"True," said Cabot.

"That is what she is worth," said the Lady Bina.

"I think," said Cabot, "she might, exhibited naked on a Gorean slave block, in an open market, bring as much as two tarsks."

"And what would I bring?" inquired the Lady Bina.

"Free women," said Cabot, "are priceless."

"Girl!" snapped the Lady Bina.

The slave looked at her, wildly, frightened.

"'Mistress'," coached Cabot.

"Mistress!" said the slave.

"You are worthless," said the Lady Bina. "You are no more than an animal, a branded animal."

"Yes, Mistress," said the girl, putting her head down.

"As you are an animal," said the Lady Bina, "why are you clothed?"

"Master has permitted his animal a tunic," she said.

"Remove it," said the Lady Bina.

The slave looked to Cabot, questioningly, and he nodded, affirmatively. The desires of free women are seldom questioned.

"That is better," said the Lady Bina, with satisfaction.

Tears sparkled in the slave's eyes, visible in the light of the small fire. One could note the path of tears on her cheeks.

"On your belly, before me," snapped the Lady Bina, "and lick and kiss my feet!"

"Excellent," laughed the Lady Bina.

"Lady Bina," said Cabot, "is well learning to be a free woman."

Lady Bina did not respond to Cabot, but stepped back, a pace from the prone slave. "Stay on your belly," she snapped. And the slave remained before her. "It gives me much pleasure to see you so," said the Lady Bina to the prostrate slave, "for in the container, on the Prison Moon, it seemed to me that you dared to compare yourself with me, and might even have dared to regard yourself as my superior." She then kicked some sand against the prostrate slave, who winced, but stayed as she was. "You were a naked slave then, as you are now," said the Lady Bina. "I saw how you attempted to display yourself to this fellow in the container, how you turned, seemingly so innocently, to exhibit your figure, how you held your head, at this attitude or another, how you extended your legs, and held your arms, how you pointed your toes to curve your calves in that delicious manner which is calculated to so stimulate the interest of men, many things. You were no more than a slave, competing pathetically, and unsuccessfully, for the attention of a free male! Speak, slut, quickly, or be beaten!"

"Forgive me, Mistress," begged the slave.

"How stupidly bold you were, how presumptuous, how insolent!" said the Lady Bina.

"And now you are as you should be, a collared slave!" said the Lady Bina.

"Yes, Mistress!" wept the slave.

"Did you, truly, in the container," asked the Lady Bina, "think to compete with me?"

"Yes, Mistress," she said. "Forgive me, Mistress! But I then thought myself a free woman!"

"And thought yourself my equal, or better?" scoffed the Lady Bina.

"Yes, Mistress. Forgive me, Mistress!"

"How foolish you were!" said the Lady Bina.

"Yes, Mistress," wept the slave.

"Rise, back away, and kneel," said the Lady Bina. "Too, don again your tiny, meaningless rag, for it goes nicely with your collar, brand, and slave's body."

"Thank you, Mistress," whispered the slave.

"She is plain, and stupid," said the Lady Bina to Cabot. "What do you want her for?"

"She can gather berries, wood for the fire, and such," said Cabot.

The Lady Bina laughed.

"Lord Grendel," said Cabot.

"Grendel," said he. "I am not of station in the world."

"Have you and Lady Bina," inquired Cabot, "entered into the Companionship?"

"No," said Grendel.

Lady Bina laughed, scornfully, at the preposterous nature of so untoward a supposition.

"But yet you protect her, and permit her to accompany you," said Cabot.

Grendel did not respond.

"Why do you not put her in a collar?" asked Cabot. "We could then have a brunette and a blonde, a nice pair, which we might then, throat-linked by a chain, sell for a handsome profit."

The Lady Bina regarded Cabot uneasily, angrily.

The slave looked up at him, frightened.

She well knew she could be sold, at a master's whim.

"I trust that you jest," said Grendel. "The Lady Bina is a free woman."

"That is true," said Cabot, "but she would look well, branded."

"Do not jest," said Grendel.

"It is true that I am beautiful," said the Lady Bina.

"If she were a slave," said Cabot, "it would be easier to assure ourselves that she would not contact Kurii and implicate Lord Arcesilaus and Peisistratus in the matter of treasonous plotting."

"I would not speak!" she said.

"You would speak instantly, and abundantly, if you thought it in your best interests," said Cabot.

"No," she averred.

"I watch her," said Grendel. "Too, there is the raft, from which she dares not escape while it is on the lake, and when we come to shore, it is a simple matter to put her on a rope, and, at night, I chain her to a tree."

"She bears no impediments now," observed Cabot.

"I am watching her," said Grendel.

"You do not trust me," said Lady Bina, reproachfully, to Grendel.

Grendel looked down, confused, hurt.

"If you loved me, as you have claimed," she said, "you would keep me free, and trust me."

Grendel seemed torn, agonized.

"And, too, how dare one such as you, a monster, aspire to the love of a free woman!"

"Forgive me," said Grendel, his head down.

"Do you think yourself worthy of such a thing?" she asked.

"No," said Grendel.

"And so much the more so of a free woman such as I?"

"No," said Grendel. "No."

"If you like," said Cabot, "I will take her into custody, binding her, leashing her, and such."

"No," said Grendel.

"I am a free woman!" said the Lady Bina.

"Even a free woman," said Cabot, "may be subjected to controls of various sorts, a limitation to specified locales, imprisonment, leashings, the restrictions of light chains, and such, if the interests of states are at stake. There is much precedent for that sort of thing."

"True," said Grendel.

"You do not truly love me," said the Lady Bina.

"I do love you," protested Grendel.

"If you truly loved me," she said, "you would trust me, and leave me to be as I wish, to do as I wish, and go where I wish."

"Please!" he begged.

She turned away from him, coldly. "Thus," she said to Cabot, "you see he does not truly love me."

"I think he loves you muchly," said Cabot, "and foolishly."

"I am beautiful," she said. "No man can love a beautiful woman foolishly."

"Those are perhaps the easiest to love foolishly," said Cabot, "and that is an excellent reason why one should not trouble oneself with them, but rather put them in collars, and own them."

"Beast!" she said.

"Do you have meat?" Cabot asked Grendel.

"Some pieces torn from tharlarion," said he.

"Excellent," said Cabot. "Let us eat, and then you can kill me afterward."

"The fire has served its purpose," said Grendel, looking about.

"Very well," said Cabot.

With the butt of his improvised spear he scattered the embers of the fire. In a moment the tiny points of light had faded into darkness.

"I do not much care for raw tharlarion," said Cabot.

"Nor Kurii for raw human," said Grendel.

"But it is meat," said Cabot.

"So, too, is human," said Grendel.

"Your mother was human," said Cabot.

"I do not eat human," said Grendel.

"That is good news for the Lady Bina," said Cabot.

"For all of you," said Grendel.

"True," said Cabot.

"Do you eat Kur?"

"No," said Cabot.

"Why?" asked Grendel.

"—I do not care for it," smiled Cabot.

"Perhaps we should withdraw into the trees," said Grendel. "The beach is muchly open."

"Let us do so," said Cabot.

"I will not eat raw tharlarion," said the Lady Bina. "We are now on land. You must find me something better."

"In the trees," said Cabot, "we have a small camp, and there are edible leaves there, some gathered roots, and berries."

"It must do," said the Lady Bina.

"I will get some tharlarion from the raft," said Grendel.

"Lita," said Cabot, "hurry to our camp, set out provisions for our guests, and later arrange bowers for them, sheltered beds of moss, grass and leaves, that they may sleep softly."

"Yes, Master," she said, and hurried toward the trees.

"See her run," said the Lady Bina, amused.

"Dalliance is not permitted to her," said Cabot. "She is a slave."

"She should be a slave," said the Lady Bina, sneeringly.

"Yes," said Cabot, "and that is what she is, and what many other women should be, as well."

"It was clever of you to send her away, while my gross cohort fetches tharlarion from the raft," said the Lady Bina. "In that way we can speak privately."

"I do not understand," said Cabot.

"I must speak to you," she said.

"You may do so in the presence of Lord Grendel," said Cabot.

"No," she said.

Shortly thereafter Grendel joined them on the beach, some blankets over his shoulder, a long ax in his right hand, and some strips of tharlarion dangling from his left hand.

The three of them then proceeded toward the trees.

At the nineteenth Ahn the cylinder was illuminated with artificial moonlight, simulating that of Gor's major moon.

"There are berries there," said the Lady Bina to Grendel. "Bring them to me."

"Yes, Lady," said he.

The slave Lita, shortly thereafter, knelt before Cabot, offering him berries, cupped in her two hands.

"How pretty!" sneered the Lady Bina.

The Gorean male, if not seated on a chair, or bench, or reclining on a supper couch, commonly sits cross-legged. The Gorean free woman may sit upon a chair or bench, or recline on a supper couch. If she kneels, she kneels demurely, with her knees closed. The female slave, commonly, is not permitted to sit on a chair or bench, and is certainly not permitted on the surface of a supper couch. Indeed, often she is not permitted even on the surface of her master's couch, for that is understood as showing her great favor. Envied is the girl so honored! Commonly the slave is used on furs spread at the foot of the master's couch, to which she is often chained, by the neck or an ankle. If she is permitted on the surface of the couch, there is often a ritual involved, in which she kneels at the foot of the couch, or toward its foot, on the side, and lifts the coverings, and kisses them humbly, and then, when permitted, crawls to the couch's surface, from the bottom, or near the bottom. In this way she acknowledges the privilege being accorded to her. The female "tower slave," though slave clad, may kneel with her knees closed, as the free woman. The female "pleasure slave" will commonly kneel with her knees open, this betokening the sort of slave she is.

Cabot was chewing on a strip of tharlarion, to soften it, before tearing it into small bits, these then to be better chewed and swallowed.

Grendel ate more in the fashion of the Kur, ripping large pieces of tharlarion apart with his hands and teeth, and then cutting them into ribbons with his fangs, and then, with movements of his head and long, dark tongue, forcing them downward into his cavernous gorge.

Lady Bina looked away from him, in disgust.

"Would you like some tharlarion?" Cabot asked the slave.

She shuddered. "Your slave," she said, "would prefer leafage, or berries."

"You gathered more berries this afternoon," said Cabot.

"Yes, Master," she said, lifting the berries to him.

"Did you eat any?" asked Cabot.

"No, Master," she said.

"We shall see," he said, and took her by the hair, and pulled her to a place where the artificial moonlight streamed down amidst the branches.

"Open your mouth, widely, more widely," he said, holding her head back, "and protrude your tongue, as far as possible."

"Good," said Cabot. "Good."

"I did not eat any berries, Master," she said, when released.

"Yes, so I determined," he said.

"Had I eaten berries, what would have been done to me?"

"If you had eaten them without permission?"

"Yes, Master."

"You would have been tied and lashed," he said.

"Could you do that to me?" she asked.

"Certainly," he said.

"And would you do that to me?" she asked.

"Certainly," he said. "You are a slave."

"Yes, Master," she whispered.

"One cannot have that sort of thing in a slave," said Cabot.

"I understand, Master."

"Though they are often sly little beasts," he said.

The slave was silent.

"But the behavior of even such a slave," said Cabot, "one who thinks she is so clever, is soon corrected, as the whip swiftly counsels against such indiscretions."

"I will endeavor to serve my master as well as I can, according to his wishes," she said, frightened.

"See that you do."

"Yes, Master," she said.

"I wish she had eaten some," said the Lady Bina. "I would have liked to have seen her tied and lashed."

"You may feed," said Cabot to his slave.

"Thank you, Master," said the slave, and bent to the berries in her hands.

"Slut!" snapped the Lady Bina.

"Mistress?" said the slave, looking up, the smears of berries about her mouth and lips.

I am told, incidentally, that Masters enjoy licking such residues from the lips and mouth of a slave, and, as it seems, one thing then not unoften leads to another.

"Your knees!" said the Lady Bina.

"Mistress?" said the slave.

"Should they not be spread?"

"She is in the presence of a free woman," said Cabot. "It is thus appropriate that she kneels in the Tower position."

"Have her split her knees," said the Lady Bina.

"Do not shame her," said Grendel.

"Be silent," she said.

"You would have her kneel in full *nadu* before me, with a free woman present?"

"She may, of course, continue to feed," said the Lady Bina.

"*Nadu*," said Cabot to his slave.

She spread her knees before her master, and, head down, fed.

"How pretty!" sneered the Lady Bina.

"Do not shame her," said Grendel.

"May I speak, Master?" asked the slave, looking up, to Grendel.

"Yes," he said.

"I am not shamed, Master," she said.

"Shame, shame, shame!" shrieked the Lady Bina, and leapt up, and would have struck the slave, but was prevented from doing so by Cabot who, himself leaping up, seized her wrists, held them, and by means of them returned her to her place, kneeling, to the side of Grendel.

"Whip her, whip her, mercilessly!" demanded the Lady Bina.

"It was you," said Cabot, "who desired to have her placed in *nadu*."

"Are you not shamed?" asked Grendel of the slave.

"No, Master," said the slave. "I am not shamed."

"Slut!" cried the Lady Bina.

"I am not only a slave, Master," said Lita to Grendel, "but I am a special sort of slave, one different from many, and to be sold as such, the Pleasure Slave. She exists for the service and pleasure of her master. Thus, as I am such a slave, it is appropriate for me to kneel as that sort of slave. The position, you see, indicates my nature, as worthless as it may be, and betokens my defenselessness and vulnerability, but, too, my readiness. Yes, Master, it is true. My readiness! I am pleased and overjoyed to have been found worthy to be such a slave, to be granted the inestimable privilege of kneeling so helplessly, so vulnerably, and revealingly before my masters, before men. Too, to kneel in this fashion not only proclaims me, shamelessly, to the world to be the sort of slave I am, but reminds me, as well, and profoundly, and shamelessly, of the sort of slave I am. Too, it thrills and excites me to kneel so before my master. It heats me. In me, so kneeling, desire flames!"

"Slut, slut!" said the Lady Bina.

"Yes, Mistress," said the slave, and put down her head.

"You may continue to feed," said Cabot.

"Put your knees together!" hissed the Lady Bina.

The slave looked to Cabot, for he had given her the *nadu* command. He nodded, and she placed her knees together, and, head down, continued to feed.

"She should be beaten," said the Lady Bina.

"Do not fear," said Cabot. "She is a slave. Thus, it is not unlikely that she will be whipped from time to time."

The slave shuddered, and the better knew herself slave.

"Come, Beast," said the Lady Bina to Grendel. "Bring me more berries, and leafage, roots, if well washed! I am hungry."

Grendel hurried to do her bidding.

Cabot, meanwhile, finished his bit of tharlarion. He did this without considerable enthusiasm.

When Grendel had returned, and served the Lady Bina, Cabot spoke to him. "The tharlarion was not much good," he said.

"No," agreed Grendel.

"Are you going to kill me now?" asked Cabot.

"Perhaps in the morning," said Grendel.

"Lita has prepared beds for you, such as she could," said Cabot.

"My thanks, Warrior," said Grendel.

Grendel and the Lady Bina then retired.

"Am I to be tied tonight, Master?" asked Lita.

"No," said Cabot. "Moreover, as there is a free woman in the vicinity, go off a bit, and prepare yourself a bower, alone."

"Master!" she protested.

"We must not disturb her rest," said Cabot, "or annoy her, or keep her up all night listening for the slightest sound like a suspicious she-urt. Thus, no thrashings about this night, no moanings, no uncontrollable gaspings, no wild, inadvertent utterances, no sudden cryings out, none of that sort of thing."

"May I not, at least, sleep at my master's feet?"

"No," he said, "for I am only human."

"Yes, Master," she said, resigned, and began to retreat into the near darkness.

"Lita," he called softly.

"Yes, Master," she responded.

"Are you going to run away?" he asked.

"No," she said.

"Why not?" he asked.

"I cannot," she said. "I am chained."

"How is that?" he asked.

"I am held in the most perfect and inescapable of all chains," she said.

"What is that?" he asked.

"That I am your slave, my Master," she said.

It was near the second Ahn when Cabot, stirring, sensed a presence near him.

"Make no sound, Lord Tarl," whispered the Lady Bina.

"Where is Lord Grendel?" asked Cabot.

"He is sleeping," said the Lady Bina.

"How is it that you are not tethered?" asked Cabot.

The Lady Bina laughed, softly. "I told the beast that I would not leave my bower, and if he truly loved me, he must trust me."

"He believed you," said Cabot.

"And so for the first night in days, I am neither a raft's prisoner, nor tethered ashore."

"He trusts you," said Cabot.

"Yes," said the Lady Bina.

"What do you want?" asked Cabot.

"I must speak with you," she said.

"So, speak," said Cabot.

"The beast," she said, "is treasonous to the world's master."

"The world's master," said Cabot, "in the view of many is treasonous to the world."

"No," said the Lady Bina, "for it is the world's master who defines treason."

"I see," said Cabot.

"You fell from his favor," she said, "but might regain it, if you exercise audacity and judgment."

"How so?" asked Cabot.

"You are strong, and have a sharpened stick," she said. "You could fall upon Grendel in the darkness, and slay him in his sleep."

"You want him dead," said Cabot.

"Certainly," she said. "He is ugly, presumptuous, repulsive, and dangerous."

"He loves you," said Cabot.

"I loathe and despise him," she said. "He is a beast, a monster, neither Kur nor human."

"Why do you not kill him yourself?" asked Cabot.

"I might fail," she said.

"Do not fear," said Cabot. "Even so, he would probably forgive you."

"You would not fail," she insisted.

"I would like to sleep," said Cabot.

"Kill him, and come away with me," she said. "Think! We know much that would be of value to Lord Agamemnon. He would reward us well for what we know."

"Lord Grendel could have killed me on the beach," said Cabot. "He did not do so."

"What is this?" queried the Lady Bina. "Honor?"

"Perhaps," said Cabot.

"Men are fools," she said.

"Perhaps," said Cabot.

"I am beautiful, am I not?" she asked.

"Yes," said Cabot. "Very beautiful."

"Come away with me," she said. "Perhaps I will let you hold me, and touch me, and kiss me."

"What of the slave, Lita?" inquired Cabot.

"Abandon her," said the Lady Bina. "Or sell the collared slut, or give her to me, as a serving slave. I will lash her into a terrified, miserable, excellent serving slave."

"I am sure you could do that," said Cabot.

"I have never forgotten your kiss, by the lock in the sport cylinder," she said.

"It was a mistake," said Cabot.

"You could not help yourself," said the Lady Bina. "You found me irresistible, irresistibly luscious, as will other men."

"You should be collared, and sold," said Cabot.

"Too," she said, softly, "I have never forgotten your touch."

"That in the breeding shackles?"

"Yes!" she said, angrily.

"I think you should return to your bower," said Cabot.

"Touch me, again," she said, "as you did then. I will permit you to do so."

"Lady Bina is generous," said Cabot.

"Do so," she said.

"No," said Cabot.

"'No'?"

"No."

"I want it," she said.

"We often want things we cannot have," said Cabot.

"But I am a free woman," she said.

"Even so," said Cabot.

"I hate you," she said.

"You could always cry out to Lord Grendel," said Cabot, "to rescue you from my foul grasp."

"He would kill you," she said.

"If he believed you, perhaps," said Cabot.

"And he would still be alive," she said.

"Or if I should survive," said Cabot, "you would then have me to answer to, would you not? And what do you think would then be your fate?"

"Do you not love me?"

"If I did not use you for bait on the beach," said Cabot, "I might sell you, or give you to Lita, as a serving slave."

"How can you not love me?" she asked.

"You are an extremely beautiful and desirable woman," he said, "and you would doubtless, stripped, bring a good price on the auction block, but, even so, it is less difficult than you surmise."

"I can bring you not only beauty," she said, "but position, honor, and riches."

"That is an obvious superiority of the free woman over the slave," he said.

"Certainly," she said.

"Strange then," said he, "how men should prefer slaves."

"A slave's beauty," she said, "is not even hers to bring—but others' to buy or seize."

"True," said Cabot.

"And she will not bring you wealth and power!"

"One might sell her for a profit," said Cabot.

"What can one have from a slave?" she scoffed.

"Herself," said Cabot, "wholly, as one cannot begin to have from a free woman."

"They would be no more than your animal," she said.

"True," said Cabot.

"And doubtless," she said, "an animal from whom one may have unquestioning, instantaneous obedience and, at one's least whim, inordinate pleasure."

"Yes," said Cabot.

"Despicable!" she said.

"Perhaps," said Cabot.

"Men wish their women to be slaves?" she said.

"That is how they want them," said Cabot.

"Such as that despicable Lita," she said.

"She lacked much on the world, Earth," said Cabot, "which she has now found, in a collar."

"Come away with me," she said. "Let us hasten to Agamemnon!"

"I am weary," said Cabot. "Return to your bower."

"You refuse to kill Grendel? You refuse to accompany me to Agamemnon?"

"Yes," said Cabot. "Now return to your bower."

"I hate you," she hissed.

"Return to your bower," said Cabot, and turned away from her, to sleep.

Chapter, the Thirty-Third:

A Return to the Habitats Is Contemplated

The light was bright on the lake, and it was not well to look too long on its waters.

"Why did we wait three days?" asked Cabot.

"I hoped she would return," said Grendel.

"You could have followed her, could you not?" asked Cabot.

Grendel reached to activate the small, disklike translator on his harness.

"You do not need that," said Cabot, irritably. "Do not put a machine between us. I can understand your Gorean."

"My Gorean is imperfect," said Grendel. "It has to do with the throat."

"I can understand you quite well," said Cabot. "Your Gorean is different, but comprehensible."

Grendel snapped off the translator, it seemed reluctantly.

"Yes," said Grendel. "I suppose I might have followed her. She was barefoot, and was indiscreet in her flight, leaving various traces."

"She did have a start," said Cabot. "Perhaps as much as three Ahn."

"Even so," said Grendel.

"Why did we not pursue her?" asked Cabot.

"She told me she would remain in her bower," said Grendel. "I trusted her."

"A tragic mistake," said Cabot. "In three Ahn she might well have come to a trail, and encountered Kur patrols."

"What is love," asked Grendel, "if there is no trust?"

"Do you think she loves you?" asked Cabot.

"No," said Grendel.

"She is a treacherous little she-urt," said Cabot, "and should have been kept on a tether, bound hand and foot, naked."

"Please," said Grendel, reprovingly, "she is a free woman."

"Blindfolded and gagged," said Cabot, angrily.

"Do not be angry with her," said Grendel. "She is beautiful."

"She might have made contact with Agamemnon's people within Ahn of her flight," said Cabot.

"True," granted Grendel.

"Look," said Cabot, suddenly, pointing to a stirring in the water.

"Tharlarion," said Grendel, resting on the mighty oar with which he propelled the raft.

Grendel then again plied his mighty lever.

"Lita," said Cabot, "lie nearer the center of the raft."

The slave crawled closer to the center of the large, rude raft, some yards in width, and lay there, supine, her left arm shading her eyes from the light, amidst the small store of supplies, one property amongst others. She was tunicked, and about her waist a rope was fastened, which rope was fastened, too, to the raft. By means of this arrangement, in the event of a storm, or an attack by tharlarion, should she be pitched into the water, she would not be separated from the raft, but would have at her disposal a means for regaining its surface. Cabot found it difficult to take his eyes off her. Her arms were bare, as is common with a slave tunic. The tunic itself was quite short, as is common, too, with such garments. Yes, Cabot thought, the slave is nicely legged, and that would doubtless, on a sales block, improve her price. How utterly marvelous are women, he thought. How excruciatingly desirable, and marvelous, they are! It is no wonder, he thought, that men want them, and want them as slaves. It is no wonder that they are sought, hunted, captured, and collared. He regarded the collar on her neck. How right it was there, unslippable, closely encircling her neck. How beautiful it was! And how beautiful she was, collared! And it was his collar!

"We will try to reach the far shore," said Grendel.

"To eventually obtain access to the habitats," said Cabot.

"Yes," said Grendel.

"I trust," said Cabot, "to join those who would stand against the Eleventh Face of the Nameless One."

"Perhaps," said Grendel.

"I fear it is too late," said Cabot. "Indeed, by now the world may be abundantly repopulated, with numerous reinforcements for Agamemnon, the fleet having returned."

"True," said Grendel, "and we may be dealt with, on sight, with power weapons."

"I advised against dalliance," said Cabot.

"I thought she might return," said Grendel.

"Why did you take her with you in your flight?" asked Cabot.

"Many wanted her life," said Grendel. "I took her with me to protect her. I feared she would be sent to the pens, as cattle."

"She betrayed you," said Cabot.

"I strove to protect her," said Grendel. "I could not continue to do so unless she were with me."

"And now?" asked Cabot.

"She may need me," said Grendel.

"Forget her," said Cabot.

"I cannot," said Grendel.

"She is your enemy," said Cabot.

"I am not her enemy," said Grendel.

"You would sacrifice a world, for one sly, cunning, treacherous she-urt?"

"I love her," said Grendel.

"I fear you are unwise, my friend," said Cabot.

"I am part human," said Grendel.

The slave stretched, languorously, and sat up, looking about.

She smiled at her master, and looked away, over the water.

What a clever little she-sleen she is, thought Cabot. Surely she knows what that smile can do to a man. How innocent it seems, and how devastating. How such a smile can twist the insides of a fellow! Well, he consoled himself, he could have her whenever he wished. She, that sinuous little Earth slut, now goods, now no more than salable, purchasable, collar meat, was his!

"Master!" she suddenly cried, pointing upward.

Cabot and Grendel looked upward.

It was very small, and somehow between the lake and the forests overhead.

"See the wings," said Grendel. "It is in the area where such things can propel one, where there is little fastening to the cylinder surface."

"As in the shuttles," said Cabot.

"Yes," said Grendel.

"Has he seen us?" asked Cabot.

"I do not think so," said Grendel.

They had been now on the lake for two days.

Cabot assisted with the oar from time to time, but it was Grendel who plied it tirelessly, sometimes when Cabot and his slave slept.

They had seen two tharlarion but neither had approached the raft. They had seen nothing further in the sky above them, save for the forests and meadows overhead, on the other side of the cylinder.

Two more days had then passed.

"Tomorrow we will make landfall," said Grendel.

It was at that point that the slave had leaped to her feet, and screamed, and pointed.

Grendel thrust the oar back on the raft and seized up the long ax.

A massive head, glistening, shedding water, on a long neck, had emerged from the water, not yards from the raft.

"That is carnivorous," said Cabot, picking up the sharpened stick he had formed into a makeshift spear.

"Master!" cried the slave, frightened, miserably.

"Get behind me," said Cabot, and the slave scurried behind him, and crouched down.

Whether she lived or died, she well understood, would depend on the courage and prowess of others. She was half naked, collared, and weaponless. But it would not have been otherwise had she been free, and terrified, quivering helplessly within ornate robes. In either case she would be a woman dependent on men, on larger, stronger, fiercer beasts, for her very survival. When there is fighting, slaves are often chained, that they will helplessly await the outcome of war, and their disposition, and free women, too, are often sequestered, that they may not by their presence compromise defenses or complicate ensuant adjudications. Women on Gor are not men. In their smallness, softness, slightness, weakness, loveliness and beauty they are either treasures to be protected, or, if things turn out badly, prizes to be distributed. They must wait to learn if they are to be rejoicing guests at a victory banquet or stripped slaves serving it.

Gor is a man's world, you see, and women are men's.

"We are closer to land," said Grendel. "Such things are commonly found closer to shore. Some beach at night. Some hunt on the beaches at night. There is more forage closer to shore, for fish, for herbivores, for their prey."

The head moved on the long neck, swaying, snakelike, which seemed odd in an aquatic creature.

"It may not take us as food," said Grendel, his ax lifted.

"It is submerging!" said Cabot.

There was a subtle, gentle subsidence in the water where the great body slipped beneath the surface.

"Master!" cried the slave, pointing back.

Another large head, similar to the first, though perhaps of a different species of aquatic tharlarion, had broken the surface.

Its head was only four feet or so from the surface. Its neck was thicker and shorter than that of their first visitor.

"There is another!" shrieked the slave.

This head was similar to that of the first, doubtless of the same species. In a moment both of these new arrivals had slipped beneath the surface.

"They are gone," said Cabot.

"Cling to the raft!" said Grendel, standing.

Cabot and the slave held to the ropes binding the huge logs together.

Almost at the same moment the raft seemed to leap upward in the water, some great back beneath it, and then, with a mighty splash that drenched the occupants of the primitive vessel it struck back down into the water.

"Master!" screamed the slave.

"Hold to the ropes!" cried Cabot.

Grendel was down on one knee, his right hand on his ax, his harnessing, and the fur beneath it, drenched with water.

He shook his massive head, to rid his eyes of water.

"It is quiet," said Cabot, as the raft settled back, rocking on the surface.

"No, no!" said Grendel.

Then a body, that of the same behemoth or one of the others, rose under the raft and tipped it to the left, sharply. The slave screamed, losing her grip on the wet rope to which she clung, and slid over the logs and plunged into the water. Cabot reached to her rope, that fastened about her waist, and dragged her out of the water onto the raft's surface, she crying and sobbing, the raft then again righting itself.

"They cannot overturn it!" shouted Cabot.

Then the stem of the raft rose almost vertically into the air and its occupants clung to the ropes on the wet surfaced almost as if clinging to a wall. The slave screamed, and Cabot extended his hand to her, which she grasped.

Then the raft again plunged into the water, with a mighty splash.

"You built this well!" Cabot called to Grendel.

"It can be overturned," cried Grendel. "If it is, get back on it, swiftly! Do not stay in the water!"

"It is too heavy to overturn!" said Cabot.

"No," said Grendel. "These things have such force."

"Ai!" cried Cabot, in dismay.

He then thrust his makeshift spear under ropes, from whence, were the raft overturned, he might, from beneath the surface, have been able to recover it.

"Surely the raft is too heavy to overturn, Master," wept the slave.

"It seems not," said Cabot.

He then bent to free the slave's waist rope from its anchoring on the raft. "If the raft is overturned," said Cabot, "the rope might hold you under the raft. Can you swim?"

"No!" she wept.

He then looped the rope about his arm.

"Cling to the rope," he told her.

"Yes, Master!" she wept.

A moment later the raft again tilted to the left, and then, half visible, the mighty back of one of the gigantic saurians, like a wet, scaled mountain, rose higher and higher, and then the raft, after a moment, slid free, and struck again into the water. "He cannot do it!" called Cabot to Grendel.

"No!" said Grendel. "He now understands it can be done!"

Again the mighty body emerged under the side of the raft, and the raft again tilted to the left, and then it was vertical, and its occupants dangled from the ropes. "Jump!" cried Grendel, and leapt from the raft. Cabot seized the slave and leaped clear of the raft, just as it struck into the water, inverted. He scrambled onto the bottom of the raft, now upward, and dragged the girl onto its surface beside him. "Grendel!" called Cabot. He saw a huge paw rise out of the water, and then Grendel was on the raft. In his harness, he had thrust the haft of the long ax. "We are safe!" said Cabot.

"No, no!" said Grendel.

Again the mighty body emerged under the raft and again the raft was almost vertical in the water, and was then vertical, and then struck down again, with great force, its occupants, as before, leaping free. Cabot thrust away large jaws reaching for him, and then he, dragging his slave with him, clambered back onto the raft. A moment later Grendel had joined them. "The supplies are gone," said Cabot.

"They are hungry," said Grendel. "They are not finished."

The raft was now upright, having twice turned, but, as Cabot had observed, their supplies were gone.

Logs were loosened, and water washed about their feet.

"The raft is heavy!" said Cabot. "It is hard for them!"

"I fear it will break up," said Grendel.

The slave screamed.

Cabot's foot slipped between parted logs, and he drew it up, swiftly, as the logs, loose in their ropes, clashed together.

The slave was on all fours, half in water.

She screamed.

A large head had lifted itself out of the water and was reaching, head turned, for Grendel, who struck its jaw with the ax. It drew back, flesh hanging from the side of its jaw, seemingly more puzzled than injured.

Blood spread into the water.

"We are done," said Grendel. "There is blood! These things can smell that from a pasang away!"

Grendel stood, the ax ready, lest the large aquatic predator approach anew.

Cabot extracted his makeshift spear from its ensconcement within the ropes of the raft, and held it, crouching down.

He saw a stirring in the water, as of a large body but a yard or so below its surface, approaching smoothly, unhurried.

Another head, the shorter, wider head, on the shorter neck, emerged behind Cabot and he, alerted by the tiny sound, spun about, and, crouched down, jabbed at the head, over the slave's prone body, and the point of the stick, blackened, and fire-hardened, but perhaps over sharpened, intended not for such an application, but for the penetration of more yielding targets, say, Kurii, snapped against the jaw, much as if it might have been plunged against rock.

Cabot drew back the splintered weapon.

The beast was peering at him, unhurt as far as Cabot could tell.

He had at his disposal no Gorean spear with its stout blade, a weapon which might have been, as the ax of Grendel, more potent.

"Master!" cried the slave, pointing, for another head had emerged form the water.

There might then have been six, or seven, saurians, curious, aggressive, within a dozen yards of the raft.

"Brought by the blood," commented Grendel. "And there will be others."

"Yes," said Cabot.

The beasts, of course, were not accustomed to men, or Kurii, both so unlike their usual prey. Too, their usual strikes would be made within the water, or near the shore. They would not understand the raft, but they could sense food.

"It is a matter of time," said Grendel.

Certainly they had tried to bring their quarry into the water.

They had met surprising resistance, however, in attempting this, due to the weight of the raft.

Again one of the predator's heads extended over the raft, jaws opened, reaching for Grendel.

He struck at it, and the ax was seized in the snapping jaws, and, with a wrench of the great head, flung away, into the water.

"I wish you well," called Grendel to Cabot.

"I, too, wish you well," said Cabot.

Cabot stood, unsteadily, on the loosened logs. He sensed the slave at his feet. She was kneeling, her head down, pressing herself against his leg.

He put his hand in her hair, fondly.

"Are we to die?" she asked.

"It would seem so," he said.

She looked up at him, her face stained with water, and tears, and smiled.

"You are a pretty slave," he said.

"Thank you, Master," she said.

"I think you are clearly worth two tarsks," he said, "and, stripped, I think you would sell for such, in almost any market."

"Thank you, my Master," she said.

"I regret only," said Cabot, "that I have had too little time as yet to apprise you more adequately of what it is to be the Earth-girl slave of a Gorean master."

"'As yet'?" she asked, startled, hopefully.

"Yes," he said.

"But there is more?" she said.

"A thousand times more," he said, "and more beyond that."

"Would that I were better apprised of that, my Master," she said, "for I long to be so helpless, so reduced, so obedient, so submissive, so dominated, so utterly and vulnerably dominated."

"There are horizons beyond horizons," he said, "mornings beyond mornings, nights beyond nights, pleasures beyond pleasures, fulfillments beyond fulfillments. A slave can never complete that journey, her journey into the fulfilling riches and beauties of helpless bondage and submission, for there is always more to learn, to understand, to do, and feel. The emotional, physical, and psychological rewards are endless."

"And yet we can be bought and sold!" she said.

"Certainly," he said. "You are a slave."

"Yes, Master," she said.

"Would you have it otherwise?" he asked.

"No, Master," she said, "for otherwise I could not know myself so much a slave, otherwise I could not be the slave I so much long to be."

Grendel, without his ax, was standing at the stem of the half-shattered raft, looking out, over the lake.

"They are coming, two or more," he said. "They will take us from the surface, or, if we enter the water, from the water."

"Perhaps not," said Cabot.

"It is over," said Grendel.

"Perhaps not," said Cabot.

"You are a fool," said Grendel.

"I am human," said Cabot.

"I am Kur," said Grendel.

Cabot then gently thrust the slave to the side, and lifted the splintered remains of his makeshift spear.

"You will fight to the end?" inquired Grendel.

"Certainly," said Cabot. "I am human."

"I will fight, too," said Grendel, lifting his hands, from which the claws emerged, like knives, "for I am Kur!"

"It is coming!" said Grendel, as one of the monsters, indeed, the first who had visited the raft, it seems, cleaved toward the raft, the water sliding from its back on both sides, sparkling in the light, simulating that of late afternoon.

But its advance was oddly, abruptly, arrested, and its gigantic paddlelike appendages churned in the water, but they did not move the tons of massive body forward, and then most of the body disappeared beneath the surface, almost as though drawn back, and down, and its head, on the long neck, rose up, for a moment, yards above the surface of the lake, as if to snap at a moon or star, and its large, round eyes, inches in width, under their transparent, encasing membranes, seemed to stare about, wildly, stupidly, and then the body, the neck, and head, disappeared, as though drawn downward.

"What is it?" called Cabot.

"It must be another tharlarion," said Grendel. "I do not understand. It was not bloody. It must be another beast!"

Suddenly the saurian rose from the water, as a whale might have breached, and one of the paddlelike appendages was a massive, bleeding stump, and its belly was torn open in a wound yards long, a wound so deep it might have reached the spine of the beast, and gut and blood, and organs, burst from the rupture. Then it fell back into the lake.

Two smaller tharlarion began to attack it, while it still lived.

"Beware!" called Grendel.

Cabot turned and, with the stick, jabbed at the second large head whose jaws, turned sideways, were reaching for him.

But suddenly that beast, too, seemed drawn back, away from the raft, its head and neck sliding back, on the logs, away from the raft.

A moment later a surge of blood and tissue reddened the lake about the raft, as though the lake itself had bled.

"There is something down there!" said Grendel.

"What?" called Cabot. "What?"

"I do not know," said Grendel.

Suddenly the slave cried out, in pain, and clambered atop one of the logs out of the water.

"What is it?" called Cabot.

"The water," she said. "The water, Master! It hurts!"

Cabot pressed his hand into the water, and withdrew it, with a cry of pain.

"Look!" called Grendel, pointing to the lake.

Beneath the surface there seemed thousands of flashing, shimmering, lights, darting about, flickering.

With bellows of pain, tharlarion, on all sides, far more than they had understood were in the area, with a churning of water, fled.

"There are charges in the water," said Grendel. He put his hand into the water and, wincing, drew it back, instantly. "It is not tharlarion," he said.

"Fish, eels?" said Cabot.

"No," said Grendel. "No."

"Surely," said Cabot.

"No," said Grendel.

"Look!" cried the slave, pointing forward.

There, some twenty or so feet from the raft a shape had arisen slowly, majestically, from the lake. It was certainly in the form of a gigantic aquatic tharlarion. There was the massive body, the huge, paddlelike appendages, a powerful, elongated, snakelike neck surmounted with a massive head, with mighty fanged jaws. But this was all of metal.

The head moved, surveying them. There were two reddish, jewellike lenses where the eyes of a natural saurian might be found. The body itself was scaled, in a way, but with shimmering, overlapping metal plates.

The jaws of the machine, and its rows of arrayed knifelike teeth, were scarlet, bearing traces of the work it had performed below the surface.

Grendel addressed the machine in Kur.

"Turn on your translator!" said Cabot.

Grendel did so, but there was no sound emanating from the immense object before them, either in Kur or Gorean.

The glowing lenses or optical devices regarded them for a few moments, and then the huge machine quietly submerged, leaving only some ripples in its wake.

"It is a body of the Eleventh Face of the Nameless One," said Grendel, "a body of Agamemnon, Theocrat of the World."

"He now knows where we are," said Cabot.

"Yes," said Grendel.

Chapter, the Thirty-Fourth:

The Storm;
The Cave

"The wind is rising," said Cabot. "How is that? Is the climate not controlled within the world?"

"It is controlled," said Grendel. "That is why it is rising."

"How could the behemoth body of Agamemnon have been brought to the lake?" asked Cabot. "I have seen little of cartage adequate to such a load."

"There are vehicles," said Grendel, "but I do not think they were used. Rather I suspect the body was housed near the lake."

"And Agamemnon came to it?"

"Or was brought to it," said Grendel.

"I do not understand," said Cabot.

"It is a thought, no more," said Grendel.

"Agamemnon is Kur, surely," said Cabot.

"Certainly," said Grendel, "but what is Kur?"

"I do not understand," said Cabot.

"Master," said the slave, shivering, "it grows cold."

"The blanket is lost," said Cabot.

"Master would have given it to me?" she said.

"Certainly," said Cabot. "One cares for the beasts which belong to one."

"Yes, Master," she said.

"Why should the temperature be falling?" asked Cabot.

"I am not cold," said Grendel.

"It has to do with humans?" asked Cabot.

"I fear so," said Grendel.

"The revolution has begun?" asked Cabot.

"Perhaps, rather," said Grendel, "this will prevent it from beginning."

"Weather is a weapon," said Cabot.

"In this world," said Grendel.

The slave suddenly shuddered, and moaned.

"What is wrong?" asked Cabot.

"I am miserable, Master," she said, "and hungry. Please forgive me."

"By morning," said Grendel, "perhaps tonight, I do not know, we will make landfall. There should be forage ashore."

The slave put her arms about herself, and trembled with cold. The small tunic afforded negligible warmth, and it was still wet, as was her hair, from the events of an Ahn earlier, those in which they had been so grievously imperiled, only to be succored unexpectedly by Agamemnon, Theocrat of the World, or by means of a body under his control.

"The lake grows choppy," said Cabot.

"There is going to be a storm," said Grendel.

The raft, mighty as it was, began to respond to the force of swift, rising swells. A wind whipped Cabot's tunic about him, and tore through the fur of Grendel.

The slave, crouched down, whimpered in misery.

The raft lifted, and fell, and tipped, and bucked, and pitched about. Muchly was it at the mercy of the lake's tumult, whether one meaningless and blind, or contrived.

How helpless are even we in the face of such masses and forces!

"Ai!" said Cabot, nearly losing his balance.

"Get down," said Grendel. "Cling to the ropes."

Cabot crouched down by the slave, and, holding to a rope, put an arm about her, and she put her dark, wet hair against his shoulder.

"It grows dark!" said Cabot.

Too suddenly it seemed that darkness fell.

A driving rain began to fall.

The wind rose further, roaring, lashing the air.

"Grendel!" called Cabot.

"I am here!" he heard, a voice scarcely heard against the wind.

Cold waters washed over the raft. Even Grendel then threw himself down and fastened himself within the raft ropes.

The raft was lifted a dozen feet into the air, again and again, and dropped, and was flung from side to side. Cabot felt the logs loosening beneath him. The slave screamed. A rope tore apart. He felt it rip through his hands, pulled away, carried off into the wind-torn, rain-driven darkness, wound about some shifted, dislodged log. He felt another log beneath his feet then, that of the lower tier of logs, and then it, too, seemed to move from side to side, and, other ropes broken apart, it slipped sideways under the raft, and was swept away, somewhere. Cabot was then in the water, between logs, and the slave clung to him.

"The raft is breaking up!" called Grendel. "Cling to a log, bind yourself to it!"

A heavy log struck against another log.

Had Cabot, or Grendel, or the slave, been placed otherwise than they were surely one or the other of them would have been crushed.

Two other logs crashed together, and one was lost in the night.

Rain continued to torment the raft and lake.

Even Grendel could not see for the darkness, and the rain.

Cold water washed over the remains of the raft, now little more than loosened timbers, held in proximity to one another by strained, then slack, scattered strands of rope.

"Hold to me!" called Cabot to the slave, and he thrust a log away and tried, clinging to another, to work his way from the raft. The slave lost her grip and cried out, but Cabot seized her by the hair and pulled her to him, and then both were clinging to a rope wrapped about a single log, and the raft might then, for all they knew, have been a dozen yards away.

"Call out!" cried Grendel, "and I will try to stay with you! Call out! Call out!"

"Here!" called Cabot. "Here!"

In the darkness, in the cold, blinding water, he thrust the slave to the log, and, with loops of wet rope, loose from the log, fastened her to it, and then he thrust his own arm amongst the ropes, and clung to the log as it pitched about, rising and falling, and sometimes rolling over, taking them beneath the surface, and then it pitched up, again, in the darkness, bringing them again to the surface, they gasping for air, trying to breathe in the ferocity of the rain and wind.

"Here!" cried Grendel, against the storm, scarcely audible.

"Here!" cried Cabot, in response, trusting that his companion's hearing, equivalent to that of a Kur, might detect the sound amidst the wash and roar of the storm.

It is not clear how long the storm lasted, as it is difficult to judge such things. Doubtless to Cabot and his companion, Lord Grendel, and his lovely beast, the slave, she who had been given the name 'Lita', it seemed a long while, perhaps even the night. On the other hand, more likely, it lasted little more than two or three Ahn.

In any event, whatever may have been the case, it was still dark when Cabot, fastened to the log, awakened, shuddering, and felt a graveled sand beneath his feet, and, then, exhausted, he thrust the log to which he had bound himself forward, foot by foot to the shallower water, and then he was on the beach, and slipped from the log, and freed the unconscious slave from her fastenings, and carried her further, higher, onto the beach, and then, putting her down, collapsed.

Later Cabot awakened in a small cave, to the heat of a fire near its mouth. The slave was still unconscious.

Grendel put a stick on the fire. It was still raining, but gently, outside the cave.

"You are awake," said Grendel.

Cabot nodded.

"Roast meat," said Cabot.

"A lake bird," said Grendel. "I brought it down with a stick."

"It is large, like a Vosk gull, is it not?" asked Cabot.

"I do not know," said Grendel. "Perhaps, the fauna here is diversely origined."

"From the feathers of the Vosk gull," said Cabot, "arrows may be excellently fletched."

The slave twisted a little, and whimpered.

"It is warmer," said Cabot, "not cold, as before."

"Doubtless Agamemnon did not suppose the cold was any longer needed," said Grendel.

"The weather?" said Cabot.

"Certainly," said Grendel.

Cabot took the girl, still unconscious, and pulled her tunic off, unceremoniously, roughly, for she was a slave.

"Let us dry this," said Cabot. "The sand can then be struck from it easily."

Grendel nodded, and arranged a stick, supported on some rocks, near the fire, over which he hung the bit of cloth.

What a lovely, skimpy little thing is a slave tunic, thought Cabot. How tiny, how clinging, how revealing, and how easily removed! And how obvious it is to its occupant and to others that its wearer could be no more than a slave. And how marvelous are women in such garments, in them as they should be, as slaves!

The girl then stirred more.

"She is awakening," said Grendel.

"In my pouch, from Peisistratus," said Cabot, "I have some articles, among them slave cord."

"Coins, too," said Grendel, "even rubies?"

"Yes," said Cabot, "worthless as they are, here no more than bits of metal, and pretty pebbles."

"Keep them," said Grendel. "They may prove valuable."

"Here is the slave cord," said Cabot.

"Your slave is a sorry sight," said Grendel.

"A washing, a feeding, a grooming," said Cabot, "would make it clearer to the average fellow why she is in a collar."

"I think such things are not necessary," said Grendel. "Look upon her."

"True," said Cabot, "even as she is, it is clear she belongs in a collar."

Cabot then fastened the girl's wrists together, crossed before her, and took the same cord down and crossed her ankles, and fastened them together. Her wrists were then fastened, bound, to her ankles, bound, and she could not lift her hands to her mouth, nor could she reach her wrist cords with her teeth. He then sat her back against the wall of the cave, her knees bent.

"She will soon awaken," said Grendel.

"Slavers," said Cabot, "often take a woman in her sleep, and bind her. She retired the night before, as usual, considering, if anything, only the prosaic routines of her next day's quotidian existence. She retires, anticipating nothing, suspecting nothing. Then, later, she awakens, doubtless to her consternation and horror, to find herself bound helplessly."

"Doubtless she cries out," said Grendel.

"Only if the captor finds it acceptable," said Cabot. "For she may have been gagged."

"Doubtless awakening so, helplessly bound, is an interesting experience for the woman."

"One supposes so," said Cabot. "On the other hand, as I understand it, most are sedated, and awaken only later, doubtless days later, to find themselves in a Gorean pen, or cell, naked and in chains."

"Doubtless it is a suitable introduction to their new life," said Grendel.

"One supposes so," said Cabot.

The girl opened her eyes, and squirmed a little.

"I am bound," she said.

She did not seem surprised. Slaves are accustomed to such things.

Sometimes they awaken while being bound, but can do nothing about it. They may then be turned to their back or belly, and put to use, as the slaves they are.

"Slave cord," said Cabot.

"I am familiar with such cord," she said.

"Certainly," said Cabot, "as you are a slave."

She struggled a little, futilely. "I cannot rise," she said. "I cannot bring my hands to my mouth. I awaken yours, and helpless."

"Not infrequently are slaves bound," said Cabot. "Few things so contribute to a slave's awareness of her condition as being rendered totally vulnerable, completely defenseless and helpless. Susceptibility to the master's bonds, at his pleasure, finding herself wholly at his mercy, whenever he pleases, well reminds her of what she is and to whom she belongs."

She pulled a little at the slave cord, wrapped so securely about her small wrists and slender ankles.

"How much I am yours!" she said. "How much you master me!"

"Do you object?" asked Cabot.

"No," she said, "I am a slave. I want to be well mastered! I need to be well mastered! I beg to be well mastered! I would be miserable were I not well mastered!"

"Any man can master you," said Cabot.

"Yes, Master," she said. "—*Now.*"

Cabot's eyes roved her, as the eyes of masters can rove slaves.

She dared not meet his eyes.

"The sand," she said, "my hair, my body."

"You are filthy," said Cabot.

"Perhaps I will be permitted later to make myself more presentable to my master," she said.

"Perhaps," said Cabot.

"I want to be presentable," she said.

"You had better be more than presentable," said Cabot.

"Of course," she said. "I am a slave."

Grendel stirred the fire.

"As a slave," she said, "I wish to go far beyond being merely presentable. As a slave I want my master to find me not only presentable, not only clean and well-groomed, and such, but appealing."

"'Appealing'?" asked Cabot.

"Attractive," she said.

"Attractive slaves are, of course, pleasing to the master," said Cabot.

"And we wish to be attractive to our masters," she said. "The life of a slave who is attractive to her master is likely to be much more pleasant than that of one who is not attractive to the master."

"Doubtless," said Cabot. "But if I am not mistaken you would like to be attractive to men, in general."

"Certainly, Master," she said, "for we are women. Even when I thought I despised and hated men, I still wanted keenly to be attractive to them."

"Do you understand the meaning of that?" asked Cabot.

"I do not think I understood it then, at least fully, at least in full consciousness," she said, "but now its meaning is quite clear. Its meaning is that we are women, and exist to be desired and sought, and that we wish, and wish desperately, despite what we might claim, to be desired and sought, and that we exist to be beautiful, and loving, for men, and that we exist to please and serve men, that we are the complementary sex to theirs, and each sex is to be a perfection to the other, and take its meaning from the other, and only as utterly different are the sexes united in the wondrous and precious perfection of wholeness, and this is what brings us to the feet of men, hopeful and submissive, to be accepted, if only we fully understood our meaning, and ourselves, as their slaves."

"And so your beauty is so important to you," said Cabot, "and, on Gor, it is a beauty that does not fade."

"So I have been given to understand, Master," she said.

"Have no fear," said Cabot, "I will eventually give you an opportunity to clean yourself, to tend your hair, as you can, to wash and press your tunic with warm stones, such things."

"Thank you, Master," she said.

"Females are such vain creatures," said Cabot.

"Would you have us otherwise?"

"No," said Cabot, "it makes it easier to control you."

"We are yours, Master," she said.

"In a thousand ways," said Cabot.

"Yes, Master," she said. "Master," she said.

"Yes?" said Cabot.

"We are attractive, are we not, Master?" she asked.

"Yes," said Cabot, "otherwise you would not be worth buying and selling."

"Yes, Master," she said.

Cabot, with his thumb, wiped some of the sand from her collar, better revealing its legend.

There were tears in her eyes.

"My master's name is on my collar," she said.

"Of course," said Cabot. "That is commonly done. The slave is goods. Thus it is important to know to whom she belongs."

"We belong to our masters," she said.

"Of course," said Cabot.

"I wonder if men can understand what it is for a woman to belong to a man," she said.

"It is not hard to understand," he said. "It is a simple matter of legalities, as owning a belt or saddle, or a kaiila or tarsk."

"To know that she is owned by him, *truly owned by him*," she said.

"It is a legal matter," he said.

"Oh, yes," she said, "it is a matter of perfect legalities, and we are well aware of that, perfectly aware of that, that we are only goods and properties, no more, but what of our feelings, our emotions, our understandings of this?"

"The feelings of a slave are of no interest, and of no importance," he said.

"Yes, Master," she said, softly.

"It is expected that the slave will be dutiful, and serve well," he said.

"Yes, Master," she whispered.

Cabot looked past Grendel, and the small fire, toward the opening of the small cave. "The weather has changed," he said.

"Yes, it is warm," she said, gratefully.

"Lord Grendel speculates that Agamemnon trusts that cold is no longer necessary to his plans, and thus, one supposes, that the temperature of the world may be returned to an equable level, one suitable for this season of the cylinder year."

"Agamemnon?"

"The cold, the storm," said Cabot, "may have been manufactured."

"It is highly likely," said Grendel. "In any event, it is surely not a natural phenomenon, of the sort with which you might be familiar. It is within the cylinder. Too, there was, for example, no lightning, and no thunder."

"No!" she said.

Grendel returned to tending and turning the meat, at the small fire.

"If Agamemnon wished to kill us," said Cabot, "he could have done so on the lake, with the aquatic machine."

"Yes," said Grendel, "but perhaps not with consequences to his liking."

"I do not understand," said Cabot.

"He appeared to save us, did he not?" asked Grendel.

"Yes," said Cabot.

"Or one of us?"

"One of us?" asked Cabot.

"I suspect the Lady Bina is involved in this," said Grendel.

"She would have importuned Agamemnon to have us saved upon the lake?"

"Or one of us," said Grendel.

"You then, her champion," said Cabot.

"No," said Grendel, looking down, stirring the fire.

"I?" asked Cabot.

"I think so," said Grendel.

"But surely Agamemnon wants us both dead," said Cabot.

"Yes, and so the storm," said Grendel. "It is speculation on my part that Lady Bina intervened with Agamemnon to protect you on the lake. In a sense, he did so, and his efforts may have been witnessed in such a way, recorded in such a way, within the machine, as to convince her of his efforts on your behalf."

"Why on my behalf?" asked Cabot.

"Lady Bina may want you," said Grendel. "Perhaps she wants you for a pet or a reward of some sort."

"Absurd," said Cabot.

"Did you refuse her?"

"Yes," said Cabot.

"This may have displeased her," said Grendel.

"I see," said Cabot.

"And the storm then would seem something in which Agamemnon had no hand, and which could not have been predicted, or defended against."

"But it could have been!" said Cabot.

"Yes," said Grendel, "but did you, at first, understand the control?"

"No," said Cabot.

"And to a lesser extent yet would have the Lady Bina," said Grendel.

"But what of you, and Lita?" asked Cabot.

"I could be disposed of later, at her convenience," said Grendel, "and she may have thought it amusing to own your Lita, who, when free, I understand, was something of a rival to her."

"Perhaps," said Cabot.

"Doubtless she would be pleased to have her under her switch, as a terrified, groveling, abject serving slave."

Lita shuddered.

"And thus I suspect we were to be finished in the storm," he said, "seemingly as the unfortunate consequence of an unforeseen accident, and thus without any compromise whatsoever to future services which the Lady Bina might render to Agamemnon."

"Then Agamemnon believes we are dead?" said Cabot.

"I think so," said Grendel. "Consider the turn in the weather."

"That gives us something of an advantage, does it not?" asked Cabot.

"Only a small one, if any, I fear," said Grendel.

"Is the meat ready?" asked Cabot.

"Yes," said Grendel. He thrust a slab of roasted meat toward

Cabot, on a sharpened stick, and he then began, with his paws, juice running between the digits, and his fangs, to feed.

The slave pulled her wrists a little upward, but they could not begin to reach her mouth.

Cabot took her by the hair, and pulled her down to her side, so her mouth was near his thigh.

He then fed for a time, and then, after a bit, he held some meat down by her mouth, only a little out of her reach.

She squirmed to it, and bit at it, desperately, voraciously.

She lifted her mouth, piteously, and whimpered a little, juice running at the side of her face. And Cabot gave her more, which she bit at, eagerly, greedily, gratefully.

"Is this the way a young lady with pretensions to station and position, even to membership in the British aristocracy, dines?" asked Cabot.

She pulled wildly, miserably, helplessly, at her bonds, but was helpless in them. And then she snatched again, and again, desperately, at the meat held out for her.

"You feed like a starving she-sleen," said Cabot, "or a hungry slave."

She did not respond to him, but seized ever more desperately, and piteously, at the food held out for her.

"Did you save the feathers of the lake bird?" asked Cabot of Lord Grendel.

"Not really," said Lord Grendel, wiping his jaws with a massive, haired forearm, "but they are about. Why?"

"They might be useful," said Cabot, "in fletching arrows."

Chapter, the Thirty-Fifth:

Lita Returns to the Cave

"Should she not be back by now?" asked Grendel.

Cabot was working with the missile, or arrow, straightener, a short wooden tool, some eighteen inches in length, with a small, round hole cut in one end. The suitable branch, properly trimmed, is seldom straight. One holds the straightener by what is, in effect, its handle, and thrusts the branch through the hole. Then, by twisting and pressing, over a small fire, one hand on the tool, the other on the shaft, thrust through the hole, the wood, now softened, now pliable, is straightened, and becomes a shaft worthy of its fletching and heading.

Cabot looked up, from his work, and put aside the branch and straightener. "I think so," he said. "I shall look."

"Better I," said Grendel. "I am Kur."

"Partly so," said Cabot.

But Grendel had exited the cave, nostrils distended.

Cabot returned to his work.

The small party consisting of Cabot, Lord Grendel, and a slave, whose name was Lita, had been in the vicinity of the cave four days now.

One gathers that ka-la-na wood, common on Gor from her wine trees, would have been preferable for the launching device, or bow, which Cabot had prepared, carved into its gentle arc with a sharp stone, but such are not found in the world. He had selected, one evening, in the dusk, two likely branches from a young Tur tree, a tree which is found on Gor, a reddish tree which, when mature, is lofty and broadly leaved, and had shaped them to his purpose. The string for this launching device, or bow, the string from which the missile, the arrow, is flighted, was easily obtained from remnants of the raft's rope, parted, unraveled, and rewoven, those remnants by means of which Cabot and the slave had been enabled to survive the storm, by means of which he had fastened himself and the slave to one of the raft's logs, after the raft's destruction. On Gor the string for the launching device is commonly encircled, bound and smoothed, being whipped with silk, this reducing fraying and wear, but Cabot, lacking this luxury, had prepared a number of strings, replaceable as needed. With these the device, or bow, might be strung and restrung as desired. The launching device, or bow, is left unstrung when not used, this retaining its resiliency, by avoiding material fatigue. He had fletched those arrows earlier finished with feathers of the lake bird, that apparently, in Cabot's mind, at least, resembling the Vosk Gull, binding the feathering to the shaft with stout threads, these obtained from the hem of his tunic, such threads being coarser, and stronger, than those which might have been obtained from the slave's tunic, for such garments are woven of lighter, softer material. He had hoped to head his missiles with that gray, siliceous rock called flint, or in Gorean, splinter stone, but none is had in the world. This lack, however, was well remedied by Lord Grendel who, several Ahn from the cave, muchly concealing his deformed hands, in a tiny habitat village, had encountered a small smithy, and, with some of Cabot's silver coins, obtained from Peisistratus in consequence of a wager, had arranged with the smith for the manufacture of a large number of alleged pendants, presumably for stringing and resale. Kurii, as is well known, are fond of ornaments, and not unoften string their bodies with them. These alleged pendants were flat and sharply pointed at one end, and, toward the other end, indented, on two sides, and flattened. A small hole was drilled in each of the putative pendants, rather near the flattish end, between the opposing indentations, or notches. In virtue of this hole, you see, the pendants might have been strung on a string or cord, for looping about the neck, or wrists, of their wearers. Each of these putative pendants later, of course, might be fitted into the leading end of a missile, or arrow, held in place on two sides by the slit wood, and lashed firmly in place, by means of the indentations, and a stout cord. Whereas a Kur familiar with Gor, and the common, fearsome weaponry of the Gorean peasant, might have easily recognized these supposed pendants as weapon points, the smith, as far as we know, unfamiliar with such things, did not do so or, at least, pretended not to do so. Lord Grendel, too, we may suppose, paid a good price for his alleged pendants. While in the habitat village he also purchased supplies of various sorts, among them some biscuits and dried fruit, some vessels, some robes, three blankets, an ax, and two knives.

The sound was subtle.

Cabot leaped up, moved to the side, behind a projection, knife drawn.

A shape hurried into the cave.

Cabot came up, instantly, half seeing it, behind it, the thing almost a blur, and his left hand went closely, tightly, across its mouth, drawing its head back, stifling any sound, and his knife was at its throat.

The girl was helpless, terrified.

"Lita," said Cabot, releasing her.

Instantly she went to her knees before him, as is fitting for a female slave before her master.

Too, she was so terrified it seemed likely she could not have remained on her feet in any event.

"Do not rush in upon a fellow like that," said Cabot.

She put her head swiftly down to his feet, contritely, and kissed them.

"Announce yourself," he said, angrily.

"Forgive me, Master!" she said.

"You might have been killed," said Cabot.

"Forgive me, Master," she begged.

She was obviously frightened. She realized then, one supposes, how foolish she had been, and how narrow her escape had been.

She might have been even more terrified if she had realized how swiftly, instinctively, Gorean warriors are trained to act.

A quarter of an Ihn can be the difference between killing and being killed, between living and dying. A swift motion in one's vicinity is likely to be the strike of the predator and he who pauses to reflect in such a situation is unlikely to reflect long, or again.

Cabot, too, was shaken.

He sheathed his knife, and struggled to regain his breath.

He let her minister to his feet with her lips and tongue, fearfully, deferently, placatingly, as what she was, no more than a slave, for a few moments.

Men enjoy owning beautiful women, wholly mastering them, and having them so at their feet.

What male is so foolish, so inert and sluggish, as not to wish to own a beautiful female, to have her as his helpless, collared slave?

She began to tremble and whimper.

"You may raise your head," he said.

She lifted her head and kissed him quickly, desperately, again and again, about the thighs and legs, and then looked up at him, shaking, her lips trembling, parted.

"You are frightened," he said. "What is wrong?" he asked.

"There is news," she said.

"Did you see Lord Grendel?" asked Cabot.

"Yes," she said. "He will be here, soon."

"Where have you been?" asked Cabot.

"I found a fallen Kur," she said. "I think he is dying. I tried to stop his bleeding, to nurse him."

"Take me to him," said Cabot, "and I will kill him."

"No," said the girl. "You could not kill him, as he is weak, and helpless."

"You do not understand," said Cabot. "He has seen you, and can inform soldiers of our presence. We must kill him, and conceal the body."

"Doubtless that is wise, Master," she said, "but you cannot do so."

Cabot shrugged, angrily. "And why not?" he demanded.

"Master well knows," she said. "It would not be honorable."

"And so we all may die," said Cabot.

"Lord Grendel is bringing him here," she said.

"Madness," said Cabot.

"Master would do the same," she said.

"Yes," said Cabot, in fury. "I would do the same."

"That is known to your slave," she said.

"And this is your news?" said Cabot.

"No, Master," she said. "I hid while foraging, before I found the fallen one, and saw several small groups of soldiers."

"They are hunting for us?"

"No, Master," she said. "They are disorganized. They do not march. Some can scarcely move. Many are bandaged, and bloody."

"Stragglers," said Cabot. "But from what?"

"I do not know, Master," she said.

"Are there many?" asked Cabot.

"Probably some hundreds," she said. "I saw many small groups, and some lines."

"There is no discipline, no order, no command?" said Cabot.

"No, Master," she said.

"The fleet has returned," said Cabot. "Agamemnon has lost. The world is in jeopardy!"

"Ho!" came from outside.

Grendel, a large Kur in his massive arms, stood in the threshold of the small, shallow cave.

"Tal," said Cabot. "Enter."

Grendel came into the cave, and, toward its rear, put down the large, wounded Kur, with great gentleness.

"Wash and bind his wounds," said Cabot to the slave.

"Yes, Master," she said.

"You have spoken with Lita?" asked Cabot.

"Yes," said Grendel.

"She speaks of soldiers," said Cabot.

"I have seen them, too," he said.

"The fleet has returned," said Cabot.

"Yes," said Grendel. "Parts of it, some of it, what little remains of it."

"The defeat, I take it, was grievous," said Cabot.

"The war is lost," said Grendel. "Agamemnon's ambition has doomed the world."

"Have you heard ought of the revolution?" asked Cabot.

"It has begun," said Grendel. "Peisistratus and his men have ferried the game humans from the forest cylinder to the world, hundreds, and he has freed the killer humans, hundreds, too, from their pens and barracks. Humans swarm about, unled, thirsting for blood. They attack and slaughter Kurii as they can, but are a slight match for them, and hundreds die on the steps of the palace, burned alive by power weapons. One Kur can destroy with his hands a hundred humans, and one with power weapons can slay thousands."

"What of the men of Peisistratus?"

"Beleaguered, trying to guard the shuttle ports," said Grendel.

"They have not taken the ships and fled to Gor?"

"The outer locks are sealed from the palace," said Grendel. "But even so, I think they are concerned to stay and fight."

"They are slavers," said Cabot.

"They are Gorean," said Grendel.

"How did the revolution begin?" asked Cabot.

"When soldiers of Agamemnon set forth upon intelligence furnished to them, to ensnare and punish conspirators, they dared delay no longer."

"And what might have been the source of this intelligence, the betrayed names, and such?" asked Cabot.

Grendel was silent.

"What of the cattle humans?" asked Cabot.

"They await slaughter, as usual," said Grendel, "with unwitting, complacent stupidity, concerned only for the filling of their feeding troughs, their water troughs."

"Peisistratus lives," said Cabot.

"It seems so," said Grendel.

"What of Lord Arcesilaus?" asked Cabot.

"He lives, as of now," said Grendel.

"He was not seized then," said Cabot.

"He was seized, but tore loose and then, though fired upon and wounded severely, losing much blood, fled from the habitats."

"How do you know all this?" asked Cabot.

Grendel pointed to the fallen Kur, lying at the back of the cave, whose wounds were being tended by the slave.

"He is, then," said Cabot, "one of us, one of the conspirators, one of the revolutionaries?"

"Yes," said Grendel, "their leader."

Cabot regarded him, startled.

"My poor, dear Cabot," said Grendel, "you do not recognize him, do you?"

"No," said Cabot.

"It is Lord Arcesilaus," said Grendel.

Chapter, the Thirty-Sixth:

Cabot Leaves the Cave;
He Is Accompanied by a Shapely Beast of Burden

"You draw it easily," said Cabot.

"It is not difficult," said Lord Grendel.

"You see that tree?" asked Cabot, pointing.

"Certainly," said Lord Grendel.

"I would like Lita's garland hung upon it," said Cabot.

This garland was woven of shrub flowers, a white Lirillium, and was in width some seven or eight inches. Such things, hung on wands, are familiar targets in rustic archery. A shaft placed within the garland scores, and one which nicks or cuts the wand scores higher, and one which splits the wand scores highest.

"Lita," called Cabot, "fling the garland!"

Lita removed the garland from her hair and tossed it away from her, and scarcely had it left her hand than the string of the bow of Lord Grendel leaped forward, and then vibrated with that sudden, intense purr, the bow's music, signaling a flight.

The roarlike hum is unmistakable.

The bow is sometimes spoken of as the peasant's lyre.

"Ai!" exclaimed Cabot, muchly pleased, for the garland rested upon the long, quivering shaft, deep in the tree.

"It is a slight weapon, is it not?" asked Grendel.

"No," said Cabot. "It is, in its way, a power weapon."

It is spoken of sometimes on Gor as the Great Bow, or the Peasant Bow. As the power of such a weapon may not be clear to everyone, it is perhaps germane to what follows to speak of its nature. First, it is a weapon which requires considerable strength and skill to use effectively. A woman, for example, would be unlikely to be able to bend the bow, and many men could not. It requires great strength even to string the bow, let alone to draw it and fire the projectile. Too, even with the strength to bend the bow it requires additional strength to keep it bent, to steady it, and to train it on a target. Too, skill in its use does not come easily to all, for there are dozens of subtleties of judgment which will affect its accuracy, judgments such as those of distance, elevation, and wind. Too, in many situations, one must take account of the motion, and likely motion, of the target. In the hands of a typical peasant, however, this weapon is formidable. It has a remarkable rapidity of fire, far superior to its common Gorean competitor, the shoulder bow, or crossbow. In the time it takes to fire and reload the shoulder bow, even with a stirrup load, as opposed to a windlass load, it can fire several missiles. A sense of the range of the weapon is given by the fact that a peasant can fire a dozen missiles into the air before the first falls back to earth. It is accurate to two hundred yards and, at that range, can sink an iron-piled shaft four inches into a wooden stump.

"I prefer an ax," said Grendel.

"That is because you want to be next to what you cut and kill," said Cabot.

"The shaft is not weighty," said Lord Grendel.

"Its swiftness compensates for its lightness," said Cabot.

"The spear can be swift," said Lord Grendel.

It is true the spear can be cast and with effect, but it is most often used as a stabbing weapon. Once a spear is cast, obviously, it is no longer available to its owner, and this is the case even if it strikes its intended target, one of perhaps dozens of advancing, threatening targets. Sometimes the spear, thrust or cast, is used to penetrate a shield, rendering it unwieldy, and a handicap to its bearer. This is particularly to one's advantage if one is faced with a given foe, as in single combat. The attack is then most often pressed with the blade, most commonly amongst Gorean warriors, a short sword, typically the *gladius*. One is trained to take the cast spear obliquely on the shield, that it may carom away. In such a case he who throws the spear has lost his weapon and the intended target remains unencumbered.

"The arrow is swifter," said Cabot. "It is not for nothing the arrow is sometimes spoken of as the bird of death. In Torvaldsland, the arrow is sometimes spoken of as the jard feeder."

This reference seems obscure, but the jard is a Gorean bird, a small, black, flocking bird, a scavenger. Its gatherings, sometimes before battles, or in the vicinity of lengthy, desperate marches, are often regarded with uneasiness, and some see it as a bird of ill omen. A saying in the Gorean north, seemingly related, is to speak of a defeated force as having been given over to the feasting of jards.

"And its range," said Cabot, "is far beyond that of the spear."

"I think it is a coward's weapon," said Lord Grendel. "One does not close with the foe. One does not face him. One does not show oneself to him. One strikes him with impunity, from a distance. It pounces with stealth. It is like a knife in the night. Is it not like poisoned wine which can do its mischief while the poisoner reclines afar, amused, upon his couch?"

"It is true," said Cabot, "that many warriors despise the bow, regarding it muchly as you have suggested, as a slight weapon, as one unworthy of a man, and surely of a warrior, even as one possibly tainted with dishonor, but I am of a contrary conviction."

"Kurii do not look for nobility and honor from humans," said Lord Grendel.

"I have shared paga with Zarendargar," said Cabot.

"Forgive me," said Lord Grendel.

"What would you think of a man who wrestles with larls?" asked Cabot.

"He would be a fool," said Lord Grendel.

"Better to use a spear, or bow," said Cabot.

"Certainly," said Grendel.

"Perhaps the larl might feel that cowardly, or unfair," said Cabot.

"Perhaps it is," said Grendel, "but each must do his best, as he can."

"And so, too, must the archer, overmatched, if unable to deal with a mighty foe on that foe's own ground and terms."

"He could choose to die," said Grendel.

"That is possible," said Cabot, "but he might prefer to live."

"I think this twig is a coward's weapon," said Grendel.

"Peasants are not cowards," said Cabot.

"I do not like the bow," said Grendel.

"It is not a child's thing," said Cabot. "It is a powerful, effective weapon, and it requires skill to use it well. A mighty warrior confronted by two foes is often doomed, one foe engaging and the other striking. The archer might slay ten before the eleventh reaches him. Who, then, is the more redoubtable foe?"

"It seems not a noble weapon," said Grendel.

"The knife," said Cabot, "outreaches the hand, and the sword outreaches the knife, and the spear outreaches the sword. Is the knife then less noble than the hand, and the sword less noble than the knife, and the spear less noble than the sword?"

"No," said Grendel.

"Perhaps then," said Cabot, "the arrow is not less noble than the spear."

"The arrow can strike from cover, the archer unseen," said Grendel.

"So, too, can the knife, the sword, the spear, even the slinger's leaden pellet or smoothed, rounded stone."

"True," said Grendel.

"Also," said Cabot, "you seem surprisingly adept with this despised weapon." He then called to Lita, that she might retrieve the garland, which hung upon the quiet shaft.

Lord Grendel did not respond.

"You have been practicing, have you not?" asked Cabot.

"Yes," said Lord Grendel.

"Why?" asked Cabot.

"This is the only match we have, against power weapons," he said.

"You would not prefer to run nobly up the palace steps and be burned alive?" asked Cabot.

"No," said Lord Grendel.

"Nor would I," said Cabot.

"Make more arrows," said Lord Grendel.

"I shall," said Cabot. "And then we must join the fray."

"I will go ahead, tonight," said Lord Grendel. "If the revolution should be successful, the Lady Bina, as a traitress, will be in great danger. She may need me."

"Forget her," said Cabot.

"No," said Grendel.

"She is worthless," said Cabot.

"True," said Lord Grendel, "but she is beautiful."

"I fear you are human," said Cabot.

"Human, perhaps," said Grendel. "Perhaps human, yes, and perhaps too human."

"Master," said the slave, Lita, kneeling before him.

It was now morning.

Yesterday evening, taking advantage of the darkness, Lord Grendel had exited the cave, taking with him a knife, the ax, one of the bows, and a sheaf of arrows.

About the slave's head was the wreath of blossoms, this of white Lirillium.

It is not unusual for slaves to bedeck themselves as they may, and to do so occasionally with flowers, sometimes a garland, sometimes with a mere blossom or two, fixed in the hair. Such things can be fetching, and it is likely they are not unaware of this. They can treasure simple things, too, a ribbon, a bangle, a bracelet, a string of colorful glass or wooden beads. Indeed, such simple things, as worn by a slave, herself recognized as goods, can be a thousand times more provocative to a male than the pearls and diamonds of a free woman.

Beautiful women tend to be vain of their beauty, and it is natural for them to nurse, guard, and enhance it, and slave girls, commonly the most beauteous of all, for commonly it is only the most beautiful of girls which are taken for collaring, are no exception. Accordingly, the slave girl, well aware of her beauty, which commonly far exceeds that of the plainer free woman, is seldom a stranger to vanity. Moreover, as a slave in a unapologetically and uncompromisingly male-dominated world, she is excruciatingly aware, as she might not be in a drabber, grayer, hypocritical world, of her femaleness, and its enormous importance. After all, it has been in virtue of that that she has been acquired, and it is in virtue of that that she will be bought and sold. Her femaleness in such a culture is not incidental to what she is. In such a culture it is not the unimportant empirical contingency, the biological irrelevancy, the meaningless anatomical fortuity, it is claimed to be in a world of anonymity and negativity, of neuterism, that of a world engineered to abet the mindless servicing of machines, technological and economic, political, and corporate. On Gor, the slave, particularly if extracted from Earth's barbarisms of fatuity and denial, discovers, usually for the first time, the enormous importance of her femaleness. It is no longer a supposed accident casually appertaining to her body but rather she herself, what she is. She is a female. It is what she is. Certainly this is clear to her when she is exposed on the block.

On Gor the woman discovers then, often for the first time, fully, that she is a female, and the specialness, preciousness, wonderfulness, and importance of this.

And, too, on Gor, she learns her desirability, and what this will mean in a world of strong men.

And she learns she has been designed in virtue of a binary sexual shaping, a complementary wholeness within which alone she can find her fulfillment, a wholeness within which there is one to command and one to submit, one to rule and one to obey.

A collar on her neck, her lips pressed fervently to the feet of a master, she rejoices to learn what she is, and would not be other than she is.

How else can she find her ultimate and perfect fulfillment?

On Gor these things are understood.

Too, on Gor, at last, as a slave, she finds she has an incontrovertible, indisputable, inexpugnable societal and cultural identity.

At last she finds she is real, quite real, and in two ways, one biological, and one societal and cultural.

Biologically she is a female, and societally and culturally, incontrovertibly, she is a slave.

And she learns on Gor what men are, and can be, and how she will be treated, and what will be done with her.

And she will have little to say about this, and this is welcomed, and it thrills her lovely belly.

Gor is a natural world.

And she finds herself a female in such a world, and the most female of all women, the female slave.

Not until she was collared did she understand the power and beauty of men, whose slave she is, and in whose arms she now longs to be enfolded.

"You are pretty, Lita," said Cabot.

"Thank you, Master," she said.

"What have you in your hands?" asked Cabot.

She put her head down and lifted and extended her arms, offering Cabot the object. "Master," she said. In the pleasure cylinder, she had been taught to so proffer items to a free person.

"What is it?" asked Cabot.

He took the object from the girl, which was a small object, weighty, and of gold.

"It is a ring," said Cabot, "a Kur ring."

"It is the ring of Lord Arcesilaus," said the slave.

"He is dead?" said Cabot.

"No," said the slave.

"How is it you have the ring?" asked Cabot.

"Yesterday," said the girl, "Lord Arcesilaus gave it to Lord Grendel, to be given to you this morning."

"Why to me?" asked Cabot.

"I do not know," she said.

"I cannot accept it," said Cabot.

Cabot made his way to the back of the cave.

He crouched down beside Arcesilaus, and turned on the Kur's translator. "Here," said Cabot, trying to press the ring into the paw of the large Kur.

His offer was received with a growl. A soft, tortured noise came from the Kur. The translator, however, rendered this in a natural volume, and clarity. "No," it said.

"I cannot accept this ring," said Cabot.

"You will fight against Agamemnon," came from the translator.

"Yes," said Cabot.

"Take the ring," came from the translator.

"Why?" asked Cabot.

"Take it," came from the translator.

"Very well," said Cabot.

"Now, leave me," came from the translator.

Cabot rose up, the ring clenched in his hand, and went back to where the slave waited. When he came into her proximity, as she was still kneeling, not having been given permission to rise, she put her head to the floor of the cave.

The former Miss Pym looked well, kneeling so.

As many times before, Cabot speculated how the young men

she had known on Earth would regard her as she now was, a collared slave.

He did not doubt but what they would rejoice.

Perhaps they would make bids for her.

But he did not think he would sell the slave, at least not now.

"Be as you will," said Cabot, absently.

She knelt up, regarding him.

"I do not understand it," said Cabot, considering the ring. "If authority is here, it is not an authority I could use. I could not command Kurii."

"He did not explain its use?" asked Lita.

"No," said Cabot. "If authority were involved, he should have given it to Lord Grendel, if only that he might give it to another."

"But he gave it to you," said Lita.

"Yes."

"Why?"

"I do not know," said Cabot. He examined the ring. It was heavy, carved, ornate, but it did not seem unusual. It did not seem a mechanism. It did not seem a key. It did not seem a container of some sort. It did not open. "It is too large for my finger," said Cabot. "I will put it on a string, about my neck."

The slave, unbidden, fetched a bit of cord, from which Cabot, with his knife, cut a strand of suitable length.

"You put it within your tunic," observed the slave, who had returned to first position.

"Yes," said Cabot, "in war, in certain lights, say, in moonlight, a glint on a buckle, a flash from an emblem, such things, might betray one's position."

She touched her collar, almost inadvertently.

"Yes," smiled Cabot, "more than one fugitive slave has been betrayed by so small a thing."

Cabot turned away from the girl, and began to gather up accouterments. He took up the unstrung bow, and a quiver of arrows, formed from part of one of the blankets which had been purchased by Grendel.

"Lord Grendel," said the girl, "left many arrows."

"True," said Cabot. "He took some, but many he left. He has greater confidence in his ax, I fear."

"Surely he left them for Master," she said.

"Perhaps," said Cabot. "But it is inconvenient, and can be dangerous, to be overburdened. It is not as though I had a pack kaiila at hand."

"Master has a girl at hand," she said.

"True," he said.

"I have never seen a kaiila, Master," she said, "but I understand I am worth far less than one, let alone the great tarn of which I have been told, but, too, have not seen."

"It is true that slaves commonly sell for less than a kaiila," he said, "and, too, usually, for the price of a tarn one might purchase twenty or more slaves, even of great beauty."

"Even as beautiful as I?" she asked.

"Vain little beast," he chided.

"Master?" she persisted.

"Yes," said Cabot.

"I see," she said.

"Perhaps you now better understand what you are, and your value," said Cabot.

"Yes," she said. "I am an animal, one animal amongst other animals, and not the most valuable."

Cabot wondered if he truly understood that. Probably not, he thought. Not in her belly.

To be sure, she had made progress, considerable progress. He remembered her helplessness, her squirming, her gasping, her thrashing about, her begging.

Surely she had begun to sense what it might be, to be a man's slave.

"But more valuable than some," he said, "usually more valuable than verr or tarsk."

"I see," she said.

"And animals such as you are special," he said. "They appeal to men."

"That was clear," she said, "from the pleasure cylinder."

"And," he said, "some men would give a dozen tarns to bring a particular woman, say, one who had not treated them well, into their chains."

"I would fear to be she," she said.

"Do not be upset," he said. "Masters occasionally grow fond of an animal."

"But she is still an animal."

"Certainly," said Cabot.

"And should that slip her mind?" she asked.

"The lash will correct such lapses," he said.

"Then she is truly an animal," she said, "not only legally, societally, and culturally, but even in the eyes of her master."

"Of course," he said.

"Good," she said.

That response interested Cabot.

The girl was perhaps on the edge of bondage. Perhaps she had begun to sense the stirring, the begging, of her secret slave, the need of a woman to be such, her master's beast, his animal, on his chain, licking and kissing, hoping to please.

It is apparently pleasant to own a slave.

Many are the wonders of the collar, many the marvels consequent upon its affixing.

"So many?" she said.

"What?" said Cabot.

"Twenty?" she said. "As many as twenty, for only one tarn?"

"Much depends on the market," he said.

"As beautiful as I?" she asked.

"You are quite vain," he said.

To be sure, this is not unusual with a beautiful woman, and it is certainly not unusual with a beautiful slave, who is probably well aware of the most likely reason a collar has been put on her.

"Master?" she persisted.

"Perhaps more beautiful," he said.

"But I am beautiful, surely," she said.

"You will do," he said.

"I was publicly chained in the pleasure cylinder," she said, "and I was not unaware of the approbatory glances of masters. They roved me well, and lengthily."

"So?" he said.

"And they are, as you may recall," she said, "slavers, professionals in the assessment of slaves."

"It is true, as I have said," he said, "that you would do. Vended off a platform at night, under torches, well displayed, your blemishes somewhat concealed, you might bring a handful of copper."

"I am extremely beautiful," she said.

"Do you think you were the most beautiful woman in the pleasure cylinder?" he asked. He recalled that she had thought herself amongst the most beautiful women she had ever seen on Earth. To be sure, at that time she was unfamiliar with a particular form of merchandise, Gorean *kajirae*.

Her eyes filled with tears. "No," she said.

"But more beautiful than some?" he said.

"Yes," she said, "yes!"

"When on my chain," she said, "I heard Master Peisistratus, assessing my lineaments and features, quite candidly as men will do, and which at the time was easily done, as I wore only a chain, commend me to another, ranking me above several of his girls."

"That is high praise," said Cabot. Certainly the girls of the pleasure cylinder had been carefully selected, chosen with the pleasure of his crews in mind.

"So I am beautiful, am I not?" she said.

"Yes," said Cabot, "you are beautiful."

"Quite beautiful!" she said.

"Yes," he said, "quite beautiful."

"And though I am not free," she said, "might not master find me of interest, if only as a slave."

"Perhaps," he said.

He found this amusing, for most slaves were once free women, and, usually, only the most beautiful of free women were collared. Accordingly, almost all slaves would be likely to be more beautiful than most free women, a fact not lost on free women. Too, interestingly, women became more beautiful in bondage, this going well beyond the garmenting, dieting, training, and exercising of the slave, but having more to do with the life of a slave, and its fulfillments.

"I would beg to serve Master," she said.

"There is little time," he said.

"I know," she said.

Amongst Goreans, though one may use a slave as carelessly, as thoughtlessly, and indifferently as one might take a drink of water, as one might take a belt to her flanks, as one might, the need on one, cuff her to her knees, it is common to take one's time with her, often a morning or an afternoon, or an evening, sometimes a day. The lengthy and patient exploitation of a slave is one of the pleasures of the mastery. She is no stranger to his favorite viands, which she, most likely nude, for masters, at such times, often keep their slaves so, will prepare under his supervision, nor to the wines which she will measure and serve, her loveliness similarly exposed for his delectation, as much as the goblet, the serving surface, and such, nor to the furs at the foot of his couch, upon which, helplessly chained, she will be forced, again and again, mercilessly, at his pleasure, she willing or not, as an object, an animal, to endure prolonged lengthy, shameful, degrading ecstasies, ecstasies beyond the comprehension of the free woman, those of the mastered slave.

"Master could use a pack beast," she said.

He regarded her.

"Surely," she said.

"It is true," he said.

"Let Lita be your pack beast," she said.

"It can be a capital offense for a slave to touch a weapon," said Cabot.

"Do not slaves sometimes arm their masters?" she asked.

"Sometimes," he said.

"And do they not sometimes struggle beneath the weight of their masters' shields?" she asked.

"Sometimes," he said. "How would you know these things?"

"In teaching me Gorean," she said, "the girls in the pleasure cylinder told me much of Gor."

"When they were not using their switches on you," he said.

"Yes," she smiled, ruefully.

"Your Gorean is coming along well," he said.

"When an error in diction or grammar brings a stroke of the switch, one learns quickly and well," she said.

"Surely," she said, "if the slave has the master's permission, she might touch weapons?"

"Such permission is seldom granted," he said.

"I might bear many arrows," she said, "all that remain here."

"You might be slain on Gor," said he, "to be discovered so, touching a weapon."

"We are not now on Gor," she said.

"The men of Peisistratus are Gorean," he said. "And there might be others."

"If it were clear I were no more than a pack beast," she said, "who might object?"

"Perhaps none," mused Cabot.

"And might they not be pleased, to see me helplessly burdened?"

"It pleases many to see a beautiful slave laboring," said Cabot.

"How might a kaiila serve Master in such a situation?" she asked.

"You are a clever slave," he grinned.

"May not a slave's question be answered?" she inquired.

"The arrows, bundled, would be upon its back, and the beast itself might not stray, being on its tether."

"Surely a slave," she said, "might be so burdened?"

"And tethered?"

"Perhaps," she said.

"But you are not a kaiila, pretty Lita," said Cabot. "You have hands, small, pretty hands, with small, lovely fingers."

"Yes," she said, "I have hands, but they may easily be made helpless."

He regarded her suddenly, sharply.

"As a slave," she said, "I am no stranger to bonds, and have I not been helpless many times, while my Master, with his patience, and skills, worked his will upon me, forcing me, whether I willed it or not, to endure ecstasies, and then ecstasies beyond ecstasies?"

"Such things may be done to a slave," he said.

"And are done to them!" she said.

"Of course," he said.

"And our will means nothing!"

"True," he said.

"And what Master may not understand," she said, "is that we wish to be choiceless. We want our will to mean nothing."

Cabot was silent.

"Our bondage is a way of life," she said. "We want to belong, to be owned, to kneel, to submit, to serve, wholly and helplessly. Our servitude, our submission, our categorical surrender, our helplessness, is important to us. We love being what we are. Our brands, our collars, are precious to us. Our bondage is our freedom, our servitude our liberty."

"I cannot understand this," he said.

"Master is not a woman," she said.

"You must remain here, to care for Lord Arcesilaus," said Cabot.

This remark was met with a roar of fury from the back of the cave, and the gigantic, wounded Kur struggled to one elbow on the stone. Its eyes were blazing. The fangs at the right side of the jaw were visible. The nostrils were distended, the ears laid back. There was moisture about the visible fangs, and the lips.

"Master forgot to turn off the translator," observed the slave, her head down, smiling.

"Vixen," said Cabot to her, apparently in English. I do not find this word in the resources.

"Do not rise," Cabot cautioned Lord Arcesilaus, for the Kur was now half on its feet, and blood emerged from beneath more than one bandage.

Cabot went to the back of the cave, and Lord Arcesilaus subsided, in obvious pain.

"The world is at stake," came from the translator.

"You must be cared for," said Cabot.

"Leave her behind," said Lord Arcesilaus, "and I will eat her, and this I swear by all the faces of the Nameless One."

"We will leave water, and food," said Cabot.

"Begone," said Lord Arcesilaus.

Cabot and the slave set supplies within reach of the weakened, anguished Kur, water in vessels which were available from the purchases of Lord Grendel earlier, and what was left of edibles suitable for Kurii, meat from huntings, and some of the processed edibles which had been chemically designed for compatibility with the Kur metabolism. The latter, incidentally, are also edible by certain forms of animal life, sheep, goats, kaiila, humans, and such.

Cabot would take few supplies with him, as he expected foraging would be available, and he retained, as well, some of the coins won from Peisistratus, and, of course, the rubies he had originally been given by Lord Agamemnon, prior to the trial of Lord Pyrrhus.

Cabot then looked upon his lovely goods, the slave, Lita.

"Master?" she asked.

"Face away from me," said Cabot. "Place your hands behind your back."

There were two swift, decisive clicks, almost simultaneous, and the slave, frightened, tried to separate her wrists.

"Master!" she said.

"Slave bracelets," explained Cabot. "From Peisistratus. I have kept them in my pouch."

"I am helpless!" she said, jerking at the bracelets. "These are metal! I cannot slip them!"

"They are not intended to be slipped," said Cabot.

"I did not expect to be braceleted," she said.

"I find that acceptable," said Cabot.

"If you must bind me, Master," she said, "do not do so in this fashion, I beg you. Rather, use slave cord. That will hold a girl well."

"It would," said Cabot, "but anyone might cut it away. Too, you might, in time, fray it, and sever it, say, on a sharp stone."

"You would have me enmetaled, braceleted, on our journey, so utterly helpless?"

"Yes," said Cabot.

"I might as well be a kaiila," she said.

"Precisely," said Cabot.

"It was a joke!" she protested.

"Not at all," said Cabot.

"And I suppose I am then to be tethered, as well," she said.

"Certainly," said Cabot.

"Surely not!" she said. "Surely not!"

He turned her about, rudely, and put the leash on her neck, over the collar. He then jerked twice on the leash, pulling it against the back of her neck. Such things are commonly done with slaves. They understand such things.

"I am tethered!" she said. "You have literally tethered me! I am literally tethered!"

"Yes," said Cabot.

Cabot then held the leash taut, his fist but inches from her neck.

He then casually examined the shapely, braceleted captive of his leash, her face and throat, and shoulders and figure, scarcely concealed in the brief tunic, and her thighs, and calves, and ankles, and small, bared feet.

"I am enmetaled, and tethered," she said. "Is Master satisfied?"

"I am considering the matter," said Cabot.

"Master regards his slave boldly," she said.

"Slaves may be so regarded," he said.

"Does Master's pack beast meet with his approval?" she asked.

"For light loads, such as you might well replace the kaiila."

"A slave is flattered," she said.

Cabot then slackened the leash, but did not release it.

"Doubtless I have little to fear now from Goreans," she said, "as my status as a mere beast of burden is well displayed."

"You are a beast of burden, true," said Cabot, "but scarcely one accountable as a mere beast of burden."

"Of course," she said. "I am a female slave."

Cabot grinned.

The female slave, you see, is wholly at the mercy of the master.

She pulled a little at the bracelets.

"And doubtless the bracelets are to make even more clear my inability to alter or modify in any way the use to which I am to be put."

"Yes," said Cabot. "In this way it should be made clear to Goreans that this is something done to you, and that you have had no say in it."

"I would be truly in jeopardy otherwise?" she asked.

"Quite possibly," said Cabot. "And in this way, too, it should be clear to Kurii that you are in no way a participant or combatant, but only goods, only an animal, and slave."

"To be disposed of as victors see fit?"

"Precisely," he said.

"I see," she said.

"What I fear you may not see, truly see, even now, given your newness to your condition, and your Earth upbringing," he said, "is that that is actually, exactly, what you are, and all that you are."

"Surely I understand all that," she said.

"Intellectually, perhaps," he said.

"'Intellectually'?" she said.

"Yes," he said, "but now you are going to better understand it, truly understand it."

"Master?"

"In your pretty little belly," he said, "as any other slave."

She looked at him, suddenly, wildly.

"Master!" she protested.

He then knelt her and, by the leash, pulled her head down, and, crossing her ankles, took the leash back, between her legs, and used its free end to fasten her ankles together.

"Do you understand?" he asked.

"Yes, Master," she said.

"May I speak, Master," she asked, with difficulty.

"No," he said.

"Yes, Master," she whispered.

He then began to gather together those arrows to the side, those not previously readied in his own blanket quiver. There were perhaps a hundred such missiles. He put them in four bundles, placed the bundles in a blanket, and fastened the whole across her back.

Later he freed her ankles and lifted her to her feet.

He then left the cave.

She followed him, staggering a little, on her tether.

Chapter, the Thirty-Seventh:

The Encountering of Small Camps

"I am weary, Master," said the slave.

"We will rest here, in this sheltering," said Cabot.

It was little more than a bower.

For two days Cabot and his companion had followed the shore of Lake Fear, and had then made their way toward the area of major habitats.

They were now six days from the cave where they had left Lord Arcesilaus.

Occasionally, concealing themselves as they could, they passed small, dispirited camps of scattered Kurii, some maimed, some nursing wounds. These were survivors of the fleet's apparent disaster, and although some of these Kurii doubtless suspected, and at times even noted, the passage of Cabot and the slave, they did not challenge or attack them.

"I am sure, Master," whispered Lita, "that twice our passage was understood."

"I think so," said Cabot. One may sense such things, from the attitudes of many organisms, the liftings of heads, the alertness, the distending of nostrils, the turning of the ears.

It was difficult to avoid these small camps, which were numerous, and the senses of Kurii, as is well known, tend to be acute.

"Why were we not pursued?" she asked.

"I do not know," said Cabot.

"What if we had been pursued?" she asked.

"Then," said Cabot, "some would die, and then later, I suppose, us."

Cabot did not understand this at the time but these Kurii,

as they had been defeated, and had yet dared to return to the world, had been refused admittance to the major habitats, and were awaiting their fates. Kurii tend not to be tolerant of failure. Too, they are reluctant to continue, so to speak, the bloodlines of defeat. Accordingly, defeated Kurii may be surgically altered, that their seed, perceived as defective, not be propagated. They are then banished to the precincts of the loathed nondominants. Alternatively they are accorded the option, elected by most, to do away with themselves in a manner appropriate to their remorse, and perceived dishonor. Indeed, in some of these camps, dangling bodies could be discerned, where some Kurii, perhaps anticipating the wrath of Lord Agamemnon, had hung themselves in shame.

"Do they not know of war in this world?" asked Lita.

"I do not know," said Cabot.

It was true, though unknown at the time to Cabot and his slave, that many of these small, scattered groups were indeed unaware of the revolution, or civil war, raging at that time in their world.

"Some Kurii," said Lita, "favor the revolution, and have planned it. How will Master know these from the minions and cohorts of Lord Agamemnon?"

"There must be ensigns of some sort," said Cabot, "arm bands, flags, scarves, something, if only for the benefit of enlisted humans, to discriminate amongst the striving factions."

"All humans would be foes of Lord Agamemnon," she said.

"Many, the cattle," said Cabot, "might be neutral, others might favor the Theocrat of the World, and seek the emoluments he might offer for their allegiance."

"Who then is friend, and who foe?" she asked.

"In war it is not always clear," said Cabot. "And a moment's hesitation may mean one's death. Indeed, the seeming friend, proclaiming camaraderie, may be the deadliest foe."

"What then is to be done?" she asked.

"There is a simple rule," said Cabot.

"What is that?" she asked.

"When in doubt, kill," he said.

She shuddered.

"Only he who is comfortable and safely removed from the

place of danger and the moment of decision can afford to grant himself the luxury of an offended conscience," said Cabot.

"Are you rested?" he asked.

"Yes," she said.

"We will then continue on our way," he said.

Chapter, the Thirty-Eighth:

The Place of War

"Master!" cried the slave.

Cabot had an arrow to the string.

The Kur was some twenty yards away, its ax grasped in both hands.

"Hold!" cried Cabot to the Kur, and this message, even at the low volume on which the translator was set, carried to it, as its ears lifted. "Do not approach!" said Cabot.

This was the first Kur they had met who stood in their way.

"Hail, Lord Arcesilaus!" called Cabot.

With a roar of rage the Kur lifted its ax and sped toward Cabot. Cabot let him approach until he had drawn back his ax for its stroke, and then killed him.

The Kur did not fully understand what had occurred, as it stopped, and, as though puzzled, looked down at its chest, and the odd, feathered thing that seemed nested there.

Then it looked at Cabot, and then fell forward, inert.

Cabot closed its eyes.

"It did not understand the bow," he said.

"Surely they will soon understand it," whispered the slave.

"The scarf, wound in the harness," said Cabot.

"It is purple," said the slave.

"That, I gather," said Cabot, "is the identifying ensign of the forces of Agamemnon."

"Master!" said the slave, aghast.

Cabot came to where she stood. There, scattered about, were several humans. Some seemed of the game world, others, from their tunicking, were doubtless from the cages of the killer humans.

All had been cut apart.

No match had such been for Kurii.

"Master?" asked the slave.

"Our journey is ended," said Cabot. "We have come to the place of war."

Chapter, the Thirty-Ninth:

What Occurred in the Afternoon

One picks one's targets carefully.

There were perhaps a hundred Kurii about the building, with its walled enclosure. Some held a large log, to be used to break through the gate or wall. Others had thick poles which might be leant against a wall, up which the claw-footed Kurii might scramble with ease.

Cabot gathered that more than one assault had been beaten back. Certainly there were Kur bodies at the foot of the wall. He could see spear points above the wall, where he supposed that a parapet of sorts had been constructed. He gathered, as was the case, the revolution was failing, the revolutionists being heavily outnumbered, and then, in their scattered, defeated, retreating groups, being punished back into a number of isolated, improvised strongholds, which might then be dealt with, one by one, almost at their leisure, by the forces of Lord Agamemnon.

One looks for isolated targets, at the rear, so that if one falls, others might not take immediate notice.

The ideal is to attack a loose, preferably straggling, single file from the rear, target by target.

This may also be done, and usually more effectively, with the knife, throat by throat.

"I see no enemy behind us," whispered Lita.

"We slew him," said Cabot. "It was he who was to protect their rear."

"The bodies?" said Lita.

"He did his job well," said Cabot. "Doubtless they were hoping to tender assistance to the beleaguered."

"He slew many," she said.

"He was Kur, they were human," said Cabot.

"Follow me," said Cabot, and withdrew some yards.

"What is master doing?" she asked.

"I am relieving you of one of the bundles of arrows," he said. "I will have to change my position frequently. Ideally they will think their foes are several."

"Thank you for unbraceleting me!" she said. "Oh!"

He had thrust her back against a tree and then fastened her hands again together, behind her, but now about the tree. He then, with the leash, pulled her head back against the tree, and looping the leash about the tree, fastened it back, against the tree. "Master!" she said, and then any subsequent sound was muffled, as the packing was placed in her mouth, and secured in place. Her eyes were wide, over the gag. Cabot then touched her, and she squirmed wildly, helplessly, pleadingly, trying to thrust herself forward, against his hand. "I see you are a slave," he said. She regarded him, pathetically, pushing her body forward, as she could. "Yes," he said, "a slave." She whimpered, piteously. "I have work to do," he informed her. "You may simmer," he said, "until I return." He then turned his back on her, listened for a moment to her tiny noises, and then left.

One picks one's targets carefully.

Eleven Kurii fell before the grunting and twisting of one alerted a fellow to a shaft's successful flight. He roared a warning to the others.

Immediately several of the Kurii began to scan the shrubbery and trees about. One Kur, ascendant on one of the poles against the wall, turned about, and, doubtless assisted by the height from which he made his observation, detected a movement in the foliage, one perhaps some seventy-five yards away. Cabot, however, at the moment of becoming aware that his assault from the rear was discerned, looked for those individuals most ideally positioned for surveying the terrain, those not on the ground, and so the perceptive Kur on the pole, scarcely raising his paw to point, fell from the pole some twenty or so feet to the ground, one of the birds of death, so to speak, nesting in its chest. A second and a third similarly perished, and then the Kurii best situated to make the determinations germane to the matter, those on the poles, leapt to the ground, preferring, if nothing else, to reduce their imminence as targets of choice. A large Kur on the ground, looking wildly about, seemingly issued orders to a fellow Kur, doubtless a subordinate, who then, instantly, as one expects a Kur to obey, climbed one of the poles, turned about to view the terrain, and died. Cabot, who had noticed the Kur who had seemingly issued the order, put him next to the dust, he spinning about, and falling against the wall. Although much depends on the city, and world, it is my understanding that many Gorean warriors, and certainly Kurii, do not, in field situations, exchange salutes or wear insignia. The person who salutes second is he who is recognized by the first, and thus is presumably he of higher rank. Thus, he is the preferred target. Also, prominent insignia of rank are best reserved for camps, headquarters, parades, and such. It is only to be expected that he who attacks will select, in so far as it is practical, those targets whose loss is likely to be the most debilitating or crippling to the enemy.

Several of the Kurii seemed disconcerted by the loss of the officer, or commander.

By then Cabot had changed his position.

Clearly the next Kur who fell had been struck from a different direction, and then another fell, too, struck from yet another quarter.

Most, if not all, of these Kurii, were world Kurii and unfamiliar with the bow, and certainly the great bow, and it was not even clear that many, at first, even understood the method of propulsion used in this attack. Similarly, at first, some supposed that these things were alive which struck their fellows. Certainly they flew through the air, swiftly, almost invisible, until they struck, and were feathered, as birds.

There was then a paucity of clear targets, as Kurii crouched down behind hurdles formed from their ladder poles, and some behind the large log, which had presumably been intended to batter at the walls or gate of the diminutive citadel, and some huddled behind ramparts raised of their fellows' bodies.

Then from behind the wall, suddenly, large stones were being cast down upon the disconcerted, apprehensive besiegers.

Roars of rage and pain greeted this barrage of weighty stones, a directed rain of gigantic rocks, any one of which, flung with the strength and force of a Kur, might have felled a tharlarion.

Too, there was a cry from the wall, as of elation, as it had become clear that succor, however minimal, might be at hand.

This cry, if nothing else, seemed to break the spirit of the besiegers, and determine them to action, for they then began to spring up, and mill about, uncertainly. Cabot's aim wavered from one to another of these distracted, erratically moving targets. He loosed no shaft. It was much as when the nine-gilled shark, in its intended, smooth hunt, finds itself suddenly startled as its quarry disappears into the midst of darting, schooling parsit fish, and loses sight then not only of its intended quarry, but finds it difficult, further, to seek out another, even a substitute, in such a frenzied, shimmering storm of massing life. So the shark draws back, and waits, until this troubling, seething brew disbands into detectible, pursuable elements.

Cabot, who knew his weapon far better than his foes, rather as the shark, stepped forth from the foliage.

He had little doubt Kurii would attack him, as they did not know his weapon, and its power.

And some would be swifter than others.

It was his hope that enough might fall to discourage the approach of others. If all advanced, clearly some would reach him.

Kurii, he trusted, are rational animals and would seldom choose certain death.

The first thing he did was wave to his left and right, backward, as though encouraging cohorts, who might be numerous, to remain concealed.

He did not doubt that his foes did not take him to be alone, for he had taken pains to construct that deception. But, too, they might not think him muchly accompanied.

Kurii moved away from the wall.

Several looked about, uneasily, crouching down, turning their heads about, ears lifted.

Then one of them lifted his arm and pointed to Cabot, and began to hurry toward him, and others followed him.

As Cabot had supposed, some were swifter than others.

As they approached him frontally, and separately, it was not difficult to pick targets. He doubted he would ever have such an opportunity again. Some would survive, and all who did would then know the bow.

In the world of Agamemnon the great bow of the Gorean peasant would have been learned.

Four fell, before the others, suddenly, stopped, none willing to continue this ill-fated journey.

Fan out, thought Cabot, fan out, and approach, spread out. Some will reach me, and they can outrun me.

Doubtless the wisdom of this had occurred simultaneously to one or more of the Kurii.

One seemed to be exhorting his fellows to such an endeavor.

Cabot admired him.

And slew him.

He put another arrow to the string.

Then, suddenly, and Cabot had not seen it, another of the Kurii spun about and rolled in the dust, scratching at it, an arrow through its neck.

Cabot lowered his weapon.

Another Kur fell.

Nicely done, thought Cabot. And you hung Lita's garland nicely on the tree as well. You have been practicing, clearly.

At this point those Kurii who had remained in the field broke and ran, two more felled before they had cover, one by Cabot and another by his unseen cohort.

A Kur cheer rose from the small citadel.

"Ah, friend Cabot," said Grendel, "you have taught your superiors that a human may be something to be reckoned with."

"They are not my superiors," said Cabot, "and perhaps we have taught them that two humans may be something to be reckoned with."

Lord Grendel grimaced, and it may have been a smile. "Perhaps," he said.

Chapter, the Fortieth:

What Occurred in the Evening

"Please, Master, please!" wept the slave.

"What is it?" asked Cabot.

"Surely Master knows what I need, and must have!" she said.

The slave had been freed from the tree, and the bracelets, and the leash, and had been put to work, preparing a meal, and a small camp for Cabot and Lord Grendel.

Obviously she had been in torment, and would have preferred to serve otherwise than in the domestic capacities then assigned to her.

Certainly she tried to put herself frequently before Cabot, and had even brushed against him piteously, more than once, but he had simply thrust her away, that she might continue her labors, gathering wood, fetching water, arranging beddings of grass, and preparing their small meal. Cabot had then fed her by hand, she in primary slave position, and with her knees spread, as she was that sort of slave. He also, in hand-feeding her, had required that she keep her hands, palms down, firmly, on her thighs. He ignored her plaintive whimperings.

It was now after the meal, and she had tidied the camp, smoothed the beddings, and such.

She now knelt in the vicinity of her master, but to one side, and back, in a place he had indicated. In this way she would be close at hand, and thus easily summonable, but her presence would be unobtrusive, outside the purview of her master, who, it seemed, might not now care to look upon her.

Had she been banished from his sight, if not from his convenience?

It is not unusual, incidentally, to put a slave in the background, so to speak, in a place from whence she may be easily brought to serve, but, too, where her presence will not intrude on the attention of free persons. Free women often insist on this. Indeed, when free women are present, at a supper, or such, the slave is likely to be demurely, modestly, clothed, even in an ankle-length gown. To be sure, she is denied gloves, her arms are commonly bare, and the collar must be clearly visible. Free women insist on that. If only men are present, matters are likely to be arranged differently, and proceed differently. For example, the slave is likely to be clothed differently, if clothed.

She strove, biting her lip, not to whimper, for her master might not care for it. Had he not put her outside the circle of his purview? Too, she did not wish to be cuffed. Yet she was sure she would soon be able to resist no longer, and would inevitably utter the soft, pleading need noise of a stressed slave, even though it might bring not the master's mercy, but the lashing of his belt.

Cabot, of course, had not been, nor it is likely any man would have been, unaware of her restlessness, her scarcely controlled agitation, her attempts, those of a slave, to call herself to his attention.

Masters, you see, do not necessarily object to such discomfitures in their slaves. Muchly thereby are their lovely bellies well heated.

He turned to regard her.

She looked at him, wildly, piteously.

She struggled to keep the palms of her hands down on her thighs. Clearly she would have preferred to turn them, so that her small, soft palms would be exposed to her master, in a slave's mute appeal.

"Perhaps I shall bracelet you for the night," said Cabot.

"Master?" she said.

"With your hands before you, so you will be comfortable," he said, "lying down, with your hands fastened about a small tree."

Tears streaked her cheeks.

"What is wrong?" he asked.

She put herself to her belly, before him, sobbing.

"Did you enjoy being braceleted to the tree," he asked, "neck leashed to it, unable to speak, gagged?"

"You touched me," she said, "when I was helpless, and could not resist! Then you left me to writhe in need!"

"It is a common way to heat a slave," said Cabot, "to make her helpless, and then touch her, and then leave her, indefinitely, if need be, until her needs master her, until she is the piteous victim of her own nature."

She placed her cheek against his right foot.

"Then," he said, "they pull against their bonds, but, of course, are helpless to free themselves, and, if ungagged, they commonly call out, piteously, begging for usage, and even for so small a kindness as a caress."

"I beg usage," she said.

"Even for the least of caresses?"

"Yes, Master!"

"Strange," said he, "for a woman of Earth."

"I am no longer a woman of Earth," she said. "Surely you know what has been done to me! Despise me, if you must, but is it not you who has made me like this?"

"If I have done anything here," he said, "it is no more than to release what was already within you, waiting, longing, begging to be freed. Have you not consulted your dreams, your fantasies? And I do not despise a woman for her vitality and health, nor for her awakened sensitivities and needs. Only a lunatic or fool would do that. One might as well despise her for the circulation of her blood, the beating of her heart. No, I do not despise you. Rather, I rejoice, as would any true man, to see you so alive, and needful."

"I need a man," she said. "A master!"

"A master?"

"Yes, a master!"

"Why?"

"Because I am a woman, a slave!"

"I see," he said.

"A slave begs use," she said.

"Earth seems now far behind you," he said.

"Yes, Master!"

"You sound like a mere slave girl," he said.

"It is what I now am!" she said.

"And anything in addition?"

"No, Master," she said, "only that!"

"I like you like this," he said.

She whimpered, piteously.

"I wonder if you know how beautiful you are in your need, how helpless and beautiful."

"Please content me, Master," she said.

"Perhaps," he said.

She moaned.

"Please," she said, "please!"

"It seems the slave fires rage in your belly," he said.

"Please, Master," she protested.

"Do they?" he asked.

"Yes!" she said.

"What?" he asked.

"The slave fires rage in my belly!" she wept.

"You admit it?"

"Yes, yes!"

"Interesting," he said.

"Please, Master!" she said.

"You are collared, are you not?" he asked.

"Yes, Master! Yes, Master!" she wept.

"And whose collar do you wear?"

"Yours, yours, Master!" she cried.

"It is on you well, is it not?" he asked.

"Yes, Master!" she said.

"It is close-fitting, is it not?"

"Yes, Master!"

"It is locked on you, is it not?"

"Yes, Master!"

"Can you slip it?" he asked.

"No, Master!" she said.

She, bellied, began to kiss his feet, piteously.

"I need your touch, Master," she said. "I need you, my master! I need you with all the desperation with which a slave needs her master!"

"It is interesting what slavery can do to a woman," said Cabot.

"I beg to be touched," she said. "Please have me!"

"As what?" he asked.

"As what I am," she said, "as a slave."

"Only that?" he said.

"Yes, Master," she said. "Please, Master!"

"Would you not prefer to be treated with the dignity and respect due to a free woman?" he asked.

"No longer," said she. "How could I, knowing what I now know, be content with something so shallow, something so meaningless, with something so tepid and absurd?"

"Would you not prefer to be pridefully resistant, inert, and cool?"

"It would cheat me of myself," she said.

"Surely you desire to be touched, if at all, only with tentative circumspection, with solicitous temerity, with hesitant, even apologetic, reluctance?"

"No," she said. "I want to be handled, and mastered, and treated, and commanded, as what I am, a slave! Rope me, if you wish! Put me under your whip, if you wish!"

"Surely you crave distance, delicacy, courtesy, and reserve."

"No!"

"You are obviously desperately needful," he observed.

"Yes, Master!"

"Perhaps I shall take pity on you," he said.

"Yes, Master!"

"Perhaps then I shall treat you—as a free woman."

"No, no!" she wept. "Do not be cruel! Do not deprive me! My needs are a thousand times beyond those of a free woman! My needs are not those of free woman, but of a slave!"

"An aroused slave?"

"Yes!"

"The needs are different?" he asked.

"Yes!" she cried. "Yes! And I am at your feet, shameless, prostrate, begging!"

"As a slave?"

"Yes, yes," she wept. "For I am a slave! She who is at your feet is not a free woman, but a slave, an abject, pleading slave!"

"And how should I treat you?" he asked.

"As what I am," she said. "As a slave, an abject, pleading slave!"

"Do you beg it?" asked Cabot.

"Yes, my Master! I beg it, I beg it, my Master!"

"Very well," said Cabot, and took her into his arms.

"Yes," said Cabot, later, "it is interesting, indeed, the effect of slavery on a woman."

"Please, Master," she begged. "More! More!"

"Very well," said Cabot.

It was some Ahn later, in the night, when the great voice was heard.

Cabot sat up, and Lord Grendel, whose watch it again was, rose to his feet, half crouched, ears lifted. Cabot's girl was at his thigh, unbound. She stirred, uneasily, and pressed her lips against his thigh, softly, gratefully, recalling perhaps the lengthy Ahn before, at the end of which her master, whose watch it then was, had thrust her from him.

"What is it?" asked Cabot.

"Turn on the translator," said Grendel.

"Can you not tell me?" asked Cabot.

"Turn on the translator," said Grendel, grimly.

The simple message was repeated, several times.

Cabot had now stood, and shaken the sleep from him. The slave was half kneeling, half sitting, beside him, on the grass, which still bore the signs of their tumult, and, later, rest.

The message, as stated, was a simple one.

It boomed within the cylinder, and must have carried even to the camps of the fleet survivors, to the remoter villages, and perhaps even to the shores of Lake Fear. If this were so, and if Lord Arcesilaus still somehow lived, he, in the cave, would have doubtless heard it, as well.

Cabot found and switched on his small translator, which he had set to a low volume, to reduce the likelihood of Gorean being detected by unwelcome ears.

"What is it, Master?" asked the slave.

Cabot cautioned her to silence, and held the device to his right ear.

"Intelligence has been brought to Agamemnon," said Lord Grendel. "And it has been sifted."

Cabot nodded.

The Theocrat of the world had obviously been apprised of yesterday's dark work.

"I fear power weapons will now be used unrestrictedly within the world," said Grendel.

"The world may be destroyed," said Cabot.

"The world is not fragile," said Grendel. "But it may be destroyed from within."

"So, too, may any world," said Cabot.

"Gor, and her sister, Earth," said Grendel, "lie within their atmospheres, but here the atmosphere lies within the world. With power weapons, Gor, and Earth, might be broken into fragments, each too small to hold an atmosphere, but here an atmosphere may be the more easily lost, escaping through vast ruptures, ruptures easily consequent upon the charges of the larger power weapons."

"It would destroy the world," said Cabot.

"Agamemnon, I am sure," said Lord Grendel, "if perceiving himself adequately threatened, would not hesitate to destroy this world."

"But he, too, would die," said Cabot.

"No," said Grendel. "There are other worlds."

"If Agamemnon wins, then," said Cabot, "he wins, and if he loses, too, he wins."

"Yes," said Lord Grendel.

"So what do we do?" asked Cabot. "Do we surrender?"

"No," said Grendel. "We fight."

"Good," said Cabot.

The simple message continued to resound throughout the cylinder.

"It seems we have made an impression," said Lord Grendel.

"True," said Cabot, tight-lipped.

"What is the message, Master?" asked the slave.

"You are short of arrows," said Cabot to Lord Grendel. "You must take half of what is here."

Grendel nodded.

"Master?" asked the slave.

"Today," said Cabot, "you will not be braceleted, or tethered."

"As Master wishes," she said, uncertainly.

"I fear there are twenty with purple scarves for one without," said Grendel.

Cabot nodded.

"And power weapons may now be utilized within the cylinder," said Lord Grendel.

"But not the larger power weapons, presumably," said Cabot.

"Not at first, surely," said Grendel.

"They are at the flat ends of the cylinder?" asked Cabot.

"In vaults, locked within," said Grendel, "with many additional weapons, smaller, manageable by a single Kur, or human."

"How can one reach them?"

"By flight," said Grendel. "By the canvas and leather wings, beating against the atmosphere."

"Flight in the absence of gravity," said Cabot.

"Much as in the shuttles," said Grendel.

"Agamemnon must be prevented from reaching the vaults," said Cabot.

"I doubt he is even thinking of that now," said Grendel. "Recourse to such things would be a last resort. Better, now, merely to keep them secure."

Again and again, in a metallic, droning, reverberating Kur, the message of Agamemnon resounded, again and again in the cylinder.

Then, suddenly, it was silent.

Cabot switched off the translator.

"Why am I not to be braceleted and tethered, Master?" inquired the slave.

Cabot shook his head.

"But such was to protect me, was it not, that I not be understood as in violation of the injunction against slaves touching weapons, and that I might be clearly understood as only goods, merely as something to be disposed of according to the fortunes of war."

"Surely," said Cabot. "But even were it not for such considerations you would have been treated identically."

"Led shamefully on a tether," she asked, "sorely burdened, helplessly braceleted?"

"Yes," said Cabot, "once I decided to take you with me."

"But, why, Master?"

"For your instruction," he said, "and my pleasure."

"You wanted me so," she said.

"Yes," he said, "it would help you understand the better your bondage, and, for my part, I find it gives me great pleasure to have a beautiful woman in my bonds, helpless, and at my mercy."

Swiftly, startled, gasping, she flung herself to her knees before her master, and, head down, kissed him, again and again, about the knees and thighs.

"Was it instructive?" he asked.

"Well was I taught my servitude," she said.

"Good," he said.

"But, too, Master," she whispered, "I felt so slave!"

"Good," he said.

"And I knew myself so yours," she said. "My belly was stirred. My thighs were hot. I was enflamed!"

"I know," he said.

"But now I am to follow you freely?" she asked.

"Yes," he said. "At least for now."

Grendel was dividing the arrows.

"But, why, Master?" she asked.

"Because, Lita," he said, "though you are collared, you are obviously human."

"Of course, Master," she said, puzzled.

"It has to do with the message," said Lord Grendel.

"Your bonds, and such, even your collar," said Cabot, "no longer afford you protection."

"The message," said Lord Grendel, "was clear."

"What was it?" asked Lita.

"'Kill all humans'," said Lord Grendel.

"We may not live out the day," said Cabot.

"Humans are safe with the revolutionaries," said Lord Grendel, "as they are regarded either as allies or neutral, but those with the purple scarves will destroy all humans on sight."

"Why?" asked the slave.

"They are suspect," said Lord Grendel, "and if one kills them all, one will surely kill those who might favor the revolution."

"And perhaps, in particular, one or two," said Cabot, bitterly.

"Precisely," said Grendel, thrusting several arrows into his quiver, and bundling others, to be carried by hand.

"What of the cattle?" said Cabot.

"They are human," said Lord Grendel.

"I must try to save them," said Cabot.

"They are cattle," said Lord Grendel.

"They are human," said Cabot.

"Where are you off to?" asked Cabot.

"The Lady Bina," said Lord Grendel, "is human."

"Forget her," said Cabot.

"I cannot, I will not," said Lord Grendel.

"I may never see you again," said Cabot.

"I wish you well," said Lord Grendel.

"I wish you well," said Cabot.

The slave put down her head and gently kissed her master's foot, and then lifted her head to regard him.

"We may not live out the day?" she said.

"I do not know," said Cabot.

"You gave me great joy last night," she said.

Cabot shrugged.

"And I no more than a slave," she said.

"Such things are commonly done to slaves," he said.

"A slave is grateful," she said.

"I found you pleasing," said Cabot.

"A slave is grateful," she said.

"Do you know what the sort of joy you experienced is called?" asked Cabot.

"Yes, Master," she said.

"What?" he asked.

"Collar joy," she said.

Chapter, the Forty-First:

The Sleen

"Do you hear it?" she asked.

"Yes," he said. "Sleen."

"They are animals," she said.

"You have never seen one," he said.

"No," she said. "Are they dangerous?"

"Some are wild, some are domesticated, all are dangerous," he said.

"It sounds in pain," she said.

"Yes," said Cabot. "It may be wounded, torn, dying."

"It is over there," she said.

"Be careful," said Cabot. He bent his bow, and set an arrow to the string.

This was not an unwise act on the part of the human, Tarl Cabot. Many sleen are clever animals, and it is not unknown for some, particularly older animals, to pretend to be disabled or incapacitated, in order to encourage curious animals to approach them, often to their subsequent instruction and sorrow.

The slave threw her hand before her mouth, and half screamed. Her eyes wide.

The large beast lifted his head and snarled.

"Steady," said Cabot to the slave.

"I have never seen such a thing!" she said.

"It is a big one," said Cabot, lowering the bow.

"Its head," she said, "it is like a snake, a viper!"

"Not at all," said Cabot, "but the width, the triangularity, is typical."

"Its legs!" she said.

"It is hard to tell as it lies," said Cabot, "but there are six."

The sleen exposed its fangs and hissed at Cabot.

The slave leapt back.

"It can't reach you," said Cabot. "The rear leg on the left, the bloody leg. You can see the teeth of the trap buried in it."

"It is wild," she said.

"No," said Cabot. "See, the collar."

"How is it loose?" she asked.

"I do not know," said Cabot, "but I suspect it, and others, were released into the habitats."

"For what reason?" she asked.

"To kill humans," said Cabot.

The slave shuddered.

"The trap may have been set by our colleagues," said Cabot, "to protect, as they could, their human allies."

The sleen lunged toward them, briefly, and then screamed with pain. There was the sound of the heavily linked chain which held it in place.

"It cannot reach you," said Cabot.

"Let us leave," said the slave, looking about.

"It will die in misery here," said Cabot. "It will bleed to death, or it will starve. The leg will never be of use to it again."

"Then kill it," said the slave.

"It is a magnificent animal," said Cabot.

"It is a monster," said the girl. "Kill it, in kindness, or come away!"

Cabot put down his bow, and approached the sleen more closely, but did not come within its reach.

He then turned about, to the slave. "I thought I recognized this animal," he said. "From the arena. It is the one called Ramar. It is a valuable beast, a fighting sleen. It might kill ten sleen, or a hundred humans. That it should be released is interesting."

"How is that?" asked the slave, keeping back.

"It would indicate, I suppose," said Cabot, "that Lord Agamemnon is concerned with the revolution, that he takes it seriously, truly, and that he recognizes that its humans may pose some threat to his forces, that their opposition is not negligible."

"Lord Agamemnon is afraid?" asked the slave.

"I doubt that," said Cabot. "But I find it encouraging that he might be concerned."

The sleen snarled.

The slave backed away, further. "Let us get away from here," she said.

"You see," said Cabot. "He may not know the extent of the revolution, of the unrest, and he may not be certain as to who is loyal to him, and who is not."

"Come away, Master," she said, "please."

"I cannot leave this powerful, beautiful thing to die here," said Cabot.

"Then kill it, Master," she said, "and come away. I am frightened. It is a terrible thing. And there may be Kurii about."

"True," said Cabot. "Keep watch."

"What are you going to do?" asked the slave. "No!" she said. "Come away, Master! Please, Master, come away!"

Cabot held his hands open, and spoke soothingly to the beast.

"It is used to Kur!" said the slave.

"Gorean will do," said Cabot. "Even English. It does not know Kur, any more than it knows Gorean or English. Some simple commands perhaps, perhaps its name, that would be all."

He continued to speak soothingly to the sleen.

It regarded him, and snarled.

"Come away, Master!" said the slave. "Come away, please, Master!"

"I will not hurt you," said Cabot, soothingly to the beast. "Be calm, be patient, big fellow."

"He cannot understand you," said the slave.

"Not as you understand me," said Cabot, "but in other ways, by the slow movements of the body, not threatening, the softness of the voice, the gentleness of its tones."

The sleen again snarled.

"It could reach you!" whispered the slave. "Come away, Master!"

"Yes," said Cabot, softly, elatedly. "It could reach me now."

"Please, Master!"

"But it has not," said Cabot.

The beast turned its head, to watch Cabot, warily, as he moved slowly to the clamped, sharpened, viselike teeth of the trap.

Cabot, for a human being, was quite strong. Doubtless many are stronger, but, for a human being, he was quite strong.

Cabot set his hands between the teeth of the trap and, sweating, straining, eased them a little open, and his hands were covered with blood and torn hair, and the sleen watched him, and Cabot, grunted, fighting for breath, and opened the teeth a bit more, and a little more, and then the sleen, with a scream of pain, drew its useless leg from the trap's jaws, leaving skin and flesh clinging to the teeth, and scrambled away, and Cabot, gratefully, reduced his grip on the jaws of the trap, and then he jerked his fingers away, and it snapped shut, the teeth fitting together, on nothing. Cabot then sat on the bloodied ground, trying to catch his breath.

"Are you all right, Master?" asked the slave.

"Yes," said Cabot. "Where is the sleen?"

"It is gone," said the slave.

Chapter, the Forty-Second:

The Ramp;
The Ladder

"The smell is frightful," whispered the slave.

"It is the stockyards," said Cabot.

"Are they truly human?" she asked.

"I am not sure," said Cabot. "I think so."

"They are meat," she said.

"They are bred that way," said Cabot.

"Can they speak?"

"No, they are not speeched," said Cabot.

"Many of the pens are empty," said the slave.

"The killing has begun," said Cabot.

"Where are the guards?" she asked.

"Guards are not needed," said Cabot, "only attendants, herders, such things."

Cabot then went to one of the pens, in which there were several of the creatures.

"Anyone could unlatch this gate," said Cabot.

"They have not done so," said the slave, wonderingly.

Cabot opened the gate, widely.

He gestured to the creatures, encouraging them to leave, but they did not much note him, save to distend their nostrils, as though smelling for food, but, as Cabot did not bear the swill buckets with him, they turned away.

"They do not wish to leave the food troughs," said Cabot.

"I had a terrible thought," she said.

"What is that?" asked Cabot.

"What if they could vote?" she said.

"They cannot," said Cabot.

"But what if they could?"

"Then fellows would rise up and make use of them, as a path to power," said Cabot.

"The smell sickens me," she said.

Cabot opened several more of the pens. "When they get hungry enough," he said, "I am sure they will wander out."

"Perhaps they will wait by the food troughs, and starve," she said.

"Surely some will leave the pens," said Cabot.

"What will become of them?"

"I do not know," said Cabot. "Perhaps some of the humans can care for them, or herd them to safety."

"They cannot care for themselves," said the slave.

"I do not think so," said Cabot.

"They are like animals, to be cared for," she said.

"And then eaten," said Cabot.

"Most of the pens are empty," said the slave.

"It took us two days to reach the pens," said Cabot.

"I am not sure they are human," she said.

"No," said Cabot. "They are human."

"Not now," whispered the slave.

"Then later, perhaps generations later," said Cabot.

"Look!" whispered the slave.

"Ai," said Cabot. "I see!"

"The line of them, being led up that ramp," she said.

"Yes," said Cabot.

"They follow, blindly," said the slave.

"See the lead human, with the bell on her neck," said Cabot.

"Yes," said the slave.

"She is leading them. They are following her, trustingly. They do not know where they are being taken."

"Where are they being taken?"

"I fear," said Cabot, "to the slaughter bench."

"She has not only a bell on her neck," said the slave, "but something on her head, as well."

"It is hard to see," said Cabot. "No, it sparkles."

"A crown?" said the slave.

"A coronet," said Cabot. "A tiara!"

"She is different from the others," said the slave. "She is not massive as they, not mere meat, encircling heavy bones."

"Surely you recognize her," said Cabot.

"No," said the slave.

"It is the Lady Bina," he said.

"Here?"

"She is leading them to slaughter," said Cabot.

The bell could be heard, even where Cabot and the slave stood.

"Doubtless she has no choice," said the slave.

"Let us hope not," said Cabot.

"I do not understand," said the slave.

"The cattle will follow the bell, and the human who wears it," said Cabot. "Such things are common in slaughter houses. There is a shoot. The lead animal, at the last moment, slips through a gate to the side, and the line behind it continues to move forward, and downward, to the great hammers, or to the ropes and slings, to be suspended, dangling, for the knives, such things."

"Can we interfere?"

"We must," said Cabot.

"What is the crown she wears?" asked the slave.

"A tiara," said Cabot.

"A tiara?"

"That of a Ubara," said Cabot.

"I do not understand," said the slave.

"It is a joke," said Cabot.

"I do not understand," said the slave.

"Lord Agamemnon, it seems," said Cabot, "has a sense of humor. Hurry. Hurry!"

Cabot clambered to the ramp, and hoisted the girl up beside him. The cattle, those near him, regarded him dully, and then continued to plod upward.

Cabot and the slave raced upward.

The passageway became narrower and narrower.

They were nearly to the top of the shoot, when the Lady Bina, now cattle, unclothed, a bell on her neck, a tiara fastened in her blonde hair, saw them.

She looked at them, once, wildly, startled, astonished to see them here, and then, regarding them, laughed merrily, and then, suddenly aware of her location and the press behind her in the now-narrowed passageway, admitting now only a single file, she turned about, and seized the small gate to her right, to slip through it.

She jerked at the gate, and then jerked at it, again.

It was locked.

She pulled at the gate, again and again, frantically.

Then she uttered a long, wild scream of terror, of protest, and was swept forward in the shoot by the press of the moving cattle.

Her screaming could be heard further down the shoot.

Her bell still rang.

"We cannot get through these bodies!" said Cabot. "We must go back, go around!"

"There will not be time!" cried the slave.

Cabot raced back down the ramp, the slave hurrying after him.

"No, no, no!" they heard, weird and shrill, then fainter and fainter, the screams behind them, as they raced down the ramp.

The throat of the Lady Bina, of course, was not constructed to utter Kur, nor would she know much of that language, saving perhaps to recognize some words addressed to her, and what Kurii might be in the facility would be unlikely to have translators, or, even, if so, would not be likely to have them switched on, as there would be no need for such devices here, for there was nothing human in the vicinity, or, perhaps more carefully put, nothing in the vicinity which was both human and speeched.

"There must be a way to the place of slaughter," cried Cabot, looking wildly about.

"There, there, Master!" cried the slave, pointing dozens of yards away, forward and to their left, to a side wall. A high ladder was there, fixed against the wall, which must have been a hundred or more feet high, and led, it seemed, to a closed ceiling. Descending this ladder were two Kurii.

"Good!" said Cabot.

The first Kur, he who had been farthest down the ladder, then leapt to the floor, and, crouching, viewed Cabot and the girl. Its ears were lifted and rotated toward them. Its eyes, like dark moons in the great building's dim light, regarded them. Then, as it rested on its knuckles, its hind legs scratched at the wooden floor.

"It is surprised, and not pleased," said Cabot.

"It thinks we wandered from the pens," said Lita.

"No," said Cabot. "We are clothed."

"It will attack," she whispered.

"Presumably," said Cabot, stringing his bow. "Presumably, and with confidence."

The second Kur then dropped down to the floor, scuffled through sawdust, and joined his cohort.

"They are handlers, or herders," said the slave. "They are not armed."

"Neither is a larl or sleen," said Cabot.

The first Kur began to shuffle toward them, sidewise, keeping his head to them.

It stopped some fifty feet from them.

"It is grinning," said Cabot. Cabot switched on his translator. "Keep away," he said to the Kur.

The Kur remained immobile.

"Where is the place of slaughter?" asked Cabot.

"You are cattle," said the Kur.

"Where is the place of slaughter?" asked Cabot, again.

"I will take you there," said the Kur. "And hang you with the others."

Cabot then loosed the shaft from the great bow.

"He is strong," mused Cabot, for the Kur was still on its feet. He then walked about the Kur, who stood very still.

"What is wrong?" came from Cabot's translator, as he picked up the second Kur's query addressed to the first.

"The stick, the little stick," said the first Kur, and he turned slowly to his fellow.

The second Kur then began to back away.

Cabot turned to the first Kur. "We are not cattle," he said.

The second Kur then turned about, suddenly, and fled, seized the ladder, and began to climb upward, rapidly.

He had managed, despite the desperation and rapidity with which he clambered upward, to ascend only thirty or forty feet on the wide rungs, when he pitched backward, to the floor.

Cabot put his bow, still strung, on his shoulder.

The first Kur regarded him.

"This, too, you see," said Cabot, "is a place of slaughter."

"But you are human," came from Cabot's translator.

"Yes, human," said Cabot. Then he turned to the slave. "Hurry!" he said, and grasped the ladder.

He looked back, once, and saw the slave, climbing below him, and, down on the floor, in the sawdust, he saw the first Kur, fallen, inert.

Chapter, the Forty-Third:

In the Vicinity of the Slaughter Bench

As Cabot climbed the ladder the shrieks of the Lady Bina came to him. "No!" she cried. "You do not understand! I am not to die! The others, not I! I am favored of Lord Agamemnon! I am high in the world! I am Ubara, Ubara!"

These noises, of course, would be unintelligible to any Kur who lacked an activated translator. He, or what, to whom they were addressed, was probably familiar with the squeals of food animals.

Cabot thrust up the trap door which led to the higher level at the height of the ladder. It was heavy, and perhaps few humans could have raised it, but Cabot, who was strong for a human, with a great effort, threw it back.

It stuck back on the flooring of the higher level.

The Kur there turned to face him.

Cabot, as he had secured the bow on his shoulder, to enable his ascent, and as he was placed on the ladder, could not bring it into play. Only his head and shoulders, as he stood, were emerged through the flat entrance to the upper level.

He saw the Lady Bina, dangling upside down, her ankles roped together, the rope slung over a hook on a pulley. Her bell hung downward, and rang. The tiara was still fastened in her hair. Her hands were free and tried to fend away the mighty, hairy arms of the butcher. He put a hand in her hair, and pulled her toward him. Her small hands futilely, weakly, unavailingly, grasped the wrist of the hand fastened in her hair. Her lovely body squirmed. The bell hung on her neck clanged. The tiara fell to the wood at the butcher's feet.

She saw Cabot. "Save me!" she screamed. "Save me!"

The butcher's right paw held a long tool, pointed and rounded, and some eighteen inches in length, which would be driven cleanly, expertly, into the heart of the suspended food animal, which would then be drawn away on the contrivance of ropes and hooks.

Cabot climbed carefully to the surface of the upper level, and crouched down. He was but feet from the butcher, who, tool in hand, the Lady Bina in his grasp, regarded him, curiously.

Cabot would not have time to activate the bow, to loose it from his shoulder, arrow it, and draw it.

His hand stole to his belt knife.

To Cabot's left he could see a number of suspended bodies, alive, dangling and squirming, some squealing, awaiting their turn, those who had followed the Lady Bina and her bell.

To Cabot's right, as he could see, there were several dangling bodies, moving and turning, with the stresses of the rope. These were the residues from earlier butcherings. And, to the side, to the right, below, he could see a number of bodies, freed from the hooks and ropes, piled like fish.

Too, oddly, he saw two Kur bodies, fallen amongst the slaughtered cattle.

"Save me! Save me!" screamed the Lady Bina.

This was picked up on Cabot's translator.

"Do not kill her!" said Cabot.

"I am the bell girl! I am the bell beast!" screamed the Lady Bina. "I am not to die!"

"We do not need you any longer," said the butcher. "You have led the last of the cattle to the slaughter bench. Now it is your turn. That is why we locked the gate."

"I am favored of Lord Agamemnon!" she cried.

"You are cattle," said the butcher.

"No, no!" she screamed.

"Do not reach for your knife," said the butcher to Cabot. "I can reach you before you can free it of the sheath. Take your hand away from it. Live a moment longer. I will have time for you when I finish here."

Cabot looked about, wildly.

"Place your hands, clasped, behind the back of your head," said the butcher, "or I strike now, this moment."

Cabot obeyed, in misery.

"You may watch," said the butcher.

"She is favored of Lord Agamemnon," cried Cabot, desperately, "Eleventh face of the Nameless One, Theocrat of the World."

"No," said the butcher. "It was he who ordered the gate locked."

Lady Bina, in pain, dangling, cried out in misery, a long wailing sound.

The butcher's arms were reddened to the elbows, the hair soaked with blood. He wore a leather apron. And a leather scarf was bound over his head and ears. That is perhaps why he had heard no sound earlier.

The butcher's mighty paw clasped the pointed tool more firmly, and he drew back his right arm, and with his left hand he drew the shrieking Lady Bina more closely to him.

"Wait!" cried Cabot, pointing down, and to his right. "Why are Kurii dead below?"

The butcher regarded him, puzzled.

"None are dead," he said.

"Two are dead," said Cabot.

"No," said the butcher.

"Look," said Cabot.

"Step back," said the butcher.

Cabot stepped back, behind the trap. He could see Lita's dark hair below, she clinging to the ladder, her shoulders. She looked up at him, but he gave no sign he saw her.

The butcher went to the ledge, where he might look down.

He did not hear the scratching, which was subtle, and came from his left.

The butcher called down to the inert bodies below.

He did not see the one paw, with its claws, which appeared over the edge of the platform, somewhat behind him, and to his left.

"They are dead," Cabot assured him, drawing his attention to his right.

"I do not understand," said the butcher.

"Perhaps you are next," said Cabot.

"I do not understand," said the butcher.

"That is perhaps why you are next," said Cabot.

"I will kill her, and then you," said the translator. In Kur this was clearly a snarl, but it was rendered, as would be expected, with calmness and precision by the translator.

The butcher turned to the dangling Lady Bina but there now stood a formidable impediment between him and his objective.

With a roar of rage, a bleeding Lord Grendel flung himself on the butcher, and with a single bite tore away the butcher's right paw, it still grasped on the tool, and Lord Grendel lifted the butcher over his head, and flung him to the lower level, where he fell among the slaughtered cattle, howling in pain, blood spurting from his right wrist.

The butcher then rose up, slipping on the bodies, fell, and rose up, again, moving away.

Cabot, by now, had freed his bow and handed it, with an arrow, to Lord Grendel.

"It will be a difficult shot," said Cabot.

The shaft took the stumbling, hastening fugitive in the back of the head.

"You have been practicing," said Cabot.

"Free me, free me, you fools!" screamed the Lady Bina.

"You are bleeding," said Cabot to his friend.

"Two, below, fought well," said Lord Grendel.

"Free me!" demanded the Lady Bina.

Lita rose up, half way, through the trap.

The Lady Bina, squirming, dangling upside down, discerned Lita. "That is a slave!" she cried. The Lady Bina's bell, as she struggled, rang. It was chained about her neck. "Go away!" cried the Lady Bina. "Do not let me be seen as I am, by a filthy, stinking slave!"

"Are you concerned?" asked Cabot.

"Free me!" she cried.

"Perhaps you feel your dignity is compromised," said Cabot, "as you are, naked, upside down, a bell on your neck. Certainly few free women are likely to be found so, except doubtless in the houses of slavers, awaiting their branding and collaring."

"Free me!" she screamed.

Lita clambered to the level.

"Send that stinking, ugly slave away!" cried the Lady Bina.

"She is not ugly," said Cabot. "Stripped, she would stand high on the price list of many slavers."

"As might you," he added.

"Insolence!" she cried.

"I must free her," said Lord Grendel.

"If I were you," said Cabot, "I would keep her naked, on a rope, and keep the bell on her neck."

"No, no," mumbled Grendel. "That is unthinkable. She is a free woman."

"You risked your life to save her," said Cabot. "Do you think she is grateful?"

He lifted her down, and bent to free her ankles.

"Do not look at me, beast," she said.

"Forgive me, Lady," he said.

"Fetch me my tiara!" she said.

Lord Grendel picked up the small object, and handed it to her. She thrust it down, in place.

"I am a Ubara," she informed him.

"I did not know that," said Lord Grendel.

"So proclaimed by Lord Agamemnon himself," she said.

"I did not know that," said Lord Grendel.

"You are bleeding," said Cabot.

"It is nothing," he said.

"Let Lita tend your wounds."

"The blood of a Kur clots quickly," said Grendel.

"And of at least one human," said Cabot.

"Perhaps," said Grendel.

"Get this terrible bell, and chain, off my neck!" demanded the Lady Bina, sitting on the platform, rubbing her rope-burned ankles.

"I cannot, without a tool," said Lord Grendel.

"Then fetch a tool," said the Lady Bina.

"First," said Cabot, "we must free the living cattle, those on the hooks, and drive those in the shoot, and in the pens, into the open, where they might have a chance to live."

"They are only cattle," said the Lady Bina.

"I will command the nondominants," said Lord Grendel. "Only they are left here. They will obey me."

"Why will they do that?" asked Cabot.

"Because," said he, "I am a dominant."

"I understand," said Cabot.

"Come back!" said the Lady Bina. But Grendel was gone. She glared at Cabot. "What are you looking at?" she demanded.

"I was wondering what you would bring," said Cabot, "—on a slave block."

"Insolent beast!" she screamed.

"It is an idle thought," he said, "but one common amongst males, when they look upon a comely female. It is quite common for them to think of them stripped, in a slave collar, roped tightly, helplessly, on the floor, at the foot of their bed, and such."

"I want Lord Grendel to return," she said.

She jerked at the bell on her neck, and it made a small sound.

"Slaves are sometimes belled," said Cabot, "sometimes for custodial purposes, for they may be locked on a slave, sometimes to enhance their attractiveness, sometimes to remind them, with the bells' frequent jangling, consequent upon their slightest movement, that they are a slave. They can humiliate and shame the slave, particularly a new slave, or stir her belly, exciting her with her vulnerability and the profound meaning of her condition. Too, of course, they can have their effect on the male. In a case such as yours, they might function differently, rather as a penalty brand, to warn others that, say, their wearer is petty and untrustworthy. Indeed, there are many reasons why a slave might be belled."

One might add, as a note, that paga girls, dancers, and such, are often belled. Indeed, one of the pleasures of some paga taverns are the bells of the slaves, jangling, as they hasten about, serving their master's custom. The most common belling site on a slave is her left ankle.

"I am a Ubara," she said.

"That is absurd," said Cabot. "Where is your city?"

"I do not need a city," she said.

"Where is your army?"

"I do not need an army," she said.

"Few Ubaras are found in the cattle pens," he said, "though I suppose a few might be."

"I was betrayed by Lord Agamemnon," she said. "Were he human, and not Kur, he would have obeyed me."

"You saw him?" asked Cabot, sharply.

"One of his bodies," she said. "A land tharlarion, he attended by Lords Lucullus and Crassus."

"I have seen that body," said Cabot.

"I have great power over men," she said.

"That is because you are not in a collar," he said. "Then they would have great power over you."

"You yourself kissed me," she said, "in the forest world."

The slave, Lita, gasped. How foolish she was! Did she not know she was no more than a slave, and thus rightless, and meaningless?

"It was a lapse," said Cabot, "but I admit you would fit nicely in a man's arms."

Lita looked up, her eyes fresh with tears.

"Particularly if you were in a collar," said Cabot. "But then that is true of any woman."

"I have never forgotten your touch," she said, softly.

"You squirmed nicely," said Cabot, "exactly as would a slave."

Lita whimpered, in protest.

The Lady Bina laughed. "You are trying to make me angry," she said. "You will not succeed."

"Lord Grendel rescued you," said Cabot. "He saved your life. He loves you."

"He is Kur," she said, "and a poor Kur, one deformed, consider his hands, his voice."

"Master," whispered Lita, "Lord Grendel approaches."

"Tal," said Cabot, rising.

"Tal," said Lord Grendel.

"Where is the tool, to free me of this hated device?" said the Lady Bina, indicating the unwelcome encirclement which graced her slim neck.

There are chain collars, thought Cabot.

As it is difficult to engrave such, these will commonly bear a small, dangling metal disk. On this disk pertinent information may be recorded, such as a girl's current name and master.

"Forgive me, my lady," said Lord Grendel, "I could not find one in the time I had." He then turned to Cabot. "Many of the cattle are now beyond the pens. This will attract attention. There will doubtless be inquiries. I think it is best for us to leave this place, and seek some camp of allies."

"I know one," said Cabot.

"I, too," said Lord Grendel.

"Let us lose no time," said Cabot.

As the Lady Bina rose to her feet the bell on her neck gave out its note.

"Master," exclaimed Lita, pointing, toward the left. "There!"

"It is one of the cattle," said Cabot.

The massive thing, perhaps six hundred pounds in weight, was in the area from which the ropes and hooks had approached the slaughter bench.

"Drive it away!" demanded the Lady Bina.

Stupidly, balefully, the creature, massive and stolid, not moving, was looking at the Lady Bina.

"I think he remembers her," said Cabot. "I think he knows what she did. I think he understands now what she was doing."

"Get rid of him!" said the Lady Bina, shuddering.

"I do not think such things are dangerous," said Lord Grendel.

"Perhaps not before," said Cabot, "but now I do not know. Things are not now the same."

"Drive it away!" demanded the Lady Bina.

"It is only human," said Lord Grendel.

"Drive it away!" she said.

"Very well, my lady," he said, and raised his arms and roared, and the creature turned slowly about, and moved away.

"What will be done with the bodies?" asked Cabot.

Lita looked sick.

"Our cohorts, I think," said Lord Grendel, "will burn this place."

"Good," said Cabot.

"Where are we going?" asked the Lady Bina.

"Blindfold her," said Cabot.

"It may be best," said Lord Grendel.

"Never!" said the Lady Bina.

"A hood would be better," said Cabot, "and a gag hood even better. I would much enjoy shoving the packing in her pretty little mouth, securing it behind the back of her neck, and then fastening the hood on her, buckling it in place, closely, tightly."

"She is a free woman," said Lord Grendel, scandalized.

"She might run to the purple scarves, and seek to ingratiate herself once more with Agamemnon, swearing her fealty to him, perhaps bartering for power with our plans and positions," said Cabot.

"Purple scarves?" she said.

"The ensigns of those loyal to Agamemnon," said Cabot, watching her.

"Oh," she said.

Cabot was satisfied then with the results of his experiment.

"You would not betray us, would you?" asked Lord Grendel.

"Certainly not," she said.

"Let us leave her here," said Cabot.

"No!" she said.

"Humans will be killed on sight," said Grendel.

"Take me with you!" she said.

"Better to put an ost in your pouch," said Cabot.

The ost, according to the resources, is a tiny, highly venomous snake. It is indigenous to certain locales on Gor.

"Let us leave her here, bound hand and foot," said Cabot.

"Never," said Lord Grendel.

And thus Cabot's second experiment came to its conclusion. He had satisfied himself that the Lady Bina, as he had supposed, could not be trusted, and that Lord Grendel, for whatever reason, might die before he would permit harm to come to her.

Cabot wished that she might be collared, for then she would be of little danger to anyone, save to herself, if she were not fully pleasing to masters.

"Are the jewels in her tiara genuine?" asked Cabot.

"I would think so," said Lord Grendel, "as that would improve the joke, Lord Agamemnon rewarding her with riches of little interest to himself, and then placing her naked in the pens. Thus she was genuinely rewarded with wealth, perhaps as promised, and then, afterwards, treated as Lord Agamemnon thought appropriate."

"Treated as the despicable, worthless, treacherous slut she was," said Cabot.

"Kurii often have dealings with traitors," said Lord Grendel, "but they feel no obligation to be fond of them, to respect them, and such."

"Let us be on our way," she said.

Then she looked at Lita, with disgust.

"If any are to be left here, bound hand and foot," she said, "let it be she, whose presence might handicap us, a worthless slave."

"She is not mine," said Lord Grendel.

"She comes with us," said Cabot.

Lita threw him a swift glance, of relief, of joy, of gratitude.

"Wait!" said the Lady Bina. "I cannot go like this. I am unclothed!"

"We will find you something suitable, as soon as possible," said Lord Grendel.

"See," said the Lady Bina, "the slave is clothed and I am not!"

"It is only a tiny, shameful tunic," said Lord Grendel, "a handful of cheap, clinging cloth."

"She is clothed," said the Lady Bina.

"But," said Lord Grendel, "it is not a garment for such as you, a free woman. It is a garment designed to designate its wearer's worthlessness, her meaninglessness, that she is no more than goods, no more than an animal. It is, like others of its kind, little more than a degrading rag. Do not think of it. Put it from your mind! It is clearly no more than the mockery of a garment. Consider its lightness, its brevity. It is brazen. It is shamefully revealing. It is the sort of garment in which a lusty man, for his pleasure, and amusement, would put a woman helplessly in his power, indeed, if he permitted her a garment at all. To such a garment, in its scantiness, in its revealing suggestiveness, in what it says about its occupant, might not a full and honest nudity be preferable? Such a garment is a public proclamation that its wearer, by it so belittled and demeaned, by it so mercilessly exhibited, by it so blatantly exposed, can be no more than a slave."

"I will have it," she said.

"Please, no, my lady!" said Lord Grendel.

"My tiara," she said, "will enhance and redeem the ensemble. It will indicate my condition, my rank."

"My lady!" protested Lord Grendel, in misery.

"Slave!" said the Lady Bina.

"Mistress," said Lita, her head down, frightened.

Lita was kneeling, as is common with slaves in the presence of free persons. She did have her knees together, doubtless because of the presence of a free woman, Lady Bina.

"Remove your garment," said the Lady Bina. "Give it to me!"

Lita looked wildly at Cabot.

"Must a command be repeated?" he asked.

"No, Master," she whispered.

A slave's obedience is to be instantaneous, and unquestioning. The least hesitation may mean the whip. They are slaves.

"Good," said the Lady Bina, seizing the garment. She then held it to her nose, disdainfully. "It stinks," she said.

Lita had, that very morning, washed the garment, and her own body, in a small stream, shortly before they had encountered the trapped sleen, subsequently freed by Cabot.

To be sure, a garment will retain the scent of a wearer, even if worn for a few moments. If this is not clear to a human, it is clear to us, and, of course, even more so to sleen, but then the sleen, as is well known, is a remarkable tracker. Goreans use them for such purposes, and so, too, do we.

"And you stink," added the Lady Bina.

"Yes, Mistress," whispered Lita.

"At least she does not have a bell on her neck," said Cabot.

The Lady Bina regarded him, with fury.

"We will remove it as soon as possible," Lord Grendel reassured the Lady Bina.

"Is the slave crying?" asked the Lady Bina, amused.

"I trust not," said Cabot. Lita's head was down, far down, almost to the floor.

The slave, who as an animal is not entitled to clothing, and may be denied clothing altogether, if it be the wish of her master, is likely to find even a tunic, even a camisk, precious. Now she had been deprived of her single garment, slight as it was, in the presence of a free woman. In this way another aspect of her slavery was brought home to her. "It is a good lesson for her," thought Cabot. "Such small things help her to better understand what she is, slave."

The Gorean slave girl is much at the mercy of free women, by whom she is likely to be resented and hated, and free women are not above petty exercises of power, ordering the slave to kneel, to serve her, to bare herself, to kiss her embroidered slippers, and such. Too, not unoften a tearful slave returns to her master with her tunic wadded in her mouth and the welts of a switch upon the backs of her thighs. The protection of the slave, of course, is the male. The better the slave pleases her master the more likely he is to intervene between her and free women. Many a blow, thus, has been prevented by the interposition of a free male between his slave and a free woman, to the fury of the frustrated free woman. This is as it should be, for a slave's whippings, should she be whipped, are most appropriately at the discretion of the master.

Needless to say, most slaves endeavor to so please the master that they are seldom, if ever, whipped. Occasionally, interestingly, a slave may beg to be whipped, that she be reminded that she is a slave. Too, sometimes, a master will bind and whip his girl, with the same object in mind, to remind her that she is a slave.

Clearly Lita, shaken, now stripped, whether she should of or not, felt miserable, reduced, shamed, humiliated, and worthless, before a free woman, and before Grendel and her master.

A tear had fallen to the boards.

"It will have to do," said the Lady Bina, holding the garment out. "It stinks of the body of a slave, but it is better than nothing."

"Perhaps not," said Lord Grendel. "Consider its lines, its lightness, what it does for its occupant's lineaments. Consider, too, its meaning!"

The Lady Bina swiftly drew on the tunic.

"Ai!" said Cabot, appreciatively.

She pulled it down, more closely, about her hips.

"Do you like it?" she asked Cabot.

"You lack only the collar," said Cabot.

"Is it attractive?"

"Yes," said Cabot. "Indeed, a master might be reluctant to allow you on the streets so clad, but then, if you were a slave, he would have no choice. It would be a matter of law."

"Poor slaves!" she laughed.

"You might be stalked, and stolen," said Cabot. "Bids would doubtless be forthcoming on you."

"I am so beautiful?" she asked.

"Certainly," said Cabot, "and such a garment much enhances a woman's beauty, which is its purpose."

"Oh?" she said.

"And such a garment," he said, "has its role, too, to play in the protection of free women."

"How so?" she asked, puzzled.

"Suppose you were a slaver or raider," said Cabot, "and you had to choose between a woman so clad, an indisputable beauty, one with an obvious sales value, one who might go for several coins, and an unknown quantity, a woman heavily robed and veiled, who, stripped, might be of little interest even to a myopic tarsk. On which would your capture rope be more likely to fall and tighten?"

"I see," she said.

"But the major reason for so clothing slaves," he said, "is doubtless for the pleasure of men."

"The beasts!" she said.

"Have no fear, my lady," said Grendel. "We will shortly obtain something more suitable."

"Too," said Cabot, "they help the slave keep clearly in mind that she is a slave, and such garments, too, have their effect on her."

"And what is that?" she asked.

"In them," he said, "she cannot help but feel female, helpless, and vulnerable."

"I see," she said.

"Accordingly," he said, "in such a garment, the slave is very much sexually aware, acutely so, and this has a common consequence."

"And what is that?" she asked.

"That she cannot help but be sexually ready, and even, frequently, whether she wishes it or not, in a state of sexual arousal."

"I see," she said.

"Shortly, shortly!" insisted Lord Grendel.

"Be quiet," chided the Lady Bina.

Cabot noted that his friend, Lord Grendel, was uneasy, and moist about the jaws.

Ah, thought Cabot, he is not unaware of the effect of that tiny garment on the body of the Lady Bina.

Surely then he will hasten to have her the sooner more appropriately clothed.

It is difficult to see a woman with dignity and respect in such a garment. Indeed, is that not another purpose of such a garmenture, that in it a woman cannot be viewed with dignity or respect, that in it she can be viewed as only a slave.

"Free women," said the Lady Bina, "are a thousand times more beautiful than slaves."

Cabot turned to regard his slave, Lita. Her head was down, and her knees were together. "Position!" he snapped. " Get your head up!"

"Yes, Master!" gasped the slave. There were tears in her eyes. She then knelt well, in first position.

Lita was apparently an extremely attractive girl, for a human. But this is common, as we understand it, for human female slaves.

"She obeys nicely," said the Lady Bina. "What a degrading position," she laughed.

"It is a lovely position," said Cabot. "Quite beautiful."

"For a female slave," said the Lady Bina.

"Certainly," said Cabot.

The Lady Bina, regarding the obedient, commanded slave, laughed derisively.

The eyes of the slave were bright with tears.

She trembled, and sobbed.

She did not, however, break position. A slave might be lashed for that.

"Lita," said Cabot.

"Master?" she said.

"You are in a collar," he said, "a slave collar."

"Master?" she said.

"Be pleased," he said.

"Master?" she said.

"The collar," he said, "is a badge of beauty, a token of excellence, a certification of superiority. It testifies that you are amongst the most desirable, the most beautiful, the most coveted of women. Do you think it is bestowed thoughtlessly, or lightly? Women such as you have been selected out from amongst others, many others. Your limbs have been found worthy of chains, your throat found fit for the clasping circlet of bondage. Do you not understand that merchants choose such as you with a profit in mind, that you are that valuable, and that you are such, and carefully selected to be such, that you might drive a man mad with desire? You have been collared, girl. You are a collared female. Understand the meaning of that. And on your part have you not dreamed of being the vulnerable, helpless object of unmitigated lust? Have you not dreamed of being so desirable that nothing short of owning you, literally owning you, will satisfy a man? And have you not dreamed of being owned, of being uncompromisingly possessed, as no more than an animal or thing, of finding yourself at the feet of a man by whom you know, to your relief and joy, your dream fulfilled, your search over, you are going to be mastered, fully mastered, whether you wish it or not, categorically and wholly?"

"Master!" she breathed.

"Kneel up, then," he said, "and keep your head up. You are

nothing, and everything. Be pleased. You are a slave. You belong at a slave ring. Men will bid for you. You, you lovely piece of goods, you delightful bit of merchandise, are worth coins."

"Yes, Master!" she said.

Cabot, you see, was well aware of much that was unknown to, and perhaps incomprehensible to, his slave, how a woman can rejoice that she has been found so beautiful, and so desirable, that nothing short of owning her will satisfy a man. And what woman does not wish to be so lusted for that nothing short of owning her will satisfy a man? What woman does not long for a master, and what man for a slave?

"In the opinion of many," said Cabot, "slaves are a thousand times more beautiful than free women. To be sure, some of it may have to do with the collar, and its meaning."

The Lady Bina turned angrily away.

"Why do we not leave here?" she asked.

"We shall," said Cabot. He reached into his pouch.

"What are you doing?" demanded the Lady Bina.

"It is for the best," said Lord Grendel.

"No!" exclaimed the Lady Bina.

Cabot, from behind, carefully placed the strip of narrow cloth over the eyes of the free woman, and then, drawing it back, wrapped it about her head, and then again, and then secured it at the back of her head.

"This is not necessary," she said. "Oh!"

Cabot had taken a doubled strand of slave cord, put it about her left wrist, drawn the free strands through the loop, jerked the loop thusly formed tight on her wrist, and then, with the free strands beyond the loop, twice encircled her right wrist, pulled the whole tight, and then knotted the cord.

And thus were the free woman's wrists fastened behind her, as simply, as easily, as might have been those of a slave.

"This is an outrage!" said the free woman.

"One more thing," said Cabot.

"Where are you?" demanded the free woman.

"This," said Cabot.

He then buckled the leash about her neck.

"This is an outrage!" she hissed.

Cabot jerked the leash twice, against the back of her neck. "It is on her, nicely," he said.

"An outrage!" she cried.

"It is for the best," said Lord Grendel.

"We do not trust you," said Cabot.

"I am loyal!" she said.

"To whom?" asked Cabot.

"To you, to you, to the allies, to Lord Peisistratus, to Lord Arcesilaus, to the foes of Agamemnon, to the revolution!" she said.

"You are a traitress," said Cabot. "It may amuse the allies to treat you as you deserve, to subject you to a lengthy and hideous death by torture."

"Do not speak to them of such things!" she cried.

"Surely the tiara on your brow," said Cabot, "makes it clear you were favored by Lord Agamemnon."

"Take it off, take it off!" she cried.

"To be sure," said Cabot, "it seems a pity to think of that pretty little body disfigured and mangled, burned with irons, torn by hooks, coated with honey, and then put out, alive, staked out naked, helplessly, for the delectation of flocks of tiny, carnivorous song birds. They feed, and sing, and feed, and sing."

"Protect me, Lord Grendel!" she cried.

"I am now Lord Grendel," he observed.

"Of course, Lord Grendel!" she exclaimed. "Do you not care for me?"

Lord Grendel was silent, fearing to speak.

"Good," she said. "You are strong, and beautiful, and may yet win my love!"

"Dare he hope for so much?" asked Cabot.

"Yes, yes!" she said.

"What must I do?" asked Grendel.

"First, kill the others, the man, the slave, now!" she said. "Then free me and take me to a place of safety, where we may await the outcome of the strife. If the allies are successful, we will join them. If Agamemnon is successful, humans may yet be permitted to live, and serve, in the world, and I myself will speak on your behalf, to win you pardon for your crime against the world."

"My crime?" asked Lord Grendel.

"Your treason to Lord Agamemnon!" she cried.

"It is time to be on our way," said Cabot. He drew on the leash of the free woman.

"Kill them!" screamed the free woman.

"Perhaps later," said Cabot. "We must now be on our way." He then drew her to the side. "Do not move," he told her, "for there is an opening here, and if you fall, it will be to your death."

She whimpered, and stood, unsteadily.

"There is a ladder," he said. "Lord Grendel will carry you down the ladder."

"You do it!" she said. "I do not want him to touch me!"

"I am weary," said Cabot, "and I fear I might drop you, some hundred feet or so."

She turned her blindfolded eyes toward him. Her lips trembled.

"Yes," he said. "Too, on the flooring below, and later, you will be in the charge of Lita, for Lord Grendel and I must remain unencumbered."

"I am to be in the keeping of a slave!" she said.

"Yes," said Cabot, "now forgive me, for I must gather some things." He then went back, near the slaughter bench, where Lord Grendel stood.

"There are no tiny, carnivorous song birds," said Lord Grendel.

"I know," said Cabot, "but she does not."

"It is a joke?" said Lord Grendel.

"Of course," said Cabot. "She is worthless, but we will do our best to protect her."

"Thank you," said Lord Grendel.

"It is nothing," said Cabot, a scion of Gor's scarlet caste, the Warriors.

Grendel then went to the trap, where the Lady Bina, and now the slave, Lita, waited.

"I am blindfolded, bound, and leashed!" said Lady Bina, angrily, when she was sure Lord Grendel was near.

"Forgive us, my lady," he said. "But it is for the best."

He then lifted her to his shoulder.

"Put her head to the rear," said Cabot.

"Why?" asked Lord Grendel.

"That is the way slaves are carried," said Cabot.

"No!" she said.

"You lack only the collar," said Cabot.

Chapter, the Forty-Fourth:

The Insurrection Is Not Yet Quelled;
A Kur Female Is Encountered;
Statius

The world itself shook, and then shook, again.

"What is it?" cried Cabot.

"Impact," said Lord Grendel. "Something from the outside!"

"Meteors?" said Cabot.

"I do not know," said Lord Grendel.

The gravitation of the world seemed momentarily altered. Cabot stumbled. Then the gravitation seemed again normal.

"It could be an attack of power weapons," said Lord Grendel, "a test of such an attack, a warning, one does not know."

"The world will be destroyed?" said Cabot.

"It would be difficult to do that from the outside, even if it were intended, with the yards of shielding," said Lord Grendel. "But with such weapons, it would be easy to accomplish that from within."

"And such weapons exist within?"

"Of course, in the arsenals," said Lord Grendel.

"It is quiet now," said Cabot.

"Yes," agreed his friend.

"Would those outside wish to destroy this world?" asked Cabot.

"Unlikely," said Lord Grendel. "Why waste a world? Only humans might do that."

"Some humans," said Cabot.

"And perhaps a Kur," said Grendel.

"Lord Agamemnon?" said Cabot.

"Yes," said Lord Grendel.

"But something is outside?" said Cabot.

"Perhaps," said Lord Grendel. "One does not know."

"We have hundreds of humans," said Cabot.

"But they are largely useless," said Grendel.

"At least they can now see," said Cabot.

Recently the light in the world had been altered, reduced to a level where only Kurii might see, this intended, presumably, to diminish the effectiveness, such as it was, of the revolution's human allies. Torches had been lit, and, where available, independent electronic lighting had been employed. Some beam devices, too, had proved of value, and flares, particularly in assisting humans to detect Kur patrols, Kur marches, the advance of raiding parties, and such. This intelligence then, usually by runners, would be communicated to rebel positions, from which countermeasures, engagements or withdrawals, might be contrived.

On the seventh night, however, one of the alternative power stations, designed to act in lieu of the central power source in the case of a failure in that facility, was seized by the rebels. This was utilized in such a way as to restore an approximation to the typical diurnal cycle, the difference being to eliminate those nights on which, in the world, no surrogate moonlight would be provided. The motivation of this departure from normalcy was conceived in order to prevent a periodic disadvantagement of the revolution's human allies.

The humans at the disposal of the rebels were ill-armed, most with sharpened sticks, and many of the killer humans, bred for the arena games, were not only unspeeched, but dangerous to their Kur allies and to one another, as well.

No contact had been made, despite the several days of the revolution, with the pleasure cylinder, and the men of Peisistratus.

It was supposed they were somewhere within the world.

Certainly they had managed to bring humans from the sport cylinder into Agamemnon's cylinder, the main world, and had released, for better or for worse, the killer humans from their cages and training areas.

It must be understood, of course, that the value of humans to the revolution was not as minimal or negligible as the hitherto-noted, disparaging assessment of Lord Grendel might suggest. For example, dozens of humans, armed with their stones and pointed sticks, suddenly swarming upon isolated Kurii were something seriously to be reckoned with. More than one shaggy head was brought back to the rebel camps.

Kurii in the field needed not be supplied, as they could feed, raw or cooked, on the bodies of their enemies. And, it might be mentioned, though with reluctance, that the protein in the diet of the humans, in particular, in that of the killer humans, was not all derived from the processed edibles confiscated from Kur commissaries.

Such unpleasantries are often associated with the altercations of rational species.

Needless to say, amongst the allies, it was understood that feeding on one another, Kur upon human, human upon Kur, was not to take place.

Indeed, interestingly, in the tensions, and the exigencies, and terrors, of war, each species was beginning to see the other in a different light, the one less as monster than colleague, the other less as food than friend.

Here and there, there were small herds of cattle humans about, rooting in abandoned gardens, gathering up fallen fruit, scavenging on the dead. Several had returned to the ashes of the stock yards, wandering about, making tiny noises, puzzled perhaps at the disappearance of the pens, and the feed troughs.

One or two of these bands, led by a behemoth of meat, became paramount, driving other groups away, sometimes seizing them, and feeding on them.

Clumsy wars were fought over patches of vegetables.

"It seems they are indeed human," said Lord Grendel once, when he and Cabot had come upon some such scene of bovine carnage.

Bleary, stupid eyes, tiny in obese bodies, had looked at them.

"It only that they do not have their feed troughs," said Cabot.

"Doubtless," said Lord Grendel.

Then they had turned away.

The cattle humans were largely ignored by the warring parties, save as the loyalists might occasionally cull the herds for meat.

* * * *

Lord Grendel, and his human companion, Tarl Cabot, were on patrol.

"Do you think it wise?" asked Lord Grendel, "to teach the bow to the forest people?"

"Yes," said Cabot, "but perhaps not to the killer humans."

Those from the forest world, it might be noted, were also being taught speech. In this way, their use of signs and certain guttural signals was significantly augmented.

"The killer humans are not stupid," said Grendel. "If the humans from the sport cylinder learn the bow, the arena humans will not be far behind."

"What are you thinking of?" asked Cabot.

"Of the cattle humans," said Lord Grendel.

"They are dangerous only to one another," said Cabot.

"Now," said Lord Grendel.

Suddenly Grendel lifted his head, and his hand.

"What is it?" whispered Cabot. His bow was already strung, as was that of Lord Grendel, for they were on patrol.

"There," said Lord Grendel, pointing.

Cabot saw nothing.

"There," said Lord Grendel, again, softly, pointing.

Then Cabot saw the head, which now lifted from the tall grass, several feet ahead of them.

He drew the bow.

"No," said Lord Grendel, putting out his paw, and Cabot lowered the bow.

"See," said Lord Grendel, "she has no scarf, no purple scarf."

"She?" said Cabot.

"Certainly," said Lord Grendel. "Can you not tell?"

The creature then approached, to within a few feet, and turned her head to the side, and snarled.

"Rather unpleasant," said Cabot. "You are sure it is a female?"

"Certainly," said Lord Grendel. "It is not large."

"I assure you," said Cabot, "it is large enough."

"See the pelt," said Lord Grendel, "the smoothness, the glossiness."

"Oh, yes, of course," said Cabot.

"That is a beautiful Kur female," said Lord Grendel.

"I am sure of it," said Cabot.

"Note the fangs," said Lord Grendel.

"Of course," said Cabot, uneasily.

"She is a beauty," said Lord Grendel.

"Indisputably," said Cabot.

The creature then snarled, again, and lifted a paw, and claws sprang from it. She snarled, again.

"Lovely claws," said Lord Grendel. "Sharp, too. One blow could take the face from a human."

"She is hostile," said Cabot. "What are those things behind it?"

There were some shaggy shapes in the background, some yards behind the nearer creature, which was glaring at them.

"She does not seem much interested in me," said Cabot.

"Perhaps she is not hungry," said Grendel.

"That is a joke, I trust," said Cabot.

"Certainly," said Grendel. "Most Kurii do not even like human."

"Probably it is an acquired taste," said Cabot.

"Possibly," said Grendel.

"She is looking at you," said Cabot.

Lord Grendel handed his bow to Cabot, and slipped the quiver from his shoulder.

The Kur snarled again, viciously.

"She thinks I am a nondominant," said Lord Grendel.

"Why is that?" asked Cabot.

"Probably because I am with a human, and one not leashed."

"I see," said Cabot.

"She is thinking of adding me to her retinue of nondominants."

"Her harem?" asked Cabot.

"No," said Lord Grendel, "to her retinue, her collection, her flock, her gaggle, her band, her small group of despised servitors. They are nondominants."

"It is not a harem?" asked Cabot.

"No," said Lord Grendel. "It is not a sexual matter, but a social arrangement. You are familiar with pleasure gardens, harems, and such, I take it."

"Surely," said Cabot.

"The females there," he said, "are used for sport, and sexual pleasure, are they not?"

"Certainly," said Cabot. "We use them as we will, frequently, and in a variety of ways, and get much pleasure from them."

"A Kur dominant," said Lord Grendel, "similarly, may keep one or more females, but what you see before you is very different. She would die before she would allow a nondominant to touch her, let alone seed her. Indeed, one who had such a thought, she might kill."

"A pleasant creature," said Cabot. "She has a rope."

The creature had unlooped from her harness several loops of soft, and pliant, but stout rope.

"She thinks to put the rope on my neck," said Grendel, "and thus add me to her servitors."

"I see," said Cabot, uneasily.

"Surely you recognize her," said Grendel.

"No," said Cabot, puzzled.

"From the arena," he said. "There were two females, do you not remember, who were to compete for seeding by the dominant male, he with rings, and she was the one who lost."

"It is the same one?" said Cabot. "You are sure?"

"Certainly," said Lord Grendel.

"Perhaps her defeat still rankles with her," said Cabot.

"I would suppose so," said Lord Grendel.

"She was almost killed, as well," said Cabot.

"Some are killed," said Lord Grendel.

"I would not turn on the translator," said Lord Grendel. "You might not like this."

"Very well," said Cabot.

"Do not interfere," said Lord Grendel.

"Very well," said Cabot.

The Kur approached Grendel, snarling, and bared her fangs. Her face was but inches from his, and she suddenly hissed at him, fiercely. Cabot noted the other Kurii behind her, at this sign of rage, or displeasure, or whatever it might be, drew back, timidly.

Grendel had shown no response to this action on the part of the female.

She bared her fangs, and hissed again, viciously.

Again Grendel did not react.

She backed away, a foot, and regarded Grendel. Perhaps he was terrified into immobility? A grimace, a Kur smile, shown about her jaws. She would add another despised weakling, another despised servitor, to her timorous, obsequious attendants. She stepped forward, and lifted a loop of the rope, to sling it about Lord Grendel's neck, but suddenly, his arms lifted, claws protruding, he uttered a roar that was unexpected, hideous, and terrible, like nothing that Cabot had ever heard, and Cabot fell back, startled.

It was as though a volcano might have burst forth at his elbow; thundering with rage.

The entire form of Lord Grendel seemed then to enlarge and become transformed. Fur crackled outward, increasing his already massive stature; his large, pointed ears were flattened back like smooth knives against the sides of his head; his enormous jaws were open, and reaching forward; his fangs were spread in width better than a foot; his eyes were as kindled furnaces.

The female Kur drew back, frightened, and was then small, crouching before him.

She began to tremble, uncontrollably.

She had unwittingly insulted a dominant.

Grendel seized her in one paw and dragged her to him, and, with his other paw, struck her head upward and back, exposing her throat, and he set his fangs across her throat, and Cabot knew well what might ensue.

He had seen more than one Kur head torn from its body by that grip.

Lord Grendel had warned him not to interfere, but that warning, as it turned out, was quite unnecessary. Cabot was no more tempted to interfere than he would have been tempted to leap between enraged, tangled larls.

Grendel's fangs half in her throat, her body helpless in his grasp, the Kur female, trembling and squirming, began to utter a piteous succession of tiny, urgent, plaintive noises.

At this point Cabot was much tempted to turn on his translator, but he refrained from doing so.

Among Kurii a mortal insult, usually followed by one or more deaths, is to accuse another Kur of being a nondominant.

To be sure, this insult is usually issued by one male Kur to another.

Grendel's jaws then closed a little more, and Cabot fully expected to see pounding, driven, surging blood, released, suddenly gush and spatter forth, drenching Lord Grendel and the grass for yards about, spurting from the opened throat of a half-severed head.

Cabot noted that the nondominants hung back, crouching down, save for one who stood half erect, watching, but making no move to interfere.

Such creatures could always attach themselves, in their parasitic way, to another female.

But Grendel did not tear her head from her.

He removed his fangs from her throat. Cabot noted their tips were bright with blood.

He then arranged the trembling, shaken female before him, held her up with one paw, for she might, in terror and weakness, have fallen, and, with his other paw, lashed her face back and forth, snapping it from side to side. Her eyes were wide, and frightened. Blood was about her mouth, from the blows. Such blows might easily have broken the neck of a human female. He then took her and threw her to the grass, contemptuously, to the side.

Most of the nondominants in the background, then began to file away. Their female had been beaten, and was now nothing. She had been reduced to the status of a Kur female in the presence of a dominant.

Lord Grendel then turned away from her, but she began to whimper, and moan, and whine, and he turned angrily to face her.

She couched down, whimpering, making herself small before him.

He went to her and, with one clawed foot, thrust her contemptuously down to the grass. He then, as she lay there at his feet, whimpering, kicked her, twice, and again turned away from her.

He was a dominant, and he had been displeased by her, a mere female.

She called out something, softly, urgently, piteously, pleadingly, in Kur. Cabot's translator was not activated.

Lord Grendel, half crouched down, turned to face her, and she crawled to his feet, and put her head down to his feet, submissively, and with her long, dark tongue, began to lick them.

"She is making amends, I gather," said Cabot.

"Turn on the translator," said Grendel, and Cabot did so.

But then she was whimpering, not speaking, her body trembling, her head still down, to Lord Grendel's feet.

"Speak," said Lord Grendel to the she-Kur before him.

"An animal is present," she said.

"Speak," repeated Lord Grendel.

"Before a human?" came from Cabot's translator.

"Yes," said Grendel.

"You would so shame me?" she said.

"Speak or not, as you wish," said Grendel.

"Are these things not our secret?" she asked.

"Speak or not, as you wish," said Grendel.

She then lifted her head to him. "Be my master," she said.

"Why?" asked Grendel. "You are of little interest. You are coarse, gross, and plain."

Cabot was surprised at this assessment, given Lord Grendel's earlier remarks, though, as a human, he was not disinclined to agree.

"Many males have sought me," she said.

"The world," said Lord Grendel, "is filled with fools."

"I will do my best to please you," she said.

"Or any male," said Lord Grendel.

"Yes," she said, "I now know they are my masters."

"Why is that?" asked Lord Grendel.

"Because I am a female," she said.

"I doubt that you would make a good submissive," said Lord Grendel.

"I will be the most submissive of all submissives," she said. "I cannot now help that."

"Turn about, and get on your belly," said Lord Grendel.

The Kur obeyed, instantly.

Lord Grendel then, with her own rope, fastened her hands behind her back, pulled her to her feet, and wrapped the rope, in several coils, about her body, and then, with the same rope, fashioned a leash for her.

This was much what had been done with her former rival, the victorious she-Kur in the arena, before she had been led forth from the sand.

Lord Grendel then led the she-Kur some yards through the

grass, so that she would know herself so led, helpless, on a male's leash.

He then stopped, and turned about, and regarded that Kur who had lingered, who had not departed with the others.

"Approach," said Lord Grendel to the Kur, and he advanced, until he stood four or five yards away, in the grass.

"Do you want a female?" he asked him.

"Yes," he said.

Nondominants, of course, are forbidden females. They are often regarded as the fourth Kur sex, the others being the males, females, and wombs. Yet the matter is ambivalent, for at times, particularly in the absence of dominants, a nondominant becomes not only capable of reproductive activity, but becomes a dominant. This transformation, too, occasionally, though rarely, takes place almost spontaneously. Even we do not fully understand this. The change, perhaps, has less to do with physiology than decision, and will. The matter is obscure, even for us.

"Take this one," said Lord Grendel, tossing the loose end of the rope leash to the other Kur.

The she-Kur looked at Lord Grendel, wildly, but was helpless.

She strained in her bonds.

"I love another," said Lord Grendel, to her. Then to the other Kur he said, "She is yours."

The other Kur jerked the female to him, she stumbling. He held her by the leash, closely, and looked down upon her. He was considerably larger than the female, and he seemed now much taller and broader, and more robust, than he had but minutes before. But minutes before he had not been a dominant. But minutes before he had not owned a female.

He kicked her feet out from under her, and she fell to the grass.

"Belly!" said he to her. "Obeisance!"

She went to her belly before him, and squirmed to his feet, which she then began to caress, frightened, with her long, dark, tongue.

He lifted his head and howled with pleasure, and she shuddered. Cabot wondered if he had not waited long for this moment. How long, Cabot wondered, had this Kur sensed the dominant latent within him?

The Kur then placed one large, clawed foot on the back of the bellied she-Kur, pinning her to the grass. Her leash looped up to his hand.

"What cause do you favor?" inquired the Kur of Lord Grendel.

"You see we wear no purple scarves," said Lord Grendel.

"You wear no scarves at all," said the Kur.

"Nor do you," said Lord Grendel.

"I was unable to fight," said the Kur.

"Now you are able," said Lord Grendel.

"What cause is yours?" he inquired.

"That of Lord Arcesilaus," said Lord Grendel.

"Then that, too, is my cause," said the Kur.

"It is a cause with ill prospects," said Lord Grendel.

"So much the better," said the Kur.

"Why is that?" asked Cabot.

"To perish while grievously outnumbered," said Lord Grendel, "is glorious."

"To succeed while so outnumbered, I trust," said Cabot, "would be more glorious still."

"Certainly," said Lord Grendel.

"Sometimes I fear Lord Agamemnon is wisest," said Cabot.

"He is more practical, surely," said Lord Grendel.

"Have you seen purple scarves about?" Cabot asked the Kur.

"Is he a pet?" asked the Kur.

"No," said Lord Grendel.

"No," said the Kur. "Not here, not today."

"Strange," said Lord Grendel.

"Not at all," said the Kur. "The forces of Lord Agamemnon are deployed in defense, for the world is under attack. That is why your small insurrection has not been crushed utterly, long ago."

"I see," said Lord Grendel.

"It is growing darker," said Cabot. "Perhaps we had best return to the camp."

Lord Grendel and Cabot then turned about, and the Kur drew on the she-Kur's leash, and pulled her to her feet, where she stood, unsteadily.

Then he put his teeth on her throat, and she whimpered.

"Please do not kill me," she said. "Please spare me, for I am now only a female, and yours."

He removed his teeth from her throat.

"Please seed me," she said.

"Have no fear," he said. "You will be well and frequently seeded."

"I think you will find her an excellent submissive," said Lord Grendel.

"I trust so, if she would live," said the Kur.

"I am Grendel," said Lord Grendel. "This human is Tarl Cabot."

The Kur then gave a name, but Lord Grendel did not accept it, as it was a cognomen fit not for a dominant but a nondominant. So the Kur chose a new name, to fit with his new being. This cannot be rendered into English or Gorean, so we will choose a name, one not unknown on Gor, Statius.

The three males then returned to one of the local, temporary camps of the insurrectionists, one in the ruins of a small, improvised citadel, two walls of which had been shaken and crumbled three days ago by minor power weapons.

The attackers, when swarming through the breached walls, found the citadel, at that time, abandoned.

It was difficult to locate the insurrectionists who, in their small, scattered groups, moved frequently.

Humans provided much intelligence to the insurrectionists, and even major power weapons are ineffectual in the absence of targets.

Several humans, too, particularly of the forest humans, were now becoming adept with the bow.

The three males were followed by Statius' bound female, on her leash. She would not be the only submissive with the insurrectionists as the Kur males were uniformly dominants, and such enjoy possessing females. These submissives did much of the labor about, and around, the camp. They were the sort of Kur female who were despised by the Kur females who knew only nondominants, but then the latter sort of females, those who knew only nondominants, are perhaps to be forgiven for their views, as they lacked certain experiences.

Chapter, the Forty-Fifth:

The Lady Bina Desires to Make Herself Useful

"How long must I wear this bell?" asked the Lady Bina.

"You are not trusted," said Cabot. "It has been decided in the camp that you will be belled. It helps to keep track of you."

"When we are outside the camp, when we march, why are my hands bound behind me?"

"That you may not attempt to silence the bell," said Cabot. "If you were to flee, its smallest sound would be heard for a hundred yards by Kurii, who could then bring you back for punishment, or execution. Too, should you escape from us, its note could easily be detected by those of the purple scarves, who would, following the edict of Lord Agamemnon, as you are human, kill you on sight."

She made a tiny, angry, fuming noise, and stamped her small, bared foot in the dirt.

This brought forth a note from the bell.

"I myself," said Cabot, "would put your pretty little ankles in shackles."

"You are a beast," she said, holding the bell.

"I would take no chances," said Cabot, "with a traitress."

"I am not a traitress!" she said.

"The tiara is pretty in your hair," he said.

"They force me to wear it!" she said.

"Surely you know why," said Cabot. "It is another sign that you are not to be trusted. It is an ensign of your treachery and shame."

She looked away, angrily.

"There are many in the camp," said Cabot, "who wanted to kill you, and several are still of that view."

She looked at him, suddenly, frightened.

"Be glad," said Cabot, "that there is only a bell on your neck."

"I am a free woman!" she said.

"Assuredly," said Cabot. "Unfortunately."

"'Unfortunately'?"

"Yes," said Cabot. "Women such as you belong in collars."

"Like that ugly, despicable slave slut, to whom you have given the name 'Lita'?" she said.

"She is not ugly," said Cabot. "Indeed, if you were both exhibited naked on a slave block, I would suppose you would go for a similar price."

"I have blonde hair!" she said.

"That is common in certain areas on Gor," said Cabot, "for example, in the north, in Torvaldsland."

"I am the most beautiful of all women!" she said.

"I do not think even Lord Grendel would believe that," said Cabot.

"But surely I am very beautiful!" she said.

"True," said Cabot. "But there are thousands in the Gorean markets who are as beautiful."

"Surely not!" she said.

"It is true," said Cabot.

"But I am a free woman!" she said.

"True," said Cabot.

"And that makes me special!" she said.

"It makes you very special," he said.

"Free women are priceless," she said.

"True," said Cabot. "But as soon as you put them in a collar, they are no longer priceless. They are then priced at what men will pay for them, some priced higher than others, as worth more coins, some priced lower than others, as worth fewer coins."

"I am a free woman, am I not?" she demanded.

"Certainly," said Cabot.

"Why then," she said, "am I dressed like this!"

"Officially," said Cabot, "with our Kur friends, in order that you not be able to conceal weapons, but unofficially, from the point of view of our human allies, because we enjoy seeing you so."

"I might as well be a slave," she said.

"Precisely," said Cabot.

It may be recalled that the Lady Bina, before leaving the area of the slaughter bench, had demanded, and received, the garment of Lita, the slave, in order that she not be unclothed. Lita, now, again, had her simple tunic. On the other hand, a similar garment, sleeveless and brief, had been fashioned for the Lady Bina. Indeed, it may have been a bit shorter than even that of the slave, which was already scandalously brief, or, as the saying is, "slave short," and, in addition, its light fabric, unshaped and loose on her body, was split at both hips, to the waist.

Cabot found it difficult to look at her and not think "slave," but that, of course, is a feature of such garments.

Indeed, it is, as I understand it, natural for any human male who sees a woman in such a garment to think of her as "slave," what she would be like in one's arms, how much she would cost, what she would look like at one's feet, and so on.

Such garments can be a terror or a joy, a shame or an excitement, a misery or an exquisite pleasure, to those females who have no choice but to wear them, and have learned to be grateful, for even so little.

Sometimes a new slave, not daring to appear on the street so clad, must be whipped from the house, shuddering and cringing, to be set upon her errands.

But soon she puts such misery and shame behind her, realizing that it is now what she is, a slave.

And some things which would be wholly shocking and inappropriate for a free woman are not only prescribed for a slave, but are fitting for her.

And slaves understand this.

And so her deportment is rapidly transformed. She soon begins to stand well, to kneel well, to walk well, and such. Indeed, she will be whipped if she does not. The slave, you see, must move beautifully and gracefully. Slovenly carriage is not permitted to her. She is not a free woman. She is in a collar. And she soon begins to take delight not only in the attractiveness of her garment, but in its lightness and softness, and in the freedom it grants her. How different it is from the gross, constricting, layered bundlings of the free woman's many robes and veils! And she surely cannot fail to be aware, and acutely, sometimes shyly, but surely happily, and soon even gratefully, though she might at first be reluctant to admit this, of the blatant public exhibition of her beauty. After all, what beautiful woman, however sweet, gentle, tender and modest, does not want her beauty recognized, noted, honored, and admired, even celebrated? And what beautiful woman, too, however sweet, gentle, tender, and modest, does not want to be looked upon by males with interest, and avid, keen desire? Let them wonder what she would be like in their arms, how she would be at their feet, in their collar! And then, as she better learns her collar, she becomes unapologetic, even bold, in the garment, and wears it, naturally, even thoughtlessly, with verve and pride, thinking nothing of it, accepting, understanding, and rejoicing in its rightfulness on her, she now well aware of, and excited by, its meaning, that she is beautiful and purchasable, that she is slave. So she now wears it with assurance, with grace, with vitality, and contentment, and joy. She may even wear it with an almost insolent, brazen pleasure, though she understands that she may be quickly put to her knees.

She now understands, you see, that she has been found to be the most desirable of women, the female slave.

In her considerable bareness, in her tiny tunic and collar, she now has little to fear, unless she should be in the least displeasing to masters, or, to be sure, unless she comes within the purview of a free female.

Surely they know how exciting and marvelous they are in such garments. In them they know they are dressed for the pleasure of men, and, in this, they find much pleasure themselves.

They, too, you see, are human.

Too, such garments, as is well known, are a badge of beauty, an emblem of desirability, of beguiling allure, of fascination and excitement, an evidence of an attractiveness so exquisite that it not only warrants interest but collaring.

Such a garment proclaims that its wearer has been found "slave beautiful," beautiful enough to be a slave.

And what woman would not be proud to be found to be "as beautiful as a slave"?

And at the feet of a master, wholly dominated, uncompromisingly owned, they learn their womanhood, and love.

"Outside," said the Lady Bina, "I saw some cattle humans. I did not like the way they looked at me."

"They probably remember you from the slaughter house," said Cabot.

"They frighten me," she said.

"They are taken to be stupid and harmless," said Cabot. "Let us hope that they are so."

"I do not like them," she said.

"Few people do," said Cabot.

"Their eyes were like those of tarsks," she said. "Small, in all that flesh."

"Lord Grendel turned them away, did he not?" asked Cabot.

"Yes," she said.

"Look," said Cabot, getting up. "Here comes Lord Grendel."

"I hate him," she said.

"Kneel," said Cabot, "and put your head to the ground."

"Never!" she said.

"You are his prisoner," said Cabot.

"Prisoner?"

"Yes," said Cabot. "Surely you know that you are his prisoner, little traitress. And it is only that which keeps you alive. If it were not for his protection, and his intervention, you would have been slain long ago."

"I cannot do such a thing," she said. "I will not do it!"

"Do it now," said Cabot.

Swiftly the Lady Bina knelt, and put her head to the ground.

"Tal," said Cabot, to his friend, Lord Grendel.

"Tal," responded Lord Grendel.

"You have been in converse with Lord Flavion?" said Cabot.

"Yes," said Lord Grendel.

Lord Flavion was chief amongst the scouts in the camp, and stood high, though not in the rings.

"He is going out, again, tonight," said Lord Grendel.

"He should rest," said Cabot.

"He does not rest," said Lord Grendel. "Had we a hundred like him I would attempt the palace of Agamemnon itself."

"I wish him well," said Cabot.

Some days ago Flavion had made his way through the enemy lines, to join the insurrection.

His contributions had proved numerous and invaluable.

"May the Nameless One be with him," said Grendel.

Then Lord Grendel looked down. "What have we here?" he asked.

"A human female, in suitable position," said Cabot.

"I see," said Lord Grendel.

He looked down at the girl.

"Do you like her like this?" asked Cabot.

"Yes," said Lord Grendel. "She is very pretty, thusly."

"Do you not wish, thusly," said Cabot to the kneeling girl, "to show your gratitude to your captor, and that you wish to be found pleasing to him, as his prisoner?"

"Yes," she said. "Yes!"

"Rise up, Lady," said Lord Grendel.

The girl sprang to her feet, and looked at Cabot, angrily, but, too unmistakably, there was something deep in her eyes, that seemed uncertain, even trembling.

She had been knelt, and in a common position of obeisance, by a man. This is common, of course, with slaves, but it is quite rare with free women. This position, of course, and the subjection to male dominance so clearly implicit in it, heats the thighs of slaves. Inadvertently, they moisten. Autonomously, involuntarily, interestingly, whether they wish it or not, their body responds. It readies itself for penetration. Women in such a position find themselves in a condition of need and arousal. They hope that their masters will soon see fit to remind them of the meaning of their collars. They are, after all, slaves.

"I think she should now report to Lita, to assist her in her duties," said Cabot.

"I am a free woman," she said. "Why should I work?"

"Many free women work," said Cabot. "Even free women of the upper castes often work. Not all have slaves or servants. Too, work is quite common with free women of the lower castes."

"I do not see why I should work," she said.

"Prisoners often work," said Cabot.

"Not I!" she said.

"Lita will help you," said Cabot. "She will show you what to do. I have given her instructions."

"Instructions?"

"As to your duties," said Cabot.

"'Duties'?" she said.

"Certainly," said Cabot.

"Duties—duties fit for a slave!" she cried.

"Yes," said Cabot.

"But I am a free woman!" she cried, looking to Lord Grendel.

"But a prisoner," Cabot reminded her.

"I will never be so demeaned!" she said. "Never!"

"You are not only a prisoner," said Cabot, "but you are a woman who has a bell on her neck."

"So?" she said, warily.

"Thus you are a belled woman," he said.

"Is that meaningful?" she asked.

"What do you think?" he said.

She shook the bell, angrily, but could not pull it from her neck.

"Commonly," said Cabot, "save in the Tahari, it is only slaves who are belled."

"Take it off!" she demanded.

"To be sure," said Cabot, "it is not a slave bell, or bells, but a leading bell, merely one to lure docile beasts to an unanticipated slaughter."

She glanced uneasily toward the perimeter of the camp.

"It might, of course, be pleasant," said Cabot, "to put you in slave bells, perhaps ankle bells, wrist bells, waist bells, neck bells, and such."

"I am a free woman," she said. "I will not work."

"As you will," said Cabot, "but our Kur friends will be watching you."

"So?" she said.

"Several of them," he said, "have urged your death by torture."

The Lady Bina shuddered.

"Including the camp master, who is watching you, even now," said Cabot.

She looked about, and saw the camp master, indeed, regarding her, and not pleasantly. She made it a point not to meet his eyes.

Women often fear to meet the eyes of those who have authority over them. What if their glance should be interpreted as boldness? What might then be the consequences?

Indeed, some masters do not permit their female slaves to meet their eyes. Commonly, however, the Gorean master wishes a slave to meet his eyes, that he may the better see the beauty of her eyes, and the better read her least expression. Indeed, few women know themselves more helplessly exposed, or more helplessly understood, or better read, than by a Gorean master.

In the presence of a master, it is difficult for them to conceal the least nuance of thought, or emotion, or feeling.

They are in his collar.

"You will work, and work well," said Cabot.

"No!" she said.

"But, yes," said Cabot.

"Lord Grendel will protect me!" she said.

"I am sure he would do so, if at all possible," said Cabot. "But he might not have time. A throat may be bitten through in a moment, a sudden blow may snap the neck, a heart, even, may be gouged out in an instant. To be sure, you might, with some luck, be avenged, and you might find some consolation in that possibility, but that only if the culprit were identified, and there is little assurance of such a thing."

"You are trying to frighten me," she said.

"I think you should hasten to Lita's side," Cabot said, "to be instructed in your duties."

The Lady Bina looked from side to side, angrily.

"There is the camp master," said Cabot. "He is still looking this way. I do not think he is pleased. He has his whip."

"His *whip*?"

"Certainly."

"He is one who wished me slain?" she said.

"Yes," said Cabot. "One of several."

The Lady Bina turned white.

"And have no fear," said Cabot, "aside from other considerations, hostility, and such, he will not hesitate to put the whip to you. You are not even of his species."

"Give me other clothing," she said, "not this thin, tiny thing!"

"You may remove it, if you wish," said Cabot.

At that point the camp master, who was not a patient sort, cracked the whip, suddenly, sharply, and the sound resounded throughout the camp.

That is a sound which is unmistakable.

Certainly it is familiar to slaves, even to those who may not have felt it, but well understand they are subject to its jurisdiction, and its remonstrances, and even to its gratuitous whims.

And, needless to say, it is a sound which even free women, as they are women, understand.

The Lady Bina then, uttering a small cry of misery, turned about and rushed from their presence.

"The human female runs interestingly, does she not?" asked Grendel.

"Yes," said Cabot, "and attractively, I think. It has to do with the hip structure."

"Doubtless," said Grendel.

"And most cannot begin to outrun males either," said Cabot.

"Doubtless," said Grendel.

"And that is doubtless why many of them end up in collars," said Cabot.

"Doubtless," said Lord Grendel.

Chapter, the Forty-Sixth:

Darkness Encroaches;
A Plan Is Formed

In Lord Grendel's small group, one of several, there were some forty Kurii and some twenty to thirty humans.

"Intelligence is clear," said Lord Grendel, addressing his group. "The enemy is massing."

"How is that known?" asked Cabot. It was difficult to attain such intelligence recently, for the cordons of purple scarves seemed ever more imminent, their patrols ever bolder and more intrusive.

"Noble Flavion has again pierced enemy lines and lived to return," said Lord Grendel.

"He is the subtlest and most effective of scouts," said one of the Kurii.

"Without him we would be blind," said another.

"Well done, Flavion," said Cabot.

"I go alone, I take care," said the scout.

"Few," said Cabot, "have penetrated as deeply into the territory of Agamemnon, and returned to report."

"I have been fortunate," said Flavion.

"The exterior enemy, that outside the world, has been driven off," said one of their group. "This releases those forces to band against us."

"Alas," said Flavion, "that is true, and is now known to all."

"It was first discovered by you," said a Kur.

"Days ago," said Flavion.

"The game is done," said a Kur.

"Might we not surrender, or sue for peace?" said a Kur.

"Never, never!" growled Flavion, fiercely. "We must fight! We must fight to the death!"

"We are too few, too weak," said one of the Kurii.

"Take courage from Flavion," said Lord Grendel. "He is the finest and fiercest amongst us."

"I wish," said Cabot, "that I had his skills."

"He is as silent as the fall of darkness, as unseen as the wind," said one of the Kurii.

"Such skills," thought Cabot, "might have been the envy even of the Red Savages, of the Gorean Barrens."

"It is strange to think that he was once no more than a scavenger Kur," said a Kur.

"I am honored to be accepted amongst you," said Flavion.

"The honor is ours," said Lord Grendel.

"My smaller size," said Flavion, "facilitates my humble contributions, if contributions they be, to our cause."

"At great risk to his life, through closely set enemy lines," said another, "he came to us."

"To fight beside you, for our cause," said Flavion, "justifies any risk."

"Welcome to you, a thousand times," said Lord Grendel. "We salute you. Few, if any, could have proved more valuable to our cause."

"We must be prepared," said Flavion, "to die bravely."

"I, myself," said Cabot, "would prefer to live, even if somewhat less bravely."

Flavion turned to regard Cabot.

Whereas Flavion was not large for a Kur, he was considerably larger than Cabot, and most human beings.

"He is human," explained Lord Grendel.

"We are too few to fight," said one of the Kurii.

"Too," said another, uneasily, "is it not forbidden, even heinous, to contend as we are, against the lawful state, against the Eleventh Face of the Nameless One."

"Arcesilaus stood against him," said a Kur.

"Arcesilaus is dead," said another.

"We do not know that," said Cabot.

"We are too few," said a Kur, again.

"Might we not recruit neutrals, nondominants?" asked Cabot.

490

"There are few neutrals," said a Kur.

"The nondominants," said Statius, "are weak, and useless. They fear only to be driven off by their queens."

"Were you not once a nondominant?" asked a Kur of Statius.

"Once," said Statius. "No more. Do you wish to fight to the death?"

"No," responded the Kur.

I have chosen the word 'queens' with some reluctance, as the social arrangements do not support the choice, but 'Ubaras' would be even more inappropriate. 'Mistresses' might do, but, as the nondominants are not, strictly speaking, slaves, though perhaps somewhat slavelike, the connotations are incorrect. The archives, abetted by one of the translation programs, though one infrequently utilized, suggest that 'queens' may convey something of the relation of a particular female to male courtiers, or servitors. The Kur expression does not translate into Gorean but the expression 'queens', as suggested, seems not altogether inappropriate. It is an expression in the language, English, which is a language of Earth. It is also the native language, as I understand it, of Tarl Cabot, compatriot of Lord Grendel. Some translators are programmed in that language. Doubtless they have their purposes.

"All is lost," said one of the Kurii.

"At least we can die bravely," said another.

"Agamemnon," said Cabot, "is cruel, arbitrary, unjust, a vain and murderous tyrant, perhaps even mad. I do not understand why so many gladly pledge their blood, their hearts and steel, to him."

"He has position and power," said a Kur.

"And weapons and soldiers," said another.

"That is not what is important," said another.

"What then is important?" asked Cabot.

"You are not Kur," said a Kur. "You cannot understand."

"Speak," urged Cabot.

"He is the Eleventh face of the Nameless One," said a Kur.

"He is Theocrat of the world," said another, dismally.

"I grant he is Theocrat of the world," said Cabot, "but how do you know he is the Eleventh Face of the Nameless One?"

"There were ten before him," said a Kur.

"How is it known that there are faces, or masks, of the Nameless One?" asked Cabot.

"It is accepted," said a Kur.

"Who is the Nameless One?" asked Cabot.

"Desist," cautioned Lord Grendel. "The plank on which you tread is weak, and the abyss is deep."

"He who is without a name," said a Kur.

"He who is before names, and beyond names, and other than names," said another.

"And before the Nameless One is the Mystery," said another.

"The Mystery?" asked Cabot.

"That which was, and that which is," said a Kur, "and that which will be."

"And none have lifted its veil," said another.

"The Nameless One has many faces?" asked Cabot.

"We do not know how many," said another Kur.

"Some see him in the ost, others in the larl, or shark, or tharlarion, or sleen," said another.

"Others in the germination of seed, the blossoming of flowers, in the unsheathing of the thorn."

"Others," said another, "in the cries of volcanoes, in the openings of the gates of earth, in the flash of lightning, the crash of thunder, in the rush of waters, in the great winds."

"There is no morality here?" asked Cabot.

"No more than in the world," said another.

"Do you worship the Nameless One?" asked Cabot.

"What is worship?" asked a Kur.

"Do not be misled into heresy," said a Kur. "There are only Eleven Faces of the Nameless One."

"Some say many," said another.

"They are mistaken," said the Kur.

"Why eleven?" asked Cabot.

"Who knows," he said. "That is the number."

"Why not five, or ten or fifteen?" asked Cabot. "Or a thousand?"

"We do not know," said another. "Eleven is the number."

"That is the teaching," said another.

"I do not understand much of this," said Cabot.

"Do not despair," said a Kur. "We, too, cannot understand it."

"Much is beyond the scope of the finite mind," said another.

"Inconsistencies are to be ignored?" asked Cabot.

"Rather, transcended," said a Kur.

"What if Agamemnon dies?" asked Cabot.

"How can he die?" asked another.

"He is the Eleventh face of the Nameless One," said another.

"But what if he were to die?" asked Cabot.

"That which speaks through the eleventh mask cannot die," said a Kur.

"It is one, the Nameless One," said another.

"Agamemnon is mortal," said Cabot.

"Perhaps," said a Kur, "but that which speaks through him cannot die."

"May not a mask die, or be discarded?" asked Cabot.

"No," said a Kur.

"But perhaps," said Cabot, "Agamemnon is not the Eleventh Face of the Nameless one. Perhaps he only pretends to be. Perhaps he is a fraud."

"Then the Nameless One would not speak through him," said a Kur, thoughtfully.

"True," said another.

"But Agamemnon has himself pronounced that he is the Eleventh Face of the Nameless One," said another.

"Agamemnon!" said Cabot.

"Yes," responded the Kur.

"Perhaps he is a liar," said Cabot.

"No one would dare to lie about such a thing," said another.

"There is a precedent for such claims," said Cabot.

"Not amongst us," said a Kur.

"Unthinkable," said another Kur.

Cabot may have had in mind the caste of Initiates, on Gor, who claim to speak in the name of the Priest-Kings, to be privileged in such ways, and so on.

"No one would dare to pretend such a thing," said another.

"Perhaps Agamemnon is more inventive, or enterprising, or less honorable, or bolder, or more daring, than you suppose," said Cabot.

"He is Kur," said another.

"But," said Cabot, "as Lord Grendel once called to my attention, 'What is Kur'?"

"Desist, desist," said Lord Grendel.

"Very well," said Cabot.

"Many of those opposed to us, the purple scarves, now have power weapons," said Lord Grendel. "We know this from Lord Flavion, and, indeed, from others, as well."

"Some could destroy the world," said a Kur.

"It would be madness to use them," said another.

"There are smaller weapons," said Cabot.

"Many," said another, "but contained in the arsenals, at the terminations of the world."

The world, as may be recalled, was cylindrical. The ends of the world, then, were the flat caps, or poles, closing the cylinder, at each end. If one might imagine a horizontal axis stretching between these caps, that would constitute what, in effect, would be a gravity-free zone, rather like that in the shuttles. To ascend to this zone by climbing the flat caps, toward their center, can be dangerous or difficult. Caught by the rotation, one could be hurled downward, and dashed to the ground, and, without aid, it could be an almost insurmountable climb to ascend against the rotation, until one had ascended far enough for it to be neutralized, and one would have approached the gravity-free, or low-gravity, axis. One of these caps, that nearest the habitats, was, however, affixed with rings and grasps, by means of which one might approach the arsenal. Agamemnon's aerial scouts utilized these conveniences, until flight became possible. One such scout, or flier, had been detected some time ago, by Cabot and Lord Grendel, while on the raft, on Lake Fear. At that time they had supposed themselves unnoted. Later events suggested that their surmise had been mistaken.

"One such arsenal has been accessed," said Lord Grendel. This would be the arsenal nearest the habitats, that nearest, as well, the palace, and enclave, of Agamemnon.

"True," said a Kur. "It is from it that Agamemnon has armed his minions."

"What of the other arsenal?" said Cabot.

"It is unreachable," said a Kur. "It is unfurnished with appurtenances."

It is interesting to note that if the ends of the world had been hemispherical, or conical, as in several of the worlds, the approach would have been, while still dangerous, yet more practical, as the rotational gravity would have pressed one against a resistant surface, it lessening, of course, as one approached the axis. The flat caps, on the other hand, provided no such purchase.

"All is lost," said a Kur.

"Two possibilities suggest themselves," said Statius, he who had once been a nondominant. "First, we storm the nearest termination of the world, utilizing the grasps at hand, and attempt to avail ourselves of weapons."

"The arsenal will be guarded," said a Kur.

"Of course," said Statius. "We expect to fail."

"If one could approach the axis," said a Kur, "one might, if winged, then attempt the far arsenal, by flight."

"Build wings," said Lord Grendel.

"The other possibility," said Statius, "is far more dangerous. It is to attempt the far arsenal."

"Directly?" asked a Kur.

"Yes," said Statius.

"There are no grasps, no rings," said a Kur. "It is reached by flight, from the vicinity of the nearer arsenal."

"Spikes, driven into the metal?" said a Kur.

"It is solid steel, feet thick," said Statius.

"Air can provide a seal," said Cabot. "Cups of rubber, pressed against the steel."

"We have no such material," said a Kur.

"Nor, if we had, even the means to form such devices," said another.

"Something similar," said Statius. "Adhesive substances. Ropes, and such substances."

"It is madness," said another.

"Let a hundred try," said Lord Grendel.

"I will lead them," said Cabot.

"And who will attempt the arsenal of Agamemnon?" asked a Kur.

"I," said Lord Grendel, "and any mad enough to follow me."

"I am with you," said the Kur.

"And what of you, Lord Flavion?" asked Grendel.

"It is madness," said Flavion, "but I, too, am with you."

"Good," said Lord Grendel. "Let us begin to build wings."

"Water, Sirs?" asked the Lady Bina, who held a ewer.

"How long has she been here?" asked a Kur.

"Not long," said a Kur.

"Kill her," said Lord Flavion.

"No," said Lord Grendel.

Chapter, the Forty-Seventh:

How the Tarns of Victory
Came to Surmount the Standards of Agamemnon

It was a long, weird cry, from Cabot's left, and he reached out his hand, wildly, but could not grasp the outstretched, clutching hand of the human, one from the cages, to his left.

He did see him descending, moving in the air, for some seconds, but did not see him strike the side of the cylinder, as he disappeared through the greenery, hundreds of yards below.

Four others had similarly fallen, who had not reached his own point. Most of those who had come with him had been unable to adhere to the flat surface. Few had managed to climb more than ten to fifteen yards onto the cap, from the cylinder surface. Cabot, and some with him, were the first to essay the climb. They had smeared their bodies and clothing, and the flats of their hands with a resinous, tarlike substance. They were climbing against the rotation. To climb with it, as they would be carried about in the rotation, courted the danger of being flung headlong from the cap before they could approach the gravity-free zone. Climbing against it was difficult but one was less likely to be swept about and dashed to the ground. One would do one's best to adhere to the surface and then, as possible, now and again, move a foot or two, at a time, closer to the center of the cap.

Cabot heard another cry of misery and saw one of his fellows slipping down the surface, scratching at it with his finger nails, and then, he, too, lost the surface, was loose in the air, turning, and disappeared in the greenery below.

"Go back!" cried Cabot to those with him. "Go back! Go back, while you can!"

Inch by inch, he saw two of his fellows, flattened against the steel, moving downward.

"Come with us!" cried a fellow, one from the forest cylinder. Cabot remembered him from the camp of Archon.

Those from the forest world, as noted earlier, were being taught speech. In this way, they might communicate the better amongst themselves, and with other humans. Already most had mastered a thousand or more words.

"Go back!" repeated Cabot, fiercely, and he, himself, moved another perilous foot toward the center.

It was little wonder this area was not guarded.

Humans were lighter, and smaller, than Kurii, and better adapted to this venture than would have been their larger, heavier, allies.

For a Kur it seemed clear this climb would be death.

For a human it might be possible, somehow.

It must be possible, somehow!

Agamemnon, Cabot was sure, in the dark gaming of war, had not anticipated humans intruding into this fearsome venue.

He moved another foot.

He felt the artificial gravity of the rotation seeming to push against him. The sensation was much like lying on a turning disk, from which one might be thrown free, but the consequence of a lost purchase here was not a slipping from the disk to the side, but rather analogous to a plunge from a cliff.

"Hold, hold," whispered Cabot to the viscous sludge by which he was held to the steel. "Hold, hold!"

And he moved another foot.

"Hold," he whispered. "Hold!"

Moment by moment, minute by minute, he inched his way toward the center of the cap.

Then, oddly, he felt less thrust against him.

He felt faint. He closed his eyes. He did not look back. He was briefly afflicted with a sensation of giddiness. He had the dreamlike sense that if he were to weigh himself the scale would be little depressed. Now it seemed hard to move against the adherent material with which he had smeared his body, his hands and clothing. It was now as if it were somehow anchoring him, almost balloonlike to the steel. Now it seemed less a salvation than an encumbrance, a nuisance. Then, sensing the possibility, he stood on the steel, his head pointing toward the opposing cap, far distant, almost invisible, at the other end of the world. The sensation now was almost identical to that of the shuttles, in free flight amongst the cylinders. He took several more steps and suddenly his feet left the steel, and he turned about, helplessly, in the air, and he spun about, and tried to thrash toward the steel, and floated some feet from it. His body was suddenly covered with sweat. Then a movement of the atmosphere brushed him, and he twisted his body to it, and waited, and waited, and, in a few seconds, one hand, covered with the adhesive substance used in his climb, struck against the steel, and he pulled himself down to it. Then, keeping at least one limb, a foot or hand, on the steel, he made his way to the arsenal gate.

The plan was to attempt the ascent to the arsenal, to determine its feasibility. If it proved feasible it was then intended for others to follow, and join the leaders, others who would, amongst themselves, bring up tools, and rope, that the gate might be forced, and the stored weapons brought down, to waiting others, who would then act as scouts and guards, bearers and porters.

But, as Cabot now saw, there was no need for these arrangements.

The gate of the arsenal was open, and, as he soon determined, the arsenal itself was empty.

"Hail Agamemnon," thought Cabot, bitterly, "Theocrat of the World, Eleventh Face of the Nameless One. It is little wonder, dear foe, that so many pledge you their heart, their steel, their blood. You are a leader amongst leaders. I wonder if you are mortal. Are you not more than man, more than Kur?"

Cabot lifted his head, suddenly, peering outward from the threshold of the barren arsenal behind him, now no more than an abandoned storeroom, its racks and shelves empty.

Approaching the arsenal, hundreds of yards away, were two figures, one seemingly several yards in advance of the other. From the distance they resembled slowly flying insects. As they approached they more resembled the winged vart, as it might appear if slowly, oddly, in an almost dreamlike progression, coursing the axis. As they neared, discernible became the slow, rhythmic beat of gigantic canvas wings, harnessed to massive bodies.

Cabot shaded his eyes.

The canvas wings sought their purchase in the world's atmosphere, thrusting against it, cleaving it, as they neared.

"Grendel!" called Cabot, as Lord Grendel folded his wings and gently came to rest on the ledge beside him.

"It is empty?" said Lord Grendel, regarding the bareness behind Cabot. His voice rang in the hollowness of the arsenal.

"Yes," said Cabot.

"We are followed," said Lord Grendel.

At that point Statius alighted on the ledge. He was covered with blood.

"They were waiting for us at the arsenal," said Lord Grendel.

"The arsenal seemed open, even unguarded," said Statius.

"We should have been warned," said Lord Grendel.

"Then suddenly purple scarves, with power weapons, sprang into view, and fired."

"It was a well-devised ambush," said Lord Grendel. "But we were fools. We thought Agamemnon's minions were overconfident, unsuspecting, otherwise deployed. We were fools."

"It seems they took us more seriously than we had supposed," said Cabot.

"We lost many," said Lord Grendel. "It was a slaughter."

"Some fell here," said Cabot. "I sent the others back."

"Others are below?" said Lord Grendel.

"Most," said Cabot. "Your quiver is empty."

"They fired from behind metal shields," said Lord Grendel. "We could do little."

"You have a bow, arrows," said Cabot, to Statius.

"Few of the birds of death are left," said Statius.

"Behold!" said Cabot, pointing down the axis.

"Purple scarves," said Lord Grendel, resignedly.

It should be understood that the control of the wings, as they are commonly constructed, requires the use of both arms, and, resultantly, it is difficult, and, in some cases, impractical, to use certain weapons while in flight.

"Flee," said Cabot. "Save yourselves."

"For what?" asked Lord Grendel.

"For Pyrrhus, for Arcesilaus, for the war," said Cabot.

"There are too many," said Lord Grendel. "Here, and elsewhere."

"We shall flight against these," said Statius, "and meet them Kur to Kur, tooth to tooth, claw to claw."

"There are too many," said Cabot. "They do not know I am here. Lord Statius, give me your bow, your quiver. Then mask my presence."

"Lord Statius?" asked Statius.

"Now!" said Cabot.

"Ah," said Lord Grendel, his features twisting into an expression of pleasure.

"It will not be only Agamemnon who can arrange surprises," said Cabot, grimly.

He took the bow from Statius, and the quiver, and grasped four arrows and the bow in his left hand, and set an arrow to the string. Other arrows he put in his belt, and others he put against the gate, at hand.

"Some may have hand weapons," said Lord Grendel, quietly.

"I understand," said Cabot.

Such weapons may be most easily used while winged.

"Do not activate your translator," said Lord Grendel to Statius.

And so Lords Grendel and Statius stood, seemingly convinced that further flight was futile, wings spread, in the great threshold of the barren arsenal.

As the translators were not activated Cabot could only conjecture the exact nature of the exchanges between the purple scarves, of which there were ten, and Lords Grendel and Statius. The general nature of the converse, however, was surely clear. Moreover, Cabot, in his time in the world, had become adept at reading not only the body language of Kurii, which is little harder, if at all, to decipher than that of the larl or sleen, but, to a large extent, also, the character or import of what was being said, for example, challenge, anger, cajolery, impatience, command, and so on. Certainly he was sure that the leader of the purple scarves, from his utterances, was insolent, contemptuous, excited, and flushed with triumph. He also heard a rattle of chain, and gathered that his friends were to be conducted back, securely tethered, to the mercies of Agamemnon.

Cabot, shielded by the wings of his friends, sensed that the purple scarves were very close, no more than feet from the ledge itself.

Cabot heard the clawed feet of a purple scarf touch the ledge, and then, rather as the two leaves of a mighty gate might swing open, outwardly, the left wing of Lord Grendel, and the right wing of Lord Statius, swung toward their bodies, and Cabot released the first shaft, point-blank, through the chest of the officer, the fletching literally disappearing into the body, and half the shaft emerging from the back, and a length of chain clattered to the metal flooring of the ledge, and a second shaft left the string, and no more than two Ehn later another, and then another. At the same time Lords Grendel and Statius pushed from the ledge and with a blow of the wide canvas wings were each entangled with a foe. One of the purple scarves freed an arm from the wing harness and groped for a hand weapon, as he spun about, loose, helplessly, in the atmosphere. By the time he could free it from its holster another arrow had found its mark and the weapon seemed to float away, as might an object in water. Cabot saw blood streaming loose in the atmosphere, like a shredding silken ribbon, and Lord Grendel, eyes half blinded with blood, spit away throat and bone. Statius and his foe grappled, spinning in the atmosphere. Cabot scanned the remaining foes who had seemed startled, almost paralyzed, at the sudden appearance of his threat. Such are commonly left to last. The foe who cries out, registering the threat, too, has hesitated. His priority is thus less than the silent foe who reacts instantly, seeking cover, drawing a weapon, such things. Needless to say, the officer had not had time to react, in any way. To be sure, other things being equal, an officer is usually given priority as a target. Accordingly, in situations of danger, as indicated earlier, at least among Kurii, insignia are often removed, salutes left unexchanged, and so on. Too, as earlier referenced, such practices are also commonly in effect amongst Gorean warriors. And, one supposes, such practices are not likely to be unfamiliar to any, whatever the world, who adopt the profession of arms, who tread the ways of war.

Statius, his teeth fastened in the shoulder of his howling foe, brought up his hind legs, ripping and gouging, tearing, digging, within his foe's belly, a reflex perhaps genetically coded in long-vanished, unspeeched ancestors of the modern Kur, ancestors not yet Kurii. This modality of aggression, interestingly, frequently characterizes the feeding attack of the smaller Gorean forest panther. It is not unknown amongst larls and sleen, but the sleen usually strikes for the throat and the larl, where practical, particularly after it has bled and exhausted its prey, bites through the back of the neck.

Cabot saw loops of gut loose amongst the beating wings, and Statius' foe, striking Statius' jaws away from his shoulder with a mighty blow, turned about, erratically, and tried to strike away. Cabot saw fur and meat in Statius' jaws. He was too weak to pursue his foe who fled, a rope of gut dangling behind him.

Cabot drew one of the arrows from his belt, and then leaped aside as a line of fire, narrow and perfect, as straight as a beam of light, seemed to stand still beside him, quiet in the air, and then, at the back of the arsenal, yards behind him, where it touched, a metal wall blackened, and drops of molten steel suddenly burst forth and floated in the atmosphere, as might have oil droplets in water.

To free the weapon, a shoulder weapon, the Kur had had to abandon his control of the wings, and he floated, without control, some yards from the ledge.

Lord Grendel thrust up the weapon with his wing, and then, spinning about, close to his foe, who floated before him, had one hand loose from the wing harness and tore the weapon from the Kur's grasp, and the Kur recovered control of the wings, and backed away, warily. Then its eyes grew wide. Lord Grendel had the weapon in one hand, had braced it against his chest, and leveled it. Cabot saw the chest cavity of the Kur disappear, as though punched into nothingness.

Two Kurii remained, other than the figure retreating in the distance.

Neither attempted to free their weapon.

Cabot aligned an arrow.

"No," said Lord Grendel, in his Gorean.

He then spoke to the Kurii, and they, carefully, removed their weapons, and thrust them, floating, softly, toward the arsenal gate.

Lord Grendel, transferring his weapon to his harnessed arm, with his free hand flicked on his translator, that Cabot might follow what was said.

Seven Kurii, dead, were in the vicinity, winged, inert, floating, in the gravity-free zone. Another, he who had fled, he muchly eviscerated by Statius, had died within moments. The body, harnessed within the wings, was now little more than some fifty yards from the ledge, drifting aimlessly, eccentrically, sometimes rolling over, a length of its entrails wrapped about a leg.

"Now you will kill us," said one of the two Kurii at bay.

"No," said Lord Grendel. "There has been enough killing."

"Kill us," said the other Kur. "Agamemnon will have us killed, if we return without the weapons."

"Free your hands," said Lord Grendel. Then he spoke to Statius. "Return to them their weapons."

The hair on the back of Cabot's neck rose.

Statius, not questioning Lord Grendel, slipped his harness, and moved the weapons to the two Kurii.

"Lower your bow," said Lord Grendel, to Cabot, who, however reluctantly, complied.

Lord Grendel then turned his back on the two Kurii, and, with one sweep of the wings, returned to the ledge.

"We have escaped," said Lord Grendel to the two Kurii, without turning to face them.

"Yes," said one of them. "You have escaped."

The two Kurii regarded one another, and then reslung their weapons, regained their harnessing, turned about, and moved away from the platform.

"They could have killed you, all of us," said Cabot.

"True," said Lord Grendel.

"Why did they not do so?" asked Cabot.

"They are Kur," said Lord Grendel.

"I do not understand," said Cabot.

"Would you have done so?" asked Lord Grendel.

"No," said Cabot.

"You see," said Lord Grendel. "You, too, are Kur."

"What now is to be done?" asked Cabot.

"We will gather the weapons," said Lord Grendel.

"Agamemnon would have killed you, instantly, without a thought," said Cabot.

"He is not Kur," said Lord Grendel.

"He is Kur," said Cabot.

"Not every Kur is Kur," said Lord Grendel.

Cabot was silent.

"We will take you to the surface," said Lord Grendel.

"They were waiting for us at the arsenal," said Statius. "They knew we were coming."

"Clearly," said Lord Grendel.

"You believe Agamemnon to have been informed of our plans?"

"Certainly," said Grendel.

"He may have anticipated such a move," said Cabot.

"It is unlikely," said Lord Grendel, "that without intelligence he would have anticipated, and prepared so carefully for, even to the removal of guards, so unlikely and bold a stroke as an attempt on the arsenal itself."

"Even we ourselves," said Statius, "regarded our attack as little more than an act of desperation, if not of madness. We expected to battle through legions of guards, in a venture in all likelihood foredoomed."

"Agamemnon is shrewd," said Cabot. "The devising of such a trap would be well within his ken."

"How would he have known where to lay it, and when?" asked Statius.

"I do not know," said Cabot.

"The Lady Bina," said Statius, "fled the camp, days ago."

"Aii!" said Cabot, softly.

"It is true," said Lord Grendel.

"She had overheard our plans," said Statius.

"How could she escape from the camp," asked Cabot. "Was she not belled. Was she not chained at night?"

"She slipped away from the camp master, before her chaining, perhaps with the assistance of a confederate," said Statius. "As her hands were not bound behind her, as in our treks, she could hold the bell silent."

"You suspect her of revealing our plans?" said Cabot.

"Certainly," said Statius.

"Agamemnon might have foreseen such an attack," said Cabot.

"There was treachery, clearly," said Lord Grendel. "Intelligence had described the security at the arsenal. It was only after the escape of the Lady Bina, and shortly prior to our attack, that it seemed to change, as though Agamemnon had decided at last, in virtue of our weakness, that such precautions were no longer necessary."

"And the ambush was laid," said Cabot.

"In all its deadliness," said Statius.

"Perhaps she is innocent," said Cabot.

"It would not be the first time she has betrayed Kurii and others to Agamemnon," said Lord Grendel.

"We will have her blood," said Statius.

"Even now," said Lord Grendel, "in robes and veils of beauty, she doubtless banquets with Agamemnon."

"We do not know that," said Cabot.

"I do not think we will see her again," said Lord Grendel.

"If we do," said Statius, "it will be the privilege of Lord Grendel to gouge out and roast the first ounce of her flesh, to be eaten before her eyes."

With proper surgical attention this mode of execution can be extended over several days, before the more grievous tortures are inflicted, with the needles, and irons, the tiny flames, the dollops of acid, and such.

"I will defend her, to the death," said Lord Grendel.

"She is guilty," said Statius.

"Yes," said Lord Grendel.

"Then, dear friend," said Statius, "you will die with her."

"It is not clear she is guilty," said Cabot.

"Why do you say that?" asked Statius.

"I do not know," said Cabot. "It is something which continues to elude me, a small something, a something I cannot place, a something that has troubled me, like a whisper not really heard, now and again."

"Perhaps," said Statius, "when, at the side of Agamemnon, in regalia, a tiara upon her brow, she presides over a thousand executions, those of our fellows, Kur and human, you might be convinced."

"Doubtless," said Cabot.

"Do you love her?" asked Statius.

"No," said Cabot. "But in my way I am fond of her. Another may love her."

"Who?" asked Statius.

"Another," said Cabot.

"Lord Grendel?" said Statius.

"Perhaps," said Cabot.

"The evidence, the incidents, the circumstances, a thousand details, are incontrovertible," said Statius.

"Perhaps," said Cabot.

"We will take you to the surface," said Lord Grendel. "My dear Statius, will you gather the weapons."

"Yes," said Statius.

Chapter, the Forty-Eighth:

The Amnesty

"You hear it?" said Lord Grendel.

"Of course," said Cabot.

Interestingly, the message was in both Kur and Gorean.

The world rang with the words of Agamemnon, pronouncing peace and amnesty.

"There is little food left," said Cabot.

"Do not feed me, Master," said Lita.

"Take this," said Cabot, pressing a rind of sul into her hands, and she put down her head and fed on it, kneeling, gratefully, her hair falling about her wrists.

How beautiful they are, thought Cabot. How desirable they are. How natural that men will take them, and make them their own, and put them in collars.

Lord Grendel's group was now small, consisting of some dozen Kurii, and some seven humans.

They were deep in the forested areas between the habitats and the far villages, those toward the far pole, and Lake Fear.

"We cannot run forever," said a Kur.

The rebellion, or insurrection, was now devastated, the revolutionary groups decimated, and scattered, in flight, pursued.

Hundreds, both Kur and human, had responded to the conciliations offered by Agamemnon.

"We had eight power weapons," said a Kur.

These were the weapons which had been acquired by Lords Grendel and Statius, and the human, Tarl Cabot, in the vicinity of the far pole, that beyond the small villages.

"Agamemnon has hundreds," said a Kur.

"Go, pledge fidelity to him," said another.

"Should we not have kept them all?" asked a human, Archon, now skilled with the bow.

"I think not," said Lord Grendel.

The reasoning had been rather as follows. The eight weapons would doubtless have made one of the insurrectionary groups more formidable than otherwise, say, that of Lord Grendel, but presumably the eight such weapons would have been of little avail against the full, massed power which might be brought against them by a reasonably large contingent of enemy forces, and, of course, given such an arrangement, concentrating the weapons in a single group, the other rebels' groups, now distributed, now muchly out of touch with one another, would have remained as before, limited to their original primitive, simple weaponry, sticks, spears, axes, knives, and such, and more dangerously, of course, and more happily for them, the arrow. Indeed, the arrow, loosed from the great bow, remained a not unformidable tool, even against foes equipped with a more sophisticated weaponry. It had then been decided, shortly after the defeats of the preceding days, on a variety of fronts, that eight of the several groups, of which Lord Grendel's was one, would have one weapon apiece, this at least, hopefully, acting as some deterrent for several of the groups, or bands, against a too rash approach by the forces of Agamemnon. Some thought had been given to the concentration of the eight weapons for a raid on the palace itself, but it was soon understood that the palace was not only closely guarded, but was, for most practical purposes, impregnable. Accordingly the weapons had been allotted amongst eight groups, of which Lord Grendel's was one. In his group, the power weapon, a shoulder rifle, in this case, to use a convenient term, one with several charges remaining, had been given into the keeping of the scout, Flavion. This seemed judicious considering his frequent departures from the camp, and the likely dangers of his encountering Purple Scarves.

Cabot was fond of his bow, and Lord Grendel, despite his skill with the small weapon, tended to prefer the weight of a Kur ax.

"How many have accepted the amnesty?" asked a Kur.

"Hundreds, I have heard," said another. "They stream to the habitats, to surrender their weapons."

"Who would not do so?" asked another.

"Some, it seems," said another.

Their eyes turned to the figure of their leader, large, as silent as rock, crouching back on his haunches, in Kur repose.

"Lord Grendel?" asked the first.

"Leave, if you will," said Lord Grendel. "Your departure will not be challenged."

"You will not hunt, and kill us?"

"No," said Grendel.

"Come with us," urged another.

"No," said Grendel.

"The amnesty is for all, Kur and human," said one of the Kurii.

"Things will be as before," said another.

"Agamemnon is tired of war," said another. "The war is done. He grants mercy, and forgiveness to all."

"To all," said another, "even to those who most fiercely opposed him."

"It is his desire to return peace to the world," said another.

"I do not doubt it," said Lord Grendel.

"Come with us, Lord Grendel," said another.

"No," said Lord Grendel.

Chapter, the Forty-Ninth:

Tracks

"Hold," said Lord Grendel, nostrils flaring.

He and Cabot were some pasangs from their concealed camp.

"There," said Grendel, "where the brush is awry. Set an arrow to your bow."

Cabot lowered the slain tarsk from his shoulders, and readied the great bow.

Half bent, head moving from side to side, ears erected, Grendel warily approached an opening in the brush.

"What is it?" whispered Cabot.

"Kur, Purple Scarf," said Grendel. "Part of a Kur, part of a Purple Scarf."

Cabot looked about, and joined his friend.

"It was killed in the open, and then dragged here, see the track, to be hidden from view."

"It is half buried," said Cabot.

"Sleen," said Grendel.

"Yes," said Cabot. The forest panther sometimes drags its prey into a tree, presumably to keep it safe from smaller predators, or from scavengers. The larl will often sleep in the vicinity of prey half eaten, thusly guarding it. Who would challenge a larl? Smaller beasts wait patiently, until it abandons its prey, and stalks away in its disinterested, lordly fashion. The sleen will commonly drag prey to a concealed location, where it may feed undisturbed, in solitude. Sometimes it buries part of the meat. The sleen is commonly nocturnal, usually emerging from its lair, or burrow, at night. It is in its way a single-minded beast and will follow a trail on which it has begun even through the midst of similar or different, even more desirable, prey animals. It is Gor's finest tracker. A common application of the sleen on Gor is the hunting of fugitive slaves.

"It is not the first," said Cabot.

"No," said Grendel.

"We have had foragers in this area, humans," said Cabot. "None have been attacked."

"I do not understand," said Grendel.

"Only Kurii have been killed," said Cabot.

"It makes no sense," said Grendel.

"It is almost as though the camp were being guarded," said Cabot.

"Absurd," said Grendel.

"Look," said Cabot. "Here!" He pointed to the soft earth. "Tracks!"

"Sleen tracks," said Grendel.

"Observe them," said Cabot. "Closely."

"Interesting," said Grendel.

"One track is lighter than the others," said Cabot. "The paw barely touched the ground."

"The rear paw of the left side," said Grendel.

"You understand this?" said Cabot.

"Certainly," said Grendel. "It is lame."

Chapter, the Fiftieth:

The Hand of Agamemnon Is Played, But Perhaps Not Wisely

"I am thinking," said Cabot to Lita, "of having you conducted to the theater of amnesty, in the habitats, where you might be spared, as the goods you are, later with others to be distributed or sold."

"Please, no, Master!" she cried, falling to her knees before him, and pressing her head to his feet.

Through her hair he glimpsed the collar on her neck, his collar. It is interesting, he thought, how one can grow fond of them, though they are only slaves, no more than domestic animals.

"You might then live," he said.

"I would remain with you," she wept.

"It is highly unlikely you would be slain," he said, "as you are nicely curved, and would have value in the markets of Gor."

"Keep me!" she begged.

"It is only a matter of time until we are located and destroyed," said Cabot. "I see no need for you to die, too."

"You care for me!" she cried.

His body tightened with anger.

How dare she so speak? What arrant presumption!

"Impudent, impertinent, presumptuous slut!" he cried.

"Master!" she cried.

With his foot he spurned her suddenly, angrily, violently, to the ground.

"Forgive me, Master," she whispered, frightened, tears in her eyes, from her side on the earth.

How dare she, a slave, an article of goods, think that her master might care for her?

Did she not know what she was?

Or, more judiciously, more carefully put, how dare she suggest such a thing? Many a woman has been bound, hooded, and leashed, and conducted weeping to a market for such an indiscretion.

This is not to deny, of course, that many a slave is well aware of her place in a master's heart, even that he might die for her. Doubtless neither, neither slave nor master, have planned it so, but so it not unoften comes about. Is it so strange? That a slave might love her master, that a master might care for his slave? Might she not, to some extent, have brought this about, perhaps lamentably, by her beauty, her helplessness, her heat, her love, her devotion, her selfless service? Too, is she not, after all, a perfection of a female for a man, a slave, what he most desires and wants, something far beyond what he might obtain from a free woman? In a collar she is, after all, a creature of love. Is the collar itself not a symbol of this? That she exists for love? So, kneeling, needful, submitted, her own love opened like a flower, she begins to hope that something of her own feelings, so deep, so profound, so overwhelming, might be reciprocated, if only to a tiny extent, by her master. Scarcely had she dared hope for this that night when, to the double stroke of a whip, she was dragged in chains from the auction block. And as time passes she begins, fearfully, trying to conceal her joy, to suspect it may be so. Has her master not, for example, of late become less patient and more strict with her, as though he might be fighting something within himself, something unwelcome, which he was unwilling to acknowledge? Surely she must now strive to do nothing which might cause him to rid himself of her. She is well aware that he would be subjected to the scorn of his peers, did they, in amusement, suspect that he might care for a slave. But might they not, some of them, in the secrecy of their own domiciles, be as deplorably guilty in this regard? Certainly the joy, the radiance, of many slaves, encountered in the markets and streets, suggested that. But she is well aware that, given the man he is, she has much more to fear from his own possible self reproach than from the jibes of others. His sense of himself, of what is proper for him, might be her greatest danger. She feels vulnerable. She may be sold on a whim. She redoubles her efforts to be his humble, pleasing slave. Surely she strives to be acceptable to him, and wholly, as she must, and desires, in the way of the slave. And of course there is no diminishment in her slave fires. Does she not, eagerly and piteously, driven by her aroused needs, as before, crawl to his slave ring, soliciting his least touch? Even were he a cruel and hated master, even of an enemy city, she could not help but behave so. Men had seen to it. But, now, even well away from the slave ring, when he returns from his labors and she welcomes him, kneeling, looking up at him, to his domicile, when she serves his supper or wine, when he observes her polishing his leather, when he orders her to light the lamp of love, has there not been something different about him, perhaps a slightly different light in his eyes? So she suspects now, as she moves before him, subtly provoking his desire, as though unintentionally, as before, as the slave she is, as she serves, that he may have begun to care for her, despite the fact that she is only a submitted, vanquished property, a slave. It is one thing, of course, in all of this, for a slave, scarcely daring to hope, grateful and rejoicing, to understand, to suspect, how she may have now come to be regarded by her master, and quite another to speak of it. Is this not a secret, not to be spoken, though possibly shared, however reluctantly on the part of the master? She will, of course, continue to kneel and serve, and please. And if she does not please, she knows she will feel the lash, as any other girl, and she would have it no other way, for she is proud of her master and his strength, proud to be owned by such a man. He is her master.

"Do not forget yourself," he said. "You are not a free woman. You are an animal, a branded domestic animal, a meaningless work and love beast, purchasable, a thing to be set to labors, a passion toy, a sexual plaything, something to be exploited at the master's will, for his pleasure."

"Yes, Master," she wept.

"If spared, some others might get some good from you."

"Yes, Master," she whispered. And then she cried out with misery, and crawled to his feet, her head down. "Keep me!" she sobbed. "Keep me, please, Master!"

"I have decided the matter," said Cabot. "You will be bound, and leashed, and taken from the camp. If necessary, you will be whipped from the camp."

"Master has never whipped me!" she said.

"I am prepared to do so," said Cabot.

"Surely not, Master!" she said.

Cabot turned to Archon, and another. "Strip and tie her," he said. "And bring me a whip."

"Master!" she protested.

In moments the slave, stripped, her wrists crossed and bound, and fastened over her head, to a stout, overhanging branch, that her beauty might be protected, that she might not be dashed against a post or tree trunk, was in whip position.

She looked wildly back at Cabot. "Have I not been pleasing?" she asked. "I have tried to be pleasing, my Master!"

"The whip has been uncoiled," he said.

She moaned.

"Hark!" said a Kur, suddenly, lifting his paw.

Lord Grendel sprang to his feet.

"Someone is coming!" said a Kur.

Cabot cast the whip to the dirt.

All eyes turned toward the gate of the small camp.

A voice came through the palings. It was registered on Cabot's translator. "For Lord Arcesilaus," it said.

"It is Lord Flavion," said Grendel. "Open the gate!"

Flavion, armed, staggered into the camp. Behind him straggled a dozen or more humans, some helmeted, all garmented in cloth.

"Peisistratus!" exclaimed Cabot.

The two men embraced.

"You are injured," said Cabot.

"Death, power weapons, fire, the screaming," said Peisistratus.

Cabot put his arms about him, and lowered him to the ground. The other humans entered the camp, haggard, pale, filthy, with torn clothing, some bloodied, and bandaged, two supported by their fellows. With them were four female slaves, including Peisistratus' Corinna.

"The pleasure cylinder has been breached," said Peisistratus. "We emerged, four hundred of us, surrendered, to avail ourselves of the amnesty."

"Wise," said Cabot.

"No, no," whispered Peisistratus. "We gave up our weapons and were directed toward the theater of amnesty, but we delayed our entry. We did not wish to do so, but we were weak, starving, and several amongst us were wounded. We were on the hill overlooking the theater. In it must have been two thousand, or more, Kurii, humans."

"Yes," said Cabot. "Joined, for the pledging of blood and honor to Agamemnon."

"Then the weapons began to fire," said Peisistratus. "The theater itself seemed a furnace of flames. They were cut down, burned alive, from all sides. We could see the blackened bodies, crowded together, bursting and smoking, smell the flesh."

"It is enough," said Lord Grendel. "It is enough."

"That is the amnesty of Agamemnon," said a Kur.

"In that cauldron," said a Kur, "would have been brethren, folk of our camp, who fought with us, our brothers, who trusted the word of Agamemnon."

"Now," said a Kur, "I am no longer afraid to die."

"There were four hundred with you?" said Cabot.

"Some such number," said Peisistratus, his head down.

"There are few here," said Cabot.

"We fled, unarmed," said Peisistratus. "We knew we would be sought. In the forest we encountered noble Flavion, who brought us here."

"There were four hundred?" said Cabot.

"Flavion rallied us, and reassured us," said Peisistratus. "He bade us wait until he had scouted a passage which might be traversed with security. We waited."

"How long?" asked Cabot.

Persistratus shrugged. "I do not know," he said. "Four ahn, five, I do not know."

"What then?"

"Noble Flavion, our rescuer and guide, returned, and we began our trek."

"There were four hundred," pressed Cabot.

"Alas," said Flavion, in Kur distress, though the voice emerged quietly enough, precisely, as always, on Cabot's translator. "We were ambushed in a defile, cut to pieces. Only the head of the column, I fear, I and some others, these, who had already exited the defile, survived."

"You were fortunate," said Cabot.

"Surely more so than others," came from Cabot's translator.

"Welcome to our camp," said Lord Grendel to Peisistratus and his fellows, and beasts. "Rest, and feed."

"In the theater," said Cabot, to Peisistratus, "all were slain?"

"Yes," said Peisistratus. "Kur, male and female, and human, male and female."

"Even your beasts, your female slaves?" asked Cabot.

"All," said Peisistratus, dismally.

"It would be the way of Agamemnon," said a Kur.

"He is thorough," said another.

Cabot turned slowly about, and went to where his own beast, the girl, Lita, was fastened, her wrists crossed, and bound, over her head.

"You heard?" he asked.

"Yes, Master," she said.

"It seems I will not return you to the habitats," said Cabot.

"A girl rejoices," she whispered.

"It would be a waste of beast," he said.

"Yes, Master," she said. "Master."

"Yes?" he said.

"Your whip was uncoiled."

Cabot reached down and retrieved the whip, and then, slowly folding its blades back, against the staff, he touched it, gently, to her back.

"My Master has beaten me," she said.

"Yes," said Cabot, wearily.

She turned her head, and pursed her lips, pleadingly, and Cabot held the whip to her lips, and she kissed it, gratefully, fervently.

He then untied her and, retrieving her tunic, tossed it to her. "Help with the food," he said. "And prepare places of repose. Our guests must eat, and will then wish to rest."

"Yes, Master," she said.

"I would speak to you," said Lord Grendel to Tarl Cabot.

Cabot joined him, to the side.

"Do you not find it surprising," asked Lord Grendel, "that the route of the fugitives was so accurately and promptly descried?"

"Doubtless a tragic fortuity," said Cabot.

"Do you believe that?" asked Lord Grendel.

"No," said Cabot.

"Nor do I," said Lord Grendel. "My friend."

"Yes?" said Cabot.

"I believe Lord Agamemnon has made his first, and greatest, mistake," said Grendel.

"How is that?" asked Cabot.

"The profession of the amnesty," said Grendel, "and then the massacres."

"Was it not clever?" asked Cabot.

"No," said Lord Grendel. "For it is not Kur."

"Many would suppose it was very Kur," said Cabot.

"No," said Grendel. "It was not Kur."

Chapter, the Fifty-First:

A Cave Is Found Empty

"He is not here," said Cabot.

Peisistratus had been left in charge of the humans in the camp of Lord Grendel's band, and Statius, who had once been no more than a despised nondominant, had been deputized to command the Kurii of the camp, and, as he was Kur, was sovereign in the camp.

Lord Grendel and Cabot had trekked about Lake Fear, on its nearer side to the habitats, in order to recover and burn the remains of Lord Arcesilaus, whom they had expected to find dead in the cave in which they had left him, long ago, sorely wounded, but, too, to replenish a supply of weapon points, for themselves, at least. Many of the humans had now accustomed themselves to the bow, of one strength or another, but there was a considerable shortage of suitable headings for these missiles, many now being merely sharpened sticks, fletched. Some heads had been made from stone and bent, folded bits of metal, but such expedients were makeshift, at best. A classical stone for such purposes, reasonably convenient to shape, was not available in the world, flint.

It had not been difficult for Lord Grendel and his human ally, Tarl Cabot, to locate the cave in which they had left Lord Arcesilaus, but, upon entering the cave, they had found it empty.

"Lord Arcesilaus bled here," said Cabot, pointing to the rear of the cave.

"The stains are not fresh," said Lord Grendel.

"Doubtless he died of his wounds, and animals, smelling blood and death, dragged the body from the cave," said Cabot.

"Let us hope he was dead before they came upon him," said Lord Grendel.

"There is no sign of a struggle," said Cabot. "The vessels are muchly as we left them. There seem no marks in the floor dust."

"It is possible he was discovered, and then captured, and returned to Agamemnon," said Lord Grendel.

"In any event, he is not here," said Cabot.

Cabot and Lord Grendel had had much better fortune with the smith who had fashioned the first weapon points, pretending, at least, that he took them to be ornamental pendants.

To be sure, Cabot's last silver coins, from the wager of Peisistratus, had now been expended in this small market.

Each now bore a sack, containing hundreds of such points.

"Do you think it was wise to have left Flavion behind, in the camp?" asked Cabot.

"Yes," said Lord Grendel. "Let him think himself unsuspected. Let him be sessile, biding his time, projecting new treacheries. We may be able to put him to use."

"What if he betrays the camp?" asked Cabot.

"It would be only one camp," said Lord Grendel. "He wishes to be of greater value to Agamemnon than that. Better, if regroupings should occur, to gather intelligence on a dozen camps, on a dozen leaders, on a dozen strategies. Let him think he lies coiled amongst us like an ost at our feet, unsuspected, unnoted, aware, listening."

"The insurrection is finished," said Cabot. "Only pockets of resistance remain, waiting to be dealt with, one by one."

"Our venture here is finished," said Lord Grendel. "We shall return to the camp."

"Excellent," said Cabot.

"Perhaps you are anxious to return to your pretty little beast," said Lord Grendel.

"The shapely collar slut, Lita?" said Cabot.

"Yes," said Lord Grendel.

"Perhaps," said Cabot, lightly.

"You spoke in your sleep," said Grendel.

"It is hard for a master to be without his slave," said Cabot.

"And one thing is harder than that," said Grendel.

"And what is that?" asked Cabot.

"Had you not put slave fires in her belly?" asked Grendel.

"It is true she is a slave," said Cabot.

"And that is it," said Grendel.

"What?" asked Cabot.

"The one thing that is harder than for a master to be without his slave," said Grendel.

"And what is that?" said Cabot.

"For a slave to be without her master," said Grendel.

"I would suppose it is really much the same," said Cabot.

"I rather doubt it," said Lord Grendel. "I have often reflected upon the mercilessness of masters, who so unilaterally and imperiously put helpless slaves into the throes of such needs."

"It does make them more desperately dependent, and easier to control," said Cabot.

"I would not be surprised," said Lord Grendel, "if the sexual needs, the helplessness, the passion, of human females far exceeded that of males."

"Only when they have been sexually awakened," said Cabot. "I know a world where many males would be surprised to encounter that speculation."

"I think I have heard of such a world," said Grendel.

"It is not Gor," smiled Cabot.

"No," said Lord Grendel. "It would be such a very different world, such a tragic, self-denying, unfulfilled world."

"In the world of which you may be thinking," said Cabot, "not all women are sexually inert, torpid, or dormant. Some have the urgent, needful bellies of Gorean slave girls."

"But that is unusual, is it not?" asked Grendel.

"It is hard to tell," said Cabot, "but the common view is that it would be unusual."

"Strange," said Lord Grendel, "given the extensive distribution of sexually vital tissue in the human female, its globality, and its subtle interrelationships with thought and feeling, and such. It would seem, as one thinks about it, that almost their entire body is, in its way, a sexual organ. Consider, for example, their sensitivity, their awareness of the subtlest colors, scents, and textures. Even their skin is alive, responsive to the slightest touch, to the least whispers and nuances of their environment."

"It is true that if you put them naked on certain surfaces, sometimes tiles, sometimes a rug, they find themselves, sometimes to their dismay, in a state of sexual arousal."

"And tied naked to a tree?"

"Of course," said Cabot.

"Human females, it seems to me," said Grendel, "are quite remarkable. It seems to me that each presents for a master's delectation a unique gift and property of emotion, consciousness, subtlety, and sensation."

"It is certainly pleasant to own them," said Cabot.

"And how vital, alive, and sensitive they are!"

"They are aware, of course," said Cabot, "of the coarseness of rope constricting their limbs, the weight of iron on a limb, a wrist, an ankle, such things."

"And the feel of a collar on their neck?"

"Doubtless," said Cabot.

"And to the brush of silk," said Grendel, "and to the scent of a perfume."

"Particularly," said Cabot, "to one they know has been prepared for a slave."

"So I fail to understand," said Grendel, "how it is, if it be true, that so many of the women of the world we may have in mind are seemingly strangers to their bodies and needs."

"Presumably there are explanations," said Cabot.

"Are they a different sort of woman?" asked Grendel.

"No," said Cabot. "Certainly not. Bring them to Gor, put them in collars, and sell them, and they are soon amongst the hottest of slaves. Certainly they bring high prices off the block."

"Then I do not understand it," said Lord Grendel.

"In the history of the world of which we may be speaking," said Cabot, "for thousands of years women were recognized, and even feared, for the intensity of their sexuality. They were the needful ones, the pleaders, the seducers, the temptresses, those to be guarded against."

"Interesting," said Grendel.

"Much has to do, I am sure," said Cabot, "with cultural prescriptions, societal dictates, requirements, influences, pressures, and such things. When a society is seized by the ill-constituted, the miserable, the sick, the self-fearing, the weak, the haters, and such, it is natural they would mold, as they can, their world in their own pathological image. Too, when a world becomes essentially a machine, with countless interlocking, dehumanized parts, practices, and procedures, there is little room or time left for the long-forgotten animals, once human, who tend to its needs, and now wander about within it, lost in its mazes."

Lord Grendel was silent.

"There is some possibility," said Cabot, "that the seeming dearth of female passion on such a world, seemingly so unnaturally pervasive, seemingly so inexplicable, is actually in its way an evidence not of the absence or weakness of female drives and needs, but of their remarkable strength, which requires for its suppression societal devices of such detail and power."

"Women must be turned against women?" said Grendel.

"Yes," said Cabot. "It is forbidden to them, so to speak, to open certain doors, to look into certain mirrors, for fear of what they might find, for fear of what they might see."

"It seems a tragic waste of woman," said Grendel.

"True," said Cabot.

"It seems they are sexually asleep," said Grendel.

"In their dreams, and fantasies," said Cabot, "I suspect that few are sexually asleep."

"They fear nature, and themselves?" asked Grendel.

"Perhaps," said Cabot. "Certainly in nature there are obvious, pervasive complementarities, and they are females."

"You speak of dominance and submission?" asked Grendel.

"Yes," said Cabot.

"They fear to find their masters?"

"I do not think so," said Cabot. "I think, rather, they long to find them."

"Interesting," said Grendel.

"And they realize, if only in their secret dreams, that they will not be whole until they kneel before them."

"I understand, from what you have said," said Grendel, "that the women of Earth bring high prices in the Gorean markets."

"Often," said Cabot. "And the prices reflect the discovered value of the goods."

"Of course," said Grendel.

"Many men seek them out," said Cabot.

"They make excellent slaves?"

"The collar frees them," said Cabot.

"Certainly you yourself have had the pleasure to own and master slaves," said Grendel.

"Some," said Cabot.

"Your Lita," said Grendel, "wept muchly, and annoyingly, I fear, at our departure from the camp."

"She was importunate," said Cabot. "She wished to accompany us, but the chain on her left ankle, she holding out her hands to us, and sobbing, held her to the tree."

"Your merest word should have been sufficient," said Grendel.

"Perhaps," said Cabot, irritably.

"You are fond of her, I fear," said Grendel.

"She is a mere slave," said Cabot, lightly.

"But surely she has properties of interest," said Grendel.

"I suppose so," said Cabot. "She is quite intelligent, and quite beautiful, that in both face and figure. Certainly she would look well, exhibited on a block. And she is vital, healthy, sensitive, aware, deeply emotional, and now, in bondage, exquisitely, helplessly, vulnerably feminine."

"And she looks well in a collar?"

"Certainly," said Cabot. "She was born for one."

"I gather she was superficial, unpleasant, troubled, confused, nasty, unhappy, insolent, vain, and petty on Earth."

"She was not then in a collar," said Cabot.

"It seems she has now grown a thousand times in character, awareness, and emotional depth," said Grendel.

"She is now a slave," said Cabot, shrugging.

"And in her belly there are now slave fires?" said Grendel.

"Yes," said Cabot.

"And they rage?"

"Frequently," said Cabot.

"And this puts her the more at your mercy?"

"Of course," said Cabot.

"It is doubtless pleasant to have a beautiful woman, naked, in a slave collar, crawl to you, begging you for your touch."

"It is not unpleasant," acknowledged Cabot.

"She would seem an excellent slave."

"She is still being trained," said Cabot.

"You think she would bring a high price?"

"I think so," said Cabot.

"Then," said Lord Grendel, "one must keep her under the fiercest and most perfect discipline."

"For what reason?" asked Cabot.

"To keep her worthy of her price," said Grendel.

"I see," said Cabot.

"She carried on, lamentably," said Lord Grendel, "when we left the camp. It was embarrassing. What were our brothers to think?"

"She was distraught," said Cabot. "I think it is healthy to let a slave give vent to her feelings, to sob, or weep, if she will."

"To an extent, perhaps," said Grendel, "but then she should be put to silence, with no more than a look, or word. She can always thrash about, and moan, and weep, and sob, later, when she wishes, in decent privacy, in her cage, on her chain, or such."

"I did not realize you were an authority on human female slaves," said Cabot.

"She needs a taste of the whip," said Grendel.

"She is a woman of Earth," said Cabot.

"All the more reason," said Grendel.

"I see," said Cabot.

"And how is she to know she is truly a slave, and you are truly her master, if you do not put the whip to her?"

"I see," said Cabot.

"She wants to be under your whip," said Lord Grendel.

"How do you know that?" asked Cabot.

"It is obvious," said Lord Grendel.

"I do not recall your putting the leather to the Lady Bina," said Cabot.

"Certainly not," said Grendel, shocked. "That would be wholly inappropriate. She is a free woman."

"Do you still suspect her of treachery, in the matter of the arsenal?"

"Certainly," said Grendel. "Clearly, she is guilty. Flavion himself could not well have exited the camp so closely before the attack, at least not for any length of time, without attracting attention, and perhaps suspicion. He arranged for her to escape from the camp. How else could it have been managed? And he sent her ahead to Agamemnon, doubtless with signs, and countersigns. Each is guilty. Each was the confederate of the other."

"And she now stands high with Agamemnon?"

"Doubtless," said Lord Grendel.

"Statius and others," said Cabot, "want her blood."

"They shall not have it," said Lord Grendel, "without mine."

"They are proposing hideous tortures," said Cabot.

"She is in little danger," said Lord Grendel, "for the revolution has failed."

"Why, then," asked Cabot, "do you continue to do war?"

"Because," said Grendel, "it is the thing to do. It is Kur."

"I see," said Cabot.

"And why do you continue to do war?" asked Grendel.

"Because it is the thing to do," said Cabot. "It is Gorean."

"I am curious to know," said Lord Grendel, "why you behaved so obsequiously to Flavion in the camp, attending so assiduously to his needs, serving him, grooming him, and such."

"It pleased him, I think," said Cabot, "to be served by a human, one of what he doubtless regards as an inferior species."

"Not wholly inappropriately," said Grendel.

"Perhaps," said Cabot.

"You even wiped down his fur with soft cloths, and to such a high gloss," said Grendel. "Perhaps this was done to seem to show him honor, to allay his suspicions, if he had them, or such?"

"Perhaps," said Cabot.

"But only for one day?"

"That would be enough," said Cabot.

"We must not spoil him?" said Grendel.

"Certainly not," said Cabot.

"In the morning," said Grendel, "we shall begin the journey back to the camp."

"Good," said Cabot. "—You said, earlier, I spoke in my sleep?"

"Yes."

"It had to do with Lita, I suppose?"

"Yes."

"What did I say?" he asked.

"I gather you had her nicely chained," he said.

"Well chained?"

"Perfectly."

"Good," said Cabot.

Chapter, the Fifty-Second:

Small Camps Have Been Found Abandoned

"Lita and I passed this way, days ago, from the cave," said Cabot. "But now the small camps are deserted."

"Surely you understand what is happening?" said Grendel.

"No," said Cabot. "I do see several bodies, rotted, no longer of interest even to birds, dangling, hanging from trees."

"The rebellion having been crushed," said Lord Grendel, "Agamemnon can return his attention to the affairs of state."

"Where are the former inhabitants of the camps, those hundreds, those who waited to learn their fate, the forces defeated beyond the world, who came here in rout and dishonor?"

"They will have been congregated, beyond the habitats," said Grendel. "To be given lengths of rope, or to submit themselves to the knife."

As may be recalled, the defeated forces of Agamemnon, the mariners who returned in the remnants of his ruined fleet, following his catastrophic, ill-starred attack on another of the worlds, had been denied access to the habitats. This was not unusual, under the circumstances, and represented common Kur practice. Kurii tend not to be tolerant of defeat, and feel that only the blood lines of victory should be maintained and propagated. Accordingly, the survivors of the defeat, or those amongst them who had been courageous enough to return to the world, to face the folk, and accept the consequences of their failure, had awaited their fate in a number of small camps. They would be given the options of self-destruction or submission to a surgical alteration which would guarantee they would never pollute the folk by the sowing of inferior seed. Many had already hung themselves in despondency and grief, unwilling to bear any longer the tarnish and stains of their dishonor. Others would accept the knife, accepting it as a warranted and appropriate penalty or punishment, one suitable to their heinous fault, one commensurate with their just deserts. Following the procedure they would be banished to the company, if any, of nondominants.

"This is a madness," said Cabot.

"You are not Kur," said Lord Grendel.

"Agamemnon was not defending the world," said Cabot. "His act was one of aggression, or such, one which, I suspect, was unprovoked."

"Do you not understand it?" asked Grendel.

"Speak," said Cabot.

"Agamemnon is the rival amongst the worlds of a great general, and vies to be first amongst the worlds, the leader of the several worlds."

"There are several such leaders, generals, are there not?" asked Cabot.

"Yes," said Grendel, "but one was most feared by Agamemnon, one whom he wished to deal with first, one whom he long pretended to befriend, but one whom he suspected well comprehended his ambitions and machinations, one whom he then conveyed from the world, ignominiously, daring to do no more at the time, and then proceeded to lay his plans, and supply and ready his fleet."

"I know the general, I am sure," said Cabot.

"It could have been any one of a number," said Grendel.

"But it was not," said Cabot.

"No," said Grendel.

"And so the mariners of the camps are to suffer for the miscalculations and mistakes, the reckless, vain ambition, the poorly laid plans, the rash, ill-fated, unjustified, personal adventure of a tyrant?"

"Certainly," said Lord Grendel.

"I see," said Cabot.

"It is such things," said Lord Grendel, "which, particularly when successful, shape the histories of worlds. The sword is the plow which furrows the soil of the future. Those who do not defend themselves die, and fall amongst the litter of their virtues. Without the spear there is no peace. Only blood can slake the thirst for violence."

"You are Kur," said Cabot, bitterly.

"I do not think you are so different," said Lord Grendel.

"I would spare these mariners, these soldiers," said Cabot.

"Interestingly," mused Lord Grendel, "so, too, would I."

"How then are you Kur?" said Cabot.

"What is Kur?" said Lord Grendel.

Chapter, the Fifty-Third:

Return to Camp;
A Surprise;
A Mystery

"Greetings, noble Flavion!" said Lord Grendel.

"Welcome to the camp, noble Grendel," said Flavion. "We have been concerned with your absence."

Peisistratus hurried forward, and pressed Cabot's hand, and touched Lord Grendel's forearm.

Heeling him was his Corinna.

"Ho!" said Statius, rushing forward. "We feared for you."

"We have brought arrow points," said Cabot, "a great many of them."

"Excellent," said Statius.

"Excellent," said Flavion.

Archon, once of the forest humans, cried out with pleasure.

Cabot and Grendel lowered the weighty sacks to the ground.

"How many charges have we left in your rifle?" Grendel asked Flavion.

"As before," said Flavion, "five. I have been sparing in their use, preferring to elude encroaching enemies, rather than reveal the nature and location of the weapon."

"Wise," said Grendel.

"There are seven others, are there not, somewhere?" asked Flavion.

"I believe so," said Lord Grendel.

"Little has taken place since your departure," said Flavion.

"We needed weapon points," said Lord Grendel.

Statius' Kur female crouched behind him, in his shadow.

Cabot looked about. "Where is my slut, Lita?" he asked. "Why is she not here, at my feet?"

The eyes of Peisistratus clouded. He looked down.

"What is it?" asked Cabot, quickly, narrowly.

"She fled," said Peisistratus. "Muchly was she distressed at your departure, that you had left her behind. Long she wept, and cried out, and then she became sullen, then angry, then seemingly resigned, and then, one night, when she had not yet been chained, she slipped away."

"She did not have the permission of a male to leave the camp?" asked Cabot.

"No," said Peisistratus.

"She was not set upon an errand?"

"No."

"Clearly, then, she fled?"

"Clearly," said Peisistratus.

"It seems," said Statius, "she does not know what it is to be a slave."

"She is naive," said Cabot. "She is new to her collar. It seems there is something of Earth left in her."

"It seems clearly she does not understand her collar, the penalties," said Peisistratus. "If she had learned her slavery in the pens, and on Gor, she would not have dared to think of such a thing."

"True," said Cabot.

The Gorean slave girl is terrified to even think of escaping. She knows she is a slave, and, as far as her own efforts are concerned, will remain a slave. She is distinctively clad, she is branded, she is collared. She is utterly helpless in her bondage. It is categorical and inalterable. She has nowhere to run. The entire society accepts and demands her bondage. It will go to great lengths to search for her, and return her to her master. The best she might hope for would be to exchange one bondage for another, and doubtless for one far worse than that from which she fled, for she would be recognized as a runaway, and, quite possibly, would be prominently branded as such, the mark seared into her forehead. She might be taken in the fields, and find herself owned by peasants, which is a quite unpleasant slavery; she might find herself placed in the mills, the laundries, or the mines, closely shackled, heavily burdened, half starved, and muchly whipped, or such. It is not enviable, for example, to be a slave illicitly, secretly vended on the black market.

"She is not on Gor," said Cabot.

"It makes no difference, at all," said Peisistratus. "She is slave."

"True," said Cabot.

"It seems she does not understand her bondage," said Statius.

"Perhaps it should have been better taught to her," said Lord Grendel.

"Doubtless," said Cabot.

"I have little doubt," said Peisistratus, "it would be easy to teach it to her."

"That is true," said Cabot.

"We could probably trail her," said Flavion.

"I do not understand why she would flee," said Lord Grendel. "How would she live? She could starve, or thirst, unable to approach water. Animals would hunt her, and feed on her. If she approaches the Kurii of Agamemnon they have no interest in her as a slave. They would simply fire upon her, to destroy her on sight."

Cabot was silent.

"It was very foolish of her to flee," said Lord Grendel. "Why would she do so?"

"She is a female," said Peisistratus, "and does not fully realize that she is also a slave."

"I think we could trail her," said Flavion.

"When did she flee?" asked Cabot.

"Four days ago," said Statius.

"The trail would now be cold," said Cabot, "particularly so, given the periodic, refreshing rains."

"Not for sleen," said Lord Grendel.

"But, dear friend," said Cabot, "we do not have sleen."

Flavion shrugged, a movement which, in the Kur, seems to course the entire body.

"Yes," Cabot thought to himself, "I think Flavion might be able to find her."

"We have formed a plan," said Lord Grendel, "to unite the rebel bands, to pool our weapons of power, and to strike at the palace itself."

"That is bold!" exclaimed Flavion.

"It will obviously require contacting our cohorts, and bringing us together, somewhere."

"All, all the rebel bands?" said Flavion.

"Yes," said Lord Grendel.

"I know a place," said Flavion.

"Excellent," said Lord Grendel. "We shall rely upon you."

"Dear Cabot," said Peisistratus. "It seems you have lost something."

"Yes," said Cabot, reaching toward his throat, which was bare. "It seems I have lost the ring, which I wore about my neck."

"It was of gold, was it not?" said Statius.

"I believe so," said Cabot.

"A grievous loss," said Peisistratus.

"Yes," said Cabot.

It had been three days after Cabot and Lord Grendel had visited some of the abandoned camps of the survivors of the fleet's disaster, those who had returned to the world.

And it was two days before their return to their own camp, the return briefly remarked on hitherto.

They had been fired on, twice, by Kur patrols, but had managed to elude them, once by taking refuge within a shambling herd of cattle humans, and once by slipping into an area within which it was unlikely, in any event, that power weapons would be employed. The latter area was one of the womb tunnels.

Too, to be fully honest, the attention of the patrols had not been zealous.

Charges are precious, and, at the distances involved, would be unlikely of much efficacy. Too, at the distance, it was not clear that the targets might not be no more than a Kur and its pet, or even a nondominant, followed by a scavenging human.

Had they realized the nature of the targets a pursuit would have doubtless been pressed with earnestness.

Before they had been detected the second time, Cabot had come upon the body of a Kur, muchly mutilated.

It was, seemingly, that of a neutral. In any event it bore no purple scarf, though, to be sure, such an emblem might have been removed, for one purpose or another, perhaps even to serve as a trophy.

"Butchery," had said Cabot.

"Killer humans," had said Lord Grendel.

Killer humans, as it might be recalled, were bred by Kurii for arena sports, and bred for energy, agility, and aggression. Some were speeched, others not. There were several such groups. Some had joined themselves to the rebels. Other groups were rogue groups, wandering about, a danger to anything in their path, even to one another. They did tend to hate Kurii, and their easily initiated murderous rages often targeted isolated Kurii, whom they would swarm upon, regardless of their own safety, and destroy as they could. They were no more concerned with their own survival than might have been a cloud of varts descending on an isolated tabuk or verr.

At that moment a burst of flame erupted in the grass near them, and Cabot and Grendel quickly slipped away, amongst rocks.

Some of the rocks seemed to splinter and burst apart, showering particles about.

"Hurry," said Lord Grendel.

"I cannot even locate the source of fire," said Cabot.

"It is far away," said Grendel.

Cabot continued to follow his friend amongst the rocks. "They have stopped firing," said Cabot.

"In here," said Grendel, and Cabot lowered his head, and entered what, from the outside, seemed no more than a lair, or the opening to a small cave.

"We are safe in here," said Lord Grendel. "Reasonably safe."

"Reasonably?"

"We will spend the night here," said Grendel. "But deeper inside."

"What manner of place is this?" said Cabot.

"Follow me," said Grendel.

"It opens into a tunnel, shaped, smoothed," said Cabot, wonderingly, "and there are lights, soft lights."

"They are mainly for warmth," said Grendel.

"Ai!" said Cabot. "I have touched something!"

It seemed to recoil from his touch. It was large, and hot, and haired. It seemed to adhere to the side of the wall.

"Kur females seldom conceive," said Grendel. "That is one reason their seeding is so important to them. When they have conceived they will come to a place such as this and deposit the tiny, fertilized ovoid."

"An egg?" said Cabot.

"If you like," said Grendel.

"These are wombs," said Cabot.

"In a sense, our third sex," said Grendel, "the third of four, if we count the nondominants as an independent sex."

"Are they not males?"

"It is a matter of definition," said Lord Grendel.

They continued to traverse the tunnel, and encountered more of the growths adhering to the walls.

"Be careful where you step," said Grendel.

A small creature, urtlike, scampered past, yet Cabot suspected it was not the presence of such small denizens of the tunnel with which Lord Grendel was most concerned.

"Many humans," said Lord Grendel, "particularly at first, have difficulty telling the Kur male from the Kur female. Did you know that?"

"Oh?" said Cabot, who himself, to be perfectly honest, was still, at least occasionally, afflicted with uncertainty in the matter.

"Unlike the human female," said Lord Grendel, "the Kur female, unless a throwback, an atavism, is narrow-hipped and breastless. The functions of gestation and nursing take place in the wombs."

"Milk?" asked Cabot.

"Blood," said Lord Grendel.

"How does the Kur female know her own offspring?" asked Cabot.

"She is seldom concerned," said Grendel, "no more than her seeder. Both contribute offspring to the folk. That is all that matters. To be sure, amongst the higher Kurii, the lords, and such, some attention is given to womb brothers, emergents from the same womb, and, more particularly, to egg brothers, namely, offspring who share at least one parent."

"They are then brothers?"

"Probably not in the full sense in which you think of brothers, being raised together, and such, but the distinction is of genetic interest, and is often regarded as germane to desiderated bloodlines.

To be sure, occasionally, a confederacy of sorts is formed amongst such brothers, in pursuit of a common concern, but that tends to be frowned upon, and is supposedly rare."

"Supposedly?" said Cabot.

"It is my suspicion that it is more common than is usually suspected," said Lord Grendel.

Cabot, softly, placed his hand on one of the wombs, which was warm, and pulsated.

The hair had an oily feel.

"Does the womb feel?" asked Cabot.

"We do not think so," said Grendel, "but it does have some irritability, for example, writhing and recoiling at the emergence."

"Emergence?"

"Something like birth."

"Birth?"

"The young one, you might say the baby, or child, when ready, tears its way out of the womb. It is bloody. Here and there you can see blood on the floor. The blood attracts the scavengers, who come to feed on it. And they are usually the infant's first kill."

"I see," said Cabot.

"The Kur, you see, is superior to the human," said Lord Grendel, "for the human is usually quite helpless at birth, and for some time afterward."

"It must cause great pain to the womb," said Cabot.

"We do not know," said Lord Grendel. "In any event the womb has no vocal apparatus."

"How are wombs reproduced?" asked Cabot.

"They bud," said Grendel. "Parthenogenesis."

"How did this begin?" asked Cabot.

"We do not know," said Lord Grendel. "It was long ago. One supposes some sort of biological engineering was involved, something intended to free the Kur female from some of procreation's more grievous burdens."

"How do the wombs live?" asked Cabot.

"They are alive," said Lord Grendel. "They have an orifice. They are fed meat, and given fluid. Yes, there are teeth, and fangs, within the orifice. Do not place your hand into one. Excretion is emitted through the same orifice, it serving for both purposes, and the waste products are exuded onto the body. Perhaps you have noted the oiliness of the pelt."

Cabot drew back his hand.

"The metabolism is very slow," said Grendel, "and the wombs are often metabolically dormant for weeks at a time. Periodically, the pelt is wiped clean and sanitized, and always when an emergence is imminent."

They continued to tread the tunnel, and the wombs became more frequent. Some moved, as what was within them stirred.

"Be careful where you step!" said Lord Grendel.

Cabot moved a bit to the side, to avoid stepping on what he took to be something dropped in the tunnel, a wad of cloth, a crumpled rag, a lump of tissue.

"What is it?" asked Cabot.

"An infant," said Grendel. "Probably waiting for a scavenger."

"Is it alive?"

"Certainly."

"It is not moving."

"I would not put my hand on it, unless you want to lose a finger," said Lord Grendel. "Just avoid it. These things are picked up, periodically, with gloves, or tongs, and boxed, for conveying to the nurseries."

They had not moved more than three or four yards when there was a sudden, frightened squeal, and Cabot spun about, to see a flurry of fur and teeth behind him. Then the mound was still, save for the sound of feeding.

"A scavenger came too close," said Lord Grendel.

It was some minutes further in the tunnel, when Cabot stopped, and stared at one of the wombs, for it seemed to shudder, and heave.

"Smell it," said Lord Grendel.

"Disinfectant, alcohol?" said Cabot.

"There is going to be an emergence," said Grendel. "Step back. Do not approach it closely, for you might be soiled."

The living thing adhering to the wall, large, and bulging, haired, began to shudder and writhe. Cabot saw its outer side, at one point, project, and pull back, and then project, again. Then a tiny whitish tooth appeared through the wall of the womb, and blood ran from the tiny aperture.

"I do not think I want to watch this," said Cabot.

"It is the way of life," said Lord Grendel.

There was then more blood and then, clearly, in moments, a tiny head appeared, with red fangs. Tiny reddish eyes then opened, perhaps for the first time, tiny, blazing eyes, and glared balefully outward at Cabot. Then a small paw, with claws, thrust through the widening hole, tearing at it, scratching at it, widening it. Then there seemed a frenzy of activity within, an energetic wriggling, and the whole head and a shoulder emerged, ears laid back, all glistening and bloody, and blood began to run down the side of the womb, profusely, and Cabot stepped back, further, and then, suddenly, a small body emerged, and clung to the outside of the womb, head downward, its claws fastened in the skin, and then it dropped to the floor, belly down, and more blood flowed about, and Cabot stepped even further away. He was then aware of movements about his feet, and several of the tiny urtlike scavengers in the tunnel rushed toward the blood, crouched down in it, and began to lap it up, and one was caught by a hind foot and pulled squealing backward toward the newcomer, and Cabot turned away, and continued down the tunnel.

"Do not be disturbed," said Lord Grendel. "Is a human birth so different? Does not life begin in brutality, just as it often ends in such, as well?"

"What of the womb, its rupture, its wound?" asked Cabot.

"It is a young womb," said Lord Grendel. "I think it will heal. Some wombs have survived as many as fifty emergences."

"How long will we stay here?" asked Cabot.

"We will spend the night here," said Lord Grendel.

"Far from the wombs," suggested Cabot.

"Certainly, if you wish," said Lord Grendel.

At last they came to the end of the tunnel. Cabot could see the darkness of the world's arranged night outside.

"We will leave, early in the morning," said Lord Grendel. "I would sleep sitting up. I would not put my head or face on the floor."

"I understand," said Cabot.

In the morning Cabot started, awake, but there was nothing near him. He breathed more easily.

Lord Grendel was already up, fastening his harness.

Cabot looked about.

"Dear Grendel," said Cabot. "What are these scratches? I did not notice them last night."

"I do not know," said Grendel. "There are many of them, they seem the effect of desperate, agitated movement. They affect an area not more than a few inches in height and width. They are not fresh."

"I do not understand them," said Cabot.

"Nor I," said Lord Grendel.

Cabot, now intent, began to examine the floor of the tunnel, near the exit. "Here," he said, pointing to the floor of the tunnel.

"Yes," said Lord Grendel. "A print."

"That of a human foot," said Cabot.

"A small human foot," said Grendel, examining it.

"See the tininess, the high arch, the delicacy of the print," said Cabot.

"A pretty print," said Lord Grendel.

"That of a human female," said Cabot.

"Clearly," said Lord Grendel. "Killer humans have been in the vicinity. It is probably that of one of their females."

"What of the scratches?" asked Cabot.

"I do not understand them," said Lord Grendel.

"Nor do I," had said Cabot.

They then left the area, and continued their journey to the camp, at which they arrived a second day later, as earlier indicated.

Chapter, the Fifty-Fourth:

There Is Converse in a Rebel Camp

"Dear Cabot," said Statius, "I find the actions of humans mysterious. I fear I will never understand them."

"You may find this incomprehensible, dear friend," said Cabot, "but humans, in their turn, do not always understand the doings of Kurii."

"You left the camp this morning," said Statius, "with a haunch of tarsk, and you returned without it. Scarcely would you devour so much meat in so short a time. What did you do with it?"

"I performed an experiment," said Cabot.

"And was this experiment successful?" inquired Statius.

"More so than I had hoped," said Cabot.

"May I inquire into the nature of this experiment?" asked Statius.

"I may respond obliquely," said Cabot, "if you have no objection."

"No," said Statius. "Do as you wish."

"Surely you are aware," said Cabot, "that more than one enemy has perished within pasangs of the camp."

"I have heard so," said Statius.

"At least four, discovered, and perhaps more, undiscovered," said Cabot.

"I have heard so," said Statius.

"The area is dangerous, clearly, for Kurii," said Cabot, "and yet our human foragers and scouts, alone, and those accompanied by Kurii, our brothers, have traversed the same terrain with impunity."

"It would seem so," said Statius.

"Indeed, even noble Flavion, alone, in his numerous and courageous excursions in our behalf, has fared similarly."

"True," said Statius.

"Do these impunities, and exceptions, not seem peculiar?"

"Assuredly."

"And perhaps they require some explanation?"

"Coincidence," said Statius, "oddities, random fortuities. No other explanation is possible."

"You are familiar with coin gambling?" said Cabot.

"Certainly," said Statius, "and stick gambling, and pebble gambling, and so on. We are fond of gambling."

"Suppose that the same face on a coin turned up repeatedly," said Cabot. Say, it turned up a hundred times, a thousand times, would you not find this surprising?"

"Surely," said Statius.

"Would you deem it a remarkable fortuity?"

"I would want to see the coin," said Statius.

"Precisely," said Cabot. "And that is what I did this morning, examine the coin."

"It had the same face on both sides?"

"So to speak," said Cabot.

"Tal," said Lord Grendel.

His greeting was returned by Statius and his human ally, Tarl Cabot.

Behind Lord Grendel, pressing closely, came the scout, Flavion.

Greetings were exchanged with him, as well.

"How go matters?" asked Cabot of Lord Grendel.

"Our plans proceed apace," said Lord Grendel.

"You have dispatched the runners?" asked Flavion.

"Yes," said Lord Grendel.

"It is unlikely all the bands will be located," said Cabot.

"It will be easier for us to locate them than for the enemy," said Grendel, "as they will not vanish before us, as before them."

"I trust that all the groups will be contacted," said Flavion.

"Surely most," said Lord Grendel.

"And those with power weapons?"

"We trust so," said Lord Grendel.

"We will need as many as possible, to conduct a raid upon the palace," said Flavion. Concern was clear in his Kur, but this concern was not, of course, evident in the dispassionate account rendered in virtue of Cabot's translator.

"Certainly," said Lord Grendel.

"Do you know the location of the bands?" asked Flavion.

"Of some," said Lord Grendel, "and of the others, generally. Would you like particulars?"

"No," said Flavion. "Certainly not! The fewer who know of such things the greater our security."

"True," said Statius. "Under torture, even a Kur might weaken. And under suitable drugs, even a Kur would speak."

"We will risk all, on this bold stroke," said Flavion.

"Your role in this is significant, Lord Flavion," said Lord Grendel, "for, as you know, we must have a secret gathering to marshal our forces and coordinate our plans."

"I have a place in mind," said Flavion, "a shallow, lonely place, which will not be suspected, yet not far from the habitats, and within a brief march of the palace."

"You will have to scout its safety, and determine its appropriateness for our purposes, before we join there, and we will depend on you in this matter," said Lord Grendel.

"You may rely upon me," said Flavion. "If there should prove to be the least danger, or even a semblance of danger, you will be instantly informed."

"Good Flavion," said Statius.

"Noble Flavion," said Lord Grendel.

Lord Grendel then, accompanied by Statius, turned about, to attend to other concerns.

"You have not groomed me of late," said Flavion to Cabot.

"May I have the honor of doing so, presently?" inquired Cabot.

"The honor is mine," said Flavion. "But it had occurred to me that you, though human, stand high in the camp, perhaps highest amongst the humans, save for dear Peisistratus, and that I, though Kur, am lowly, and no more than a scout."

"But you are Kur," said Cabot, "and I am only human."

"True," said Flavion. "But I, more appropriately, I think, now command such services from certain of the female slaves of the camp, the Corinna of Peisistratus, for example."

"I have seen her, naked, combing you," said Cabot.

"I like her naked," said Flavion.

"That is understandable," said Cabot. "Too, it is appropriate for her. She is a slave."

"You require such services of female slaves, do you not?" said Flavion.

"Surely," said Cabot. "We use them to bathe us and towel us, to comb us, to dress us, to tie our sandals, which they bring to us, naked, crawling, on all fours, in their teeth, and such."

"I have seen the female of Statius humbly grooming him, as well," said Flavion.

"She has been conquered," said Cabot.

"A worthless she," said Flavion.

"Statius does not think so," said Cabot.

"Worthless!"

"She seems now content, and happy, and fulfilled," said Cabot.

"Worthless!" repeated Flavion.

"I suspect," said Cabot, "she would now die for him, and he for her."

"I do not understand these things," said Flavion.

"It is simple," said Cabot. "She is his slave, and he her master."

"But they are Kur!" said Flavion.

"All rational species have slavery," said Cabot. "Females seek their masters, males seek their slaves."

"I see," said Flavion.

"Incidentally," said Cabot, "in the case of the girl, Corinna, did you speak to Peisistratus, concerning her service?"

"Should I have done so?" he asked.

"One does not put another's slave to use without his permission," said Cabot.

"But I am Kur," said Flavion.

"It is a matter of courtesy," said Cabot.

"I did not know," said Flavion. "I must hasten to apologize to Peisistratus."

"Your civility is impeccable," said Cabot.

Flavion hesitated. "With respect to your Lita—" he began.

"Yes?"

"Would you like to recover her?"

"The trail is cold," said Cabot. "It is no longer possible."

"But would you like to recover her, if it were possible?"

"Certainly," said Cabot. "She is naive and stupid. She has much to learn about what it is to be a female slave. And I would not mind if she learned it at my feet."

"Perhaps you should not be impatient with her," said Flavion. "Perhaps she did not fully understand what she was. It seems she was angry, and proud, and terribly upset, and not thinking clearly. Doubtless she felt abandoned. Desolated. In anguish. Doubtless she was swept away by her emotions. Indeed, it may have been from the very love of you that she fled."

"There are no excuses for her," said Cabot. "She is in a collar."

"Of course," said Flavion.

"And now she is lost," said Cabot. "And so let us now put the worthless slut from our mind."

"Perhaps her trail might be found," said Flavion. "What would you give for her?"

"If we were on Gor," said Cabot, "perhaps a handful of tarsk-bits, merely to bring her again to my feet."

"She means so little to you?"

"She is only a slave," said Cabot.

"If I knew where she was," said Flavion, "I would not charge you so much as a single tarsk-bit."

"You sound," said Cabot, "as if you knew where she was."

"Certainly not," said Flavion. "But I have wondered, sometime, if it might not be possible for one to find her trail."

"Not even a sleen could trace her now," said Cabot.

"Doubtless," said Flavion.

"But I might be interested in recovering her," said Cabot, "if only to have her learn what it is to be a female slave, and then, doubtless, to sell her."

"I thought so," said Flavion.

"Do you think you might be able to find her trail?" asked Cabot.

"It does not seem likely," said Flavion.

"Then, let us forget the matter," said Cabot.

"Very well," said Flavion. "But forgive me now, for I see noble Peisistratus, and I must hurry to him, to beg his forgiveness for imposing upon him, however innocently and inadvertently, in the case of his Corinna."

"Do not overly concern yourself," said Cabot, "for she is only a slave."

"True," said Flavion. "But, as you have reminded me, she is not mine."

Chapter, the Fifty-Fifth:

What Occurred on the Plain

It was now some ten days later.

The runners had returned, and had met with unexpected success. To be sure, the groups were now muchly reduced, for many of the opposition to Lord Agamemnon had availed themselves, ultimately to their sorrow, of the proffered amnesty. The place of meeting had been made clear, and in accord with Flavion's arrangements. The groups then, unless otherwise informed, would meet at the place designated, which was a broad, sloping, shallow place known as the Vale of Destruction, from an incident which had occurred there more than a hundred years ago, between rival factions for the Theocracy, adherents of the Tenth and the Eleventh Faces of the Nameless One. It was now an isolated area, save for a modest memorial stele, stating the outcome of the dispute. Its location apart from the major courses of the world doubtless recommended it to Flavion. Despite its isolation, and practical remoteness, it was, however, as indicated earlier, not altogether removed from the vicinity of the habitats, and it lay within a night's march of the palace. From it, as a *point d'appui*, the palace might be attacked at the world's dawn. Certainly it seemed suitable for its purpose, and, as it turned out, this proved to be the case.

The gathering was to take place in six days.

"The arrangements have been made, have they not?" asked Lord Grendel.

"I set forth our proposals," said Cabot. "One does not know if they will be acted upon or not."

"You did all that was possible," said Lord Grendel.

"I think so," said Cabot.

"I would," said Lord Grendel, "that the burdens of command rested upon another."

"I am pleased that they repose where they do," said Cabot. "There is no other so fit as you for these risks, and so able to bear the weight and terror of command."

"I am afraid," said Lord Grendel.

"I, too," said Cabot.

"I am weak," said Lord Grendel. "Doubtless it is the human in me."

"Who knows?" said Cabot. "The human in you may prove to be a strength."

"How could that be?" asked Lord Grendel.

"Doubtless it is foolish," said Cabot.

"I think so," said Lord Grendel.

Lord Grendel suddenly lifted his head, and the large, pointed ears turned, as one, in a given direction, cupped, leaning forward, intent, toward the open plain, that not so far from the hemisphere of rocks, amongst which lay, concealed, a womb tunnel, indeed, that very womb tunnel in which Lord Grendel and Cabot, earlier, eluding a Kur patrol, had sought shelter.

A moment afterward Statius' head, as well, lifted, ears erected, and turned similarly.

Cabot was with them, and the three were reconnoitering, far from their base camp. Through this area lay the route proposed for certain of the groups invited to the gathering. Several diverse routes had been delineated, largely to minimize the danger of discovery, and, in the case of discovery, to minimize consequent losses. The rebel forces were not to be concentrated until the gathering, and the subsequent march in force upon the palace.

"What is it?" asked Cabot, softly, for he had heard nothing.

Lord Grendel motioned for Cabot to come forward.

"Look," said Lord Grendel. "But stay back, in the trees."

The three were at the edge of one of the many forested areas outside the major habitats.

Kurii tend to like cover.

From their position they could see down into a plain, and to the rocky outcroppings, and the cliffs, beyond.

"Cattle humans," said Cabot. "You heard their bleatings?"

"Not that," said Grendel.

"They seem to stir," said Cabot. "They are restless!"

"Look there," said Lord Grendel.

"I see," said Cabot. "Humans."

"Yes," said Lord Grendel.

"They seem to be coming out of the cliff," said Cabot.

"As we did," said Grendel, soberly. "They are coming out of the womb tunnel."

"Killer humans," said Cabot.

"Yes," said Grendel.

Cabot could see several of the humans, who moved with stealth and agility, very differently from the lethargic, shambling motions of the massive cattle humans, bred for stupidity and meat.

As Cabot watched, he saw more and more of the humans emerging from the tunnel.

"There must be twenty or more, all males," said Cabot.

"Wait," said Grendel. "There will be females."

"What are they doing in the tunnel?" said Statius. His body language, and the rasp of his phonemes, suggested extreme agitation.

Lord Grendel put out his paw, to restrain his confrere.

"I do not think they are harming the wombs," said Grendel. "I doubt that they even understand them."

"Perhaps they are hunting cattle humans," said Statius.

"I do not doubt they cull the herds when hungry, as would the minions of Agamemnon," said Lord Grendel, "but I think they are otherwise intent at the moment."

"But they are hunting?" said Cabot.

"Not us, surely," said Statius. "They would not know we are here."

"No," said Lord Grendel. "Not us."

The twenty, or so, humans, now emerged from the cave, had arrested their advance, and now seemed to be scanning the plain, surveying the herd of cattle humans.

"Look," said Cabot, pointing. "There are females. Coming out of the cave now, females!"

"Of course," said Lord Grendel.

"They are being driven, herded, with sticks," said Cabot. "They are naked, and roped together, by the neck."

"Certainly," said Grendel. "They are the females of killer humans."

"See how they turn them," said Statius, "and mill them, and they do not know what to do or how to move."

The females were then crowded together.

Sticks struck them, sharply, and they recoiled in pain, trying to turn away from the blows.

"They are crying out, in fear, and in misery," said Statius.

"I cannot hear them, at this distance," said Cabot.

"We can," said Statius.

The females then, presumably at the utterance of some command, or in response to some gesture, all went to all fours, in the grass.

The men, with long, sharpened sticks, continued to look about.

"You think they are hunting?" said Cabot.

"I think so," said Lord Grendel.

"What?" asked Cabot.

"Women," said Lord Grendel. "Indeed, I would not be surprised if some of those women were taken from other groups, killer humans against killer humans."

"I see," said Cabot.

Kurii, it might be mentioned, are not the only species which take the females of other groups for mates, thralls, servants, slaves, and such. It is common amongst rational species. The female has always been an attractive and desiderated object of predation. Indeed, for a male, what other object of interest can compare? Out-group females, in particular, have often been regarded as subject to barter, to sale, to capture, and such. The female has always been regarded as goods, or booty, and energetic and powerful groups have always understood this, and seldom hesitated to act upon this understanding, bringing women, or at least the more attractive women, of weaker groups, or enemy groups, when raided or conquered, to the slave markets.

"See how the women crouch down in fear," said Lord Grendel.

"Yes," said Cabot.

"It is not so different from Gor, is it?" asked Lord Grendel.

"No," said Cabot. "—That is, with slaves."

"Good," said Lord Grendel. "Slaves are to be understood as slaves, and treated as slaves."

"Certainly," said Cabot.

"Even a Lita?" said Lord Grendel.

"Of course," said Cabot.

"The important thing," said Lord Grendel, "is that the order of nature be scrupulously observed, whether primitively, or enhanced with the amenities of civilization."

"Certainly," said Cabot.

"Locked collars are useful," said Lord Grendel.

"That way one, at least, knows to whom they belong," said Cabot.

"Those below," said Statius, "may be held in common, but, too, they might be individually marked, that one know their owner."

"It probably depends on the group," said Grendel.

"It must be much easier to be a slave in civilization than otherwise," said Statius.

"No," said Lord Grendel. "Much to the contrary. A slave in civilization is a thousand times more a slave, a thousand times more helplessly, inalterably, and perfectly a slave, than one in a different venue."

"I do not understand," said Statius.

"Consider something as simple as collars," said Lord Grendel.

"They are attractive," said Statius.

"Of course," said Lord Grendel, "but they are also locked on their necks, and they cannot remove them."

"I see," said Statius.

"Too," said Lord Grendel, "as an additional consideration, as an additional assurance, convenience, and precaution, the slaves are nicely marked."

"Marked?" said Statius.

"Branded," said Lord Grendel, "given beautiful brands, which not only enhance their beauty, but separate them unmistakably from free women. Too, they are forced to wear, if clothed at all, a distinctive garb which could only be that of a slave, a garb so brief, revealing, and provocative that in it, as some see it, they are more naked than naked."

"Still, is their slavery not easier in a civilization than in a rude culture?" asked Statius.

"No," said Lord Grendel, "not at all, for in a civilization, as may not be the case in a barbarism, the truths of nature are recognized, understood, accepted, and explicitly celebrated."

"It depends on the civilization," said Cabot.

"Perhaps," said Lord Grendel.

"A civilization," said Lord Grendel, "is far superior to barbarism. It supplies advantages and benefits unknown to barbarism. In a civilization the ways of nature are not only understood and accepted, even embraced, but, further, beyond anything known in barbarism, they are refined, enhanced, and incorporated deliberately and inextricably into the very nature of society."

"I see," said Statius.

"In a civilization the slave is a particular sort of thing, and understood to be that, and nothing beyond that, nothing further, or other. It is what she is. It is she. She has a recognized nature, condition, status, and identity, which she is incapable of altering or qualifying in any way whatsoever. She is an accepted article of commerce, or form of animal, valued for the labors she can perform and the manifold pleasures, intimate and otherwise, which she must provide. Her appearance in society is no accident. She is no mere accretion or happenstance in society. She is a part of it, an important part of it, and fully ingredient within it. That must be understood. She is implicated in a venerable institution, that of bondage. It is an ancient institution, historically founded, socially proven, honored, and unquestioned. And it is a matter not simply of time and tradition, you must understand, but of mores, customs, practices, an *ethos*, and abundant and tested law."

"I can see," said Statius, "where the slave in a civilization is more helplessly and inalterably a slave than one in a simpler, ruder, more primitive situation, but, still, would their lives not be easier?"

Lord Grendel snorted, a derisive Kur laugh.

"Lord Grendel?" said Statius.

"Perhaps if they strove desperately and mightily to be absolutely pleasing, in all ways," said Lord Grendel.

"I see," said Statius.

"One buys them for a purpose," said Lord Grendel. "They will be kept with perfection."

"They are slaves," said Cabot. "It is the Gorean way."

"But, surely," said Statius, "they will not be cruelly roped, as are the cowering properties below, those of the killer humans."

"More likely they would be chained by the neck, perhaps to a master's slave ring, at his couch's foot," said Cabot.

"But they need not fear the brutality of simple sticks, surely," said Statius, "as those below."

"No," said Lord Grendel. "Seldom would they need to fear the blow of a simple stick."

"That is as I suspected," said Statius.

"But civilization," said Lord Grendel, "improves considerably on such things, advancing far beyond a stick."

"I do not understand," said Statius.

"Surely far superior to a rude stick," said Lord Grendel, "is an article devised to fulfill a similar purpose, and far more effectively, say, a lovely, sturdy, pliant, attractively beaded, well-crafted slave whip."

"A whip?" said Statius.

"Certainly," said Cabot.

"And do the slaves understand such things?"

"If they do not understand them at first," said Cabot, "they will soon understand them."

"I am to understand then, am I not," said Statius, "that the slave in civilization is not only more a slave than a slave in another venue, but that she is in far greater jeopardy, has more to fear, and is likely to be more sharply and perfectly disciplined."

"Yes," said Lord Grendel.

"But they have little to fear, actually," said Cabot, "if they are perfectly pleasing, in all ways."

"But if they are not?" asked Statius.

"Then," said Cabot, "they have a great deal to fear."

"I understand," said Statius.

"The important thing, however," said Cabot, "is not the whip. Indeed, one would hope, on the whole, that it would not be necessary to use it on her. The important thing is the girl's recognition of the whip's jurisdiction over her, that she is subject to it. Her fear of the whip, and her understanding that it will be used on her if she is not pleasing, is usually all the motivation she requires to do her best to please."

"I see," said Statius.

"And interestingly," said Cabot, "after a time, fear of the whip becomes less of a motivation for her than the desire itself to be found pleasing by her master."

"I see," said Statius.

"It is then, in her heart," said Cabot, "that she understands that she is truly a slave."

"Interesting," said Statius.

"There is little point," said Cabot, "in whipping a good slave, save perhaps, occasionally, to remind her that she is a slave."

"They want that," said Lord Grendel.

"It seems so," said Cabot.

"The whip is useful in keeping women in line," said Lord Grendel.

"Yes," said Cabot, "and I trust you remember all this, should the Lady Bina be snatched from the side of Agamemnon, and come into our power."

"She is different," said Lord Grendel. "She is a free woman."

"Some of the killer humans," said Statius, "seem to be threading their way amongst the cattle humans."

"Only two," said Lord Grendel.

"Surely they are not interested in cattle females," said Statius.

"Scarcely," said Lord Grendel. "Not even cattle males are interested in them. In the pens the cattle humans were reproduced by means of artificial insemination."

Suddenly Lord Grendel's ears lifted, and he turned to the field, and he began to gaze intently toward the mingled cattle humans, and he began to tremble, uncontrollably.

"What is wrong?" said Cabot, alarmed.

Statius suddenly uttered a sound, clearly of astonishment, but it was no word, or at least none programmed into Cabot's translator.

"What is it?" asked Cabot, in earnest.

"He heard it," said Statius. "I, too, heard it. Can you not hear it?"

"No," said Cabot. "What is it?"

"Down there," said Statius, intent, pointing.

Cabot shaded his eyes, and narrowed them, but he saw little other than the grass, the cliffs and rocks behind it, the massed cattle, forward, in the plain, and two, only two, killer humans beginning to move through the herd, slowly, deliberately, watchfully, thrusting or striking one beast or another from their path.

"Surely you heard it then!" said Statius.

"No," said Cabot. "What is it?"

"See, toward the nearer part of the herd?" said Statius.

"They are restless, surely," said Cabot.

"Agitated, disturbed," said Statius.

"Something is amongst them!" said Cabot.

"Clearly," said Statius.

Cabot then heard a cry from below, from one of the killer humans, who now pointed toward a portion of the herd, rather where the stirring had been remarked. He, and his fellow, then began to press more vigorously, more intently, roughly, amongst the gross, sluggish bodies of the herd.

Then Cabot, for the first time, heard the sound which had been noted earlier by Lord Grendel and Statius, and, at almost the same time, saw a small, struggling body in the grasp of one of the cattle humans, and he then heard the sound again, and again, as the small body was lifted and shaken in fury by its obese captor, the sound of the bell from the pens, the bell which the cattle humans were to unwittingly follow to the slaughter bench, and Lord Grendel, with a roar of rage, had sprung from the shelter of the trees, and was bounding, on all fours, on feet and knuckles of forepaws, in Kur haste, toward the herd.

The cattle human, massive even for a cattle human, doubtless the herd leader, soon noted the approach of a gigantic Kurlike figure moving toward him with great rapidity.

He instantly flung his prize, rolling to the grass, bell jangling, from him, and backed into the herd.

Cabot had little doubt Lord Grendel was intent upon tearing his throat out.

Lord Grendel stopped, though, at the edge of the herd, lifted his mighty arms, and roared, a Kur roar that echoed back from the cliffs beyond.

The two killer humans were not unaware of his arrival, and they, exchanging cries, something between speech and signals, ceased to prosecute their passage through the herd, and made their way back, almost as though through chest-high water, to the company of their colleagues, nearer the exit of the womb tunnel, and on the herd's far side.

At the same side the small figure freed by the massive cattle human, flung from him, regained its feet, and fled through the grass.

Lord Grendel was then between the fleeing figure and the herd, and, farther back, the killer humans.

Nothing moved from the herd, and the herd leader, bleating in fear, and protest, moved further back into the herd, using it as a wall to separate himself from the angry, hostile figure who was threateningly close.

Some of the herd held rocks, and three or four held branches, but none ventured to engage Lord Grendel.

Indeed, in moments, most of the beasts of the herd, in their doltish fashion, had returned to their pursuits, as though nothing had happened, scratching for grubs and worms, digging here and there to uncover edible roots. From the mouth of one dangled a small snake.

The killer humans, on the far side of the herd, had now congregated together, and were regarding Lord Grendel, who roared once more.

Cabot then, bow strung, an arrow to the string, a quiver at his hip, laden with the birds of death, emerged from the forest. So, too, did Statius.

Whereas the killer humans might, or might not, have surprised and attacked a single, preferably unarmed Kur, it was a different matter altogether to attack two who were aware, ready, and aroused. Also, although they did not themselves possess the bow, they understood it. They would not go against a bow with sticks, and certainly not across a distance, in full daylight.

Accordingly, the killer humans brought their neck-roped females to their feet, placed themselves between the females and the herd, and Lord Grendel, Cabot, and Statius, and, with a few cries and strokes of their sticks, herded them away, withdrawing behind them, with an occasional vigilant glance cast backward.

Lord Grendel stepped backward, and then looked about. He was still visibly agitated. His body shook. His nostrils flared, and fangs protruded, glistening with saliva.

Cabot was unwilling even to speak to him in his present state.

Lord Grendel crouched down, and fastened his paws in the grass. His mighty chest heaved, his head was down.

Then he lifted his head. "Where is she?" he asked.

"Gone," said Cabot, looking about.

Lord Grendel uttered a long, strange noise, less of disappointment, or anger, as of the ventilation of some wracking agitation.

The small figure which had fled away, bell jangling, was blonde and shapely. Too, interestingly, its small wrists were pinioned behind her back.

"They would have killed her," said Lord Grendel. "They would have cut her with stones, thrust sticks into her, broke her with rocks and clubs, chewed the skin from her bones."

"Understandably," said Cabot. "Some, at least, would remember her from the pens."

The fugitive was, of course, the Lady Bina.

"It is surprising to find her here," said Cabot. "I would have thought rather that she would have been silked, bejeweled, and veiled, and regally ensconced at the side of Agamemnon."

"How has she lived, thusly?" asked Lord Grendel, rising up, now again himself.

"Not well, I would suppose," said Cabot.

"Her hands were held behind her, were they not?" asked Lord Grendel.

"Fastened there," said Cabot, "in steel, in slave bracelets."

"I understand now the scratches in the cave, the print of the foot," said Lord Grendel.

"Yes," said Cabot. "The print was doubtless hers, she having taken refuge in the tunnel, and the scratches were doubtless the results of her attempts to free herself of the light but effective impediments which constrained her."

"Stone will not conquer metal," said Lord Grendel.

"And slave bracelets are not designed to be slipped by their occupant," said Cabot. "They are manufactured to guarantee a female's utter helplessness."

"Doubtless such things are known to any slave," said Lord Grendel.

"Sooner or later, surely," said Cabot.

"They had to be put on her," said Lord Grendel.

"Yes," said Cabot, "but for what reason, and by whom?"

"How insulting," said Lord Grendel, "that she, a free woman, should have been put in slave bracelets."

"Insulting, perhaps," said Cabot. "But one notes that they will hold a free woman with the same perfection as a slave."

"It seems clear," said Lord Grendel, "that she was in hiding, for some reason, and perhaps for some time, and was then discovered and flushed out of concealment by the killer humans."

"One can understand how she would seem an excellent catch for them, in their hunting of women. Indeed, they may have noted her, and been searching for her, for some time."

"She sought refuge amongst the cattle humans," said Lord Grendel. "That must have taken great courage, for she has feared them, terribly, since the pens."

"Her act, I suspect," said Cabot, "was one less of courage than of terror, of sudden and thoughtless desperation, an irrational flight at any cost to escape capture by the killer humans."

"It is true," said Lord Grendel, "that we had attempted to assure her of the harmlessness of cattle humans."

"In that," said Cabot, "we were mistaken. It might have been true once, but it seems untrue now. Some cattle humans in any event now arm themselves, however primitively, and attack others, and encroach on the feeding territories of others, and so on. Indeed, they have now exceeded, it seems, their former bovine placidity, now that they are not cared for, and fed. Now, it seems, they have learned cruelty, predation, and war."

"They are becoming more human," said Lord Grendel.

"Or more Kur," said Cabot.

Grendel looked about.

"The Lady Bina has again eluded us," said Cabot. "She has escaped."

"Nonsense," said Lord Grendel. "The trail is fresh. A Kur child could follow it."

There was, at that moment, a cry of Kur elation, and greeting, and Cabot and Lord Grendel turned about to see Statius approaching, dragging behind him, by means of a stout rope on her neck, stumbling, filthy, terrified, only the remnant of a stained tunic left to her, her wrists pinioned behind her in slave bracelets, the Lady Bina.

"The Lady Bina returns," said Cabot.

Statius hurled the Lady Bina triumphantly, contemptuously, to the feet of Lord Grendel. "Here," cried Statius, "is the traitress, the Lady Bina!"

The Lady Bina, helpless at the feet of Lord Grendel, squirmed in misery, and terror. The shred of tunic remaining to her was filthy. Her hair was tangled and unkempt, and caked with dried blood. Her body was muchly soiled and her knees were red, too, with dried blood. With one foot Statius put her to her belly and then pulled her wrists up, behind her, so that their confinement might be obvious.

"Slave bracelets," said Cabot.

Statius then thrust her wrists down, angrily, and put his clawed foot on her back, pressing her against the earth.

She wept.

"Here she is, the traitress," said Statius, "now ours!"

"She is in the presence of Lord Grendel," said Cabot. "Kneel her, fittingly."

Angrily Statius drew her by the hair to a high kneeling position before Lord Grendel, and then thrust her head to the ground, before him.

"Kiss the feet of your lord," said Statius, "before justice is done to you."

Terrified, the Lady Bina began to desperately kiss and lick the feet of Lord Grendel.

"Shall we kill her now?" asked Statius.

"Let me see her," said Lord Grendel.

Statius seized her by the hair and pulled her up, kneeling, so that Lord Grendel could see her face.

"Bend her backward," said Cabot.

This was done and the body of the Lady Bina was then placed in the position of the slave bow.

Many times Cabot had so positioned women. In this position they are helpless and the nature of their figure is well exhibited.

This position, while one of great indignity for a free woman, is one with which a slave is likely to be familiar.

"She is nicely formed," said Cabot. "Perhaps if she were cleaned up, if she were soaked and scrubbed, if she were thoroughly washed, and combed and brushed, and silked, she might be made a slave."

"No!" said Statius. "She is a traitress. She must be put to the slowest and most terrible of all deaths. She must be brought to the bar of justice. Recall our fallen friends and comrades! Recall our betrayal, the slaughter at the arsenal!"

"Such things will be well recalled," said Lord Grendel. "Kneel her up."

Statius pulled the Lady Bina up, to an upright kneeling position, before Lord Grendel.

His rope was still on her neck.

The lips of the Lady Bina quivered. She trembled. She was too frightened to speak.

"Should she not kneel with her knees spread," asked Cabot, "that she might thusly plead to be spared, that her life might thereafter be devoted to the service and pleasure of men?"

"No!" said Statius.

"She is a free woman," said Lord Grendel.

"Many free women, in dire straits," said Cabot, "so plead, and in a thousand other ways, as well, to escape the edge of the sword. Have I not seen them, in burning cities, strip themselves, and kneel, and grovel, and belly and squirm, and kiss and lick fervently at the feet and legs of conquerors, begging to be spared, begging to live, begging mercy, begging desperately and with their whole heart to be granted the collar of a slave?"

"That is what they want anyway," said Lord Grendel. "That is what they all want."

"And so?" said Cabot.

"The Lady Bina is different," said Lord Grendel. "She is a true free woman."

"There are no true free women," said Cabot. "There are only women who have not yet met their master, only women not yet in their collar."

"The Lady Bina," said Statius, "is not a slave. She is a free woman and as a free woman must accept the penalties incurred by her crimes, crimes both obvious and grievous. Such crimes cannot be ignored, or eradicated, by something as simple as the snapping shut of a close-fitting metal circlet."

"True," said Lord Grendel.

It seemed the Lady Bina would collapse, but Statius, a hand in her hair, held her upright.

"Her face," said Cabot, "is filthy, and her hair. There is dried blood about her mouth."

"Too, on her legs, and knees," said Lord Grendel.

"Yes," said Cabot.

"That is muchly how she lived," said Grendel, "at least in the tunnel. After emergences she knelt in the blood, bent over, her hands helpless behind her, and lapped at the blood, competing for it with scavengers."

"A cheek is marred," said Cabot, looking closely at the kneeling girl.

"From the bite of a scavenger, competing with her for the blood," said Lord Grendel. "It is tiny. It is not serious. It will heal. If it had been from the bite of a child it would have gone through to the bone, or she might have lost an ear."

He then regarded the Lady Bina, sorrowfully. "You had the wisdom to avoid the children, did you not?" he asked.

She nodded, head down, numbly.

Statius jerked at the rope on her neck. She made a tiny sound, of misery. "Let us bind her and cover her with blood, and put her in the tunnel for the scavengers," he said.

"But," said Lord Grendel, "that would be too quick, would it not?"

"Yes," said Statius, thoughtfully. "You are right. That would be too quick."

"We will take her back to the camp, for judgment," said Lord Grendel. "Then we may be judged together."

"No!" cried Statius.

"It can be no other way," said Lord Grendel.

"I will stand by you to the death," said Statius.

"I, too," said Cabot.

"But I do not think the others will," said Statius.

Lord Grendel then turned away from the captive, in grief, and Statius, with one clawed foot, impatiently, angrily, spurned her to her belly, where she had knelt.

"Lord Grendel," she whispered. It was the first time she had spoken. Lord Grendel turned to face her. She lay on her belly before him, miserable and filthy, in the tattered and stained shred of her tiny garment, weak, doubtless starving, her small hands fastened behind her in the slave bracelets, Statius' rope on her neck. She lifted her head, weakly, just a little. "I am innocent," she whispered.

Chapter, the Fifty-Sixth:

What Occurred Within the Vale of Destruction

"It is dark," said Cabot. "Perhaps we are unexpected."

"Statius," said Lord Grendel. "Send Flavion to us."

"He is not here," said Statius.

"Then," said Lord Grendel to his human ally, Tarl Cabot, "we are expected."

"It will be several hours until dawn," said Cabot.

"There may be an early dawn, even an early noon," said Lord Grendel, looking about.

In the darkness, about them, were tense figures, several, silent, not much moving.

"Flavion believes we are conjoined to march in force on the palace," said Cabot.

"I wonder if he thinks we are so stupid as to actually intend that," said Statius.

"I do not doubt that Agamemnon is a genius," said Lord Grendel. "But a common fault amongst those of genius is to assume that all others are fools."

"The others were informed of our plans, and the risks?" said Cabot.

"Yes," said Lord Grendel, "and offered the opportunity to withdraw."

"How many were lost?" asked Cabot.

"None," said Statius. "Neither Kur, nor, surprisingly, human."

Cabot could not see much about him, for the darkness. His Kur brethren were better adapted to absorb and profit from the minimal light, but even for them, he gathered, the darkness was limiting and opprobrious.

As Cabot and Lord Grendel, and others of their group, had

arrived earlier, in the arranged dusk, he had assessed the terrain, rather as might have been expected of one of his caste. They were in a broad, shallow valley, rather like a gentle, expanded, wide bowl of grass. It was rather oval, something less than a half pasang in length, and little more than a quarter of a pasang in width. At one end of the valley was a simple, memorial stele, recounting what had once occurred there, something over a hundred years earlier, a victory in which the forces of a Tenth Face of the Nameless One had succumbed, and those of an Eleventh Face of the Nameless One had emerged victorious.

"There was a massacre here, was there not?" inquired Cabot.

"It was long ago," said Lord Grendel.

"It seems a good place for a massacre," said Cabot.

"So, it does," said Lord Grendel, "and I do not doubt but what Flavion selected it with that thought in mind."

"It would be hard to climb the slopes, to escape," said Cabot.

"We will be encircled," said Lord Grendel. "One would climb into the very muzzles of weaponry."

"The depression, too," said Cabot, "makes a splendid crossfire possible, from which oppositely situated cohorts would be in little danger."

"I trust, too," said Lord Grendel, "you are aware of certain resonances here which would be savored by Lord Agamemnon."

"I was informed of the message of the stele," said Cabot, "that it was here, in this very place, though long ago, that an Eleventh Face of the Nameless One became Theocrat of the World."

"Flavion and Agamemnon, it seems," said Lord Grendel, "could not resist having their moment of theatricality."

"Is that you, Archon?" asked Cabot.

"Yes," said Archon.

"Are you all right?" asked Cabot.

"I feel like a tethered verr," said he, "staked out by hunters, hoping to lure in a larl."

"The analogy is apt," said Statius, "save that there may be no hunters."

"How many are here?" asked Cabot. Reports had come to Lord Grendel from time to time, consonant with the arrivals of diverse groups.

"Most, if not all," said Lord Grendel.

"Four then, or five, hundred," said Cabot.

"Three hundred and fifty, perhaps four hundred," said Lord Grendel.

"The trenches have been dug," said Statius.

This had been done easily enough, and presumably unnoted by an enemy, for it would approach later, utilizing the cover of darkness.

"They will provide little protection," said Archon, "if the minions of Agamemnon stand over them, or enter them, filling them with fire."

"How long until dawn?" asked Cabot.

"Not long," said Lord Grendel, "as we are now well gathered."

"No," said Cabot. "Surely Ahn."

"My dear Cabot," said Lord Grendel, "you are not now on Gor, but within a Steel World. Dusks, dawns, nights, days, are muchly subject to discretion."

"Yes," said Cabot.

"And weathers, and such," said Lord Grendel.

"I see," said Cabot.

"I wonder if the daylight will come brightly, instantly," said Statius. "Our human allies would then be briefly blinded, as they are so tardy in their optical adjustments."

"Given the graduality of dawns and dusks on the worlds in which the human evolved," said Lord Grendel, "there was little need for rapid optical adjustments."

If I might add a note here, it should be understood that the human being is primarily a diurnal form of life. More importantly, the Kur might emerge suddenly from the darkness of caves into bright sunlight, to hunt, and, say, the sleen might similarly emerge suddenly from darkness, though commonly from its burrow. It seems reasonably clear then that the Nameless One, in its wisdom, or its blind, adventitious lotteries, casting its cards as it pleased, favored swift optical adjustments in the Kur, and the sleen, and doubtless in several other forms of life, as well. The sleen, incidentally, is predominantly a nocturnal animal. The Kur, we note, can function efficiently, and comfortably, in both light and darkness, provided the darkness is not absolute. In this respect the Kur is clearly superior to the human, at least. As the human is predominantly a diurnal animal, its dark vision is, we suppose, relatively unimportant. To be sure, it can make adjustments to varying light conditions, but, as noted, these adjustments are relatively slow, or slow, at least, compared to those of the Kur and sleen.

"If I were Agamemnon," said Lord Grendel, "I would in my arrangements lighten the world somewhat but, on the whole, keep it rather dark. In this way his folk may function effectively, directing their fire efficiently, and our humans will be essentially helpless, effectively neutralized."

"Aii!" cried Cabot, suddenly, in pain, and shouts of dismay rang through the field, from both Kur and human, for the world was suddenly, instantly, flooded with an intense light.

"Trenches!" cried Lord Grendel, and others.

And those in the valley, Kur and human, flung themselves bodily into these narrow, rude shelters.

Then, just as suddenly, it seemed, certainly from Cabot's perspective, the world was plunged into complete darkness, and, then, at the same time, lines of fire, traceable as streaks from all sides, many crisscrossing, tore into the valley.

Even the Kurii in the valley were temporarily blinded.

The forces of Agamemnon, forewarned, had, at a signal, it was later determined, closed or covered their eyes, opening them, adjusted as they had been for the darkness, a moment later, and opened fire.

It had taken the forces of Agamemnon a moment after the blast of light to align their weapons and begin to empty a thousand charges into the valley, but, to their amazement, a moment later, it seemed that the valley was empty.

This caused consternation in their ranks, but this was decidedly temporary, as the nature of their foes' disappearance was readily explicable.

Indeed, very shortly, the firing ceased.

"I cannot see," said Cabot. "Grendel, are you here? Where are you?"

"We must congratulate Agamemnon," said Lord Grendel. His voice came from Cabot's right. "His brilliance is unparalleled. Not even we could adjust from darkness to that light in so brief a time. Had we not prepared the trenches most of us would now be dead."

"Can you see?" said Cabot.

"What a splendid enemy is Agamemnon!" said Lord Grendel, rapturously. "Let us salute him! Great enemies make for great wars. To be opposed to so great an enemy does our small and lowly cause infinite honor. To challenge larls is noble, to stamp on urts is inglorious, even embarrassing."

"I fear we are the urts," said Cabot. "Can you see?"

"Certainly," said Lord Grendel. "Can you?"

"No," said Cabot.

"Wait a few moments," said Lord Grendel.

Some desultory fire came from one side or another, but it did little more than gouge up buckets of earth, and, here and there, as later became clear, tear and blacken grass.

Then, again, the firing stopped.

"Charges are precious," said Lord Grendel. "They will not waste them. They will come down to finish us off."

"I cannot see to use the bow," said Cabot.

"Do not concern yourself," said Lord Grendel. "Those who rise from the trench with weapons will be the first targeted."

"They will not meet you with axes?" said Cabot.

"Certainly not," said Lord Grendel.

"We have failed," said Cabot.

"Do not despair," said Lord Grendel.

At that point it became lighter in the world.

Even the humans could see.

But no enemies descended into the Vale of Destruction.

The rebels waited in the trenches.

Some moments later they were addressed by a loud, mechanically reproduced voice, smiting the vale with authority. It spoke in Kur, but those humans with translators, as Cabot, had no difficulty in following it.

"That is not the voice of Agamemnon," said Cabot.

"No, it is not," said Lord Grendel. "I am pleased that you can discriminate amongst Kur speakers."

"Amongst some," said Cabot, not altogether pleasantly.

"Still, it is an achievement for a human," said Lord Grendel.

"Thank you," said Cabot.

The voice, as it turned out, was that of one of Agamemnon's high lieutenants, that of he whom, for convenience of reference in Gorean, we named Lucullus. The message was simple, and direct.

It was a summons for the rebels to surrender instantly, submit to the chains of prisoners, and await the mercy of Lord Agamemnon.

"They do not wish to risk approaching us," said Statius, "while we have weapons, however few and inadequate they might be." There were, at that time, seven power weapons in the trenches. An eighth weapon, we may recall, had been entrusted to the scout, Flavion.

"The trenches provide some cover," said Archon.

"Not much," said Lord Grendel. "This generous offer, I suspect, is motivated less by considerations of tactics, mercy, or military courtesy, than the desire to bring us helplessly and humiliatingly before Agamemnon's tribunal of retribution."

"Are you good at resisting prolonged and extreme tortures?" asked Statius of Cabot.

"I rather suspect not," said Cabot.

"Would you like me, then, to kill you now, mercifully?" asked Statius.

"Not really," said Cabot.

"My dear Statius," said Lord Grendel, "there are sophisticated tortures available to Agamemnon to which even a Kur might object."

"Would you like me, then, to kill you now, mercifully?" asked Cabot of Statius.

"Forgive me, dear friend," said Statius. "I trust you did not take offense. In a moment of weakness I thought of you more as human, and less as Kur."

"I am human," said Cabot.

"What is human?" said Lord Grendel.

"Perhaps it would be churlish," said Statius, "to deny Agamemnon his pleasures."

"There are limits to my civility," said Cabot.

"And mine," said Statius.

"And so what is to be done?" asked Archon.

"When they come to kill us, we shall meet them, as we can," said Statius.

The message of Lucullus had now echoed several times throughout the valley, and no answer had arisen from the trenches.

Each time the message had seemed more severe, and less patient.

"Should we not respond?" asked Cabot.

"We are waiting," said Lord Grendel.

"What for?" asked Statius.

"For victory," said Lord Grendel.

"You are mad," said a Kur. "Let us emerge from the trenches, and rush upon their weaponry, thus dying as befits Kurii."

"Wait," said Lord Grendel.

"Look!" said Cabot.

Here and there, on one side or the other, some Kurii, and some humans, perhaps some twenty or thirty, emerged from the trenches and, weaponless, arms lifted in surrender, began to climb upward, toward the perimeters of the vale.

"Come back!" called Lord Grendel, and others, but their cries, if heard, were unheeded.

"Fools, fools," said Lord Grendel. "Piteous, trusting fools!"

Those who had emerged from the trenches were allowed to climb almost to the very rim of the vale before the orders were given and they were incinerated on the slopes.

The light then began to dim, and soon, again, Cabot, and other humans, found themselves in practical darkness, save for some fires on the slopes, brief, soon-extinguished fires, marking places where the grass, here and there, in half circles of some yards, had been ignited by sheets of blazing, discharged weaponry.

"They realize now," said Lord Grendel, "that we will not surrender."

"Their chains will remain empty," said Statius.

"What is going on?" asked Cabot.

He sensed Lord Grendel rising in the trench, and looking about. "Yes," he said.

"Yes," said Statius.

"What is going on?" asked Cabot.

"They are coming now, from all sides," said Lord Grendel. "They descend into the valley, in ranks, weapons leveled."

"We are lost," said Cabot. "I failed."

"This is the moment," said Lord Grendel. "They are intent on us. They are unaware. There is limited visibility, even for them. They have their backs to the vale's perimeter. They no longer have the height of the vale. They are caught between the height and the trenches."

"I cannot see!" said Cabot.

"Now! Now!" said Lord Grendel. "They are coming over the rim, hundreds, multiply armed. Dear Cabot, you were successful! The minions of Agamemnon are only now aware that there are others behind them."

Cabot could now hear cries of surprise, of questioning.

"They turn about! They are confused," said Lord Grendel. "They do not know if they are friend or foe! They understand nothing! Perhaps they are reinforcements, additions to their numbers!"

Suddenly there were cries of rage, and the crackling, and streaming of weapons.

Lancets of fire cut through the darkness.

Cabot could hear the sounds of fighting, of grappling, the hiss of weaponry, the striking of blades, axes, doubtless, into shoulders and flesh.

"Rise from the trenches, attack, attack, Kur brothers!" called Lord Grendel, and his cries were echoed, from trench to trench, and coursed down the lengths of trenches, and Cabot, and the humans, confused, bewildered, were aware of mighty bodies, howling with cries of war, scrambling out of the trenches.

It was perhaps a quarter of an Ahn later that it began to grow light, again, gradually, and the routine of the world, adjusted to its timers, certain obstructive circuitries destroyed, returned to its normality.

Cabot, and other humans, wonderingly, slowly emerged from the trenches, to thread their way through soft, furrowed earth, soaked with blood, through seared grass and lost weapons, amongst fallen, scattered bodies, contorted and awry, some blackened by fire, others dismembered. Here and there lay a Kur, moaning, bleeding. Elsewhere a line of sullen Kurii, disarmed, were being fitted with chains.

Cabot sought out Lord Grendel.

"It is victory, is it not?" he asked.

"The tide is turned," said Grendel. "Those from the small camps, the survivors of the fleet's disaster, in their hundreds, are now with us, and have armed themselves with the weapons of our foes. Lord Agamemnon is now on the defensive. For the first time we may hope for success."

"I am pleased," said Cabot.

"It is to you we owe this victory," said Lord Grendel.

"I did only as you advised," said Cabot.

"It was to you that Lord Arcesilaus entrusted his ring," said Lord Grendel.

"I know not why it was not to you," said Cabot.

"You were the ideal herald of his hopes," said Lord Grendel. "Were you not, in your way, proof that there might be amity betwixt allies, Kur and human? Too, you could make clear the value of human allies, and the nature of our common interests. That these species could be allied at all would astonish Kurii, and the more so that their alliance might prove fruitful. Who better in such a cause than a human warrior to bear to Kur warriors the ring of Arcesilaus, mightiest of Kurii, mightiest of the foes of Agamemnon?"

"I think," said Cabot, ruefully, "that they might have been shamed to face a fellow Kur in such role, one still with pride and status, who did not share their dishonor and degradation. A lowly human, thus, I fear, might prove a less embarrassing visitor to their great gathering, that beyond the small camps, where they were to await the ropes or knives."

"Too," said Lord Grendel, "with all due respect, I suspect few Kurii would care to soil themselves with such a mission, with contacting the defeated, the unworthy, ruined, and fallen."

"It was due to the ring," said Cabot, "that I was enabled to enter their great camp, that of the gathering, engage their attention, and certify my authority to speak, and plead, on behalf of Lord Arcesilaus."

"You did well, friend Cabot," said Lord Grendel.

"Your subsequent contacts with their agents, secretly accomplished, enabled their intervention in the affairs of the world."

"We gave them the opportunity, if not of redemption, in their own eyes," said Lord Grendel, "at least that of striking a blow for the world."

"I fear many still feel it incumbent upon them to submit to the rope or knife," said Cabot.

"That is madness," said Lord Grendel, "though this, I recognize, may be no more than an evidence of my weakness, a hesitation due to the human in me."

"I tried to convince them," said Cabot, "that defeat in a struggle well waged cannot be accounted dishonor."

"And were you successful?"

"I fear not."

"What then brought them to the field?"

"To do honor to Lord Arcesilaus," said Cabot.

"They are Kur," said Lord Grendel, proudly.

At this point Statius joined Lord Grendel and his human ally, Tarl Cabot. Statius carried a weighty Kur ax, double-headed, and each blade bore blood. Statius, as other Kurii from the trenches, had been active in the field. The Kurii of Agamemnon had not only been taken unawares, but had been found themselves trapped between the fleet's survivors and the forces under the command of Lord Grendel.

"Four hundred are chained, and ready to be slain," said Statius to Lord Grendel. "To be sure, fearsome tortures may be arranged."

"Those are the very chains, I would suppose, which had been brought for us," said Cabot.

"Yes," said Statius, "and now they wear them themselves."

"Only four hundred?" asked Cabot. "We must have been encircled by two to three thousand foes."

Lord Grendel did not immediately respond.

Then Cabot looked about, at the broad field. "I see," he said.

"Kurii seldom take prisoners," said Lord Grendel. "Too, you must understand that the attack of a Kur is commonly fatal."

"What of our wounded?" asked Cabot.

"They will be attended to," said a Kur.

"And the enemy wounded?"

"They will be killed," said a Kur.

"Lord Grendel!" protested Cabot.

"It is the Kur way," said Lord Grendel.

"Let the Kur way change," said Cabot.

"Do not be weak, commander," said a Kur.

"They were defeated," said a Kur. "It is a disgrace for them to live."

"Tend their wounds," said Lord Grendel. "If they wish, they may kill themselves later."

"Would you tend and heal a foe whom you might then face again, and less successfully?" asked a Kur.

"You need not follow me," said Lord Grendel. "I am weak."

"You are lord," said the Kur.

"Obey him," said Statius. Then he turned to Lord Grendel. "What of the four hundred? Surely, even should you not subject them to the tortures which they in turn would have inflicted upon us, you will have them slain, swiftly, if you would prefer."

"Remove their chains," said Lord Grendel.

"Madness!" cried Statius. "None will follow you, if you do this!"

"I will follow him," said Cabot.

"I, too," said Archon.

"I, too, of course," said Statius, "but who else would do so?"

"I believe Lord Lucullus commanded the forces of Agamemnon," said Lord Grendel. "Is he accounted for?"

"He is not among the dead, or the prisoners," said a Kur.

"Some escaped," said a Kur.

"What of our scout, Flavion?"

"He, too," said a Kur, "is not accounted for."

Lord Grendel then turned to a Kur. "Please convey my greetings, and thanks, to Mitonicus, and ask him to attend us at his convenience." Mitonicus, who had commanded the fleet's survivors, was a minor admiral. He had brought his four ships, damaged as they were, back to the world, that they not be lost to Agamemnon's navy. He was one of the few surviving officers, as most, if they had not perished in the fray itself, their ships destroyed about them, melting and fragmenting in the silent fields of space, had hung themselves in shame, some aboard their returning vessels, others, having made worldfall, in the groves about the small camps.

"I cannot do so, commander," said a Kur, "as he has returned, with his men, to the gathering."

"The work here is not done," said Lord Grendel.

"He has departed, commander," said the Kur.

"Mitonicus has the ring of Arcesilaus now, does he not?" asked Lord Grendel.

"Yes," said Cabot. "It seemed fitting that he should bear it."

"I agree," said Lord Grendel.

"The four hundred must now, surely, be killed," said Statius.

"No, free them," said Lord Grendel, wearily.

"What are we do to?" asked Archon.

"We will return to the forests," said Lord Grendel. "A precarious stasis now exists. With the departure of Mitonicus, we are unable to force our war to a favorable resolution, but, too, I think that Agamemnon, as well, now lacks the power to dislodge us from our retreats. Further, he must be wary of Mitonicus and his cohorts."

"Not if Mitonicus and his fellows all hang themselves," said Cabot.

"I do not think they will do that," said Lord Grendel.

"Why not?" asked Cabot.

"Because," said Lord Grendel, "they have now tasted victory."

Chapter, the Fifty-Seventh:

What Occurred in the Camp of Lord Grendel

The gate of the forest camp of Lord Grendel swung open, and an astonished, elated Peisistratus, who had governed the camp in the absence of its lord, rushed forward, stumbling, half-speechless, bewildered.

"Dear Grendel!" he cried, "we had report that your plan had failed, and your command destroyed, wiped out, each and every one of our fellows, in the Vale of Destruction! Praise the Priest-Kings! You, and Cabot, and some others, Statius, I see, and some few, have escaped!"

"Praise the Nameless One, if you will," said Lord Grendel, "if it pleases you to do so, but do not praise Priest-Kings, not in this camp, for they had, I am sure, little influence on the day, nor had they had influence, would it have turned out as it did."

"Forgive me, Lord Grendel," sobbed Peisistratus, "but I am overcome with joy, that you have escaped the slaughter."

There was, behind him, as well, elated denizens of the camp. His Corinna was eagerly heeling him, Statius' female hurried forth, to kneel at his feet, rubbing her head against his leg, and other slaves crowded about, kneeling, weeping with joy, and the seven or eight humans and Kurii who had been commanded, to their sorrow, to stay within the camp, to protect and hold it, with its goods and slaves, now pressed forward, jubilantly seizing comrades in arms, and crying out with pleasure, and some of the Kurii bounded about, and turned in the air, and then scratched in the dirt and flung spumes of celebration yards into the air.

"It is true there was slaughter," said Grendel.

"You are followed, surely," said Peisistratus.

"I do not think so," said Grendel.

"But Agamemnon would surely follow up his victory and press a determined, vengeful pursuit."

"I am sure he would do so," agreed Grendel.

"But you were not followed?"

"I do not think so," said Grendel.

"How fortunate that you have escaped!" said Peisistratus.

"We have not escaped," said Grendel. "We have returned."

"But it was reported you did not even reach the palace," said Peisistratus.

"That is true," said Grendel.

"The massacre, it is said, took place in the Vale of Destruction," said Peisistratus.

"That is true," said Grendel.

"Hundreds must have perished," said Peisistratus.

"That is true, and even more," said Grendel.

"You have returned with few," said Peisistratus.

"And left with few," said Grendel.

"The others?"

"Returned to our several camps," said Grendel.

"I do not understand," said Peisistratus.

"The victory was ours," said Grendel. "Slaughter befell, but it was upon the minions of Agamemnon."

"I cannot believe it!" said Peisistratus.

"We are hungry," said Grendel.

"Slaves," cried Peisistratus. "Prepare a feast!"

The slaves sprang to their feet, scurrying away.

"But it was reported that you perished in the Vale of Destruction," said Peisistratus.

"And who conveyed this report?" asked Cabot.

"The sole survivor," said Peisistratus.

"Flavion," said Cabot.

"Yes," said Peisistratus.

"Flavion was mistaken," said Grendel. "As you can see he was not the sole survivor."

"Happily!" said Peisistratus.

"Thanks be to the Nameless One!" cried a voice. "Glory to our cause!"

In the threshold of the camp, startled, and seemingly jubilant, stood Flavion, who then rushed forward to embrace Lord Grendel,

Cabot, Statius, Archon, and others, and then he bounded about, leaping into the air, uttering screeches of pleasure, and then, alighting, again and again, he reached down and cast flags of dirt into the air, and then, struggling to govern his emotions, he returned, fawning and cringing, to the presence of the Lord Grendel.

"Joy! Joy!" he cried. "Did I not see you die?"

"It seems not," said Cabot.

"I waited with you in the Vale of Destruction," said Flavion, "but grew suspicious, and withdrew to confirm my suspicions. Unnoted, I ascended the rim of the vale, where, to my horror, I saw minions of Agamemnon, countless minions, converging on our position! I was cut off! I could not return to warn you! Discovered, I fought and slew six enemies, but, turning, saw what could only be the initiation of a most complete and grievous slaughter. I saw them descend, our terrible foes, in their thousands, into the vale, heavily armed. Only one outcome could proceed, given a position so untenable, and odds so fearful. So, stricken in heart, anguished, I must return to the camp, that our fellows be apprised at least of the danger in which they must then stand."

"Noble Flavion," said Grendel, "how brave you are, how well you did."

"I should have fought my way back, to die with you," said Flavion.

"No," said Grendel. "Of what avail could you have been? Obviously your duty was to attain and warn the camp."

"Better I had died with the others," said Flavion.

"Few died," said Cabot. "Of our forces."

"Many of those of Agamemnon," said Archon.

"The victory was ours," said Statius.

"Ours?" said Flavion. It seemed a shudder spread through his fur. "Splendid!" he said, suddenly.

"Mariners intervened, survivors from the fleet's ruin," said Cabot.

"Afterward," said Statius, "they withdrew to their place of ignominious gathering, the place of ropes or knives, and we could not follow up our victory."

"How unfortunate," said Flavion. "How tragic!"

"We are pleased to see you again," said Grendel.

"Very pleased," said Cabot.

"But it is clear we were betrayed!" said Flavion.

"Very clear," said Lord Grendel.

"We were unable to march on the palace," said Flavion. "We were surprised in the Vale of Destruction! Agamemnon must have had intelligence of our plans."

"Clearly," said Lord Grendel.

"And the spy, the traitress, is in this very camp!"

"How can that be?" inquired Lord Grendel.

"Come, I will show you!" said Flavion, and led Grendel, and others, about the camp, to a small, low, open shelter, backed against palings. In the center of this tiny shelter two heavy stakes, some four inches in width, had been driven deeply into the ground, and attached to these stakes were heavy chains, one to each stake. The termination of each chain ran to a ring, one on the left side of a heavy iron belt, the other on the right side. This belt, itself, was hammered shut.

"Come out, traitress!" ordered Flavion.

There was the sound of a bell, dangling from a fair throat, locked on a chain about it.

"You see," said Flavion. "She answers to the name of traitress."

"Come out, traitress," he said. "Come out, and kneel, head to the dirt, before your superiors and judges."

The Lady Bina crawled slowly, painfully, from the tiny shelter, against the weight of the chains, lifted her head briefly, saw Lord Grendel, cast a look of terror at him, and then knelt shuddering before the group, her head down, to the dirt, as commanded.

Shortly after her capture and return to the camp, Lord Grendel, with a tool, had widened one of the links on her slave bracelets, so that she might separate her hands, but the rings of the bracelets, each with a bit of dangling chain, were still locked upon her wrists. In this fashion, if it were desired, the opened link might be once more closed, and her small wrists might then be confined as wished, either before her body, or behind it. Gorean masters commonly fasten a girl's wrists behind the body not merely that she will be more helpless, but that her beauty will be more conveniently exhibited, and be the more vulnerable to, and the more accessible to, say, the idlest caress of the master.

"It was you, yourself, who captured her!" said Flavion to Lord Grendel.

"Those chains," said Cabot, "would hold a tharlarion."

"I did not have her so burdened," said Lord Grendel.

"It was done to assure that she not again escape," said Flavion.

"Remove them," said Lord Grendel.

"As you wish," said Flavion.

"I had her cleaned up," said Lord Grendel. "Why is she filthy?"

"To clean her, a traitress, would be a waste of water."

"Wash her, brush and comb her," said Lord Grendel.

"It will be done," said Flavion.

"She is a free woman," said Lord Grendel. "Why is she naked?"

"That she may not conceal weapons," said Flavion.

"Give her a tunic, as before," said Lord Grendel. "You need not fear, my dear Flavion, that such a tunic will conceal a weapon, lest it be, and surely to no more than a tiny, almost mocking extent, the beauty of the female herself."

"It will be done," said Flavion.

"She is to have the freedom of the camp," said Lord Grendel.

"Surely not!" said Flavion. "She betrayed Peisistratus and Lord Arcesilaus, and doubtless others, to Agamemnon, long ago. Then, escaped from the camp, she betrayed the attack on the arsenal, that encompassing the slaughter of so many of our brothers, and then, clearly, returning, spying, she must have somehow become apprised of our plans involving the palace, and the Vale of Destruction, and betrayed those to Agamemnon, as well."

"I see," said Lord Grendel.

The girl whimpered, negatively, but dared not speak.

"She was brought to the camp, a prisoner," said Lord Grendel, "before our march to the Vale of Destruction."

"But not before the plans were laid," said Flavion.

"That is true," said Lord Grendel.

"We captured her, pinioned, ragged, dirty, and starving, in the vicinity of a womb tunnel," said Cabot.

"Doubtless she had, in her espionage, perhaps returning from the palace, to do more mischief, inadvertently fallen into the grasp of our peers, whom she later eluded, but found herself unable then either to return to the palace or, braceleted, to secretly frequent again the environs of our camp."

Cabot may have been about to speak, but Lord Grendel put a hand upon him, and then, it seemed, he refrained.

"Excellent, Flavion," said Lord Grendel. "What you say makes a great deal of sense, and explains much in a satisfactory manner."

"Thank you, Lord," said Flavion.

The Lady Bina lifted her head, a little, to regard Lord Grendel. There was a tiny sound of the bell. Then she thrust her head down, again.

"Shall we keep the bell on her?" asked Peisistratus.

"Yes," said Lord Grendel, "as before."

"And when," said Flavion, anxiously, "shall she be put to death?"

"Do you not think it best that she be interrogated first?" asked Lord Grendel.

"I would think that unnecessary," said Flavion.

"Might she not, under torture, as she is seemingly a valued and esteemed agent of great Agamemnon," said Cabot, "be encouraged to betray his secrets?"

"She is human," said Flavion. "To no secrets would she be privy."

"One might be curious to hear her own account of her treacheries," said Lord Grendel.

"What could her own words do," asked Flavion, "other than seal her fate the more securely, other than serve to more fiercely heat the very irons which will burn her?"

"Has she said nothing?" asked Cabot.

"As her guilt is clear," said Flavion, "she has been forbidden to speak."

"It seems a shame to burn and tear such sweet flesh," said Cabot. "Might it not be better to auction it off on a slave block?"

"Certainly not, dear Cabot," said Statius. "Loathsome and despicable as she is, she is a free woman. Surely you would not reduce her to the unutterable shame of bondage. Nothing so shameful for her as chains, a whip, a collar, and a feared master."

"When we captured her," said Lord Grendel, "she was starving, and I am not sure she is much better off now."

"She is a traitress," said Flavion.

"What has she been fed?"

"She has had a pan of water, and, from time to time, has been thrown a handful of garbage."

"I see," said Lord Grendel.

"We knew you would wish for us to keep her alive, that she might face your justice."

"You are thoughtful," said Lord Grendel.

"I am eager to see her under the irons, the pincers and knives," said Flavion.

"Feed her, decently," said Grendel.

"I see," said Flavion. "Yes! That she will be restored to health and vitality, this enabling her to better suffer, to experience more fully even the least and most exquisite nuances of agony. Too, Lord Grendel, I now understand, as I did not before, your seeming lenience to the traitress, permitting her clothing, such as it might be, the freedom of the camp, and such. It will be almost as though she were free, but she knows she is not free. Things might seem near and possible, but are far, and hopeless. To what tantalizing anxieties, to what false hopes, to what terrifying uncertainties, she will be subjected, not even knowing at what moment she will be roped and carried to the torture table!"

But then Lord Grendel had turned away, with Statius, and others, to confer on matters of policy, diplomatic and military.

Flavion went to accompany them, but Cabot bid him pause, however briefly.

"I had a slave," said Cabot, "who has displeased me."

"I know the one," said Flavion.

"I would like to recover her."

"Surely you do not care for her," said Flavion.

"It is true she is only a slave," said Cabot.

"I think," said Flavion, "you would do much, perhaps anything, to get her back."

"Perhaps to teach her what it is to be a slave, and then sell her."

"I am a poor judge of slaves," said Flavion, "but she is exquisitely curved, is she not?"

"She would probably sell for at least two tarsks," said Cabot.

"That is a high price, is it not?"

"Yes."

"She fled, days ago," said Flavion, warily. "Doubtless, by now, she has perished of exposure, or starved, or fallen to wild animals, or has been killed by Agamemnon's Kurii, for they had orders to fire on all humans."

"Doubtless," said Cabot. "But, as I recall, you suggested that her trail might be found."

"It has been so long," said Flavion. "How could that be?"

"Find it," said Cabot.

"What?" said Flavion.

"Find it," said Cabot.

"I do not understand," said Flavion.

"Amongst your things," said Cabot, "before the trek to the Vale of Destruction, I found a purple scarf."

"Of course," said Flavion. "I needed such to penetrate enemy lines, and prosecute my duties as scout."

"A most satisfactory explanation," said Cabot.

"Certainly," said Flavion.

"And did it sometimes prove of use?"

"Yes," said Flavion, more easily. "Several times."

"Interesting," said Cabot.

"Why, interesting?" asked Flavion.

"You then, I take it, had contact with Kur patrols, guards, and such."

"Occasionally, inadvertently," said Flavion.

"You were stopped?"

"Seldom, but sometimes," he said.

"And you were not killed."

"Obviously not," said Flavion.

"Why not?"

"I had the disguise," said he, "the false uniform, the purple scarf."

"You would have to have had more than that," said Cabot.

"What?" asked Flavion, stiffening.

"The signs, and countersigns," said Cabot.

"—What do you want?" said Flavion.

"What have you to give?" asked Cabot.

A Kur smile eased the face of Flavion. "I might have much to give," he said.

"I thought so," said Cabot.

"The least of which might be a female slave," he said.

"You can find her?"

"I can try," he said.

"Do it," said Cabot.

"I am pleased," said Flavion, "to learn that you are a wise and practical person. I had feared otherwise. Some are not."

"We shall speak further of this tomorrow," said Cabot.

"Very well," said Flavion.

"Perhaps you would like me to groom you?" said Cabot.

"No," said Flavion. "You are a trusted confidant of Lord Grendel, and stand high in the camp. I am only a lowly scout."

"Perhaps," said Cabot, "you are less lowly elsewhere."

"Perhaps," smiled Flavion.

"Come to the feast! Come to the feast!" called Peisistratus.

"Let us go to the feast," said Cabot.

"Certainly," said Flavion.

"Have you ever attended a feast served by female slaves?" asked Cabot.

"I have been served by them," said Flavion, "as have all in the camp, but not at a feast."

"I think you will find it quite pleasant," said Cabot. "I note that Peisistratus will have them serve typically, as they frequently do on Gor."

"And how is that?" inquired Flavion.

"Humbly, and stripped," said Cabot.

"I see," said Flavion.

"You will sit next to me," said Cabot.

"I would be honored," said Flavion.

Chapter, the Fifty-Eighth:

Cabot Contemplates a Rendezvous

"Flavion is not in the camp," said Grendel.

"He is out, doubtless attending to the arrangements," said Cabot.

"As I understand it," said Grendel, "I am to be betrayed into the hands of Agamemnon's agents."

"That is it, precisely," said Cabot.

"I did not understand I was so important," said Lord Grendel.

"You are quite important," said Cabot.

"There are others, in other camps," said Grendel.

"Your authority is foremost, clearly," said Cabot. "You are leader."

"There are others," said Grendel.

"It is the view of Agamemnon that without you the revolution will fail."

"You have this on the authority of our friend, Flavion?"

"Yes," said Cabot.

"Interesting," said Grendel. "And what are you to gain from all this?"

"Incidentally, a meaningless slave, of course," said Cabot, "but more importantly the favor of Agamemnon, riches, power on Gor, such things."

"He is renewing his original offer?" asked Grendel.

"It would seem so," said Cabot.

"His ambition is insatiable," said Grendel, "even after the disaster of the fleet."

"The attacking navy, it seems, was repelled," said Cabot. "Thus it may be dismissed."

It may be recalled that there were attacks, in the recent past, on the world. These had impacted the shielding, but had not penetrated to the interior of the cylinder.

"It is not like Kurii to abandon fresh meat, not when it is torn, not when it is run to ground, weakened, exhausted, panting, hot and bloody," said Grendel.

"Nor is it like them to rush into flames or leap from cliffs," said Cabot.

"Your own actions, of late," said Grendel, "have provoked curiosity."

"Suspicion?" inquired Cabot.

"No," said Grendel. "Curiosity. Why, upon occasion, have you carried meat from the camp, and returned without it?"

"It seems I made a friend, long ago," said Cabot. "I have only recently renewed my acquaintance with him."

"A friend with a considerable appetite it seems," said Grendel.

"No more than some Kurii," said Cabot.

"Can you communicate with your friend?" asked Statius.

"Originally with the help of the translator," said Cabot, "which produces recognizable Kur. Too, many commands are standard. What is most significant is he who issues the command. A command issued by one individual may be ignored, while the same command, from another, will be acted on, instantaneously. What I then did was to associate commands in Kur with commands in Gorean, and then reward only the Gorean version of the original command."

"So your friend, now, will respond only to Gorean?" said Grendel.

"He will doubtless understand both," said Cabot, "but respond, hopefully, only to Gorean."

"And it is to your commands only that he will respond?"

"I think so," said Cabot. "If you like, I shall introduce you, and you may test the matter."

"Perhaps another might make the test," said Statius.

"This has been done over several days?" said Lord Grendel.

"Yes," said Cabot. "And often I have not taken meat from the camp. A kind word, a hand knotted in the fur, affectionately, and shaken, is as effective, and seems more savored, I learn, than even roast tarsk."

"Your friend seems unusual," said Lord Grendel.

"I do not know," said Cabot. "I suspect, rather, it is that few take the trouble to understand such friends, let alone accord them friendship, or affection."

"I think your friend," said Statius, "is hideous, and dangerous."

"He is in his way beautiful," said Cabot, "as the shark, or larl, is beautiful, but it is true he is dangerous."

"I suspect your friend is quite intelligent," said Lord Grendel.

"He has long been noted for that," said Cabot.

"And loyal?" asked Statius.

"I fear so, even unreasonably," said Cabot.

"I think I know your friend," said Lord Grendel.

"He has long protected the camp," said Statius, "has he not?"

"I think so," said Cabot.

"How are we to proceed?" asked Grendel. "Am I to serve as bait in some trap?"

"No," said Cabot. "I would not put you at risk."

"Is that decision not mine?"

"No, dear friend," said Cabot. "In this instance, it is mine."

Chapter, the Fifty-Ninth:

A Rendezvous Takes Place

"I see," said Flavion, stepping forth from the trees, "you have not brought weapons."

"In accord with our agreement," said Cabot.

"My colleagues," said Flavion, glancing to the left and right, "are armed."

"I see no colleagues," said Cabot.

"They are there," said Flavion. "You were to bring Grendel with you, as though hunting or on patrol, delivering him to us, at this place. Where is he?"

"Where is the slave, and gold?" said Cabot.

Flavion bent over, and one of his feet scratched angrily, suddenly, at the ground. Cabot watched, imperturbably, as leaves and dirt settled.

Cabot heard a rustle in the brush to his right.

Flavion was not the only Kur displeased.

"Do you think to insult us?" came from Cabot's translator.

"Do you think to insult me?" asked Cabot.

"We do not care to be tricked," said Flavion.

"Nor do I," said Cabot.

"Where is the monster, Grendel?"

"Where is the gold, the slave?" said Cabot.

"You do not trust us," said Flavion.

"My mistrust, it seems," said Cabot, "is abundantly justified."

"Where is Grendel?"

"I suppose, in camp," said Cabot.

"You are making a test of us?"

"And perhaps you of me?"

Flavion brandished his rifle, one of power. "I could kill you now," he said.

"That would not bring Lord Grendel to you," said Cabot.

"I must consult with my superiors," said Flavion. "Return to camp."

Cabot turned about, and withdrew.

Behind him he heard a howl of Kur rage.

Chapter, the Sixtieth:

The Ways of Kur

"Our cause is lost!" exclaimed Flavion, entering the camp.

"How so?" cried Grendel, rushing forward. Others, too, rushed forward, to be apprised of whatever dire intelligence might be conveyed by their scout, Flavion.

"The men of Mitonicus have entered the theater of death," said Flavion.

"As in the amnesty?" said Statius.

"They are true to the ways of the Kur," said a Kur.

"Speak!" demanded Cabot.

"Speak!" demanded Archon.

"Tell them," said Statius, "for they are not Kur."

"As you well know," said Flavion, "the despised wretches, the arrant cowards, of the great defeat have the obligation to do away with themselves or submit to the knife, that their dismal, unworthy seed not pollute the folk. Great Agamemnon, in an act of seeming mercy, has called them to the theater, that of death, where they expect to be forgiven, and their penalties revoked, merely for joining his forces."

"That will be the end of it," said Archon, "for we cannot long resist such a coalition."

"No," said Lord Grendel. "It is the same trick. They have been brought there to die."

"I fear so," lamented Flavion.

"How so?" asked Statius.

"They have been forbidden to bring weapons with them," said Flavion.

"How is this known?" asked a Kur.

"It is common knowledge," said Flavion. "I learned it in the habitats, which I recently infiltrated at great personal risk."

"Brave Flavion!" said a Kur.

"They filed like docile verr, slowly, in long lines, heads down, to the theater of death," said Flavion.

"Madness," said Cabot. "In their numbers they could balance the very forces of Agamemnon, which are intent upon their destruction."

"We are lost either way," said Flavion. "If they are spared, Agamemnon will be invincible. If they are destroyed, all hope for our cause is doomed."

Lord Grendel was silent.

"What then, noble Lord Grendel," said Flavion, "is to be done?"

"What would you suggest?" said Lord Grendel.

"We have no choice," said Flavion. "We must surrender, surrender completely, wholly. We must submit to an abject, unconditional surrender."

There were moans of misery within the camp. Slave girls wept. Statius' slave howled, and then crept to his feet, frightened, seeking comfort. He put his hand gently on her shaggy head.

"Humans will be killed, surely," said Peisistratus.

"All rebels," said Statius.

"No, no," said Flavion. "We must not despair. The future is unclear. The only thing clear is that we must surrender our cause, and place ourselves at the mercy of Agamemnon."

"When," asked Lord Grendel, "were the mariners to gather in the theater?"

"Yesterday," said Flavion.

"Then," said Cabot, "the thing is already resolved."

"But how?" asked a Kur.

"Does it matter?" asked another.

"Poor Mitonicus," said Cabot. "Loyal to the Kur paths despite to what horror or madness they might lead."

"We have other things to think of," said Flavion.

"True," said a Kur.

"Weapons will not be permitted," said Flavion. "We must put them aside. I will lead you to the habitats. Doubtless anyone, Kur or human, found hereafter, unaccounted for, in the forests, will be outlawed, hunted down, and destroyed."

"Much in the Kur way is foolish, perhaps insane," said Cabot.

"No more so than much in some human ways," said Statius.

"You do not understand Kur," said Lord Grendel.

"Surely you do not approve," said Cabot, angrily.

"As Kur I understand it," said Lord Grendel. "Kur ways, such as striking first, retaliating instantly, seeking vengeance, annihilating an enemy, eliminating weakness, punishing failure, improving the folk, pledging loyalty, and keeping it, unquestioning obedience to command, ruthlessness, breeding for Kur virtues, power and energy, savagery, if you like, are hard ways, but they have brought us to a supremacy amongst species. They have made us Kur."

"They are our ways," said Statius.

"If we surrender the ways," said Lord Grendel, "we cease to be Kur."

"At the arsenal, dear Grendel, you spared two agents of Agamemnon, allowing them to return to their base with weapons, in the Vale of Destruction you permitted a tending of enemy wounded, after the battle you freed four hundred prisoners."

"I was weak," said Lord Grendel.

"No," said Cabot. "You were human."

"Yes, weak," said Lord Grendel.

"Yet," said Cabot, "I think few are as Kur as you."

"What is Kur?" said Lord Grendel.

"Let us cast down our weapons, emerge from the forests, and place ourselves before great Agamemnon," said Flavion.

"As surrendered, helpless penitents?" asked Lord Grendel.

"Sadly, needfully," said Flavion.

"Someone comes, someone comes to the gate!" cried Archon.

There was a pounding at the gate.

Weapons were leveled at the gate, cover sought, defensive positions occupied.

"Who is there?" called Lord Grendel.

"Word, word from Mitonicus!" cried a voice, gasping.

"Open the gate!" said Lord Grendel. Two Kurii hurried forward, and opened the gate a yard, and assisted a Kur within. He was gasping, and was scarcely able to stand. He was held by the two who had opened the gate and was brought before Lord Grendel.

"It is a runner," said Statius.

"How did you find us?" asked a Kur.

"I was searching for you," he gasped. "I could not find you. I was lost. And then I was driven here, brought here, by a giant sleen."

"One lame!" cried Cabot.

"Yes," gasped the runner.

"He was not attacked," said Statius.

"Speak, speak!" cried Lord Grendel.

"I bring word from Mitonicus," said the Kur.

"Speak," said Lord Grendel.

"Victory!" he gasped. "We brought concealed weapons to the theater of death, and when they readied their weapons, to fire upon us, it was we who first fired, and attacked. We slew hundreds!"

"How would you dare to do this?" cried Flavion.

"In vengeance for the slaughter of the amnesty!" he gasped. "And we were joined by others, some four hundred, and others, as well."

"Four hundred!" said Archon.

"So what is the situation now?" pressed Lord Grendel.

"Agamemnon has withdrawn to the habitats, and the palace!" said the runner, who then collapsed, shuddering, into the arms of the two Kurii who supported him.

"Tend him," said Lord Grendel.

"What do we do now?" said Cabot.

"We march on the palace," said Lord Grendel.

Chapter, the Sixty-First:

A Stability of Positions;
The Report of Flavion;
The Accosting of the Lady Bina;
A Reference to Omens

"There," said Lord Grendel, pointing, "off there, in the valley, to the right, see the dome? That is the palace."

"I see," said Cabot.

With Lord Grendel and his human ally, Tarl Cabot, were several others, Kur and human.

The habitats lay muchly below them, some pasang or so away.

The revolutionaries controlled most of the world's territory, but this was primarily forested area, even wilderness, the remoter villages, and such.

The industrial cylinder and the two agricultural cylinders were largely automated; the pleasure cylinder, with its sealed locks and ports, was effectively emptied; and the sport cylinder, commonly used in less troubled times for the hunting pleasure of Kurii, was now depopulated of its human game, though continuing rich with other forms of animal life.

The outcome of the conflict betwixt Agamemnon and his adversaries would be decided in the world.

"They have excellent defensive positions," said Lord Grendel. "We have probed them. It would be madness, at this time, to undertake a frontal assault. Beyond this, consider the habitats themselves. Who would risk a door-to-door, habitat-to-habitat, war?"

"Agamemnon, if he were in your position, and had the forces," said Cabot.

"I suppose so," said Lord Grendel. "One would expect him to be lavish in expending his resources, but he is no longer in a position where he can spend so freely."

"It is a stalemate," said Cabot.

"A siege, at least," said Lord Grendel.

"On Gor," said Cabot, "a fortress, a city, might be starved into submission."

"Not so here," said Lord Grendel, "the habitats are, in their way, a land, a territory, at least, for most practical purposes, a world in itself. Supplies, too, have been stored there against investments of the world itself. It would take a century to reduce the habitats to surrender with the resources at our command."

"So a stalemate," said Cabot. "Or a mad rush to certain death, either on our part or on that of Agamemnon."

"Agamemnon will not order such a charge," said Lord Grendel, "as he, in his wisdom, would well understand not only its futility, but its implicit fatality, the doom to which it would subject his own cause."

"I recall a war, on another world," said Cabot, "in which leaders flung their forces repeatedly, meaninglessly, for months, into the muzzles of one another's weapons."

"They were insane," said Lord Grendel.

"They themselves were of course far removed from the fighting, secure in positions of safety, and thus had little to fear personally. Also, they had abundant resources, it seemed, which they did not mind squandering, doubtless in the hope that each would prove to have more to squander than the other."

"This war of which you speak was between humans?" said Lord Grendel.

"Yes," said Cabot.

"Of course," said Lord Grendel. "And was this matter resolved?"

"Through the employment of machines, unusual for the times," said Cabot.

"There are machines here," said Lord Grendel, "primarily in the habitats, but none I think which will prove effective here, for none could resist the direct discharge of a power weapon."

"Stalemate," said Cabot, glumly.

"Agamemnon is impatient," said Lord Grendel. "He will not submit to your stalemate."

"What will he do?" asked Cabot.

"I do not know," said Lord Grendel. "I know only that he will act."

"Lo," said Archon, "Flavion approaches."

"Lord Grendel!" said Flavion.

"It seems you are wounded!" said Lord Grendel.

"It is negligible," said Flavion. He seemed to waver, slightly. There was blood at his left temple.

"Have your wound treated," said a Kur.

"It is nothing," said Flavion.

"Stout Flavion," exclaimed a Kur.

"You bring us intelligence?" said Lord Grendel.

"Yes," said Flavion, "intelligence of enormous, and, I fear, transitory, import. I have scouted the habitats and have discovered a route within their defenses, a long path overlooked, and consequently undefended, betwixt high structures, one much shielded from observation, that will lead us to the palace itself, where a certain lightly guarded gate, known to me, may be easily forced."

"This puts the palace in our hands!" said Archon.

"Brave and noble Flavion!" cried a Kur.

"But," said Flavion, "we must act immediately, as soon as darkness falls."

"Why?" asked Statius.

"This weakness in their defenses is certain to be soon remedied, surely by daylight, when the streets are reconnoitered by the guard."

"Our humans will be at a serious disadvantage in the night," said Statius.

"Let them be led, clutching strings," said Flavion. "This moment must not be lost."

"And what forces might we invest in this venture?" asked Lord Grendel.

"As many as possible," said Flavion. "All, if necessary. Once the palace falls, all opposition will cease."

"Act now, Lord Grendel," urged a Kur.

"Yes!" cried others.

"Go, dear Flavion," said Lord Grendel, "and have your wound tended."

"There is no time for delay, Lord Grendel," protested Flavion. "Prepare! Summon the forces! It will be dark soon. This opportunity may never come again! We must act, act!"

"Have your wound tended," said Lord Grendel.

"You must act!" said Flavion. "The situation demands it! Otherwise you are casting away the war! If you do not do this, who will care to follow you? Mutiny will assail your camps!"

"Have your wound tended," said Lord Grendel.

"Yes, Lord," said Flavion, and, angrily, departed.

"So," smiled Lord Grendel, to Cabot, and Statius, who was of late, from a conversation the reader may recall, one in which an ally, or friend, figured, now well apprised of their suspicions with respect to a certain member of their company, "shall we cast away the war?"

"Do as Flavion urges," said Statius, "and the war will well be cast away."

"I suggest," said Cabot, "that Flavion himself lead the secret march."

"Yes," said Statius, "chained, and with bells attached to his hands and feet, and neck."

"Did you see his wound?" asked Cabot.

"Yes," said Lord Grendel. "And I think dear Flavion was correct, it was negligible."

"There was a good deal of blood," said Cabot.

"Given the wound," said Lord Grendel, "it is not likely the blood was his."

"He will try to stir up dissension amongst our forces," said Cabot.

"Then," said Lord Grendel, "we will have to kill him."

"I would rather you did not do that," said Cabot.

"Why not?" asked Statius.

"I think he knows the location of a certain female slave," said Cabot.

"Forget her," said Statius. "She is meaningless, nothing, only a female slave, no more than a piece of vendible collar meat."

"She is nicely curved," said Cabot, "and is appealing in a closely fitting locked collar."

"Slaves are cheap," said Statius.

"She might bring two tarsks in the open market," said Cabot.

"Forget her," said Statius. "We can give you slaves who would bring ten tarsks in an open market."

"Better than she?"

"Certainly."

"I shall have to think about it," said Cabot.

"If you recover the slave," said Statius, "you would not mind our killing him."

"Certainly not," said Cabot, "and if we do not find her, I would insist on it."

"At least, my dear Statius," said Lord Grendel, "you cannot blame this projected treachery on the Lady Bina."

The Lady Bina, as might be expected, was with the rebel forces, as were the others who had been in Lord Grendel's camp, which had now been abandoned. In accord with the orders of Lord Grendel she had now been freed of the thick, broad, heavy, hammered-shut waist belt, with its heavy chains; had been cleaned, and brushed and combed; had been clothed, however excitingly and minimally; and had now been given an ample and nourishing diet, though one somewhat simple; and certainly some of her curves had now filled out and returned to their state of former interest, curves which, had she not been a free woman, would have been vulgarly referred to as "slave curves." As she was no longer within the camp, confined within its palings, a number of adjustments had taken place in the nature of the security to which she was subject. The widened link on the slave bracelets, which had permitted her to separate her hands, had now again been closed, in such a way that her hands, again, were pinioned behind her back; she had also been placed in ankle shackles, with a linkage of three horts; and chained by the neck to a stake. Also, of course, she still wore the bell. Thus, even had she been free of the shackles and chain, she could not, as her hands were confined, have impeded the sounding of the bell, which would make her easy to follow and locate, even for a human.

"She has treacheries enough to her account to justify a thousand deaths by the most harrowing of tortures," said Statius.

"You have no intention of acting on the recommendations of Flavion, I trust," said Cabot to Lord Grendel.

"Certainly not," said Grendel.

"Flavion does stand high in our war," said Statius. "Most take him as indispensable, and courageous, and, I fear, he will attempt to undermine the authority of Lord Grendel."

"That of one who is at best no more than a monster," said Lord Grendel.

"And one who acts in concert with a human, and even with one who was once a despised nondominant," said Statius.

"He will doubtless insidiously, as he can, capitalize on such things," said Cabot.

"I fear he will find a ready field for the sowing of such seed," said Statius.

"Yes," said Lord Grendel, "particularly as the war does not soon proceed to some clear resolution."

"Too," said Cabot, "it is clear he wants the death of the Lady Bina, on whom many are eager to impose justice, indeed, of a most hideous sort, and he may, thus, use your dalliance in this matter, and your reluctance to expeditiously prosecute her, as further grounds to undermine your authority, to insinuate your weakness, and such."

"Surely that can await the outcome of the war," said Lord Grendel.

"Not indefinitely," said Statius. "And many suspect that you will die before you permit harm to come to her. Thus, if her prosecution is forced, you may both die, she by torture, and you, as well, should you attempt to interfere, and the insurrection is then deprived of its ablest leader."

"And in his place, doubtless," said Cabot, "would appear our friend, Flavion."

"And that," said Statius, "would guarantee the victory of Lord Agamemnon."

"It would be easy," said Cabot. "He might simply order a full-scale frontal assault on impregnable positions, and thus seem to many a courageous and audacious captain, one perhaps to be honored even in defeat."

"And Kurii would follow him," said Statius.

"Yes," said Lord Grendel, "if the orders were given. It is the Kur way."

"Then the orders must not be given," said Cabot.

"You must permit the torture and death of the Lady Bina," said

Statius. "Even if you attempt to flee with her, Flavion will come to power."

In Cabot's translator there was an indecipherable, unintelligible, staticlike sound. It was responding to an inarticulate rumble of sorrow and misery, scarcely audible, from Lord Grendel.

Then he was again, or seemed again, himself.

"Dear Grendel," said Cabot, concerned.

"It is nothing," said Lord Grendel.

"It is clear," said Statius. "You must sacrifice the Lady Bina. Our very cause depends upon it."

"I cannot," said Lord Grendel.

"Our cause is then lost," said Statius. "Our defeats, our deaths, our struggles, our hopes, our deprivations and hardships, will be for nothing."

"We will wait," said Lord Grendel.

"Kurii are not patient," said Statius.

"And Agamemnon is Kur," said Lord Grendel.

"I do not understand," said Statius.

"That is my hope for victory," said Lord Grendel.

"There is some movement below, in the fields," said Cabot, "between the habitats and our lines."

"The enemy is moving?" asked Statius, eagerly.

"No," said Lord Grendel. "It is a herd of cattle humans, only a herd of cattle humans, foraging."

"Nothing then of interest," said Statius.

"No," said Lord Grendel.

At this point, from the rear, there was a scream.

"The Lady Bina!" cried Grendel, turning about, and hurrying to the rear. He was followed by Cabot, his human ally, and Statius.

There was another scream.

Moments later Lord Grendel pressed through a circle of Kurii and humans, and discovered the Lady Bina on her back. Her ankle shackles had been removed. They lay in the dust to one side. She was struggling in the grip of a killer human, one of their allies, who bent over her. With a hand on each ankle he had spread her legs widely. She squirmed, futilely, and screamed again.

None in the crowd about her seemed disposed to interfere.

One great paw of Lord Grendel closed on the back of the neck of the killer human and tore him from the Lady Bina, and then his fangs went to his throat.

"No, no!" cried Cabot.

Lord Grendel threw the killer human from him, he rolling yards away in the dust.

He then scrambled to his feet, and withdrew.

But Cabot discerned that he had first cast a look at Flavion, who stood in the vicinity.

Grendel cast a wild, belligerent look about him.

"Kneel, head up, near the stake," said Cabot to the Lady Bina, and she, wild-eyed, shuddering, hastened to comply.

"What is wrong?" inquired Flavion.

"Shackle her," said Lord Grendel.

One of the Kurii reapplied the close-fitting restraints, joined by their short linkage, with two clicks, to the slender ankles of the Lady Bina.

"Who removed her shackles?" asked Lord Grendel.

"The human," said Flavion calmly, "but I authorized it, thinking it would be appropriate, and that you would approve, as she is a free woman. Otherwise it would have been simple enough to kneel her, turn her about, and put her head to the dirt."

"She is not a slave!" cried Lord Grendel.

"Certainly not," said Flavion. "That is why I authorized the removal of her shackles."

"How dared you permit this!" said Lord Grendel.

"Do you disapprove?" asked Flavion, innocently.

Lord Grendel roared with fury.

"You grow bold, dear Flavion," said Statius.

"It was not my intention to displease anyone," said Flavion. "I regret only, Lord Grendel, that you were disturbed, when graver matters, matters of command, concerned you. I should have had her gagged."

"But then," said Cabot, "we could not have heard her scream."

Lord Grendel motioned that Cabot should be silent.

"Surely," said Flavion, "a prisoner, and certainly an arrant traitress, should do something to earn her keep, should provide some service in exchange for her food. Certainly we should strive to find some use in the camp to which she might be put."

There was a murmur of assent to this from the Kurii about,

and from the humans, as well, which response Cabot could well understand.

"Surely you have no personal interest or concern in this female," said Flavion.

"Who was the human?" asked Lord Grendel.

"Cestiphon," said Flavion. "But do not blame him. Blame me, if you wish."

"No!" cried several about.

"Too," said Flavion. "Is it not well past the time the traitress was judged, found guilty, and put to an appropriate death?"

Kurii present murmured assent.

Lord Grendel did not respond.

"But that may wait until tomorrow, after our secret march, our assault on the palace, and the glory of our inevitable victory," said Flavion.

"We are not marching tonight," said Lord Grendel.

"I have scouted the terrain," said Flavion. "Many know this. Many are eager to march. This is a brief moment of advantage, which may never occur again. It is in our power to win the war this very night."

"We do not march tonight," said Lord Grendel.

"But why, Lord?" asked Flavion. "What could possibly be the reason?"

Lord Grendel did not respond, but appeared stricken.

"If I may answer that," said Cabot, "it is because the omens are inauspicious."

"What omens?" said Flavion.

"I feared it," said Cabot, "when I first heard the screams of the Lady Bina, and grew more fearful when she screamed thrice, for that is the number of screams. I only hoped then that a fellow would not be involved whose name consisted of three syllables, as well, and my heart sank, when I learned her accoster was named Cestiphon. For the omens are unfavorable when a free woman screams thrice and he who accosts her has a name with three syllables, such as Antiphon, or Leander, or, say, Cestiphon. No action of import is to be undertaken on such a day."

"That is absurd," said Flavion.

"I do not doubt it," said Cabot, "and I myself take little stock in omens. I merely call attention to the omen, for I should feel remiss did I not do so."

"I myself," said Lord Grendel, "am similarly dubious of such portents, but one hesitates to risk a great enterprise when the signs are against it."

"Clearly, surely," said Statius, "the signs are against marching tonight."

Several of the Kurii exchanged uneasy glances, and the humans, too, looked to one another, apprehensively.

"Return to your duties," said Lord Grendel to the Kurii and humans about. The group disbanded.

Lord Grendel, Statius, and Cabot then regarded the Lady Bina.

"You do not have to kneel back on your heels," said Cabot to the Lady Bina. "You may kneel up."

She did so.

"She is beautiful, is she not?" asked Lord Grendel.

"Yes," said Cabot. "Quite beautiful."

Cabot would have preferred for her to remain kneeling back on her heels, for that was more like a slave. But she was, after all, a free woman. If she were a slave, the proper modalities of kneeling before free persons would be taught to her. For example, such things are taught in the pens.

"For a human," said Statius, for he perhaps had his mind on his own female.

"You must not think too badly of Cestiphon, and other male humans," said Cabot, "for such a female is like delicious food to a starving man. Though she is a free woman, yet, secured as she is, clothed as she is, she has something of the allure, the inadvertent seductiveness, the sensuous vulnerability, the helplessness, of a Gorean female slave, or *kajira*."

"Interesting," said Statius.

"She should be collared," said Cabot.

"She is a free woman," said Lord Grendel.

"That can be easily changed," said Cabot.

Lord Grendel and Statius then returned to a place of vantage, forward.

"May I speak?" whispered the Lady Bina.

"You are a free woman," said Cabot. "It is not necessary for you to ask permission to speak."

"I am not supposed to speak," she said. "My tongue may be torn out."

"Who says so?" asked Cabot.

"Lord Flavion," she said.

"I see," said Cabot.

"Despite his public demeanor," she said, "I think he is my only friend."

"Secretly, of course?" said Cabot.

"Yes," she whispered, looking about. "He dare not reveal his concern for me."

"I see," said Cabot.

"And Grendel," she said, bitterly, "is my secret foe."

"I doubt that," said Cabot.

"It is true," she said.

"You have that on the authority of Flavion?" said Cabot.

"Lord Flavion," she said.

"I see," said Cabot.

"I am beautiful, am I not?" she asked.

"Yes," said Cabot, "quite beautiful."

"I am a free woman," she said. "I will use my beauty. I will dangle it before men, and entwine them in its toils, and they will obey me, unquestioningly, for gifts as small and costless to me as a glance or smile."

"You know what should be done with you, do you not?" he asked.

"What?" she asked.

"You should be put on a block and sold," said Cabot.

"Kiss me," she said. "No one is looking. I will permit it."

"Kneel there," said Cabot, who then turned his back on her, and went forward to join Lord Grendel and Statius.

On the way he met Flavion.

"You think quickly, for a human," said Flavion.

"Thank you," said Cabot, and continued on his way.

Chapter, the Sixty-Second:

The Conversation in the Redoubt

"We may speak here," said Flavion.

Cabot was on watch, at one of the forward outposts. He had a power weapon at this place, but it was not assigned to him but to the post itself.

It was four days following the accosting of the human female, the Lady Bina, in Lord Grendel's camp.

"Yes," said Cabot.

They were alone in the small redoubt, but the ground they surveyed also fell within the purview of two similar redoubts.

Each watch in each redoubt contained either a human and a Kur, or two Kurii. Flavion had arranged to be posted with Cabot this night.

"I still have much to offer," said Flavion.

"Oh?" said Cabot.

"You were very troublesome earlier, in the camp," said Flavion.

"What need would you have had for me," said Cabot, "if you had had the war won in a night, with the ambush amongst the habitats?"

"You are very clever," said Flavion.

"I fear far less clever than you," said Cabot. "Had the secret march been undertaken, victory would have been Agamemnon's. And, if it was not undertaken, many in Grendel's forces would be convinced that it should have been undertaken, and thus the standing of the generalship of Grendel is reduced."

"Your subterfuge of omens was transparent," said Flavion, "an obvious stratagem to buy Grendel time."

"You are certain it was a subterfuge?"

602

"We consulted with several of the men of Peisistratus," said Flavion.

"It proved useful at the time," said Cabot.

"That must be admitted," said Flavion.

"It seemed to me wise to appear to favor the cause of Grendel," said Cabot.

"You are aware that many favor a frontal assault on the habitats?"

"That would be madness," said Cabot.

"Perhaps," said Flavion, "but many feel that it is now the only chance for victory, and despise Grendel for not ordering the assault."

"And in the abeyance of such an order seeing him as timid, even cowardly."

"Certainly," said Flavion.

"You have done your work well," said Cabot.

"It would be useful if Grendel were removed," said Flavion.

"Have you not planned for that," asked Cabot, "by demonstrating his concern for the welfare of the much-hated traitress, the Lady Bina, his defense of her against the human, Cestiphon, and urging her trial, conviction, and execution, confident that Grendel would defend her, and thus die with her?"

"He delays the trial," said Flavion, "and he is still too much respected in the camp to be gainsaid in the matter."

"But this does further undermine his stature," said Cabot.

"Certainly," said Flavion. "But it is too slow."

"Agamemnon is impatient?" said Cabot.

"His patience is not endless," said Flavion.

"And how may I figure in your plans, and for what recompense?"

"When the forces hesitate to acclaim me commander," said Flavion, "I want your support."

"I am so important?" said Cabot.

"You are more important than you know," said Flavion, "with humans, with Kurii. Too, you are close to Grendel, and if you turn on him, this will weigh heavily with many."

"I see," said Cabot.

"Only you know my allegiance to Agamemnon," said Flavion.

"Your treachery might be broadcast," said Cabot.

"None would believe it," said Flavion.

"I suspect that is true," said Cabot.

"Power on Gor would be yours, and palaces and cities, and armies, and gold."

"I must trust you on this?"

"Perhaps you would like a token, of good faith?"

"Perhaps," said Cabot.

"One, say, cast naked, in chains, to your feet?"

"That is a small token," said Cabot.

"Perhaps such a one with a sack of gold tied about her neck?"

"I wonder if you could find her."

"One can always try."

"I had thought," said Cabot, "that you might be interested in something other than my support in some coup. I had supposed you would be interested in something other, something as simple as an assassination, a knife in the night, plunged into the heart of a commander."

"That will not be necessary," said Flavion.

"Oh?" said Cabot.

"Arrangements have already been made," said Flavion.

Chapter, the Sixty-Third:

What Took Place in the Field

"The Lady Bina has escaped!" cried Archon, rushing forward.

Lord Grendel leaped to his feet, wildly.

"How can that be?" said Statius.

"Some confederate in the camp!" said a Kur.

Lord Grendel was already at the stake to which the lovely prisoner had been fastened.

Tools had been used on the slave bracelets, for they lay to the side. The neck chain and the shackles had been opened. They, too, lay to the side.

Lord Grendel howled in rage, his eyes raised to his far sky, where one could see the heights of the trees descendent, so far above him, visible through wisps of clouds. Then, wildly, he crouched down and scratched at the dirt, gouging it. His visage was terrible. Cabot feared to address him as he was, for it seemed maddened Kur had suddenly somehow become his friend.

"What is wrong?" cried Flavion, hurrying forward.

"The traitress is gone!" said a Kur.

"No!" cried Flavion. "It is impossible!"

Then Flavion leaped back, for it seemed Lord Grendel would leap upon him, as to rip his throat from his body.

"Dear Lord Grendel, beloved commander," said Flavion, "believe me, I know nothing of this!"

Lord Grendel shook with rage, his fangs emerged, his ears darted back, smoothly against his head.

"Surely it is Cestiphon, the human, who has done this!" said a Kur.

"Spare Flavion!" cried a Kur.

"Lord Grendel resents the wisdom of our Flavion," said a Kur.

605

"He would destroy him, the most valuable and courageous of scouts," said another.

"Kill me if you wish," said Flavion. "I had rather die than be suspected of some part, however small, in this foul deed."

Lord Grendel seemed poised to hasten forward in the savage, bounding rush which Cabot knew well from his dealings with enraged Kurii.

"Flavion would be the last to wish her freed," said a Kur.

"He has always urged that justice be meted out to her," said another.

"He is innocent," said another.

Cabot put his hand out, gently, and touched the arm of Lord Grendel.

Lord Grendel spun about and Cabot feared his arm would be torn from his body. It was terrible to look into the raging eyes of Lord Grendel.

Then, with a mighty effort, almost as though an exploded cliff, tumbling and showering boulders, might arrest itself in flight, and then, slowly, carefully reassemble each pebble and each stone in its place, Lord Grendel slowly straightened his body, and looked about himself.

"Forgive me," said Lord Grendel.

"It seems, dear Flavion, you will survive the day," said Statius.

"Lord Grendel is perhaps not himself," said Flavion, uncertainly.

"He has gone mad," said a Kur, softly.

"This," said another, "is our commander, in whose hands lie our fates?"

"Where is Cestiphon?" asked Lord Grendel.

"Bring him here," said Flavion, "in chains!"

"No," said Lord Grendel. Then he looked about himself. "Has anyone here seen anything, does anyone here know aught of this?"

Only demurrals greeted this inquiry.

Shortly thereafter, ushered forward by two Kurii, came Cestiphon.

"Lord Grendel?" he said. Then he looked about himself, and then to the ground. "Where is the pretty little chain slut?" he said.

"Beware," said Flavion, "you are speaking of a free woman."

"She is gone," said Archon.

"Where?"

"We do not know," said a Kur.

"Do you know aught of this?" demanded Flavion.

"No," said Cestiphon, "but I am not displeased. There are better things to do with an exquisite female than tear her to pieces."

"Put her up for sale," suggested Cabot.

"I would have liked to have had her on my neck rope," said Cestiphon, "with my others."

"Kill him!" said Flavion.

"No," said Lord Grendel.

"Why would anyone free her?" asked Cabot. "She is nothing to Kurii, as she is human. At best, they would want her blood. And why would humans free her, unless they could have her for their own? But there is nowhere to keep her, or hide her."

"I do not see her bell here," said Lord Grendel.

"It is not here," said Statius, looking about.

"Then it is still on her," said a Kur.

"No one heard it sound," said another Kur.

"She could hold it silent, in her escape," said Lord Grendel.

"Perhaps," said Flavion, "one who wished her blood made off with her."

"It would have been easier to remove her head, in a single bite," said Statius. "And who would steal her? And where, if she were stolen, could she be taken?"

The confluence of these realities and speculations whirled about in the mind of Tarl Cabot, Lord Grendel's human ally. It seemed the hand of his mind reached out to grasp something, but it slipped from his grasp.

"Where is the tiara?" suddenly asked Cabot.

It was shortly discovered that it was missing.

"She must be making her way to the lines of Agamemnon," said Flavion, "for she was his human."

"He would have had her on the slaughter bench," said Lord Grendel.

"Is that worse than dying on the torture table?" said Cestiphon.

"It seems clear she must have had a confederate in the camp," said Flavion. "Who knows what she might have been promised?"

"Of what use could she now be to Agamemnon?" asked a Kur.

"To the forward lines!" said Lord Grendel.

So the Lady Bina was missing.

That she was missing, however unaccountable this might seem, was less disturbing to Cabot than why she might be missing.

On the surface there seemed little that was rational here.

But there must be, he was sure, a concealed rationality, a rationality awaiting some intelligible elucidation.

Threads of thought, like strands in water, like half-visible snakes, coiled and uncoiled in Cabot's mind.

Certainly the Lady Bina would have welcomed any opportunity to escape.

But she would have had to have help to effect her escape, help to elude her constraints, and presumably help to pass through the insurrectionists' lines.

There would thus have to be a purpose other than her own involved in all this.

And what purpose could that be?

"Of what use could she now be to Agamemnon?" had asked a Kur.

He then recalled, suddenly, sharply, his conversation in the redoubt with Flavion.

"Arrangements have already been made," had said Flavion.

With a cry of alarm Cabot hurried to the forward lines.

"Where is Lord Grendel!" he cried.

"There, there!" cried a Kur, pointing to the wide, long field separating the near side of the habitats from the forward lines. "We could not stop him!" said the Kur.

"The glass, give me the glass!" cried Cabot, and the instrument was placed in his hands.

"He heard the bell below, from a half pasang distant," said Statius. "He leaped over the parapet and sped below, to rescue the Lady Bina."

"Down there," said a Kur, "in midst of the cattle humans."

"He will fetch her back," said another.

"He should have sent others," said a Kur. "He is commander."

"He is mad," said another.

"We could not stop him," said Flavion. "He will return shortly."

Cabot peered anxiously through the glass. "I know that herd!" he said. "Its leader is the cattle human from the time of the slaughter bench, he who noted the Lady Bina, he who understood in his simple, doltish, stupid way her role in leading others to the slaughter bench, he who would have her blood!"

"No!" cried Flavion, in dismay.

"It is no coincidence that it is that herd and not another which is foraging below!" cried Cabot.

"Surely it is a mere coincidence," protested Flavion.

"No, no!" cried Cabot.

"They will kill the Lady Bina!" said Statius.

"Nonsense," said Flavion. "Lord Grendel will have her before they even realize she is amongst them."

"He will return shortly," said a Kur.

"We will then learn who abetted her escape," said another Kur.

"Certainly," said Flavion.

"No, no!" cried Cabot. "Seize power weapons! Follow me!"

"Are you mad?" said Flavion.

"This is not about the Lady Bina!" cried Cabot, taking a rifle. "This is about Lord Grendel! The herd is cover! Mingled in that herd will be the minions of Agamemnon!"

Cabot then scrambled over the parapet, and began to run, wildly, toward the herd.

"He is mad!" cried Flavion. "Do not follow him! Remain here!"

Concealed amongst the cattle humans were somewhere between twenty and twenty-five Kurii, these picked minions of the elite of Lord Agamemnon's forces, each armed with a power weapon.

Lord Grendel had entered the herd unarmed, save insofar as a Kur can be said to be unarmed, given their size, might, agility, fangs, and claws.

We might suppose that given the odds involved and the importance of Lord Grendel that the Kurii of Agamemnon would have been charged with his capture, that he might be later exhibited and dealt with according to the dictates of the war and day, but it seems they had no such charge.

In any event, shortly after Lord Grendel entered the herd, two Kurii rose up from amongst the cattle humans and fired.

In this action may perhaps be detected the astute recommendation of Flavion, whose grasp of politics, diplomacy, and war was of a most direct, simple, and practical sort.

The head of one of the cattle humans was burned away but

inches from the chest of Lord Grendel, and another cattle human's chest was burned through, in such a way that a portion of Lord Grendel's harness was blackened, and hair singed from his shoulder.

Lord Grendel then took cover amongst the cattle humans, precisely as had his foes.

Had Lord Grendel not been overwrought, or had he been less concerned with the safety of the Lady Bina, he might have chosen to remain within the safety of his lines and allowed her to perish as she might, and would, at the hands of the cattle humans.

The leader of the cattle humans, of course, was not privy to the machinations of Agamemnon's minions, nor would he have understood their concerns even had they attempted to explain them to him.

He did have his hatred, of course, and his memories, and a single-minded program in mind, to deal with a bell human, a human who would have led him, and others, to the slaughter bench.

The other Kurii then rose, too, weapons readied, from amongst the cattle humans, their heads now clearly visible amongst those of the unkempt, lumbering, shambling, obese, bovine herd.

This must have been obvious to those in the revolutionists' lines, as they had access to more than one optical instrument of the sort with which Cabot had made his earlier determinations.

One of the Kurii suddenly seemed to sink into the herd.

Lord Grendel's jaws were foaming with blood.

The Kurii then, in pairs, for these were elite Kur warriors, began to thread their way through the herd. No longer might Lord Grendel isolate a foe, and the likelihood of taking two at once, given their spacing, which was considered, for they were elite warriors, would be negligible.

There was the sound of the Lady Bina's bell and her scream was heard in the field.

Lord Grendel then, unwisely, as most would agree, tried to make his way to her, to afford her succor.

Whereas the hunting Kurii had not the least interest in the Lady Bina herself they had been well apprised of her importance to their target, this information having been supplied by Flavion, and so they began to converge on that locality from which had emanated the sound of the bell, and the scream. It resembled that of a shrill, terrified, caught animal, something similar to that perhaps of one of the womb tunnel's scavengers suddenly seized in the teeth of a Kur infant.

Lord Grendel, unwisely, began to thrust cattle human after cattle human from his path, hastening to the relief of the Lady Bina, who was in the midst of several cattle humans squealing and stamping about her, some with stones, and others with sharpened sticks. The herd leader had a large club, with which he was trying to turn her to her back. She screamed, several times, and began to choke, and sob, as they dealt with her.

The leader of the herd pushed his confreres back with the club, and raised it high over his head, to strike the torn, and bloodied, piece of flesh at his feet.

The blow did not fall because the club was torn from his grasp and then Lord Grendel, the massive club in his hands, began to strike about him, and the cattle humans fled back before these blows, limping, arms dangling, faces a mass of bones and blood.

The leader of the cattle humans, blood about his teeth, where he had bitten his prey, was seized in the mighty paws of Lord Grendel, lifted high in the air, and then flung to the earth, this breaking the back and neck of the leader of the cattle humans, who was then, as Lord Grendel had not loosened his grip, jerked upward, and the head was seized in Lord Grendel's jaws, and torn away from the shoulders, and then, with a movement of his head, flung fifty feet away.

Meanwhile, the two foremost of the Kurii of Agamemnon, these first through the cattle humans, intent on their target, and now having isolated it, leveled their weapons.

By this time Cabot had reached the edge of the herd.

The Kurii of Agamemnon, concerned with their priorities, were unaware of his presence.

Indeed, the following Kurii were not even aware, immediately, that two of their number, those closest to Lord Grendel, were no longer with them, but had been, for most practical purposes, with two charges from Cabot's weapon, incinerated.

Lord Grendel crouched down, jaws red with blood.

Cabot fired three times more.

With these three charges, he had managed to hit one other Kur.

Cabot's rifle, as most of its model, contained five charges, one in the bore, four in the magazine, which five had now been expended.

His foes having now clearly discerned his presence, and the nature of his weapon, and being quite as well aware as he of the likely expenditure of ammunition, began to approach his position, though warily.

Cabot, naturally, shifted his location, as he could. His rifle now was of little more use than would have been a metal club.

There was a bleating from the herd as Kurii now began to burn their way through the massive, obstructive flesh, almost as one might have set fire to a palisade, in order to clear a line of fire to its garrison. The herd then, many of its members stung and burned, several now no more than smoking meat, confused and tormented, finally alarmed, wildly bleating, piteously squealing, began to hurry away.

Some of the Kurii were buffeted one way or another, but then the herd was muchly scattered, and Lord Grendel would not move from his place, which was near small, torn flesh, and Cabot walked to join him, presumably that they might die together.

The remains of Agamemnon's Kurii then raised their rifles, but were almost immediately cut down in a withering torrent of flame.

"Are you all right?" called Statius.

Archon raised his rifle and brought down one of the two fleeing Kurii. The other made it to the habitats.

With Statius and Archon were more than a dozen Kurii and humans, armed with power weapons.

Lord Grendel reached down and lifted, tenderly, in his arms the limp, lacerated form of the Lady Bina.

He stood there, in the field, silent, in the grass, amongst bodies, those of cattle humans and Kurii, holding her.

"Is she alive?" asked Cabot.

Lord Grendel was looking toward the habitats.

"She is still bleeding," said Archon.

"She is alive," said Statius.

"It might be better were she not," said a Kur.

"What is wrong with our commander?" said a Kur.

"There is water on his face," said a Kur.

"Those are tears," said Cabot.

"Kurii cannot weep," said Statius. "They lack the means."

"He is partly human," said Cabot.

Lord Grendel turned about and slowly made his way back to the insurrectionists' lines, the unconscious, torn body of the Lady Bina in his arms.

Cabot, bending down, picked up a tiara, and followed them to the insurrectionists' lines.

Chapter, the Sixty-Fourth:

Thoughts Behind Thoughts

"She is no longer beautiful," said Archon.

The bell had been removed from the neck of the Lady Bina.

For four days she had been unconscious, and had then awakened raving, in delirium, her body burning with fever. In all this time Lord Grendel had remained at her side, watching over her, tending her, while the governance of the camp was surrendered to the human ally, Peisistratus, and the rule of the insurrectionists' lines, the orders of the day, the arrangements of signs and countersigns, the inspection of weaponry, the postings of guards, the arrangement of patrols, and such, was accorded to Statius, who had once been a nondominant.

"If there should be any sign of enemy activity," had said Lord Grendel, "I am to be notified, immediately."

But the habitats were quiet, and the field below was largely deserted, save for some cattle humans who had drifted back, to scavenge.

Flavion was missing.

This had been discovered shortly after the return to the insurrectionists' lines.

Some ten days after her escape and recovery, and six days after it had begun, the Lady Bina's fever broke. She then, after imbibing some broth administered to her by Lord Grendel, slept soundly for a full day. When she awakened her delirium had passed, and she looked about herself, wonderingly, trying to gather together her thoughts, and comprehend what had happened to her. She then suddenly half sat up in the coverlets and screamed, but was gently pressed back by Lord Grendel. She felt about her neck for the bell, but it was not there. "Sleep," he advised her, tenderly, and she again slept. Once she thrashed in her sleep and screamed, and awakened, but he again soothed her, and she again slept. It was on the twelfth day after her return to the insurrectionists' lines that she awakened, lay there awake, not moving, for a long time, and then dared to touch her fingers to her face, and she then cried out, a long, wavering wail, one of horror. She then demanded a mirror. Lord Grendel demurred and tried to soothe her, but she would not be soothed, and would have the mirror. She looked into the mirror and then flung it away and begged to be brought a knife. This request Lord Grendel refused. "Kill me," she begged. "Kill me!" This request was also refused.

"She is hideous," said Peisistratus.

"Lord Grendel does not think so," said Cabot.

"Then he sees something other than we see," said Peisistratus.

"I think he does," said Cabot. "I think he always did."

"I could not sell her for a pot girl, let alone a kettle-and-mat girl," said Peisistratus. "She is good for nothing now but sleen feed, if that."

"She was refusing to eat," said Statius, "until our friend Cabot spoke to her."

"What did you say?" asked Archon.

"Not a great deal," said Cabot. "I merely informed her that if she did not eat she would be stripped and lashed, and then force fed, as might be a slave, and that her hands would be fastened behind her, that she not be able to rid herself of the food, that she would not be permitted to starve herself any more than a new slave, who does not yet understand that the will is her master's and not hers, one who does not yet understand fully, as she shortly will, that such things are not permitted to her, and that she is truly a slave, is to be treated as such, and will be treated as such, in short, that she is no longer hers, but is now the master's, that she is now property, his property."

"And Lord Grendel permitted this?" said Statius.

"He authorized me to do whatever I thought useful, or necessary, in the matter."

"How did it turn out?" asked Statius.

"When he entered with food," said Cabot, "she fed, with neither protest nor dissent."

"Good," said Peisistratus.

"But you treated her, in effect, as a slave," said Statius.

"Every free woman, from time to time," said Cabot, "should be treated as a slave."

"They are all slaves," said Peisistratus. "The only difference is the collar."

"She may be quiet now, but I fear she will watch," said Archon, "and, when the opportunity permits, destroy herself."

"She will not be given the opportunity," said Cabot.

"How is it to be precluded?" asked Archon.

"We will keep her in slave chains," said Cabot.

"But she is a free woman," said Statius.

"She should be a slave," said Cabot. "Thus it is appropriate that she be placed in the chains of a slave, and become accustomed to them."

"Cestiphon, who is a killer human, inured to the sights of the arena, and such, caught a glimpse of her, and cast up his food," said Statius.

"She need no longer fear then," said Cabot, "her stripping beneath his appraising glance, his accosting, the callous, imperious grasp of his strong hands on her defenseless beauty."

"I questioned Cestiphon," said Peisistratus. "It was Flavion who encouraged his advances to the Lady Bina."

"I was sure of it," said Statius.

It may be recalled, the look, perhaps one of puzzlement, or resentment, that Cestiphon had cast at Flavion. Cestiphon had not anticipated the intervention or fury of Lord Grendel. It had only recently become clear to Cestiphon that Flavion had put him to use, to further his own ends, to bring Lord Grendel hurriedly to the assistance of the Lady Bina, thus betraying his concern for a traitress, and, thus, he hoped, undermining and compromising his position in the camp.

"Not that he would have required a great deal of encouragement," said Cabot.

"No," said Peisistratus, "no more than any other healthy human male."

"She need no longer fear a rope on her neck, fastening her amongst his other women," said Archon.

"Unfortunately," said Cabot.

"It is my understanding," said Archon, "that she has begged a sheet, a covering of some sort, with which to conceal her face and body."

"That is true," said Cabot. "And I have no doubt it will be granted to her."

"Good," said Peisistratus. "It sickens one to look upon her."

"At least Kurii no longer call for her blood," said Peisistratus.

"Why should they?" said Archon. "What could they do to her now that she would not welcome?"

It would be injudicious, and certainly unnecessary, in a reportorial narrative of this sort, to delineate in any detail the terrible moments which were spent by the Lady Bina in the clutches of the cattle humans. They had, of course, their nails and teeth, small stones, sharpened sticks, and such. With these there had been a brief frenzy of tearing, poking, stabbing, gouging, and cutting, such things, which attentions had not been restricted to any particular portion of her small body, but had been delivered almost randomly, with a violent, vengeful, doltish zeal.

"Many," said Statius, "feel she should be turned out of the camp."

"To die?" asked Cabot.

"Presumably."

"Lord Grendel would not permit it," said Cabot.

"Her presence depresses many in the camp," said Statius.

"She will cover herself," said Cabot.

"Have any heard aught of the traitor, Flavion?" asked Archon.

"No," said Statius.

"I should not like to be he, should Lord Grendel learn of his whereabouts," said Archon.

"Nor I," said Statius.

The reader notes that Archon referred to Flavion as a traitor. This was now common knowledge in the camp, given the freeing of the Lady Bina, the attempt on the life of Lord Grendel, his flight, and such.

The Lady Bina had confirmed, as was scarcely necessary, the collusion of Flavion in her escape. She had regarded him as a secret friend, concerned to protect her, as possible, from the wrath of Kurii. After all, had she not once served Agamemnon? She had thus been overwhelmed with gratitude at having been accorded an opportunity to escape. She had not understood, of course, her unwitting role in the attempt on the life of Lord Grendel, who was certain to follow her. Nor did she understand the nature of the cattle humans through which she was to make her way, identified in her tiara, to the lines of Agamemnon, of whose shelter, contrition, gratitude, and affection she had been assured by Flavion. It is true she had betrayed Peisistratus and Arcesilaus to Lord Agamemnon long ago but the profit she had hoped to accrue from that act had been persuasive, and, of course, although this consideration would do little to mitigate or extenuate the treachery of her act, it might be recalled that she was not a member of a party to which she would have owed an allegiance. Her act then could be conceived of as primarily one of shrewd calculation. Greed for significance, importance, power, and wealth is a motivation to which many humans are susceptible, and we must, in all honesty, acknowledge that it is one to which some Kurii, perhaps surprisingly, are not immune. That motivation, too, we might speculate, might be particularly acute for a certain type of human female, perhaps one at war with herself, self-estranged, self-alienated, discontented with her sex, envying males, or such, as she often finds herself precluded in virtue of her slightness and body from utilizing the usual routes to such advantages, leadership, dominance, aggression, charisma, violence, physical superiority, prowess with weapons, and such. Gorean males, in particular, it seems, prefer women on their knees, stripped and in collars, their lips pressed to their feet. They feel that is where they belong, by nature, and they will have them there, that nature's loveliest gift to them is the natural female; their slave. Too, many females, despite disparaging and alienating acculturations, sense that they rightfully belong at the feet of masters. Often they silently beg for the collar. Many is the female who has brought herself to the feet of a master. Many is the female who has knelt, lowered her head, and extended her arms, piteously, beggingly, wrists crossed, for binding. "I am a slave, Master. I beg to be yours. Please, I beg you, accept me."

Too, how is a woman a woman, truly, until she kneels, ineradicably submitted, hopelessly and irredeemably feminine, in the fullness of her vulnerable femininity, before a man, her master?

How tragic it is that many human females, the product of pathological cultures, cultures and civilizations at war with nature, are unhappy with their sex, even resentful of it. What an astonishing epiphany it is for them, then, to accept that they are females, and are profoundly different from males, that they are gloriously and wonderfully other than males, and come to understand the value, preciousness, and delicious specialness of their sex. Certainly this becomes clear to them when they find themselves being auctioned, offered to heated, competing, eager buyers.

Too, of course, considering matters of motivation, it seems the Lady Bina may have been displeased that Cabot had not proved more amendable to her considerable charms, that whilst both were clasped in breeding shackles.

Beyond the matter of the betrayal of Peisistratus and Lord Arcesilaus, she had, incidentally, as it turned out, no particularly active role in either the debacle of the arsenal or the projected massacre in the Vale of Destruction. Her first escape, that following her acquisition from the place of the slaughter bench, prior to the ambush of the arsenal, had been arranged by Flavion, that all suspicion would fall upon her, whilst he himself, in a putative scouting excursion, had earlier informed Kur patrols of the plan. The girl herself had been picked up shortly after her escape by a Kur outpost, and remanded to the palace. There, taken before Agamemnon, who had viewed her from one of his bodies, her hands had been pinioned behind her, though she was a free woman, in the shameful, but perfectly effective bracelets of a slave. She had then been taken into the forests and released, to be hunted down by, and devoured by, one or another of the sleen which had been released into the world to prey on humans. There were fewer such sleen, however, than Agamemnon realized, as traps had been set, one of which, we may recall, had snared the giant sleen, Ramar, and, too, humans, and their Kurii, had often defended themselves with vigor, often killing the animals, or, if their scent had not been taken, driving them away. After several days, miserable and half starving, still helplessly braceleted, she had stumbled upon a womb tunnel, in which she took shelter, and in which she managed to feed on the remains of small scavengers and compete with them for the nourishing blood ensuing so liberally from the rent wombs, consequent upon a Kur birth. She had been noted by killer humans, and was fleeing them, when she was apprehended by Lord Grendel, Statius, and the human, Tarl Cabot, which party brought her back, a prisoner, to the camp. It was Flavion's expressed speculation that she had earlier lurked about the camp, and learned the plans for marching on the palace, after first meeting at the Vale of Destruction, and that then she had conveyed these plans to the forces of Agamemnon. Supposedly it was after this that she had been captured by human patrols and back-braceleted, patrols from which, however, she had managed to escape, this accounting for the condition in which Lord Grendel and his confreres had found her. Thus, most in Lord Grendel's camp had considered her guilty of three betrayals, the first of Peisistratus and Lord Arcesilaus, the second pertaining to the arsenal, which was costly, and the third, which turned out well due to no fault of hers, given the intervention of the mariners. It was thus no wonder that many Kurii had hungered for her blood. In Lord Grendel's camps, that of the forest, and that later within their lines, she had been terrified to protest her innocence or even to speak, as she had been warned that her tongue might be torn out. Too, as she had no translator, and few were in her vicinity, and she could understand very little of Kur, she was not even clear as to what the nature and extent of the charges against her might be. It had been made clear to her, of course, by Flavion, the dreadful danger in which she stood, information which, if nothing else, would motivate her desire to escape at all costs.

There were four females on the personal neck rope of Cestiphon, all women of killer humans. These were Cestiphon's own women, as opposed to the women held in common by his group of killer humans. On that rope there were fourteen. Cestiphon was the leader of his group, which contained some twenty males. It was his group which had flushed the Lady Bina into the open, earlier, when she had been noted by Lord Grendel, Statius, and Cabot, in the vicinity of a womb tunnel.

Perhaps too close to them a small, concealed figure moved, timidly, slowly, trying to pass about them, its motion impeded by the shackles it wore on its slim ankles. It was bent over and clutched a sheet about itself with closely braceleted hands. The sheet was clutched in a such a way that the face was effectively hooded, the opening on the sheet sufficing for little more than a lowered head to survey the next patch of ground on which it might dare to tread.

One of the women of the killer humans sprang to her feet and snatched at the sheet but the small figure hastily, frightened, drew back. But the other women of the killer humans, on the rope, had sprung up, and encircled her.

In a moment the small figure had cried out in misery, the sheet ripped from her, and she knelt in the dirt, cowering, covering her face with her hands, that none could look upon its horror.

Beneath the sheet she had been as naked as the women of the killer humans.

The killer humans keep their women naked.

Surely this is not unusual for the women of primates.

One supposes the hostility of these women of killer humans was the natural hostility of one type of female toward another, say, one of a certain race, breed or group to that of another race, breed, or group, or perhaps it was something like that of the glorious free woman toward the degraded, vulnerable female slave. In any event, these women clearly did not understand that the Lady Bina, for it was she whom they had entrapped, was a free woman, or, more likely, they had no concept at all of a free woman. Too, it is certainly possible that they remembered her from the pursuit of her in the vicinity of the womb tunnel and recognized that she might have been captured and put on their rope, and might perhaps have been more favored of food and caresses than they. Indeed, they may have been aware of her earlier accosting by Cestiphon. But clearly there was little they had to fear from her now.

Two of the women pulled the Lady Bina's hands away from her face, and a third drew her head up by the hair.

They made gleeful noises, the leader pointing to her, and all spat upon her. Their leader danced and posed before her, exhibiting her superior attractions, and lifted and flung her hair about, indicating its sheen and length. And then the Lady Bina's captors pulled her to her feet, and turned her about, and about, displaying her to the camp, but the men turned away, disgusted, and the women shrieked and laughed the more. But then, suddenly, the switch, for he had now obtained such a device, useful for the control of women, of an angered Cestiphon fell amongst them, and they went to all fours, and cowered, sobbing under the blows. "Master!"

begged their leader, now on her knees, trying to fend blows. "Master!" The killer humans, this group, were scarcely speeched, but the word for a male, any male, was "Master." Similarly, their word for a female, any female, was "slave."

Cestiphon hooked the switch on his belt, where he was accustomed to keep it. He glowered at the neck-roped women of the killer humans. They cringed under his gaze, not daring to meet his eyes. The switch had done its work well, its supple, stinging slash, far better than its humble predecessor, the stick, which, less yielding, was more likely to damage a woman than punish and instruct her. The stick was a makeshift device, crude and barbarous; the switch was an artifact, a boon of civilization, a tested, refined, efficient implement, one explicitly and intelligently designed for the management and improvement of slaves. Cestiphon then picked up the sheet and threw it about the Lady Bina, who gratefully, with her small, closely braceleted hands, clutched it about her.

"Begone, beast, monster," said Cestiphon, angrily, and the Lady Bina, sobbing, clutching the sheet about her, fighting her shackles, moved away, as swiftly as she could.

Men withdrew from her course.

Female slaves slipped back, and knelt, their heads to the dirt, that she might pass, unimpeded.

The Lady Bina was, you see, despite what might be her misfortunes or fate, a free woman, and thus a thousand times, and more, above them.

The Lady Bina went to where Lord Grendel was in conference with Peisistratus, Statius, and Cabot, and, with a small sound of chain, lay down at his feet.

"Kneel up, knees together, in suitable fashion," said Lord Grendel to her, kindly. "You are a free woman. You are not a slave, to lie curled at a man's feet, as a pet sleen."

"It is appropriate," said Cabot, "for a slave to lie at her master's feet. They look nicely there, and it is where they belong. Too, most female slaves are worth less than a sleen, certainly less than a good sleen."

"But she is a free woman, dear Cabot," admonished Lord Grendel.

"Ah, yes," said Cabot, resignedly.

"She belongs in a collar," said Statius.

"No one would want her now," said Peisistratus.

The Lady Bina sobbed, softly, and knelt as she had been encouraged to kneel, as a Gorean free woman, demurely, erect, gracefully, her knees together. To be sure, even a tower slave will kneel with her knees together. The pleasure slave, of course, must kneel with her knees spread, as she is a pleasure slave.

"Lady," suggested Peisistratus, "draw the sheet about you."

"You are free," said Lord Grendel. "Do as you wish."

The Lady Bina carefully, closely, drew the sheet about her, and knelt beside them, her head down.

From time to time, from within the carefully arranged sheet, was heard a small noise, a soft noise, a sob.

The men then returned to their concerns.

"It has been too quiet," said Lord Grendel.

"Many of our men grow impatient," said Statius. "Many urge a rush upon the enemy ramparts."

"Perhaps we should have simply taken Flavion's advice," said Lord Grendel, "and marched into a carefully laid trap."

"I would suppose," said Cabot, "that there is a similar unrest amongst the forces of Lord Agamemnon. They, too, are Kurii."

"Let us hope," said Statius, "that they will make the first such move."

"Agamemnon must manage his forces as well as we ours," said Lord Grendel, "and he will be subject to similar influences and pressures."

"But he will not be mad enough to order a frontal assault," said Cabot.

"No," said Lord Grendel, "but he will do something, I am sure."

"He is subtle," said Cabot.

"He has thoughts behind thoughts," said Statius.

"And doubtless, too," said Cabot, "he now has at his ready disposal the advice of a most astute counselor."

"One familiar with our lines, our leadership, our thinking," said Peisistratus.

"Do not concern yourself with Flavion's knowledge," said Lord Grendel. "As the positions are stable, it will do him little good, no matter how extensive it is. Fear rather his cleverness."

"I do not understand," said Statius.

"There will be a new initiative," said Lord Grendel. "It is only that we do not know what it will be."

"It will be conceived by Flavion?" asked Cabot.

"No," said Lord Grendel. "It will be beyond Flavion. It will be of Agamemnon himself."

Shortly after this conversation, indeed, the next day, the nature of Agamemnon's initiative became clear.

To the insurrection's humans its potency was not evident.

Its potency, however, was quite clear to Kurii.

It depended, you see, on the ways of Kur.

Chapter, the Sixty-Fifth:

The Delegation Returns

"You have heard the proclamation," said Lord Grendel.

"Who could not?" said Cabot, angrily. "The world rings with it."

The proclamation had been repeated several times, in both Kur and Gorean.

"Surely," said Statius, "he does not have Lord Arcesilaus."

"He may," said Cabot. "Lord Grendel and I found the cave by Lake Fear empty."

"Lord Arcesilaus would surely not have us comply with the proclamation," said Archon.

"No, he would not," said Lord Grendel, "but he cannot change the ways of Kur."

"It is not clear he is in the power of Agamemnon," said a Kur.

"That would have to be determined," said another Kur.

"What would it matter?" asked Archon.

"You are human," said a Kur. "You do not understand."

"Perhaps one might die for a cause," said Cabot, "but surely not for a leader."

"Surely humans have died for leaders, as well as causes," said Lord Grendel.

"Not in this way," said Cabot.

"No," said Lord Grendel, "I suppose not in this way."

"Have humans not chosen to die for friends, for brothers, even for slaves?" asked a Kur.

"Not in this fashion, surely, or seldom so," said Cabot.

"The proclamation is clear," said a Kur. "It is our lives or that of Lord Arcesilaus. He will be put to death if we do not slay ourselves. Our only way to save him is to slay ourselves."

"Surely he would not wish that," said Cabot.

"His wishes in this matter are not decisive," said Lord Grendel.

"This is utter madness," said Cabot. "Our Kurii cannot be serious."

"They are quite serious," said Lord Grendel.

"Do not fear," said a Kur. "Humans are not involved in this."

"They would be hunted down, and killed later," said another Kur.

"Our Kurii will die, that Arcesilaus may live?" said Cabot. "The war teeters on some bizarre irrationality?"

"It is not bizarre to us," said a Kur.

"It is the way," said another.

"To die for a leader is to betray the cause," said Cabot.

"The cause is the leader," said a Kur. "The leader is the cause."

"That is madness," said Cabot.

"You are not Kur," said a Kur.

"It is alien to you," said Lord Grendel, "but it is not alien to us."

"We are not as you, nor are you as we," said a Kur.

"Surely we have rationality in common," said Cabot.

"We are rational," said a Kur. "It is you who are not rational. It is rational to die for the leader, to whom one is pledged. What could be more rational? It would be irrational, an act of insanity, not to do so."

"Life is first," said Cabot.

"No," said a Kur. "The way is first."

"Surely, Lord Grendel," said Cabot, "you will not betray humans, and the Lady Bina amongst them, to the vengeance of the minions of Lord Agamemnon."

"I can die with them," said Lord Grendel.

"Humans will continue to resist," said Cabot.

"The winter can be brought," said Lord Grendel, "and humans will be immobilized, perhaps frozen, in temperatures which, to Kurii, are merely severe."

"Suppose," said Cabot, "many, or most, of our Kurii kill themselves. What, then, is to prevent Lord Agamemnon from killing Lord Arcesilaus?"

"Nothing," said a Kur.

"One supposes he would do so," said another.

"Recall," said Lord Grendel, "the mariners awaited the noose or knife, in dismal, patient resignation, as befitting their degradation."

"That, too, was madness," said Cabot.

"No," said a Kur. "It is the way of Kur."

"Without the way of Kur," said Lord Grendel, "we are not Kur."

"I suspect," said Statius, "Agamemnon does not have Lord Arcesilaus."

"I have sent a delegation, lifting above their heads the broken spear," said Lord Grendel, "that they may be permitted through the enemy lines and conveyed to the palace, that a determination may be made in the matter. I expected their return by now."

"Doubtless they have been slain."

"I think not," said Lord Grendel, gazing beyond the rampart, to the field betwixt the habitats and the lines of the insurrectionists.

Small figures could be seen in the distance. Some small groups of cattle humans moved slowly from their path.

"It is the delegation," said Statius.

Several Ehn later some four Kurii were admitted to the insurrectionists' lines.

"Well?" said Lord Grendel.

The leader of the delegation cast aside the broken spear.

"Well?" said Lord Grendel.

"Lord Agamemnon, Eleventh face of the Nameless One, Theocrat of the World," said their leader, "has Lord Arcesilaus in his power."

Chapter, the Sixty-Sixth:

Winter Has Been Arranged;
Time Has Run Out

Cabot crouched down within the ramparts, a robe clutched about him, shuddering with cold. He could not even hold the bow, nor finger arrows from the quiver, so stiff and useless were his fingers.

Wind tore about the ramparts, and blinding snow.

Lord Grendel brushed snow from his face and eyes, and examined the wintry terrain extending to the habitats.

"The weather may be localized," said Lord Grendel. "I have given permission for the humans to withdraw."

"Sharpen blades, and form lines," had said a Kur. "We will begin the cutting of throats."

"And the last alive may then drive the knife into his own breast," said another.

"May I speak?" had begged Cabot, and Lord Grendel had bidden the others listen.

"I do not understand the ways of Kur," had said Cabot. "I do not understand how my friends, my compatriots, and brothers, can contemplate the ruination of a cause for which we have long and well fought. Are we really to abandon our war and accept a defeat which we may ascribe only to ourselves? This seems to me not only an error, a dreadful mistake, but a lapse into abject madness. Further, it is clear to me, as well, that Lord Arcesilaus would not wish this monstrous act, this self slaughtering, to take place, and, indeed, that he would forbid it, and categorically, had he the opportunity to do so. All this, I take it, is clear."

There was general assent to his remarks, but little evidence that his peers were to be dissuaded from their woeful intention.

"Let us suppose," said Cabot, "that the way of Kur is not to be changed."

"It will not be changed," said a Kur.

"Why should it not be changed?" asked Lord Grendel.

"It will not be changed!" said more than one Kur.

"Very well," said Cabot. "Let us suppose the way of Kur is not changed, that this lethal pact, so peculiar and incomprehensible to mere humans, is to be brought to effectuation."

"As it must be," said a Kur.

"But when?" asked Cabot. "Is there anything in the way of Kur which insists upon a particular hour, or day, or moment?"

"No," said a Kur.

"The mariners, after their defeat," said Cabot, "did not all immediately hang themselves or rush to the knife. Days, weeks, passed, before they went to the place of gathering."

"They have still not submitted to the noose or knife," said a Kur.

"Nor will they," said Cabot.

"They have changed the way of Kur," said Lord Grendel.

"This is different," said a Kur. "Another life is at stake, that of the leader, Lord Arcesilaus."

"Yes," said Lord Grendel, "it is different. But, I take it, the point of our friend Cabot is that we need not act on this precipitately."

"Why should we wait?" asked a Kur.

"Let us be done with it," said another.

"Let us wait," pleaded Cabot. "Must we instantly gratify Lord Agamemnon? I, for one, would not care to do so. And what will Lord Agamemnon do, if we wait? His forces are doubtless as anxious as ours to bring our conflict to a favorable resolution. May they not eventually swarm forth as irrationally as many of you seem to propose to do, and might not they then, rather than us, be cut down in the intervening fields?"

"Waiting would disconcert Agamemnon, at least," said Lord Grendel. "And certainly it will put pressure on his commanders, as their forces grow ever more restless."

"He may kill Lord Arcesilaus," said a Kur.

"If he does so," said Lord Grendel, "then he is no longer in a position to bargain with his life."

"Let us wait," said a Kur.

"Agamemnon will be angry," said a Kur.

"Excellent," had said Lord Grendel.

When the Kurii had filed away, Lord Grendel turned to Cabot. "Thank you, friend," he said.

"We have bought a bit of time," said Cabot.

"Do you think it will be enough?" had asked Lord Grendel.

"No," had said Cabot. "I do not think so."

It was four days after the return of the delegation that the weather changed.

It began with the wind, and then the temperature.

"You should withdraw, friend," said Lord Grendel to Cabot.

"I will stay," said Cabot.

"And others?" asked Lord Grendel.

"Some," said Cabot.

Wind tore at the cloak of Peisistratus, whipping it about his shoulders. He shut his eyes against the fierce sting of flighted ice.

Archon struggled to breathe, turning away from the wind.

"You are useless here," said Lord Grendel. "In these temperatures only Kurii might live."

"No," said Cabot. "We will clothe ourselves against the cold, build fires."

"It may be warmer elsewhere, perhaps in the vicinity of Lake Fear," said Lord Grendel. "I have ordered several of our humans to withdraw, searching for warmth."

"And what of the slaves?" asked Cabot.

"They will herd the slaves before them."

"Good," said Cabot.

It is a common practice of humans to care for their domestic animals, taking, say, bosk, kaiila, verr, and such to better pastures, more temperate climes, and such.

"What of the Lady Bina?" asked Cabot.

"We have bundled her well," said Lord Grendel. "And I have had a litter prepared, which will be dragged by the women of Cestiphon. They, too, are now well bundled, and their feet wrapped."

"The women of Cestiphon?"

"It would amuse you to see them," said Peisistratus. "They are miserable with cold, and the very rope on their neck is stiff and frozen."

"But they hate the Lady Bina," said Cabot.

"They are now terrified of her," said Lord Grendel, "for they have now been taught the difference between free women and slaves, and that they are slaves."

"Interesting," said Cabot. "Then they now have more than one word for female."

"Yes," said Lord Grendel. "Whereas they, like Goreans, tend to think of all females as slaves, particularly as they consider their bodies in comparison with those of men, they do recognize that some females, however unaccountably, or irrationally, have a far superior status than themselves, that of the free woman."

"You dare entrust the Lady Bina to them?"

"Yes," said Lord Grendel. "I assure you they will be zealously solicitous of her welfare. If aught befalls her they will all be killed, and most unpleasantly."

"Do they understand that?" asked Cabot.

"Clearly," said Lord Grendel. "Very clearly."

"If the Lady Bina had retained her beauty," said Peisistratus, "perhaps she could train them as serving slaves."

"Do not forget they belong to Cestiphon," said Lord Grendel.

"True," said Peisistratus. "But perhaps he might sell them. At least two might bring a tarsk and a half."

"They are beautiful," said Cabot, "but little more than Kur pets, inarticulate, scarcely speeched."

"Some men like them that way," said Peisistratus.

"I have seen them in the hands of Cestiphon," said Lord Grendel, "writhing, squirming, bucking, crying out, begging for mercy one moment, and for more the next."

"Perhaps two tarsks," mused Peisistratus.

"I see no cattle humans below," said Cabot, half shutting his eyes against the snow, the swirling wind, the pelting of bits of ice.

"They have the memory of their pens, and the feed troughs,"

said Lord Grendel. "I would suppose they would return there and huddle together, for warmth."

"In weather such as this," said Cabot, "the forces of Agamemnon might well advance, seeking cover in the storm."

"No," said Lord Grendel. "Perhaps they would do so if the ramparts were held by humans, half blinded, scarcely able to move, but we have many of our folk here, well armed, strung along the ramparts. The blasts of our weapons would in moments destroy regiments, flood the plain with boiling water."

Lord Grendel suddenly lifted his hand.

The wind at the same moment ceased to blow, and the snow to fall. Cabot watched its last flakes gently descend to the white plain. The plain itself now seemed icy and still. The air was sharp and clear.

"Listen," said Lord Grendel.

The announcement, as before, was in both Kur and Gorean. It would be broadcast throughout the cylinder, throughout the world, even to the shores of Lake Fear.

"Agamemnon's patience is at an end," said Peisistratus.

"Lord Arcesilaus is to be executed tomorrow, at noon, on the palace steps," said Cabot.

"The time you purchased us," said Lord Grendel, "has run out."

Chapter, the Sixty-Seventh:

Cabot's Journey;
An Acquaintance Is Renewed

Cabot did not care to accompany Lord Grendel to the palace, to watch him die, as Kur, before Lord Arcesilaus.

It was a demand of Lord Agamemnon that all power weapons of insurrectionists be defused, gathered together, and destroyed. Not one power weapon was to be left in the camp. This, too, was a portion of the price for Lord Arcesilaus' life.

It was with a bitter heart that he watched his Kur brethren defuse and stack their weapons, prior to their destruction.

It was with a bitter heart that he watched his Kur brethren, one by one, unarmed, depart from the ramparts to file to the palace.

This time there would be no concealed weapons.

"Agamemnon has won," had said Lord Grendel, resignedly. "I knew that he would."

"How is that?" had asked Cabot.

"He is the Eleventh face of the Nameless One, Theocrat of the World," said Lord Grendel.

"But you fought against him," said Cabot, "and many others, too."

"It was to have been done," said Lord Grendel.

Cabot, though a warrior, had wept, parting from his friend.

Humans, whose ways were surely not the ways of Kur, left the camp, to seek what shelters, what concealments, they might.

Mostly they scattered, to live as they could, until the hunters, abetted by sleen, might find them.

To be sure, as many had now mastered the bow, they would prove dangerous game.

This risk, of course, would be welcomed by many Kur hunters. Such things increase the sport. They add considerable zest to the chase.

The hunters, of course, wary of the birds of death, it should be noted, would not go into the forests subjecting themselves to the self-imposed limitations to which they had been accustomed in the sport world. One would not expect that. They would therefore carry power weapons. With these they might burn out a swath of forest, yards wide, with a single charge. Too, they would wear body armor, capable of turning an arrow at point-blank range.

In such ways, one trusts, might their risks be reduced.

In this respect, one effects nothing critical.

Who would care to hunt otherwise masters of the great bow?

The heads of males might be tied to their harnesses as trophies, to be later properly mounted. Human females had their uses, even to Kurii, and could be brought back, stripped and bound, and dragged on a handful of leashes, almost as though they might be slaves. The prettier ones might be put again in high collars, to serve as pets, groomers, filers of claws, cleaners of caves, and such. Plainer ones might be used for the scouring of sewers, the cartage of wastes, the scavenging of garbage, such things, or, if fortunate, be put to work in the pens, cleansing them, filling the feed troughs, and such, hoping that they would not themselves be sent to the ramps, for they would understand the ramps, as their gross, lumbering charges would not.

The weather, for humans, was still bitterly cold. There was much snow on the ground. Overhead Cabot could even see it on the trees which, from his vantage point, though so far away, seemed to be growing downward.

Cabot had no particular destination in mind but he found his steps tending toward Lord Grendel's abandoned forest camp.

It was now some five days after his departure from the ramparts that he heard an astonishing, unaccountable message, one somehow, as several others had been, on the great speaker system, a message which seemed to emanate, as they had, from a thousand points in the world. The message was astonishing to Cabot. He did not understand it. It made no sense to him. If there were to be such messages he would have expected them to be, say, warnings to Kur loyalists, even nondominants, to beware of humans, or renegades, or calls to humans, or others, if there were others, to come in and surrender, perhaps to be spared for lowly services, groomings, and such, or, most likely, some gloating, or matter-of-fact announcement, pertaining to Agamemnon's glorious victory, perhaps the announcement of some holiday, or festival, or such. But such was not the message.

The message, incomprehensible to Cabot, was very simple. It was repeated three times, and only three times, but each time more insistently, more urgently.

Bring me a body.
Bring me a body.
Bring me a body.

Shortly thereafter Cabot became less concerned with his trail, which had been obvious in the snow.

As a warrior, or as anyone actually, who might be concerned with such things, Cabot had some sense of the value of remaining both alert and undetected, while in certain milieus. One moves with some stealth, naturally, often taking advantage of cover, and one tends to be very alive to one's surroundings, as the smallest suggestion of something perhaps seen, the tiniest sound perhaps heard, the faintest odor perhaps discerned, may be burdened with significance. Similarly, to the extent possible, one avoids the breaking of branches, the tearing of leaves from a bush, the crushing of a twig, the dislodging of pebbles or debris, such things. A stone turned, for example, may reveal a dampness for better than an Ahn, which bespeaks its recent movement. The edging of a footprint, its sharpness or lack of sharpness, may have its tale to tell. The tiny tracks of a night insect across the footprint may be a chronometer of passage.

Commonly it helps to utilize snow-free, windswept rocks, but there were few to be encountered in his journey, save in the vicinity of the womb tunnel. Too, it is common to utilize stream beds, for even the sleen cannot scent through flowing water, but must peruse the banks for an emergence. But the small streams which in a more equable time might have provided some trail's concealment were of little value now. If the ice was thick, it was laden with snow; if the stream moved, however slowly, beneath a ceiling of ice, that ice, if thin, too often broke beneath a man's weight. Too, to plunge into the icy water, in the cold, without a prompt application of warmth, the availability of fire, a toweling and change of gear, might within an Ahn result in incapacitation.

But as recorded, shortly after the strange message heard within the world, Cabot became less concerned with the obviousness of his trail, hitherto so obviously broken through the snow.

He had for Ahn, you see, waded through snow, much of it to his thighs.

But shortly after the strange message the snow ceased to be deep and dry, and began to subside into dampness, and, where it had been flat, and hard, and icy, he could see water beneath it, in bubbles, and tiny rivulets at the side.

He stopped, and put back his hood.

There was a cracking sound, and he crouched down, alert, but it had been ice fallen from a branch.

He moved to a higher place, for the wrappings with which he had swathed his legs were now dark, wet from softening snow.

At his feet he saw a trickle of water, moving through damp leaves.

Some yards away he heard the small sound of moving water, sluggish, undeniable.

Investigating, he detected a small stream pursuing its course. In it, twisting about, drifted some branches, some small blocks and plates of ice.

He removed his cloak.

Clearly, remarkable changes were occurring in the world. It seemed that a winter had been set aside, to be replaced with a damp, fragrant spring.

Wet, fallen leaves now appeared beneath his feet.

Here and there there were tiny ponds of water.

He could see branches of trees reflected in them.

The ground, here and there, for a time at least, would be wet, muddy.

When he resumed his journey, he would avoid such ground, insofar as it was possible.

He had feared to string the bow for days, for fear it would snap in the cold. He thought that it might soon be safe to do so, perhaps by noon. He shook the arrows in the quiver, and they moved well.

They were loose, ready. The fletching was now damp, no longer stiff, cold to the touch. He had kept the strings wound about his body, for warmth.

Cabot shuddered, as though to throw the remains of cold from him, as a sleen might shudder, to rid itself of snow or water.

Light, sunlike, blazed within the world. Water began to drip from snowy branches.

Cabot stretched, and moved his hands and fingers. Now they felt as they usually had, and responded as he wished. His feet no longer ached with cold, were now no longer wrapped in crackling, frozen cloth.

Cabot pondered the unusual shift in the weather.

Presumably there might be many explanations for this change. They would not, of course, be entirely meteorological, for this was a steel world, and weathers and climates, droughts and storms, light and darkness, heat and cold, or the initial conditions for such, which might then produce their natural consequences, could be planned and produced, both with respect to their frequencies and durations.

The unnatural winter, Cabot supposed, had cessitated, as it was now no longer necessary, or, perhaps better, useful, given Agamemnon's victory. The weapon of the weather, a very effective and terrible weapon, with its devastating impact on the insurrectionists' human allies, and surely even its seriously inconveniencing impact on its Kur allies, might now be put aside. The establishment secure, all things in their place, the world might now be returned to its normality.

The only thing Cabot did not understand was the strange message, repeated three times, consecutively, each time more insistently, more urgently, which had been earlier broadcast throughout the world: "Bring me a body."

Two days later Cabot had arrived at the abandoned camp of Lord Grendel, that in the more remote recesses of one of the world's farther forests, that from which they had long ago departed.

The gate was open, the palings were in place. Shelters had remained much as they had been, save for the effects of weather. The snow had melted and Cabot could find the ashes of cooking fires. There were some vessels about, one of them an overturned, dented metal bowl. In one place he found a stick, partly carved, not yet drilled. Such would have been intended for an arrow straightener. The small open-sided shelter in which the Lady Bina had been chained was still there. The stakes between which she had been fastened were also still there, but the chains, and belt, were gone.

This is a strange place, thought Cabot, for a human to end his life, on a steel world.

On the other hand, he supposed it was as good as any.

He might have preferred a field on Gor, with long green grass, with the wind rising from the east, in the morning, or perhaps a crag in the scarlet mountains, the mighty Voltai, or perhaps the stem castle or helm deck of a lateen-rigged galley, perhaps the *Dorna* or *Tesephone*. The thought crossed his mind of the mad shipwright, Tersites, filled with his dream of a ship so sturdy and mighty that it might see what lay on the far side of Thassa, to go so far that no mariner who had attained only to the first knowledge would dare to ply one of its oars, for fear of plunging over the world's cliff.

He thought of Lord Pyrrhus, slain in the arena, of Lord Arcesilaus, of the slaver, Peisistratus, of his dear friend, Lord Grendel. He thought of the forest humans, of the men of Peisistratus in the pleasure cylinder, of killer humans, bred for arena games, of the ponderous cattle humans, bred for stupidity and meat. He thought in sorrow of the beauty of the Lady Bina, and how she was now little more than a broken, torn, hideous, shapeless thing. Lord Grendel alone, it seemed, could bear to look upon her. He would, as though she were but a child, enfold her in his arms, and whisper to her, and try to comfort her.

Cabot looked up, quickly.

The animal was moving through the gate, a large animal, dragging something. It was making no effort to conceal its presence. Clearly it was not hunting.

"Ho," said Cabot. "Tal, welcome, friend."

Cabot went to greet the large, sinuous thing.

He would not close the gate behind it, for such things can become uneasy, even dangerous, if they feel closed in.

Cabot knelt down and fondled the large, triangular, viperlike, furred head. It was better than eighteen inches in width at its widest point. He held it against his chest.

"You have continued to guard the camp," observed Cabot, "though it is empty. Perhaps you were protecting it, perhaps you were waiting, patiently, for our return, wondering what had become of us, and it is only I who have returned."

There was a rumbling in the chest of the beast. This sound is not formed in the larynx. The noise is seldom heard by a human being.

"I am pleased to see you, as well," said Cabot. "You bring me a gift, I see. It is part of a tarsk, which was buried, and you have dug it out of the ground for me, to share it. I think I may not eat it, but I appreciate the thought." Cabot, curious, did wipe some dirt and leaves from the meat, which smelled, and put it to his tongue. After a time such meat, as it spoils, will form cadaverine alkaloids, which are potently toxic. Animals who might, long ago, have found the taste of such things agreeable would fail to replicate their genes. Similarly, animals who happened to find the taste disagreeable, say, in the case of humans, offensively bitter, would survive. It is not an inexplicable happenstance that foods which nourish beasts tend to have an agreeable taste to them and those unlikely to nourish them tend to have a disagreeable taste to them. The tastes may originally have been randomly allotted in a population, distributed with indifference, but the consequences of these tastes would weigh quite differently in the scales of life and death. A trail of misery and death in one case, and of health and vitality in another, lies at the roots, here and elsewhere, of what might seem to be a thousand matters of coincidence, but are no more coincidences, or inexplicable accidents, than the scimitarlike sharpness of the larl's fangs, or the erratic, bounding fleetness of the tabuk. Is not each the artist and designer of the other? Does not each, in his way, make the other more beautiful? And thus are played out the dark games of the Nameless One. The meat was not yet bitter, and so Cabot supposed it edible, if not palatable. Once the cadaverine alkaloids are formed not even the flocking, despised jard will feed. Cabot pretended to partake a bit of the meat and Ramar, the giant arena sleen, lamed in the left hind leg from a steel-toothed trap, began to tear at it contentedly, holding it down with his paws, and pulling at it, bit by bit, with his teeth. The rumbling in the animal's chest continued, as it fed, undiminished, for, as noted, the sound does not emanate from the animal's larynx, or throat, but its chest.

"I am hungry for meat, friend," said Cabot. "After the supplies brought from the war camp, I have had little but berries, and, near the womb tunnel, some roots dug out from under the snow. So perhaps we will go hunting in the morning. I think you would like that. We may even make a fire. I would suppose you have never had cooked meat. I wonder if you would like it."

Ramar continued to feed, contentedly.

Chapter, the Sixty-Eighth:

An Encounter in the Forest

"Do not loose your arrow, if you are so armed!" called the Kur.

"We know you are out there, away from the fire!" called the second.

"We are starving," called the first. "We smelled the cooking meat! Do not fire upon us, from the shadows, from the brush."

"We lift the broken spear," called the second. "We come in need, and peace."

There was no carried broken spear, of course, but the meaning was clear, that a truce was sought.

"Put aside your power weapons," called Cabot.

The first Kur looked about. He had no way of knowing how many might be in the vicinity. Perhaps a dozen bows might be trained upon them. Too, he seemed weak, resigned to what might ensue.

Each unharnessed a power weapon and put it down to the side. Near the weapons they placed a metal box, something about a cubic foot in dimension. They placed this box on the leaves tenderly, as with great solicitude.

Cabot then emerged from the brush, his bow relaxed.

At his side, low, crouched, crept a great sleen. Cabot had little doubt that any harm done to him would be at great risk to an assailant, particularly with the power weapons to the side.

"You are hungry," he said. "Eat."

Roast tarsk, brought down but an Ahn before, in the dusk, skinned and gutted, was on the spit, and grease hissed, when it fell to the fire.

The two Kurii crouched down by the tarsk and watched Cabot.

"I have fed earlier from this, and my friend," said Cabot. "Eat."

Both Kurii piteously seized at the meat. They clutched it, hot and burning, and crammed it into their jaws.

Cabot was puzzled at their hunger, for Kurii have a storage stomach. But perhaps they had not had an opportunity to fill it, or had long ago exhausted its contents.

Cabot wondered at what might be the contents of the metal box, which contained, he supposed, some artifact, some device, perhaps some treasure.

Ramar did not take his eyes from the pair of Kurii.

"I think I may know you," said Cabot. "I am not sure. Have we met?"

"Doubtless we look much alike to humans," said one of the Kurii.

"We know you," said the other. "And we have met."

"Where?" asked Cabot.

"Does it matter?" asked the first.

"I suppose not," said Cabot.

"Agamemnon," said the first Kur, "was the greatest of all Kurii. Never before, and never again, will there be such a leader."

"Hail Agamemnon," said the second, reverently.

"I do not understand," said Cabot.

"May we have our weapons?" asked the first, eying Ramar.

"Have I your word you will not use them against me?" asked Cabot.

"You would trust us?" inquired the second Kur.

"Certainly," said Cabot, "for you are Kur."

"Yes," said the first, "we are Kur."

Neither seemed disposed to linger by the fire. Each retrieved his weapon, the first to carry it, easily, the second to sling it on his back, while he picked up, with great gentleness, the metal box.

"We give you our word that we will not use our weapons against you—now," said the first, he with the weapon most ready.

"But perhaps later?" said Cabot.

"Yes, perhaps later," said the first.

"You need not fear," said the second. "Were we to fire now the smell of the charge would linger, and brush might be blackened and burned."

"I do not think you are hunters," said Cabot. "Why are you here, alone? What are you doing, here, alone, in the forest?"

But the two Kurii had then disappeared into the darkness, amongst the trees. Ramar looked after them, and growled, softly.

"I wonder if they are criminals, or thieves," thought Cabot. "There must have been something in the box, perhaps something precious, as it was handled. They were hungry, and needful. They feared to leave signs of their passage, seared brush, even the brief odor of a discharged weapon. Clearly they are fugitives. But from what are they running? And what were they carrying, with such care? They seemed to know me. Who might they be?"

Chapter, the Sixty-Ninth:

Cabot Will Hunt;
First, He Will Feast

Cabot, from behind, slipped his hand over the female's mouth, and then held her helplessly, tightly, back, against him. She squirmed, and made tiny, helpless noises. She was barefoot, and nicely tunicked and collared. Her hands were braceleted before her, closely together. Slaves are often kept braceleted, or chained, bound or such, for no other reason than that they are slaves. "Do not struggle, well-formed beauty," whispered Cabot, and she, commanded, was instantly quiet, not daring to move in the slightest.

"You may use her, if you wish!" called a merry voice. "Feel free to make her squeak and sob, and cry out!"

"Peisistratus!" cried Cabot, and released the slave. "Corinna!" he said, now recognizing her. But the slave was now kneeling, head down, shuddering, trying to overcome her terror at having been seized.

"We thought we might find you here!" said Archon.

Peisistratus and Archon, and others, rushed forward, to seize Cabot's hand, to embrace him, to weep with gladness at this reunion.

"We feared for you," said Peisistratus.

"And I for you, and others," said Cabot. "I see Kurii outside the gate. Are you prisoners?"

"Weaponed prisoners?" laughed Archon.

"They are our Kurii," said Peisistratus.

"Yes," said Cabot. "I see! Some I know!"

Ramar, the sleen, lay outside the gate, watching the arrivals, contesting the entry of none. The female slaves edged through the gate, knowing they must enter, but did their best to keep as much distance as was possible between themselves and the huge, watchful, six-legged, viperlike carnivore. The female slaves who were familiar with Gorean civilization were particularly wary of the sleen. They knew they were such as might be hunted by them, and torn to pieces by them, or might be apprehended by them, and then returned by them, being driven, herded, mercilessly, relentlessly, back to the mercies of dreaded, waiting masters. Too, it is one thing for a female slave to enter through such a gate, in the presence of such a watchman, if set there for such a duty, and quite another to exit through the gate. Similarly a verr might be admitted to a verr pen by a guard sleen, but would not be permitted to leave it, except in the company of a herdsman.

Here, in this camp, as on Gor, slaves would well know themselves slaves. They would be kept and managed with perfection. It is the Gorean way.

"We have brought stores with us, abundant supplies, even wine, and paga," said Peisistratus. He then clapped his hands together, sharply, joyfully. "Get busy, you worthless pot girls, you tarsk-bit sluts, prepare a feast, a mighty feast!"

"Yes, Master!" they cried, and hurried to the crates, and stores, which had been brought into the camp.

Cabot thought that not one of the slaves would have gone for less than a silver tarsk. He knew no slaver, even a Tenalion of Ar, who would not have been pleased to have them on a slaver's necklace.

"What has happened?" cried Cabot. "How are Kurii here? Are they not all slain?"

Just then he glimpsed Cestiphon, the killer human, and Cestiphon's four beauties, neck-roped.

How different they were now!

No longer were they filthy, crouched, and slovenly.

Now they were washed, and brushed and combed, and walked erectly, and beautifully, if fearfully. They approached abreast and, responding to a curt, sharply issued verbal command, they knelt, as one, in line, hands identically placed on their thighs, heads lifted, to the same angle. At another word they half knelt, half lay, the left leg beautifully extended, a common posture for exhibiting brands, but, Cabot noted, they were not yet slave-marked, and at another word they sat down, knees partly flexed, hands on their knees, heads lifted. Another word released them from their discipline and they gratefully reclined, as they would.

"They are learning," said Peisistratus. "I have been helping Cestiphon improve their value. Soon, I think we can take them off the neck rope. Soon, I suspect, they will be ready for pretty brands and nice, close-fitting metal collars."

"I see they are still naked," said Cabot.

"Yes," said Peisistratus. "They are still essentially primates. As they grow in bondage and learn how beautiful and desirable they are, and how men see them, they will strive zealously for as little as the shielding of a slave strip."

Modesty, though officially not permitted to a female slave, as they are animals, is often important to them. Whereas they think nothing of being bared before their master, who may keep them in no more than a collar, it is quite another thing to be nude in public, on the streets, in a market, and such. One can well imagine their shame, their consternation, to be, say, on the streets, where they might be seen by strangers, and, in particular, might fall beneath the contemptuous gaze of free women, their eyes flashing in disgust and fury over their veiling. In any event, a skimpy, rent, castoff tunic may be more precious to a slave than a vast, expensive wardrobe to her free sister. Whether a slave is permitted clothing or not, and, if so, its extent and nature, is not up to the slave, of course, but her master. She cannot own as little as a slave strip. She can own nothing. It is she who is owned. A slave's desire for clothing, and her hope that it will be permitted to her, even a slave strip, gives her master additional control over her. Some think this is quite as effective as the whip.

"Where is the Lady Bina?" asked Cabot.

"In the palace," said Peisistratus.

"With Agamemnon?" said Cabot.

"We do not think Agamemnon is any longer in the palace," said Peisistratus.

"Where is he?"

"We do not know," said Peisistratus.

"What has happened? How is it that you are here?" asked Cabot. "I understand nothing."

"Much has happened," said Archon.

"The loyalists," said Peisistratus, "acted."

"The world was invaded," said Peisistratus. "Those forces which attacked the world, after the defeat of the fleet, and seemed to withdraw, only drew back to turn about and, when not expected, renew more vigorously the attack which, before, had been little more than a feint."

"The world has fallen?" said Cabot.

"Agamemnon has fallen, not the world," said a Kur.

"Lord Arcesilaus is the Twelfth face of the Nameless One," said Peisistratus, "Theocrat of the World."

"I understand nothing of this," said Cabot. "I thought our Kurii were to sacrifice themselves for the life of Arcesilaus."

"They were prepared to do so," said Archon. "It was what we expected."

"What happened?" asked Cabot.

"Our Kurii were unarmed, as you recall. Thus, in the presence of Lord Arcesilaus, who was chained, and was still weak from wounds, standing on the steps of the palace, begging them to neglect him and renew the struggle, they must petition the loyalists to fire upon them."

"And they refused to do so?" said Cabot.

"No," said Peisistratus. "They are Kur. They petitioned the loyalists to destroy them where they stood, in honor, before the protesting, pleading Lord Arcesilaus. The loyalists saw that Lord Arcesilaus did not wish to have his life purchased at such a cost. This was Kur. They saw, too, that our forces were prepared to give their lives for Lord Arcesilaus, and this, too, was Kur."

"What then must be the might and worthiness of a cause so served, by adherents and partisans of such nobility?" said Archon.

"The treachery of the amnesty betrayal still rankled with many," said a Kur, "for that was not Kur."

"Too," said another, "the luring of Lord Grendel into an ambush, with odds of more than twenty to one, was not pleasing to many. It is one thing for a Kur to challenge a Kur, Kur to Kur, as in the rings. It is quite another for what are in effect no more than armed brigands, concealing themselves like vermin amongst beasts, to suddenly, unexpectedly, rise up to slay a single, unarmed foe, one not set for battle."

"It is not Kur," said another Kur.

"No," agreed another.

"Our forces," said a Kur, "waited, surrounded by loyalists, rung in tiers about us."

"We were prepared to die," said another Kur.

"Fight!" cried Arcesilaus.

We did not move.

"Then he cried, 'Down with Agamemnon!'"

"The great voice of Agamemnon then rang out," said a Kur. "'Kill them, kill them all!'"

"'Fire!'" called out Lucullus, high captain to Agamemnon, who stood near Arcesilaus, amongst his many guards and jailers. "'Fire!'" cried Crassus, as well, high lieutenant to Agamemnon.

"The weapons were leveled," said a Kur. "But then there was a hesitation."

"And in that moment of hesitation, that one moment of hesitation," said another Kur, "we triumphed."

"'Fire, fire, fire!' called Agamemnon," said another Kur, "but none fired, and it became clear, moment by moment, that none would do so."

"A voice then from somewhere amongst the loyalists," said a Kur, "we do not know who it was, cried out, 'Hail Lord Arcesilaus, Twelfth Face of the Nameless One, Theocrat of the World!'"

"This cry," said another, "was taken up by a thousand voices. Guards beside Lord Arcesilaus raised their weapons to slay him, but they were burned alive beside him. A hundred weapons began to fire. The steps of the palace were gouged with flame, chips of stone showered aflight, exploding from the steps, dark lines of flame laced them, the very air was smoking and burning, and Lucullus and Crassus, and several others, those who could, fled in rout back to the shelter of the palace."

"The palace, then," said a Kur, "was invested."

"The chains of Lord Arcesilaus were struck off, and he was carried to the habitats, that he might be treated," said another.

"Rejoicing took place," said another.

"Insurrectionists and loyalists embraced, crying out with joy," said another.

"But then terror seized all," said another, "for locks were blown and swarming into the world, to the rolling of drums and the blast of war horns, from a hundred ports, were warriors from the world which Agamemnon had menaced, and whose fleet, so beautifully generaled, had decimated ours."

"All seemed lost," said a Kur.

"Surely, surprised, taken unawares, all would be slain by that fleet's general," said another.

"The world had fallen!"

"No quarter would be given, no mercy shown!"

"But it was not to be," said another Kur. "When it was clear that Agamemnon was no longer in power, that this reversal had come about, the enemy put up its arms, for their foe, you see, was not we, the folk, but he who had been the misleader and tyrant of the folk, Lord Agamemnon. Their war, it seems, was not with us, at all, but with our common foe, Lord Agamemnon."

"The great general, their formidable leader, one of the fiercest and most formidable in all the many steel worlds, ordered his banner furled, the drums and war horns silenced."

"Fraternization took place, and rejoicing," said another Kur, "but the palace remained apart, invested."

"What is the name of this foreign general, so adept, so feared, so renowned and terrible?" asked Cabot.

"Zarendargar," said a Kur.

"It is said he asked for you," said a Kur.

"Do you know him?" asked a Kur.

"Yes," said Cabot.

"How can that be?" asked a Kur.

"Once," said Cabot, "long ago, in another place, far away, we shared paga."

"When the palace was forced," said another Kur, "it was found empty."

"Many secret passages were located, which led from the palace," said another.

"Thus, Agamemnon, and many of his adherents, escaped."

"Twice," said a Kur, "the world was again in jeopardy, for minions of Agamemnon were surprised in the planting of mighty charges, which, if detonated, would have opened the world to the outside."

"He would destroy the world, rather than have it no longer his," said Cabot.

"But even his own Kurii, elsewhere in a dozen places, surrendered themselves, and the charges which had been committed to them, rather than perform so hideous and monstrous a deed."

"It would not be Kur," said a Kur.

"I am pleased," said Cabot.

"But Agamemnon himself," said a Kur, "would prefer the forfeiture of a world to the loss of a throne."

"Perhaps even to the least diminution of his power," said another.

"Such a deed, the destruction of a world, would be his last, grand act," said a Kur, "a fitting conclusion to his reign."

"Even were such a charge detonated," said a Kur, "it would not necessarily entail the end of the world."

"No," said another. "Certainly meteoritic impacts have been anticipated, and prepared for."

"Agamemnon is gone?" said Cabot.

"Yes," said a Kur.

"Where might he be?" asked Cabot.

"We do not know," said a Kur.

"Where is Flavion?" asked Cabot.

"The scout?"

"The traitor?"

"Yes," said Cabot.

"We do not know," said another.

"In hiding," said another.

"He cannot be found," said another.

"I know one who can find him," said Cabot.

"You have been called for, by Zarendargar, currently the military governor of the world," said a Kur.

"You should proceed to him, at once," said another.

"Surely you will do so," said Peisistratus.

"Convey to him my regards," said Cabot. "I have something to attend to first."

"But he is governor, he is Zarendargar!" exclaimed a Kur.

"He will understand," said Cabot. "We have shared paga."

"What will you be about?" asked Archon.

"I think I will go hunting," said Cabot.

"Perhaps Lord Grendel might like to join you in your hunt?" said Peisistratus.

"I would prefer not to risk him," said Cabot.

"The hunt will be dangerous?" asked Peisistratus.

"I think so," said Cabot.

"I am sure he would wish to accompany you," said Peisistratus.

"Perhaps," said Cabot.

"Lord Grendel is in the palace," said a Kur, "assisting in the reorganization and distribution of power."

"Do not inform him of my absence," said Cabot.

"As you wish," said Peisistratus, reluctantly.

"Put up a discipline post, somewhere aside, in the camp," said Cabot, "to which a slave might be tied."

"Excellent," said Peisistratus. "It will be good for our girls to see such a post."

"You have in mind a particular slave?" asked Archon.

"Yes," said Cabot.

"It might serve for any of them," said Archon.

"Certainly," said Cabot.

"You will not leave until the morning," said Peisistratus.

"No," said Cabot.

"Tonight," said Peisistratus, "we feast."

"In the Gorean manner, I trust," said Cabot.

"Certainly," smiled Peisistratus.

"I have not seen Corinna dance since the pleasure cylinder," said Cabot.

"If she does not dance well," said Peisistratus, "she will be thrown no food."

Chapter, the Seventieth:

Flavion

It may be recalled, from some time ago, that Cabot, perhaps surprisingly, given that he stood high in the forest camp, and was of the scarlet caste, had tended to the grooming of the scout, Flavion, an office commonly attended to, amongst the lords, by clients and sycophants, and, most often, in most cases, including that of the lords, by menials, in particular, human females, pets, and slaves. Cabot had performed this office with diligence, cleaning the fur with his fingers, and then brushing and combing it. Indeed, he had even wiped the fur down with a soft cloth, for several Ehn, until it shone with a high, oily gloss. The cloth with which he had performed this task he had saved, wrapping it tightly in a leather wrapper which had been kept in his wallet, or pouch. It may also be recalled that his colleague, Ramar, so to speak, was a carefully bred domestic sleen, of unusual size and ferocity. Indeed, such animals are often used to hunt and kill wild sleen. Ramar, who had served as an arena animal, successful again and again, had also been trained, as would have been expected of most domestic sleen, in a number of other behaviors. He could, for example, hunt a quarry, keep it in place, drive it, and kill it.

The sudden snap of the metal was followed, almost instantly, by a long, weird scream of Kur pain.

"Well done, Ramar," whispered Cabot.

The sleen had grasped Cabot's intention, as he had hoped. First, Ramar had been given the scent from the cloth, and, though the scent was old, it was not difficult for a sleen to follow once it had picked it up, which it had, in the forest. They had then, at a distance, trailed their unsuspecting quarry. A mere word from Cabot dissuaded the mighty animal, once it was within some hundreds of yards of its prey, from rushing forward and attacking it. At this point most domestic sleen would require a leash. Ramar was doubtless muchly puzzled by this arrest of the chase, but he offered no resistance to Cabot's will, though he doubtless suspected that some fault or inadvertence lay within it. That night, giving the sleen the "stay" command, Cabot had made his way to the quarry's camp, and, silently, attended to its reconnoitering. The quarry was alone. This did not please Cabot, but it did not dismay him either. It made sense to him that the quarry would be alone. Had he been in the quarry's place he would have behaved similarly.

The next morning Cabot with his hunting companion made his way to a locale familiar to them both, but one the companion was reluctant to enter, except upon the most urgent, quiet bidding.

Ramar crouched back, watching, while Cabot, with a considerable effort, struggled with the huge spring which, if one of its several pedals was tripped, would fling shut the sharpened teeth of the device. It clicked, and was set, and Cabot, sweating, sat beside it for a time. He then beckoned Ramar closer and the giant beast warily, reluctantly, approached. Cabot did not let him come too close. Cabot then wiped the cloth with the quarry's scent liberally about the sharp metal teeth. He put the cloth to the beast's snout, and then, again, rubbed it on the metal teeth. He pointed to the cloth and then to the teeth, again and again. Ramar backed away, belly low. Cabot then, carefully, to the best of his ability, concealed the trap.

"Do you understand, friend?" Cabot asked the sleen.

Ramar lifted his head, and peered at Cabot. Then he looked at the trap, and growled.

"If not, I suppose it does not matter much," said Cabot. "But you may understand. I wonder if you do."

The sleen had been taught to drive, of course.

The common termination of the drive, of course, is commonly a pen, or cage. Many is the female slave who, to save her life, driven, has fled to the cage, scrambled within it, and flung down the gate, locking herself helpless, weeping, within it. Later, when the master checks the cage, he will find her within, at his pleasure.

"Drive," said Cabot to the sleen, softly. To a trained animal it is not necessary to speak commands sharply, or harshly. Often one wants to issue them quietly, very quietly, even whispered, that a quarry may not be alerted to its presence. It may be recalled he had retrained the sleen in the forest, beginning with the translator, to substitute Gorean for Kur, such that the animal would now respond only to Gorean, and, as is usual with a sleen and single trainer, only to the particular trainer's commands. It would not do, obviously, for just any individual to be able to set so dangerous a beast into its behaviors. When masters change the beast must be retrained, or, if this proves impractical, killed.

Ramar padded away, amongst the closely set trees.

Cabot had good reason to believe the sleen would not be in much danger. This had to do with his activity the preceding night in the quarry's small, rough camp.

Too, the quarry would be reluctant to expend charges except in cases of the utmost necessity.

Where might he find others?

Too, whereas many Kurii, large Kurii, might manage, at least with good fortune, to survive the attack of a typical sleen, say, a smaller, wild sleen, the quarry, though large for a human, was not large for a Kur, and Ramar was an unusually large, dangerous animal.

Cabot followed the drive, but unseen, and at a distance. It gradually became clear to him, to his gratification, that the quarry was being encouraged to move in smaller and smaller circles, centering on a particular area.

"Excellent, excellent, Ramar," Cabot breathed, to himself. "How intelligent you are. What a joy you are, what a champion amongst beasts you are."

In a few Ehn Cabot had come to the trap.

In it the Kur writhed.

Blood flowed about the clamped leg. It struggled to its feet and tried to drag the trap on its chain to where it had lost the rifle, flung from his hands, when the teeth had unexpectedly, viciously, snapped shut. It could move the trap, his leg bleeding in the grass and leaves which had concealed the trap, only to the end of the chain, which encircled a nearby tree, and was locked about it. The Kur threw himself prostrate and reached toward the weapon, scratching toward it. But it was a foot beyond its grasp.

Cabot sat down, cross-legged, near the rifle, and Ramar crouched down, placidly, beside him.

The beast had been given the 'drive' command, not the 'kill' command.

Cabot switched on his translator. "Tal," he said.

"You!" said Flavion, scarcely able to speak, for the pain. "Open the trap! Help me! I am caught!"

"We lost track of you, after the escape of the Lady Bina, and the business of the cattle humans, the killing squad, and such."

"Free me!" screamed Flavion, his visage contorted with agony.

"Why?" asked Cabot.

"I will lose my leg!" screamed Flavion. It was interesting how the urgency and horror of his utterance was rendered by the translator, calmly, precisely, unemotionally.

"That is possible," agreed Cabot. Surely the metal teeth had bitten deeply.

"I will reward you, richly!" cried Flavion.

"Oh?" said Cabot.

"Yes, yes," screamed Flavion, then daring not move, lest he further injure his gripped limb.

"Perhaps you think I am not aware of what has occurred in the world," said Cabot. "I am aware of it, however, as you doubtless are, as well. Agamemnon and the riches of the world are no longer at your disposal. Too, I suspect Lord Arcesilaus, Lord Grendel, and several others, would be pleased to see you."

"Is the sleen yours?" said Flavion.

"No," said Cabot. "It is a friend."

"It is Ramar, is it not?"

"Yes."

"Restrain it!"

"I do not think he needs restraining," said Cabot. "He seems contented. He is not hungry."

"I did not know it was he," said Flavion, in pain. "I thought there were more than one."

"Just one," said Cabot.

"Free me!" demanded Flavion.

"Are you going to faint?" asked Cabot. Clearly the Kur had lost, and was losing, blood.

"Let us bargain!" said Flavion.

"What have you to bargain with?" asked Cabot.

"Something soft, in a collar!" said Flavion. "Help me! Free me!"

"I thought you were clever enough to hold that in reserve," said Cabot. "You would not risk having it with you."

"It is worth my life, is it not?"

"She is worthless," said Cabot. "That I discovered when she fled. One can buy women like her, and better, in any market on Gor."

"You want her back!" said Flavion.

"Why?" asked Cabot. "That she be taught her collar, that she be beaten, and sold?"

"I know you men of Gor," said Flavion. "You hunt and capture women, you buy them, and trade them, and sell them. You desire them and are content with nothing less than owning them, and with utmost totality! You risk your lives to bring them to your feet in chains, to be mastered. Wars have been fought for them. Ships ply the slave routes to Earth, to bring the most delicious and needful to the collars of Gor."

"What do you want for her?" asked Cabot.

"My life!" said Flavion.

"That seems little," said Cabot. "Before, I thought she was to have a sack of gold tied about her neck."

"I have gold!" said Flavion. "Open the trap! Release me!"

"Cannot you open the trap yourself?" asked Cabot.

"No," said Flavion. "I will die here! Help me!"

"It seems you will," said Cabot.

"No!" protested Flavion.

"I think you will soon lose consciousness," said Cabot. "I wonder if you will awaken. Perhaps you will, in a few Ahn, at night, to agony and weakness, to hunger, and thirst, and such. Perhaps you might live for a few days in the trap. One does not know. Some sleen do. In any event I do not envy you."

Cabot then made as though to rise to his feet.

"Do not go!" cried Flavion.

"Why not?" asked Cabot.

"The slave!" cried Flavion. "The slave!"

"A worthless slave for a worthless life?" asked Cabot.

"Yes, yes!" said Flavion.

"It is a possible exchange," said Cabot.

"Yes, yes!" cried Flavion. Blood was about his jaws where he had bitten himself in his pain.

"Perhaps," said Cabot.

"You want her back," said Flavion.

"Do I?"

"You desire her," said Flavion.

"Better can be purchased in the markets," said Cabot.

"But I think it is she whom you want," he said.

"Perhaps, to teach her that she is a slave, a mere slave, and nothing else, and then beat and sell her."

"I will include gold," said Flavion, "staters of Brundisium, tarn disks of Ar!"

"It seems you are well prepared, should the opportunity present itself, to buy your way to Gor."

"One must prepare for contingencies," said Flavion. "It seems it is you who chose the winning side."

"As I am of the scarlet caste," said Cabot, "I do not care to haggle."

"One hundred staters then, and ten tarn disks," said Flavion.

"The girl herself, stripped, on a block," said Cabot, "would not be likely to go for more than two silver tarsks. She is not even pen-trained."

There are professional slave trainers, of course. For a fee, they will train a girl. It is said that some can take a pot girl, a kettle-and-mat girl, a mill girl, a laundress, or such, and return a needful dream of a pleasure slave. This is often a good investment, obviously, as one might then sell them for a higher price, that would more than cover the trainer's fee. To be sure, no woman can thrive except at a man's feet.

"The exchange is obviously much to your advantage," said Flavion.

"Considerably so," said Cabot.

"We are then in agreement?" said Flavion.

"It seems so," said Cabot. "You will lead me to the slave?"

"Certainly," said Flavion. "Release me."

"Might it not be better for you to tell me where she is," said Cabot. "Then, if you are telling the truth, and I recover her, in block condition, salable and such, I could return for you."

"No, no!" he cried. "I will die here!"

"Some sleen," said Cabot, "survive for days."

"My presence would be necessary," said Flavion.

"Then there must be others, to recognize you," said Cabot.

"—Yes," said Flavion.

Cabot then, with much effort, lifted the teeth of the trap a few inches, and Flavion, with his hands, lifted his torn, bleeding leg free.

"We have an agreement, do we not?" asked Flavion, in pain.

"As I understand it," said Cabot, "a slave—for a life, and gold."

"Give me my rifle," said Flavion.

"I have your word, do I not," asked Cabot, "that it will not be used against me?"

"Surely," said Flavion.

"May I trust you?"

"My word has been given, and I am Kur," said Flavion.

"Very well," said Cabot, and pushed the weapon across the leaves, so that it would lie within the reach of Flavion. "You had best staunch the bleeding," said Cabot.

Flavion reached to the weapon, in pain, grimacing, and then swung it to his shoulder, pressing the detonating mechanism twice, once point-blank at the large sleen, once at Cabot.

"I removed the charges in your camp, last night," said Cabot. "If you are to be of much use, you had better stop the bleeding."

In desperate fury Flavion cried out with rage and flung the rifle at Cabot, who moved to the side, permitting it to pass, which it did, spinning into the brush.

"I will cut a branch, to be used as a staff," said Cabot. "That leg will not be of much use to you, not for some time, perhaps never."

Chapter, the Seventy-First:

A Destination Is Approached

"We are close?" asked Cabot.

"Yes," said Flavion. "I keep my part of the bargain. You will not turn me over to Lord Arcesilaus, and others?"

"No," said Cabot.

Ramar was at Cabot's side.

"They may, however," said Cabot, "seek you out."

Flavion was no longer in need of the makeshift crutch which had been supplied by Cabot in the vicinity of the sleen trap.

He was however, lame, and could do little more than hobble, lurching from side to side.

Two days ago Cabot had conducted his prisoner to a smithy, in a remote village. There he had had a chain belt and manacles prepared for his prisoner, which would hold his hands close to his body. Too, he had a heavy iron collar, with a ring, hammered shut about his neck. He also purchased some heavy chain, which he slung about Flavion's body, and by means of which he could tether him at night. Cabot also scratched, in Gorean, on the collar: "I am Flavion, adherent of Agamemnon, traitor to the cause of Lord Arcesilaus."

The smith had been quite cooperative, particularly as he had received for his work a ruby, one from the trial of Lord Pyrrhus, long ago.

It was equivalent to more than he would be likely to earn in more than two revolutions of the steel worlds about Tor-tu-Gor, or Sol, the common star of Earth, Gor, the steel worlds, and a wheel of worlds, satellites, fragments, and debris.

Cabot had two power weapons, one from the forest camp, and

one which had been Flavion's. Between both, he had only five charges, three designed for one weapon, two fitted to the other.

"Free me of these encumbrances," said Flavion, shaking the manacles.

"You were doubtless making your way to some enclave or post when caught," said Cabot. "Too, I have little doubt that is where you, and others, are holding one or more prisoners, and slaves. You will have compatriots there. They will doubtless have tools."

"I will explain our agreement to them," said Flavion, "and they will hand over the slave."

"And the gold?"

"Of course."

"And they will not be concerned that their enclave has been detected?"

"There is another," said Flavion.

Cabot stopped.

"What is wrong?" asked Flavion.

"A slave is only a slave," said Cabot, "and gold is only gold. I am thinking it might be more pleasant to turn you over to Lord Grendel, or others."

"We have an agreement," said Flavion.

"True," said Cabot. "You are certain that it will be safe to approach the enclave?"

"I will guarantee you safe passage," said Flavion.

"That sets my mind at ease," said Cabot.

Chapter, the Seventy-Second:

The Treachery of Flavion

Cabot flung himself to the leaves and fired twice, and one blast struck a tree, cracking it open, setting it afire, as if it might have been smitten with lightning, and the other charge took off the head of a Kur.

"Kill him! Kill him!" Flavion was shrieking, with a rattle of chain, the translator conveying this imperative in Gorean with its customary passionless professionalism.

Another Kur raised his head, cautiously, warily, only feet away. It would have been better for him had he been more patient, and waited even Ahn, or until night, but he had not. And so he died, and Cabot changed his position again.

It was quiet then in the glade.

Cabot discarded one rifle, and had at his disposal then only two charges, those configured to the second weapon.

Cabot was then within the enclave, and saw the vessels, the stores, the half-buried amphora for water, the mats for sleeping. There were six such mats. Cabot detected no sign of chains or cages.

"Draw his fire, find his position!" he heard Flavion screaming.

But Cabot had made the determinations he wished. What he had sought, something soft, in a collar, was clearly not here, nor any sign that it had been. Nor was there any sign of coffers, or sacks, which might have bulged with coin.

Fire from various quarters burned into the grass. Some of it blackened and burst into flame just over his head.

Cabot might have obtained a kill with one of the charges, as he placed its source from the pencillike fire stream, but, had he done so, his own position might have been similarly revealed, and the power weapons could sweep out swaths of terrain, and there had been six sleeping mats. Thus, not counting Flavion, he supposed there might be four, or more, Kurii left in the vicinity.

Cabot withdrew.

With him, more silent in the grass than he, came Ramar.

"Better, dear Flavion," Cabot thought, "I had left you in the trap. Perhaps, however, we will meet again."

Chapter, the Seventy-Third:

There Will Be an Institution of Festivals

"What is in the box?" asked Cabot.

"Agamemnon," said Lucullus.

He slid back the protective metal lid of the box and, through the glassine ceiling, Cabot could see, within, below, bathed in fluid, complexly wired, a mass of gray tissue.

"Through these ports," said Crassus, indicating a variety of apertures on the outside of the box, to which wires led, "Agamemnon could utilize his bodies, see and hear through them, speak through them, control them, and so on."

"You should have seen him, you should have known him," said Lucullus, "when he had his own body."

"He was the most magnificent of the folk," said Crassus. "How splendid he was, how massive and swift, how splendid of visage, so clear of eye, so quick of hand."

"He was first in the rings," said Lucullus. "We loved him."

"He was champion, he was first," said Crassus.

"Never before, and never after," said Lucullus, "will there be his equal."

"We extended the amnesty," said Lord Arcesilaus, from his throne in the palace, "and they came in, surrendered."

"You may now kill us," said Lucullus, indicating himself, and Crassus.

"That is not my amnesty," said Lord Arcesilaus. "My amnesty is an amnesty. You served Lord Agamemnon well, and it is my hope that you will so serve me."

"We shall, Lord," they said.

"I think all have come in," said Lord Grendel. "The amnesty has been general."

On the finger of Lord Arcesilaus was a large ring, heavy and ornate, a symbol of authority. Once Cabot had worn it about his neck on a string, and he had given it to Mitonicus who, later, had returned it to Lord Arcesilaus, who had been the early champion of the revolution, and the chief conspirator who had brought it to its beginning, before he had been betrayed to Agamemnon by a shapely Kur pet.

"At a crucial moment," said Cabot, "as it was reported to me, in a far camp, one cried 'Hail Lord Arcesilaus, Twelfth Face of the Nameless One, Theocrat of the World.' Was it ever discovered who it was who first so cried?"

"Yes," said Lord Grendel, looking to the side.

"It was I," said a Kur.

"And I then, as well," said another.

"Surely you recognize them?" said Lord Grendel.

"From the far arsenal!" said Cabot, suddenly.

"Yes," said Lord Grendel, "the two we spared, and to whom we returned their weapons, that they might return without jeopardy to the habitats."

"We had other adherents, as well," said Statius, "adherents, and dissenters, many, from those spared, at the Vale of Destruction."

"It seems, Lord Grendel," said Cabot, "that in a human weakness is sometimes found a wisdom, and sometimes a strength."

"But often not," said Lord Arcesilaus.

"True," said Cabot.

"I think there is now little need of me here," said Zarendargar, war general of Kurii, "and I shall withdraw my people and my ships."

"Pray, remain for a time, noble ally," said Lord Arcesilaus, "for I shall decree a mighty festival, with days of rejoicing and feasting, which I would that you and yours, your splendid, numberless adherents and crews, shared with us."

Zarendargar, war general of the Kurii, no longer military governor of the world, as Lord Arcesilaus had now been ensconced in the palace, inclined his head, in ready, gracious assent.

"Our two worlds," said Lord Arcesilaus, "will be as one."

"No," said Zarendargar. "Each will be its own."

"Good," said Mitonicus, admiral of mariners.

"It is the Kur way," said Statius, who stood high in the councils of Lord Arcesilaus, Twelfth Face of the Nameless One, Theocrat of the World.

"The ports have been unsealed," said Peisistratus. "Our ships are now free, to wharf here, or to return to our lairs on Gor, or our secret places, our islands and dens, on Earth."

"My people," said Archon, "may return to the forest world, or remain here, or voyage to Gor."

"I will provide ships," said Zarendargar.

"You remembered me," said Cabot.

"I returned for you," said Zarendargar.

"Human will no longer be eaten here," said Lord Arcesilaus, "nor hunted."

"What of the cattle humans?" asked Cabot.

"Some will be shipped to Gor, others will remain here," said Lord Arcesilaus. "It makes little difference. As they are reproduced only by artificial insemination, they will be allowed to live well, in their bovine simplicity, and then perish. We will see to it that they are cared for, and have their feed troughs filled. That is all they want, to be fed, and have their needs supplied by others."

"Why should they live at the expense of others?" asked Archon. "Should they not produce, and work?"

"They are too simple, too stupid, to do so," said Statius. "If they are not cared for they become frightened, confused, and dangerous. They become cruel, and mean, and warlike, and will fight for roots, and will feed on, and kill, one another, and others."

"They are human," said a Kur.

"A sort of human," said Cabot.

"What will be done with Agamemnon?" asked Cabot.

"Without a body, he is harmless," said Lord Arcesilaus.

"Should we not now remove his victory stele from the Vale of Destruction," said a Kur, "and put there our own, to commemorate our victory?"

"No," said Lord Arcesilaus, "let his victory there, of more than a century ago, be recalled. He was a great commander. Let it stand."

"He was the Eleventh face of the Nameless One, Theocrat of the World," said Lucullus.

"He will be remembered for what he was, not for what he became," said Crassus.

"Is he conscious?" asked Cabot.

"There is activity," said Lucullus.

"We do not really know," said Crassus.

"The amnesty is general?" said Cabot.

"Yes," said Lord Arcesilaus.

"And all came in?"

"All."

"I have in mind, one," said Cabot.

"Yes," said Lord Grendel. "Flavion came in, and availed himself of the amnesty."

"And you did not tear his head from his shoulders?" asked Cabot.

"No," said Lord Grendel.

"The amnesty is the amnesty," said Lord Arcesilaus.

"He is vicious, cunning, murderous, and treacherous," said Cabot.

"Yes," said Lord Grendel, "but the amnesty is the amnesty, and he has availed himself of it."

"There is no punishment for him?" said Cabot.

"No," said Lord Grendel. "It is the amnesty."

"But the Lady Bina," said Cabot.

Lord Grendel's body shook, and Cabot feared, once more, as he had once feared it in the camp, that he might become something other than he would recognize, something terrible, fanged, merciless, stormlike, predatory, something unmitigatedly and primitively Kur, Kur as Kur might once have been, emerging howling, ravening and hungry, from the first primeval caves of a raw, far, pristine world. Then Lord Grendel recovered himself, again. "It is the amnesty," he said, quietly.

"The amnesty," said Cabot, "is not mine."

"It is ours," said Lord Grendel. "Thus, it is also yours."

"No!" cried Cabot.

"Yes, dear friend," said Lord Grendel.

"Perhaps," said Lord Arcesilaus, "he has in mind a pet."

"I have something in mind far less than a pet," said Cabot. "I have in mind a slave."

"Had you not so precipitately sought Flavion," said Lord Grendel, "had you waited for me, had you not rushed off, into the forest, as I learned, I might have spared you some effort."

"I do not understand," said Cabot, uncertainly.

"I gather," said Lord Grendel, "you believed that a certain slave, who had fled our forest camp, certainly an unwise thing to do, and a most serious offense, one whose gravity she may not have fully understood, had fallen into the company of Flavion."

"Certainly," said Cabot.

"And he encouraged this view on your part."

"Yes," said Cabot. "He even bargained with her, or seemed to do so, for services, and, later, for his life."

"Flavion is clever," said Lord Arcesilaus.

"He never had her," said Lord Grendel. "I found that out, in the victory."

"I do not understand this," said Cabot.

"She was picked up by one of our other groups," said Lord Grendel, "and, as a loose slave, was well roped, hand and foot. After the victory she was brought to the habitats."

"She is alive?" said Cabot.

"Yes," said Lord Grendel, "and is even now nicely, if somewhat uncomfortably, caged in one of the stables, with some others similarly caged, in individual, small shipping cages, waiting to be claimed by their masters."

"Given her collar," said Peisistratus, "you will have no difficulty claiming her. She is clearly yours."

"Take me to her!" said Cabot.

"There is no hurry," said Lord Arcesilaus.

"She will wait for you, dear Cabot," said Archon.

"She is not going anywhere," said Statius.

"I want to see her," said Cabot.

"Doubtless she is eager to see you, as well," said Archon.

"I will change that," said Cabot.

"Her pleasure will soon turn to terror," said a Kur.

"She was a flighted slave," said another.

"Perhaps she does not understand that she has been displeasing to her master," said a Kur.

"Doubtless she will soon understand it," said another.

"Yes," said another.

"She is a slave," said another.

"There is no mercy for a runaway slave," said another.

"They will be treated as they deserve," said another.

"Put from your minds vengeances on foolish animals," said Lord

Arcesilaus. "I am planning several days of celebration, of feasting, and such, and Lord Zarendargar and his forces, I am pleased to note, will revel with us. They will share our joy, and participate in our games, and festivals. Departures may take place thereafter."

"Will there be female Kur slaves?" asked Zarendargar.

"Female Kur slaves!" exclaimed a Kur, shocked.

"Certainly," said another.

"Surely there are no such slaves," said he who had expressed astonishment.

"Do not be naive," said another, to he who had expressed that astonishment.

"Yes," said Statius, to Lord Zarendargar. "And if you wish we will put them in collars."

"And free Kur females will be denied entrance to the festivals," said a Kur.

"Unless they submit themselves as slaves," said a Kur.

"Yes," said another.

"And will serve as slaves."

"Yes."

"And will be slaves."

"Yes."

"And will be denied harnesses."

"Certainly," said another Kur.

"And they will serve with human female slaves," said another Kur.

"They will be so degraded?" asked a Kur.

"Yes," said a Kur, "and they will be well taught what it is to be a slave."

"Human female slaves often serve unclothed," said a Kur.

"Save for collars," said a Kur.

"If no free females are present," said Cabot.

"They will be denied harnesses?" asked a Kur.

"Yes," said a Kur.

"Then they will be naked," said a Kur.

"Precisely," said another.

"Let them learn what it is to be a slave," said a Kur.

"Excellent!" said more than one Kur.

"Our females, many," said Zarendargar, "are quite beautiful.

Why should we, who are Kur, not have the same pleasures from our females which the men of Gor enjoy from theirs?"

"From those who are slaves," said Cabot.

"Very well," said Zarendargar.

"Perhaps," said Lord Arcesilaus, "our folk will become less precipitate, and driven, and become somewhat more civil, less inclined to hasty, violent response, if their needs and desires are fulfilled, if vessels are at hand, properties, which they may subject to their will, which they may rule, and on which they may conveniently slake their lusts."

Cabot supposed something of the sort might be true. Contented men, in any event, are unlikely to rob, to kill, to practice cruelties, and such. Cabot wondered if the congeniality and civility of some fellows might have so simple an explanation as the full, pleasant, and convenient satisfaction of their most acute, recurrent masculine needs, those for dominance, ownership of the female, mastery, and sex. Their peace, and perhaps the safety of their neighbors, he speculated, was kept within the collars which encircled lovely necks.

A man wants nothing so much as a slave, and nothing so pleases a man as a slave.

It is no wonder they are brought to the markets.

"Return now," said Lord Arcesilaus, "to your habitats, your shelters, your tents, your ships, your bivouacs, and refresh yourselves. Prepare jewelries and festive garments, for tomorrow there will be music, enactments, martial dances, and games. Tomorrow we feast!"

Outside the palace Cabot and Lord Grendel paused, on the steps.

A figure, small for a Kur, lurched toward them. It had apparently been waiting for them to emerge from the palace.

Cabot, with all his strength, held Lord Grendel in place.

"Peace, noble sirs," said Flavion, saluting them with great ceremony. "Greetings, and may the peace of the amnesty be with you." He then, with another bow, and flourish, took his leave.

"No," said Cabot. "No."

A moan, almost human, of rage, of grief, of helplessness, came from the shuddering, hirsute massiveness of Cabot's companion.

"No," said Cabot, gently.

"Does he think we have forgotten?" asked Lord Grendel.

"No," said Cabot, "he does not think that, nor has he, in his turn, forgotten."

"Will you now forth to the stables, to claim a slave?" asked Lord Grendel.

"I think," said Cabot, "that I will wait a bit. What I would like, however, is for you to see to it that she comes to understand, and quite clearly, the changes that have taken place in the world, the new arrangements, and such."

"She is a slave, of course," said Lord Grendel.

"But she is to come to this understanding," said Cabot, "seemingly in a manner appropriate for a slave, a manner seemingly innocent of intention, as if none were interested in informing her. Let her obtain this information from the actions of diverse, seemingly unconcerned, casual intermediaries, perhaps from guards, attendants, even passersby, in the vicinity of the cages, bit by bit, from, say, a word dropped here and there, to which she, in her cage, desperate for knowledge, would be eagerly alert. Let her assemble this understanding then from seemingly inadvertent scraps, which she will zealously scrutinize, that she may put pieces together, as in a puzzle. Let her suspect nothing."

"Then she is to be informed, without suspecting that she is being informed."

"Yes," said Cabot.

"But even so you would have her informed?" said Lord Grendel.

"Yes," said Cabot.

"Even though she is a slave?"

"Yes," said Cabot.

In order that this may become clearer to a reader, one perhaps unfamiliar with the ways of masters and slaves, it might be kept in mind that the slave is an animal. Would you, for example, stop to explain politics, or the events of the day, to kaiila or verr? To be sure, the female human slave, although an animal, is an extremely intelligent and curious animal, and one much interested in her milieu and its prospects. This is an aspect of her often considerable intelligence. Keeping her in ignorance then is one of many means, perhaps one somewhat cruel, by which she may the better be informed of her bondage. It helps her to feel it, often keenly. She is not a free woman. Let her be kept then in darkness, squirming and frustrated, her eager, high intelligence deliberately left without enlightenment. Often important events are not spoken of before her, even events which might affect her profoundly, raids, excursions, shortages, closings of trade routes, marches on cities, the approach of armies, and such, and even lesser things, as well, for example that offers have been made for her, perhaps by handsome young men of whose presence on the street or in the bazaar she was only dimly aware, or, say, that they are thinking of breeding her, or that her master's companion wishes her sold, or that, according to quotas imposed by the city, she has been selected for a tribute slave, that she and two others are to be exchanged for a kaiila, that one of her master's recent guests was a slaver, unbeknownst to her, by whom she was being appraised, and so on. This ignorance, of course, is also helpful with respect to her control. On the other hand, despite the best efforts by masters, there is often, one fears, slave to slave, one overhearing something here, another hearing something there, and so on, often a rapid transmission of the most exquisite and detailed information amongst them. After all, they traverse the streets, draw water at the fountains, bargain in the markets, kneel at the laundry troughs, and so on. A well-known Gorean saying has it that curiosity is not becoming in a *kajira*. Nonetheless, it is also commonly understood, often to the surprise, and sometimes chagrin, of masters, that *kajirae*, in a thousand ways, however mysteriously, are often well informed.

It may be supposed then that the slave in the stable, despite the handicap of her incarceration, was already well aware of certain profound alterations in the world, political, and otherwise.

Nonetheless, as this was not known to Cabot and Lord Grendel, or not known for certain, Lord Grendel, by means of intermediaries, guards, and such, made certain that the slave was well aware of the victory of Lord Arcesilaus, the appearance of Lord Grendel in the capital, that of a human commander, Tarl Cabot, as well, and so on.

"Then she will look for you," said Lord Grendel. "She will expect to be claimed at the first opportunity."

"That is my supposition," said Cabot.

"But she will not be?"

"No."

"Excellent," said Lord Grendel.

"We shall let her wait for a few days," said Cabot.

"Excellent," said Lord Grendel. "But she is also to know that you are well aware of where she is, and such?"

"Of course," said Cabot.

"I thought you were earlier interested in her most swift recovery."

"I have rethought the matter," said Cabot. "Let her remain in her cage."

"The better to know herself a slave?"

"Yes," said Cabot.

"I thought she was important to you," said Lord Grendel.

"How could that be?" said Cabot. "She is only a slave."

"So let her learn that she is without importance?"

"Yes," said Cabot.

"And a cage is an excellent place for her to learn that?"

"Yes," said Cabot.

"Shall we meet here, tomorrow, in festive regalia?" asked Lord Grendel.

"Such will be provided, I trust," said Cabot.

"Of course," said Lord Grendel. He then turned to leave, but Cabot, a hand on his arm, stayed him, briefly.

"I do not understand the matter of faces of the Nameless One," said Cabot. "How could both Lord Agamemnon and Lord Arcesilaus be faces of the Nameless One?"

"Why not?" said Lord Grendel. "They are different faces."

"The Nameless One has faces of both evil and good?" asked Cabot.

"The Nameless One has many faces," said Lord Grendel. "Agamemnon doubtless viewed his face as rightful and just, as good, if you like, and so, too, though the faces are quite different, does Lord Arcesilaus. Perhaps it is you who find the faces good and evil, and not the Nameless One."

"I do not understand," said Cabot.

"I think," said Lord Grendel, "the Nameless One is neither good nor evil, as you think of such things, but that he is beyond such things, or other than such things. I do not think he is concerned with such things. They do not interest him. Is the venomous ost good or evil? It is the ost. Is the prowling sleen good or evil? It is the sleen. Is the harmless verr good or evil? It is the verr. I think the Nameless One is indifferent, even to whether or not it shows itself. It is itself, that is all, visible and invisible, public and private, secret and revealed, shown and concealed; it is as it was, and is, and will be."

"I will return to the quarters assigned to me," said Cabot.

"Let us meet here, tomorrow," said Lord Grendel.

"At noon, the tenth Ahn?"

"Agreed," said Lord Grendel.

Chapter, the Seventy-Fourth:

**An Earth Female Finds Herself Kept in a Slave Cage;
Feasts, Festivals, and _Agons_;
A Slave Is to Be Taken into the Forest**

"Tarl! Tarl!" she cried. "Where have you been? My body aches! Free me, immediately!"

She was fetching in the cage, naked and collared, kneeling, bending over, holding to the bars. It was a tiny, shipping cage. It had bars on four sides, that the slave may be conveniently viewed. The ceiling and floor of the cage were of quarter-inch steel. The bars were something like three-eighths of an inch in diameter, quite enough to hold a female. It was something like a yard square, and the slave could not stretch her body within it to her full length, even her small, deliciously curved female body.

She shook the bars, angrily, futilely. "At last you have come for me," she said. "You should have been here days ago. Release me!"

She did not notice that the other slaves, of which there were several, like herself, naked and collared, were kneeling in their cages, heads to the floor, palms of hands, too, down on the floor, in first obeisance position. They knew themselves to be in the presence of a free man.

Cabot then turned about, and left.

"Come back!" she cried, shaking the bars. "Come back!"

But he was gone.

The festival would last several days.

Much of the music was lost on Cabot, as he could hear little of it, and what he heard was little to his liking.

The martial dances were more fascinating, particularly the convolutions of Kurii, which were hitherto unknown to him.

He was familiar with martial dances from Gor, of course, which are used not simply for public displays, and such, but in the training of infantry, the turns, advances, withdrawals, the liftings and lowerings of spears, the rhythmic clash of blades on shields, the stamping of feet, the glittering of light on helmets, and spears. On level ground nothing could stand against the weight of a thousand spears, of different lengths, bristling before the advance, rushed forward with the weight of a thousand running, screaming men behind them. On rough ground other formations were more effective, smaller, coordinated groups of men, groups which, to the movements of standards, the blasts of horns, could break apart from other groups, rejoin, slip to the rear, be replaced with fresh groups, and so on. Such groups, for example, might be tactically divided, to accommodate themselves to the exigencies of terrain and battle, and then seamlessly rejoin, as though by magic, when desired. They were not like a great chain whose links, shattered by rises or defiles, break apart into disjointed segments, with openings, gaps, between them. Commanders choose their ground carefully.

The martial dances, in part, supposedly assisted in spacing, and the maintaining of spacing. In actual battle, in the great formations, there is an almost inevitable drift to the right, as soldiers attempt to obtain some protection under the shield of the man to their right. As a consequence, it is common for each formation, as the battle continues, to be overreached, and outflanked, on the left. The right wing of each formation is almost invariably victorious, and the left wing of each almost always finds itself in jeopardy. Commanders commonly lead the right wing. Aside from matters of morale, exhibition, training, spirit, and such, the martial dances, then, with their emphasis on order and symmetry, are intended to compensate for the rightward drift of the great formations. In actual battle, of course, with the press and crowding, the buffeting, the noise, the shouting, the screaming, the shedding of blood, the dying, the rightward drift is seldom arrested.

Tarn cavalries, as it is explained to me, have similar exercises, and maneuvers, to the beating of drums, these often coordinating the stroke of the great wings. Although I have never seen this, I am informed that these evolutions are remarkably beautiful, hundreds of birds, with their riders, ascending, descending, whirling about, separating, rejoining, and so on.

Each night there was a feast.

More than once raucous killer humans had to be separated, flung from one another.

Once a knife had sped past him, and lodged deeply in the wall behind him. Somewhere in the hall he knew was Flavion, but he did not know where. He thought the knife had probably been intended for another. Or perhaps it had been flung for no more than delight, or sport, to a mark on a wall.

He probably drank too much.

Once he was startled to be served by a female Kur, collared. A dominant stood behind her, whip in hand.

She wore no harnessing.

From Cabot's point of view, in the glossiness of her oiled and scented coat, she was as concealed as ever.

From the Kur point of view she was naked.

From her diffidence, serving even a human, Cabot was well aware she knew herself a naked slave.

Cabot preferred the human females, hurrying about, serving both humans and Kurii.

How beautiful human females are, he thought. It is no wonder that men make them slaves.

Lord Arcesilaus sat on a dais, at the head of a hundred tables, with Lord Zarendargar, Lord Grendel, and Statius; and Archon, of the forest humans, and Cestiphon, of the killer humans, sat with them.

He found himself being served by one of Cestiphon's slaves.

She was now collared.

It was lovely on her neck.

Collars much enhance the beauty of a female, aesthetically, certainly, but also in their meaning.

Cestiphon's chosen sign for his females, the petal of a flower, was on the collar. There would thus be no doubt as to whom she belonged.

When she turned away Cabot noted that she had been tastefully marked, high on the left hip.

Many are the enhancements with which a civilization may acknowledge and express the primitive realities of nature.

Some female slaves, who had been of the pleasure cylinder, danced, to music supplied by the men of Peisistratus.

The humans were well pleased.

Some of the slaves had been granted dancing silk. They were high-haltered and bare-bellied. The silk was low on their hips and swirled about their bangled ankles.

How it enhances the dance, thought Cabot, and how easy it is to remove it.

At a gesture from Peisistratus, his Corinna came and writhed before Cabot. Peisistratus, this evening, had chosen to deny her clothing. She was skilled, and danced well. Cabot was pleased and threw her a piece of hot, greasy meat, which she clutched to herself, gratefully, and swirled away.

He gestured to a slave to kneel beside him and put down her head, that he might use her long hair to wipe his hands.

"Master," she begged, daring to look up at him.

How needful they are, thought Cabot. How much they are in our power, once slave fires have been lit in their bellies.

Excellent, he thought. A most pleasant way to bring them to our feet.

The girl whimpered, piteously.

Several were even now serving, on belly or back, moaning, squirming, crying out, begging for more, on cushions cast about the floor of the hall. Others knelt, head down, on the tiles.

"Master, please, Master!" petitioned the girl.

"Petition another," said Cabot, and left the hall.

"I understand you have been very busy, Tarl," said the slave, peering through the bars.

He did not respond to her.

"I spoke perhaps too earnestly, too directly, before," she said. "I understand that you are a commander, that you have been important in the war, that you may have many duties to attend to, that you must have many duties to attend to, but now you have returned."

The bottom of the cage was wet, as were her knees, where she knelt in the dampness. One of the cleaning slaves had cast a bucket of water into the cage, to wash wastes from it, to be later cleaned. To one side, where she could reach it, through the bars, was a small bowl, in which lay a piece of fruit, and a crust of bread. On a nearby post hung a damp, bulging bag, and, on a nail driven into the same post, on a small string, hung a small metal cup. The cup was small enough to be passed through the bars.

"I am understood to be a slave," she said. "Accordingly I will need to be claimed. I am now ready to be released. I trust you will see to it, and soon."

Cabot glanced to the other cages, in which the fair occupants were in first obeisance position, knowing themselves in the presence of a free person.

"Tarl," she said. "Please, Tarl!"

Then he left.

"Come back!" she cried after him. "Come back, Tarl! Come back, Tarl!"

She then looked to the other slaves, and saw that they had now resumed positions of their choice, in their small, cramped quarters.

Some were regarding her, curiously.

"Well done," said Flavion.

Cabot did not respond to him.

"Yes, well done," said Flavion, and then politely withdrew.

On the steel world in question, as well as on Gor, most festivals included a large number of competitions , *agons*, of one sort or another, usually races, spear casting, wrestling, log hurling, and such.

Although it had not been cultural on the world until recently, archery had been included in the *agons*. Cabot had done well, coming in second in the contests. Lord Grendel had not competed in that *agon*. His skill, as suggested earlier, was remarkable, but he declined to draw attention to it, perhaps being somewhat embarrassed by it, and certainly feeling that the ax was a more respectable, Kurlike weapon.

The winner of the archery contest was one of the men of

Peisistratus, who had originally been of the peasants, of the village of Rarir.

Cabot, however, was not unskilled. He could, reportedly, draw a bow with most peasants. His preferred weapons, however, as was expected of his caste, were the sword and spear. His skill with the former tool was said to be deft, exquisite, and lethal.

On Gor, I am told, poetry of various sorts, literary efforts, musical compositions, choral dancing, enactments, and even song dramas are included in the *agons*.

It might be mentioned, in passing, that Lord Grendel won the *agon* of the ax. That is, as you doubtless know, a weapon of high repute amongst Kurii. It is popular too, I understand, in certain areas on Gor, particularly in the north, toward, and in, Torvaldsland. He could split a post with an ax hurled from fifteen Kur paces, which is approximately twenty human paces.

The crossbow and power weapons were not included in the *agons*. It was felt that the use of neither weapon, however dangerous and effective it might be, required enough skill to qualify it for inclusion in an *agon*. In the case of the crossbow this seems to the writer a mistake. The writer feels that, beyond a certain point, skill with the crossbow is as respectable and rare as that with the great bow. The prejudice against the crossbow, the writer suspects, is due largely to the fact that it is, for obvious reasons, the assassin's weapon of choice.

The next time Cabot visited the tiny cage of a brunette slave, she knelt as the other slaves had, with the palms of her hands down on the cage floor, and her head down to it, as well, in first obeisance position.

"I gather," she said, acidly, "this is the way you want me."

But when she looked up, he had gone.

"Is he your master?" asked a slave.

"Do not think of me as a slave," she snapped.

"I think you are in a slave collar," said one of the slaves.

"Clearly she is in a slave collar," said another.

"Thus," said another, "we would suppose you are a slave."

"Few free women are in slave collars," said a slave.

"Crawl out of your cage, free woman," said one of the slaves.

"Perhaps in some sense," said the brunette, "I am a slave."

"You are either a slave or you are not," said another.

"And you are obviously a slave," said another.

"Fully," said another.

"Completely," said another.

"Totally," said another.

"Yes, slave," pronounced another, with finality. "Slave, and only slave."

"He is of another world," said the brunette slave, "as I am. He will not think of me as a slave. He cannot so think of me."

"Is he not Tarl Cabot?" asked one of the slaves.

"Of Gor?" asked another.

"Once of Earth," said the brunette.

"But now of Gor," said one of the slaves.

"Yes," said the brunette, "now of Gor."

"And you are a woman, are you not?" asked another slave.

"Obviously," said the brunette.

"And you are in a collar."

"Yes," said the brunette.

"Be afraid," said one of the slaves.

"Why has he not claimed you?" asked another.

"I do not know," said the brunette.

"Perhaps he is going to sell you," said a slave.

"No!" cried the brunette, frightened, grasping the bars.

"I would sell you," said another of the slaves.

"*Sell me?*" stammered the brunette.

"Certainly," said one of the slaves.

"Who would want you?" asked another.

"No one," said another.

"After first well beating you," said another.

The brunette turned pale.

"What did you do?" asked a slave.

"You must have displeased him," said another.

"That is it," said another. "She is a slave who has displeased her master!"

"She spoke to him other than as a slave dares speak," said another.

"We heard her!"

"She used his name to him, putting it on her slave lips!"

"What did you do?" asked a slave, she who had earlier asked this question.

"I left a camp, without permission," said the brunette.

"A beating perhaps," said one of the slaves, "but that would scarcely keep you in your cage."

"I ran away!" said the brunette.

This announcement was met with a silence, one of disbelief, of shock. The slaves regarded one another. Clearly they were frightened. More than one then looked at the brunette, frightened. And it was then, perhaps, that the brunette first began to grasp the nature of what she had done, and that she was one to whom such things were not permitted.

"And now you have been caught!" said one of the slaves, peering at the brunette through the bars of her own cage.

"Yes, I have been caught!" said the brunette, and flung herself down, legs drawn up, to the floor of her cage. "I have been caught," she sobbed.

"What if he should be of Gor, truly?" she thought. "And what if I should be a slave, truly?"

She began to tremble, lying in the cage.

"I have been caught," she whispered, frightened, to the floor of the cage, to the bars. "I have been caught!"

"I am going to claim a slave," said Cabot, to Lord Grendel.

"There are still days left of the feasting time," said Lord Grendel.

"I am going to venture into the forest," said Cabot. "I am going to seek out our old camp, from which, long ago, we were to march on the palace."

"I think I understand," said Lord Grendel.

"There is to be no secret about my departure," said Cabot, "nor about my destination."

"And what, supposedly, is to be the reason for this journey at this time?"

"A journey," said Cabot, "may have more than one reason."

"And what," asked Lord Grendel, "is that reason which lies open, and comprehensible, to all?"

"To take a slave into the forest, far from civilization, and do with her as I will," Cabot said.

"That she may learn she is a slave?"

"Yes."

"I do not think I would care to be she," said Lord Grendel.

"When I am through with her," said Cabot, "she will know what she is."

"I do not doubt it," said Lord Grendel.

Chapter, the Seventy-Fifth:

**A Slave's Scent Is Taken;
An Earth Woman Is Tortured by Her Needs,
And Understands the Meaning of This;
No Fire Has Been Made**

"May I speak, Master!" begged the slave.

"No," said Cabot.

She stumbled behind him, naked, back-braceleted, drawn on her leash.

They were deep in the forest.

Two days before she had been claimed.

There had been no difficulty about it, as Cabot was now well known in the habitats, and the legend on the slave's collar was clear: *I am the property of Tarl Cabot.*

A single glance, when he had entered the stable, had informed her that he had come for his slave. He was no longer in festive regalia, but a simple tunic, mottled with greens and browns, colors such as might be found in certain natural backgrounds, say, that of forest, a traveling cloak, similarly configured, and the bootlike sandals common to soldiers, and travelers. At his waist was a belt with pouch and knife. On his back, slung in straps, was an ax, long-handled, but of a size manageable by a human. A pack, which might be shoulder slung, to lie at the left hip, had been left at the stable gate. From his left hand dangled a pair of light slave bracelets, and the loops of a chain leash.

She went to first obeisance position.

She heard the attendant summoned and, in moments, heard the key turn in the two locks which secured the cage. The door was then swung open; she saw the shadows of the bars moving on the wooden floor.

She saw before her the two heavy sandals. They had thick straps, wound high about the legs, almost to the knees. They had a blunt, brutal look about them.

She lifted her head a little, saw his eyes, and then put her head down, again, quickly.

She saw that he was to be addressed, as only a slave would address a master.

There was so much she wanted to say to him, to tell him, to explain to him, to make clear to him, to pour out to him.

He must understand her.

She must make him understand her!

"May I speak, Master?" she whispered.

"No," he said.

The first day in the forest, Ramar, the great sleen, had joined them. To her terror, and horror, she had been put on her back on the leaves, and the sleen, at Cabot's urging, had taken her scent. She felt the hot breath of the beast on her body, the hairy snout, the licking tongue, the inhaling nostrils. She cried out with misery, and squirmed, and was turned, and positioned, in one manner or another, to facilitate the beast's work. "Oh!" she protested. "Oh!" And then again, "Oh!" and "Oh!" And then, "Please, no! Please, no! Oh! Oh!" "Be silent, slave," she was told. And the beast continued its work. Then she was again supine, and the beast was to the side, and Cabot stood over her, looking down on her. Her scent had been taken, as a slave's scent is taken. She felt raped. But, did she not know she was a slave?

Cabot then crouched beside her, and took her by one arm, its hand braceleted behind her. He looked to Ramar, and then shook the slave, and said, "Cecily, Cecily."

She looked at Cabot, with horror.

This was a name she despised, a name fit, in her view, only for a shopgirl. Too, she knew, by now, that it would be recognized in Gorean markets as an Earth-girl name, the sort of name to be fastened on only the lowest and most degraded of slaves. Such names are sometimes given to Gorean slaves as punishment names. Gorean men often bid intensely for Earth girls, but not because they wish to show them respect, and such. Rather they want to have on their chain one of the lowest and most helplessly delicious of slaves.

"Your scent has been taken," said Cabot to the slave. "Too, it has been associated with a particular name. The purpose of this should be clear. The name, together with a given command, initiates the sleen's behavior. For example, given the "kill" command the sleen will locate and destroy the quarry, given a "drive" command, it will conduct the quarry to a predetermined location, or, if the quarry should prove recalcitrant, tear it to pieces. There are other commands, too, as you may suspect, but most are obvious, and I decline to make clear their nature. If you understand the purport of what I am saying, nod affirmatively."

The slave, miserable, nodded, affirmatively.

"What is your name?" asked Cabot.

The slave looked at him.

Then she said, tears in her eyes, "Cecily, Master," adding "—if it pleases Master." Then she blurted out, weeping, "May I speak, Master?"

"No," he said. "You will relieve yourself, and then sleep."

"Yes, Master," she whispered.

"There," he said, pointing.

"Yes, Master," she whispered.

He then fastened her to a tree by the chain leash, bade her recline, and placed a blanket over her.

Later she sat up a little, and was sensible of the pull of the leash on its collar, and the tiny sound of its links, and she then lay down, on her side.

"Please, Master, let me speak," she begged.

"No," he said.

Ramar, the great sleen, lay nearby.

She tried the bracelets a bit, fastening her small wrists behind her body, and knew herself, as she knew she would, slave helpless.

"I want to be in his bracelets," she thought, scarcely daring to believe her own thoughts. "How long can I pretend to myself I am a free woman? Have I not learned by now I should be a slave, and am a slave? Why does he not touch me? I want his touch. Does he not know what was done to me before, how my body has been changed? My mind cries 'free woman'! My belly cries 'slave'! How foolish is my mind! How wise my belly! Dear mind, how you desire to dictate to me! Do you still listen only to others, dear mind, and not to me? Why do you not look upon my truth? Is it not your truth, as well? Dear mind, surrender, unite with my body! Dear mind, is the truth so terrible, so unfamiliar, so unreasonable, so alien? I want to be one with my body, not its foe. I want to be whole! Let the gates be forced, let the walls collapse; please, dear mind, see to it that I am led in chains, helpless, choiceless, rejoicing, to my master's couch!"

The slave noted that her master had made no fire.

This puzzled her.

He sat nearby, not sleeping, considering the forest.

Chapter, the Seventy-Sixth:

The Forest Camp

Tarl Cabot and the slave came to the abandoned forest camp without incident.

He inspected the camp and found it much as it had been, when he had come here last, through the snows of the arranged winter.

He did not close the gate.

He freed the slave of the bracelets and leash, and sent her to gather firewood.

She wore only her collar.

This was sufficient, and the collar would mark her as what she was, should she encounter anyone in the forest.

A brand may be concealed by clothing, if it is permitted the slave, but the collar is commonly visible. This badge of servitude is not only attractive, but it is to be prominently mounted, on the neck of the slave. There must be no mistaking of her for a free woman. If the weather is of inclement ferocity and the slave is muchly bundled against the cold she is expected to kneel immediately in the presence of free persons. In this way she makes her status unmistakably clear. To be sure, regardless of her dress or lack of it, the slave is expected to kneel, at least initially, in the presence of free persons, for example, when addressed, when entering rooms in which they are present, and so on, until, and if, permitted to rise. Interestingly, the slave collar, which might be thought a badge of shame, is often regarded, rather, by its wearer, and certainly by men, to the jealousy, hatred, and envy of free women, as an indisputable emblem of female desirability, a token or insignia of appeal and interest, of attractiveness and allure. Not just any woman is worth a collar; not just any woman is worth buying and selling, or having at your feet. The collar then is, in its way, a public certification of female excellence, a mark, like the brand, of special quality. It says, in effect, "This is excellent goods. Look upon her. Is she not well worth chaining?" Thus, it is not surprising that many slaves, after a time, are not only well pleased with their collars, but find themselves proud to be collared. There are two elements here which many who are unfamiliar with these matters may not understand. First, what many understand as "freedom" has never been essential to happiness, and may actually prove inimical to it. What is important to happiness is that the individual is as she wants to be, and desires to be. She is thus to be permitted to find her happiness where she does find it, in fact, and not where someone else would have her find it. It is also helpful, of course, if the society recognizes her status, accepts it, and approves it. The ideal then is that she finds herself fulfilling a recognized, accepted, approved, and valued societal role, and finds her personal fulfillment and happiness in doing so. And this role may, of course, require the collar. Second, there are many sorts of freedom, not just one. And the slave, though she is the property of a master, and is wholly his, may in her way find more freedom, and be a thousand times more liberated, so to speak, and more joyous, than the free women who fear and despise her. This is sometimes spoken of as the "paradox of the collar," namely, that she who is least free may, interestingly, be the most free.

To be sure, there is much to fear in being a slave, for masters are not patient, and will have much of her.

She must be concerned to please, and, to the best of her ability, to please superbly.

Ramar was in the woods somewhere, perhaps hunting, or renewing a burrow.

Cabot wondered if the slave would return.

She returned in some twenty Ehn with an armful of dried branches. She was then sent forth twice more.

Following her return, the third time, he took her to a stout post, some six feet high, with two rings, one high, one low, at the side of the camp, one he had had placed there earlier, indeed, with she, the errant slave, in mind, knelt her before it and then braceleted her hands behind the post, and, with the chain leash, pulled her head back against it.

He then closed the gate, built a fire, the first since their journey had begun, and prepared food.

After he had eaten, he rejoined the slave, and fed her some small viands by hand, and gave her of drink, water from a bota.

"May I speak, Master?" she begged.

"No," he said. He had not permitted her to speak, even from the time of the cage.

Tears sprang to her eyes.

She tried to pull out a bit from the post, and thrust her belly toward him. She whimpered, piteously.

Thus, he thought, were the women of Earth, if brought to the comprehension of their sex. But so, too, were the women of Gor. The differences between them were not biological, but cultural. Interesting, he thought, how the women of Gor look down upon, and despise, the women of Earth as aroused, salacious barbarians, and yet themselves, identically, will whimper and squirm in slave bracelets, pull against chains, writhe in ropes, and lift their bellies pathetically for a master's touch. Cabot saw little to choose between them. Both, reduced to essentials, were the same, human females.

The slave fought the bracelets; she turned her head back and forth, in frustration, in the chain leash that held her head back, against the post. In her eyes were tears. Again and again, struggling, she thrust her belly toward him, supplicatingly.

"She would sell well," he thought.

He thought, too, of the young men of her former world, how well they might be pleased to see her so.

"No," he said.

He then went to the opened gate, and peered into the woods. He smiled. He then swung the gate closed.

He returned to the vicinity of the fire and, with a stone, sharpened the two edges of the ax he had brought with him.

This took some time.

Before retiring he again visited the slave, and rebraceleted her hands before her, and about the post, and fastened the chain leash in such a way that she could lift her head no more than a foot from the ground.

She turned, as she could, to view him, and raised her head to the extent permitted by the leash, it shortened and locked about the lower post ring.

"May I speak, Master?" she begged. "Please, may I speak?"

"Tomorrow," he said.

"Thank you, Master!" she said, bursting into tears. "Thank you, thank you, Master!"

"Now, be silent," he said.

"Yes, Master," she said.

She then, at a gesture from Cabot, lay swiftly down, for she well knew how a slave is to obey, immediately, and unquestioningly, and he threw a blanket over her. He did this in such a way that it covered her head, as well.

Slaves are often kept in ignorance.

Curiosity, after all, is not becoming to them.

Chapter, the Seventy-Seventh:

What Occurred Later in the Forest Camp

"May I speak, Master?" she asked.

"And how are you to speak?" he asked.

"As I must," she said, "as what I am, as a slave before her master."

"You may speak," he said.

It was morning. She knelt before him. Her knees were in the position of a pleasure slave.

"How clever they are," thought Cabot.

Cabot had his back to the gate, which he had opened.

"I will not whip her for that," thought Cabot, "though I know what she is trying to do. Indeed, I think that within that extraordinarily tantalizing body which so stirs me, which I could almost hate for the effect it has on me, there lies concealed, unknown even to she herself, piteously needful, a pleasure slave."

"Master?" inquired the slave.

But Cabot was considering the delicacy, sensitivity, and beauty of her features, the clearness of her eyes, the sheen of her hair, still somewhat shorter than would be ideal for her marketing, and the sweet, tender, vulnerable femininity of her, to which she might not yet be fully reconciled, but which was she, and which would muchly improve her price; how wondrously, he thought, does the femininity of a woman emerge and manifest itself when she is collared, no longer needing to be hidden, or denied, no longer a source of embarrassment, shame, or regret, and how nicely on her lovely neck appeared that collar, his collar, close-fitting and locked. Yes, they should be slaves, he thought. And, he thought, too, while considering her various characteristics, which might appeal to buyers, though she is naive, confused, uncertain of herself, a stranger to herself, in some ways alien to herself, yet she has surely a fine, supple mind, quick, and, even, within its limits, those of Earth, educated. Such things add to a slave's value. To be sure, she was woefully ignorant of Gor, but so, too, are most Earth females brought to the Gorean markets. What need they to know, other than that they are slaves, and must please their masters? How beautiful she was! He decided he would keep her illiterate. Reading and writing was the province of free persons, not of such as she, a slave.

But she has a considerable intelligence, he thought, the sort of intelligence which a man can appreciate, the sort of intelligence he wants at his feet.

"Master?" she asked.

He sat cross-legged, regarding her. The ax lay beside him, at hand.

"You may speak," he said.

In moments then, tears running down her cheeks, to her collar, and body, stammering, half-choked, words tumbling out one upon another, piteously, only half-coherently, she addressed her master, and as what she knew she was, a slave.

"Forgive me, Master!" she wept. "I was a miserable and foolish slave. I did not realize what I was doing. I felt abandoned! You did not take me with you! You left me in the camp! Better you had bound me, and whipped me, to hurry me before you! Better you had put me on a chain and dragged me behind you! I could not bear to be left behind! Could you not better have burdened me and struck me with switches if I lagged? I wanted so to go with you! You did not permit it! Had I not accompanied you before? Had you not taken me with you before? I wept, grieved, I was outraged, I would teach you you could not treat me in that fashion, you could not do that to me, not to me! I was not thinking clearly! I was foolish! I made a terrible mistake! I should have realized that it was your will, and that I am subject to your will, but I did not! I did a foolish and stupid thing! I ran away! Forgive me, Master! Please, forgive me!"

But Cabot listened to her, impassively.

"I did not understand I was in a collar," she said. "I did not realize there was nowhere to go, nowhere to run. I did not understand then that there was no escape for me, nor for any girl in a collar! I was soon picked up by partisans, and found myself roped, and sequestered. After the resolution of the war I was taken to the habitats, where I was caged, as was fitting for me, caged, to await my master, and my fate. You are my master! Please, forgive me, Master!"

She put down her head, sobbing.

"Did you ever expect, on Earth, to be as you are now, before one such as I, speaking so?"

"No, Master," she said.

"In the cage," he said, "initially, you showed me too little respect. You did not assume first obeisance position. You did not speak to me appropriately, as a slave."

"Forgive me, Master," she whispered.

Cabot had his back to the opened gate. The girl had her head down.

"Did you think you were still on Earth?" asked Cabot.

"Forgive me, Master."

"You were not on Earth," he said.

"No, Master," she whispered.

"In several respects," said Cabot, "it seems you were insufficiently respectful."

"Yes, Master."

"Are you aware of the penalties for showing insufficient respect?"

"No, Master," she said, "but I fear them."

"A slave," said Cabot, "may speak the names of free persons in certain fashions, and in certain situations, obviously, such as 'My master is Tarl Cabot', 'I am the slave of Tarl Cabot', 'Mistress Publia desires that you would call upon her', 'Master Gordon desires your opinion on the breeding of a young female slave', 'Master Clearchus has repaired the kaiila saddle', 'It is expected that Master Turik's new coffle will arrive in the city tomorrow, by the tenth Ahn', and so on. But the slave does not address the master, or other free persons, by their own names, unless having permission to do so."

"Yes, Master."

"And that permission is rarely, if ever, granted."

"Yes, Master."

"Did your master give you that permission?"

"No, Master."

"And he will not do so."

"Yes, Master."

"The names of free persons are not to be soiled in such ways, by appearing on the lips of slaves."

"No, Master. Forgive me, Master."

"Your faults," said Cabot, "are numerous and heinous."

"Yes, Master."

"Perhaps you think you are a free woman?"

"No, Master, I do not think I am a free woman!"

"What are you, then?"

"A slave, Master, a slave!"

"Anything else?"

"No, Master, only that! Nothing else. Only that!"

"And most seriously," said Cabot, "and as you have acknowledged, you did something preposterously foolish, something incomprehensibly stupid, the seriousness of which I doubt you understood, something the gravity of which you, unfamiliar with your collar, no more than an ignorant, naive slut, fresh from Earth, newly under the whip, could perhaps not even have begun to comprehend, something foredoomed to failure, impossible of success, something fraught with inevitable and profound peril, something of which an informed, knowledgeable girl, aware of her collar, and its meaning, and the realities of her world, would not even dare to think."

"I was angry," she said. "I was foolish. I made a terrible mistake. I did not know any better. I fled."

"What could you have accomplished, other than perhaps to fall into the power of another master?"

"Nothing, Master," she said.

"Perhaps you thought you might escape," said Cabot.

"I did not even think," she whispered.

"There was no escape for you," said Cabot.

"No, Master," she said.

"I gather you now know that," he said.

"Yes, Master," she said. "I know that now. I am branded and collared, and am a slave. There is nowhere to run, nowhere to go. Even were I to escape one master I would fall to another. I am slave, and must remain so. This world will have it so."

"And so would Gor," said Cabot.

"Gor?" she said.

"It is a world more beautiful than you can imagine," said Cabot.

"And on that world would I, too, be a slave?"

"More securely and perfectly, and more helplessly, than you could conceive," said Cabot. "On Gor they know what to do with Earth women."

"As on Earth they do not?"

"Yes," said Cabot, "as on Earth they do not."

"Will you take me to Gor?"

"Perhaps," said Cabot. "Certainly there are better markets for selling you on Gor."

"Selling me?"

"Yes," said Cabot. "You are a slave."

"Please do not sell me, Master!" she cried, lifting her head.

But then, as she lifted her head, her eyes suddenly widened, and she flung a small hand before her mouth, and screamed, shrinking back.

Cabot turned, in an unhurried fashion, and picked up the ax, and rose to his feet, to face Flavion.

"My dear Flavion," he said.

"Lord Flavion," said Flavion.

Flavion carried a Kur ax. It was of solid metal, and of a piece. A human could not easily lift such a tool, let alone put it to practical use.

"I have been waiting for you," said Cabot.

"You were a fool to not face the gate, and to leave it open," said Flavion.

"How better to lure you within?" asked Cabot.

The slave, at a gesture from Cabot, scrambled, on all fours, to the side.

"You positioned the slave, that you might be warned," said Flavion. The slave, it may be recalled, had faced the gate. But in her misery, distracted, sobbing, her head down, scarcely daring to raise her eyes from the dirt, she had not immediately detected the presence of the Kur.

"No," said Cabot, "your left foot drags in the dirt. This scratching, this slow scuffling sound, which you so vainly tried to conceal, is as readily detected as the stroke of a broom, the dragging of a rake."

"The sleen let me pass," said Flavion.

"Of course," said Cabot. "You were once of this camp, and so you would be admitted, as before."

"You counted on that?"

"Certainly," said Cabot.

"I could have killed it," said Flavion, lifting the ax a bit.

"How easily he handles that tool," thought Cabot.

"That is possible," said Cabot, "if you knew it was about, were expecting an attack, and such."

"But I came through, without difficulty."

"As I wished," said Cabot.

"I think you are mad," said Flavion.

"Should you raise that weapon against me," said Cabot, "you have repudiated the amnesty."

"You are a fool," said Flavion, "to rely on the amnesty for your security. Do you truly think I would fear to violate it, here, far from the habitats, here, in the forest?"

"My intention," said Cabot, "is not to rely on the amnesty for my security, but rather that matters be so arranged that I may see it explicitly repudiated."

"None will know," said Flavion, "or none who matter," he added, glancing to the slave, crouched fearfully to the side.

"Run!" cried Cabot to the slave, and pointed to the opened gate.

With a cry of misery she sprang to her feet and ran toward the gate.

Flavion intercepted her, seizing one arm by which she was swung about, and hurled yards away, tumbling over and over in the dirt.

Doubtless Cabot wished that the slave might have reached the safety of the forest, a desiderated outcome, where she might, a fleet, collared human female, have managed to elude a lame Kur, but he was not surprised when she failed to do so.

He had, of course, gathered some intelligence from her attempt. The Kur, despite his lameness, had moved with great agility. This was noted by Cabot, and gave him a better idea of what he might expect from such a foe.

"Ah, dear Flavion," said Cabot, "you are quicker than I might have supposed."

"Lord Flavion," said Flavion.

Cabot shrugged, and watched while Flavion went to the gate, swung it shut, and secured it shut. It would take some moments to undo that latching.

Flavion then stood before the gate, his back to it, and regarded Cabot.

"You are a fool to have come here alone," said Flavion. The slave, of course, did not count.

"I did not think you would care to resume your games amongst the habitats," said Cabot.

"If necessary, I would have," said Flavion. "I owe you much."

"Was it you who threw a knife, in a feast?" asked Cabot.

"That would not have been enough for me," said Flavion. "That cast was flung to a wall by a drunken rowdy, to test the balance of a throwing blade, offered to him by another rowdy, another drunken ruffian, for a coin, both killer humans. I feared only it might strike you."

"I appreciate your solicitude," said Cabot.

Killer humans, successful in the arena, were awarded coins, with which they might purchase women, commonly penned naked within their view, prizes awaiting the victorious. This is not that unusual on Gor, either, I am told, that a successful arena fighter, say, may be awarded a lovely slave. On Gor, however, as I understand it, she is not purchased but bestowed, rather as might be a wreath, or a piece of gold. The killer humans, then, had this additional difference, or advantage, that they might, out of a pool of women, buy she who might most please them. The female, of course, had no choice as to who might purchase them, no more than other slaves. They could, of course, through the bars, attempt to interest one male more than another, hoping that he might then spend his coins accordingly. Gorean slaves, exhibited on slave shelves, often behave similarly, eager to be purchased by a particular master, perhaps a handsome fellow whose eye they hope to catch. And their owners, the merchants, might upon occasion indicate a particular fellow in the crowd, who looks well robed and affluent, to be accosted with posings, assurances of pleasure, the customary "Buy me, Master," solicitation, and such. To be sure, the master's choice might not be the slave's choice, but she does not wish to feel his whip either. The women of the killer humans, it might be noted, were not expended in the arena, nor trained in any form of combat or weaponry. They existed merely to encourage greater diligence and zest in the males, that they might have an additional motivation for success in the arena. They were commonly taught to go to all fours before males, to be neck-roped, and such. They were subject, like cattle, to the will of the male. It maybe recalled that Cestiphon, the leader of his group of killer humans, had four such women. The killer humans, now, of course, the males, were no longer arena animals matched for the sport of Kurii. They were now, the males, free men, dangerous, formidable, and armed. No longer pitted against one another in blood sport they had become comrades in arms. Many would in time seek their fortunes on Gor. The women, of course, as suggested earlier, were to be much improved by the refinements of civilization, cleanliness, grooming, brands, collars and such. The filth, neck-ropes, and sticks of their savage condition had now been well superseded. For example, a collar and chain is a considerable improvement over a neck-rope, which might be chewed through. In time Cabot did not doubt but what many of the women of the killer humans, who were very lovely, would be indistinguishable on a slaver's necklace from their hitherto more-civilized sisters. After the loosing of the killer humans in the revolution coins would be of less import as the women might then, man against man, or group against group, be fought for openly. The number of women on a fellow's rope, or a group's rope, would then become a mark of prestige, rather as the number of kaiila in one's herd, or in one's tribe's herds, would become a mark of wealth and status amongst the warriors of the Red Savages. To be sure, they might also keep white women, in their beaded collars, identifying their masters, as slaves. Coins, of course, were not now unknown, either, amongst the killer humans. Many a slain Kur's pouch had been rifled for such goods.

"Do you think you can stand against a Kur, with an ax?" asked Flavion.

"I do not know," said Cabot.

"First," said Flavion, "I will cut off your left foot, that in vengeance for what you did to mine. Then I will cut off your right foot. Then your left hand, and then your right hand. I will try to staunch the bleeding, for a time. Then, when it pleases me, and I am tired of your screams and pleas, I will open your stomach and hang you from the gate by your own intestines."

"I am impressed," said Cabot, "that you have given some thought to the matter."

"A great deal of careful and delicious thought," said Flavion. "I owe you much."

"Spare the slave," said Cabot.

"Who would kill an animal, which has some value?" asked Flavion.

"Indeed," agreed Cabot.

"She is, I gather," said Flavion, "the sort of thing which is not without interest to human males."

"To some human males," said Cabot.

The animal was to the side. She had risen to all fours, and was regarding the males fearfully.

"I have ascertained, from human males," said Flavion, "men of Peisistratus, that she might well bring in the neighborhood of two silver tarsks."

"Perhaps on a good day," said Cabot.

"Too," said Flavion, "I gather that such things have been done to her that she, no longer capable of controlling herself, will now leap obediently in the arms of any human male."

"Commanded, properly caressed," said Cabot.

A sob escaped the slave.

"It is true," said Cabot to her, sharply.

"Yes, Master," she said.

"She is a slave," said Cabot, matter-of-factly.

"I will take her to Gor with me, to sell her," said Flavion.

"You must obtain her, first," said Cabot.

"Of course," said Flavion.

"I see you have your pouch," said Flavion. "And there is a pack, too, if I am not mistaken. Perhaps you have some rubies left, from the trial of Lord Pyrrhus."

"Yes," said Cabot, "several."

"Why not offer them to me, to buy your life?" suggested Flavion.

"Would they suffice?" inquired Cabot.

"Who knows?" said Flavion.

"To what purpose might they be put?" asked Cabot.

"On Gor," said Flavion, "we will form a new enclave of Kurii, unreconciled adherents of Lord Agamemnon."

"You will join them?"

"I will lead them."

"As rubies are rare," said Cabot, "and valuable, I doubt that you would choose to dispose of them here, in the world. There might be questions raised, as to their provenance, whence they were obtained, such things."

"True," said Flavion. "But on Gor, you see, they will be unquestioned, and, on a street of coins, will have great value."

"You, and some others, then, will buy passage to Gor?"

"I, and several," said Flavion. "Do not fear, we have the coins. We find ourselves unwelcome in the habitats. Political reservations obtain against us. Gor will be better for us, more open, providing some advantages denied us here, affording us greater opportunities for political activity, more scope for intrigue and ambition. In our plans the rubies will obviously have their role."

"But you must obtain them, first," said Cabot.

"Of course," said Flavion, "but I anticipate no difficulty in that regard."

"I would suppose that there must be already on Gor some such enclaves as you mention, doubtless established there in the past by Agamemnon, long before the war, to assist in his several projects."

"For a human, you are perceptive," said Flavion.

"You will make contact with them?"

"Certainly."

"But will form, as well, a new enclave."

"Of course," said Flavion, "for I must be first, I must be leader."

"Lord Flavion?" said Cabot.

"Yes," said Flavion. "Lord Flavion."

"Shall we adjudicate our differences now?" inquired Cabot.

"Would you not like, first, to kneel before me, offer me rubies, plead for your life, and such?"

"No," said Cabot.

"If you plead nicely, I might be persuaded to finish you quickly," said Flavion.

"Let us fight," said Cabot.

"I will have you on your knees quickly enough," said Flavion, "when your feet have been cut off."

"Let us proceed," said Cabot.

"Be patient with me, dear Cabot," said Flavion. "I have waited a long time for this moment."

"You seem confident of the outcome," said Cabot.

"No human can stand against a Kur, with the ax," said Flavion.

"How unfortunate for you that power weapons have been outlawed in the world."

"Let us fight," said Cabot.

"Very well," said Flavion. He then looked to the slave, to the side.

"Chain her," he said.

Cabot went to the slave, and pulled her to her feet, his hand on her left arm. He dragged her to the post of discipline. "Please, no, Master!" she begged. That she, a slave, had dared to speak, angered him. He struck the ax lightly into the post, that its handle was within an easy grasp, and it was lightly held in the wood. He then turned the back of the slave to Flavion, so that he could see him. He was some yards away, behind the ashes of the fire, and the gate was some yards behind him. Cabot then took the hair of the slave in his left hand and held her head up, before him. Her eyes were wide with disbelief. Did she not know she had spoken without permission? He then, sharply, cuffed her thrice, first her left cheek, and then, with the back of his hand, her right cheek, and then with the palm of his hand, her left cheek, again, the triple cuffing, a common cuffing for a slave. He then turned her about and thrust her, belly to the wood, against the post. In a moment, passing the slave bracelets through the high ring, he had fastened her to the post, her hands above her head. He then freed the ax easily, and returned to his side of the fire pit. She jerked at the bracelets, again and again, futilely, in misery, and frustration. How well she was held in place, the steel snugly encircling her small wrists! Cabot and Flavion, who was well pleased, measured one another. The slave, helplessly fastened, looked over her left shoulder, to see what events might ensue, events of great consequence to her, but events on which she, as is commonly the case with slaves, was absolutely incapable of exerting the least influence. She would await the outcome, as the tethered animal she was.

Cabot had come to the forest camp, that Flavion would follow. He had little doubt that Flavion would act, sooner or later, and thought it best to bring the matter to a conclusion sooner rather than later. After Flavion dealt with him, Cabot had little doubt but what Lord Grendel would be next, either in the habitats, or not. Thus, in a way, Cabot hoped to protect his friend. Certainly Lord Grendel would not violate the amnesty by killing Flavion without provocation, nor, indeed, would Cabot. For example, it would presumably have been easy enough for Cabot, bow in hand, and a quiver filled with the birds of death, to have slain Flavion days ago, in the forest. But that, obviously, would have violated the amnesty. This business has to do then, rather clearly, with a sense of honor, well acted upon, or not. Accordingly, it was important to Cabot that Flavion be the first to violate the amnesty, and thus voluntarily deprive himself of its sheltering. Whereas Cabot was familiar with the ax, from Torvaldsland, he was uncertain of his ability to withstand the onslaught of the mighty ax of the Kurii, which a human could scarcely lift, in the grip of a Kur. His uncertainty, as it proved, was more than justified.

A Kur smile, grimacelike, contorted the broad muzzle of Flavion, and moist fangs protruded from the sides of his jaw.

"I have waited long for this," said Flavion.

Cabot moved to Flavion's left, and Flavion lurched after him.

Flavion's ax was some seven feet in length, and outreached that of Cabot by some two feet. Too, it was of solid metal, and the blades were forged from the haft itself.

A swift flight of this mighty tool swept toward Cabot and he sprang back. Such a blow would have cut off two legs. It could have split apart the palings of the stockade, could have shattered the gate of the compound into a dozen pieces.

"You cannot escape," said Flavion, grinning, lurching after Cabot. "How long can you run, little thing? Do you call that little stick you carry an ax? You cannot even reach me with it! You are human! I am Kur! Close with me! Close with me! Hold still! Stand! Fight!"

Cabot circled, as he could, to the left, looking for an opening, but now Flavion held the ax more closely, was more guarded in his movements, in his strokes, even poked at Cabot, trying to force him backward, to fall, or to pin him against the palings.

The slave, braceleted at the post, jerked and jerked at the snug steel on her wrists. The links of the chain joining the bracelets scraped again and again at the iron ring, and pulled futilely against it, but her frenzied efforts were not in the least availing. The steel, the links, the ring, the post, such things, were not designed to concede the least possibility of escape to their selected prisoners. They are designed to hold them, and do hold them, with perfection.

She sobbed, and screamed, and jerked at the bracelets, and was helpless, a slave, fastened in place, as masters would have her.

Cabot lifted his ax above his head, such a comparatively tiny, frail thing, to hold back the haft of Flavion's pressing ax, and Cabot was forced down, to one knee, miserably, and then he rolled to the side, and Flavion's struck at him sidewise and a great shower of dirt leapt from the ground, scattering even to the post where the slave was fastened. She turned her head aside, against the dust, and then, tears streaming down her face, turned again, to look with terror and horror upon the battle.

Again Flavion, lurching about, was stalking Cabot.

"I am Kur. You are human. I am Kur!" chanted Flavion.

Flavion's great blade again swung in a mighty arc and Cabot caught it on the double head of his own ax, and a blast of sparks burst into the air, and the head of Cabot's ax hung in its bindings, loose, against the haft of his ax. Cabot lifted the ax, again, the head dangling, and a second blow broke the haft of his ax, and tore it from his hands, and Cabot, defenseless, the head of the ax, and the parts of the ax, in the dirt, yards away, stood at bay.

Flavion then stood in the compound, grinning, and lifted his ax. "I am Kur!" he said. "You are human! I am Kur!"

At that moment there was a terrible sound, a crashing and splintering of wood, and then another such crashing and splintering, and then another, and Cabot backed away, and looked wildly behind him. The sound came from the back of the compound, opposite the gate. Then, to his amazement, he saw parts of palings thrust to the side, and there was a mighty roar, and a terrible figure stepped into the compound through the great, jagged, wrought aperture in the wall.

"I am Kur!" it cried, in a terrible voice.

"Lord Grendel!" cried Cabot.

Chapter, the Seventy-Eighth:

A Conversation Takes Place
between Two Ankle-Chained Slaves;
Some Account Is Given of Lord Grendel's
Meeting with the Kur, Flavion

"I would please him so," said the brunette slave to the Corinna of Peisistratus.

Both were chained by an ankle to the discipline post.

We have noted, briefly, the arrival of Lord Grendel at the forest camp. Four days later, Peisistratus, with several of his men, arrived, together with some of their slaves, for Gorean men are fond of slaves, and seldom wish to do without their services and pleasures. This is easily understood, as I understand it, by any human male who has, as the saying is, "partaken of collar meat." Once a fellow has, as it is said, "tasted slave," it seems he is content thereafter with nothing less. Perhaps this is one of the reasons that free women so hate slaves. It seems they should not really blame the slaves, however, for the slaves are in collars, are subject to the whip, and such. Yet, perhaps their feelings are comprehensible to some degree, as they cannot help but take note, doubtless with some irritation, of the seemingly unaccountable contentment, fulfillment, happiness, and joy of the slave, a contentment, fulfillment, happiness, and joy of the absence of which in their own lives they are too acutely aware.

"Teach me to be a slave," begged the brunette, "dear Corinna. I am a slave, and I want to be a good slave. Teach me how to please my master! I want to serve him, and I want him to care for me!"

"Beware," said Corinna, looking about. "Do not dare to speak so. Masters might hear."

"I do not understand," said the brunette slave.

"I would not speak to the master of being cared for. You are a slave. Why should you be cared for?"

"But is that not what we want, dear Corinna, that our masters might care for us, if only a little?"

"Of course," said Corinna. "It is what any slave desires, and dreams of, but do not speak to the master of such things. You might be quickly beaten and sold. What master would admit that he is fond of so low and worthless a thing as a slave? Suppose a free woman should hear of it?"

"We must fear free women?"

"Terribly," whispered Corinna.

"I have known only one free woman," said the brunette slave, "the Lady Bina."

"It is true she is free," said Corinna, "but she does not even count. She is unfamiliar with Gor. She has no real conception of the haughtiness and power of the Gorean free woman, in her pride, in her regalia, her robes and veils. We are nothing before them, only lowly, half-naked, shapely, collared beasts, who must kneel, and grovel, in terror at their sandals."

"I want to be loved," said the brunette slave.

"Oh, be silent, foolish slave," cautioned Corinna. "What if a master should hear? Do you wish to be whipped? Do you wish to be marketed? Concern yourself rather with being an abject slave, wholly submitted. It is yours to serve, and be pleasing."

"Do you not want to be loved?"

"With my whole heart, but one dares not speak of such things to the master. One is only a slave."

"I love being a slave," said the brunette.

"We all do," said Corinna. "Your name is Lita, is it not?"

"It was," said the brunette. "But the master has named me anew. I am now 'Cecily.'"

"That is an Earth-girl name, is it not?" said Corinna.

"Yes," said the brunette.

"Do you like it?"

"I hate it!"

"Perhaps that is why you are now 'Cecily,'" said Corinna.

"Doubtless," said the brunette, petulantly. "I do not like the name. It was one of my names, when I was free."

"It is not the same name," said Corinna. "It is now only a slave name, put on you as one might name a sleen, or kaiila."

"Perhaps it is not so bad, then," said the brunette, "if it is only a slave name."

"That is all it is," said Corinna, "and I think it is a rather pretty name, an excellent name for an Earth-girl slave."

"'Corinna' is an Earth-girl name," said the brunette. "Your Gorean is beautiful. Could you be from Earth?"

"No," laughed Corinna, "I am Gorean, and many of my Gorean collar sisters would look down on me for even speaking to an Earth-girl slave. The name 'Corinna' was put on me that I might see myself as no better than the lowliest of slaves. Too, I think my noble master, Peisistratus, finds the name sexually stimulating on a Gorean girl."

"I want to be sexually stimulating to my master," said the brunette.

"Oh, you are," said Corinna. "I have seen him. He must struggle to keep his hands off you!"

"He has not touched me in months," said the brunette.

"I find that hard to believe," said Corinna. "Is he readying you for a sale?"

"I trust not," said the brunette. "Teach me to better please him!"

"What are your feelings?" asked Corinna.

"I flame," wept the brunette. "I kneel appropriately, I place myself before him, as the mere slave I am, I beg! But he does not touch me! I want to scream with need."

"Have slave fires been set in your belly?" asked Corinna.

"Yes," cried the brunette, softly, piteously, "and they torment me, and torment me. Fiercely they burn, and I am left untouched!"

"Poor slave!" said Corinna.

"Dare I ask, dear Corinna," said the brunette, "if such fires have been set in your belly?"

"Of course," said Corinna. "It is something men do to us. I now have a slave belly. In it my fires burn frequently and deeply, but my master, Peisistratus, contents me."

"He loves you!" said the brunette.

"Surely not!" said Corinna. "I am a mere slave, no more than an object he uses for his pleasure!"

"He does love you," said the brunette.

"Surely your master has put you to his purposes," said Corinna.

"Muchly, long ago," said the brunette, "but not since I ran away."

"That was a very stupid and foolish thing to do, Cecily," said Corinna.

The brunette touched her collar. "I know," she said.

"And how were you punished?" asked Corinna.

"I was not punished," said the brunette.

"Not punished?"

"Yes."

"That is very strange."

"Many times I writhe in need," said the brunette.

"Perhaps that is your punishment," said Corinna.

"Tell me of pleasure and the masters!" begged the brunette.

"The masters need not be concerned with our pleasures," said Corinna, "for we are slaves. They may slake their lusts upon us, peremptorily, and as they choose, unilaterally, without the least consideration for us, no more than for a sandal in which they might press their foot, for we are slaves. To be sure, they sometimes, for their amusement, are patient with us, inducing in us feelings we may not, and cannot, resist, feelings which transform us into helpless, rejoicing, sobbing, grateful, begging toys."

"I would," said the brunette, "be touched by my master, though he had no more interest in me or no more cared for me than a carpet beneath his feet. And if he would deign to be patient with me I would love to be his dominated, helpless, yielding, begging toy."

"Oh, yes," breathed Corinna, softly.

"You, too?" said the brunette.

"Certainly," said Corinna. "Do not reproach yourself. We cannot help ourselves, nor do we wish to."

"We are in collars," said the brunette.

"Yes," said Corinna.

"And slave fires burn in our bellies."

"Yes," said Corinna, smiling, "the masters have seen to that. How much now, and how helplessly, are we theirs!"

"But might they not, sometimes, be kind to us, and grant us a caress, and more, for our own sake?"

"Surely," said Corinna, "much as one might pat a kaiila, or pet a domestic sleen."

"More than that?" asked the brunette.

"Let us speak softly," said Corinna. "Many times, doubtless more often than they care for, or would admit, masters grow quite fond of their slaves."

"Doubtless free women would object to this," said the brunette.

"It is surely another reason they hate us," said Corinna, "and with such ferocity."

"Might they not envy us?" asked the brunette slave.

"Doubtless they do, and cruelly," said Corinna, "but one would dare not even suggest such a thing, lest they would see to it that the flesh were lashed from our bones."

"The master who is fond of his slave," said the brunette, "would surely be concerned, at least to some extent, to assuage the needs of his property, to relieve the miseries of her tensions, to attend to her slave fires, which he has done so much to ignite and stoke?"

"Certainly," said Corinna, "but he may keep her in suspense, see to it that she begs prettily, and such, and sometimes, the monsters, will bring us to the brink of ecstasy, for which each particle of our hungering, raging body cries out, and then pause, that we may the better know ourselves as subdued and helpless slaves, fully at the mercy of our masters, and then, if they wish, when they wish, if we beg desperately and piteously enough, they might grant us the tiny kiss or touch which sends us weeping amongst the stars."

"My master does not touch me," wept the brunette.

"How cruel are the masters!" exclaimed Corinna.

The brunette pulled against the chain on her ankle. "If I were not chained," she said, "I would crawl to him, cover his feet with kisses, and beg for his least caress."

"Of course," said Corinna.

"But then he would not respect me," said the brunette.

"Perhaps that is what he is looking for," said Corinna.

"From an Earth girl?" asked the brunette.

"Why not?" said Corinna.

"My master does not desire me," said the brunette.

"Do not be absurd," said Corinna. "What woman can be desired, as a slave is desired?"

"I would be pleased to find myself of interest to my master, and would be grateful, and pleased, to be desired," said the brunette.

"I am sure you are desired," said Corinna.

"I want to yield, and yield," said the brunette. "I want to yield so, and as no free woman, being free, could possibly yield, and how could I yield thusly, save to one who was my master?"

"You could not," said Corinna, "nor could any woman. You must understand what it is for you to be owned, truly owned. The slave must yield with absolute fullness, and without reservation, to he who is her master. She is choiceless; she has no choice but to yield as she must, wholly, helplessly, and without reservation. No woman can yield with the fullness of the ravished slave to one who is not her master."

"Teach me to be a slave!" begged the brunette.

"You are a slave," said Corinna. "Be what you are."

"I do not know how," said the brunette.

"I am not sure you know you are a slave," said Corinna.

"I am a slave," said the brunette. "I want to be a good slave!"

"I am sure you are a good slave," said Corinna.

"My master does not desire me," she said. "He has chained me to a post!"

"Wait until tomorrow night," said Corinna.

"I do not understand," said the brunette.

"We will be returning to the habitats," said Corinna, "and will be leaving the day after tomorrow, in the morning."

"I do not understand," said the brunette.

"Tomorrow night," said Corinna, "will be the last night in the camp, at least for some time."

"I do not understand," said the brunette.

"There will be a feast tomorrow night," said Corinna. "And do you think you will not be serving at that feast?"

"As a slave serves?"

"Of course," said Corinna.

It may be recalled that some days ago Lord Grendel, well in advance of certain human allies, arrived at the forest camp.

Whereas Cabot, as a human, had shortly found himself in immoderate difficulties with the Kur, Flavion, adept with a great Kur ax, Flavion, himself, found himself at a severe disadvantage when unexpectedly confronted with Lord Grendel, who was much larger than Flavion, much stronger, was similarly armed, and was a champion, who had earned several arena rings.

Whereas it might be conjectured that Flavion would have defended himself with vigor, even in so desperate a situation, the fact was that he flung down his ax, turned about, and lurched to the gate of the compound, the gate which, as we recall, he had securely latched, and fastened, in such a way that it might not be easily opened by Cabot, should Cabot have sought to avail himself of it, attempting to exit from the compound. The same precaution to which Flavion had had recourse, to ensure Cabot some inconvenience in leaving the compound, militated against his own rapid departure. He had torn away some of the fastenings when Lord Grendel's ax, flung with considerable swiftness and accuracy, struck him in the back, rather parallel to the spine, on the left side. Lord Grendel had won one of the *agons* of the ax in one of the festival games, splitting a post, at a distance of some fifteen Kur paces, which would correspond, approximately, to some twenty human paces. Following this cast Lord Grendel dragged Flavion, who was still alive, as Kurii are robust and tenacious of life, by his lamed, left leg, through the dust back to the center of the compound, where he turned him to his back, and looked down upon him. He then, with two blows of the ax, smote away the left foot and the right foot of Flavion, and then jerked him upward, that the two bloody stumps would be placed in the dirt, where the flow of blood might be slowed, if not staunched. The dust was like red mud, the stumps partly sunk into it. "Remember the arsenal," said Lord Grendel. Lord Grendel then flung Flavion down, again, on his back, and stepped on his left forearm to hold the arm in place, and then smote away the left hand of Flavion, and then, similarly treated the right hand. "Remember the treachery contemplated at the Vale of Destruction," said Lord Grendel.

Flavion lay in the dust, flopping and screaming.

"Finish him!" cried Cabot, in horror. "For the sake of Priest-Kings, finish him!"

Lord Grendel seemed transformed into something alien and terrible. "What are Priest-Kings to me?" he asked.

Flavion was piteously begging to be slain, but Lord Grendel put aside his reddened ax, and put his large, fanged mouth close to the left ear of Flavion. Cabot's translator barely registered what was said. "Remember the Lady Bina," Lord Grendel had whispered to the fallen, shuddering Kur, and then he had straightened up, and backed away, and lifted his head to the far ceiling of the world and howled, as a primeval Kur might have howled, a cry of rage, of hatred, of victory, and satisfaction.

Cabot backed away.

Flavion managed to turn himself to his stomach and began to crawl on the bloody stumps, leaving prints and tracks of blood in the dust, toward the gate, but could approach it no more closely than some four or five yards.

As the Kur is robust and tenacious of life, it took Flavion several Ehn to die. He spoke much, though doubtless incoherently, but Cabot did not know what he said, for he had, long ago, turned off his translator.

Lord Grendel later cut off the head, and then sacked the body, and its parts, and dragged them into the forest, where he emptied them, for the feeding of birds, and small animals.

Ramar, the great sleen, investigated the remains, but did not feed.

It is probable that he recognized them as belonging to one who had once been a member of the camp, and was thus to be allowed to pass, unmolested.

Chapter, the Seventy-Ninth:

The Litany; Cecily Better Learns Her Collar,
At the Discipline Post; The Feast; Cecily Dances;
Some Account of What Later Occurred
Between a Master and His Slave

"Kneel," said Cabot, "there."

"Yes," Master," said the brunette slave, and knelt before him.

"Now," he said, "you are kneeling, before a man."

"Yes, Master."

"Is it appropriate?"

"Yes, Master."

"Why?

"Because I am a woman, Master."

"And what else?"

"A slave, Master."

"Keep your knees together," he said, "closely."

"Yes, Master," she said, and pressed her knees together, closely.

"What is your name?"

"Cecily," she said, "—if it pleases Master."

"And what name would you like?"

"Whatever name Master wishes," she said.

"You are Cecily," he said.

"I am Cecily," she said. "Thank you, Master."

"I believe," he said, "you received some training in the pleasure cylinder."

"Yes, Master," she said.

"There are many litanies of servitude," he said. "I believe you were taught one of these in the pleasure cylinder."

"Yes, Master," she said.

"We will now recite it," he said.

"Yes, Master," she whispered.

As Cabot noted, there are many such litanies, or exchanges of questions and responses, or such. On the assumption that the reader might be curious as to the litany used in this particular instance, it went as follows:

Q: What is that on your neck?
A: A collar.
Q: What sort of collar?
A: A slave collar.
Q: Why is it on you?
A: It is on me because I am a slave.
Q: What is a slave?
A: Property.
Q: And what are the duties of such a property?
A: To please her master, in all ways, to the best of her ability.
Q: Whose collar do you wear?
A: I wear your collar, Master.
Q: And what does that mean?
A: That I am your slave, Master.
Q: What, then, are your duties?
A: To please you, in all ways, to the best of my ability.
Q: Do you beg to be permitted to do this?
A: I do so beg, Master.
Q: And are you aware of the penalties for failing to be found fully pleasing, in all ways, to the best of your ability?
A: Yes, Master.
Q: And are you afraid?
A: Yes, Master.

"You did well," said Cabot. "If you had not done well, you would have been switched, and then, later, examined again, and if you did not do well then, you would be switched, again, and so on. Soon, you would do it well. You would do it perfectly."

"I was switched, more than once, in the cylinder," she said.

"Do you recall the sting of those blows, even now?" he asked.

She shuddered. "Yes, Master," she said.

"Spread your knees," he said, "kneel straight, back on your heels, head up, palms of your hands down on your thighs."

The slave began to tremble.

"Head up!" he said. "Do you wish to be put in a high collar, to keep your head up?"

"No, Master," she said, quickly.

Such collars are common with Kur pets. They are also used from time to time in slave training.

"Do you know in what position you have been placed?" he asked.

Certainly this was a rhetorical question, for she would have learned this position in the pleasure cylinder, and Cabot, himself, in the pleasure cylinder, near Lake Fear, and elsewhere, had put her in it often enough.

"The position of a Gorean pleasure slave," she said. "Am I a pleasure slave?"

"Are you?" he asked.

"I would hope to give pleasure to my master," she said.

"You," he said, "a woman of Earth, desire to give pleasure to a master?"

"Surely that is not unusual for a woman of Earth," she said. "In the history of that world millions of women have been held in bondage, and even now it is not known how many are in bondage. And in countless places, throughout that world, there are countless slaves, secret slaves, at the feet of their masters. It is not so rare, really, for there are men and women, and where there are men and women, there are masters and slaves. And untold millions of women fantasize themselves helpless in the chains of masters, fearing the whips of their owners, and millions, as well, are the slaves of their lovers, as they wish to be, though they dare not acknowledge this truth even to the unsuspecting lover. She fears being scorned for her realities and needs. She knows it is a slave he holds in his arms, but she is afraid to tell him so. How her heart cries out to kneel before him, to kiss his feet, to be bound by him, to feel the stroke of his switch, to be mastered by him, and yet she dares not speak. It then is only she who knows that about her neck, unseen, quite invisible, but as real as steel, is the collar of a slave."

"You seem to have inquired into these things," he said.

"I have long known myself a slave, Master," she said.

"As I recall," he said, "your name was once Virginia Cecily Jean Pym."

"Yes, Master," she said, "but I am now Cecily."

"That is a slave name," he said.

"I understand that, Master."

"And you are a slave."

"Yes, Master," she said.

"A slave's duties," he said, "are to serve and please her master, in all ways, to the best of her ability."

"Yes, Master," she said.

"Have you done so?"

"Master?"

"To all fours," he said, angrily, "and crawl to the post of discipline."

"What are you going to do?" she said, frightened. Then she said, quickly, "Yes, Master!" And crawled, her master on his feet beside her, to the foot of the post. She was familiar with the post. She had been fastened to it her first day in the camp; she had been fastened, standing, to it, belly facing it, during the duel of Cabot and Flavion, and during the arrival and vengeance of Lord Grendel; and she had been chained to it often enough since then, sometimes with other slaves, usually by an ankle, the left, which is the customary chaining ankle for a female slave.

When she had reached the post, he said, "Kneel, facing the post."

"Yes, Master," she said, uncertainly.

He braceleted her left wrist and passed the other bracelet through the post's lower ring and then snapped it about her right wrist. She was then before the post, kneeling, fastened to it.

"What are you going to do?" she asked.

"Whip you," he said, and then left her there, leaving to fetch an appropriate implement.

He did not return for some time.

When he did return she could see that he carried a five-stranded Gorean slave lash, with broad blades. She had seen such a thing in the pleasure cylinder. It is designed for the disciplining of female slaves. It punishes nicely, but does not mark, for that might lower the slave's sales value.

"You are of Earth," she said. "I am of Earth! You cannot be serious!"

"I have not fastened you standing at the post," he said, "your hands over your head, for I feared you might be driven against the post, and injured."

She scarcely registered what he had said. It was only later that she better understood its import.

She jerked at the bracelets, angrily. It seemed she might wish to rise, but she could not, of course, fastened as she was, have stood erect.

"Remain kneeling," he said, "or go to your belly."

"You are joking!" she insisted.

"If you wish," he said, "you may brace your hands against the post, or your shoulder, to prevent being dashed against it. Later, you may wish to go to your belly in the dirt. It is permitted."

"I am of Earth!" she cried.

"No longer," he said.

"I am sorry I ran away!" she said. "I am sorry if I spoke to you with insufficient respect! I am sorry if I did not perform obeisance when it was appropriate to do so! I am sorry that I foolishly used your name in addressing you! I am sorry if I have displeased you in any way! Forgive me! Please, forgive me!"

"Do not do this!" she said. "You cannot do it, for I am from Earth, and such things are not for me. I am from Earth and such things cannot be done to me! Do you think I am no more than a Gorean girl, some simple slave, to be put without a second thought beneath the lash? I am from Earth, from Earth!"

"Do not fear," he said, shaking out the blades of the supple tool. "You will not be beaten as a man is beaten, with the fullness of a man's strength, and such, nor with a whip such as is used on men, say, the snake. This whip is for female slaves, and has been developed over a long period of time, perhaps centuries, to attend nicely to their discipline. Similarly I will not whip you at great length, but only to the extent you deserve, so richly, and to the extent which I hope will rectify your behavior."

"Do not whip me!" she pleaded.

"A crossbar fastened between two posts is often used, to which the slave, kneeling or standing, may be fastened," he said. "In this way they will not be bruised, or torn, as they might be, against a post, or a wall, such things. An overhead ring might also be used with the same end in view. Such rings are found in many Gorean dwellings."

She then recalled that before, in the forest, when she had been put in whip position, she had been fastened, her hands over her head, rather in the open, to a thick, overhead branch. Only now was the purpose of that, in virtue of the remarks of her master, earlier and now, fully, consciously clear to her, as she might writhe and try to flee the whip, to protect her from forcible contact with a hard surface.

"You cannot whip me!" she cried. "You did not punish me before! You will not punish me now!"

"It is true," he said, "that I did not punish you before."

"Just touch my back, if you must," she said, "as you did before. That is enough! It is more than enough!"

He did not respond.

"I need not be punished," she said. "It is not necessary to punish me. Punishment is not necessary. I will mend my ways!"

Again he did not see fit to respond to the anxious declarations and protestations of the lovely, distraught, braceleted beast.

"I will strive to be pleasing!" she said.

"I trust so," he said.

"I am sorry I was displeasing!" she said.

"But you were displeasing," he said. "You are a slave. Did you expect to be displeasing, and not be punished?"

"You cannot punish me!" she said. "I am from Earth!"

"You may find this quite unpleasant," he said. "Accordingly, it is my hope that in the future you will go to great lengths to avoid incurring repetitions of this experience, at least too frequently, and will be muchly concerned to monitor and improve your behavior, that in such a way as to better serve and please your master, in all ways, to the best of your ability."

"Let me go!" she said, jerking the linkage of the bracelets against the ring.

"To be sure," he said, "it is often difficult for the slave to avoid displeasing her master, even inadvertently. And occasionally a slave slips somewhat, and becomes lax, and such things are inappropriate, and are not to be tolerated."

"Let me go! Let me go!"

"She is always subject to the whip, you see. Too, as you may not realize, the slave, as she is a slave, may be whipped at any time, for any reason, or for no reason. That helps her to understand she is a slave. Also, occasionally, she may be whipped for no other reason than to remind her that she is a slave."

"You cannot whip me," she cried. "I am from Earth!"

"From Earth," he said, "you should be clearly aware, here, as would you be on Gor, that you are only a slave."

"Surely you are not going to whip me, truly, not as a slave!"

"You are a slave," he said, "and it is as the slave you are that you will be whipped."

"Master!" she cried.

"You are *kajira*," he said.

"Please, no, Master!" she wept.

He then put the whip to her.

"Viands, Master," she said, kneeling and lifting the plate to him, her head down.

He took what pleased him, and dismissed her, and she stood, near him, for a moment, uncertain, and then another called to her, from across the great fire, about which the men sat, being served, and she, casting a forlorn glance at him, hurried to serve the other, to whom she had been summoned.

She served identically, as all the others.

There was the music of flutes, and a tabor, and one kalika, and a slave, she of one of Peisistratus' men, stamped her feet, and turned, and danced in the firelight. Bangles clashed upon her bared ankles. It is beautiful to see a slave dancing in the firelight. Or in the light of torches, or candles, in some such natural light. How beautiful are women, thought Cabot. It is a rare Gorean camp, incidentally, which does not have its slaves, for, as noted, Gorean men are fond of them, and reluctant to forgo their services and pleasures.

"Wine, Master?" inquired Corinna, kneeling before him, lifting the goblet in two hands, her head down, between her extended arms.

In the goblet, of course, was actually paga.

"Peisistratus sent you to me?" said Cabot.

"Yes, Master," she said.

"Thank him for me," said Cabot, "but I think I will have wine later."

"Yes, Master," said Corinna, smiling. "Later in the feast I will send her to you."

Cabot nodded, dismissing the beauteous Corinna. He hoped to see her dance, later.

"Paga!" called men. "Viands!" demanded others. "Bread, meat!" cried others.

It was a small feast, with no more than twenty men, and some five or six slaves, but it was a ready, merry one, with the usual raucous gusto of strong, healthy, uninhibited men. Cabot thought that many of Earth might have regarded such as barbarians, but they, Goreans, had much the same views of those of Earth. Who but barbarians would poison their foods, pollute the air they breathed and the water they drank, would live lives of unhealthy deprivation and misery, would wrap their bodies in clumsy, malformed, constricting garments, would congratulate themselves on denying themselves the natural gratifications of their species, would feel unworthy, belittled, and ashamed for having the most natural impulses and feelings of their kind, would allow free women to go about unveiled, as though they might be slaves, and would unthinkingly sacrifice themselves for foolish, preposterous, and contradictory ideologies and creeds? Too, they did not speak Gorean, an infallible sign in many Gorean minds of barbarism. Still, despite the many faults of that barbarian world there was something to be said for it. It was a source world for superb slaves. Certainly its women sold well in the Gorean markets. But that was not to be wondered at, for it is common knowledge that from barbarian shores are not unoften harvested the finest of slaves.

Lord Grendel was not at the feast, for he had returned to the habitats, doubtless on business, say, with Lords Arcesilaus and Zarendargar, or perhaps to participate further in the festivals, or, perhaps, more simply, to be near the Lady Bina.

Near the gate the great sleen, Ramar, had been given a huge haunch of roast tarsk.

Muchly about the fire were conversations, shoutings, songs, recitations, games, proposals, projections, and plans.

Some discussion concerned the respective merits of weapons, particularly the crossbow and the peasant bow. There was discussion, as well, of poets. I trust this is not surprising, that hardy men, skilled with weapons, who often lived with peril, might have such concerns. On Gor and in the world poetry is not the labored, esoteric possession of a delicate, pretentious minority, as it might prove to be in less civilized or more decadent climes, but is a matter of life, robust pride, and zestful living. In any event, in the world, and on Gor, as well, poetry, like music, and song, is familiar, public, and popular. It has not yet fled into eccentric byways. It has not yet been taken away from the people. To be sure, much of the conversation was far more prosaic, involving matters of trade, commensurabilities of currencies, tharlarion versus kaiila races, pen procedures for acclimating new girls to their collars, the best seasons and cities for the marketing of women, whether or not the slave girls of Ar were superior to those of Turia, and what not.

Cabot observed the slaves, serving, the firelight reflected from their bared skins, and glinting and flashing at times, suddenly, from their collars.

How beautiful they were, and how well they served.

And she of most interest to him moved amongst them, no more or less than any other.

Cabot mused, that she had been put with him in the container, on the Prison Moon. She had been selected with care by Priest-Kings, doubtless from many thousands, with him in mind. She would doubtless constitute for any male an almost irresistible temptation, but for him, Tarl Cabot, she had been actually picked out, chosen with all the insidious wisdom and callous astuteness of an advanced science, the science of Priest-Kings. If she was an almost irresistible temptation for any male, what must she be then to him, he for whom she, unbeknownst to herself, had been selected, readied, and prepared? Cabot wondered if in a sense she had not, unbeknownst to herself, been bred for him. Too, clearly she was a slave, to those who could remark such things, the sort of woman to be seized by the hair, thrown to a fellow's feet, stripped, and collared. And, too, of course, the matching, to be most successful, would presumably be one of designed reciprocation, not only she to him, but he to her. She was to have been, as a free woman, a challenge to his honor, the means by which, sooner or later, it must be inevitably lost, but now there was no longer a need to concern oneself with such things, for now, as a slave, she was as open to him or to any other who might own her, as any other slave.

He watched her serving, and he supposed that many of the young men she had so belittled and tormented, led on and then frustrated, for her vanity and amusement, would have enjoyed sitting with others at that feast, seeing her serve with others, as what she was, a slave.

Perhaps, too, they would have enjoyed seeing her at the post, earlier in the afternoon, being punished for having been displeasing.

After only the second stroke she had gone to her belly.

Cabot had left her there for an Ahn, and had then freed her from the post, that she might assist her collar sisters in preparing the feast.

One of the fellows started up a song, and it was taken up by the others, a song of Cos, a rowing song, from which island Ubarate derived Peisistratus and some three or four of his fellows. The song, however, was well known, certainly on Tyros and Tabor, named for its shape, and in other places. Cabot had heard it in Port Kar, but attributed there judiciously to another origin, as little love was lost between Cos and Port Kar. It must not be supposed that the crews of Peisistratus, which composed somewhere between four and five hundred men, most of whom were still in the habitats, enjoying the festival, were all Cosian. They had been recruited widely, and carefully. That is common with the slavers of the ships. The men he had brought into the forest, to abet the mission of Lord Grendel, were thus a tiny fraction of his men; but they were picked men, men muchly trusted, men often relied on.

"Paga!" called a fellow, and a slave, with her vessel, hurried to him, to serve him.

There were no free women present at this feast, of course, so the slaves need not be attired in decorous tunics, or even gowns, nor needed they serve so deferentially and unobtrusively that they might almost not be present, in order that free women not be distressed or disturbed. Too, of course, this was a remote forest camp, away from the habitats, and free Kur females, and the men were, after all, Goreans.

Accordingly the slaves served as one would expect at such a feast, naked, save for their collars.

He observed one of the slaves, she whom he had named 'Cecily', hurrying to one of the fellows, to replenish his plate.

He was pleased.

She would learn to serve masters unquestioningly, thusly.

If he had her back on Gor, in a holding, and was entertaining, and free women were present, she would, of course, rather as suggested, serve quite differently. Indeed, in a refined supper, or entertainment, female slaves, if not gowned, are usually tunicked rather demurely, the tunics often reaching to the knees. The common slave tunic, on the other hand, usually comes well above the knees, because men enjoy seeing the legs of slaves. In some houses the slaves, in serving, as indicated, might be clad in gowns, indeed, in long, lovely, flowing gowns. When kneeling unobtrusively to the side, or in the background, waiting to serve, the slaves in the long gowns will lift and arrange the gowns in such a way, gracefully, that they are about and over their knees, that in order that it will be their knees which are in direct contact with the tiles, and that the gown, thusly, not be pressed to the tiles by their weight. This protects the gown. The serving garments, whether tunics or gowns, are almost invariably white. This is supposed to make it clear to the free women present that the slaves are modest, quiet girls, bashful and retiring, of a sort a fellow would scarcely notice. It would not do to have them serve in, say, slave red. The arms of the serving slaves are almost always bare, however, as this tends to be cultural for slaves. Too, the collar must always be visible to free women, for they like to see collars on slaves. On such occasions, too, of course, if free women are present, the slave, even if she is her master's pleasure slave, will kneel with her knees modestly closed. Indeed, to look upon her there, so quiet, so decorous and demure, one would scarcely guess what she is like, stripped and chained, begging, at the foot of her master's couch. The free woman at such entertainments, too, will usually have her customs and preferences. A common custom is to scarcely notice the slave, and have her serve, in so far as possible, almost as though she did not exist. And the free woman will often prefer to have the serving slaves be women obtained from some enemy city. This assures them of the nature of such women, that they are worthy only of wearing collars and serving their betters, and, thus, in the same way, in this, they find, inversely, evidence of their own incomparable worth and innate superiority. Sometimes they will buy such a woman, to have her as a serving slave, or, as it is sometimes put, a sandal slave. Slave girls dread to be purchased by a free woman. A man is likely to punish a girl only if she has failed in some way to please him, but a free woman may whip her for no other reason than that she is a lovely slave and men might desire her. It is well known that it is much harder for a girl to please a mistress than a master. The master is, after all, a man. The sandal slave is likely to be whipped if she so much as looks at a male. On her leash she may be expected to keep her eyes modestly down, on the pavement. Too, even if a slave fails to please a master in some way she may well succeed, it must be admitted, in averting his wrath, in managing to placate him, in a variety of ways, by tearful contrition, the display of her beauty, by covering his feet with kisses, and such. But such stratagems, often so effective with males, are unlikely to prove availing with an owner of her own sex. The beauty and the thousand tender, sweet, ingratiating charms of the female slave, as timid and fearful as she may be, often so effective in dealing with masters, are likely with a mistress to earn her only angry, additional strokes of the switch.

Lastly it might be mentioned that free women, at suppers, banquets, and such, also enjoy being served by Earth-girl slaves. Many would like them, as well, it seems, as serving, or sandal, slaves, to demean and abuse, as they seem to hate them almost as much, or perhaps even more, than their Gorean collar sisters, but most Earth-girl slaves, given their reputation as terrified, but hot, trainable sluts, starved for sex on their old world, are purchased by males. In Gorean collars they soon learn what it is to be a man's slave.

Corinna was now dancing.

Rhythmic clapping accompanied her dance.

She had been granted a veil and used it superbly, even tormentingly, until it was torn away by her master, Peisistratus, who had had enough, and he dragged her from the fire, into the darkness.

Cabot hoped she would soon return to the feast, as he did not think that she had, as yet, informed another slave that he was to be served wine.

Another girl, and another girl, was summoned to dance.

Cabot summoned the brunette to him. Naturally, she knelt, instantly. But he indicated she should stand. She then, frightened, for she did not know why she had been summoned, and she had felt his whip, stood before him, stood as she had been taught in the pleasure cylinder, as a slave before a master, soft, graceful, and submissive, sweetly lissome, supple, and lithe, displaying for his appraisal a property, the lovely property which was she, her back straight, her shoulders back, her small hands at her sides, her head up, turned slightly to the left, that she not meet the master's eyes directly.

Cabot then walked behind her, and after considering the delights of her form, gave his attention more carefully to her back.

It was facing the fire, and the fire light danced upon it.

He then held her from behind, by the arms, that she would not move, and would know herself held.

His grip was stern.

He could feel her begin to tremble in his grasp.

"Master?" she said.

She had no understanding of his intent.

"Please do not whip me," she begged.

"You are not marked," he informed her, and then let her go.

With a cry of fear, she fled from him, away, to the other side of the fire, whence she turned to look at him, her eyes wide, her hand, palm out, before her mouth.

She now feared her master.

She had not been pleasing.

She had then, of course, been whipped.

She would be muchly concerned to better please him in the future.

She had now learned, you see, what it was to be under a man's whip. That simple, supple, tool is an excellent device for encouraging attention, care, and dutifulness in a girl.

That a slave is subject to the whip is commonly all that is required to obtain the marvels which are at her disposal to dispense. She will go to great lengths to see to it that it remains quietly on its peg.

Too, she soon desires to serve her master not from fear, but from emotions into which she dares not inquire, and which, surely, she dares not reveal to her master.

After she had been whipped she had lain in the dirt, at the

post, "I have been whipped," she had whispered to herself. "I am a whipped slave. He is my master. He is my master."

Too, her name, 'Cecily', had now, with the whipping, been well associated with her bondage.

It was she, Cecily, who had been whipped.

"Cecily has been whipped by her master," she then whispered to herself. "Cecily now well knows who is her master. Cecily now well knows whose slave she is."

She had learned, too, of course, that if a girl is not pleasing to her master, she may expect to be punished.

"Cecily," she had then whispered to herself, "now knows herself a slave, and she is well content."

"Cecily," she whispered to herself, "I will tell you a little secret, which, I trust, does not alarm or disconcert you. You wanted to be whipped, Cecily. You wanted him to whip you. Now you know that even if he is not yours, that you are his. There is no doubt now that you are his slave. His whip is over you. It is he who is your master."

Well had the whip, you see, taught her to whom she belonged.

And that is why, it seems, she had wanted to feel his whip, that it would confirm upon her his unique and indisputable ownership.

Yet, too, as noted, she mightily feared the whip, and would surely do much to escape the renewed kiss of the slashing leather blades. How small and soft she was, and how terribly they hurt her! She had wept, a punished slave, and had yet been reassured by the pain of his interest and attention. That he was concerned to punish her, and thereby improve her, bespoke a possible intent to keep her on his chain. She might not then, she hoped, be sold, or gambled away, perhaps this very night. She now well understood that could be done. But it seemed he cared enough for her to punish her, to see to her discipline. But how the whip hurt! If he cared to admonish her in the future, she hoped he would be content, at least for the most part, to use a stroke or two of the switch, as had the girls in the pleasure cylinder, charged with improving her Gorean. Surely the instruction of the switch's swift, stinging admonitions would be more than sufficient for her control, management, and improvement. Assiduously would she attend to its lessons and strive to correct her behavior, that she might become more pleasing to her master. In short, the slave, as most slaves, had very ambivalent feelings toward the whip, that unmistakable symbol of the mastery, that he was master and they were slave. They loved and revered it as a symbol of their treasured bondage, of the preciousness of their collars, put on them, and kept on them, by masters, but would do much to evade its stroke. Yet, too, oddly, through their whimpering and tears, they might sometimes rejoice as it might be applied to them, as it left in them no doubt that they were truly in their collars, truly the slaves of their master. Their status, their condition, their reality was then well confirmed upon them. So Cecily feared the whip, but was pleased that she was subject to it, and that it would be used upon her if she were not pleasing. She now well understood, given the events of the afternoon, that she, though an Earth girl, was the abject slave of a Gorean master. The slave fears the whip, but is thrilled to be subject to it.

She sees the simple device, always present in her milieu, suspended on its peg. She sees it with apprehension, and yet, too, with reassurance and ecstasy. She is profoundly reassured of her specialness, her worth, her importance, her identity, slave, her desirability, her womanhood. She is now, perhaps for the first time in her life, overjoyed to be a female, now acknowledging herself, openly and honestly, as a member of the suitably submitted sex, the slave sex. She finds her natural fulfilment in bondage. She is grateful to be wanted, grateful to be a property, grateful to be goods, grateful to be a slave, grateful to belong to a man, his, like a sleen or kaiila, her master, at whose feet she will kneel, whose collar she wears.

From time to time, commanded, she will kneel, and lick and kiss the whip, it held to her lips by her master, licking and kissing it as his slave, in which simple, familiar ceremony, that of kissing the whip, in lingeringly, attentively, obediently, and humbly caressing it with her soft lips and delicate tongue, she acknowledges that she is subject to its rule.

So the slave notes it, the whip, suspended quietly on its peg. She smiles. She knows the best way to keep it on its peg. She is to be diligent in her duties and strive, to the best of her ability, to please her master.

Is that not what a slave is for?

And what slave, eventually, does not wish to please her master as a slave, for the inexpressible joy of serving him as what she is, his slave.

This transcends the whip, but, to her joy, this reassuring her, she knows the whip is always there, in the background, ready should it be needed, there like the world, her world, for she is a slave.

Be strict with me, my master, thought Cecily. It is to such a man that I, a slave, wish to belong. It is such a man's collar I wish to wear. It is such a man whose chains I wish to weight my limbs. It is before such a man I desire, naked, collared, and chained, hand and foot, to kneel. It is such a man whose feet I beg to kiss.

A girl who had been writhing before her master, in the firelight, was seized by him, and pulled to the side, away from the fire.

Other fellows then looked around, drunkenly, for another dancer. There must surely be one, somewhere. "You!" cried more than one, pointing to the brunette. "No, no!" she screamed, and fled into the darkness.

Cabot rose from his place, and followed her, and found her crouched in the darkness, shuddering, against the wall of the palisade.

"The slave! The slave!" he heard, from the group about the fire. Too, he heard the flute skirl an invitation.

"They wish to see you dance, Cecily," he said, kindly.

"I cannot dance, Master!" she wept.

"It is true you are far from Oxford," he said. "But many maidens of Oxford might envy you the opportunity to dance before such men."

"I am naked, Master," she whimpered.

"So, too, are the others," he said. "Think of the many fellows you knew on Earth. They are not here, but do you not think they would like to see you dance naked before them, in a collar? You might imagine them here. Do you not think it would be a nice restitution to them, for how you treated them?"

She put down her head and moaned.

"The slave! The slave!" they heard.

"It would be nice," he said, "had you a scarlet halter, earrings, bangles and bracelets, necklaces, a belt of coins, a scarlet skirt, one of Turian drape, such things, but you do not, and so you must do without, and do the best you can."

"The slave!" they heard.

"They want to see you," said Cabot.

"The Earth slut!" they heard. "Let us see barbarian collar-meat! Let us see the shapely she-tarsk! Five tarsk-bits for the slut! Six, if she is pleasing! Put her on her back! Kneel her, give her to us!"

"You will dance," Cabot informed her.

Cecily then sprang up, and, in tears, ran to the fire, and stood before the men. "I cannot dance, Masters!" she wept.

Cabot followed her to the fire, and sat down, cross-legged, in his place.

He was pleased to see that Corinna and Peisistratus had rejoined the group. Peisistratus had not kept her long. Perhaps Corinna had only herself to blame, as her veil work had driven her master mad with instant need. Doubtless, after the feast, as he had regained his composure, she would serve him again, for perhaps one or two Ahn, or more, perhaps until the forest, in its softness, and dampness, was ready to awaken.

The tabor joined the flute, and then, suddenly, too, the kalika.

"Dance!" cried men.

And then, in tears, terrified, as she could, Cecily, a naked Earth-girl slave, danced before masters, Gorean men, men who knew what to do with women, and would have uncompromisingly what they wished from them.

It was true the Earth girl was not skilled in slave dance, but it takes years to master its subtleties.

But she was young, and beautiful, and stripped, and collared, and in the firelight.

The darkness doubtless covered many flaws, but then she was not really dancing, in any event, as dancers might think of dance.

She was naked in the firelight, and moving, in such a way she hoped might be found acceptable.

"Whip her!" called a fellow.

"Please, no, Masters!" she cried.

"She has felt it!" laughed a fellow.

"Only this afternoon," said another.

"Whip her, again," laughed a man.

"No, Masters!" wept the slave. "Please, no! I am trying to please you!"

"You are not a bad-looking piece of collar meat, you shapely slut," said a man. "Make us want you!"

"'Want me'?" she said, aghast.

"She is stupid," said a man.

"She is from Earth," said another.

"What do you think slave dance is about?" asked another.

"Show them you are worth owning!" called Cabot, laughing.

"Here, before me!" laughed a fellow. "Here! Show me your belly! Beg with it!"

"Let it jerk in need!" said a fellow.

"Surely you have experienced slave spasms!" said another.

"Rotate your belly, slowly!" called another.

"You are a slave," called Cabot. "Writhe! Let your body beg to be caressed!"

"Here!" called a fellow.

"Here!" called another.

She moved, as bidden, terrified, trying to please, about the circle.

She was then before Cabot.

She tried then to obey the others, but before her master.

Suddenly, reflexively, beyond her control, unexpectedly, her hips jerked, and she cried out with misery.

She then fled about the circle, frightened, trying to writhe before others.

There was much laughter.

"Let me dance!" cried out another girl, leaping to her feet, and Cecily fled to Cabot's side, and lay down, small, and frightened, trembling, beside him.

"Forgive me, Master," she whispered.

"You are not a dancer," said Cabot. "You gave us what we wanted, to see you in the firelight, naked, a slave, in the music. Do not mind the men. They were pleased. All were pleased."

"Was my master pleased?" she asked.

"He was pleased," said Cabot.

"I am not to be whipped?" she asked.

"No," said Cabot, "but if, in six months, you do not do better, I will put the lash to you."

"Do not whip me," she said. "Please do not whip me."

"Slaves are not free women," said Cabot. "They are subject to the whip. To be sure, much of this is in your control. The more pleasing you are, the less likely you will be whipped. If you are displeasing in some way, you must, as a slave, expect to be whipped. Too, a slave may be occasionally whipped, if only to remind her that she is a slave."

"My hips, once, when I was before you, moved suddenly, strangely, Master," she said. "I could not help it. I did not do that on purpose, as with my other movements, my deliberate, intended movements of hips and belly. It just happened. I could not control it."

"Do not concern yourself," said Cabot.

"I do not understand it," she said

"It was a simple slave spasm," said Cabot.

"May I speak, Master?"

"Certainly," he said. "As before you unwisely left the compound, months ago," he said, "I now, again, accord you a general permission to speak, but this privilege must be used with discretion."

"Yes, Master," she said. "But I must always speak as what I am, a slave."

"Certainly," said Cabot, "for you are a slave."

"And that permission may be instantly revoked, at any time, at your least discretion."

"Yes," said Cabot, "and then you would have to ask specifically for permission to speak."

"Yes, Master," she said.

"What did you wish to say?" asked Cabot.

"I feel so strange," she said. "I lie beside you, helpless. I am frightened. My whole body seems alive. If you were to touch me, I would cry out, and sob, and squirm in the dirt beside you! My belly is hot, and begs! Please touch me, Master! Give me the surcease my body pleads for! I am your slave! I knew I was your slave from the first moment I saw you, in that cruel container, in that terrible place."

"The Prison Moon," said Cabot.

"I have tried to fight my bondage," she said. "But I have failed! It is what I am, a slave, and yours! Touch me, my master! I beg it! When first I saw you I knew you were my master! Did you not, as well, know I was your slave?"

"It was no accident," said Cabot, "that we found ourselves together there."

"I do not understand," she said.

"Perhaps I will one day explain it to you," said Cabot. "But this is neither the time nor place. I will tell you, however, that our conjoint presence in that small receptacle was no accident. We were matched."

"Matched?"

"Yes, by a vast intelligence, one beyond our grasp."

"How matched?" she asked. "As lovers?"

"As beasts entrapped by the will of others, placed together for their purposes, not ours."

"Beasts?"

"Biologically paired," he said.

"As lovers, Master?"

"Of a sort," he said.

"It is a complementarity, is it not?" she asked.

"Yes," he said.

"Long ago," she said, "I read of something like this, in an Asian philosophy, a harmony, a rightness, a propriety, a balance and reciprocity, a way of the world. It was spoken of as *yin* and *yang*."

"I gather there are many such complementarities," said Cabot.

"One," she said, "is man and woman, and there is another, which I fear is the same."

"What is that?" asked Cabot.

"Master and slave," she said.

"Interesting," said Cabot.

"I know nothing of such things," she said. "But I do know I am your slave."

"That is clear," said Cabot. "My collar is locked about your pretty little neck."

"I was your slave when first I looked upon you," she said, "long before you closed that device upon me."

"Perhaps, in a sense," he said.

"And you whipped me," she said.

"That is meaningless," he said.

"It was not meaningless to me," she said.

"What is important," he said, "are the legalities, the brand, the collar, such things. It is those things which are important. They are what make you wholly and perfectly a slave. A lashing is nothing. It is merely something which may be done to a slave, a mere hazard to which a slave is subject, particularly if she fails to be pleasing in some way."

"Yes, Master," she said.

"To be sure, a slave may have an emotional reaction to many things, a lashing, a cuffing, clothing, caging, food, errands, commands, almost anything."

"I had an emotional reaction to my beating," she said.

"Oh?"

"I sensed then how much I was yours."

"You were no more or less my slave before or after the beating," he said.

"My emotions seemed different," she said.

"Such things are irrelevant to the realities involved," he said.

"Yes, Master," she said.

"It does not matter what you feel or do not feel. It does not matter whether you are beaten or not, cuffed or not, clothed or not, chained or not, kept as a house slave or a field slave, kept as a pot girl or a pleasure slave, pampered or well ruled. You can be bought and sold, and done with as might please me."

"Yes, Master."

"Any master who owns you might be expected, at one time or another, to give you a lashing."

"Any master?"

"Certainly."

"I do not want to be sold," she said.

"I am thinking of selling you," he said.

"Why?"

"You are not a bad-looking slave," he said. "I think I could get a good price for you."

"Please, no!" she wept.

"Do not fear," he said. "Many slaves have had several masters. And I assure you, you will be zealous to please any master whose collar is put about your neck and snapped shut."

"But have we not been matched?" she asked.

Cabot looked at her, suddenly, angrily.

"How then were we matched?" she asked. "If you are the master to my slave, as I knew when first I looked upon you, must I not be similarly matched, to you, as the slave to your master?"

"It is true," said Cabot, "that I find you, as would most men, of interest as a female, and a slave."

"Only that?" she said.

"I do not like being manipulated," said Cabot, "even by vast, incomprehensible intelligences."

"And so you would reject me?"

"It would be a way of mocking them, of defying their will."

"What then will be done with me?"

"I might give you away," said Cabot. "But I think I would sell you. I would be curious to see what you would bring, objectively, apart from my interest in you, amongst other women."

"You do have an interest in me!" she said.

"You are a comely piece of collar meat," said Cabot. "What man would not?"

"Am I not special to you?"

"That is what I fear," said Cabot, "and what angers me. I would that it were I, and not others, who had picked you out. I would rather I had collared you amongst the collapsing walls of a burning city, that I had bought you off a block in Ar! A thousand times better I had discovered you for myself, in an exposition cage in Venna, or as you were being marched naked down the gangplank of a corsair in Port Kar, having been taken as a prize with others on gleaming Thassa, or as you were being whip-herded, blistered and burned, neck-chained and belled, with a thousand others, on a great Tahari coffle!"

"You might never have found me," she said.

"There are doubtless thousands who would be as special to me," said Cabot.

She touched her collar. "It is true we are slaves," she whispered.

Cabot made an angry noise, a fist was clenched.

"But what difference do such things make?" she asked. "What difference does it make, really, how I came into your collar?"

"It makes a difference," he snarled.

"Could you not suppose you had found me in a hundred other places, in a hundred other situations?"

"But I did not find you so," he said.

"But I am still the same!" she wept.

"You were put in my way by intelligences you cannot even conceive of," he said.

"I rejoice," she said.

"For purposes beyond your comprehension," he snarled.

"I gather," she said, "that as a free woman I was to be a temptation to you, one which would somehow bring about your downfall. But clearly that is over. I am no longer a free woman. I am a slave, and if I remain a temptation, it is certainly one which need not frustrate you; it is one which you can command to your feet, and enjoy at your leisure."

"I did not find you myself!" he said.

"What difference does that make?" she said. "Millions of women have throughout the history of Earth, and doubtless of Gor, been picked out for others, for marriages, companionships, and such. And doubtless millions of female slaves have been picked out for others, matched to others, to the best of the purchaser's ability, a slave who sings and recites, and plays the lyre, for a fellow who loves poetry and music, a skilled dancer for a fellow who is fond of dance, a brilliant, informed, educated slave, perhaps once of the scribes, who, now collared and without caste, would be a delightful little beast to have in a scribe's house, affording her master many pleasures, those of conversation and intellectual engagement, as well as those which she, inevitably subdued, will provide at his slave ring, moaning and thrashing in his arms."

"It is different," said Cabot. "There are forces involved here which you do not understand, forces concerned even with worlds."

"What of my feelings!" she cried.

"They are unimportant," said Cabot. "They are the feelings of a slave."

"Yes, Master," she said.

"You were picked for me, and put with me, you must understand," he said, angrily, "in accordance not with my will, or yours, or ours, but in accordance with the will of others."

"What difference should it make?"

"Should it not make a difference?"

"No!" she cried.

"Perhaps it does," he said, angrily.

"Surely their schemes were foiled," said the brunette, "when we were removed from the Prison Moon. Perhaps I was once the tool of someone or something to demean or destroy you, or serve some purpose not known to me, I do not know, but I am no longer such. I am now only a female slave, though perhaps one still well matched, through no fault of her own, to your bracelets and chain. So, can you not now accept me as a gift, if nothing else, as a pretty pebble you might stoop to pick up, as a small silken animal you find at your feet, her neck on your leash?"

"I think, indeed," said Cabot, "we were well matched, I as master to your slave, you as slave to my master."

"You can do with me as you wish," she said, "for I am a slave. But if we were so well matched, I know you must find me pleasing."

"I think I will lash you," he said.

"Please do not," she said.

"I have had, and have, many slaves," said Cabot, musingly.

"Keep me then amongst them," she said. "Let me be the least of the slaves in your house. Set me the most disagreeable of tasks. I want you for myself alone, but I would rather share you with a hundred slaves more beautiful than myself, if I am beautiful, than be apart from you."

"One of my slaves, though I have not claimed her," said Cabot, "was once, until disowned, the daughter of a Ubar."

"What is a Ubar?" she asked. "A king?"

"More powerful than a king," said Cabot.

"Until disowned?"

"She shamed him, her father, the Ubar."

"How so?"

"Once, enslaved, she begged to be purchased, a slave's act, and so, once purchased and freed, she was disowned."

"I do not think I understand this," she said.

"Conceive of it," said Cabot, "first, the daughter of a Ubar a slave! Is that not shameful enough?"

"Master?"

"Consider the shame to the Ubar!" he said. "Put such daughters aside! Leave them in their collars! Let them be sold thousands of pasangs away! Their bondage must not be allowed to besmirch a noble house! Let them not be spoken of, seen, or heard of again! Leave them on their chains. Let it be as though they had never existed!"

"But many must be the daughters of Ubars who find themselves slaves," she said, "given the fortunes of war."

"Certainly," said Cabot. "The victors make them slaves, and some are even marketed."

"Doubtless they bring high prices."

"Sometimes, for the amusement of the victors, they are sold for almost nothing."

"A considerable alteration in their circumstances," she said, "from the luxury of a court to the exposure of the auction block."

"But, too," said Cabot, "she begged to be purchased."

"I could conceive of myself begging to be purchased," she said, regarding him, "if it were a certain man."

"But you are a rightful slave," he said.

"Yes, Master."

"Sometimes," said he, "slaves must beg to be purchased. Indeed, a common phrase expected of an inspected slave is, 'Buy me, Master'."

"I could conceive of a man," she said, "to whom I might address such a plea, and in a most heartfelt manner, and with earnestness and hope."

"But you are a slave, you see," he said.

"Yes, Master," she said.

"I think you cannot even conceive of how the free Gorean views the slave," he said.

"But surely girls in their collars are of interest?" she said.

"Certainly," said Cabot. "What Gorean male does not find female slaves of interest?"

His she-beast trembled at his side.

"Clearly the girl was no longer fit to be the daughter of a Ubar, and so, when freed, she was disowned. She was then sequestered, and kept from public view. But the Ubar disappeared. None know his whereabouts. The city, betrayed by many within, who sought advantage, fell to foes, and the former daughter, a conspirator as well, was brought forth by the traitors and victors and placed as a puppet on the throne."

"How is she a slave?"

"She fell afoul of a law, one of her own father's laws, that she who couches with, or readies herself to couch with, a slave, becomes the slave of the slave's master, the couching slave in this case, whom I had purchased in order to compromise and entrap the Ubara, was a famed and handsome actor. Afterwards, as had been my intent,

I freed him, but this, in accord with the law and my plan, left her my slave. The matter was duly witnessed and processed, but then I permitted her to be recovered, and returned to the throne of the city. So now she who sits upon that throne, supposedly a Ubara, is only a slave, who must with uneasiness await her reclaiming."

"It is hard to understand how her father could disown her," she said.

"She fell slave, and begged to be purchased," said Cabot. "This was an enormity, twice an unconscionable affront to her father's honor, and shamed him. Doubtless he was merciful to have her sequestered, and not slain."

"Is it such a shameful thing, to be a slave?" she asked.

"Certainly," said Cabot. "The slave is only a beast, as you are, a nothing, an object, mere goods, to be bought and sold."

"And you hope to reclaim her?"

"Why not? I own her, legally. And once she was unkind to me. And so I hope to have her naked on her knees before me, in slave bracelets."

"Doubtless she is very beautiful."

"Quite so," said Cabot. "Certainly worth a collar, as many others."

"But is she not a great and noble woman?"

"Doubtless she seems so to the world," said Cabot, "but now, under her father's own laws, she is only another slave."

"She sits upon the throne?"

"And desecrates it," said Cabot. "Can you conceive the ignominy of this? Commonly, even in low-caste households, a slave is not permitted to sit on a bench or chair, and certainly would not be permitted to recline on a supper couch. Indeed, in many domiciles, a slave is not even allowed on her master's couch, but is used at its foot."

"Yet," said the slave, "she sits upon the throne?"

"Uneasily, I trust," said Cabot, "in terror, lest her secret be discovered."

"In the garb of a free woman?"

"Did the girls in the pleasure cylinder not speak to you of such things," he asked, "when they were measuring you for a tunic, teaching you how to belt a camisk, and such?"

"Yes, Master," she said, "slaves must be distinctively garbed, that there be no mistaking them for free women."

"It can be a capital offense," said Cabot, "for a slave to present herself as a free woman, to pretend to be a free woman, to garb herself as a free woman, or such."

"Surely she must know this," said the slave, fearfully.

"Of course," said Cabot.

"And you hope to bring her to your holding?"

"Certainly," he said.

"Let me be her sandal slave," said the brunette.

"No," said Cabot. "You are clearly a man's slave."

"Yes, Master," she smiled.

"Trust that you never become the sandal slave of a free woman," said Cabot.

"I gather from Corinna," she said, "that that would be unpleasant."

"You have little to fear there," said Cabot, "as you are ignorant of the intricacies of the free woman's toilette, the arrangements of robes, their foldings, drapings, and closures, the subtleties of various veils, the choice of scents, many things."

"Yes, Master," she said.

"A not unknown punishment for a slave," said Cabot, "is to sell her to a free woman."

"I see," she said.

"The mere fear of that," said Cabot, "motivates many a slave to increase many times her efforts to please her master."

"The slave, being a slave," said the brunette, "must in any event strive to serve and please her master!"

"And?" said Cabot.

"—in all ways, to the best of her ability," said the slave.

"Yes," said Cabot.

They were then silent, for a time. Cabot seemed angry, and lost in thought, and the slave was at first reluctant to speak.

"I grieve that Master is distressed," she said, at last. "And I fear I do not, at least to my satisfaction, understand wholly the causes of his concern. The considerations which seem to motivate him do not seem to me coercive, even weighty."

"You are not a man," he said, "nor are you of my caste, the scarlet caste, nor are you Gorean."

"It seems, to me," she said, "that I am like a piece of fruit, in some lovely orchard, dangling on a branch before you, perhaps luscious fruit, certainly within reach, which you might pluck or not, as you pleased. Why then would you not reach out your hand, and seize me, and pluck me from the branch? Some men, I am sure, would enjoy having me at their feet. I knew men on Earth who would, I am sure, have reveled in my bondage, and striven to buy me."

"I did not seek you in the markets, or hunt you, or capture you," said Cabot.

"Release me into the forest," she suggested. "With a word to Ramar he will bring me back, bleeding, to your feet."

"I did not choose you," said Cabot.

"Choose me now," she said.

"—Now?" said Cabot.

"Choose me now," she said. "See if I prove satisfactory. Slave girls, surely, are often tried out by masters, to see if they are satisfactory, and, if they are not, the master may seek another. Can you not try me out?"

"—Perhaps," said Cabot.

"Are not some girls rented, or put out, on a trial basis?"

"Yes," said Cabot.

"It is now your free choice," she said, eagerly, "to choose me or not."

"Interesting," said Cabot.

"Others may have brought me to your attention," she said. "But the choice is yours. You may accept me or not, and for a given time or not. It is up to you."

"True," said Cabot.

"You may then, later, if you wish," she said, "give me away, or, better, as I understand it, sell me, to get some better sense of my value, what I might bring on the sales block."

"True," said Cabot.

"Put others, and their thoughts, or plans, or projects, from your mind," she said. "If you let such things, their fulfillment, or their defiance, the acceptance of their views, or the repudiation of their views, influence you, it is they, you see, who determined you, not you yourself. You are Master. Not they! If you find a slave of interest, keep her, if only for an Ahn, or if you do not find her of interest, it is a simple thing to rid yourself of her. She is a slave. Return her to the markets. Perhaps another might find her of interest."

"You are a clever slave, Cecily," he said. "But that is not unusual for a girl in a collar. It is a pleasure to have them under our whips."

"I do not know if I am clever or not," she said, "but I am a slave, and yours."

"True," said Cabot.

"I am a human female, at your feet," she said. "Is this not where you want us?"

"It is," said Cabot.

"And it is where we want to be," she said.

"As an abject slave?"

"Certainly," she said, "and the more abject the better, the more abject the more owned, the more helpless, the more possessed, the more as we want to be, the more as we want to know ourselves, the female of a master!"

"Interesting," said Cabot.

"We do not dream of weaklings," she said. "We dream of masters."

"What you say is true," said Cabot, "that is, that it is I who should decide, as I wish, and not be forced, or guided, in one way or another, into, or from, channels wrought by others."

"You are Master," she said. "Not they, whoever or whatever they might be."

"Men are sometimes blinded by their vanity," said Cabot. "Sometimes they fear being tricked or manipulated, of being lured into pathways and projects not their own. Sometimes they stumble over themselves. Sometimes, too often, I fear, they are their own most grievous foes."

"Sometimes, Master," she said, "what lies in plainest view, most open to all, is most concealed to some, who refuse to see it."

"I think that is true," said Cabot.

"A stranger, a bystander, a child, might see such things," she said.

"Even a slave," said Cabot.

"Yes, Master," she said, "even a slave."

"And perhaps particularly," said Cabot, "one who is keenly

motivated, one who fears to be put into the markets, who is reluctant to ascend to the height of the auction block."

"It is true," she said, "that I hope my master will keep me. I will strive zealously to please him."

"Why do you wish to be kept?" he asked. "Perhaps you fear being exhibited naked, under the torches, standing in the sawdust of the block, being bid upon, being displayed by the auctioneer?"

"Perhaps, Master," she said.

"Millions of women, in numerous cultures, on various worlds, have had this experience," said Cabot, "some of them several times."

"Yes, Master."

"The female is a familiar and popular commodity," said Cabot.

"I know enough of the history of Earth," she said, "to be well aware of the market value of my sex."

"And if you knew more of Gor," he said, "you would be even more clearly aware of it."

"My master may exhibit me, and put me up for sale," she said. "I know that. But I hope he will not do so."

"Why?" he asked.

She looked away. "Please do not make a slave speak," she said.

"You need not speak," he said.

"Thank you, Master."

"I think I should lash you," he said.

"Please, do not, Master," she said.

"I do not think men alone are plagued by such self-deceit," said Cabot.

"No, Master," she said, "I knew long I was a slave, before I was knelt before masters. Thousands of times I screamed aloud in my mind against the quiet, insistent whisper, the amused, mocking whisper, which came, again and again, from the mind beneath my mind. 'You are a slave,' it said. 'Do you not know it? Look in the mirror! Strip yourself and kneel. Do you not see a slave there, and it is you who are the slave!' Long I denied the needs of my belly. Long I fought my heart's pleas! And then, strangely, fragments and planets away from Earth, in a cylindrical world, a world made of steel, I found my lips pressed at last to the whip. It was there I was rightfully knelt."

"As you should have been, on Earth," he said.

"Yes, Master," she said.

"In a way," said Cabot, "one could see all this as a splendid joke."

"Master?"

"In attempting to manipulate me," he said, "they, whom you need not know, for you are a slave, they, in all their wisdom and cunning, may have succeeded in little other than putting in my way a pleasant little slave, one on whose neck my collar looks well, and with whom I may do as I please."

"Master?" she said, suddenly frightened.

"For that is all you are, now, in my view," he said, "a pleasant little slave."

"Surely more than that, Master!" she wept.

"To be sure, one who is nicely curved."

"Master!" she protested.

"You do have nice slave curves, Cecily," he said.

"Surely I am more to you than just any slave!" she said.

"Why?" he asked.

"Have we not been matched?"

"Certainly," he said.

"Have I not been selected, with you in mind?" she said.

"Yes," said he, "and my thanks to those who have done so."

"Surely, then," she said, "I am not just another slave to you!"

"You have been nicely selected," he said. "And that is very nice. Certainly I appreciate that. Who would not? But when all is said and done, that is all you are, just another slave to me."

"Please, no, Master!" she wept. "Please, no, no, Master!"

"Perhaps you understand better now, what it is to be a slave."

"Master!"

"Get up," he said. "The feast is not yet done. Return to your serving."

"Master!"

"Now."

"But my needs, Master!" she wept.

"Needs?" he asked.

"My needs, my slave needs!" she cried. "Please! Be kind! Have mercy! Surely you have some sense of my misery, what I feel! I am only a slave! Is it not you who put slave needs into me? Is it not you who have done this to me? Do you think I am any longer a free woman? I am not! I am a slave! I beg you! Be kind! Please be kind to me! If nothing else, touch my arm, my hip, my thigh, that I might cry out, and weep!"

"Resume your service, slave," he said. "Now."

"Yes, Master," she wept, and leapt up, and hurried to resume her duties.

"Paga!" called a fellow.

"Yes, Master!" she wept, and went to the vat, to obtain a pitcher.

It was something like an Ahn later, and more than one fellow had retired from the circle, to his blankets.

Cabot had watched the brunette in her service. Her movements now were stiff, almost wooden. Tears had coursed down her cheeks. She did not meet his eyes. He did not summon her to him.

Only seven or eight fellows, mostly half asleep, were still about the fire. Some three slaves were about, in case anything might be needed.

Corinna, who had remained at service, looked to Cabot, and he nodded.

Corinna then fetched a goblet of paga, and went to the brunette slave, and spoke to her. The brunette shook her head piteously, negatively, but Corinna was firm, and was not to be gainsaid, and pressed the goblet into her hands, and indicated Cabot.

The brunette approached Cabot, and knelt before him. She lifted the goblet toward him, holding it in both hands. Her head was down, between her extended arms.

"Wine, Master?" she said.

"It seems paga," said Cabot.

The slave looked up, and drew back the goblet a bit.

"We have no wine," she said.

"That is known to me," said Cabot.

Again she put down her head, and offered the goblet.

"Wine, Master," she said.

"You understand this, do you not?" asked Cabot.

"Yes, Master," she said.

"You offer me your wine," said Cabot.

"Yes, Master," she said. "But reject my wine, as I know you will. Do not play longer with me. I have suffered enough. I know now you despise me. You have not touched me. I know I am only an ignorant Earth-girl, who finds herself unaccountably in a man's collar. I cannot dance. I do not know the kisses. I cannot compete with the Corinnas of the camp. I am not Gorean. I am only an ignorant Earth girl."

"You might try to interest me," said Cabot.

"Please do not mock me," she said.

"Kiss the goblet," said Cabot, kindly. "Lingeringly. And regard me while you do so. Now lift your head and touch the goblet, lightly, to your collar, so that you hear the sound."

"Please do not make me do these things!" she said. "You do not know what it is doing to me, how it makes me feel!"

"You have lovely breasts," said Cabot. "Now touch the goblet lightly to each of them, first the left, then the right. Make certain you clearly feel the touch, pressing it in a bit."

"Master!" she protested.

"Now lower the goblet to your belly," he said, "and, while first looking at me, and then, secondly, down to the goblet, press the rim into your belly, firmly."

Tears coursed down her cheeks.

"You may now," he said, "offer me wine."

She then put her head down, again, between her extended arms, the goblet grasped with both hands.

"Wine, Master?" she said.

Cabot did not respond, and the slave kept her head down.

"I offer you my wine, Master," she said. "Please accept my wine, Master. Please, Master, accept my wine!"

She gasped as Cabot, gently, took the goblet from her hands. She looked up at him, lips trembling, tears in her eyes. He took a tiny sip of the drink, and then handed the goblet to a fellow next to him, who seized it gratefully, groggily, drunkenly.

"You stupid girl," called Corinna to her, laughing, from across the fire. "Hurry to his blankets!"

The slave sped into the darkness.

Cabot rose, and went to his blankets, where the slave, in the darkness, was waiting for him.

He took the slave in his arms.

"Choose me, choose me," she begged.

"Perhaps," he said.

She lifted her lips to his.

"What are you?" he asked.

"*Kajira*," she whispered. "*Kajira*, Master."

"Anything else, or other, or different?" he asked.

"No, Master," she said. *"Kajira,* only *kajira."*

"Good," he said. "That is how we want women."

"And that," she said, "is how men such as you will have us, and how we would be!"

"Speak," he said, softly.

"La kajira," she said. *"La kajira!"*

"I am a female slave," she said. "I am a female slave!"

"I am a slave girl," she said. "I am a slave girl!"

"And whose?" he asked.

"Yours, Master," she said. "Yours, Master."

Chapter, the Eightieth:

They Will Soon to the Tables

"My dear Cabot," said Lord Arcesilaus, "it is so good to see you again, here in the habitats. We have missed you. Lord Grendel returned a few days ago. And there you are, Peisistratus! I see you have several of your fellows with you. I take it you know our colleague and ally, Lord Zarendargar. I gather you, with others, and friend Zarendargar himself, and his people, will soon be leaving us, returning to your various duties and destinations. You and your ships, Peisistratus, of course, may continue to wharf upon our shores, as you wish, for purposes of shelter, supplies, repair, the temporary housing of your goods, or whatnot. Many of your men have been anxious about you, and have earnestly inquired as to your whereabouts. You passed a few days, as I understand it, in the quiet of the forests. It is perhaps just as well. I almost envy you. The festival days are now, as you know, drawing to a close, and it will be a good thing, as I see it, to return to some congenial normality, here. Certainly we will welcome some quietude, after the tumult of the festivals. Matters go well in the agricultural cylinders, and in the industrial cylinder. They were little affected, if at all, by our recent difficulties. Arrangements have been made for various transportations and relocations."

"Where is Lord Grendel?" asked Tarl Cabot.

"He will be here, shortly," said Lord Arcesilaus. "I have asked him to drop by."

This conversation, and meeting, was taking place outside the palace, on its broad porch, to which led a long flight of wide stairs, some fifty yards in width. The palace grounds themselves were within high walls, but the great gate was now opened, and humans, and Kurii, might come and go within the grounds, and gardens, as they wished.

"I would like to do something nice for Lord Grendel," said Lord Arcesilaus to Cabot. "What would you suggest?"

"He is muchly concerned with administrative duties, and such," said Cabot. "I fear there is little in which he would be interested, in the way of emoluments."

"His contributions have been richly recognized, and in detail," said Lord Arcesilaus. "Without him and his services the world would have been much different from what it is. He has been given several rings."

"He deserves much," agreed Cabot.

"But he seems little impressed with our gratitude," said Lord Arcesilaus.

"He is mindful, and grateful, I am sure," said Cabot, "but he has, for some time, been saddened, and much distressed."

"Surely it has nothing to do with the triviality of his small pet's fate, anything so unimportant?" said Lord Arcesilaus.

"She is not his pet," said Cabot, "though I can see how you might think of such things, in particular, since she was once your pet. She is, to be precise about the matter, if I may, not his pet, but a free woman."

"Very well," said Lord Arcesilaus, agreeably. "Very different then, from these others?"

"Yes," said Cabot, "but these others, to whom you refer, these human females, kneeling, tunicked, and collared, are not pets either. They are less than pets. They are slaves."

There were several such amongst the men. Two we are familiar with, one who had been named 'Corinna', who was the slave of Peisistratus, and one who had been named 'Cecily', who was the slave of Tarl Cabot. Both were tunicked rather briefly, as human males like to see the legs of their slaves.

Tarl Cabot had been offered as much as three silver tarsks for his Cecily, but he had chosen, as yet, not to sell her. He was perhaps waiting for a better offer, on Gor.

She knelt at his thigh, and occasionally pressed her cheek against it. He shoved her away.

Enamored slaves can sometimes be a nuisance.

How helpless they are, once well mastered.

It might also be mentioned that some Kur females were present, kneeling. They wore harnesses, but, too, metal collars were on their necks. It seemed that several of the suggestions and innovations of Lord Zarendargar, in the matter of handling female Kurii, had been implemented. The bondage of some Kur females was now public. No longer was it a secret, though suspected, thing, found amongst isolated Kurii. Already several had been attacked by enraged free female Kurii, which attacks, as they were slaves, they were not permitted to resist. Having the slaves publicly recognizable, of course, delighted male Kurii, for they might now look lustfully upon them, desire them, make offers for them, and so on. Soon, Cabot had heard, there would be a slave market for such established on the world, and soon thereafter, he supposed, some of these slaves, doubtless in chains, would be carried to others of the steel worlds, and then it would be but a matter of time until the useful and practical, and delicious and prized, institution of female slavery would be as familiar and popular on the steel worlds as on Gor itself.

Male Kurii had chosen to act.

No longer would they content themselves with less than the men of Gor.

"Have some Kurii departed from the world, for Gor, recently?" asked Cabot.

"Yes," said Lord Arcesilaus. "Some before your return, some afterwards. They were former adherents of Lord Agamemnon, and so it is perhaps just as well for the world, that they take their departure."

"Where is Lord Agamemnon?" asked Cabot.

"He is in the palace," said Lord Arcesilaus.

"Have no fear," said a Kur. "He has no body."

"Friend Cabot," said Zarendargar, "sometime before we part, before we diversely take ship, perhaps this evening, I would enjoy speaking with you."

"That would give me great pleasure," said Cabot.

"Perhaps we might once again share paga."

"That would give me great pleasure," said Cabot.

"Look," said a Kur. "Lord Grendel, I believe, is approaching the gate."

"Excellent," said Lord Arcesilaus. "We may all go in then, soon, to what I have had prepared, a state breakfast."

"May the slaves come?" asked one of the men of Peisistratus.

"Certainly," said Lord Arcesilaus. "They may kneel behind you, or to the side, and you may, if you wish, feed them, or throw some food to the floor for them, whatever you wish."

The throwing of food to the floor for an animal, incidentally, is not that unusual. For example, it is commonly done with sleen. Slaves, too, may be fed by hand. Usually they have their food in a dish. Often they may feed from the dish much as a free person would, though their head is usually to be lower than that of their master. For example, if the master sits upon a bench at table, his dish will be upon the table, whereas the slave's dish, as she kneels near him, is likely to be on the bench itself; similarly, if the master reclines on a supper couch, the slave, kneeling, is likely to have her dish upon the couch's step, where footwear may be placed. Sometimes the slave's food and water dish is placed on the floor, and they must partake, heads down, on all fours, without the use of their hands, rather as would a sleen, another form of domestic animal.

This is not uncommon in the training of a new girl.

It helps her to understand that she is a slave.

As the inquiry of the man of Peisistratus might have seemed to some readers somewhat anomalous, it should be mentioned that on Gor slaves are not permitted in many public buildings, rather as other animals would not be permitted in them. Accordingly, public slave rings are frequently available in piazzas, plazas, squares, forums, agorae, and such, and along public streets, for the convenience of masters, to which their slaves may be conveniently chained. One sort of building in which slaves are never permitted, and may be slain if found within, are temples. It is felt by Initiates, the alleged representatives and servants of Priest-Kings, understandably enough, that the presence of a slave in such a place would be a profanation of sacred precincts. Provisions are made for their caging or chaining outside such places, in nearby lots, removed to a decent distance.

"Lord Grendel was somewhat distressed at the disfigurement of his pet, as I understand it," said Lord Arcesilaus.

"At the gross tearings and multiple mutilations of the free woman, Bina," said Cabot.

"Yes," said Lord Arcesilaus, "that is it."

"You are from Earth, are you not?" asked a Kur.

"Yes, once," said Cabot.

"If those of Earth, or Gor, wished to bother with such things, despite their unimportance," asked the Kur, "how might they address themselves to the business?"

"What business?" asked Cabot.

"The repair of the pet," said the Kur.

"They would use knives," said Cabot, "and various metal implements, to cut tissue, relocate it, and such."

A small, weird sound came from Cabot's small translator, which was not really a word. It was not clear what it was.

Lord Arcesilaus, whose translator had, of course, assisted him in understanding Cabot's response, shuddered.

"That is disgusting," said the Kur.

"Barbarous," said another.

"I have looked upon the Lady Bina," said Cabot, with a shiver. She is beyond even such help."

"Help?" said a nearby Kur.

"Knives?" said another.

"Our science," said Lord Arcesilaus, "is not public, as is yours, and as is, to some extent, that of Goreans. We recognize the dangers of science, and how it may be misused, and so we reserve its knowledge and techniques to a carefully chosen few."

"The Priest-Kings," said Zarendargar, "as I understand it, behave similarly, at least where humans are concerned."

"That is true," said Cabot. "The Priest-Kings prohibit certain areas of science and technology to humans, certain forms of weaponry, and such, for they fear the stupidity and aggression of humans."

"Justifiably," said Zarendargar.

"Certain other areas," said Cabot, "are apparently deemed unobjectionable."

"They have not put space flight at the disposal of Gorean humans," said a Kur.

"No," said Cabot. "They have not."

"We have," said another Kur.

"I am aware of that," said Cabot.

"Even many Kurii," said Lord Arcesilaus, "are kept ignorant of our science, and what it can accomplish."

"I suppose that is a good idea," said Cabot.

"Some at hand, indeed, at your elbow," said Lord Arcesilaus, "are amongst our scientists."

"I am honored," said Cabot.

Two of the Kurii present inclined their heads, acknowledging this compliment.

"Lord Grendel," said a Kur, "is within the gate, and at the foot of the stairs."

"Good," said Lord Arcesilaus, "when he joins us we may soon to breakfast."

"I feel," said one of the Kurii to Cabot, "that you may not appreciate the nature, extent, and quality of Kur science, as it is often concealed."

"You are a scientist?" said Cabot.

"Yes," said the Kur.

"Much of it is obvious and impressive," said Cabot. "There are the steel worlds themselves, the vacuum ships, the power weapons, the translators, even such seemingly simple things as the heat knife, the customized weapon sheath, and such."

"Such things are trivial," said the scientist. "They are applications of engineering, largely matters of budget, the allocation of resources, and such. Other things are more interesting."

"Doubtless," said Cabot, uncertainly.

"Biomolecular studies, for example," said the scientist.

There is, incidentally, no exact equivalent, as far as I can determine, for the Kur expression actually used. As the studies involve levels of life, subtle architectures, hereditary coils, and such, I have chosen, with reservations, and considerable uneasiness, the term 'biomolecular'. My reservations are largely founded on what, from the Kur point of view, is a false dichotomy or division, between the living and the nonliving, between, say, the living biological and the nonliving molecular. Kurii certainly recognize a distinction between, say, a rock and a sleen, but our science tends to think less of life and nonlife, as of levels, or strata, of energy, of activity, or, as we think of it, life. In this sense, even the stone, properly understood, is a mysterious thing, in its way alive, vibrant with invisible latencies, churning, twisting, in its depths.

"Consider the wombs," said the scientist. "You are familiar with them?"

"Yes," said Cabot.

"Welcome, Lord Grendel!" said Lord Arcesilaus.

And he was muchly welcomed by those on the dais.

"Am I late?" inquired Lord Grendel.

"Not at all," said Lord Arcesilaus.

"Let us repair to the great hall," said a Kur.

"A state breakfast has been prepared," said another.

Lord Grendel, with others, including Cabot, turned then toward the large doors, of heavy timber, better than a foot thick, perhaps brought from the northern forests of Gor, adorned with mighty brass studs, doubtless from the industrial cylinder.

"But a moment, Lords and others," said Lord Arcesilaus. "But a moment." He then raised his hand, lifting it toward the outer gate, well beyond the foot of the long, wide stairs leading upward to the dais.

Down at the gate a Kur, who had perhaps been waiting for this signal, turned aside, disappeared for a moment beyond the wall, and then, in another moment, reappeared, together with another Kur, and another figure, one much smaller.

These three figures then began to approach the foot of the stairs, the small figure first, and then a Kur on each side, and slightly behind it.

"No!" cried Lord Grendel.

"What is it?" asked a Kur.

"See," said another, pointing.

"It is a human," said another Kur, shading his eyes.

"A small human," said another.

"Do not do this, I pray, Lord Arcesilaus," said Lord Grendel.

"What is his concern?" inquired a Kur, puzzled.

"Ah!" said Corinna, frightened.

Cecily gasped, in misery.

Both remained on their knees.

The small figure was now, flanked by the two Kurii, ascending the stairs, slowly.

"It is a human female, is it not?" asked a Kur.

"Are you certain?" asked another.

"It is surely dissimilar from these," said another Kur, indicating several of the kneeling slaves.

The Gorean slave tunic not only leaves little doubt about the sex of its occupant, but it proclaims it blatantly.

A free woman may be guarded with respect to her body. She may even be embarrassed by it, or ashamed of it. She may fear to show it. Certainly she may conceal it. How frightful if she were to be thought of in terms of it, her body, that embarrassing, troubling thing so appropriately concealed, rather than, say, in terms of her mind and personhood, or, perhaps, her clear, fine features, if her veil were to become disarranged, inadvertently. But beneath those robes and veils her body is there, embarrassing and troubling or not, in all its loveliness, as though waiting for its exposure or disrobing. And surely she knows it is she, ready to flame alive in its exposure, as much as any other aspect of her, her mind, her features, her emotions, the needs of her belly, all such things which constitute the wholeness of her. Does she, enclosed in those ornate blockades, wonder from time to time what it might be to feel a man's hands upon those stiff enwrapments, and wonder what it might be to feel them ripped from her, abruptly, imperiously, and feel the sudden flash of air upon lovely, startled skin?

Does she wonder what it would be to be a whole female, loving her sex, and rejoicing in it?

In any event the bodies of slaves are commonly well, if not entirely, exposed. They are, after all, are they not, the bodies of animals?

The garmenture of the slave is, in effect, another of her freedoms, though she may well regard it with some trepidation, realizing how well, how boldly and excitingly, it reveals her to men, and her vulnerability. The garmenture makes it clear what she is, property. A common justification of slave garmenture, though surely not the only one, nor the primary one, is that it is supposed to make the slave the desiderated object of raiders, thus supposedly diverting attention from precious, priceless free women. Some slaves have been stolen several times, from one city, or caravan, or another. Many are the cages whose bars they have grasped, many are the chains they have felt on their necks, many are the blocks from which they have been auctioned.

In any event, in slave garmenture, the slave, and others, are never in any doubt that she is a female, and that she has that remarkable gift of nature to males, the female body.

The slave, commonly, unlike the enrobed free woman, is happy, and pleased, to be a female. If she were a man, such a coarse and brutal beast, she could not be the marvelous thing she is, vulnerable, perhaps, but desired, and marvelous.

How could the slave not be frightened of her body, and yet thrilled with it? It is soft, beautiful, yielding, and alive. It is obviously a source of great pleasure to masters, who command it and put it to their purposes, as they will, and if the masters consent, and are kind, it is a source of untold rapture to herself, as well.

It is little wonder that the slave loves her body, and her tunic.

"It is a human female, a woman," said Cabot, observing the approach of the small figure up the stairs, flanked by the two Kurii.

"She is so hidden," said a Kur. It might be recalled that Kur females, free and slave, wear usually only some harnessing. To be sure, there are great differences amongst the harnessings, most of which would be lost on our friend, Cabot, with respect to quality, arrangement, ornamentation, and such. The Kur female who is an open slave commonly wears a collar, her master's collar. Commonly she would be denied harnessing only in the privacy of her master's dwelling, while being exhibited for sale, while serving certain feasts, and such. If she is not harnessed she is, in effect, naked. Cabot, and some humans, it might be noted, do not seem fully aware of the momentous distinctions involved in such matters.

"She is clad in the robes of concealment, and veiled," said Cabot. "Such things are common on Gor with free women, particularly with those of high caste, particularly in the high cities."

The high cities, as it is explained to me, are usually larger cities, with many towers, and bridges amongst the towers. Many regard them as citadels of civilization. Ar, as I understand it, would be such a city.

The small figure approached, climbing the stairs.

"Send her away!" cried Lord Grendel. "Do not do this to her! She has suffered enough! If you care for me, spare her this humiliation!"

"What is his concern?" asked a Kur.

"The ears and nose, the cheeks, the eye, shattered bones, the crookedness of the body," said Cabot.

"It is only a pet," said a Kur.

"If you care for me, Lord Arcesilaus," said Lord Grendel, "have pity, not only upon her but upon me, as well! Spare her this! Spare us all this horror!"

"It is only a pet," said the Kur, again.

"Be patient, Lord Grendel," said Lord Arcesilaus.

The small figure then, flanked by her two attendants, was upon the dais. She stood before the group. She was resplendent in the multicolored robes, so carefully assorted and arranged, of concealment. As noted, she was veiled, as well. The veiling was heavy, and opaque. Clearly a street veil was worn. Beneath it, Cabot conjectured, might be a house veil. Too, her head was almost entirely concealed within an ample hood, this well matched to the colorful robes.

"Stay, Lord Grendel!" pleaded Lord Arcesilaus.

Lord Grendel had turned away, and a moan escaped him.

Cabot's heart was torn for his friend, and he, too, turned aside, that he might tender him some minim of comfort, however inadequate it must be.

"Oh!" cried Corinna, softly.

"Ahh!" breathed Cecily.

"Ai, well!" cried several of the men. The Kurii were largely silent, having little or no reaction. Cabot then heard the striking of hands on the left shoulder, surely from the human males present.

Cabot steeled himself, and turned about.

The small figure had lifted back her hood and lowered her veils, of which there were indeed two, a street veil, and a house veil. They now hung about her neck. She shook loose long blond hair, and looked upon the group.

She smiled.

"Lord Grendel!" cried Cabot. "Lord Grendel!"

"Your barbarous knives," said the scientist to Cabot, "could not accomplish that. It is done with the hereditary coils, with their innate equations. One stimulates the hereditary coils, and the restoration is accomplished from within. Too, in this fashion, one does not risk changes which might be brought about by knife work, whether clumsy or not. If you wish changes, of course, that can be arranged, by the insertion of fresh elements into the hereditary coils, but we supposed it appropriate, and sufficient, in this case, to let things develop naturally. Who are we to guess what humans would or would not regard as an improvement? So we contented ourselves with a simple restoration. It was not difficult. Growth is stimulated. It is rather, again, then, as though childhood became adolescence, and adolescence became youth. We would have preferred a long, glossy pelting but then she is a human female, and we felt that it would have been improper for us, in her case, to simulate the beauty of a Kur female. Too, it would have required a great many adjustments. It is done, as I mentioned, by means of the hereditary coils."

"Lord Grendel!" said Cabot. "Lord Grendel, turn about, and see! Look, Lord Grendel, look!"

Lord Grendel slowly, trembling, turned about.

"You are in the presence of a free woman!" said Cabot to Cecily, and Cecily quickly put her head down, to the dais. At a sign from Peisistratus, Corinna did so, as well, and the other slaves, even the Kur female slaves, did so, as well.

The Lady Bina smiled, again.

"How beautiful she is!" said a fellow.

The Lady Bina stood before the group, her veil descended, her hood put back, and was again as once she had been, incredibly fair, and marvelously beautiful.

She was, again, then, as she had been in the container, in the collar of Lord Arcesilaus, when she was his pet, as she had been elsewhere, in the game world, in the camps, as she had been in many places, before her encounter with the lumbering, bestial cattle humans.

"We hoped you would be pleased," said Lord Arcesilaus.

A sob escaped Lord Grendel.

"You are pleased, are you not?" asked Lord Arcesilaus, concerned.

"Yes," said Lord Grendel.

"You are looking well, Lady," said Tarl Cabot.

"I trust you, too, are well," she said.

The Lady Bina then said to the slaves, "You may lift your heads, girls."

"Thank you, Mistress," said Corinna, and the other slaves.

The Lady Bina then looked directly upon Cecily.

"Thank you, Mistress," said Cecily.

"What is your name?" asked the Lady Bina.

"'Cecily', Mistress," said Cecily, "—if it pleases Mistress."

As the Lady Bina was not the owner of the brunette slave, she would not, of course, be authorized to name her. The slave's response, however, was not an unaccustomed one to such an inquiry, and, in its way, acknowledged that she was such as might be named as masters, or mistresses, might please.

"You are pretty, Cecily," said the Lady Bina.

"Thank you, Mistress," said Cecily.

"Very pretty, Cecily," she said.

"Thank you, Mistress," said Cecily.

"I seem to remember you from a container," said the Lady Bina, as though with some difficulty attempting to recall the matter, "when you naively, in your presumptuous and foolish vanity, dared to consider yourself a free woman."

"Yes, Mistress."

"That was foolish, was it not?"

"Yes, Mistress."

"You have a pretty collar, slave girl," said the Lady Bina.

"Thank you, Mistress," said Cecily.

To be sure, her collar was no different, essentially, from that worn by thousands of other slaves.

Yet there is no doubt that such collars are extremely attractive on a female.

It is said that no woman knows how beautiful she is until she has seen herself in a collar.

And it is said, as well, that no man knows how desirable a woman is until he has seen her in a collar.

What man, seeing a beautiful woman, does not imagine her in a collar, and want her?

It is, accordingly, not surprising that Gorean masters keep their girls in collars.

To be sure, Merchant Law, in any case, prescribes the collar, the brand, distinctive garmenture, and such.

In no case is the female slave, goods, an animal, to be confused with her incomparably exalted superior, the free woman.

The Lady Bina, the free woman, then looked away from the slave, disdainfully, and looked at Cabot. She then arranged her robes a little differently about her throat, drawing them down, a little. In this way it was made clear, however briefly, however inadvertently, that her throat bore no close-fitting metallic encirclement. Then, as though scarcely noticing what she was doing, she rearranged the robes, in such a way, modestly, that her throat was again concealed. Gorean free women commonly conceal their throat, which, of course, is easily done with the robes of concealment, the veils, and such. If a woman's throat is bared, how does she know that a fellow, say, that one, sitting across from her, in a public cart, or such, is not idly fancying what it might look like in a collar. Indeed, it is natural for a Gorean male, seeing the bared throat of a woman, to think "collar." The throats of slaves, of course, are commonly bared, save, of course, for the collar. As they are slaves, they are expected to display the collar, obviously, and publicly, such a lovely badge of servitude.

Indeed, as earlier noted, this display, as certain others, is prescribed by Merchant Law, which is a general, intermunicipal body of law regularly promulgated by the Merchant caste at the great fairs, and tending to be shared by disunited, often hostile, Gorean communities. Even were it not for such law, of course, practical considerations would dictate some obvious ways of marking the distinction between the female slave and the free woman. One might think in terms of a slave bracelet or a slave anklet, or such, but the collar is almost universally preferred, possibly because of the prominence of its mounting, its unmistakable visibility, its way of clarifying the nature of its wearer, as a collared animal, and its beauty.

"Lord Grendel," said the Lady Bina, acknowledging his presence.

"Lady Bina," he said.

He extended his hand, to touch her, but she recoiled, moving back.

"Do not touch me!" she said.

"Forgive me, Lady," he said.

She drew her robes more closely about her.

"Lord Arcesilaus," she said. "It is my understanding that you have had prepared a state breakfast."

"Yes," he said.

"Shall we then to the tables?" she asked.

"There is no place prepared for you," said Lord Arcesilaus. He, naturally enough, still muchly thought of her as a pet, and so no place would have been prepared for her, no more than for the slaves.

"She shall have my place," said Lord Grendel. "I will stand behind her chair."

There were cries of anger and dismay, both from Kurii and men on the dais.

"It is my wish," said Lord Grendel, and none would gainsay him.

"I think this is a world of Kurii," said the Lady Bina, "not of humans. I have heard of Gor. I think I will see what it is like. I think it would be interesting to live on the surface of a world, rather than within a world."

"Lady?" said Cabot.

"I shall wish," said the Lady Bina, "to be given transportation to Gor. Others, as I understand it, are being indulged in this particular."

"Gor is dangerous, Lady!" said Cabot. "You are attractive, and you have no city, no village, no Home Stone. You might end up in the markets."

"In the markets?" she said.

"Being sold," he said.

"I," she laughed, "being sold! Absurd! I am a free woman!"

"I assure you," said Cabot. "There is danger."

"I am a free woman," she insisted.

"So, too, once, were most slaves," said Cabot.

"Then they were not true free women," said the Lady Bina. "They were only uncollared slaves." She then looked at Cecily, who feared to meet her gaze. "Is that not true?" she asked.

"I do not know," whispered the slave.

"But it is true of you, is it not?" asked the Lady Bina. "You were merely an uncollared slave."

"Yes, Mistress," said Cecily. "It was true of me. I was only an uncollared slave."

"And the collar belongs on you, does it not?" asked the Lady Bina.

"Yes, Mistress," said Cecily. "The collar belongs on me!"

"Are you insolent?" asked the Lady Bina.

"No, Mistress," said Cecily, quickly. "Forgive me, Mistress!"

"Slave," sneered the Lady Bina.

"Yes, Mistress," said Cecily. "I am a slave, and should be a slave."

"Quite true, slave girl," said the Lady Bina. Then she looked at Cabot. "I will need funds," she said.

"If you are determined," said Cabot, "I will provide some rubies, and I would suppose that Lord Grendel might contribute something, as well."

"Surely," said Lord Grendel.

"You will accompany me," she said to Cabot. "I will need guidance, and protection."

"Not I," said Cabot.

"I will reward you richly," she said, "for I intend to become a Ubara."

"Do not be absurd," said Cabot.

"My beauty," she said, "will win me influence, and soon a throne."

"Do not be foolish," said Cabot. "There are thousands of women on Gor as beautiful as you, if not more so, and a great many of them are in cages, on shelf chains, and in coffles."

"Am I to understand that, despite their beauty, they are for sale?"

"It is largely because of their beauty," said Cabot, "that they are for sale."

"They are slaves?"

"Of course," said Cabot. "They are slaves."

"Then," she said, "it is appropriate for them, as they are slaves, that they be for sale."

"Certainly," said Cabot.

"Slaves?" she said.

"Yes," said Cabot.

"Men have made them so?"

"Of course."

"I am a free woman," she said.

"Yes," said Cabot.

Cabot thought it a shame that the Lady Bina was a free woman. Was there not there a waste of slave? Cabot thought that at a man's feet, naked and collared, under his switch, she might be much improved. Certainly she was beautiful, even slave beautiful. Many free women are slave beautiful, of course, but they have not yet been brought to the feet of men, and put in their collars.

Only then, mere slaves, reduced and exalted, in love and fulfillment, might they become truly beautiful.

Many a free woman, naked before her sandal slave, might inquire, "What do you think? Am I not beautiful enough to be a slave? Would I not sell well?" And to this the sandal slave, kneeling before her mistress, might well respond, and truthfully, "Yes, Mistress." The sandal slave might then be lashed, and informed that the beauty of a free woman is far superior to that of a slave, any slave, to which she had best reply, "Yes, Mistress," one of the few lies which a slave might safely utter. After all, what could a collar do for her mistress, really, other than enhance her beauty, and make her a thousand times more desirable to men? The sandal slave might think, "Be sold, great lady. I would bring more on the block than you!"

"I wish you to accompany me," she said.

"I will ship with you," said he, "to the surface of Gor, then we part."

"I will accompany you, Lady," said Lord Grendel, quietly.

"No!" cried Lord Arcesilaus, and several others, amongst the Kurii. "Remain with us," said a Kur. "Here you stand high in the rings," said another. "Here you are champion, and hero!" said another. "Stay with us!" begged another.

"On Gor," said Cabot, "you will be seen as no more than a beast!"

"What am I other than that here?" said Lord Grendel. He lifted his hand, which bore only five digits, not six. Some of the Kurii looked away. "And my voice," said Lord Grendel, "is different. It is not fully Kur."

"You have rendered great services to the world," said Lord Arcesilaus. "We will cheerfully overlook such deformities."

"Keep the slut here, and chain her to a ring," said Cabot.

"No," said Lord Grendel.

"Go to Gor, yes," said a Kur, "but later, and only in war, to win her, and claim her, for the folk!"

"Stay with us, and help us to conquer Gor," said another.

"No," said Lord Grendel.

"Perhaps he should go," said one of the Kurii.

"Perhaps there is, truly, no place for him here," mused another.

"It is true, he is a monster," said one of the Kurii. "There is no gainsaying that."

"But we salute him," said another.

"Yes," said another.

"He must be permitted to go, if he wishes," said Lord Arcesilaus. "I, for one, will cruelly regret his departure, but I would not oblige him to remain, nor attempt to influence him to do so, against his will."

"You may accompany me then," said the Lady Bina. "I may have need of you, if what friend Cabot suggests is true, that some peril might obtain. You may be my protector, rather like a sleen, my beast, my pet."

"Collar her," said Cabot.

"She is a free woman," said Lord Grendel.

"I may need a serving slave," said the Lady Bina. She then looked upon Cecily. "That is a pretty slave," she said. "What do you want for her?"

"She is not for sale," said Cabot, "not now."

"Later?"

"Perhaps," said Cabot.

Cecily looked at her master, in fear. She was property, of course, and could be disposed of, as the master might please.

"I think you want her," said the Lady Bina, "—perhaps for slave use."

"Of course," said Cabot. "Why do you think men make slaves, buy them, and such?"

"That they may have slave use from them?"

"Of course."

"Doubtless you make her grovel and squirm," said the Lady Bina.

"Certainly," said Cabot.

"She seems quite modest, and quite demure now," said the Lady Bina.

"Now," agreed Cabot.

"Doubtless she is different, in your arms, or under your whip."

"Of course," said Cabot.

"She is a pleasure slave," said the Lady Bina.

"Yes," said Cabot.

"Why is she kneeling, then, with her knees together?"

"She is in the presence of a free woman," said Cabot.

The Lady Bina then looked at Cecily. "Show what you are, slut," she said.

"Before a free woman, Mistress?" said Cecily, frightened.

"I like the word 'Mistress' on your dirty little slave lips," said the Lady Bina. "It belongs there."

"Yes, Mistress," said Cecily.

"Now!" said the Lady Bina.

Cecily spread her knees.

The Lady Bina then laughed, merrily.

"Grendel," said the Lady Bina.

"Lady?" said he.

"I do not too much care for this hood, and all these veils," she said. "I think it better if my hair were seen, attractively flowing, and if my face were visible, that my beauty might be the better noted."

"Lady?" said he.

"And some adornment would be appropriate, for my head and hair," she said.

Lord Grendel was silent.

"I will need my tiara, again," she said. "You can find it, can you not?"

"Yes, Lady," he said.

"Well then," said the Lady Bina, to Lord Arcesilaus, "shall we now to the tables?"

"Yes," said he.

Chapter, the Eighty-First:

Departure

In the narrow, steel corridor, Cabot knelt Cecily, and snapped the short chain about her neck, which would fasten her to the bulkhead. Cecily's eyes were wide, and we fear she was uneasy, but Corinna was similarly secured, near her, and so, too, were several others; all were girls who had been in the pleasure cylinder. This form of custody was not unfamiliar to them.

Each had been accorded, prior to boarding, when they had been stripped, a brief, gray, shipping tunic, which had a number clearly inscribed in Gorean on the upper left side. Cecily's number was 27, and Corinna's was 28. These numbers were correlated with identical numbers at the bulkhead's chaining rings, number 1 with ring 1, and so on. In this manner ship's records might be kept in order. Also, if a girl were to be removed from a ring, say, for pleasure, it would be clear to what ring she was to be returned.

Cabot jerked Cecily's chain against the collar ring, twice, this ring attached to the bulkhead's holding collar, which was rather heavy, which was closed over her slave collar.

In such a way the slave is reminded she is chained, not that they truly need any such reminder. With their small hands they can, if they wish, pull at the chain quite well themselves, and pull it against the ring to which it is fastened, and so on.

"Master?" she said.

"We will be leaving soon," said Cabot, and left her.

The chain was some three feet in length, as were the others.

Peisistratus, as Cabot, and his slave, had never been, at least consciously, in such an environment, had led them about, the preceding day, introducing them to at least some of the ship's several divisions and systems.

764

They had visited, for example, the bridge, galley, pantries, mess, crew's quarters, officers' cabins, engine room, weapon cubicles and turrets, the diverse holds, and such.

Cabot noted that the ship carried propellant, which consumed much space, and functioned on a principle of reaction. In short, the propulsion system of the ship was relatively primitive, at least when measured against what he understood to be the capabilities of the ships of Priest-Kings. For example, if the ship were to lift away from a planetary surface, even one such as Gor, a great expenditure of propellant would be required. This expenditure need not take place, of course, in leaving the steel world. Cabot suspected that certain ships, larger ships, might remain in orbit, while communication to and from a planetary surface might take place by means of shuttle craft. On the ship of Peisistratus, however, which Cabot supposed might be typical, there were no shuttle craft. There were, however, some escape pods. The ships of the Priest-Kings, as Cabot understood, did not carry internal fuel, but drew on the forces of gravity for their propulsion. In this way there was no difficulty in leaving a planet's surface, nor need they face dangers such as the exhaustion of the ship's source of power, the risk of its volatility, and so on. Whereas the force of gravity as normally encountered is, so to speak, a very weak force, widely distributed, obviously it is, in its extent, a titanic force capable of holding moons to a planet, planets to a primary, stars in a galaxy, and so on. The Priest-Kings, Cabot speculated, had discovered a way to gather together or focus this universally distributed force, multiply its effects exponentially, and utilize it for their purposes. Indeed, it was speculated that Priest-Kings could use a planet as what, in effect, it was, a space ship, and shift it, if one wished, from one primary to another, a competence possibly of great value, should alterations or disturbances take place in its local primary.

In one of the holds Cecily was fascinated by closely arranged racks of transparent cylinders, outfitted with various forms of tubing. There were a hundred or more of these cylinders, or containers. Each was now empty.

"What are these?" she asked.

"Slave capsules," she was informed.

"Earth-girl slaves," said Peisistratus, "are normally sedated on Earth, brought to collection points, stored in such capsules for the journey to Gor, disembarked unconscious on Gor, and then brought unconscious to the pens. Thus, in a typical case, a girl might retire as usual, in the comfort of her sheets, with no thoughts save for her quotidian existence of the morrow, totally unaware of her selection, and then, later, to her astonishment, awaken in the pens. To be sure, there is a great deal of variation in these matters. Sometimes, for example, if a girl has been somewhat annoying, she might be surprised in her bed, gagged, stripped, bound hand and foot, and then left there for a few hours, to ponder matters, after which she will be sedated, and things will continue in a more routine matter. Sometimes girls are not taken directly to the pens but, particularly when the patrols of Priest-Kings are unusually zealous, are disembarked in the wilderness, and, while unconscious, coffled. Thus they awaken in the grass, naked, on a slave chain, thence to be marched to some predetermined house or rendezvous. In this way they appear no different, to satellite surveillance, than other such coffles, being taken between cities, and such."

"You, however," said Cabot to his Cecily, "would have been selected by Priest-Kings and brought in one of their ships to the Prison Moon."

"Might I," Cecily asked Peisistratus, "have been found of interest by you, or your colleagues?"

"Certainly," said Peisistratus.

"How are your acquisitions selected?" she asked.

"There are usually a number of parameters involved," said Peisistratus. "Obviously feminine desirability is important, for they are to be sold. One looks, then, for unusual beauty, high intelligence, helpless sexual needfulness, and such."

"It might be understood, however," said Cabot, "that one is looking, most essentially, for women who will make superb slaves, women who have slave dispositions, who desire to be slaves, who want to be slaves, who need to be slaves, who will not be happy until they are collared, and such."

"They need not, of course, be fully aware of this on Earth," said Peisistratus. "It will, presumably, however, be clear enough to them in their dreams, dreams which may frighten them, or in their fantasies, which they will perhaps fear and keep as their most closely guarded secret."

"Some of these women are scouted carefully, as I understand it," said Cabot.

"True," said Peisistratus. "Our agents often scout them for days, weeks, even months, observing their characteristics and dispositions, considering what they might look like in tunics and shackles, such things, and careful lists are kept."

"You have some sense of their latencies?" asked Cecily.

"Certainly," said Peisistratus, "we are skilled in the evaluation of slave stock, such as yourself. One can, certainly after a time, sense their needs, and the fires which burn within them, scarcely concealed by their idiotic garments."

"You have lists?" said Cecily.

"Yes," said Peisistratus, "there are possibility lists, which are, in effect, inspection or assessment lists, and then, if the female is deemed suitable, she is put on an acquisition list. Once on an acquisition list it may still be weeks or months before she is acquired. It is amusing in its way, how they go so naively, so unsuspectingly, about the boring, meaningless trivialities of their daily lives. They do not know that they are already Gorean slaves. They lack only the brands and collars."

"One thing which might be mentioned," said Cabot, "though you have doubtless noted it in most of your sister slaves, is that almost all of them have the bodies of the natural human female, in height, size, shape, and such."

"With the exciting slave curves of the natural woman," said Peisistratus.

"The Gorean male," said Cabot, "tends to find such women pleasing. They are the sort he wants in his collar, at his feet."

"They sell well," said Peisistratus.

"Cargo the ships," had called Peisistratus. His men had then carried various supplies aboard. Shortly thereafter, to the crack of a whip, the slaves had been herded aboard, to be put by one of the corridor bulkheads, to be chained in place before departure.

Another object had been loaded as well, a large cage, in which a mighty beast, snarling, wary, impatient, twisting and turning, paced angrily back and forth.

"Are you sure you wish to make this journey, Lord Grendel?" Cabot asked.

"Do not call me Lord Grendel any longer, dear friend," said

Lord Grendel. "Call me by the name of 'Grendel' alone, for that is the name of a monster, and I go where I shall not be "lord," but, at best, a deformity, a beast."

"Remain in the world," said Cabot. "Here you have prestige, and power."

"I must accompany the Lady Bina," he said. "She may need me."

"She is a pretentious, treacherous, worthless ingrate," said Cabot.

"She is very beautiful," said Grendel.

"She does not care for you," said Cabot. "She does not even respect you, despite all that you have risked and suffered for her. She loathes you. She despises you."

"Justifiably," said Grendel, "for I am a monstrosity."

"Strip and collar her, and put her on a chain, here, on the world," said Cabot. "Put her in a high collar, if you like, and keep her as a pet."

"No," said Grendel. "She is a free woman."

"Where will you be disembarked?" asked Cabot.

"If all goes well," said Grendel, "in the vicinity of Ar, perhaps Venna."

"Why is that?" asked Cabot.

"The Lady Bina has made inquiries," he said. "She seems to feel that her ambitions might have their best play, the greatest scope for their activity, amongst the highest of the high cities."

"Venna is not a high city," said Cabot.

"Ar, then," said Grendel.

"You had best encourage her to veil herself, and well," said Cabot.

"The Lady Bina is a free woman," said Grendel. "She does as she pleases."

"Perhaps she hopes to catch the eye of a Ubar," said Cabot.

"Perhaps," said Grendel.

"There is no Ubar in Ar," said Cabot.

"Then perhaps that of a high general, or wealthy merchant," said Grendel, "until a Ubar may be found."

"She has no Home Stone," said Cabot. "If she catches anyone's eye, she is likely to be seized and put naked in a pleasure garden."

"Thank you for the rubies which you have given us," said Grendel.

"It is nothing," said Cabot.

"Where will you be housed?" asked Cabot.

"With the crew," said Grendel.

"I, too," said Cabot. "And the Lady Bina will perhaps be chained in the corridor with the slaves?"

"The Lady Bina," said Grendel, "will be cabined in the private quarters of Peisistratus, who will then share quarters with his officers. She is a free woman, and should be accorded privacy and luxury, at least such that the ship may afford. Peisistratus is amenable to this, as a personal favor to me."

"It is my understanding," said Cabot, "that the ship, if it eludes the blockade of Priest-Kings, will make more than one landfall on Gor."

"It will elude the blockade," said Grendel.

"How do you know that?" asked Cabot.

"I have spoken to Lord Zarendargar," said Grendel, "four days ago, on the evening before he and his ships left. It has been arranged."

"How can that be?"

"There are intermediaries betwixt the Sardar and the worlds," said Grendel.

"Initiates?" asked Cabot, skeptically.

"Certainly not," said Grendel. "They have nothing, truly, to do with Priest-Kings. They merely inhale fumes, starve themselves, interpret dreams, and such, and think the Priest-Kings communicate with them."

"Many ships come and go on Gor," said Cabot, "but the blockade is surely a standing danger."

"Not this time," said Grendel. "The ship will have safe passage."

"Why?"

"Because of you," said Grendel.

"I do not understand," said Cabot.

"When you spoke with Lord Zarendargar, on the day of the great breakfast, that night, did he not speak to you of these things?"

"We spoke of many things," said Cabot, "of war and weapons, of beasts and ships, of stratagems, of honor, of codes, and such, and we again drank paga."

"But you spoke not of the Sardar, of Priest-Kings, and their will?" said Grendel.

"No," said Cabot.

"It seems then," said Grendel, "that I have news to convey to you, which you may welcome."

"Speak," said Cabot.

"No longer," said Grendel, "are you outlawed by Priest-Kings. No longer are you to be hunted down by them. No longer need you fear the containers of the Prison Moon."

"How is this?"

"Agamemnon, and his ambitions, it seems, were of some concern in the Sardar," said Grendel. "Lord Zarendargar made clear to the Sardar your refusal to accept his plans, and your role in his downfall."

"I did nothing by intent for the Sardar," said Cabot. "I owe it nothing, lest it be the bitterest of enmities."

"I see," said Grendel.

"In any event, I am pleased," said Cabot.

"Do not be too soon pleased," said Grendel.

"I understand," said Cabot, "the outlawry lifted, that I am free to return to my holding, free to go where I will, and be as I will."

"Let us hope so," said Grendel.

"I have a slave in Ar," said Cabot, "whom I am thinking of reclaiming, and collaring."

"Interesting," said Grendel.

"The Priest-Kings," said Cabot, "have no more interest in me."

"Perhaps not," said Grendel.

"Nor Kurii," said Cabot.

"Let us hope not," said Grendel.

"I am to be returned to Gor, am I not?" inquired Cabot.

"That is my understanding," said Grendel. "Somewhere on Gor."

"Somewhere?"

"Yes," said Grendel.

"In the vicinity of Port Kar, surely," said Cabot, "in the vicinity of my holding."

"That is not clear," said Grendel.

"I do not understand," said Cabot.

"Much is unclear," said Grendel.

"Am I not free, if the outlawry is lifted, free to return to my holding, free to go where I will, and be as I will?"

"Perhaps," said Grendel.

"But you are not certain?"

"No."

"In this you see the hand of Priest-Kings?" asked Cabot.

"Perhaps," said Grendel.

"I hate Priest-Kings!" cried Cabot.

"Perhaps you are no more than a piece on their kaissa board," said Grendel.

"I move myself!" said Cabot.

"Perhaps," said Grendel, "that is why they want you on their board."

"We will soon be ready to lift away!" called Peisistratus. "Make haste!"

"Dear Cabot," said Grendel.

"Speak," said Cabot.

"There is restlessness in the high councils, suspicions, moves and counter-moves," said Grendel. "I fear things are afoot."

"Are you not privy to their deliberations?"

"No longer," said Grendel, "as I have chosen to accompany the Lady Bina to Gor."

"What are you suggesting?" asked Cabot.

"Others may not yet be done with you."

"I do not understand," said Cabot.

"You are suspect."

"How so?"

"It is feared you may yet be upon the kaissa board of Priest-Kings."

"No!" said Cabot.

"What if it be their will?" said Grendel.

"I repudiate their will!" said Cabot.

"It might be dangerous to do so," said Grendel. "Are they not world masters, the gods of Gor?"

"If their laws are respected," said Cabot, "they dabble little in the doings of human beings."

"Or Kurii," said Grendel.

"Yes," said Cabot, "or Kurii."

"So it seems," said Grendel.

"There is no board," said Cabot.

"I think," said Grendel, "there may be such a board, but that, unbeknownst to Priest-Kings, two sit at that board."

"I do not understand," said Cabot.

"Do you think that my people, the Kurii," asked Grendel, "are merely the messengers of Priest-Kings?"

"No," said Cabot.

"Might they not, too, see uses for you?"

"No," said Cabot, angrily.

"Might the game, perhaps one of dozens, not prove interesting?"

"There is no such game," said Cabot.

"Perhaps," said Grendel, "it is even a new game, or a changed game, pieces subtly removed, or even swept, from a surface, a different board, even, a game not even of Priest-Kings, but, now, rather, one of Kurii."

"There is no game," said Cabot.

"But perhaps you are right," said Grendel. "Perhaps the Priest-Kings have no further interest in you, nor Kurii, and that you will be returned to your holding, freed from the obligations of worlds."

"Certainly," said Cabot.

"But the rumored coordinates," said Grendel, "suggest not Port Kar, but a location farther north, a remote beach, far from civilization, in the vicinity of the northern forests."

"Perhaps that Ramar may be freed, in a suitable venue?"

"Perhaps," said Grendel.

"But you do not believe that?"

"No," said Grendel.

"But why?" asked Cabot. "To what end, for what purpose?"

"I do not know," said Grendel.

"And who then might know?" asked Cabot, angrily.

"Perhaps Priest-Kings," said Grendel.

"Or Kurii," said Cabot.

"Yes," said Grendel, "or Kurii."

"Games may be afoot," said Cabot.

"Perhaps," said Grendel. "Do you really object?"

"No," said Cabot.

"I thought not," said Grendel.

"I see, beyond the port," said Peisistratus, joining them, "Cestiphon, Statius, Archon, Lord Arcesilaus, many noble humans and high Kurii. They have come to see us off. Several of the humans will take another ship to Gor. Lift your hands to them, and board."

And so hands were lifted, and then Cabot, and Grendel,

preceding Peisistratus, entered the lock, which was then closed, behind them, and, in moments, they were within the ship.

"The capsules, below, are empty," said Cabot.

"After our departure from Gor," said Peisistratus, "we will make planetfall on Earth. We will stay there as briefly as possible, for little longer than it takes to fill the capsules, as my men do not care to spend much time there, given its various pollutions and poisons."

"With what are the capsules to be filled?" asked Grendel.

"With female slaves, of course," said Peisistratus. "They have received something of a reprieve, it seems, given the sealing of the ports here, and the war, but that is over now."

"They suspect nothing?" said Grendel.

"Nothing," said Peisistratus. "They do not yet know they are Gorean slaves."

"We are prepared to cast off?" said Cabot.

"Yes," said Peisistratus, "momentarily. Have you chained your slave?"

"Yes," said Cabot.

"I did not show you, in our small tour," said Peisistratus, "as I saw no point in alerting your slave, but there are small chambers on the ship, furred and suitably equipped, where slaves may be ingeniously fastened for the pleasure of men."

"Excellent," said Cabot.

"Now," said Peisistratus, "I must to the bridge."

Shortly thereafter, scarcely noticeably, the ship left the dock, and took its course for the unspoiled, green, fertile world of Gor.

Epilogue

This tale is now finished.

I have entitled the tale, *Kur of Gor*. That seems to me an acceptable title. It is a tale of several individuals, and several events. It deals with a war, and honor, and friendship. Two individuals figure particularly in the story, one a human, interestingly, and one a Kur, or partly a Kur.

One is a member of an inferior species, or, perhaps more kindly put, a lesser species, the human, and the other is, when all is said and done, a monster, yet one who well served the world.

It is interesting that the shape of the world should have been to some extent a function of two such unlikely agents.

But the subtleties of the Nameless One are difficult to predict, and even to discern.

In any event I have tried, on the whole, to tell this story not only with some objectivity, but also with some sympathy, despite its unlikely protagonists.

I think we can learn something of the mysterious nature of the world in mysterious ways.

And so, are not both, despite the species in one case, and the genetic deformity in the other, in their way, worthy of being considered, say, in courage and honor, however surprisingly, Kur of Gor, and so the title of the tale.

About the Author

John Norman, born in Chicago, Illinois, in 1931, is the creator of the Gorean Saga, the longest running series of adventure novels in science fiction history. Starting in December 1966 with *Tarnsman of Gor*, the series was put on hold after its twenty-fifth installment, *Magicians of Gor*, in 1988, when DAW refused to publish its successor, *Witness of Gor*. After several unsuccessful attempts to find a trade publishing outlet, the series was brought back into print in 2001. Norman has also produced a separate, three installment science fiction series, the Telnarian Histories, plus two other fiction works (*Ghost Dance* and *Time Slave*), a nonfiction paperback (*Imaginative Sex*), and a collection of thirty short stories, entitled Norman *Invasions*. The *Totems of Abydos* was published in spring 2012.

All of Norman's work is available both in print and as ebooks. The Internet has proven to be a fertile ground for the imagination of Norman's ever-growing fan base, and at Gor Chronicles (www.gorchronicles.com), a website specially created for his tremendous fan following, one may read everything there is to know about this unique fictional culture.

Norman is married and has three children.

OPEN ROAD
INTEGRATED MEDIA

Open Road Integrated Media is a digital publisher and multimedia content company. Open Road creates connections between authors and their audiences by marketing its ebooks through a new proprietary online platform, which uses premium video content and social media.